Angel of The Maya

By

Ruth Lee

ANGEL OF THE MAYA

Copyright © 2007 by Ruth Lee

Published by:
    Femme Osage Publishing
    1301 Colby Drive
    Saint Peters, Missouri, USA 63376
    FemmeOsagePublishing.com
    Publisher@FemmeOsagePublishing.com

Printed in the United States of America

ISBN: 978-1-934509-12-8

Library of Congress Control Number: 2007938943

First Printing 2007
Second Printing 2008

Author Contact:
    Ruth Lee
    www.RuthLee-Scribe.com

Cover Design by:
    Sarah Van Male
    cyanotype.com

Angel of The Maya

By

Ruth Lee

Also by Ruth Lee

We Are Here ~
The Teachers of the Higher Planes

The Work Begins

The Art of Life ~
Living Together in Harmony

Now is The Time

The World of Tomorrow

The Word of The Maya

The Making of a Scribe
How to Achieve a Life You Can Write About

Can You Pray?
We Are All Here to Seek the Way

Within the Veil:
An Adventure in Time

It's About Time!
Work for a NEW You

Dedicated to my brother,
Charles

☼ CHAPTER ONE

Sitting all day at a loom is not easy, but Wanda figured it was a lot easier than what her daughter did for a living. All her prayers and hopes had been to raise a child to womanhood who would be popular and happy, someone the world wanted to see and be near, but her dreams never extended to watching her daughter pose in furs in tropical settings and bikinis in Antarctica, while constantly landing in trouble because of her poor choice of friends. She hated Teri's lifestyle as a super model and how it affected her personally, but did not feel like doing anything about it right now.

Moving from the dining room to the kitchen, Wanda thought she saw a 'hooded, doomed figure' standing in front of the refrigerator. Crossing herself, she walked quickly toward the table shouting to anyone who might be present: "Get out! Go away!! I do not want anyone bothering me now! I have work to do! Leave me alone!! Go home!"

Hearing her mother's raised voice Teri panicked and ran to see what was happening. When she saw there was no one in the kitchen but her mother, she burst into laughter. This was not a good response.

Wanda barked, "Don't laugh, Teri. You have to let them know you don't want them bothering you when you're alone—or they'll take over and run the show. I know!"

Tickled by Wanda's explanation of what she neither saw nor believed, Teri chose to act as if she understood and accepted her mother's logic and turned to look at the garden in full bloom just beyond the kitchen window. Staring in silence a long moment Teri said softly, "What would you say to moving away from here? Wouldn't you like to live somewhere else for a change?"

Waving her hand absentmindedly, Wanda smiled while sorting through hanks of yarn that had fallen to the floor and gotten mixed together. Keeping her reply vague, she said with a sigh, "I don't know, Teri. I used to want to move or travel and see everything this side of the moon, but anymore…I don't know…I guess I just want to weave and be left alone. You know how it is."

Unexpectedly, Teri snapped back, "No, I don't know how it is! When did all this happen? When did you get depressed again? I don't like it one bit how often you're getting upset and depressed now. Why don't we move? The weather here is always messy—cloudy and hazy, and the women around here are too lazy or stupid to study with you and learn how to weave as you do." Without a trace of her famous smile, Teri switched tactics and cooed through carmine lips that had sold millions of tubes of lipstick and gloss, "Let's move—now!"

"Again?" Was all Wanda could say before Teri threw her mind into high gear and began arguing in earnest.

"What do you mean, again? When did you move last? I've been living all over the world for more than ten years and you've stayed here—apparently doing less and less and getting more and more depressed. How can you say you aren't ready for a change? You have to be tired of this house and the way it needs painted every other year or it looks dingy and dirty?" Satisfied for now, Teri sat down at the table and pretended to read the morning paper lying open as if Wanda intended to continue reading it.

Doubting that Teri would miss the headlines she had read and cast aside earlier, Wanda mumbled, "I think maybe you forgot to mention that crime is rising around here, too. I read that article you're looking at and they say it is just a bunch of kids whose parents did not pay enough attention to their after-school activities, but I doubt it. It sounds like gangs to me." Normally Wanda could glibly manage conversations and swiftly change topics, but this time she was intent on going over her inventory of yarn and did not notice the disconnect immediately. When she did, she asked Teri, "What do you think?"

Teri was scanning the news about foreign affairs rather than local crime scenes, mumbling incoherently until it became obvious that Wanda could not hear her, so she spoke louder. "Can you get me a glass of iced tea?"

Relieved that the subject had changed—somehow, Wanda grinned and said, "What? Do you think I'm one of your assistants?" As she spoke, she put down her yarn and walked to the refrigerator. Pulling out a pitcher of iced lemon tea, Wanda noticed it dripping when it hit the room's heat and humidity—even thought about getting the mop, but it slipped from her mind as she poured the sweet, sticky tea into a glass sitting on the island.

As she extended the glass, Teri said with a wicked grin, "I think maybe we should go to Mexico and visit Mandy again."

Unable to conceal her alarm, Wanda blurted out, "Mandy? That freak! She looks way too weird for me. What do you see in her anyway? And why doesn't she take better care of her skin? All that sun is turning her into a Mayan—way too old before her time. I don't know what gets into women like her. If you do, please explain it to me."

While returning the pitcher to the refrigerator, Teri's response stopped her dead. "Mandy is no freak! Mandy's a great friend and ally of The Maya. She can do anything she wants. She's one of The Chosen, and you know she quit her high-powered corporate job to continue her Mayan quest because she wants to learn how to leave this world better than we found it--" Pausing as if to catch her breath, Teri regrouped her thoughts before adding, "Anyway, you like Mandy. You know you do! She always makes you laugh."

She was about to push her argument further when she noticed her mother walking toward a puddle of water. Unable to move or scream she watched in horror as Wanda slipped across the tiles and crumpled to the floor with one leg jutting out at a crazy angle.

She saw it all happen in slow motion and heard Wanda scream before she got to her and tried to help her get up. One pull and they both knew Wanda's leg was shattered. It was obvious things were going to get worse because the bone had broken through her skin just above the knee. Thoughts of osteoporosis and splintered thighs leapt to Teri's mind unbidden, but her mother was too deep in pain to think of any remedy other then to call 911 and get an ambulance immediately.

Rushing to get the message across to the dispatcher, Teri gave the wrong address the first time and had to reconnect and go through it all again. It took a few minutes to undo the initial damage and get the crew headed in the right direction, but the ambulance arrived in what seemed an amazingly short time.

As the experienced rescue team worked on Wanda's leg, Teri danced around the room humming a tuneless sound. Her behavior seemed more than just strange to the two medics who had recognized her immediately. High expectations lead to disappointment. Instead of appearing in clothes that accented her famous curves or beautiful face, like in her cover girl days or even her dismal TV movies, Teri was decked out in faded jeans and a baggy denim shirt. Her long blond, shampoo ad hair was now pulled back in a sloppy knot that drooped at her nape—and there was no sign of the makeup she sold everywhere—including QVC.

As the men wheeled the gurney out, Wanda seemed strangely relaxed and said matter-of-factly, "Teri, get my clothes out of the dryer, and don't forget to pack my deodorant. I'm allergic to antiperspirants."

Teri nodded, still chanting, ignoring how it might sound to those escorting her mother to the nearby hospital emergency room. Unable to relax until she achieved a high G, she made it—just as her mother's gurney was pushed into the ambulance. She believed it was a sign that her mother would be back on her feet soon.

♓ ♓

Before Teri could rejoin her mother, many people had to be notified about this unexpected turn of events, and much advice had to be sought on how to lessen its adverse effects on both their busy careers. When she finally arrived at the hospital several hours later, she headed straight for the operating rooms, and then remembered to stop at the admitting desk to see if Wanda was out of surgery and doing okay, or what to expect.

The hushed response from the Physicians Assistant was not what she expected. Told that her mother was not doing as well as could be expected, and not responding to medication as well as they had hoped, Teri was startled to hear that the leg had been saved. Overcome with panic, she shouted, "Saved? You mean there was a chance she might have lost it?" This was said with a toss of her now beautifully-coifed blonde hair that caused the hearts of gossiping men standing nearby to race into high gear.

The young African-American clerk assigned to Customer Service hid behind a somewhat bored expression when she saw the famous model approach her desk. She decided to interrupt Teri's exchange with the Physicians Assistant by way of a snide aside. "You do know that your mother is diabetic, don't you?" She said it without blinking, talking non-stop, without any evidence of sympathy or interest in the tragic event that had brought them all together.

Teri managed to say quite civilly, "No, I did not know she was diabetic." She paid little attention to the clerk then, but later wondered why the woman had talked to her with such disrespect. Whatever her reasons, she caused Teri to stop obsessing and stressing out. She was used to people being rude and thinking she was stupid because she was a super model. At such times she quietly intoned her mantra and calmed herself down. She started intoning her mantra as she backed away from the counter that separated her from the blinking computer terminal and the officious clerk.

Her confession apparently annoyed the clerk, because she said angrily, "You haven't provided us with her insurance cards, and I've asked you twice—quite nicely."

This further assault on her nerves and lack of consideration was too much for Teri. She snapped back, "Here's your damn cards! You can give them to the nurse when you're done with them." Intending to stomp her way toward the elevators, she was stopped by the clerk's loud demand.

"Wait a minute—not so fast!! You have to sign here that you're taking full responsibility for any charges not covered by her insurance!"

Tired of needless theatrics, Teri smiled at the glaring woman and pretended not to notice the strident tones and what they implied as she picked up a chained pen and waited with it poised over the counter top until the contract was ready to sign. Neither woman was happy with the other, yet there was no apparent reason for this instant dislike and tension. Later each would wonder what came over them and made them act so tough and unyielding—as well as disinterested in the other's problems, but not right then.

When Teri finished the paperwork, she went to the nearby waiting room and paged through a fashion magazine that had provided her with millions of dollars in revenue over the years. Before she finished browsing through it, her name was announced over the intercom, along with instructions to visit the nurses' station on the ground floor stat. With her mind now lost in time, Teri headed out without noticing the offensive clerk waving insurance identification cards at her. Later she would remember that confrontation and recognize it as the first sign that her mother's leg would not be 'just fine,' but then she still believed that nothing done in such a modern facility would hinder her mother's complete recovery.

✺ CHAPTER TWO

Without much thought, Wanda struggled to walk on her leg now swathed in a hip-to-toe cast. It was healing none too fast and she had received no confirmation from her doctors that the pain had been contained and would leave when the cast was removed, so her leg ached and complained most of the time. She somehow made it through days of worshiping her daughter for taking time off from her thriving career to be with her and worrying about others doing the same, because she was not raised to expect such consideration.

Each night Wanda talked to friends and clients over the phone or in person, always trying to figure out what would happen if she moved to Mexico. She fretted that she could never accomplish all the marvelous things proposed by her daughter and others who were building a mission of some kind there. She felt she had nothing to give others. Whenever she mentioned it, she was greeted by gales of laughter, but no real plan or confirmation of what she might do to help others there.

As the days slipped into weeks, she saw her home given away to people who would love it as much as she did, but it was still not set in concrete that she had to move and stay away. Why did she have to go anywhere anyway? No one said she had to leave. No one said she had to go to Mexico to get better, but she felt it within every conversation and every situation she discussed with her therapist. She worried because her mind could no longer connect with people she just met. She was not registering them in her memory, perhaps because she instinctively knew she would never see them again? Was it a premonition or just the realization that once you move from a place you never again are connected to it, except in memories of the past?

What made her laugh was realizing that there were others who were also groping to understand how a woman of such wealth and great work would move away or start over. They, too, saw her as losing everything and gaining nothing if she moved to Mexico.

Her daughter was the only person on Earth closely tied to her now, and she wanted her to start over and do more with her life now, so Wanda gave the move more careful thought. What more could she tell Teri about her work and the people she once knew that would convince her that the move would not do her good? Nothing biographers or students in Master of Fine Arts programs had written about her work helped deflect their growing determination to get her to sign on to teach Mayan women how to make money from their own designs and update their lives. Eventually, with no conviction that she needed to do anything new and totally different now—and absolutely no need to flee anything, Wanda packed up her art and yarn and departed.

⋈　⋈

　　The new woman who reentered that room a few hours later was not so very different from the old Wanda, except that this one did not limp or feel pain. It was not due to a mood swing, she had changed spiritually and suddenly realized she had to leave immediately, and she was eager to get moving! The only unresolved worry left was how far she might be guided to help this strange woman of The Maya, Mandy. In the past she had not liked to talk about Mandy much because she did not want to ask a lot of questions and be told that there were no ready answers; however, she intuitively knew now what Mandy could do and would do soon. It was all there inside her mind! If she had to know what was going to happen immediately, she could look within at a spot on her forehead right below her hairline. Everything that is about to happen could be viewed there like watching a slide show, but she could not picture Mandy.

　　When Wanda left her old personality behind and slipped into a new disposition, she walked away with a new slant on time and felt absolutely unique. She was sure she was the only woman on Earth who could walk out of one life and find a better one, but she was wrong. You can see what she did not: Wanda moved up a life or two and was no longer down and out, sad and blue, but you can do it, too.

　　When her work moved her to go out and about, Wanda used crutches that strained her arms so much that she worried she might be unable to work on her art as she did in the past, but in her mind she saw canvases of brilliant colors stretched out before her for years to come. Wanda saw colors she had never used in tapestries or fabrics that now commanded high prices and knew what was to be. She saw it instantly!

　　As that day ended and Wanda's life mended, creating a new woman, Teri stood at the dining room window waving to a family departing from the house where they would stay a few days. She was undecided about what to do until the ship moving all their things to Progresso on the northern coast of Yucatan sailed. She was ready to leave immediately because her hands ached to heal the mistake made when setting her mother's broken leg. How could she help Wanda manage the pain when she finally realized that the leg would not make it all the way? Nothing came to her, so she did nothing.

　　As flowers arrived each and every hour, Teri would kneel and mentally embrace them as if their aroma could heal her sorrows—and it did. The tincture of roses and sweet attars she had created and enhanced over the years helped her see the world in a more positive way, but it was not her way to push that view on others. She sold nothing produced by her own hands, promising God that one day she would find a way to mass produce aromas that could help everyone suffering from sore throats, runny noses, or rose fever and other allergies.

　　She let her mind wander about the house one last time, looking at vases of flowers produced by a woman who once lived nearby. The silk roses and lilies were so pure and natural that few could tell them from those created by God's mind. She wondered only a moment before deciding to promote these beautiful flowers. Since she no longer knew the woman who created them, what should she say about them?

When Teri wanted to know something about another, and the person was nearby, she normally rushed to chat them up as if they were best friends who would never meet again—and sometimes that was true, but this time she could not find the old neighbor who turned silk into lilies equal to those admired by a king who loved wisdom more than power. Sniffing the flowers individually, trying to catch their unique fragrances, she missed their scent. Her mind worked through time and she saw perfumers painting fragrances into the center of each flower, but that would happen in another day and another country, if it was to pay.

Working with demanding, cold, bold, even evil people was not what Teri wanted to do until she grew old. However, such work had paid for most of her fabulous possessions and great adventures, so she could not scold herself for doing such work. Instead she chose to forget what she did. Her work as a model was so easily forgotten that it humbled the world, but not La Petite Teri.

Instead of waiting to be told that she was over the hill or getting fat, Teri decided to depart the runways for a decade or two or whatever it takes—yet deny that her career was over. Wanda once told her what would happen in the end, but she did not believe her because her career was established and plotted out for at least ten more years. She was not a foolish daughter who blurted out what she thought, because she could see her mother was not worried by what she saw in a vision. She thought: 'How ironic that Mom is the one most upset when her prophecies come true.'

Working with earth was what Teri had always wanted to do, so if the flowers of Earth were erased and forgotten, as seemed to be their destiny, she wanted to leave silk clones behind for future generations to see and picture what was once her reality. She mused that flowers given now are not gifts of love but doubt. Only when men were concerned that they might not be approved or their sexual appetites would be ignored did they think to give bouquets, often opting for one single bloom because it was a lot cheaper to produce an atmosphere of caring where there was very little sharing involved. This flash of intuition goaded Teri to transform silk flowers—especially roses, into a gift of love…but where to start?

Working on projects in her mind at home enabled Teri, because of her stage presence and many male friends, to plan a big production and get it operational in no time at all. Having always maintained equal distance with every man in her life, her male friends willingly did miraculous work, even when resettling her and her girl friends in another community far away from New York. It was not that men did such things more easily than women, but because they actually wanted to help—not just talk. It was Teri's opinion that men choose to cooperate, while many women mistake acting bossy as managing others. She fretted because modern work was never meant to become a way of life that caused pain or strife between the sexes or cause many to leave their spiritual path—ending in grief and sorrow when retired or when times were less than prosperous.

Tossing down her mental pen, picking up a catalog instead, Teri studied cloth woven all over the world and began envisioning a huge collage created from all sorts of fabrics. Such art would combine acts of love with the hands of time or whatever her fertile mind might divine when she took time to sketch and work out all the details. Her mundane mind saw millions to be made in everything around her community—or any town, but residents always claimed they could not make it pay. She continued to be astounded by Americans who believed they could not achieve a goal that was well conceived and worked at diligently, preferring instead to deceive themselves by saying everything worth doing has already been done—except making money from it. For that very reason, she was prepared to leave the country where she had achieved success and formed her present belief system.

Her pace had slowed down to one-step-a-day, but Teri knew it always paid to follow her gut instinct—and not look back even once. Accompanied by a woman relying on crutches, she planned to leave America behind, equally determined to stick to a simple belief for the time being: *Always follow your inner wisdom and be patient with those you love.*

Not only was Teri giving up a huge income and all its perks, she was also determined to financially enable a Mayan shaman to erect buildings to house thousands of women, lots of kids, and some men, so she could work safely there, too. She could *see* Mandy teaching ancient ways to those who would pay for today's needs. This enigmatic woman was not a demented being or a demon, but she had to put up with people who used such words when trying to downgrade her contributions. To make any real progress immediately, Teri realized she must find a way around a very serious blockade that was holding women back—all over the world.

Until recently in The States, women were unable to achieve much outside of traditionally feminine career paths, because they posed a threat to women who did very little and liked it that way. To stop working women from wanting more of the pie, or possibly luring away their guys, ambitious women continually cut up and cast out women who managed to make it to the top—or close enough. Businessmen seldom befriend women once they discover other women appear to dislike them. Few men are wise enough to always take into account the ever-present jealousy factor. Add to the problem of intra-gender jealousies the fact that many American women do not *really* want to rise in their careers now because they intuit that the world as we know it is about to explode. As if removing such thoughts from her mind, Teri shook her head hard enough to loosen her long blonde hair. As it cascaded around her shoulders, it helped her relax but not forget the most important reason why their Grand Plan would succeed: *Mandy is a wise woman who can see what will be!*

Mandy chose to leave the city capitalism built and maintained, New York, for a better climate and a society less dominated by deceitful and dishonest people hell-bent on making a profit off other's hard work. Her desire when she moved to Mayaland was to erase pressure and stress lingering from an intense career. In time she arrived at the same moment another was ready to include her in work she already knew how to do. These two shamans worked in a way not known today, in order to help The Ascended Maya.

When Teri reviewed Mandy's bio and recent history again, her mind rejected some of it. She wanted to explore more than what she could read. She wanted to know how one person could live within many people or times and yet not really exist. Was Mandy such a person—one who would change the Earth; or was she a mirage that came and went, then appeared to stay only until the vision had been perfected?

The vision Mandy helped them create was such that Teri was driven to give up her modeling career—at least for now, to relocate with her friends and mother to another part of the world to do work that none of them had ever done before. Within this vision that Teri held in her mind, she suddenly spotted an owl. It was not the kind of symbol you would expect to find in a sage's mind, because it was not considered wise. The owl was white and stood out from the trees as if in the brightness of day. It was working at twilight—spotting mice and vermin and such, trying to take them out before night.

This same owl appeared within Wanda's mind at the very same time. She was sitting and waiting for the dawn to creep across the front lawn. She did not appear to be in the same time frame as Teri, yet she apparently was. How could they both spot the same owl from another time and space?

Both lost in contemplation, neither paid attention when the clock sounded off the hour noisily, because divine intervention had intercepted them in time. The two women now sat patiently waiting to hear from their mutual friend in the Yucatan, Mandy. What would be *their* final destination? Where would they live in Mexico? Would it be a lark or a walk in the dark? Was it really to be the next step in a lifelong lesson on time?

In less than a flicker of the cursor on an active computer the two women simultaneously heard the magic words: "You've Got Mail." Both woke from their semi-comatose states in different rooms and turned to read the incoming message together. They both laughed and mentally danced as they dreamed of even grander lives.

☼ CHAPTER THREE

When Mandy opened the letter from her old friend, Teri, she paused to wonder about the contents before she read it. It appeared to be only a few lines asking for her assistance, but it contained much more. What was it? The note was handwritten on paper emitting hints of lavender and familiar spices meant to delight the reader's mind, but the scent did not mask the writer's feelings, nor did it dilute the energy or how her friend tried to hide behind some lines what she wanted Mandy to do once she read the letter all the way through.

Without a doubt now, Mandy discerned that her friend was upset and very concerned that her mother might lose her right leg. It was not written that bluntly, rather hidden in the way she framed the page and carefully chose her words. Although still not able to know exactly what was wrong, Mandy knew she was close to the truth when her right leg started to shake. With one leg shaking and the other stable, Mandy drifted into a reverie or dream as she reread the letter and began to pray for her friends elsewhere.

Dear Friend,

I am writing to you today to ask a great favor of one who has no reason to grant my request. I am busy, as usual, with my career and what is here, and I sometimes forget to keep up with yours and what you do…but that isn't really true, as you know.

I am busy as usual doing what comes easiest to me…in order to amass enough wealth to do what I really want to do very soon with you—and only you know what that is now. I want to do something new! Can't keep working as I do without at least a glimpse of what comes next. Can you help me with that? What do you see? Please write or e-mail me…Give me a preview, please.

I would love to move my mother and a couple of friends into your new compound and work with you and them, too…doing more for The Maya. We are not as gifted as you spiritually, but each of us is able to do work that will enhance the power wherever you are, and give you a lot to do, too. I know you want more work and more energy, and we are willing and able to do this for you… Smiling at that because I know how busy you are, yet I still want to come and stay with you this Spring.

My mother's leg is a real work of art. The surgeon is so proud of what he did in a few hours, but I believe something is still not quite right. If we could visit you asap, working together, I think we might be able to heal it, which I doubt because just as she slipped to the floor and broke it, I had a vision of her walking with only one leg. I did what I could to dispel the vision, but it didn't go away easily. Do you see something different?

Am so confident you will welcome us into your new home that we are packed and ready to go as soon as we hear from you. (You do remember inviting us for an extended visit when we met at Christmas?) I didn't think then that you 'knew' we would actually be coming now, but I am laughing about it now… You knew then, didn't you? You always do! Thanks for all you do and being you.

Love and Light, Teri

Turning the stationery over, Mandy noticed the watermark and realized that Teri's logo of a single rose had always marked her as a special power. Did she have power over plants, too, she wondered? Mandy often thought of Teri as a saint dressed in the latest high-fashion. Only a few close friends noticed the beauty of her soul.

When the day ended, Mandy felt totally relaxed for the first time in months. She had mailed letters to several Mayan elders in her area advising them that a super model would be moving into her compound soon, along with her equally famous mother who would teach weaving on floor looms, as well as what it takes to successfully market Mayan designs. Mandy never regretted that her work grew more difficult when advancing the art of others who richly enjoyed life, too. It actually inspired her to work even harder!

Working daily in the way of a shaman of the Maya of this time and space was not what made Mandy feel great. She was inspired by whatever work came through to her, but also needed to be around people who reminded her of what she went through to reach this state of mind. Her time alone was never enough to cover all of the *stuff* she said she wanted to accomplish before leaving 'the world' behind, but she could do more in an hour than four others who did the job before her.

Comparing one person to another is never a good way to begin a new day, but whenever she greeted anyone for the first time Mandy wondered who would stay and who would leave immediately. She knew that Wanda would be a wonderful ally to the work of The Maya who lived on the other side of this parallel of time, but she was not sure if it would work out in such a way that today's tribe would know what to do with her. Mandy did not *have* to worry about it, but she worried because it was a way of gaining acceptance without inflicting pain.

Mandy tended to everyone entering a room and later weeded out the bad seeds or those foolish enough to contemplate doing evil deeds. At times this created problems for those who worked differently than she did, especially those who upon spotting evil moved to rid themselves of it immediately—refusing to associate with such fools. This was not the only difference in the way Mandy lived and worked among today's Maya, as opposed to those born and raised in the present day tribe living in the Yucatan and Guatemala, but the most controversial. Most Maya denied it was a problem, so it remains a big issue for some even now.

Working with strangers, or those she knew only slightly, was something Mandy usually did not enjoy, so she prayed and meditated as she waited for the plane from the States to
arrive. She prayed that all would be supportive of her work and none were enemies dressed
as friends. She intended to meet Teri's mother and casually touch her bad leg before deciding
if her herbs and such could cure it or just give them the impression that time would heal
her leg. However, when the plane arrived and the excited women stepped off the curb into
waiting cabs, she knew immediately without laying her hands on Wanda's leg that it would be
amputated. She did not wish to think about it, so she followed the noisy group back to the
compound in a cab filled with Mayan elders who had stood at the back of the waiting room
watching the crowd of American women arrive in style.

Wanda looked brave and happy at the same time as she nodded toward Mandy, as if
she were merely an acquaintance. Mandy did not notice her coolness since she was predis-
posed to like Wanda simply because she was Teri's mother. However, the Mayan elders who
appeared to view the arrival of the women were not pleased to see that this famous American
weaver was less than friendly toward Mandy—and appeared to extend her antipathy toward
themselves as well. As a result, they were unwilling to be impressed by the news that Wanda's
tapestries hung in museums world-wide or that everything she wove was eagerly sought after
by wealthy patrons.

In the weeks that followed their reunion, the two old friends met daily and did much
with the women from America and other visitors, as well as the tribal elders. All the while,
Mandy gently freed her friend's mother of the belief that her leg could be saved through
prayer and application of herbal medications. Only then was it able to be amputated.

When that fateful day arrived, Teri was left without any doubt that it was God's
will. She sensed something strange stirring within her abdomen and then creeping upward
toward her heart where it burst from her chest and fled the hospital room in a vaporous way,
just as her mother was being prepped for the operation. It was the wave of energy Teri had
suppressed ever since she had the vision that her mother would lose her leg as she fell to
the kitchen floor months before. She had the first awareness that fateful morning as Wanda
walked toward the refrigerator door—before the doctors said they could save the leg. She
wondered, 'How is it possible to believe in the spiritual side of life when what you see every
day seems concrete or more definite than dreams or visions?' She did not know, but tried to
understand what was happening anyway.

✳   ✳

As the work associated with the business of weaving and teaching concluded, their
plans for reaching many more students world-wide, in addition to native women, were final-
ized. Mandy left her two friends and their group of designing associates to visit the beach in
order to relax alone and think about what she thought needed to be taught to all the weavers
first. Leaving her home, she felt no resentment toward anyone about anything because she
considered these women to be friends of The Maya. However, any time Mandy left town,
the elders who ran the compound in her absence were not pleased with the woman who no
longer was able to stand without a stick to support her. They saw Wanda as limited in many
ways—not just her leg, but did not wish to say anything about it to Mandy just yet.

Within a month or two of her arrival in Mexico, Wanda started writing about her past life in The States because she felt fit, but tired of living as is. She was bitter, but not upset enough to take it out on her daughter or her friends, yet delighted with whatever she found in the way of art and how willing Mayan weavers were to talk to her; but she was upset that her leg might be lost due to something never explained in terms she could understand.

After delving into self-pity relentlessly, Wanda emerged to see herself standing with one crutch, believing that she would soon walk with a cane, and then not even need that, when she suddenly fell backwards, hitting her head on something quite hard. She awoke two days later without her leg. It was all too strange! She loudly rued that the Mexican government did not provide adequate training for its doctors and nurses and that if she had only remained in The States she would still have her leg. She did not speak of it again later, but the thought remained lodged in her brain and her self-pity flowered.

While Wanda wondered and worried about her life in this place, the elders plotted to get rid of her and the others who had arrived with Teri. They decided that the way to chase away these American women was not to discourage them from working harder, but to diminish and discredit whatever they accomplished. This turned out to be impossible for the men to pull off without Mandy noticing it.

Upon arrival at the compound, Teri's friends had immediately set up computers linked to many cities, thereby enhancing their own personal work as they helped the tribe. Their links to the outside world were not unique, but to the elders it was a kind of magic that could destroy their way of life and not help them or The Maya. The elders were not all old or beyond the age of adapting or assimilating new behavior patterns, but their traditional training and lessons since birth were never verbalized enough to explain what had to happen today to prepare for tomorrow.

Within a month of her arrival in the compound, Wanda was talking freely to every-one, yet still avoided Mandy. This was not the best way to ingratiate herself with the elders, but she did it anyway. When she walked into a room and sat down to visit with the native women, many times she could not smile but they felt her pain. The women of the tribe were usually relaxed but laughed only when everyone present felt good, too. Since Wanda was often sad, they prayed and started working on her as soon as she hobbled into a room, so they might all be happy.

Since work on the spine aligns you in time, Wanda began to feel so powerful that they cut back work on that particular line so her body would not wear out her 'good' leg trying to compensate for the loss of the right leg. Learning to never move faster than she was physically able to walk was the lesson Wanda most resented, but she rose to greatness once she mastered it. Each day she appreciated the women around her more than she had the day before, and they quickly grew to love her in a way that would not have happened if she had not lost her leg.

Taking her moods into consideration, yet envying her the power she had over their women, the local men tried to resist rebelling against what was said when she entered any discussion with them. They discovered she did not work like the weavers of their tribe, even though she had been weaving for many lives, too. Their shared history was enough to help each man realize that in time Wanda was not to be told what to do or how to work, because she, too, was there to do whatever it took to help the tribe ascend again when the calendar was at its end.

Over weeks and months Wanda worked diligently on her new life with only one leg, she grew in stature and won a leadership role in their daily work and within the mind of the tribe. She was named leader of the weavers because she earned it, without realizing she was being tested. Working in the weaving parlors was not hard for her by then, but whenever she walked alone or talked privately to outsiders, she immediately felt the strain of having only one leg left to stand on then. Such weariness with the world wore her patience down at times, but she did not give up on doing her new work.

⽊　⽊

When the men finally reached the point where they knew that they, too, had to do something new, plus help this woman from outside their tribe, their brotherhood came unglued and began to fall apart. Some did not believe it was necessary to promote the work of women who came from other parts of the Earth—not while their women and children had so little of what Americans preached was absolutely necessary for success. However, more and more men believed and even insisted that the new weavers were there only to help The Maya—not to hurt their tribe.

When Mandy returned to the compound from her brief respite by the sea, she noticed immediately that the men from the nearby villages were not nearly as interested in setting up schedules and working with her as they had been before this last group of women arrived at her compound. She wondered why, but said very little because she spotted another more serious problem that required her immediate attention.

Within a few days Mandy went to the eldest elder, and after greetings and a series of secrets were shared, she asked him what he thought was happening within and around the compound. The old man muttered the one word she was afraid he would say, "Lust!"

Staring into the air, Mandy asked him how lust had been able to gain a footing in the compound in such a short time. He laughed and pointed to Teri and the other models surrounding her. He told her that the men did not trust a woman who exploited her beauty and took off her clothes to please men for money. Without coaxing, he added his personal thoughts that Teri was far too complicated and difficult to understand, as well as too spoiled to be of much use in the future. With that he put on his jaunty Panama hat that only partially hid his wide smile and glittering eyes and departed.

As she drifted off into her own time and space, Mandy could hear him humming a mantra or whatever he mumbled all day when he was pleased. Long after he left her office, she remained seated in deep meditation. She appeared to everyone around her to be in a daze, so they did not disturb her with what they wanted to say.

Shaking up her head and mind at the same time, Mandy looked through time and realized that the woman she now regarded as Thérèse was still 'Teri the Super Model' to these men—not a saint sent to help the tribe celebrate the coming new world. In deference to the men, because she knew something that they did not, she decided to get rid of Teri immediately—on the next plane to leave Merida for The States.

Mandy suddenly appeared before the group standing nearby, as though awoken by a bolt of lightening. Thérèse flew to her side to see what had happened. Before she could ask, Mandy said casually, "Hey, Teri! How's it going? Are you getting tired of life in the Yucatan, too? You do not look as happy as when you arrived." Grinning impishly as she spoke, she extended her hand and gripped Thérèse's outstretched hand and let herself be pulled toward her. This was to be the only embrace she would permit before bidding her old friend to sit down and watch the black birds bathe in the swimming pool before them.

Thérèse appeared to be surprised, but readily sat and watched the grackles cavorting in the shallow water. Finally she said slowly and lowly, "I guess I am tired. Funny, but I never thought about it until now. Maybe we should all go back to New York and clean up old business—at least get it off my back. Will that be okay, Mandy, or do you need us around here to do more work?" Although Thérèse laughed easily, she knew she was being asked to leave, in a way that had never happened before. She also recognized that she wanted to return to New York, so she let everything drop.

As though reading her mind, Mandy said, "You've got a lot to do before you can return to live with us here in the Yucatan as we planned. Why not go back and start up the fund-raising bandwagon again? You know how everyone likes to hear about our artists and weavers and their work—and what we're all trying to accomplish. You can help us a lot that way, probably more than before."

Thérèse cocked her head, noting the poetic lilt to Mandy's words, sensing that her friend was talking in Spirit once again, not just jawing away about what she wanted done by someone. This realization caused her mind to open to time right then. She immediately saw that it was not appropriate for her to strut about the compound when so much work had to be done in the world to promote Mayan art. This intuitive flash was not what she expected or wanted to see, but it propelled her mind into the future faster than she had ever flown through time before now. After a few moments, sounding a bit groggy, Thérèse almost whispered, "We'll all leave on the afternoon plane out of Merida—provided we can get tickets at a good price. Is that okay with you, Mandy?"

Noticing for the first time that the other models and friends of Teri were listening intently to their conversation, Mandy laughed and said that the Mexican government could arrange flights for such lovely ladies at whatever price they could afford—without any problem. That immensely pleased the anxious women immediately! They all hurried away to pack their bags and arrange to get to the airport fast.

It was suddenly obvious to Mandy, as well as Thérèse and Wanda, that if these women willingly packed that fast that they were not as happy as they claimed to be. Laughter immediately healed any breach that might have produced a break in their internal communication system. The three women believed in each other and in what they would do together when Today was over.

When that day ended, Wanda found Mandy lying on the ground under the great Guardian Tree noisily breathing into the air as if she were imitating a floundering whale. She took a seat nearby under another huge tree, laughing and talking joyfully as she watched the birds flocking together for the night. It was not just another relaxation ritual. Whenever they hung out together, it intensified their relationship, but only shamans understand what happens within then.

Over the next few weeks the weavers and their teachers completed several new business ventures including opening another line and giving it a new name. This was cause to celebrate, but no one could decide which Maya of the nearby clan could run the business best. The way the natives arrived at their business decisions was initially viewed by their American counterparts as not the best way to make money, but seeking a consensus was not thrown away. It would always be used by the tribe.

Through consensus, the women decided that each of them would practice a bit of political campaigning during their meetings and while they worked, in order to make the best decisions for the tribe. Each had to develop a new line or a new name or select the one to run the business, and then sell it to others—without saying or doing anything that might defame anyone. Being so unlike what Americans are used to, some toyed with the idea that Communists might be at work within the tribe, but Mandy laughed at the idea—and continued to laugh loudly.

When Mandy realized that local elders did not like the idea of outsiders influencing the governance of their tribe, she cut back on what was said outside the compound and started holding evening meetings with the weavers that appeared to be focused only on their work. Since weaving was not of interest to men who liked to drink or mingle and talk about whatever they thought, they gradually left the weavers with only those men who were willing to let their minds be changed by listening—not participating in such meetings. The few elders who stayed were open to anything new; and as it turned out, they were the only ones able to celebrate the old ways.

♓   ♓

At one such meeting Mandy passed out candy to drowsy toddlers who followed their mothers everywhere. She then poured cups of hot chocolate that had a bit of pepper to warm it even more, saying over and over again as she handed them out: "Today is a day of great celebration! We salute our youth!"

The room suddenly became silent, even the children refused to whine. The oldest elder present said, "Thank you, Mandy, for all you do." He spoke with sincerity, but because he always thanked everyone profusely for whatever they said or did, no one believed him. He may have regretted this reputation, but it kept him out of many arguments, thus granting him greater peace of mind than he might otherwise have achieved when communicating his views in the usual way.

Working with waves of energy ebbing and flowing through the crowd during such sessions was what another elder did best. He would sit alone intoning a sacred sound, followed by humming or drumming or doing something just for fun. The weavers paid little or no attention to these men, but never forgot that what they wanted to accomplish required their approval since they were in the foremost ranks of elders unwilling to let them move ahead with new designs and modernization plans.

Distance created depth within pictures they wished to reproduce, thus the mood of the group changed as the weavers rearranged their family life more and more to accommodate the work they loved to do on their looms. Their men were not always asked if some action was best, instead told more and more often that weaving was part of The Great Plan, and they had to get on track so The Ascended Maya would not get mad again. The Grand or Great Plan was never discussed much, so elders present during these evening events assured their clans that nothing had been decided yet.

Whenever Mandy had to visit another compound, the weavers easily ran everything—better than they did before the Americans arrived on the scene. There were changes—some differences in management style, but no problems surfaced until Mandy returned and could take over and sort things out.

Unlike Mandy, Wanda did not stand up and walk around as she talked or lectured, preferring to sit and chat about whatever came to her, as well as the minds of the women and girls gathered around her. She intuitively discovered quite quickly that each woman, child, and teen wanted something from her. She could tease, laugh, or make them sad, so no one doubted she was their leader, but the men never knew. They were clueless about what the women would do next, too.

The motto of each woman weaving her thoughts into fabric became, "As the weeks and months of a year come to be, can you see what I used to be?" As their dexterity and ability grew in more directions, the weavers understood more about what they did in the past and added pieces of wisdom to their work at home, as well as the fabrics woven in the compound almost continuously now.

The artists who designed basic patterns and experimented with new materials were better than ever. Colors suggested and preferred were bolder than what was used in recent times, but the older weavers had no regrets because they worked better than ever. These artisans had such a definite way of working that it had to have always existed, so no one really noticed the greatest changes take place.

When Mandy returned to the compound from her most recent trip abroad, she was swept away by the waves of energy stored and now ready for use in changing the mood of the elders who hung around the women far too much. Without a lot of thought, Mandy decided to invite all the men to a meeting of the weavers and ask them to contribute something new to the patterns and fabrics woven by these women.

The men readily accepted her invitation because the elders wanted to tell these women about the past—not discuss their future. Elders often stated angrily that women could not understand the traditional ways of the tribe without losing their desire to be better wives and mothers. Other men were more covert in their attempts to change or coerce the women into returning to the life they lived before Mandy and groups of outsiders moved into Mexico and Guatemala. Each male speaker took pains to blunt their pointed comments in ways that any elders present could agree was nicely done. However, all the weavers balked at congratulating any of them or commenting on what they said. Instead, they continued with their own handwork as if waiting for the party to start.

Finally, it was Mandy's turn to speak. She crossed the room and took a seat in the middle of the women and began to laugh—just to clear the air. The men flashed their eyes and moved their hands as they intuitively shouted that she was ignorant of what they were *all* there to do. Directing her laughter at the men only, Mandy flashed back to them that she was there to help The Maya of other times. She added intuitively, 'The Maya want to get into the minds of artists, dyers, and weavers, so work can accelerate within tribal members, thus the outside world will be better able to understand time, too.'

Those who got the message resented it, but knew better than to mention her offense. No one present knew for sure who Mandy was or how long she existed before she arrived to explore time—which was several years before The Maya of other times announced The Grand Plan or Great Idea, depending upon who was talking about it.

Mandy sat and laughed almost continuously for a minute or two while the weavers admired her exclusively—or until their thoughts drifted toward Wanda who was able to sit back and not lead that evening. They suddenly realized that Wanda, like Mandy, was accepted by their men. They wondered how women of other nations could sit with the elders and speak in their strange dialects and make sense of it, but they did not ask about it or about the pain Wanda might be enduring to remain among them now. They at first admired her, and then they accepted her work as superior, but now they realized they were all one tribe of women—and some happened to be Maya this time.

At the end of this lengthy meeting, the tribal elders spoke one-by-one about the way women of today lived without men. Their women, as well as others, started laughing, and soon the room boomed with hilarity, but no one said a word against them. Unable to discover what was so funny, yet wishing to claim credit for being witty and wise, men let everything discussed pass as it was—not as they wanted it to be when the evening began.

Within a week of that meeting the men unanimously decided they had to do more for the tribe—particularly make a greater effort to assert themselves, because their women were outstripping them economically, thus no longer seeking them out for money or help with the children. "Is this what they want?" The men asked each other over and over again.

It was what these men complained about for years—even prayed about, but when released of such responsibilities, they hated it. They had not noticed that many started doing work only they wanted to pursue. Their original intent was to show up the women and put them back in their past places, but it turned out to be too much fun to give up what they enjoyed now, so change occurred in many places without anyone becoming afraid of it.

♓   ♓

As time went by the tribe was more than able to pay its own way, while enjoying waves of Maya coming through the veil to help them assume duties for the last group ascension in this time. Many clans thought they were ready to ascend until reminded that much remained to be done to help those who were lost in the sun.

The weavers and their friends set up booths in nearby fairs in order to give the public a taste of what they made, raised, or thought. This plan involved no major expenditure—yet was fun for the young and made extra money for the weavers, the potters, the scribes, and other artisans and businesses throughout Mayaland.

Once money was no longer everyone's major concern, because they had enough, the gamble they thought they were willing to take was no longer a risk they could all condone, so they banned games of chance. When men and women have the ability to do whatever they want, and they can become whomever they aspire to be while achieving goals through hard work, they no longer want to use others or take their goods—or at least not as much as they did in the past.

Love grew ever brighter when the weavers got together to work and have fun. So it came to be that men were no longer trophies sought by women, as they had been in the past. Now when a man was truly loved, he was given her thoughts—not just an ounce of her time. The tribal elders and others could not believe the changes that quickly came to be as a result.

Since Mandy was not around as much as when she established the compound, the men came to love the weavers, potters, scribes, and others without the need to control their lives. This was truly the greatest blessing bestowed by God and moving through The Ascended Maya. Many men never noticed it, but the women did.

Working on what glorified Earth was always first. Their art was such that each and every artisan had to take time out to think about the Divine—not just about the lines and designs. Each day the ways of The Church were renounced less and less, and the depth of meditation grew deeper and more pronounced. It was not until the priest announced that the chapel was the only place the Maya could safely meditate in good faith, knowing that no evil could enter into them while there, that the women and some men returned to sit and pray in the pews every day. It did not take waves of energy to bless the priest and what he did, but The Holy Spirit helped him build a better school within a year.

Doing business in other countries was not sought initially, but it helped news spread to those living within the tombs of time and unaware that the time had arrived when their group must move on or be left behind again. The Maya were able to thrive in any land at any time, but only the few left in the region of the Yucatan through Guatemala were recognized by the world as Maya now. It appeared that The Ancient Ones were stating in various ways that this was not good. They wanted more work created to help those able to ascend at the end of this time to come together now.

The Ancient Ones asked: "Is the recognized tribe able to pretend it has only one leader at a time?" It had never been acknowledged that any one person was able to lead the Maya in 'modern' times. In fact, this harks back to when the last group of Maya rose into time. Those left behind were not kind. They were not wise. They had to live and survive until the next time the tribe could meet and the ascent begin again—only this time without a royal leader to guide them. They had believed that they would suffer much until the next great day came to be because no leaders stayed behind the last time. The Maya left on Earth have no royal leaders to preside over them now and announce when it is time to ascend again. Instead, they must work on their own at home to get in line to ascend in Spirit—possibly link with others who are ready to go home, too.

One afternoon, soon after these grand revelations first appeared, Mandy finished making huge exhalations and began dancing with her arms lifted high. She rose above the ground where she had been standing. Surprising Mandy even more than that, Wanda lifted her crutch above her head and stood easily on one leg without any support. Wanda was finally ready for a new leg!

☼ Chapter Four

When the teachers and weavers gathered in the inner room of the loom wing to work together on a new way to help The Maya of this tribe, as well as those lost in time, they were not consciously aware that this was why they were there. After all, it took a lot of work by everyone to make it to this point on Earth. So many were into change and what needed to be done, and how to win, and so on…without stopping to size up what might be growing out of bounds now or in need of being trimmed a bit.

The men and women within this group most likely to plan ahead were usually American by birth, but stuck in a rut. Since the group most likely to understand the project was unhappy with their lives since birth, they overlooked what they could do together now. As the room overflowed with what might be done or should be done, and who could raise others' esteem, their combined power and energy dipped to a point where The Maya did not wish to participate—and then it suddenly spiked higher. Why?

Everyone present stood at attention as Mandy stepped up to the altar recently constructed in the center of the room. Everyone could easily hear her without altering her vibrational levels via a microphone. They were ready for her, but she was unwilling to give away anything about her present mission—at least not yet. When they grew restless and fretful, Mandy suggested everyone meditate and think straight. No one admired her request, but some tried it anyway. Those few found themselves immediately in a time line that was easily described as Today, followed by another day and several weeks ahead, but no future beyond the farthest point in that line.

As the meditators within the group *awoke*, they excitedly spewed their news and views. Several others then tried to meditate, too, but were unable to assume the inner calm needed to experience visions in time. Those who had meditated for just a few minutes felt so refreshed and recreated that they enthused that it was the best time ever spent in this kind of work, and they wanted to do it again. Mandy said nothing to them.

Working within this group's atmosphere, Mandy spotted only a few who could help her lure the ancient ones out of space and entice them to come back and work with her thereafter here. She felt it was not worth the *Ancients'* time if only one or two in the group would benefit from the work. So she dropped the line she normally used when approaching The Ascended Maya and sat still waiting for everyone else to become quiet within once again.

When everyone finished talking about 'their special moment,' Mandy laughed as if she just heard a funny story. No one else present could laugh as she did, but some tried to imitate her now, while others wondered why she mocked them. The sound she intoned rose and then fell in a regular pace or beat as it celebrated her faith.

Suddenly aware that most present did not know why she was laughing, or that it was necessary if they were to also follow a line into time, Mandy stopped laughing and explained the lungs' capacity to uplift the physical body. She told them all to open their mouths and lungs as far as possible and hold that expansion before letting the lungs collapse in a slow, deep exhalation. She talked quickly about breathing. Now very interested in what they were able to believe at this stage, Mandy demonstrated several times how much energy was lost if you never adequately exercised your lungs. She did not mention again the need to meditate and go within to find time, instead she spoke for exactly one hour and a half before returning to her own home to be alone.

♓ ♓

In the weeks and months that followed this event, many of the women and some of the men present were challenged by the fact that they could not achieve that *special moment* again. They wondered why, even argued about it behind Mandy's back because they believed she had lied to them and practiced magic. Why else would they not be able to easily replicate that experience again?

Without much sense used, and no idea of the disrespect they incited, these few women and one man refused to talk about what they did to get into that space. Instead, they said Mandy was able to do it too easily—especially when she was in front of a crowd—for it to possibly be 'the real thing' and what they had experienced then. They accused Mandy of abandoning many of The Maya within the various clans who had taught her everything she knew. Values drifted and Mandy became suspicious of what these would-be shamans were doing with her work during their idle fascination with what was easily achieved by anyone practicing their intuitive interests frequently.

Whenever Mandy returned from any trip, she unpacked and settled in as if she would never leave them again. This never came to be because within seconds—on any given day, she might have to leave immediately to minister to one who lived far from her compound. No one knew how she became aware of being needed—perhaps unaware of the cellular phone hidden in the folds of her gown, and she chose not to enlighten the talkers very often. If they wanted to believe that The Holy Ghost worked in the dark, she did not try to stop them. After all, it was not her place to tell others what to believe or practice in these last days.

In the minds of some training to become great weavers, the source of mystery surrounding Mandy stemmed from the man she spent so much time with then—Jorge. He was seldom seen locally, but when he did appear, all the American women ran to see him. They described him as coming out of a dream they had had about a soul mate. He took little notice of most of his female fans, but kept close to the men who seemed to know a lot about the women working around them—as well as their achievements.

If Mandy was bothered by the unwillingness of some women and a few men to meditate in order to more fully develop their intuitive connections within, she did not normally show it. However, she did begin dropping such women from her study groups and often dropped in unannounced during the week to look at their work.

The weavers were not averse to showing off their work, but only a few regularly received compliments from Mandy, the elders, or Jorge. Most could not understand why they were not praised when their work was great and getting even better, but the initiated of the clan knew what Mandy and the elders were looking for and that they would compliment more and more until all the work was under their control.

As weeks pass into months and years arrive unbidden in time, the people within any tribe age and grow in grace or fade in faith. This guild became greater with the influx of power generated by new weavers producing fabric whenever Mandy needed to channel The Mayan Teachers of Time. Since these sessions were unannounced, very few could boast that they knew when The Ancient Ones would arrive in this space.

⋈ ⋈

Over the course of several months' work, according to an internal plan they had developed privately, certain Mayan elders decided to hold a feast and invite only a few of those who could work with them as well as with the weavers. They did not expect much to happen immediately, but news exploded over the world that Mayan Teachers were going to introduce a new kind of work that would more easily explain the final days. When asked to comment on this broadcast, the elders refrained from boasting and said that it would be just another meeting—nothing new. Then no one believed them!

At times during the days surrounding this celebration the trees growing around the pavilion bent dramatically due to the pressure of high winds. According to elders, these trees sensed things and delivered messages to them, thus eliminating the need to get news by more traditional routes. This is how The Maya learned that an Essene elder was unhappy that he had not been asked to contribute to the ceremony, and he had anticipated doing so. Who could still channel the Essenes? They asked the trees.

When Mandy came back to the family she had created in this estate, she walked over to Wanda's place and asked her to believe that the new leg being created would be superb, even though it needed more work. The head weaver was not angry about the delay, but her disappointment was evident in the way she later stood at her door and weakly waved away anyone who wanted to visit or even called out a greeting to her.

Mandy did not wish to upset Wanda or her friends from both ends of the continent, but she knew the ultimate fit would be such that the leg would appear and react as if it had grown in place of the amputated limb, but only when the time was right. This was not magic! It was what any healer could produce if the bone was not good. The bone of contention between them now was about what needed to be reduced or eliminated within the woman's home—not within her body.

As she approached Wanda, Mandy carefully examined her body as she stood right of her front door. She could see that what remained of her right leg had not shrunk at all. She also saw immediately that her friend's body was as firm and strong as the day it was hacked at by would-be butchers and lost its main stay. Wanda lacked the ability to walk easily without her right leg, but her balance was much improved. Her spine was as straight as it had ever been in this time, and because of this, Mandy knew Wanda could channel The Maya of Ancient Times, too, if ever such a need arose. She said nothing about it to Wanda then, but became even more determined to help this woman, who was now her closest ally in this work, to settle down within the tribe and create beauty within the eyes of everyone in this time.

⋈ ⋈

As beautiful weaving processes continued to develop and expand, many seemed to lose interest in keeping up with the work that Mandy insisted had to be done while still on Earth. They got into what *they* wanted to do—not what was good for their guild or clan. Some even left the country, but what Mandy did not suspect was that a group of her own kind would try to undermine her from time-to-time.

The weavers worked on patterns in time, but some worked on only one article and used only one pattern. That was all they did because someone else completed their work. This produced dissension in people who were used to working their own patterns and designs through to the end of that line.

With artisans working within—discovering that their hearts could fill with love over and over again and were able to give more then ever before, the weavers' guild began work on developing patterns that could easily be replicated whenever they had to produce woven art quickly. One pattern was to be the logo of their guild, but not that obvious. It was to stay hidden among the threads so only those who were aware of it being woven into the fabric would discover it later. Then if anyone tried to counterfeit their work, they would know it immediately because the logo had been added and the pattern overworked—not done only once by the last master weaver in that line.

Weaving was not the only business moving forward in the compound, but it occupied the minds of most of the residents to the extent that they did not notice what Mandy did or where she went. What everyone did know was that Mandy did not permit ambulances to enter the compound with sirens howling. She also insisted that the dead, dying, and others who came from many places to confer with her be admitted to a place separate and away from where the artists and weavers worked all day. She insisted on this because it helped everyone remain calm and able to go within to see what had to be done to stay in business for another year.

The weavers often saw the sick, the decrepit, and the dying who had fallen apart in time disappear within a week—happy and content—not upset. They witnessed this even as they continued to pine over their own lovers, clothes, or even cosmetics—if immature. Such life and death matters did not erase the need of some to gripe when not recognized as great by those higher up the ladder of textile designers. In fact, it seemed to increase anxiety among some who had never worried about their careers and personal affairs in the past.

As time wove its web, deceit crept into their daily work. Weeks passed with no one complaining that Mandy did not listen to them enough. Why? She learned how to symbolize what was going on in each mind and heart in a meeting. She could now sit and say one word to each person and watch them flip out over it. It was obvious she knew what she was doing, but how she did it was the continual worry of those trying to undergo a transformation that would enable them to lead the present Maya tribe and take on the Mexican government at the same time. Mandy was not unaware of their efforts, but unconcerned about it now.

What if people attacked and killed a Mayan man and a fight arose over it? It was not that Mandy was disinterested in what might play out after such a drama, rather that she was aware the government would soon quit working on 'the Maya problem' and would soon let them all alone. Why? The Maya were better off than those who lived in other states and daily wanted money from their government. The Maya were able to grow and prosper as they worked at home creating what tourists, as well as many others using the internet, wanted for personal use or to retail in stores and on E-Bay. Commercial web sites now advertised the plight of the Maya better than their previous bloody, political struggles had ever been able to accomplish.

Visitors noticed how the Maya lived and how happy they were to give back to anyone asking about them, thus the world discovered that their art was spiritual in nature and the work of these Maya was linked to time. How did they work and what did they believe? Tourists and others asked so many questions that it became imperative for Mandy to make contact once again with her artistic friends in Los Angeles and New York, as well as those who write legends in space. She invited them all to come to her place for a meeting with The Maya.

⊁ ⊁

Within a few months of the day the first group sat and let the door to space close without attempting to use it for more than a mere stepping stone, Mandy related her version of what lay ahead for the tribe. She talked to each and every man and woman who asked if there was something he or she could do for the tribe. She gave each of them many insights, in order to get them even more interested in improving their work, so a healing could take place that enabled some present to move into the next world. None of these intervention efforts was enough to stop those who plotted against Mandy or her work in order to get her to leave the compound.

Working hard, doing what you know has to be done is never easy, but when you attempt to change the way the Maya of today work, while rearranging the way the public perceives them to be, it is extremely difficult and takes longer to get through the really tough stuff of life. There is a sinew or tissue that runs throughout works of art that is not easy to expand or make more elastic over and over again.

Mandy's plan was to help each woman and man master the easy stuff of everyday life so as to be able to do something for the universe once they saw their own work through to the end. However, that was not the way some weavers expected her to behave. They became discontent and advertised that she was broke because she never charged people enough for her work and she never promoted return visits from those seeking private consultations or laying on hands to heal, as she purportedly did in the privacy of her home or office.

When the subject of money came up in conversation, Mandy immediately pleaded for money from that group or person. This ploy enabled her to downplay money all day. No one wanted to hear her lament about expenses or pay more to be allowed to associate with the weavers and such to learn their trades, so critics learned to keep quiet when the subject of work or wealth came up in a meeting.

Whatever was going to happen happened! Mandy lived in a time warp that enabled her to do almost anything she dreamed about, while Wanda worked very hard to learn how to get along with only one arm when walking or standing long. Wanda did not quarrel with anyone about how long it took to get her artificial leg, but she did wonder why Mandy had not ordered one from The States and have it delivered immediately.

As Mandy saw it, the day would come when Wanda would no longer be afraid, which in turn would produce the group and mood needed to give her a new leg. She knew it would happen soon, but not until everyone in her group was able to leap into space. She had to get the group moving soon!

☼ CHAPTER FIVE

Seeing the police car sitting in the driveway, Mandy surmised that someone had tried to raid them again on the sly and would now be unhappy having found that nothing illegal was going on here. Thus she was not prepared to discover that the Mayor of the nearby town was visiting and had confiscated their Police Lieutenant and taken him away from his duties in order to escort him to see Mandy.

The Mayor shouted, without bothering to salute Mandy as everyone in his town did before asking her any questions on any given subject, "What do you expect to gain from all this work with the women of this village?"

The Mayor was rude in a way that implied he was afraid, or so Mandy thought. He was unaware that she could stare deeply into men such as him and determine what they thought and would become. Shaking hands, she asked about his plan, without moving toward him or the Lieutenant, who commanded a local band of roguish policemen. Neither man smiled now. The Lieutenant was definitely on full alert, not about to blurt out his business to her.

In a stentorian voice befitting a campaign stump, the Mayor announced, "I came to see if anyone is doing work here that they are not being paid for. It's rumored everywhere around here that you are exploiting our villagers. What do you have to say to that?" He looked down his nose, over his reading half-glasses, at Mandy.

Although Mandy was amused, she did not laugh. Instead, she addressed the policeman with great respect, taking him off guard just long enough to let him know how offensive and wrong his boss in this town was now. The officer laughed, but the Mayor did not notice because Mandy took the papers out of his hand right then. While she looked them over, she continued to maintain her silence toward him—not speaking even when he pointed out specific articles of his agenda that declared war on her and her entire compound. When she finished reading, she sniffed the air and said loud enough that the women and men standing around them could hear, "What is that smell? I think I detect the leaf of the cocoa plant. Do you not notice it, too?"

Immediately the policeman looked at the Mayor and shook his head in disbelief. 'What is going on here?' he transmitted intuitively to Mandy and her group. They all knew instinctively that he regretted having been so ill used. Without much thought, he stepped in front of the Mayor and said, "What do you have in your pocket, Senor Mayor? Are you trying to plant a cocoa leaf here?"

The Mayor stared at him, then gulped as if there was not enough air to support his thoughts. He plunged his index finger into the pocket of his shirt and something exploded with a powerful energy. The cocoa leaf is unique in that when squeezed it releases its energy and implants in fingers a smell that cannot be washed away in a day. The mayor did not know this and thought that by wrapping the solid leaf very carefully in a tissue that the police and Mandy would never know what he planned to do when their backs were turned away from him.

Since everyone in the compound used processed cocoa in drinks and food, no one noticed the faint rush to the touch, either. Everyone appeared to be amazed as Mandy reached over and pulled the Mayor's hand toward her and then opened his fingers with a gentle touch. He seemed unable to withstand her command, but was nevertheless upset that his plot had been ruined and she was not the one who looked dumb or corrupt now.

The Lieutenant called the Chief of Police, who arrived with several others from the closest village to look over the situation as described over the phone. Each officer knew it had been intended to be a mockery of justice, but it would be advertised as a mistake on the Mayor's part that might end one of their careers if he was not provided with some way to escape this unexpected entanglement. No one wanted to point a finger at such a man with so much power, since his only crime seemed to be his inability to adjust to people around him becoming financially independent. Ironically, because the Mayor was given an easy way out that day, he lost his power over the law. Anyone who assumed then that he was beaten by Mandy never forgot how easily all was lost for that politician.

As the day drifted into night, the weavers, scribes, and artists gathered to praise Mandy for her amazing grace under fire from so many powerful people, which resulted in yet another stunning victory for their tribal work. Since no one there read what a crime reporter wrote about the encounter, they could not imagine why so many politicians soon started campaigning that something must be done for the Mayan tribes and that Mandy was the perfect ambassador to help them out now. It was not what anyone expected, but it was accomplished without a single gun being brandished by anyone.

The local town now admired Mandy and Jorge and everything they created, as well as what the women made and sold in the zocalo every Sunday. This unexpected outcome was truly amazing to everyone in the compound and demonstrated that luck has two sides—one you can see and one that just happens when you are in touch with your intuition much.

♓ ♓

Within the day and night that followed that fight and the flight of the Mayor, the Mayan elders prepared for a meeting to be held in the inner rooms of the compound. It was their intention to encourage others to follow their art. Mandy was proud of the men who could sense what was needed now and did not have to have things spelled out about how much artists, weavers, and scribes could be paid now. She trusted them and they knew she could *see*, which made everything as good as it could be.

When the scribes arrived at the weavers' compound, Mandy noticed that only one of them wrote down the words while the rest of the men mumbled a repetition of each sentence, as if memorizing what was said. The oral history of the tribe had survived many disasters when the written word had been erased or defaced, so they spared no efforts in recording work in as many ways as possible today. However, they were unwilling to use computers to record what came through the veil for them now.

Chatting first with the scribes and then meeting with the dyers who had gathered together in the aisles to talk about the colors they had chosen to use in certain ways and on certain days was interesting to Mandy and Jorge, since it was next on their agenda. But several of the elders who accompanied them as they walked about the room acted as if such talk was of little worth and of even less interest to them. It then became obvious that Mandy had a lot of plans in mind and wished to lead them through the next few years without any apparent envy or jealousy between the men or toward the women, but some were still unwilling to let it happen.

Those guilty of conspiracy within any group are usually the ones who stand or sit in the middle of the row and mumble under their breath, or so Mandy believed then. She watched the way their backs swayed and knew which man would say nothing in her defense again and which man was determined to make a change in the way he envisioned the tribal work. All of this was accomplished as she wandered about and chatted with everyone. She now knew who would attempt to upset her work and when.

Mandy made good use of her central life plan and ended it successfully, but working in the first person was no longer easy for her. She had to use all her earthly gifts to sense what could go wrong and react to it before anything adverse actually happened. Without a word to Jorge or the others who stood with her long before this evening came to be, Mandy moved across the room and took a seat in the deepest section of the stage apron in order to watch the audience unobserved. At first the men watched whatever she did, but soon forgot her. The women standing along the walls were not friendly, judging from their frowns and folded arms, but Mandy knew them to be fair—and always in her corner when she needed them. These women were afraid of the men, so they often stood rather than taking seats, so as not to be cornered or picked upon. Mandy, however, never worried about the men when it came to whether or not to select a chair within their area.

When the dyers demonstrated their deep purple shades, Mandy was sure the main perpetrator or traitor would do something strange right then, because he strained his lips into a grimace and spat on the floor near several women who were standing aloof from their group. They were unaware that he was near until he spat. One woman jumped at the splat and looked about her as if scared, while his face registered smug satisfaction at her reaction. His thoughts seemed to then dart into another line, but Mandy followed him easily since he was a man without a great mind and his spine was as crooked as a weak sapling often buffeted by strong winds. This elder did not yet understand that his stance was no longer one of pride and righteousness within the tribe, but that of a malcontent, thus a danger to everyone. The other men intently watched him now.

Working in the second person within the group took much patience. Mandy waited to see what might come to her naturally when she looked into time and there it was. This man was not the rightful heir to the rulership he wished to achieve among The Maya. He was not well liked because he had been given his work when quite young, thus not seen to be as 'Maya' as many others in the tribe. Mayan wisdom was not what he chose. More often than not, he inserted words to paraphrase what The Maya might say about any given situation on any given day. He was truly into ego and tried to make sure no one knew by attacking everyone else about *their* pride.

The business of the tribe was making slow progress when a man shook his finger at a little girl standing next to her mother near the back of the room. He said with brutal frankness, "You should be home in bed, instead of standing here watching your mother and her friends ignore their husbands and families and homes." His anger infected only one other man, and proved to be deleterious when it reached others seated nearby. He was unaware that he was not wanted anywhere after that night, because he was deemed to be from another tribe and not Maya.

When the Maya of today and The Maya of other times meet on any given street, they shake not a hand but use a signal that completes the relay of materials given from different worlds. Many proved to be unequal to that task and were unable to fully comprehend what they were to do as men, so the women laughed at them. Women often used laughter to keep men at bay or make them upset and afraid. For that and several other reasons, the men straightened up in their chairs immediately and left the women alone. They even clapped for the ladies in black who were truly brilliant in their selection of patterns, but those ladies never opened their minds to them again after that night. Fools once discovered seldom have any power over the wise again.

The tribe was able to improvise and make a few wise to what they planned to do with the weavers and the scribes, but the artists were unable to provide others with any ideas about what they could accomplish in any given day or two. Art is not something you can take to the bank and arrange for financial backing based on when it will be done. If you can do that, you are dealing with craftsmen and not artists.

Quickly the crew of engineers who pursued design lines as well as power and such were able to trip up all who were unequal to the tasks at hand, so everyone could clap their hands and stand erect. The power was completely turned off when Mandy stood up again and raised her hand. She would not burn for saying what she had learned, if she blurted it out now.

Standing, Mandy raised her right hand and arm toward the ceiling. All the men understood she was about to channel someone walking among them now. The energy level required to do that had been achieved—finally! Mandy speaking: "I see the need for men and women to work in a way that is not seen today. You will create a pattern of beauty. You will all know what to do, but only what *you* do will matter to You. Our art will be so unique that many will want to collect it from the very first week, but you will never give up perfecting the art and making it better. Do not let money ever again harm this tribe!"

Now without a word, some women looked down at their feet—squirming just a bit. They had sold more than ever before and decided to hide some of the money on the side—not share it with the tribe. The old ways were slow to die, but this tribe had to survive and do things the old way if it was to ever again be able to produce a pyramid great enough to end this time and move into the new line. Suddenly, they all saw it!

Working out a kink in her spine, Mandy squirmed and thrust her left hand high. She moved from side to side without a word until a man in the midst of the group yelled: "Get on with it! What do you think you're doing?"

The hushed silence was enough to inform this unfortunate man that he would never again be permitted into the inner sanctum of this guildhall—never again hear things before others about what would be grown or known or done within and with the outside world. He immediately regretted his impatience, but never again was able to realize how little time he gave up to pay for this lack of trust. He was dead without ceremony within ten years and never realized that his fate was sealed the night he displayed such rude behavior and mocked someone who spoke for The Ascended Maya.

The truth of the inner group's purpose rose and fell without anyone able to stop the rush of energy to the outer circle. Mandy was not upset by it, but Jorge was furious that what should have happened that night was aborted due to the less fortunate. He never saw that some people were so human they could not give up greed and envy as he did, instead he saw them as lacking in ability to love.

Jorge's voice echoed through to the time zone Mandy was preparing for everyone present to walk into with her now, but she heard nothing more than a hushed request from someone on the other side who wanted to talk to Jorge—not her. The group remained attentive as Jorge thundered down the line that everyone should stay exactly as they were or the mood would be broken and nothing left for them to use. The Maya and all the men and women of the tribe sat in silence; the rest of the group followed suit because they did not know what else to do.

Forgetting that the power had shifted from where it had been when they started, Mandy shifted and her hand was immediately burned by energy not of Earth. She cried out in pain and dropped her hand to the floor, igniting the stage. The fire was quickly put out by the Mayan elders who had seen this sort of thing before.

As Mandy checked out the burn on her hand, others came forward to examine her more closely then. To them she was not the same woman they had named Teacher of The Maya. She was now seen as greater, and thus her mundane chores were over. She would walk in the way of The Lord forever—as far as these elders could see now. Mandy was immediately given the highest status of Mayan elder by those gathered to work on the designs of the tribe now. She never again sat without everyone else present sitting, too.

Mandy's world was circumvented by a life she was not prepared to accept when she first moved into this area, but today she was going to be wise—whether she believed it or not! The tribe moved to make Mandy head of everything they intended to do with other countries—and they would stop the feuds. She knew about the feuds, but had no idea what they wanted her to take over since she was now cold and unable to think.

⌬ ⌬

Over the next few days mundane tribal work came and went without anyone asking Mandy what they individually had to do with it. This provided her great relief, and she slowly felt totally released from the spell she had been under since that great meeting when the power of God was given to her by The Ascended Maya.

Since The Maya of old were unable to do anything new with people who were unable to view time and move into it now, Mandy, Jorge, and several others constantly helped this guild move into a better state of mind. The work they did at home was never enough for some, and definitely not what was wanted by one.

The youngest Mayan elder hated Mandy! He was not about to change his mind because she had been elevated in the tribe above him once again. He was unwilling to accept that she could walk into the veil and out again without any harm done to her mind or body. He could not admire her because she was unlike any other woman he knew, so he aspired to retire her before she was hired because he saw her as a threat to his manhood. She would not take 'no' for an answer and refused to yield precedence to him simply because he was a man. This was not the best time to work around him, but Mandy easily resisted any interest in him and was equal to anything he might try to do to break into her mind over time.

The Maya are not a tribe as you might see in the World of Today. They are greater, wiser, and more into what is worldly than ever before. Yes, the world is not what you think it is. This world is created by scribes, artists, and gifted people everywhere. The tribes identify themselves with uniforms and such that weavers are delighted to create and give away. These weavers are not seen as powerful women, but they are.

Within each woman is a totem that works for her. That totem may be a flower or the power of an animal that is not very big or tall, but most weavers use their intuitive source and follow their Spiritual Guides to the other side before creating an inch or two on any loom. They know how to pray, but they do not use their totems every day.

♓   ♓

While walking through the gate at the end of the last day of healing rites, Mandy wanted to run away and never come back to stay with the weavers again. She was just about to flee down the road when suddenly confronted with Wanda and her best friend, Jeanne, as well as a few weavers walking with them toward the Guardians who lived in the ancient trees surrounding the compound. She waved and then realized that Wanda's leg was still not what it must be if she is to end all thoughts of loss and misery and toss in her lot with The Maya of thought.

When Wanda was close enough to whisper what Mandy thought, she said softly, "What is happening with my new leg? I thought it would be here by today."

Forcing herself to smile, Mandy said, "It's going to be a surprise, Wanda, but only if you're patient." Intuitively she was aware that the hour to give the leg enough room to move into the new prosthesis had to be soon, because her own leg ached now—which was a sign that it was time.

Wanda spoke with a wince, as if her leg pinched and refused to move another step or two, "I'm patient. I'm patient. What weaver isn't patient?"

As if talking to one of the other sages who knew in an instant what she would do, Mandy said, "I see you've found the spot that needs adjustment now. Let me massage the stump and see when the angels will deliver your new leg."

Wanda knew what she would do and Mandy suddenly realized this woman was not just a weaver, and Jeanne was not just a scribe! Both of them knew what to do when it was time to leave this world alone—and to grow or not. She made no movement as she examined the stump of Wanda's leg, but the leg seemed to move toward her of its own accord—rotating in a direction that followed the sun. Then it changed direction and turned the other way. Only a few witnessed this since most of the group were headed toward the dining hall—eager to eat dinner. The impatient diners never again felt quite as happy as those who stayed and witnessed the miracle. Due to their lack of interest, they never passed along what passed between Mandy and the leader of the weavers then.

Without any thought, Mandy motioned for Wanda to sit down on a tree stump left in place for anyone who felt the need to seek out the Guardians on any given day or wished to rest there. Not everyone present was able to see the pain Wanda felt then, but it was sensed in other ways by her family of weavers, as well as the scribes who had gathered to see what was happening outside the compound.

Suddenly all the weavers present began to hum, later they said they could not do otherwise. The scribes opened their minds wide to read lines of poetry and study works of art they would write in time. The work of one artist was brought out and put on display, as if it were the reason they were all standing under the ciba trees. The ruse was arranged so others would not stop and listen to them as they prayed over Wanda's leg then. Once again it worked well enough to confuse many men, but not all of them.

Without thought as to where the prosthesis might be, Mandy called to a man at the back of the group to go and get the mail. He was not happy to be told to do a child's errand, but headed toward the gate—unafraid to grumble all the way. When he opened the gate he was shocked to find a man in a postal uniform standing there ready to announce his presence. He was unable to speak before the postman pulled the gate open wider and handed him a huge box that contained the leg ordered from Chicago over a month or two before. Everyone was impressed, but not as much as he was. Never again would this lazy man be able to say he did not believe in The Ascended Maya, which is to say, he changed completely then and remains changed today.

The new leg was carefully examined by each and every one who could fit under the lofty branches of the tall tree that was central to this process. The tree shed one leaf—and then ten, until each person standing beneath it had a leaf to hold and wave in the breeze. When the breeze they created circulated through the leaves without seeming to make a sound, the weavers' humming stopped. The women's waving arms and men's clenched fists were no cause for alarm then, but when the leg was passed around so each weaver could pray and treat it with respect, something magical happened that caused many to wonder about it years later. Their prayers helped this beautifully molded prosthesis blend in and mend what remained of Wanda's mangled leg.

Wanda's leg was never again put on display. She wore long dresses and pants only after that. She could do whatever she wanted and no one said wearing pants was disrespectful to their men. Now able to wear pants while weaving, the group that studied and worked with her was granted dispensation and allowed to do the same. Thus, another miracle occurred—the Mayan women were able to do more weaving than ever before, without losing their femininity, and able to work better than any man they knew who also worked on the floor looms. Wearing trousers did not block their creativity! It gave the weavers a sense of security that they could work like men if they wanted to do so. The women never, of course, gave up the feminine side of life. Why would they? They have it made today!

☼ CHAPTER SIX

The weavers were no longer able to contain their work to a day or two a week as they did when the compound opened, so The Teachers offered to show them how to put down on paper or in the computer the patterns and weaves they did each day or wanted to save or do next. Initially, most refused to comply; but once they learned how to download power in an hour, they were ready to review what others did and they could use—once they were assured they would not forget designs over time.

The Teacher who came through in Spirit was channeled by a woman who was not a Maya this time, so the natives resisted accepting her direction initially, until most of them realized that whether or not you live as a Maya today, or in another time, means nothing on the other side of time. They could not fully comprehend the enormity of this work until it was interpreted by a Scribe—a woman or man able to handle such work or words with integrity, and let others decide what to do with it as a group of individuals.

The weavers' work greatly improved by the time their guild held its first public viewing of new designs, colors, and weaves, as well as what the tribe previously had never revealed to those they felt were not actually real now. Yes, Maya in the past had been all about tribal rights! They were not immune to negative words used in high places judging their minds and their daily lives, so they always and in all ways hid whatever they held sacred from outsiders.

"After all," as Mandy explained, "how many times have the Mayan tribes been raided over time in attempts to make them appear less than what they are, and how many times did they have to put everything back into shape and remember what had been tossed out or into a fire?" The tribe's thoughts were not something Mandy shared with outsiders, but she often received messages as if they were free to everyone, everywhere.

Those who wanted to learn more than what was given to them as spiritual gifts completed their duties easily every day, but those not blessed since birth with much spiritual work had to learn all such skills and it took time. Once proficient, such students often felt that they did not need to learn anything new ever again! They were satisfied with what they had mastered in the past, but Mandy and Wanda and others were there to teach weaving as a spiritual art and refused to let them stop and not develop further.

Master weavers could command assistants to lend a helping hand with their work, but only after they, too, worked as laborers in the compound. If an artist did whatever she or he did best and never pressed others to help them with their work, they did not have to offer to help others. However, many artists supported the kitchen staff more than anyone had ever expected would happen. Why? Mandy revealed that many artists came through the veil from lives where they did not have enough to eat. That kind of 'life' experience is something you cannot explain away today, even though some try. So artists starved for food and drink worked behind the scenes to gain more rations—unwilling to appear greedy or gluttonous to others.

As separate clans dwindled when their craftsmen vied for supremacy and acceptance of tribal plans, the weavers pulled their work together in a pool large enough to gain full acceptance of Mayan art in the outside world. They shied away from men and women installed in high places within their countries, but had no wish to secede or run away from paying taxes when due. They did, however, want to discover for themselves if everyone was as rude and ignorant as their central government's agents when they visited and inspected Mayan products and working conditions.

⋈ ⋈

The local tribe was not as into The New Age Movement as many tourists who flocked to visit this latest group of artists thought them to be. So many visiting now wished to stay, so 'Settlers' were temporarily housed in a block of homes in a nearby town. Artists working within this latest group did not produce work as the Maya of old did, rather as admirers and copy artists who wish to make a living reproducing ancient art and relics.

The weavers reluctantly welcomed tourists and other outsiders into their studios, but were unsure about the new breed of artisans with their skillful use of computers that enabled them to detail any piece of art. Were they pure enough of heart to produce spiritual art or even copy such work? They hesitated to let them into their lives now because of what their teachers had said in the past about such seekers and their art.

Words left within minds are unlikely to define all that can be done within a short time, but they can guide a generation to the next time. What these Maya remembered most readily from past lives were patterns—and generations of laughter. They could easily see pictures in trees and clouds, as well as whatever was on earth, but were unwilling to teach strangers about such things—or how to laugh.

Mandy was not in need of help from this compound, which was readily seen by elders and others working closely with her, but her *power* continued to mystify many who lived in communities surrounding them now. Time denied Mandy many things that she would normally have done as a human being, but she was compensated by being able to see into the future and know when she would need help and who would provide it, and usually it was the men of the tribe who came forward to help her then.

Why did men enter her work when she was there to help Mayan women of all time? It is no exaggeration to say that many men are not wise to the minds they use daily and accept as inferior in certain ways, but none of them wants to give away his *gifts* to someone who may never use them. Women, however, are often spotted doing very little with their spiritual *gifts*—apparently not equal to the task of meditating and spending days studying their dreams as done in the past. Thus, it was the men who came forward to help Mandy more and more while the women lingered in self-depressing thoughts and confusion. Power-filled men of the Maya wanted to teach their women how to pray, fully aware that this had to be handled by someone not exactly like them, because they expected someone to return from the past and appear as a woman of modern times.

⋈ ⋈

As Mandy continued to grow in her own way, others created myths and stories about her arrival among the Maya, based on where they were when they first met her. She was not surprised by this, but disliked being lied about or not given a chance to defend what she did or planned to do one day. Her own man was not the same as she had thought he might turn out to be, so she left him and joined a clan. She accepted that her lot in life was to teach and not be led by the nose to the trough of slop provided by governments created by men—and even some tribes. She was not a commodity and she taught that concept, along with the wisdom of the ancient sages, thus it was no wonder to her that Mayan elders were the first to consort with her when she came to stay in Mexico and set out to learn their ways.

Usually no one very different from a group's members—especially if not producing a sizeable income—is wanted, but Mandy's reception by the Maya was warm from the very beginning. At first she could not converse constantly as they did. Her English was similar to what she used daily when a wealthy New York stockbroker, but veered into various archaic Mayan dialects that even some elders could not remember. When that happened, she was 'trance relating' with them. According to Mandy's teachers, this *gift of tongues* comes directly from The Holy Spirit and was the first thing she wished she could explain, but *interpreting* was not her calling. It was up to others, interpreters, teachers, and elders, to explain her work today.

Working with Mandy, Jorge and Wanda, as well as master weavers was not so grand that Guild members would not find fault with them, especially when work was returned to them late in their day. They often argued about who caused delays, but never placed any blame on those who worked hard. This guild of weavers was one of great power! It gave off an aura of richness unseen in recent Mayan history. The men of the tribe felt invigorated by this success, and the women strived to be as equal to the work as Mandy saw them able to be.

Time changed and no one alive could look back without laughing. As each artist worked diligently on her share of weaving that must be done beautifully if the tribe was to sell it easily, the women laughed—a lot. Their laughter was usually high pitched, but at times erupted from deep within their throats. These trills and melodic sounds thrilled any man able to listen in on the weavers' conversations, but few ever got that close because men were forbidden inside the women's compound. The men never complained about being excluded from this inner sanctum—once they were included and spent a few days fetching materials and taking orders from Wanda and the others.

⋈ ⋈

As time disappeared and work appeared that was equal to that of the finest machines ever created by the human brain, workers began to realize that change was in their hands. For perhaps the first time, they were able to plan their own lives. Since the pain of hunger was not to be seen again in their land, they were able to place a few dimes away for education and recreation.

Within a month of the day Wanda returned to easy standing, the tribe gave her a salute on the side. She was given the recipe for a familiar dye. Overcome with gratitude, and humiliated to find she could not do anything like it for them, she cried. The length of this session was such that many men thought she was a broken woman, unworthy of the task of teaching Mayan weavers, but when she opened to them at the end of the day and spoke, no one ever again doubted that she was Maya. Here is what she said to them then:

"I am Maya! I have arrived from a time and space where the artist is not disgraced with material that is shoddy and not fit for use… I am here to help you produce the same kind of life you had in that time and place where you were able to rise to new heights… It is time to rise! You will find that my hands are not tied. I am able to stand up and salute you with my work, but it will be visions that I see that will help you do what you alone know how to do at home to prepare for the ascension everywhere…"

The men revealed to no one not present what was said, but it was apparently enough to confirm that Wanda was heaven-sent, and not merely pretending to be one of them. She was indeed Maya! They never again doubted her position among the teachers and weavers, but she was still given challenges usually not given to Mayan men. Discrimination masked as prejudice is something that cannot be changed in some minds until something grand comes into view.

As Wanda's visions grew, she was able to see into other countries and know what many of the foreign leaders planned to do and how they would move. For this reason, she did not speak of anything she saw until she first talked to Mandy or Jorge about it. Her own life was such that she despised reading newspapers and following TV news and gossip, so she did not have the proper background to evaluate these views and use them or let them go. She was able, however, to provide Jorge with much knowledge that he used daily while working within the community of men.

Mandy received profound insights all the time and often wished that she did not, because they were very unsettling to her mind. She mulled them over and only then said whatever came out. At the last session of the elders, she said, "Politics is not something most women are willing to put their minds into now, but some will pretend to want to do such work soon, and then leave it to men. What harm can they do? You cannot assume the position of an elder and then drop it when you spot something else you would rather do… Women have too many options now. It's not easy for them to stop and select only one path and do it very well—seeing it through to the end. Men have fewer options, so they work harder on whatever they can do to prove themselves to other men. Thus it is easier to be a man!"

When Mandy made pronouncements that sounded more like psychology than phi-losophy, she would place them in the context of a societal movement or a more of the local village or nearby clan, but most of the women she addressed did not hear it, preferring instead to believe she was 'being intuitive.' This often bothered Mandy in the early days when she was attached to the final outcome of her work on Earth, but it left her in later years—never to disturb her again. She said, "The effect of your words and what you leave to others to interpret can hurt the work, but you can't imagine what harm would come to everyone involved if the words were never heard."

Following Mandy's work in wisdom, Wanda spoke of her visions each week to Jorge or Mandy, or both of them. They would help her interpret how these insights fit into the world of today, but Wanda was not very interested in what they said then. Later she came to understand it, and even later she began to use this work to benefit her own crew and what they had to do, too.

During the initial offering of Wanda's channeled work, seeds of wisdom were planted and plans initiated to work together even better. The stage was set, and their play was never sad, if Mandy was allowed to change the cast to produce more laughs. She admired the honest, hard-working men a lot and especially loved their cook. No one ever was as close to Mandy as the woman she placed in the kitchen to advise all newcomers about the work they would have to do if they decided to become new recruits.

The distance between Mayan cities and world capitals was great in the beginning, but less with every passing season as they grew in ability to communicate through e-mail and videos. It became commonplace for a clan to perform a ritual they would normally never do again or let outsiders into, just so they could teach seekers what to do when the final time arrived.

Each clan possessed a ritual, or piece of the puzzle, or clue to the mystery that was necessary to preserve for the end of time. All the material needed to protect the world had been placed in their minds and in their hands over time. Each clan knew only what they alone had to do then, because no one until now was willing to place their own mind on hold and help the Mayan tribes become bold. The old cheered from the sidelines and hoped that this year would be the year when all would see the world that was coming to be, but it was not to be.

Mandy said with spirit, "Each and every single being has to be able to decide now if they want to go or stay."

Wanda agreed with her, because she once saw it in a vision. However, most visitors did not wish to portray today the way the end was once done. They only wanted to talk about it, or pretend to believe in God, or welcome those who accepted *their* God as being able to ascend when the end came one day.

The group that would next ascend was huge, according to Mandy and Jorge, but very few were actually present and able to meet with the men and women of the clans that represented the Maya of Yucatan through Guatemala. Their clans prepared for danger and all manner of hatred and intimidation, because trust in others had faded so much that they could not accomplish all that had to be done to raise the level of power within the entire tribe higher than it had ever been raised in the past.

Elders recalled several fables of the past where secrets were deposited among shamans in a limited way so as to reveal what had to be said and done before the planet would permit you to rise into the skies again. They knew how to use the gravity of any situation, but not enough was known now about the time that it takes for an entire tribe to ascend in time. After all, this was not what they were trying to do as a tribe, it was just part of this group's work.

As the team of leaders and teachers taught each weaver, potter, scribe, and artist what to do with their art, their compounds grew materially. They each became more and more secure in their own minds, vying over time to be the very best one in line.

〤 〤

Since Mandy often arrived at a compound without any warning, each tribe, guild, or clan became wise to how to connect with her in ways not known by them until then. She was traceable, but only until she became wise to the fact that they were trying to lie behind her back or get things in shape only when they expected her back. She laughed at that—even howled at times. Mandy was wise to just about any prank they could imagine pulling when she was absent. Her mind was sharp and her wit not diffused by a bad attitude.

The Maya, however, were not willing to laugh as much as they once did due to the attacks they had sustained over many millennia, so they often complained that Mandy did not understand the gravity of their situation. She would laugh even harder then. Understanding the gravity of any situation was unique to Mandy. She noticed that powerful, ambitious men and women were inclined to use up an energy field if they worked in a line, so she gathered her people together in circles all over the world and asked them to lighten the load of everyone else wherever they might go. The growth of the electrical field that seemed to support Mandy and her world was not seen as a burden to anyone but her. She was often unable to speak as loudly as she wished, and at times even lost her voice if she was asked a question whose answer would be ignored by the person asking it.

This was not a good time not to be Maya! However, most of the world refused to realize The Ascended Maya were in this world and could find their own lines in time and greet everyone in the way of the Mayan tribes of today. In fact, some misguided tribes sent emissaries to the Yucatan with designs to build power and water plants or teach the Maya how to till their land, while remaining totally ignorant of them as men and women. They tried to understand The Ascended Maya without buying into the mind of the people alive today within the tribe.

At such times Mandy would say, "You can't understand a man or woman without being one of them for at least a day, so try not to act like you know what they're doing when you're not able to explore your own dreams more." Whenever Mandy said such things, at least one person would rise to her side, but no group was able to produce enough energy to rise en masse as they sat together or danced in time with her.

〤 〤

On one occasion Mandy peered into the gloom and saw how much Wanda missed her daughter, Teri, and immediately put a plan into action. She asked the men to set up a camp near the compound where the weavers could go and visit with their families and be alone with them in order to talk about whatever they did in the past or was going on at home now, and so on. Mandy knew there was something she could not see within the work of Teri and her mother, but she was prepared to let it go since her work was to simply *know*—not to show what she knew or tell others what to do. Mandy just did it!

While the men set up a better camp than Mandy had designed and asked them to build, Jorge spotted that the area was not secure against the attempts of unwanted men visiting the women and possibly getting into trouble there. He asked the men to promise not to ever go there and got a few laughs in response. The men who laughed were never trusted again by Jorge or the tribal elders who supervised the lives of the women, their children, and old men in this compound.

As time barely survives, the sun dips further into the Western Hemisphere and the Yucatan seems to disappear. During such times, Mandy and Jorge would sit and talk as a pair of missionaries might who work in rarefied air. They were not known to each other from the earliest times on Earth, but were able to sense that while on Earth this time they were a pair who did better work when together than working with others, but passion between them was not to be. This was what kept them apart from others and made them sense within the power and energy of a man and a woman who did not act upon urges that often caused the downfall of many others while living on Earth. This was very interesting to Mandy, but not nearly as intriguing as it was to Thérèse and Wanda who did not miss a thing.

☼ CHAPTER SEVEN

The men and women who stayed behind in the compound when the students left for the nearby town refused to open the compound's gate to a station wagon driven by a man hidden behind its dark windows. Unwilling to trust people in such vehicles, because lust and crime prefer to exclude the sun as much as possible, the natives thought this shrouded vehicle brought them no good. A woman standing in the front line farthest from the gate opened her middle eye to scan the driver and decided it would not present a problem to open the gate to him then, but the men refused to accept her view.

Without thinking, Mandy walked in silence to the gate and opened it with a crank and lever that could withstand a gale, but not so secure that the poor or needy could not open it easily. All the men stared fiercely at the car as it crept into the pavilion and parked under the Guardian Tree. No one wanted to move toward the vehicle or look directly at the man who would appear, because only Mandy knew what to expect.

Once parked, Mandy walked over and opened the car door, again without thinking about what the others might want her to do. She waited for the driver to enter the light, and when he stood with the help of a cane and looked at everyone, no one said a word because he looked extremely frail. In fact, he looked like a skeleton misplaced from Day of the Dead celebrations in the nearby town. He did not look like anyone they had ever seen before. Mandy, however, seemed happy to see him and hugged him as if he were an old friend. He was not, but she spotted that he was about to cross into another world and needed protection from whatever was after him there and then.

Even though the others moved closer to hear what Mandy said to the man, they lost out on what came to be known later as The Blessing of the Dead. Because she spoke softly, he understood everything she had ever done or become. He walked only a few steps before stopping to breathe deeper, and than he seemed to be able to walk more easily. Without thought, or so it was described later to members of the tribe, Mandy took his hand and guided him to a spot beneath the huge Guardian Tree and sat beside him. She leaned into his body and smoothed away the lock of hair that had strayed over his brow into his right eye.

She did not ask him anything, but crooned a song that the Maya standing close by knew to be centuries old. Elders picked up traces of the dirge and began to intone along with Mandy. Everyone else moved away to give the singers and seer more room to pray.

Within an hour or two Mandy signaled the cook to come and talk with her and their visitor about what he should eat now. This woman, Louisa, whom Mandy admired as much as she admired any man in the tribe for his strength, stood with her hands on her hips and listened as he talked of his pain and sorrow. Having advised Mandy which of three things he needed to eat before leaving Earth, Louisa started working on the soup she would feed him as soon as it was ready.

As the elders waited patiently for the man to do something or for Mandy to relate something, the group surrounding them shrank in size. Everyone has a time limit set that once reached leaves them impatient to tell another what they learned so far. Thus the elders were the only ones left watching Mandy when Louisa called to the sick stranger to enter her kitchen and eat his soup.

The elders suddenly perceived what rituals had to be done to help this man move into the next world, but the youngest shaman was displeased, as usual, with Mandy's behavior. He demanded proof that this man was about to die and deserved to be served by them. Mandy did not heed his demand. Her look commanded the men to bend and they all hurried to get fire and water enough to complete work that normally took days to reach the point where the eldest shaman was invited to speak over such a feast. He said the few words needed to help a soul pass from this room into the next view and on into the next, until the man's soul passed through the veil. The eldest shaman was pleased to help but the youngest, being mischievous, tried to foil Mandy's plans again.

♓   ♓

Meanwhile, next door to the dining room the tribe's Scribe sat writing a Letter to the Editor of a newspaper far away in America. A tall, dark man stopped and knocked on her office door and waited to hear what she would say when he asked to see her privately. She did not notice his presence or hear his rap. Something had come over her that caused her to stand and walk to the door and throw it open right then. They both blinked at each other in surprise, and then backed away quickly as if embarrassed by the bright light that struck both of them in the eyes from somewhere other than the sky. Apparently the motion detector was overloaded with whatever stimuli it took to trip off its spotlights, which made them laugh.

When Jorge left the ceremony, Mandy was not aware of what errand took him elsewhere, but assumed he was going to ask the tribe's Scribe to write the deceased man's obituary. Hearing the two of them laughing heartily, she wondered what had happened that made that solemn task funny, but then heard chanting from somewhere close at hand.

The words being chanted became clearer. "Take this man. He is now a friend. He was lost from his tribe, but he came here to end his time among his fellows and friends. He is not seen as ancient or Maya, but he is wise and dedicated to the many lives he saved while working on the northern plains. He is a chief of great experience! He needs to be free of the grief he experienced over the years when he was unable to feel alive within his tribe. He wants the alcohol he drank in his past to evaporate forever so he can face the long trip home—purified … His water is low and he wants to go… His life is now over."

As Mandy listened intently to the shaman's chanting, she noticed that the stranger's fingertips were not like hers or anyone else's in their tribe. They were long, spatulate, and callused as if he had played a guitar or flute for hours every day. She noticed a hump on his back and reflected on what she had seen in dreams until she was sure she could see into the next life. The switch was made because it was this dying man's wish. Mandy was grateful to receive his spiritual gift of power and insight, but amazed that he would have traveled for days to die with her at his side.

"Who was this gifted individual who claimed to be a Great Plains Chief?" Mandy mumbled and explained in prayer what she needed to know and what she would love to have explained now. No one present took notice because Mandy spoke in an unknown dialect understood only by the Guides of the man who died as she spoke them.

When Louisa came forward with more broth and more herbs, she quickly saw that the soul had departed and would never eat turkey again. She dipped her finger into the pot of broth and with the tip of her finger proceeded to draw a cross on his brow as if the soup was holy water. She was not ordained to touch anyone dead, but the men said nothing. Even the youngest was wise enough to keep his mouth closed then. Later he would say Louisa was given far too much credit by Mandy and others, but by then he too knew Louisa was asked to do the final blessing by the elders.

When the Chief totally understood that he had passed through the veil, he stood up straight and walked into the next room where the women sat and shook hands with two cooks. They knew it was an honor of sorts, but did not feel good about a *spirit* asking them to dance, until Mandy indicated with a shake of her head and a rattle of beads that it was right and proper and good to do. The night passed and the man's body was thoroughly cleansed. His spirit was taken in hand by the men and women celebrating the dance of the dead. It was unlike anything they had ever done in the past, so each one present remembered differently how it began.

Later, many stories circulated about Jorge and Mandy lifting a dead man and helping him dance and how he danced in circles and so on, but no one really knew what happened then. Only the 'dead' man was able to report accurately that all was good and because of their dance with him that day, he was able to review his life without any problem. The energy produced by the men and women then was equal to the thrust he needed to leap into the future of the man he seemed to have been. He smiled when he was laid out in his shroud.

The car he arrived in was registered to a man from San Francisco, so they called the local police to report that a man had died the previous night and they wondered if it might be from AIDS. The police did not whisper about it, but shouted and wanted to know what the Maya intended to do with his body. No one knew what to do, so Mandy assumed responsibility for everything. She told the police that the man was related to her and would be buried beneath the ciba trees near her home immediately. No one in power really wanted to know anything more about it, so they let Mandy do whatever she decided was best. She wisely assumed that when others are not paid to think things through to the end, it is a blessing for them not to interfere or cause any problems for such people. However, she often wondered why it was true.

The dead man was not a man of the cloth but a man of many faiths and spiritual blessings. He could have given his power and spiritual gifts to anyone close to him, yet he chose Mandy to be his beneficiary. In addition to such bequeaths, a gift is given to each and every person who helps those who lose their way or need help crossing over at the end of their day here. In some instances there is so much to give that the recipient cannot accept it without experiencing an overflow of emotion—possibly feeling physically ill. Mandy was used to accepting much power and knew what to do to survive such surges, but his gift was so awesome and intense that even she had to go to bed immediately in order to absorb everything and stay well.

⋈   ⋈

As the week weakened and the men returned to whatever they usually did during the day, Mandy experienced many dreams at night and in her own time. She had to be weak from no sleep and nothing to eat, but no one bothered her—not even Jorge. When she finally raised her head and pulled at the lamp cord to brighten the room, the cook standing sentry in the kitchen saw her light and boomed to everyone nearby that Mandy was awake. Hurrying toward the room where Mandy had slept deeply, secure from anyone bothering her, Louisa prayed all the way that her boss was okay. She had been unwilling to say aloud that Mandy was a Mayan elder until now, but she would continue to smile and refer to Mandy as 'the boss' so the younger cooks would understand that Mandy was in charge—not her.

Without hesitation, Mandy stood up as Louisa entered the bedroom and almost fell into her out-stretched arms. She gained her balance immediately by some strange constriction of her spine that no one else seemed to be able to do to get the same result. Extending her arms wide enough for Louisa to walk between them and hug her to her breasts, the cook took a moment to thank God for Mandy's recovery and granting her the rest she so badly needed.

As the two friends chatted nonstop in Mandy's room, the rest of the kitchen staff prepared dinner. When the workmen entered the dining room no one was so indiscreet as to speak about what the two women might be saying to each other about a week in which Mandy slept and the Cook worked the staff endlessly—cleaning everything that had ever been used in the kitchen at any time this past year. When Mandy and Louisa finally walked into the kitchen to bless the food the elders would eat, the youngest women and some of the men continued to sit and chat as if she were not present. This did not upset Mandy. In fact it reassured her that she looked about the same as always—sort of Mayan, but way too tall to be a woman of the old tribe. She knew that to the young she seemed wise but laughed too much to be an elder.

Mandy's laughter was not rough or raspy, but it was not as sweet as Jeanne's nor as hearty as Wanda and her daughter. She looked to be 38 to those who were young in age and 56 to most others. But who was she? No one ever asked after her first class, but report-ers constantly showed up trying to get 'the lowdown on Mandy' and were never successful in such gross attempts. The entire tribe was protective of Mandy, as well as Louisa, who was probably the only member of the local clan always admitted to Mandy's inner sanctum, regardless of the time.

Within minutes of the blessing being given, Mandy whispered that she would sit in the kitchen and watch everyone else cook and clean pots and sinks and whatever. She often relaxed there, saying that it reminded her of her youth. She claimed that whenever she sat for any length of time in the kitchen of any friend that her mother would arrive and stand close-by. Her mother reminded her how hard women worked before electricity made America lazy.

They had wondered about electricity and the power that coursed naturally through everyone in a room and usually made them energetic. It could also be leashed to create energy to do the chores of everyone who applied their minds to such work, thereby reducing physical energy output. 'Hmmmm,' Mandy would just hum and wonder about such things and no one knew what she was thinking.

When Mandy sat in the kitchen she usually regaled the women who worked around her with stories of her youth and later years in New York—trying to get ahead and succeeding only as far as making a lot of money. At such times the women would grow bold and ask her about her past. She usually started out the same way to let them know she was approachable and willing to answer questions then, but this time there was a little twist in the line. Her usual way was to share herself first, and then listen to them.

Today, she sat at the kitchen table and said she was back and as hungry as the proverbial bear after a long winter's nap. The Mayan maidens knew nothing of hibernating bears, but laughed anyway. Within a short time, Mandy was brought up to speed about all the babies and the older children's behavior. That always preceded every conversation with her staff. It was talked through with the greatest urgency if there was any emergency or serious problem she was unaware of until then.

Yes, Mandy noticed that one woman was pregnant again and not able to name the father—again, but she said nothing. Her mind worried about the young women and the ways they misunderstood men, but more wisdom would come to them as they worked out their place at the table than could be said in a day or two by family and tribe.

While everyone listened, they watched the cook, whose hands were now very strong from working with clay, beat eggs viciously as she prepared a surprise dessert for Mandy. Each woman loved to treat her to things they knew Americans loved to eat—based on what they saw in movies and TV. Mandy never fully understood why they wanted to make so many goodies for her, but accepted them eagerly since the other women truly loved treats of any kind—and desserts were their absolute favorite.

When the men finally realized that Mandy would not be spending her first night back in this reality in the dining room with them, an elder grumbled about it, and the rest laughed at him—again. He was jealous of women and their children and did not realize it. In stark contrast, Jorge was not that kind of man. He seldom showed interest or concern in Mandy or the women who lingered about him, too, instead he was into what everyone did all day. According to him, his concern for Mandy was equal to what teachers and artists feel about their latest masterpiece or protégé. No one ever asked him why he worried so much about her, as he obviously did; but if anyone had ever dared to ask, he would have said he was just doing his job as a guide.

Their day ended with the women busy in the kitchen and the men equal to the task of digesting their dinners along with many laughs. The energy within the two rooms took away the sense of doom and gloom that had hung over them for days as Mandy slept and seemed to exist in a daze. They were equal to most tasks, completing them in a few days even if they were huge and complex, but erasing worry left room for laughter and new ideas, which was the case tonight. Everyone was eager to hurry back to their work now.

♓ ♓

Work in the world is equal to the mind that provides such work at any time, but many men and women really prefer being slaves—not thinking much while they work. Some prefer to be given small pieces of a big picture and told how to put those few pieces together and announce when they are done with a task—rather than creating art. Within this compound many worked with artistic values in place but were unwilling to complete the details needed to keep the work flowing, thereby enabling everyone to be paid on a timely basis. This problem was often discussed but never resolved, until Mandy opened up to the women meeting in the kitchen that night and told them what she had seen in her dreams that week. She spoke at length about what they all needed to do immediately.

"I saw in my dreams that we need to help those who are over-burdened with raising children who don't listen when spoken to. We need to educate everyone, and we need to help families more. I suggest that we build a child care center in the middle of the village so women can see their children as they work, and the children can be trained as they play. We'll have no TV stuff, either. We'll help them learn colors and the basics of language and mathematics to a limited degree, since it's going to be their work when they reach six or seven years of age. We will not burn out our babies delight in life on work that can be more easily learned when they reach the right age." As she spoke, Mandy stood up and walked among the mothers who seemed most eager to hear about her dreams, since dreams made sense to them immediately, while others sat and wondered why children were always considered first when it came to education.

By the end of the next day, the elders entered the schoolroom to talk about a way of life they were sure was ending for the clan. They were not as thrilled about educating the children as Mandy, but they were always hopeful that she was right and they were merely tired of life.

Mandy often used an overhead projector to teach lessons to children or their mothers or the cooks or even the teachers and artists and weavers who were close to her heart, in order to increase their participation in work or to make needed changes more easily understood. Everyone can participate, but only a few ever want to work hard. Since the few who loved to laugh and chat often had no mind for facts, it usually took positive recognition to get those fit and able to speak their wisdom, so Mandy usually let the silly minds sit for a time before she began to speak seriously to them.

⋈ ⋈

Within and around the compound the trees often broke apart and shed their leaves or sent a limb to the ground. This fact of life might be ignored most places today, but not in Mandy's world. Any dead wood was examined immediately by her and the elders to see if it was diseased or just old age. No one else knew for certain why they did this, but many thought that the decaying body of the strange man who had died and been buried under them might have something to do with it.

As the trees dropped leaves and went into a time when they could refresh themselves and do very little for a month or two, Mandy and the others who knew about such things waited with bated breath to see what kind of leaves would return to these trees. Surprisingly, the trees did not wait as long as usual to replenish their leaves.

Mandy and the elders prayed and sat for a day asking the Guardian Tree what to do about the soil placed over the dead man's casket, and what to do about AIDS, too. The tree was not equal to the task and withdrew. It would not give them what they asked, but The Maya of other times knew what to do to help such people improve. They were the first to speak and the last to leave once this work was over and this day was seen as complete.

Apparently only Mandy understood why the trees did not wish to speak. She said they saw the planet needing to cleanse the man now and remove his old ways—not the other way around, as many say today. Man is most responsible for wasting what was freely given, but Earth cannot get out of assuming responsibility, too, by always blaming man. According to Mandy, "Earth will shed its work never again. Earthly rearrangements and changes created by man will never be catered to again. Frequent equivalents of storms and such will clear the air more. People will be given less water than before, so as to make them more able to explore other ways to live than they followed before the great drought. Work will be reduced so as to include more poor, handicapped, or disabled than ever before. The world is going to cleanse itself—and AIDS is nature's way of fighting pollution and such."

As always, Mandy would not defend what she predicted or channeled, but put it out to others to seek out answers or to rip it apart and do it over better than she did. Her work was not used as a catalyst now, but she was revered as a teacher of great worth and highest integrity. She pushed and she moved and she yelled if she had to, but she always smiled when everyone was doing the right thing—the will of God at that time. Her own life was not equal to all the people who came into or went through the workrooms, offices, or dining hall, but she managed to easily maintain her equilibrium for days and weeks at a time, regardless of the interruptions to her thoughts.

♓ ♓

When the time of the month when the elders cross their minds with time came around again, Mandy stopped to watch and worried not. Her own home was secure from harm, but some Maya were said to be plotting against her—again. She did not for one moment believe anyone who was Maya would harm her or her work, but she knew that all men could plot if they were not able to share in what they believed to be the best that could be achieved.

For reasons unknown, Mandy began lecturing the men and the women again, without mentioning that her first words were always directed at women who bred the children. She told them she was back from the land of her ancestors and theirs and had many things to compare, but she would not share her dreams with them again.

The idea that she would talk to The Scribe and release messages through her to others who were not Maya was not advised as good to do, but she did it anyway. Mandy did not ask the elders for their input when it came to what she wanted to drink or eat, either, but the fact that she was weird in what she liked to eat and would not drink was not a problem for them. Coffee was never seen in her presence, but she drank much tea during the day. It turned out that cocoa was her drink of preference when she was about to speak of what she could *see*. At first only a few recognized this change of habit, but later almost everyone knew that to be invited to drink hot cocoa with Mandy would elevate your mind and your spirit at the same time.

Days and weeks are bound together and the year they bring to be is not always clear even when it is over, but Mandy was able to make progress with the work she did in her home. Her compounds were accepted here and there and she maintained separate quarters everywhere she owned a home for others to work in or rent out to strangers. The houses she was prone to visit stood alone, and though she often could travel in limos and such, she usually drove a green Jeep. She never announced her plans, but the cook, Louisa, usually knew when she was leaving and how soon she would return. No one knew why Mandy told this woman so many things, because it was never wise to ask Mandy why she did anything.

The group that once barred passage to a great chief of another tribe realized that they had come close to harming one who would guide them in future times. This caused many to pray that they would never again bar the gate to someone because they seemed alien to them. Mandy was so grateful for that change in this clan's mindset that she resided there more often than at any other compound as she roamed from place-to-place in her usual way.

☼ CHAPTER EIGHT

Many assume that when a woman and man enter a room together that they are a couple—some even check for further proof that their first impression is correct. But when Mandy and Jorge join any group, they do not provoke a mood or mindset that impressionable women can easily weave into romantic dreams and visions about what their relationship may be. They present a united front of energy and cooperation that is difficult for dreamers to comprehend initially, and their entrance usually presages a burst of energetic enthusiasm that moves through everyone present. Some wonder, "What is going on with them? How do they combine their energies with a partner over time? Is it something they do together only in public and are they more than just friends or lovers or whatever? Does anyone else notice the after-effects of their performances?"

Since the combined energy of Mandy and Jorge is usually atmospheric, many people experience miracles in their daily lives immediately after merely watching the 'truly dynamic duo' work within their group. Working within groups is not easy to do, but these two can so easily combine their work in such ways as to appear to be divine. They appear to speak without any idea of what the other will say—without ever repeating themselves or each other.

All the local women and men wanted to build a community wherein there was work enough for each of them. In addition, they wanted time enough to spend repeatedly in family situations without losing lives to malnutrition or lack of passion caused by little food or money enough to buy what is needed from the outside world. These people do not wish to become capitalists—an easy slogan to repeat, but not an easy ideal to maintain when they can so easily view how the rest of the world lives now. Some remain confident that the old ways are still the best ways, while others firmly believe that the best of both worlds is too infrequently incorporated and used to help them become the best any Maya can be while residing on Earth.

In a culture imbued with respect for spiritual guides or shamans there is a state of grace in which such elders walk easily, without putting on airs or berating others to listen to their wisdom. In a contemporary culture where you can see clearly into the future and know what will happen if you follow through and do what you propose, it might seem easy for the Maya to comprehend that if they seek to change too many things they love about their lives now, it could possibly threaten the lives of *all* who are Maya. What to do about it now?

Rearranging a room is not the same as changing your mind and creating a new wave of energy, but for some it helps to rearrange their outside lives in order to see if it works or is a comfortable fit. Some do not believe that outer walls are walls you can use to conceive dreams, yet others see it immediately.

What Mandy did for the folks who loved her most was create a life in which they could excel and work at whatever they did well, but she never said that their work or life was great as is. Her comments, if offered, were meant to instruct and help others do better than they did before and not become conceited or too content. She seldom said someone did poor work, instead she pointed out ways they could improve or excel. Although this teaching style was her way, she was not a slave to it now. Meanwhile, critics reported that Mandy used Mayan women as slaves and then wasted their time attempting to prove their libel was true.

⯎ ⯎

Within three weeks of the last meeting of the elders Mandy was unable to sit in the weavers' compound and read or meditate without being interrupted by someone new to the belief and faith that she helped establish that day with Jorge. Her mind was no longer able to rest during the day, but she felt blessed, even when attacked by those who originally smiled on her views but now ridiculed behind her back. As the weavers paraded before her that day, she *knew* what was going on, but never said a word. At such times she merely laughed or smiled as if nothing was wrong or bothering her mind.

In the wee hours of the day that followed the display of supposed solidarity, Mandy awoke, dressed quickly, and then drove out of the compound alone without saying a word to anyone. Spirit prompted her to leave immediately! She was told not to contact or speak to anyone, and as always, she obeyed the warning—without any idea why she had to steal away during the night. She left her bed unmade and did not pack a suitcase. Everything had been prearranged for such situations, so she was not without cash and other resources, as well as a computer secured in its traveling case.

When the entire household awoke hours later and gradually became aware that Mandy was no longer there, some immediately assumed she had been kidnapped. Why? Because she never left her room without making her bed and rearranging her closet and drawers in order to keep everything neater than any maid would. There were always a few around her who strove to impress others that they knew Mandy intimately because they were aware of a few of her personal habits and foibles, and these self-appointed intimates now said Mandy never felt that the women acting as maids did less than their best—and she enforced that thought, but she still cleaned up after herself because she did it better than others. It was not a behavior the maids understood, but it impressed them enough that they worked harder to keep everything clean throughout the many rooms of the public areas where Mandy and others spent most of their time.

When Jorge was informed by staff that Mandy had been kidnapped, he responded by going back to sleep and not reawakening until much later in the day. He was obviously not dismayed when he awoke, nor when he joined the folks who had gathered in the outer compound to await news of Mandy and what ransom might be demanded. As he walked toward them he was unaware that most of the crowd was scared, so he sat down at an umbrella table and awaited his usual cup of chocolate to be served. Only then did he notice that one or two of the cooks were neither upset nor sad, even though everyone else was crying or trying to hide their tears.

♓ ♓

Within a day of Mandy leaving without saying where she would be a note arrived. It demanded payment of $1,000,000 and stated that Mandy was being held captive in a place they could not find on any map. As Jorge examined the note he laughed and shouted, "Can you believe this?" He turned the paper over and over while surreptitiously watching the faces of those closest to him, in order to determine if there was an enemy within the inner circle once again. Since they all believed Mandy had been captured and taken hostage again, no one smiled or acted indifferent, so Jorge shouted even louder, "This is an absolute hoax!" He laughed, but no one else followed his lead.

Looking carefully at each man, Jorge counted ten willing to pay the ransom—in some way not yet imagined. It was assumed by everyone present that it was within Jorge's power to create whatever money was needed now. He was amazed that they were willing to pay out money *they* did not have! Believing they did not value money enough to realize that a million dollars was far too much to pay anyone for anything, nor did they understand it would never be paid, even if the ransom note was legitimate and could return Mandy to them immediately.

Stroking the top of his head with both hands, Jorge said without looking at anyone, "What I can see is that Mandy knew someone in this compound cannot be trusted, and rather than stay here and wear down her faith in the human race, or worse—become cynical, she removed herself to a mountainous place where she is safe…and she's happy now. Just visiting her room should have been enough for any spiritually-developed person to sense that Mandy didn't leave with someone she hates or doesn't trust. Didn't anyone sense this?" Jorge enjoyed using such ploys to get some of the old boys to confirm that they were aware of what had happened. However, none of the men confirmed his interpretation of Mandy's present condition, so after a few moments, Jorge spoke quietly to a young Mayan woman who had settled down beside him at the table, "What do you see, Nita?"

Unbeknownst to Jorge, he often intimidated Nita with the power of his intellect and wisdom and frightened her with his decisiveness when he spoke to her during private meetings held after dinner most evenings. Perhaps this is why she now refused to answer him? Without meeting his eyes, Nita mutely shook her head, refusing to reveal anything or possibly admitting that she saw nothing.

Suppressing his disappointment in his student's reaction to the pop quiz, Jorge almost missed spotting the truth within his vision. It caused him to pause and not speak aloud. He thought, 'I see now! You, too, Nita, believe that something evil has happened to Mandy—and it doesn't interest you—at all.' Wincing at the thought of how badly he had misjudged this lovely woman, his mind recoiled with the truth he could see quite clearly now.

Several of the women and girls watching Jorge assumed he was sleeping with this Mayan maiden rather than teaching her the ways of a spiritual guide or shaman. Without revealing his thoughts, Jorge dropped Nita from ever being considered as a shaman in train-ing. From then on she would do office work only! He also decided not to speak to her again outside the confines of the compound…or at least until she changed her thinking about Mandy. With a sense of disgust with himself for having failed to notice Nita's pride and vanity, he realized that she must be the one who was misleading the young.

The voice of the head cook broke into Jorge's dark thoughts right then. "What do you want us to do, Jorge?" Louisa reigned supreme in the kitchens and was the only woman trusted enough to take food to Mandy when she lay in a dream state. She was the most admired of all the Mayan women, because Mandy trusted her, but she knew she was not the only woman Mandy trusted much.

With a curt gesture, Jorge commanded everyone's attention and said, "What do *you* women want to do? Do you want to pray all day or go out and act like Mandy's still here?"

No one spoke. The uncomfortable silence continued until a melodious alto voice reverberated from the loud speaker above them saying, "What do you think Mandy is going to say if we don't meet our individual and combined quotas this month?"

Startled, all eyes turned toward the woman standing at the back of the patio. She appeared to be laughing at some unknowable vision or specter. A halo of pale golden light surrounded Wanda and caused everyone to gawk to see if she was standing and talking to them or, as was often the case, talking to no one visible to them.

Jorge greeted her words with a wide, wide grin and a chuckle as he said, "I think you can take over now, Wanda! I'd like to go out and about and find out who is trying to cash in on Mandy moving out."

Quickly, without glancing at anyone standing between them, Wanda said, "Don't look for a man!" Wanda had quickly learned how to stay balanced in her mind all the time so she no longer was seen weaving or struggling to maintain her balance. Her mind learned to compensate for the loss of her leg to such a degree that she no longer wallowed in self-pity, although others assumed she still suffered from it. She used this misconception to her advantage—rather than correct some men's beliefs or advise many women that losing her leg to diabetes and osteoporosis was no longer her problem. Wanda now added, "I think I can help, Jorge. Go to the city and wait around until you run into a pretty girl/woman who does something to attract you—is flirtatious like a prostitute. When you spot her, ask Spirit to remove all your inhibitions so you can follow her to her room immediately. This woman can tell you where Mandy is and how to get in touch with her."

Stunned and embarrassed, Jorge felt his face redden with the implication that he must follow someone beneath his mind's interest through the city streets. Recovering quickly, he nodded in agreement while thinking, 'Who is this I will meet? Will this prophecy cause someone here to meet me or alert others to accost me like that?'

Her last words were lost on those who were wailing ever louder that Mandy was dead. They refused to believe either Jorge or Wanda, preferring to assume that Mandy could not be saved, even if the huge ransom was paid today. This was not to be her fate, but some wanted it to be true so they could ascend into her position. No one in power sits there in ease during times of need.

There are times when even a known thief can walk into a room and take away the doom and gloom, making light of a dark subject—and thrive. So when the youngest kitchen helper spoke up and made sense of everything, she immediately became a shamanic candidate, replacing the now-deposed Nita. All she had to say was, "I think Ms. Mandy would laugh if she saw us now. She would giggle about how solemn all of us are now. After all, she's not dead! Can't you all feel her presence now?"

As Juanita finished her speech, Louisa, the head cook, rose from her seat on the sidelines and danced about with her hands held high in a gesture of merry abandonment. Her feet skipped over the clay tiles without touching the ground at times. Everyone stared, realizing that Louisa was now able to do something that only Mandy did that easily previously—although Wanda miraculously achieved it once or twice, too. Dancing in circles at a very fast rate, without getting dizzy, Louisa began to levitate a few feet off the ground, laughing loudly. After a few moments, her feet settled down and made slower circles over the smooth tiles. As she ended her dance, Louisa sang out, "I think we can safely say that Mandy is going to be back someday, but for now we have to carry on as if she never left—as if she left instructions with each of us about what we have to do every day until she gets back!"

Jorge appreciated what Louisa said, but was not sure her words were pure. He let his fears go, though, because it was time to visit the city and walk the streets in pursuit of a beauty destined to lead him to Mandy. He left when no one was looking in his direction.

♓ ♓

As Jorge walked through the streets of Merida, revisiting places where he and Mandy had been well received and entertained in stages, he thought about her and what she must be doing now. As if by the miracle of teleportation, he immediately spotted Mandy walking down the street in front of him. Jorge called several times, "Mandy!" She did not heed him and continued walking away from him. He stopped calling her name, wondering about the improbability of this woman actually being Mandy and the very real possibility that he might be following someone who was dead or worse yet, trying to take over his mind. After all, this is an ongoing problem for the spiritual guides and shamans who walk both sides of the thin veil of time.

When the woman stopped to cross a street she glanced around and met Jorge's eyes. Looking into his eyes, her message was succinct, though unspoken: 'Meet me in the zocalo. Do not speak to anyone else!'

Sensing that this woman appeared very real but was only part human, Jorge was rattled that she had looked directly through him as if with X-ray vision, without calling attention to herself. Nothing about her stood out enough that a passersby would recall seeing her, if ever asked to bear witness. Parting his thought waves just enough to keep her in his mind's eye as she outdistanced him and he followed her down the crowded city streets. Her undulating walk was very sexy. He was amazed that this might be Mandy, even wondering, 'What if this is Mandy?'

Just then, within a minute of ten, he watched her cross the boulevard in order to meet a tall, thin man wearing horn-rimmed glasses. She pecked him on the cheek, which amazed Jorge because he knew how much Mandy hated such conventional affectations. They stood talking as if he were an acquaintance of long standing.

While Mandy stood talking on the street corner, her mind was not on Jorge—much. She had been startled into being alive to today by meeting a man she once worked with in New York—someone who used to share the stoop of her old brownstone and talk about 'stuff' and dreams and when they would retire from the world—never having to work for anyone again. Martin was not surprised to meet Mandy! In fact, he expected to run into her here, but could not understand why she was not as he remembered. Little had changed in his everyday life and within his mind, so he believed Mandy had remained the same, too. In fact, he began this conversation with exactly the same line he used the last time they met, rather than picking up where they left off on their almost daily e-mails.

As Jorge approached Mandy, she turned away as if he were a stranger and meant nothing to her. Her eyes were focused on another time, and she seemed not to recognize him now. That is when Jorge realized she was not the one he was to follow and that Mandy was living another adventure in time!

Without a word to either Mandy or the man she was talking to, Jorge continued his walk down the avenue. Strolling, as if digesting a heavy meal, without any thought of being intercepted or blocked, he relaxed and absorbed the atmosphere. The trees around him began to waver as he examined them, noticing that the leaves were not as they had been. The bougainvillea wept and the floral spray above a gate drooped and looked to be decayed. He wondered if he was in the presence of evil again. If so, where should he go to escape it?

As time closed in on midnight, he saw no one who might be able to guide him to a rendezvous with Mandy or whoever it was he should follow, so he let himself be steered by his inner pilot. His brushes with evil were not as deep as they were wide, so he did not worry that something new would happen now—so it did!

With no wave of energy misplaced, Mandy suddenly appeared and spoke to Jorge, without mentioning what she had been doing since he pursued her to the broad avenue. She did not laugh as usual, but smiled to possibly reassure him that she was the woman he wanted to meet. She was not. She was not Mandy. She was evil personified!

We could follow Jorge on his trip through time and space, but we will save that for another day. Today, we are not fit to travel that far and leap into those feats while keeping our feet on the ground, so to speak.

☼ CHAPTER NINE

A class of potters, along with their Master, visited the weavers in order to watch anyone who might still be working at their looms in the late afternoon. Jorge accompanied the group and interviewed the Master in charge of their work. He asked her, "What do you think about our dropping our usual work to begin moving into what people really want to do? Do you think it would improve their views of why they are here…and what they are here to do? Would it help us teach them what to do?"

Although Jorge was not working hard, beads of sweat stood out on his brow as if he was. Wiping his forehead, he suddenly realized that someone in spirit was working through him again. It was one way to locate others of like mind and explore what they were doing, but it meant that he had to let himself open to those who could blow his cover on Earth. At times it took a lot of work to remain undercover—even hurt him to accomplish whatever needed to be done at times, but he usually submitted and did every assignment handed down to him now.

The Master Potter, Julie, taught mostly women, and a few men, the basics of her art, so she had rich experience to call upon as she replied. "I think we could work a lot closer to each other, and see if it works. Then, if it reaches the point where we're all able to communicate and cooperate and work for The Lords the way we were born to work, maybe we can try it out on others, but then I could be wrong—again." She smiled up at Jorge. When he said nothing to indicate that she was wrong, she knew she was.

Julie was originally from The States, but like many others she left that province to work with Mandy in Mexico in her own special way and was a huge success in every way possible. She had lost nothing by walking away from her past, because she learned from every task. Today, for example, she was leading her class in the first of many sessions they would spend with Jorge and Wanda, the Master Weaver, as well as others who were blocking out time in order to unite spiritually in ways not yet defined.

By the time daylight drifted into a gorgeous sunset, everyone who had been clinging to Jorge or Julie had dropped away to seek other pastimes in which to release their pent-up physical energies and creative ideas. The two old friends took this time to embrace once again and reiterate that their faith had brought them back together and would mend many fences once again.

Julie had worked hard delivering a new kind of material to her potters—quite different from what they were used to working with in the past, and they disliked it. The oldest potters laughed and refused to work with her for days on end. No progress was made until one woman in a breakaway state offered to introduce Julie's work to others who were far away from their homes. That was enough to get the initial work off the ground and enable Jorge and Julie to stand together and launch the entire program into orbit now. They refused to abort the retraining mission, intending to uplift every woman and man to a higher level, including those who had previously severed connections to this work by laughing and ignoring instructions.

United in this uncommon dream, Jorge channeled another mind or time and said softly, "What you need within any view of life is a tool that opens wide the gates of a mind. Once you get inside that mind, you need to be careful not to let the gates stand open too long on any given day."

Without thought to what he had said, Julie gestured toward Wanda, who was standing with a group of weavers near the front gate, and said, "Why is Wanda waiting on her friend, Teri? Doesn't she have faith that she is okay?"

As if batting a fly away, Jorge pushed aside whatever he had intended to say and answered her. "No, that's not it. She's just anxious to see Thérèse again. She wants to tell her all about her new plans. She's so into a pattern, but not able to teach it yet because she can't find the right words. When Teri arrives, she'll fill in the blanks then and be as open and frank as always when she teaches how to weave and what to leave."

Squinting into the distance where she *knew* a car would soon appear, Julie said, "I notice that you say Thérèse and then Teri, interchangeably. I've never met anyone who used two names quite like that before. Why does she use two names?" When the car appeared, Julie smiled as if congratulating herself on the fact that she was not losing her precognitive touch.

Noticing Julie's unease for the first time, Jorge spoke quickly to dispel any illusions that she might have about Thérèse's legitimacy. "That's easy to explain. She's a Saint at times—but not much of one at other times." He chuckled softly and then added, "Our Thérèse is often used by the famous Saint of that name. The one who says you need do only a little each day, and then add a little to that, and eventually you're able to do anything you ever wanted to do or wanted to become."

When Julie said nothing, he continued, "You see, Thérèse speaks and gets into the spirit of this Saint. At such times light appears over her head like a crown or a halo—as if she were illuminated by a painter of saints in the Renaissance. You'll see what I mean. She's coming now and I can tell it's Teri, because her smile is Teri's smile, but she'll change. Watch and see what I mean."

As Jorge spoke he turned toward the group hailing the new arrival and decided to add his greetings now, before he went inside to dine. Julie, however, stood rooted to the spot watching without speaking to the two or three women who rushed by asking if everyone had met Teri yet.

Unaware that she was not wholly welcomed, Teri waved at the group crowding around her and said without formality, "Hi, everybody! I'm so bushed I could sleep for a week, but I won't! I've brought back with me all the sheep in Australia—actually just their wool or whatever. You can use it or not, but I think it'll keep the ranchers busy there if you work into each thread a thought about what they need to do to get ahead. Such people! They drink and forget and drink and forget, and pretty soon another week is down the creek without anything new being done to help them work out of their classic views of what people can create together."

Wanda did not say much, because she knew Teri was extremely tired and wanted to sit without talking now. She knew this because Teri was talking a lot! Most people would not notice that particular contradiction in terms, but she did. She knew that when Teri offered opinions and social commentary without being asked that she was really asking people not to ask questions. She would offer fans something to think about so she could slip out of her shoes or go to bed—anywhere away from the public eye.

Today, as always, when she arrived at Mandy's compound she flew into the arms of Wanda, hoping to say nothing that would be misinterpreted as misleading, but as always, she was doubted. Her thoughts were on what she had to do very soon, but now she could let her guard down and talk to her Mama without letting on that their true relationship was such as it was.

Speaking over the heads of the young women now pressing in on Thérèse, Wanda said as much. "I think you need to take a nice long, warm bath with mimosa floating on the water. What do you ladies think?"

At that moment, Nita popped up in front of Teri and said, "I'll get the hot water! You two take your time. We can always talk later, Teri. You both have a lot to share about what we're doing here. Don't you?" Nita had assumed a sweetness she did not possess, and she did not know their true relationship, so she did not as yet regret that she often e-mailed Teri that she did not like Wanda.

Ignoring Nita, Wanda ran her hands over the sacks of wool now standing around the small truck that had delivered her daughter. Apparently satisfied with what she saw, Wanda spoke with finality to the weavers still clinging to the scene: "What we need now is space and time to get everyone onto the next line of the scarf we're weaving—then we can decide what to do about the yarn we have to card from all this wool."

Suddenly Wanda broke down and laughed so merrily that everyone joined in, even though they had no clue why she was so happy. She then smacked Teri on the hind end hard enough to determine that her bottom was as solid as ever, and said with feeling, "I feel great, and you're the reason!" From just that pat she was sure no one else had touched her daughter's bottom recently, but that was not why she trusted her now to be wise about men.

"I feel great, too—and it's because of you!" Teri shouted. She laughed as if it was a great relief to be home among friends again. Her thoughts were best expressed when alone with her mother, but she was seldom able to stay with Wanda as much as she wanted, so they often carried on private conversations within public meetings by acting like they were talking about something else. No one ever heard what they were really saying to each other—until now.

Standing and solemnly watching them, Jorge was stunned to discover that this woman who graced so many magazine covers was the daughter of his friend, the Master Weaver. No one else present knew it, so the two assumed he was still in the dark, too, but he was not. Light filters out darkness and lets in friends of the soul as well as those gifted enough to read into such things. Since Jorge was able to read just about anyone alive, he could see into their words and hear what was left unspoken in the outer context, but embedded within their conversation. His discovery would not be shared or mentioned until he had time to figure out why Wanda would lie—or had she never said anything, merely let everyone assume a lot about her life?

Wanda pulled a hair out of Teri's head and held it between her fingers as she said gleefully, "I see a gray hair, and it's on your left side! It will now go into my new pattern. I'll weave it in before I go to bed."

"Oh, Wanda, you're too much! When I get a head of gray hairs are you going to weave each and every one into it?" Teri was not swearing or mean spirited, but her mother looked as if her feelings were hurt.

What happened between them, as well as why only Jorge figured out their true relationship, was to be saved, but he could not stop and file his thoughts immediately. He spoke to them while they stood alone with him in the pavilion, before filing Wanda's words in a safe place so they could be reviewed later and not erased by mistake—or so he thought. His thoughts were too disarranged to help him end his present state of confusion concerning their true relationship to each other, so Jorge smiled as they stood in front of him, not sure what was going on between them now. He said to himself, 'What was I thinking when I approached them?' Since he could not remember, he began again, determined to say whatever came to his mind next, which turned out to be: "I think it's time to eat, ladies. We're having American-style steak for dinner—not our Mexican-style, thinly sliced beef that can be used later to resole your shoes."

Wanda retorted, "Men! Always thinking about food!" It appeared that she often teased Jorge, but in reality she never spoke familiarly to Jorge unless he started a conversation with her. Now she acted like they were very close friends, and she discovered that Jorge was definitely not displeased, but Teri was.

The trio talked and walked until their conversation came to a complete halt in front of the compound's main showroom window. After a moment of silence, Teri said with forced enthusiasm, "I see the new robes you're making turned out great, Wanda. When did you decide to put them in bags? I think that'll turn them into best sellers! I took some of the ones you sent me to my favorite boutiques and everyone said they were nice, but no one was willing to buy. With that ditty bag and the robe inside, I know it will sell now!" Ignoring the other displays, Teri began prodding her mother to walk in front of her toward the kitchen garden.

Jorge stayed behind at the showroom window watching the two women walk toward the kitchen. He waited to see if they would wash their hands when they got to the lavabo and they did. Straining his ears, he caught a few words, but none were coherent enough to make any sense. He decided to meditate and reiterate what he heard when his mind went blank and he lost time. He knew it had something to do with mysteries—but what he could not even imagine.

♓ ♓

Usually after saying grace, Jorge led everyone in a guided meditation throughout the meal in order to feed both their minds and bodies at the same time. This time when everyone became still, their commercial happiness was cherished by all. Many women raved about

Jorge's wisdom—talking about him whenever he was near, but he knew some never listened to anything he said. They were more interested in what they thought he might do for them in bed. He did not say it, but he wished Mandy would lay down the law once again.

As the women separated after this great dinner in Teri's honor, and the men gathered in the living area to think and talk about their private religious views, Mandy suddenly appeared as if out of thin air. No one said anything about it, but two men ran to bolt the doors and pull the curtains so others could not see Mandy standing there. She immediately addressed the men now struggling to appear as if nothing unusual was taking place. "I've come to see you without any body-armor and without any guards, so it has to be quick! I have something you need, and you have to do something for me!"

Having said this, Mandy stopped talking while each man moved forward and peered into the middle of their circle as if someone else was there with her now. No one else could be there, but if someone was, the air was still as pure and clear as if no one else was present. Such puzzling events were occurring more and more often, so these elders saw nothing strange in what just happened. However, they wanted information that only Mandy could communicate about wherever she was—provided everyone present could combine their work in the ether to build a vessel strong enough that it could safely hold her here for an hour or more. She could enter through spiritual portals, but usually left in the flesh, and no one could remember how she did it.

"As I stand here and talk to you again about the war and what we have to do to save them, you may not understand what I'm conveying to you now. I regret that it can't be explained again, but we have to move and do something new or we lose."

Stirred by Mandy's words, the elders stood and began chanting as they walked in a circle around the center of the room. Some women standing outside their circle smiled condescendingly at what they believed to be the silliness of old men—even mocked their ritual because it meant nothing to them.

Mandy's voice boomed and then faded before it could be heard beyond the confines of the inner group as she said, "As you gain status and fame, more and more will want to study with you and become elders, too."

Most of the men smiled, and one or two laughed out loud at her expression of appreciation, but they did not believe her. They kept smiling until they realized what she was saying. "You have worked for centuries… and today there are those who seek only instant gratification. They want what you have, and they want it now! They are like cows waiting to be milked—mooing loudly." Mandy was not smiling as she pulled at the imaginary teats of a cow. Thus the men realized they would be milked dry if they let everyone coming here to continue demanding, as if entitled to it, the shamans' work, without providing sustenance for the community of spiritual guides and elders present.

When Mandy stopped talking, the elder standing in front of her at that moment said, "Maybe we can give lectures and seminars and classes and help these people learn our ascension rituals that way?"

Mandy continued standing in their midst, without drifting, while other elders mumbled that teaching those who were totally ignorant of The Maya was a hopeless way to begin another day. Their doubts drifted into her mind through time.

"What can we do, Ms. Mandy, to help these outlanders learn their place in the world and why they exist now? Is there anything we can do? Are we to lead or just hold this place in time?"

Startled, Mandy said emphatically, "That's a great question—and the answer is that we must lead them. We must be able to take a few aside and guide them into the work of The Lord. We can't be too sure that we are who will be helping them. Once we find out what they have to do or why, we can step aside and let them follow their own inner Spiritual Guides then. Does that make sense?"

As Mandy said this, Jorge took a step backwards and appeared to collapse. Without a word, four men picked him up by his extremities and dragged him over to a couch where he could rest undisturbed by anyone present. He did not speak, but Mandy spoke loudly, using stronger words than they had ever heard her use before.

"I'm going to ask that you not talk about this to anyone! You are Spiritual Guides and elders who have powers that others deny are available at this time. Don't say you aren't able to do whatever you do, so as to elude these people, because you could possibly trigger the lose of spiritual gifts. Instead, push *them* to do something! Make *them* work! Get *them* to confess what they are tired of doing or why they want to change their way of life. But don't give them an hour of your time to do it! People who whine are mean with your time and won't pay you back with respect. If you need to meet with someone again and they don't recognize that you're teaching them, then you're the one wasting your time—not the tyro. But if someone comes to you and talks about what they will do—and they never do anything they say, turn them away and never be burdened when they pray or chant or do a ritual in front of you again."

Mandy did not stop for air but to rethink what she had to say now. For a few moments she stood as if glued to one spot, unable to melt the icy core of the group enough to leave them in tact, so she taught what she felt. Her mind was now excited, but her soul was not. She was in a fight for her life and knew this battle would be one that could end her life, so she did not wish to work hard with these men or say another word. Her body shook involuntarily and her feet danced an intricate pattern before she spoke again. Very calmly, Mandy spoke, "As I said, don't worry about those in a hurry *or* those who don't do what they say every day. Be yourself and work on your own work. Share what you dare, but don't give away your day!" The men's expressions changed dramatically, to indicate that her message was clear and understood by them all.

With finality, as though answering a question, Mandy said, "If anyone sells their time to others, it's their work they're denying." She then whirled about the room and when she stopped, she started talking rapidly. The room began to shake as if a major earthquake had hit nearby.

Everyone was shocked by this manifestation of power and energy, some opened their minds even wider than when Mandy arrived. An ancient elder said, "I will help you get to the other side, Miss Mandy." The other elders joined in then to help her sink within their work deep enough to rebound and leap over the threshold into time again.

☼ CHAPTER TEN

"Thinking about doing something and actually doing it is never done at exactly the same time, because each requires about the same degree of mental application. So you should decide on your work and begin doing it immediately, rather then think or dream about what you want to do next, or doing something else before you start working on a new design."

As Jeanne listened intently to the lecture and thought about the lesson being taught, she disagreed with the premise and wanted to leave, but she could not stand up and walk out, because she had to lead everyone in prayer at the end of the session. After that she had to return to her hotel suite and get ready to meet her friend, Julie, for lunch. Just at that moment she felt urged by Spirit to stand up and speak out to the crowd...and just as suddenly she had a hunch that someone else in the room would carry the day and speak out and deliver Spirit's message instead of her.

In a flash, a woman dressed all in white threw open the double doors at the back of the room and an invisible movement or shift in the energy system challenged the speaker's ability to keep everyone looking forward. Most of the audience turned to check out the late arrival because the new woman spoke just loud enough to carry across the crowd. The interloper asked everyone to sit back and relax.

Jeanne recognized the stranger to some degree—perhaps on another plane, but she could not put it together now. Perhaps it was her voice? That is one thing that never changes.

In Tucson, it is either cold or hot—extreme, seldom a medium setting. The sun was broiling hot more often than not, but the woman in white coolly reflected the light from the sun—or was it emanating from her inner life? She appeared to represent the positive world, which contrasted with this gathering of negative outsiders and imitators of life. All present had been called to meet in Tucson to critique the art of indigenous peoples of the Americas in order to determine what could be auctioned at profit, once this convention developed further interest in such art. The speakers and judges present were basically there to criticize artists. Unable to create such work themselves, but full of stinging comments about how it should be done or who did superior work, etcetera, etcetera. Some in the news described them as 'glitterati,' but Jeanne referred to them as 'etceteras,' because it was traditionally their way to end most sentences whenever they were into something way over their heads.

As long as Jeanne remained still and let her mind unwind, her timing was always superb, but there had been too many unexpected twists to this vacation to allow much time for meditation. Her schedule had been changed constantly, so she now felt unable to concentrate and connect within as she normally did. Pressure had been building in her mind, and she was experiencing anxiety over a secret threat, but outwardly nothing appeared to be amiss. Jeanne felt now that she was being rescued by this woman in white. Weird!

Lightening quick that thought brought her back to the present in a flash, just in time to hear the headline speaker from a large art gallery in New York say: "I believe indigenous people need to harness their imaginations and keep their minds on what people of other climates and lifestyles want and use now. However, even if they become half as practical as we are, they will never rule the world of art." With this sentence ringing over the audience, the speaker sat down and began fiddling listlessly with her rings. She obviously did not want anyone to ask questions or make comments.

Either the audience was stunned or asleep, because everyone sat in silence a few seconds before one or two decided to applaud politely. A few others began to clap half-heartedly and everyone else looked at their programs to see what was next on the agenda. When the small applause died away, the art dealer from New York made no move to leave the stage, nor did anyone else appear to take charge, so the audience sat, apparently mulling over whether or not they should stay or move to another room. Most chose to wait for another speaker to orate.

Speaking to the audience from her seat at the back of the room, the woman in white said, "Three things are missing when you don't debate an issue."

Most assumed the stranger was addressing the last speaker who slumped in her chair, apparently paying no attention to the intruder. Her posture caused alarm bells to go off in the minds of a few. Several thought she might be suffering an attack of some kind and prepared to go to her rescue, but Jeanne could not move. She just looked on while the woman in white approached the podium to fill the void in leadership.

Speaking pleasantly, but firmly, the *brilliant* woman said, "Let her alone. She's extremely tired. She wanted to inspire all of you to work harder on your art, but became so fatigued she couldn't continue. That happens when you yourself are not inspired."

Without introduction, the unknown woman spoke with authority, as if she had been invited and expected to speak. She was neither, but that did not stop her from talking. "I see you all have a lot to do now, and many are wondering about how I just walked in and took over when your headline speaker pooped out and left you flat." She snapped and clicked her fingers loudly as she spoke, which woke a few in the audience who had lost their places earlier and were now sitting in a stupor of their own making. The stranger smiled as the dazed ones rejoined the group. They believed that they alone had missed her introduction.

This turn of events was so unexpected that the audience quickly became interested in what the stranger had to say. Many had assessed the way she was dressed and decided that she had to be some kind of shaman from one of the Mexican tribes, but no one put his or her mind far enough into time to figure out which tribe.

Ignoring their whispers and sighs, the woman said, "I see two of you are here to pray, meditate, and let your hearts embrace time, but everyone else came to have a good time—or whatever passes for fun among art critics." No one laughed, but they could see that she was having fun. "The reason I'm here is to reach out and touch those of you who want to do a lot more for the arts than you ever did before." Now looking very serious, possibly about to say something profound, everyone stopped moving about to listen intently as she said softly, "I am the leader of a group of people who need your help."

Now everyone watched her closely, as she paused and then began to stride across the stage while telling them about what her group wanted and needed. Her actual speech was quite reserved, even elegant, but her dramatic sweeping motions as she grandly delivered each sentence convinced the audience that she knew what had to be done to help starving artists—and had done it a lot!

What no one could figure out was her name or what group she represented. Some were so overcome with curiosity that they could not listen any longer. They were so busy framing questions they alone wanted answered. However, most listened and enjoyed her refreshing insights about artists, life, and people who worked with both sides of life—the spiritual and the material—expressing their belief systems in artistic mediums.

Throughout the lecture, Jeanne sat beaming, always agreeing emphatically with what was said. Finally, she recognized that the speaker was none other than her enigmatic friend of many lives, Mandy. It had not been easy to figure out who she was until now. But her style and her way of speaking emphatically and directly to the heart opened memories of their past associations. Mandy never let anyone relax when there was work to be done! 'Aaaahhhh, yes,' thought Jeanne, 'this is exactly what I needed right now. My old friend, Mandy, lecturing me about working harder and doing things better than anyone would ever believe could be achieved… I feel better already…I feel like I can go out right now and write the greatest All American Novel ever…and still have plenty of things to editorialize about life hereabouts …but it will fade. It always does. Whenever I leave her space I'm suddenly defeated by a lack of energy. I feel drained in my brain, and today will be no different. I can see it now… Mandy has so many way-out beliefs that are soooo weird and strange, yet indigenous people always know what she means… Meanwhile, I end up feeling strained to the limit or an inferior without a brain… She changes things or makes me change—and that's hard work…. Yes, I guess I do need her now….'

Jeanne's musings suddenly broke apart as she heard Mandy say: "I feel that you all need a break—as well as a new way of life that will bring you back to true faith and belief in God—and your own humanity. You can wait to see if something better is going to appear, but I can't. I have to leave!"

As if exhausted from lecturing for hours, Mandy plopped down in the chair next to the dozing moderator. Unlike the previous speaker, she could not get away with sitting down and shunning all questions. The first one to ask questions spoke so rapidly that the audience's enthusiasm did not peak for another hour. The conventioneers eventually wore themselves out asking for all they wanted to know, expressing their feelings, and telling everyone how great they felt, but Mandy was still 'raring to go' as she said in her native, nasal accent.

Finally, Jeanne was called upon to end the symposium with either a prayer or a salutation—depending upon each participant's philosophy. She stood and shared a few brief thoughts that sounded like elegant prose to her, but were not. When she completed her assignment, unbidden her hands traced a cross on her chest as she watched. Totally fascinated to watch what appeared to be an automatic response, she wondered why she made the sign of the cross when she was not Catholic. The audience followed suit automatically, too. Instead of leaving then, many stood as if riveted in place.

Unable to move beyond the first few rows of seats because friends from the past blocked her path, Jeanne stood patiently and waited to see if Mandy would also approach her—perhaps ask her to lunch or wish to speak to her alone. Within five minutes Mandy appeared nearby and motioned to her to head toward the door. The two women left the room together as many watched them exit in silence. A few cried out that they wanted to talk to Mandy as she disappeared into the light of outside.

"What are you doing in Tucson?" Jeanne asked as she slipped her arm through the crook of Mandy's elbow, seemingly her oldest and best friend. "You look great, but you have to be exhausted! I heard somewhere about you being run out of Mexico—again. It's getting to be a habit. Isn't it?" She laughed and poked at Mandy as if she were not real or perhaps only half-baked.

"As a matter of fact, I'm going back to Mexico today. But I had to stop and help out a friend who was blocked. Wonder who that could be?" As Mandy said this, she stroked her chin as if it was covered with a long beard. She glanced away before giving Jeanne a wide smile that expressed more than could be explored in ten volumes about friends of many lives sharing past experiences, together and apart, with those who stand just beyond the threshold waiting for you to take your next step into space or time.

"I think maybe I did ask for you to be here today, Mandy, but how did you get the message so fast? I was just sitting on the stage wishing—and presto, you appeared!"

"I was on my way to my next interview and caught your scent." Mandy chuckled at the shocked expression on Jeanne's face. "Yes, I smelled *you*. You wear a kind of lavender veneer. Very healthy scent—not easy to forget! I caught a whiff of it and then took a quick look around the hotel, and it turns out you're in the conference room next to where I was scheduled to speak. Who really cares if I talked in one room or the other? No one listens, so no one in the other room will figure out I didn't speak to them until they compare notes later and discover that some dull guy without any original ideas spoke to them twice!" Mandy laughed away her prank and motioned to hurry. She had to catch a plane to Merida within a few hours.

Since both women were elated as they walked out of the convention center, they did not notice a man standing alone at the back of the lobby as he turned and followed them, without hiding it from anyone who might be watching him or them. Seemingly, they randomly selected a restaurant and asked for window seats to more easily watch the street-life. Once ensconced in a huge booth, they prepared to talk for hours. The watcher was probably hungry, too, but he did not enter the restaurant after them.

Mandy's pager started vibrating in her bag, but she resisted its urgent appeal. Who was trying to save her this time? What could they do anyway? She rejected the summons, purposely neglecting to send out a warning that they were being watched, but angels arrived anyway, apparently just in the knick of time.

When the waitress offered them dessert menus, Jeanne pointed across the street to where a bus was backing up and moving too close to the curb. She said, "Wow! Did you see that?"

"Yeah, and I also noticed a guy walking up and down the block—crossing back and forth several times. At first I thought he might be watching us, but I guess he was just waiting for the bus." As Mandy said this, an ambulance with siren blaring slammed to the curb directly in front of the bus.

"No, Mandy, look, the bus hit him! It's the same guy. I saw him, too. Can you believe it? He was hit by a bus while I was thinking that he was watching us! Wonder what that means?"

Worried beyond anything she could imagine possible at this stage in her shamanic work, Mandy dropped her voice to whisper to Jeanne. "I think I've made a serious mistake and better not leave The States right now. Can you take me to your room or let me in later?"

As casually as possible, Jeanne whispered assurances that she was welcome to stay with her as long as she wanted. Mandy nodded and quickly resumed talking—only louder, as though the accident outside no longer held their attention once their desserts arrived. They ate slowly—commenting about their desserts and how many calories they needed to work off now…time slipped by. Since the waitress had been tipped generously, she did not care how long it took them to dine.

Once outside the restaurant, Mandy said her good-byes loudly in case anyone might be listening in then. She said she was headed to the airport, making no mention that they would meet again later in Jeanne's hotel room. Grinning, Mandy waved good-bye as Jeanne turned toward her rental car. Just then a thought struck her and she yelled after Mandy, "Yoo-Hoo! Mandy! Let me drive you to the airport. I have time."

As she turned to look at Jeanne, Mandy noticed a dark man standing near the rear of a nearby van. She did not think he would take Jeanne hostage, but after the bus incident, she was not going to take any chances, so she called back, "Why not?"

Walking quickly toward Jeanne, she watched the man hurry toward a car already in motion. She glanced at the license plate and put it to memory. She was not about to be negligent twice in one day and risk her friend's life.

As they scrambled into the rented sedan, Jeanne said, "How about you and I driving out of town—not staying at my suite?"

"No, I think that's exactly what they would want us to do… If we split up now or go into the desert, they could pick us off easily and no one would ever know what happened to us or where we were. If we both stay in your room, but you appear to be alone while I stay hidden, I can hide out for a few days, and whoever it is will think they lost me along the way and that I fled Tucson. I know how to do that, but I need you to feel okay with getting involved in my plot."

"No problemo, Mandy, I can see it all now! I don't mind if you want to stay in my room. I'm sure the maid can be paid off not to say anything, but I think it's best if you appear to be a visiting relative—not a girl friend. The maid's Mexican and wouldn't think much about it, and we wouldn't have to talk to the front desk then."

"We don't have to pay off the maid or talk to the front desk. I can easily remove or move my material being anywhere I please. I'll demonstrate when we have to move." Obviously, Jeanne was shocked by this revelation, so Mandy patted her arm reassuringly and said, "As soon as we get to the airport, I'll hop out, grab my bag, and walk into the nearest ladies room and disappear."

Jeanne's eyes were now as big as they could get without popping out of her head, so Mandy patted her arm again and crooned soothingly, "Not long after I enter the ladies room, I'll leave again—dressed as a nun. I'll be wearing a large, plain gold cross and a navy blue business suit—like they do."

In a way, the thought of Mandy becoming a nun made sense to Jeanne, but when she later saw her friend coming out of the ladies room dressed like one, she wanted to laugh. Her thoughts had gotten mixed up enough that she forgot she was not to act as if she recognized her friend when they met again. It did not matter. No evil was around them then.

Bubbling over with enthusiasm—not entirely an act, either, Jeanne said to the businesslike nun, "So you flew in to speak tomorrow about living your life in faith? That's so very interesting! I was just dropping off another friend of mine who spoke about the same thing today—I think."

Mandy did not reply. Instead, she primly pursed her lips and walked with a black leather purse clutched in front of her as if it contained a few million dollars that someone nearby might want to steal. When she finally replied, her words were few and far apart, without any nasal nuances, not at all lyrical or rhyming—as usually happened when Mandy talked while in another state of mind. She was so transformed from her usual self that Jeanne began to think she had mistaken a Mother Superior for Mandy and was now leading the wrong woman out of the airport terminal. Managing to whisper without moving her lips, Jeanne said, "Are you here to speak at a conference?"

This unexpected remark caused Mandy to laugh out loud. Attempting to recover her composure, she said as severely as she could, "Obviously! I'm here to make an accounting for all the foolishness you hear in Church—about how women are not to be revered or held dear unless they produce children."

Jeanne only had time to say, "Hush! You're out of your field. Be as nice as you can and we'll be out of here before anyone realizes you're not a nun." Her last words were aimed at the back of Mandy as she hurried toward the rental car parked near the ramp closest to the exit.

As they climbed into the hot car, Mandy said with severity, "I am a nun! Don't you get it yet? I am or have been every personality that I have ever created in this age or space… It's time to put everything together and flee this place. I have no intention of staying behind again to help any more people ascend. I've had it! I'm ready to go!!"

Mumbling was something Jeanne was prone to do when she was alone, so it never occurred to her that she was mumbling again as she drove the car out of the garage and onto the Interstate.

"What are you saying? Anymore you mumble all the time, Jeanne. Are you upset and afraid that we'll meet our just end today?" Mandy's laughter was abbreviated as she watched her friend maneuver the car into lines of fast flowing traffic where everyone was determined to break the speed limit, even if they made no progress.

As soon as they were speeding along, too—way beyond what was safe for all involved—'just keeping pace,' according to Jeanne, she finally answered Mandy. "I'm okay! But since I live alone and write out of my home, I've developed the habit of talking things out with myself—out loud, and I even get great answers sometimes."

Mandy was no longer laughing as she said sagely, "You're wise and you do have a brilliant life inside, but remember I'm in the car with you and we're being followed—or maybe you already noticed."

"What?" Jeanne immediately glanced into the rearview mirror and saw without difficulty a car that had not been there a moment before. It was rapidly advancing on them. It was not easy to see into due to very dark windows, so she prepared for trouble. Her rear-view mirror had a special coating on it that enables the driver to see in the dark, but this would be her first use of it. Thinking back, she decided that the rental agent who had demonstrated how it worked must have been a secret agent—or an angel. She had not thought anything about it then, but now??

"What kind of light do you need to see inside that car?" Mandy asked.

"I have it. It's in the mirrors. If you look closely you can see there are three men and a woman inside, and they're aiming a gun at us now! It's a semi-automatic, and it's not going to be funny if it hits us. I think I'll use my only weapon—speed." As she said this, Jeanne tramped down on the accelerator and tore up the road with the other car in hot pursuit, barely managing to keep pace.

After a quarter of a mile, driving fast enough to make the car shimmy, Jeanne abruptly pulled over to the far right lane and stopped on the wide berm. Meanwhile the huge sedan remained locked in a stream of racing cars that forced it to maintain too great a speed to easily merge and make a quick exit. Headed into the setting sun, the driver had difficulty maneuvering into either right lane. Once they got over to the far right he was traveling too fast to pull off onto the narrowing berm as it banked into a turn. The car was stopping, so it would not be long before someone headed toward them on foot…and there was no way they could drive by the car without getting caught.

Just as their fate seemed sealed, Mandy laughed and pointed upward. A helicopter suddenly appeared right over them, seemingly out of nowhere. It lowered a rope toward them. Not a scene out of an action movie, more like a rescue operation on the high seas orchestrated by someone a lot higher in this world than Jeanne was accustomed to meeting and greeting. As they scrambled into the cockpit, no one said a word. The pilot motioned for them to sit back while two women dressed in business clothes swiftly descended the ladder and entered their rental car. The rest is history as far as Mandy and Jeanne could see. They never knew what happened to the two women (and neither do we), but it was very interesting to see.

As their day ended, the two women moved up their work alone. A group of new arrivals met them at the airport, all eager to help them with whatever they wanted to do, but strongly urging Mandy not to go back to Mexico just yet. They felt a lot had to be done before she could be totally supported in her work there and be allowed to move freely about the countryside and see everything. Jeanne was asked to consider taking a risk and go back to Mexico with them instead of Mandy. Often described as impulsive, Jeanne seldom was, but she quickly decided that it was a great way to visit Mexico and not have to pay. As a mumbler in good standing, Jeanne saw nothing odd in Mandy stammering when she said she was not prepared to do whatever they had in mind.

Several members of Mandy's elite group hastily decided not to tell Jeanne anything about the web. Her thoughts were entangled enough! Within days, we will be able to easily see what happens to Mandy and friends, but for now we will do nothing until we see what happens to Jeanne. Will she flee Tucson? Will she take her books and things to Mexico to please people who are not perfect strangers?

☼ CHAPTER ELEVEN

Standing at the back of the hall, Mandy could not see what was going on in the front rows, but she could see from the dark hue of the speaker's aura that this shyster was trying to pull something over on the audience. Watching closely as he pranced across the stage—mentally reviewing his commitment to them, she suddenly laughed when she realized he could not add.

Apparently used to hecklers, he continued his harangue to all unfortunate enough to be trapped in their seats now. "Thrifty people seldom have to be told how to work well with others, but sometimes they're miserly—scrimping constantly—never spending freely—and that makes everyone else restless! So today we're going to help them do something unique, and it won't cost them a dime. Can you guess what it is?"

Two suited and tied businessmen sitting in the middle of the room stood up immediately to call his attention to the math errors. He told them to sit down and keep quiet! This self-anointed expert was not to be sidetracked by facts. As though nothing happened, the fast-talker said, "I have three hundred million people who can use this product, but only ten families in each community will be allowed to sell it. Do you catch my drift? I'm going to make someone in this room a millionaire today! You can decide among you who'll make a million—while we discuss the best healing cream you've ever seen—and it's produced only in the Andes! It's an ancient Incan remedy that heals the sick and infirm. It keeps for weeks without refrigeration—as long as it doesn't sit out too long once opened."

Listening to his shtick, Mandy began to shake with laughter. Looking around to see how he affected others, she was shocked to realize that no one else nearby was wise to him…and they were obviously irritated by her reaction to his lies. Their gullibility caused her to call him out and state that The Inca never used creams like he described; but before she could speak, she intuited that somehow this huckster was on to something the Incas *did* use! She pondered and thought, 'How did this charlatan find out about it? Why was he given such wisdom?'

Hidden deep within the audience, Mandy opened her mind to time and saw greed take over the scene. Around her the audience was groveling at his feet, eager to find treasure and more money than they could make through honest labor. She could clearly see how this one man conned the greedy and the needy without ever seeming to be a fraud. Angered by thoughts that tumbled from her mind, end-over-end, she thought, 'How can these nice people be bought so easily by a con man? Is it because they want a piece of the American pie—and they want it now? What does it mean anyway, and why does this guy keep saying it over and over again like a mantra?'

His harangue increased in intensity. He was growing hyper as he emphasized what he believed would be the cincher—the irresistible point that he must make. "As you know, most people don't buy homes they want to live in for the rest of their lives and pass on to their children. Why? Because they don't make enough or have enough money saved to buy houses they really want! So they have to buy whatever is out there in their price range. Those rules won't apply to you ever again!!! You'll be able to buy million-dollar houses in five different states and live off the profits of others' labor—and the best part of all this is that you don't have to do a darn thing—except use this fantastic salve just once…and then tell all your friends about it."

Apparently the two men in the middle of the room he had rebuffed were unwilling to drop their discovery of an error in his math, so two beefy ushers appeared out of nowhere and escorted them outside, along with their wives. It was Mandy's belief that they had been rescued, but everyone else in the room apparently thought they would never be able to live it down and always regret missing out on getting rich quick.

'Why would anyone buy into such far-fetched ideas? Why would anyone believe success and prosperity were so easy to achieve?' Thinking these thoughts and others, Mandy decided to slip out now, because no one else seemed ready to leave.

As the glib promoter revved up for the final whirl of his sales pitch, Mandy decided to unhitch her powers—only for a moment or so. She asked God to arrange the final outcome of this day in such a way that The Holy Spirit would descend and save these stupid people from pain, sorrow, and poverty. She sat still, waiting for something to happen, but nothing changed. In fact, the huckster spoke even more eloquently than before she prayed. He realized the audience was eager to please him and would gladly spend whatever he wanted on his 'miracle salve,' but just as the thought of his imminent success sunk into his mind, he felt something within his brain change in a weird way. One thought popped up and stayed.

All he could hear now was a resounding voice or echo saying: 'There is nothing within you that will be saved if you take all these people with you today—even if everyone makes more money than ever before.' Right after that thought he saw a flash and felt a stab in his back. His conscience had suddenly arrived in his mind, and it made him stop selling the crowd. He suddenly felt so weird that he thought maybe be was dying on the spot. Gone in a flash was his euphoric mood!

Standing in silence, he looked out over the crowd and recognized for the first time in his adult life that no one can afford to lose money, nor should people bankrupt their families in their old age by buying into his highly-inflated miracle salve pyramid scheme. As he watched his mind warp into a thin wavy line that was not solid enough to hold his audience's attention, he could not stop babbling.

Seeing his impending collapse, Mandy urged it on by laughing loudly. Because she was laughing so hard that tears ran down her cheeks, the entire audience noticed the woman in white was leaving then. Several women ushers quickly escorted Mandy to the ladies room where they stood and watched her wash her face.

But what happened next? Why do things seem to break up when Mandy is on the move? Those who can move easily through such a lesson on time will look back over it later in order to rate if what Mandy did next made any sense. Everyone else will have to work on it in time because Mandy has no desire to talk about how she looks back or how she grades the behavior of others—unless there is very good reason to do so. According to those who work with Mandy behind the veil, teaching wisdom is not reason enough to lead every one away from what they believe today.

"What a smooth operator!" One woman called after him as he left the auditorium, because she could not see inside his mind.

A few hours later, when he talked one-on-one with Mandy about his various natural products, she could easily see what he wanted, but he did not know what she thought, so he said, "As you can see, Mandy, you and I aren't any different inside. You and I can pitch better now than ever before—and audiences always agree with us! Don't you see? If you team up with me, you can have everything you ever dreamed of—while saving the entire world."

In a perverse way, Mandy felt sorry that his greed made him desire so very little from life—and that he had no dreams, so she decided to string him along a bit longer, preventing him from ever again bothering the people in this town. Her day was not over and she was not tired, so she suggested that they walk about the city and spot what they might do together soon.

He agreed instantly! This man with iron-gray hair, wearing a silky vest, had to take the lead always. The salesman within him responded with great enthusiasm: "As you can see easily, Mandy, I'm a huge success!"

Mandy waited for what he would say next, but he said nothing more because he could not identify who he was in his own mind's eye or even the image he saw in store windows as they walked and pretended to look at wares set up to trap the unwary. Lifting her chin a bit higher so he could not see into her mind, Mandy smiled at the successful grifter and said, "I think you'll find it harder to sell people in the new millennium than you did in the last century. But then again, it's all about time, isn't it?"

Looking perplexed, he blurted out, "What do you mean? Our business can boom forever! Drops in the economy are caused by people getting confused. They stop believing that they can achieve everything if they dream."

She could not fault his reasoning, but Mandy suddenly felt something strike at the pit of her neck. She looked back at their path and saw that they were being followed. Her mind could not locate anything handy that she could use immediately to stop this invasion of her inner world, so she began jamming whatever listening device might be in place by whistling through two fingers—very loudly.

The huckster looked away from her unseemly display—into his future or perhaps down the street, while Mandy peered at shop windows reflecting the presence of two or three people who were holding their ears and appeared to be screaming in agony. That was all she needed to leave this man immediately. She raised her voice and said, "Have to run, Alex. You can do whatever you want, but making a living by high-jacking the universe and demanding huge sums of money for your exclusive use—at the expense of others, always leads to far different outcomes than what you're predicting. Take care, and don't be afraid if you're asked to review your income with the IRS. I think that's about to happen now."

Having warned him, Mandy could no longer contain her smile as she watched the man struggling internally with his accounting records. She left him gaping and escaped into the wind. He would never know why he was audited, but she knew that the FBI always uses the IRS when things are tough to prove. Too bad she could not trust them, either.

♓ ♓

An old lady said to the bus driver who was only half listening to her. "As I was saying, I think we should ban people from buses who eat or read dirty books or yell at cars or people standing outside as we drive by. Don't you agree?"

The driver put a new spin on the old company line when he replied, "I have to agree that they're a nuisance—not very nice to be around at times, but I'm the one who has to enforce the rules…and there are already too many rules to follow to be able to enjoy working—like I used to. Now I have to be a father to kids going to school—and especially afterwards when they get so rowdy you have to worry about all the people they're willing to run over to get on or off the bus…Hey, wait a minute, that woman over there is running like somebody's chasing her. Let's see if she needs help…." As he said this, he pulled the bus over to the curb and jerked it to a stop that did not bother the old woman and only slowed down a few of the children out of their seats and annoying others. As the doors folded back, he called to the running woman and asked if she needed a ride or wanted him to call for help. She motioned that she needed a ride.

Gasping for air, she dashed onto the bus, there and then. "Thanks, so much! What a day! Some guy suddenly appeared out of nowhere and I started running because I'm not sure if he's a gang-banger or a dirty old man just trying to make his day. Anyway, I sure appreciate your stopping for me!"

The bus driver wasted no time putting distance between the bus and the unscheduled stop, all the while checking his mirror and looking over his shoulder to make sure he lost the man who had been chasing her. He was now enjoying himself, talking as if he would take on the challenge of fighting off the man if necessary.

At first sight he had thought the running woman was pretty, but when he checked her out more carefully, she appeared exhausted and about the same age as the old woman who had been talking to him before the incident. He was puzzled because he had never seen anyone that old run that fast.

The old woman who had made room for the woman to sit down beside her asked, "What are you going to do now?"

Very calmly, Mandy said, "I'll walk back from the next stop and see if anyone comes after me again."

The boys who had been acting up in the back of the bus were now watching Mandy and how she moved. What she said amazed them enough that they decided she had to be an undercover cop—and they were not that far off the mark. Only a few blocks after having rescued Mandy, the driver pulled the bus over once again and she hopped off. She said with a wink, "You're an angel. Do you know that?" The driver grinned and waved and she added, "I'll make sure you get that raise—and you *will* live to a very old age." Then she sent him a message telepathically, 'Don't ever let anyone on the bus get the drop on you again."

Without thinking much about what just happened, the driver looked into his mirror to survey the back of the bus and discovered that three boys were playing with knives as if they were toys. Immediately stopping the bus, he helped the old lady get up and escorted her down the steps. While doing this he told her that he would have to take the bus to the police station and she was to trust that he would be okay. She loved it! She was thrilled that he was going to help the entire community—and she only had to mention it to him once that they needed help now.

When one man or one woman takes a stand, can everyone else sit back then? That is not what Mandy did in this land she had at one time called home. She felt a chill, as if she had to do something now or the entire country was doomed. What could she do that would not hurt the work and would help everyone who really worked?

In the time it took Mandy to walk back from the bus stop to her car, she thought of several different options and laid them out side-by-side in her mind. Her first thought was that she should stop and move everything out of The States forever and never again say that she is an American. She could do that very easily, but her mind said that it was not right to stop a life that was not over and change its venue into something else, a life that she was not yet prepared to say she had come to Earth to live now.

Mandy thought about this for quite a while because it was a very confusing idea, until she deduced that it made a lot of sense. She said softly to herself, "If you're here to live through one life in this time, but as you begin to discover who you are, you change your venue or your religion or the people closest to you, you have to live this life over and over again—because you have to end each and every life episode that you opened while on Earth before you can leave."

With no doubt about her purpose now, Mandy strode into the parking lot. Spotting her car, she strode toward it with a power-filled mind set. No one noticed her as she exited the garage at 28 miles per hour, but by the time she hit 70 and turned toward Interstate 10, everyone was watching her head out of town. Although she knew this car was equipped for speed, she continued to be amazed at how quickly and easily it achieved peak performance. Since her present lifestyle was no longer rooted in what she appeared to be but who she is, Mandy was no longer aware of the cost of such a vehicle, so she had accepted the Porsche as a gift without giving it much thought. She was also unaware that many thought she had raced cars for a living in the past. If she had known, she would have laughed—heartily!

As her wheels spun out, they seemed to change direction instantaneously as she turned away from the Interstate and drove through the maze of Tucson's backstreets. Mandy knew she had to make a life-altering choice now! She could either go to Mexico immediately or stay in The States indefinitely, so she decided to stay. Her mind cleared just as the skies opened to reveal a sun as large as anyone could imagine a star to be. She felt her heart leap at the sight of it! She knew this was going to be one of those really, really strange days, but she was ready for anything now.

Within three blocks a new pursuit began, but this time Mandy did not worry. She did not worry because her car was now being guided by something other than her mind. She was steering—not driving the car. Her thoughts were engaged, but not very much. She was alert, but not thinking about what was going on in Tucson as her hands whipped the steering wheel around and downshifted to take sharp curves—never aware of what she was doing or where she was going. The work was now in place, so all she had to do was physically get to the starting line.

A few minutes of high-speed chase took place before two Ford Crown Victorias pulled up beside her and pressed badges at her from behind dark tinted windows. She could see both cars simultaneously, without turning her head toward either. Without acknowledging that she would stop, Mandy began downshifting, so the officers in both cars seemed to relax their grip. One car pulled in front of her, but the other car was unable to control the rate of deceleration and shot beyond her. In a flash, Mandy spun the steering wheel and accelerated enough to create a high-pitched screech audible for blocks around as her high-performance Michelin radials prepared for take off. She was far down the road before either Crown Vic could turn around and give chase.

To no one visible, Mandy said, "What's with these guys in Tucson?" She liked to talk aloud as she drove and often sang off-key just to vent her vocal chords with what others might think was a country rendition of today's hits. With her mind wide open, she always willingly abided by the law, but apparently not everyone working with her today cared about such limitations.

During those tense moments when her car appeared to be jet propelled and free-wheeling, the men in hot pursuit of Mandy yelled into unseen ears somewhere, "I thought we were supposed to be chasing a woman?" No one apparently had any explanation for what had happened, so they checked her plates—again. It turned out they were not supposed to be chasing this car, and it barely even resembled the one they were supposed to pull over. How did that happen?

Smiling broadly now that she had ditched the police or g-men or whomever they were, Mandy knew she could walk into any restaurant in Tucson without being recognized, but she was still not sure if she personally could be detected by the police. She continued to wonder why they had chased her or her car or whatever?

Within a day of this case of misidentification coming to light, Mandy created a list of what she wanted to do before she gave up her American citizenship. The list was not very long, but seemed to reflect a new state of affairs. Nothing listed could be said to be strange or weird, but she felt something was not quite right, so she double-checked it to make sure there were no creditors anywhere who would say later that she owed them money. She wanted to be sure that every friend she had ever met along the way was able to live without her and did not require any help. As a result, her list turned out to be longer than expected, but easily checked out. She reasoned aloud, "Friends are no longer friends if you never see or hear from them again."

As her plan for the final day moved into another and yet another, Mandy began to feel that she was living undercover in the United States and hiding in Mexico—and now being chased by unknown parties in both places—so she might as well go home. Home to Mandy was Mexico now, but she was still an American to those who knew her best. Wondering how she could change her homeland without losing face, she decided that it was just not that big a deal. The issue at stake now was pride—not faith.

Her final, final decision was to let her citizenship sit and not bother to change anything just yet. So whenever Mandy spoke to friends about her plans to permanently relocate, she usually said just about the same thing: "I have a dual relationship with two countries that are truly one. If anyone doubts it, let them contact people who live along the border and see for themselves what's really going on now."

If any friends refused to accept her decision, she lectured them. Her favorite argument went like this: "If America was as poor as Mexico is, and the government didn't give out huge welfare payments to farmers, ranchers, and politicians, as well as a meager existence to the disabled, our Southwest constituents would be the ones fleeing into Mexico to find a better life. When poverty is confronted with greed, it usually loses, but in a time of great plenty, those living in poverty can move up and not be lost if they move fast to greener pastures."

According to Mandy, today and every day is a wave of energy, so she wanted to catch this wave and ride its crest before it crashed in the surf. She was unwilling to fetch and carry and deliver or do whatever others wanted unless the end justified the means, and she deemed it to be worthy of her time. Mandy knew personally that the work done well today or completed yesterday need not be done over again on another day, but she had to constantly teach that lesson to others—over and over again.

The US Government wanted her to act as a courier and do whatever she could to help them fight a world revolution, but she could not see such an international conflict happening and refused to do any more than she did before. Once the tide turned and an event was over and done with, Mandy returned to her own moment and looked into time.

Standing alone in the desert, she felt something chilling emanating from a distance and flying toward her. She shivered. Her work was not over here, but she knew then that she was no longer needed in Arizona. Las Vegas planners and other huge cities are busy enhancing the desert around them at the expense of everyone else. The fact that potable water was needed elsewhere bothered no one in the central government. It was rumored and believed that nobody with enough influence to make any real change cared, once they were paid well to look the other way. Mandy decided that this was too big a battle for one woman and one warrior to win, so she backed away from it once again and moved on with her work in Mexico.

Only later when she looked back did she remember the effect that one bus driver had on the world when he took it upon himself to wage war on the homeboys and blocked their bullying people who ride buses.

What humanity might do next or how humans choose to live now is not meant for angels to handle, according to those who say they know such things. But when we live with angels and demons and others, we quickly find out that some exist and others are mere figments of fertile imaginations. Which ones exist and which ones do not? You will pay a high price if you believe in something that will never be or has ever been or is now, but not nearly as much as you will pay if you never see and believe even less.

Working on her life without delay was what Mandy had planned to do that day, but she was swept away into the night. The desert life she chose does not provide clues about what happened then, but we know she was not seen for years by anyone who remembered her from that time in Tucson.

☼ Chapter Twelve

My mother used to say: "Whatever you worry about never happens."

Jeanne sat staring at the words and thinking about her mother as she was when she was a child…She felt her mind then drift into another time. As she slipped away, her hands started typing again. She had only a few seconds to watch in amazement before she was totally unaware of what was happening to her. Her fingers typed without apparent thought:

Only twice in a life are you able to think before you leap, but you do whatever you want anyway. So why worry? What do you think we should do together, now that We Are Here working as a group in a unified field—trying to discover the reason for life before we die?

When her fingers stopped moving she sat and reread the lines several times, then began putting her work away for another day, but her mind would not turn off. She kept thinking about the work she had signed on to accomplish with Mandy and the others she loved working with, too. 'How can a writer of classic prose and poetry, as well as self-help books about living successfully–within the constraints of a career, prepare me to work with people who keep mentally fit by meditating while they work at a potter's wheel all day or at a loom? How do I reach them? Most of the native artists are disinterested in formal education after the sixth grade, so I'm unable to reach them through my books.' Jeanne finally came to the conclusion that she was there to learn from the artists, rather than to teach them. It was a shock to her mind—possibly her ego, but not her soul, which was eager to live a more awe-inspiring life.

Mumbling, "If I'm to ever reach You, my Higher Self, what do I have to do?" Instead of turning off her computer or exiting the existing screen, her hands flit quickly over the keys once again, but this time she was able to easily read what she wrote.

You firmly believe that you must excel in order to do well, whether working on your Higher Self or teaching another how to succeed, but here you are without enough language skills to teach much and you find that no one else is very interested in speaking English only for your benefit. They care nothing about how many books you have written and sold to millions.

Rereading the message, Jeanne erased it when she realized she was whining, full of self-pity, and deserved to be reproached. The idea made her wince! What had become of her past? How did she end up in Mexico with two friends constantly reaffirming why she was here, because she constantly said she was lost—without a clue about what to do with her life?

Jeanne sat still a few minutes more before deciding to take a walk to relax and erase whatever was chasing a blues line through her mind. Exhausted, but not physically tired enough to sleep, wanting to read, but the books available were not what she wanted to remember forever. Thoughts about what to do next and how to work now kept pursuing her throughout the house until she said, "The house! That's what I can do! I was born to be a decorator. I can sell others my views on color and shape, too. If I rearrange the display rooms with little fuss and bother, and we sell more wares, then everyone will want to know what *I* do, too…I think."

♓   ♓

In the days that followed, Jeanne closely inspected many items she found stacked behind bushes and inside storage sheds. She dragged whatever she found to be interesting to her into a large area off the verandah, then got some of the men to build shelves and put up tables, all without any effort, because she had a special way with men who worked for a living. As she talked with them, her face lit up and her jaw relaxed until they could see and feel her life force issuing through her mouth. In the past these same men had often commented about how unconfident American women appeared, even though they controlled their country's economy.

Even without a degree in anthropology, Jeanne could easily see that the art of the ancient Maya spoke loudly through the art of today's tribes, making it brilliant and vibrant. She realized then that The Maya never died! Today it was unseen as history or even oral tradition as having been ordered by royalty in the past, but the true hues of their ancient world and tribal history surrounded her here and now.

Daily Jeanne met people in the 'new' old showroom and adjacent area who eagerly chatted about their lives and art while delivering supplies, but she was too preoccupied with her own troubles to listen attentively to any of them. She had no interest in figuring out why some traders took a lot of time and trouble to travel deep into the Yucatan to deliver only a jar or two of something she would never use or care to sell. However, when she heard that Mandy would be in the area again, she began creating one of her infamous long lists of things she needed to share with her. Jeanne did not wish to waste a precious minute of their time together, and knowing from experience that Mandy could flit through lists with great speed, she cut and pasted and printed out a revised list daily in a vain attempt to keep it brief.

Was it because Mandy reportedly was born to be a leader or because she had been a great success on Wall Street that enabled her to know in an instant what to do in any venue related to revenue? That thought teased Jeanne's mind, even though she was not jealous or envious of Mandy, like so many others obviously were. She just wanted to be of greater use to the mission and The Maya, so she ran down every stray thought now trying to figure out how she could improve. Thinking: 'Humility doesn't usually get you to the top, but with The Maya you can't tell who is a leader and who isn't. They all achieve a brilliant beam and seem to follow it around the world without stopping to talk a lot. I wonder how they do that?'

♓ ♓

Work usually stopped about one o'clock so all the workers could rest and gain sustenance and talk together about what they would do next. It was a great way to live in this climate. They all prayed before eating, but far differently than Mandy or Jeanne experienced in America. No one appeared to bless the food so much as take it all in quietly, showing no ambition to take the best pieces, or eat only preferred food, or even talk about the food itself, as they moved through their meals. Jeanne was still trying to understand the process and adopt this new etiquette, but found that in its simple elegance it was not easily mastered.

The arcane, often weird methods used by anthropologists to study Mayan tribes came to mind as she worked side-by-side with the natives. She immediately rejected their ways as unsuitable and inconsistent with her views on life, as well as her experience with others. One question haunted her, 'How can you believe you understand others when you don't really live within your own tribe?'

With that in mind, Jeanne decided to visit the capitol city of Yucatan State, Merida, and discover what was preserved there from the past. She was confident that a trip to that provincial city would provide her with enough contrast to her daily work in this remote outpost to keep her mind busy for weeks after she returned. That was her plan, anyway, until she heard that Mandy was en route to visit her soon.

As the news spread through the compound, Jeanne ran quickly without thinking toward the compound's mailbox to wait with letters in hand for the postman's arrival. She continued to wonder what she would do with her everyday thoughts if her readers bored of what she liked to write. She decided to write another letter to yet another friend or colleague, just as she did when she submitted manuscripts to publishers—or entered college or sought new jobs. With all this in mind, Jeanne flitted through the minutes until she saw the postman's old car creep through the village, continually stalling every hundred feet or so. Her patience was never obvious, so living in Mexico gave her a greater appreciation for her life when it was not lived at this slow pace. She felt as if she could never again manifest anything quickly, that things would materialize only if she slipped into deep reverie first.

The postman came close to running Jeanne over as his dented side-view mirror nicked the post holding the mailbox, but he totally ignored her presence. Instead, he cursed his car as he sorted through letters and cards until he suddenly remembered that the bulk of his mail was for this address and maybe he should enter the gates and deliver it to the office. He hated driving in the compound because all the pretty girls laughed when his car stalled and would not restart without a lot of effort, so he decided to dump all their mail on the ground outside, beside the big mailbox. As he got out of the car, he finally realized that Jeanne was standing beside the mailbox with letters in hand. With no idea that his gallantry might not be needed or wanted, the mailman winked and said, "Hey, you really a lady! I need no more mail, but for you, Senora, I will stop and take it myself straight to the postmaster."

Jeanne smiled and handed him her letters, then moved forward to inspect his vehicle more closely. She said, "I think you're leaking oil. I can see it dripping on the ground. Want me to put some gum in the crankshaft?" Jeanne was joking, but he took her seriously, because she was not smiling as she spoke.

"I have much trouble with this car, but I cannot buy another one. I have to take care of my brother's children. He is very sick." The man spoke softly—his deeply lined face could pass for a classic mask of tragedy.

Without thinking, Jeanne placed her hand on her heart and then on his car. She did it without speaking while the postman watched and wondered about her powers. He decided that if his car started up easily with much power, he would never again mess with these women and their men. He would deliver their mail first, and never steal the loose money he found. Without realizing it, he made a promise that would keep him in check—always.

Nudging the car a little with her index finger, Jeanne said, "I see the car is very sick. You have to take it into town and get it checked. But until then, try to stay in second gear—don't drive in high gear. Can you do that?"

"I will remember, Senora. I am not a reckless driver—ever, but I will now take more time and not hurry like I always do to deliver mail to you."

Unable to hold her humor in check any longer, Jeanne laughed and the postman grinned as he opened the door and slipped behind the steering wheel. Right then a butterfly flew out the back window, as if it had been trapped in the car. This frightened him, but he said nothing. Jeanne was delighted to see a sign that confirmed her belief that this man would change his ways, but she did not mention it to him.

Watching as he pushed in the starter and lightly applied the manual choke, she was pleased to see his car roar into full power and move forward without jerking and coughing. Inspired by this small miracle, the postman crossed himself and said a small prayer in thanksgiving. Jeanne watched the car move away a bit too quickly before she let her mind collapse into time. Although she never quite remembered what took place next, something strange did happen that day.

⋊   ⋊

Sitting cross-legged as she talked about a vision with Mandy, who was swaying in a hammock and sipping a glass of tea, Jeanne said, "I was stooping to pick up the mail sack when a strange being came into sight. He, or it, asked me if I wanted to write a book about life. I said I would love that, but my new computer isn't hooked up. Looking at this Being more closely, I read between the lines on his brow what needed to be done now. Instead of alibis and lies about what I might do with the rest of my many lives, I suddenly realized that I could get my computer installed easily now."

Mandy had been about to leave her body when Jeanne made this confession and began recounting events from the past day or two. No one else in the compound knew what had happened to Jeanne when she went out for the mail, but most suspected she had suffered from Montezuma's revenge and did not want to admit it. Instead of entering time or another life then, Mandy let her mind ease into the recent past so she could more easily remember what she had seen when she spotted Jeanne standing outside the compound by the mailbox several days earlier.

She had recognized immediately that Jeanne was in a deep trance then and unaware she was near. Unwilling to expose her to anyone who could not accommodate the energy field surrounding her and the power surging through her body, Mandy had slowed her Jeep down to a crawl to ensure no one would see what was going on. When she examined Jeanne, her dress became a shining robe of light. There was no vision in her eyes and she mumbled, as always, but said nothing intelligible. She had waited and watched over Jeanne until a couple became aware that she was back. She pretended that she had just arrived and was unable to go any further due to the huge mailbag blocking the road, thus she was able to wave them away before they got very close.

Lolling in the hammock, Mandy watched Jeanne as she released energy and opened her mind to time. Smiling, she wished Mandy a great day. That is the accepted way to leave this life for a time, but Mandy added a wish that whatever wisdom Jeanne received could be shared with everyone who lived within these walls with her.

Her reverie remained undisturbed as Jeanne mumbled, "I think I'll go to bed now. I feel so sleepy…What day is it? When did you arrive?"

Sipping the warm tea, Mandy moved her head side-to-side, as if wagging her mind, and said nothing for a few minutes. She hummed a haunting melody as she picked up a rubber mallet and hit the giant gong, indicating that Family Hour was to begin now. She never missed this event when she was in the compound, but tonight she had no intention of joining in or leading them in any kind of joke or story—even listening to gossip. Jeanne needed her here and now.

As the last echoes of the gong cleared the area, Mandy folded her legs into a yoga posture she had learned years ago in New York. Believing she could sit as is for days, she was surprised to find that her body refused to assume the pose longer than a few minutes. She could not imagine why, but listened to her body—not her mind. Shaking out her legs and flicking her finger tips, as if about to compete in a swimming meet, she almost missed Jeanne saying softly: "Mandy, you don't have to sit with me. Go and find out what they're all up to…what's happening in town…I'm fine, I can stay here alone…but if you remember, send me a cookie or cup of chocolate…I'm just fine."

Mandy made no move to leave her. She stood with arms spread out as if suspended from a marionette's grasp—not the puppeteer's apparatus. Her feet disappeared, then her legs…eventually she, too, was lost in time, but Jeanne never noticed because her mind was in another place and time, unable to sense what was happening in Mexico or the United States. She could not feel her life as it existed now, but as it was. Her thoughts moved into the *past* and she coexisted with it now.

♓   ♓

The two dreamers seemed to be standing in a clearing somewhere in the Yucatan jungle when Jeanne said, "I see that the Maya are not going to exist in the future if they don't learn to feel at home now in this existence."

Shaking her head, Mandy replied. "You're a worrier, Jeanne. I don't worry about being Maya or about the tribe flying when it's time to leave. The Ascended Maya don't worry about people who are left behind...I don't get it yet, but I'm not worrying about it either."

"You're able to forget, but I always remember! I see things in my dreams about the life we had in Chichen Itza and in the fields that are now Merida. I feel lost now. I want to go back, but I know that if I do, this will become a time of great confusion and I won't be able to help anyone leave again."

Bending her neck and moving her head side-to-side, Mandy prayed loudly that the Lord of Time would appear now and not force them to stay any longer. Unwilling to stand out from the tribe, she was aware that she had to leave or be taken somewhere else and possibly harmed by enemies of The Ascended Maya. Her gift was one of far sight, so she looked into the future as if she were an eagle soaring over the earth. She spotted tiny 'birds' thousands of feet beneath her. She was powerful and could easily become a man, but she did not wish to land in another life without the power to change what she was unable to believe now. Her power was sound—not only rooted to planet Earth, even though in this life she was not of high birth. This life they existed in now was one of slavery and strife for Mandy. She did not wish to live it again—at least not now.

Raising her eyes to see what her slave was creating with twine made of vines, Jeanne saw a face peering at her through the trees, then another, and another. She let out a cry, "Mandy, look! They're here! They're going to kill us—or worse!"

Jeanne immediately left the others sleeping on the ground and moved toward the dense bushes that gave cover to the invaders. Her mind was clear and alert. She would sacrifice herself to save the tribe. The look of amazement at her own decision was mistaken by the watchers as a mask of fear. When her body started quivering and shaking, they realized she was not crazy or stupid, and definitely not without power. She was obviously a shaman!

Such a turn of events shocked those waiting to take this clan as slaves. They saw that Jeanne's eyes were wide open, yet blind. As far as they could tell, she was neither woman nor man, and then someone remembered that there was an ancient curse if you harmed such a person. Immediately, the invaders changed their plan and began plotting to coerce this woman or man into helping them. They usually help others before defrauding them, but Jeanne was not to be a slave to any man ever again.

Since Jeanne's thoughts were transparent, she did not want her enemies to get too close, so she emitted a beam of light stronger than any star of the night. Unaware that her ray had seared the enemy, she was surprised when they leapt high into the air and appeared to be dancing there. Her power was clearly of God, so they hurried away without saying another word.

♓   ♓

"Jeanne, wake up! You have to go to bed. You're all cramped up and hunched over. Your shoulder won't be able to handle all the typing if you don't release the tension now." Shaking her friend and yelling to awaken her immediately, Mandy pushed Jeanne to return to today, but she did not wish to awaken. Her arm dropped out of the hammock and wrote in mid-air that she was a scribe, not a shaman.

Realizing that she was unwilling or unable to remove this cloud of whatever now, Mandy decided to invade Jeanne's space and check it out, so as not to lose another friend to the Past. She was unwilling to repeat what she had done when others left her—never to return, because she had never really believed that it happened—until now. Sitting with her arms folded across her chest and her back pressed against an adobe outer wall, Mandy began praying to the wind. Her voice carried through the window to the women waiting outside her door, and they shivered with its intent. She prayed that her home would not be entered until she gave a signal that all was clear. These women were expected to keep watch so no one on this side of time could try to take over the tribe.

As the two old friends met once again in time—or was it space, they embraced and acted as though they were ancient in many forgotten ways. The distance between them was always equal from one to the other, yet one seemed to be all about business and the other concentrated on art. What would happen to them now was not whispered but imparted in their breath.

"Look," whispered the one working diligently on her art. "I see colors in different vibrations! They're unlike anything we ever saw before. I want to take them back when we decide to leave this place. How do we do that?"

"I don't know, but maybe we'll be instructed in the ways of The Ascended Maya and be able to take it back now—but maybe not. We can't ask. We can't make any demands. We have to accept what is here and being given—or leave. Do you understand? We can't have a plan!"

"I understand. Do you think I would have planned to do this?"

While Mandy and Jeanne beamed their feelings back and forth, another being approached them. It was a man whom they both wanted to see—yet they did not agree on what he might be.

Jorge stood in front of them looking about the same as always. He was not angry, upset, or commanding them to be still. He seemed totally at ease as he spoke. "Without saying a word, please adjust your levels of trust. You're both afraid, thus unable to fly today. Take care not to be upset when you are asked to give up your family, your money, and your life—be aware that it is all still there. Okay?"

His friendly gesture and use of slang was all they needed to follow him, but they did not get very far. They were unable to move as fast as Jorge. When he finally stopped, they told him that they felt as if they were being blocked.

Jorge's tone was severe as he said, "Don't let anyone into you again! Do you understand me, Jeanne?"

"No, Jorge, I don't understand what you mean. Are you saying not to have sex—or something else?"

Jorge grinned in a strange way and said he was not even aware they could have sex here. He explained that their vision of the Future or the Past was just that—a vision; and if you let someone else interpret it for you, you lose your own path. Others took over and led you—and no one is supposed to do that. All he added then was: "You actively participate in any coercion to lose your way or your soul, if you practice witchcraft or anything like that."

Mandy asked, "If you can walk erect and have no trouble while on Earth, does it mean you're more powerful than The Maya?"

"I am Maya! I have lived in many times, but always as a Maya. You are able to be a Maya, too, but often try to combine two lives. You're not of the faith you were born into when you arrived this time, but you try not to break with that faith, either, in order to be Maya. You want it both ways! You can't have two gods, and you can't discuss God, yet you're willing to try. That is when you cannot fly! Never forget that God is inside you and able to take care of you in every way imaginable, then you will be happy."

Jorge seemed to be smiling, but neither Mandy nor Jeanne could follow his steps or his thoughts closely. In fact, they were beginning to crumble and bend in half again and again, instead of holding their heads erect and observing what he wanted them to understand now.

Suddenly Jorge laughed and said good-naturedly, "Okay, Okay, you two have had enough for one day. I can see that when you are finally ready you'll let me know…But obviously I'll have to watch out or you'll take over my mind and leave me sitting in full view of my ego, which will destroy my ability to fly as well as I do now." As Jorge laughed, Mandy and Jeanne collided with each other and awoke with a loud bang.

♓ ♓

While Jeanne and Mandy were journeying through time, Nita entered the house surreptitiously. She was suspicious that they were conspiring to do something in opposition to the army. She had listened intently, but heard nothing of any consequence when discovered by a sentry making his rounds later than usual. The man was not happy to catch Nita spying, but was willing to let it pass if she gave him a glass of strong drink and sat on his lap. Instead she laughed and quickly moved to the middle of the verandah and announced loudly that Mandy and Jeanne were awake and able to see everyone now.

The fact that Nita knew they were awake, yet neither had announced it, worried both women, but neither said a word. This woman, the beauty of the village, would no longer be assigned to counting money, working with supplies, or greeting strangers. She sealed her fate this day and would have to leave if she wanted to lead. Nita would decide to leave, but not just yet.

As Jeanne and Mandy opened the door to welcome in the women waiting for them, they saw Nita leave with a strange man—walking quickly toward the outer world. They both understood that she was an enemy and never to be trusted again and wondered simultaneously, 'Why do women place men above their family, their country, even their God?' That was a mystery they intended to investigate before they ended their work undercover.

☼ CHAPTER THIRTEEN

"Whatever you're doing, stop! I've got something to tell you. It won't take more than a minute, I promise." Wanda was shouting to a woman across the room who appeared to be leaving. Her plea was such that three women and a man stopped what they were thinking to wonder if she wanted them to listen now, too. At a glance they saw she was calling out the beautiful woman known to be a famous fashion model.

Since the familial tie is stronger than all others, Teri stopped and made a sign that she would not leave and would wait at the back of the room. Wanda picked her way through the empty chairs scattered everywhere until she was at her daughter's side and able to speak without raising her voice. She said, "Don't even think about driving to Merida tonight. I have it on good authority that the highways are going to be flooded with tourists, and you don't have to be caught up with them—as well as the thieves who steal whatever is available when tourists unwind with wine and such—supposedly having a good time."

Smiling only slightly, Teri said, "Okay, Wanda, you've made your point, but why the big windup before the pitch? What's really going on now? Are you having trouble with your leg again? I don't know how you work as hard as you do with it like that? I worry about you all the time, but you never say anything personal to me anymore. What's wrong?" While talking, Teri checked how her mother was dressed and her hair, then began to smooth her coat lapels—even tried to straighten her tie and blouse collar.

This display of preening in public upset Wanda enough that she erupted with what she had wanted to keep hidden from others. "Don't fuss like that! I'm okay. I have to really rush because the boys—even some of the girls—are going to make a presentation to the President the day after tomorrow when he comes down to look at what we're doing. If you'd stay and wait on his *highness*, we'd be sure to secure government funding. I kid you not."

"Oh, yes, I know all about guys like him, but he's not the womanizer he pretends to be. His wife won't let him give away money if any woman encourages him to do it, so don't think I'd be an asset when you meet him. You wine and dine his staff yourself."

Unsmiling, Wanda looked around the room at what still might need her attention and could find nothing wrong—only her inherent need to always be perfect was alarmed by what she saw.

Knowing her mother so well prompted Teri to say with great pride, "I think the place looks great! You've outdone yourself—again, and the flowers are just what our new-style bowls and pitchers needed to celebrate opening day. Our favorite floral person should be getting quite a few orders, if this party is any indication of how great she has become in her art. Why just look at this white rose!"

As she examined the rose, a luminescent glow descended upon Teri and her mind left this space. Anyone willing to look at her while she digested the workings of the rose could easily see she was now in a deep trance state, but because she was surrounded by strangers, most present never noticed her glow or saw her go.

When Wanda noticed that Teri was no longer able to firmly plant her feet on the floor, she murmured, "Look out for that vase," as Teri started swaying in the same strange rhythmic way that usually preceded her assuming the pose of a queen and saying the strangest things. Wanda did not wait to see what would happen next before hurriedly ushering everyone out of the room.

As Wanda bolted the doors to the kitchen and main office, Teri took a seat and placed her hands together in a replica of the now-famous 'Praying Hands' statues Julie created years back and now produced with the help of Mayan artisans. Once Teri seemed satisfied that every finger was in its proper place, she gazed into space. As if on cue, her golden hair tumbled down over her shoulders as though the comb holding it in place had been removed, but it never moved. Her eyes opened wider, and a light unlike anything Wanda had ever seen before shone out to the world. It first appeared around the outside of her irises and quickly moved inward to the pupil. The blue faded to almost white. Although Teri remained still and calm, Wanda felt shivers run up and down her spine and extend into her mind as her daughter spoke in a voice unlike her own.

"Thérèse is my name. From this day forward I will be called Teri only when in the outer world—never here. I will help you more once a position is offered—in a very short time. My patrons will be politically motivated, but not greedy. Power is the name of their game, and what we do for them will benefit us here and now, as well as The Maya. I am through…I can move into the room now. Can you help me move?"

Although stunned by this exhibition, Wanda positioned herself to accept the risk of Teri collapsing or falling as she extended her hand toward her. She was shocked to see that her daughter easily recovered from her trance-formation and stood with no assistance—even attempting to dance. It was a tribal-style dance, yet she appeared to be a nun attempting to learn new steps rather than a native performing a ritual or leaping with laughter. When she returned to her seat, Wanda whispered, "Do you suppose Ste. Thérèse knows about The Maya?"

With great confidence Teri announced, "I know! Ste. Thérèse is Maya. I felt it in my glands. She has this long, long wave of energy that seems to take over right here." She pointed at the middle of her neck and drew a line upward across her face directly to her crown. Smiling even more, Teri said everything was okay because she could see all of Today and knew who would be in the compound the day after tomorrow.

Wanda asked, "If you can see today, can you see tomorrow, too?"

"Today isn't a 24-hour period of time. It's the time it takes to complete a task. This day—Today, begins with work you want to complete with the President—and me. It'll be done when they leave—not today, but when they move away. Can you see that?" As she continued explaining the concept of time, Thérèse waved her arms about as if painting a magical scene that anyone could see or believe, but Wanda was not able to look into it and see Today, too. In fact, she stood in a daze looking into space unable to detect anything!

Touching her shoulder, Thérèse pantomimed an astronomer showing a telescope to a dull student. She patiently directed her mother to focus on a distant point. "Look up—over to the left. Look harder," she said.

"I can't see anyone. I just don't get it. How do you see so much, yet I'm older and probably wiser?" Wanda was smiling, but her tone projected serious doubts about her daughter's ability to connect to whatever might be *out there* now.

"You're not able to see what I see because you don't believe in God. I see many things and have been able to move into this work gradually, because I am Maya, too. I don't fight life, like you do. I don't have to have everything explained to me or see something in print to believe what I can easily see within my mind—but apparently you do. You work with color and deliver designs from the other side to this side all the time, without really believing in what you're doing—like now."

Wanda walked toward the window and pulled back the curtain as if to check if anyone was there. She felt lonesome, suddenly worried, and in no hurry to leave Teri. She mused about her need to be free of people versus her need to stay close to her daughter while never letting others know of their close association since her birth. At times she felt that she was a liar, but then joked about the need to keep some things private or you would end up in the tabloids—treated without respect.

Reading Wanda's mind, Thérèse interrupted her thoughts by asking, "Why don't you want anyone to know I'm your daughter?" She had never really wanted to know the answer before, but at this moment it seemed extremely important to hear it.

Saddened immediately by thoughts of the past, as always, Wanda sighed and hoped Teri would change the subject. When she did not, she took a deep breath and said, "I was only 18 years old and your father was not someone who would strike any mother or father as a wise choice—and they were right. So I never let anyone know I was pregnant and had you at a home. I was so ashamed of the way I handled it that I never wanted anyone to know just how stupid I can be... As you know, you were raised by people who were very different from my parents—and me. They came to the house, very polite and nice, but I didn't think Mexicans could raise a white child as well as I wanted it done. You see, I was very prejudiced then...Raised by racists of a type that you never know they are unless you live in the same house. The problem with racism is that it always, always coexists with sexism...so that's how we lived then, and what I was taught." Wanda smiled as if the memory revealed a huge joke, which it did. She motioned toward all the Mexican and Mayan artwork surrounding her loom and filling the room as she spoke the last words she ever intended to say on this subject.

When her mother dropped her head and looked away, Thérèse waved her hand at someone she saw in space and time before resuming her walk around the room. Looking more like a model than a saint now, she said, "To think that I was raised as a Mexican... when my dear ones were really Maya...Forced to live then as if they were not Maya. It seems that everything about my childhood is a mystery. Does it not?"

Revealing her deep concern, Wanda said, "Who do you see now? Are you able to see Saints—or just ghosts or Maya or whatever?"

"I see many beings, Mother, but The Maya are not able to transmit their bodies into the sky now. They are lost to sight, but not lost to time. Do you realize why? Do you know why The Ascended Maya are able to transmit information to those who possess *the gift*?"

Shocked that Teri had called her 'Mother' for the first time, Wanda stammered, feeling ashamed again. She could find no words to express her thoughts, let alone her belief system.

"Don't worry, Mother. I won't say a word. You'll always be 'Wanda the Wonderful Witch of the East' to me, and I will always be the daughter of friends you met while traveling in Mayaland. Remember?"

"Oh, Teri, I feel so insignificant and unreal when you start talking about these things. I've worked on so many ideas and beliefs, and my own background is Celtic, so I figured I could weave everything into something useful for me to do and maybe help others, too. I just wanted to produce what came to me in dreams, but not you! You're so real, yet completely surreal now. I wonder at your beauty and your ability to skip over subjects like sex as if they're insignificant. You never really need men, do you? Are you gay? I always wanted to ask you that, but was afraid of the answer."

Thérèse looked closely at the rosy hues playing across her mother's face as she stepped out of the shadows and into the sunlight pouring through the window. She could easily see that her mother was truly afraid of what she would say next. Although she felt no need to keep secrets or to lie, she now believed her mother to be too far to the left to understand her rights, so she said simply, "I am Maya. I don't exist as woman or man in this life. I have nothing to hide. I'm able to take men or women at a glance and see inside them and let them be—or not, but I don't want to die, have a child, or meet unpleasant people who would rule over me as a family might. So, to avoid in-laws and outlaws—and others who would waste my time, I choose the divine path of the past as my way of staying alive and sane today."

Totally amazed, and more than a bit confused by this news, Wanda peered into the air around her daughter to see if anyone was there in Spirit. She had grown used to Saints who often came through and talked to her, too, but this Maya business was news to her. What do you do with a woman who is *of you*, but not able to relate to you? How do you compare your states of mind and how you lived in the past, when one of you is Maya and the other is not?

Reading her thoughts again, Thérèse said plainly, "I think you're afraid that this will change our relationship in some way, but it isn't. We're still the same. It won't change—unless you decide to make a change of some kind. I won't. I like this time and life. I want to be a super model and laugh and talk and make fun of how people live now, but I do worry about women who try to be as thin as I am. I don't eat less. I just need less, because I meditate and live in the blessed way of Sainte Thérèse today. I need very little need to eat, but if I were hungry, I would eat as much as I wanted."

"You always had a social conscience, but some of the tabloids say you have sex with every man on the set. I can't understand why they would say it if you weren't doing it, but if you say it's not true, I'll believe you."

Raising an eyebrow as if to question her mother's motives, Thérèse said, "Worried that one day I might have a child I don't wish to raise?"

"You're right, I'm projecting my life onto yours again! I try not to see things that aren't actually here, but it's become embedded in everyone's mind that all models are wanton and simple-minded—and that all actresses are willing to do anything to get a part, and that every woman secretly wants to be a sex object and act like a prostitute. So what's a mother of a beautiful daughter to do?"

Thérèse laughed as she adjusted the curtain, letting it fall back into place. She moved to erase the knots in her mother's face by running her fingers lightly over her forehead and talking softly to her. "You're the best! You don't have to worry about me—ever. I'm not a mess. I'm not in therapy or into drugs and sex, and I don't need to lower my standards to get work. My calendar's always full and it's hard to stay away from work an extra day, so don't worry about what people who willingly libel others might write. They don't know anything about me and you, so how deep do they ever dig? When you *really* don't want publicity, you usually don't get much. One day I'll drop out and no one will remember me six months later. It's happening even now."

With hands folded, Wanda stood and began swaying to the faint strains of mariachi music coming from the pavilion where the children were playing. She was ready to stay exactly as is and talk for hours, but one look at Teri and she knew how tired she was. This realization embarrassed Wanda, so she said too quickly, "Here I'm taking up all your energy and you need it for yourself. You work too hard! Let's go and get something to eat and then retire. I want to catch up on all of this stuff about The Maya, but it can wait until tomorrow."

"No, Wanda, you're not going to wait another day. The Ascended Maya never hesitate to show their colors when we're ready—and you are. You're finally able to believe and I won't leave you without a trial run on how The Maya may call and visit or do whatever they have to do within you now, so sit and let me adjust your leg."

Embarrassed that she was unable to adjust her leg easily, Wanda tried to push Teri's hands away but found she needed help. As the pain subsided in her leg, the peace that comes directly after pain helped her submit to what came next.

Seemingly transported and able to sing and dance with lords, Thérèse started chanting. Wanda had never heard her chant before. She suddenly realized this tune was always playing on the stereo or in the car whenever Teri was around. The chant was plaintive and very high in intensity. She felt the pain leave her leg immediately. It ascended from her mind and was lost in space for all time. No more would she have to take pain pills or lay down for half a day. The pain was gone miraculously and Teri tried to explain what was going on around her now.

"I'm not a prostitute, or a lesbian, or a man-eating hellion, but I am a woman and able to choose whomever I need and want to see. I don't have to wait on anyone or serve others who are bored by life, but it may seem to you that I do that now. I've amassed enough fame to keep men at bay who would normally go after The Lords…. You see, there are levels of life that you can't see and can't comprehend, but I can. For example, I was raised to observe and study the rose and the way it grows, but Sainte Thérèse's appearance now is a surprise to me. After all, she was French. I never realized that many of the Saints were Maya, too. I don't know why, but it surprised me!"

Hesitantly, Wanda tried to say that she could not understand a word Teri was saying, that it had to be her mind blurring what was spoken and making the words sound like some strange Mayan dialect rather than English.

Thérèse continued, "I can now move through you to You, your Higher Self, because you're in a trance and providing a portal for me to use, but if you want to work with The Ascended Maya on your own, you'll have to produce a new set of views, and you have to reduce *you* in size, too."

Wanda laughed as she said, "Am I getting fat? Are you saying that will keep me from rising above this life to be Maya like you?"

Thérèse was amazed that her mother still interpreted her words literally, totally missing the meat of what was said, but she let it go until she was inspired. Almost instantly, she began channeling divine thoughts entering the world around her. It was not something she could stop and start and interrupt, so she let her mother wonder.

Suddenly Wanda said, "I'm Maya! I now see my mind as a defective instrument that can't do what it's supposed to do—due to *my* neglect. I can't see into time, because of it. I didn't understand much that the seers said in the past because I couldn't register it in my mind…Now and then I read something or heard something that made a lot of sense, but if I made notes and read them later, there was nothing there—nothing that made any sense to me anyway. Why?" Only then did Wanda notice that Teri was no longer singing, dancing or talking. She was addressing an empty room. Teri was gone! How long had she been rattling away, and where had her daughter gone?

"I'm high above you," called Thérèse.

Wanda looked up to the rafters and started laughing, before asking, "How on earth did you get up there? You're as bad as Mandy. Do you two meet The Maya this way, or do you do it just to get a rise out of me?"

"No, we don't meet The Ascended Maya this way. We're grounded then, and we don't lose our way. We're Maya and able to lead today's tribe, but we're not wanted. So we float on our own—practice flying alone, and learning the way of Mayan power still available now. When we're able to get it all together and teach others how to do it, too, we'll practice making passes into the work of The Maya first, then try to escape time. Do you want to try now?"

"Not today, Teri. You've given me way too much to think about already. I don't see how I can ever breeze into space and walk on the ceiling like that!"

The two women looked at each other from their opposing positions and laughed. Most men avoid hysterical women, unless they are unwise. Suddenly an elder opened the door and walked in on them. He knew something was not quite right because he heard two women laughing, but only one woman was present in the room.

"Hey, how are you?" Wanda yelled to the old man. She was not able to tell if he was a shaman or not, so she assumed he was a local and would not notice much. "Why don't you go outside and look around while I change my clothes? When I'm done laughing and listening to the echo, I'll be out."

The nosey man frowned as he continued looking around the room. He was paid to set the stage for the President's cavalcade and to project suspicion onto everyone he met. Glancing upward, not expecting anything to be there, he assumed the ceiling was painted—until it moved. Without a thought, he drew his weapon and aimed at Thérèse.

"Don't shoot!" cried Wanda, while Thérèse laughed unmercifully at both of them.

The man was dumbfounded. There were no procedures to follow when you spotted a woman sitting on the rafters. Just then his earphone went berserk and he had to rip it out of his ear or go deaf.

"Don't listen to the phone," whispered Wanda to the secret service agent, since he appeared too upset to be able to decide what to do next. "We're not the Mayan spies you're sure are hiding in our compound waiting to shoot the President—or you." Wanda was now laughing because her words were so blunt and not at all what she meant to say. She could not stop what came out of her mouth now.

Swiftly regaining his composure, the agent said, "Yes, you're going to have a visit from the President and his friend, and I don't want to be guilty of letting the Maya take a part in any of it. Do you know any of them?" He seemed doubtless that they would be instantly on his side because they were white, but he was not wise. How can anyone know The Maya? How can anyone tell who is Maya and who is not? The Maya know, but they do not talk—at least to those at this level of intelligence.

"I think you better get down from there—and try not to break a leg." As he spoke, he noticed Wanda standing on one leg because her prosthesis had fallen to the side when she tried to dance. He blushed and stuttered so much that neither woman could understand what he was trying to say.

Wanda took pity on him and said, "Oh, don't be upset. People say things like that to me all the time. Anyway, Teri's an acrobat and can jump really high. Does it all the time!" Since he could not speak coherently, she added, "Come on down, Teri, and meet the President's right-hand man."

Blushing even more than before, the agent stared at the graceful woman now standing in front of him. She was so beautiful! There was something about her that made him think he already knew her. With no success, he struggled to get that across to them.

Thérèse gave him a million-dollar smile and said, "How are you? I'm Teri. I'm staying here until your boss arrives, so we can talk. Do you have to clear me or frisk me or things like that?" She made her artful little speech with turned-on smile while tossing her long, flaxen hair from side-to-side.

Stumbling over his words, the agent assured them both that The President would be delighted to talk to them—both, and see their work! He assumed Thérèse to be a weaver, too. Little did he know!

☼CHAPTER FOURTEEN

"When you watch someone climb on top of a wall and look over, but not follow through and fall to the ground on the other side, you know they are intruding—not up to anything good, or can you tell?" As Jorge spoke, he moved through the crowd of young people gathered to hear him teach arcane subjects that directly affected their future. Stopping to look into their eyes, as if they were all wise and good—not as if they were about to leave the tribe.

Jorge never let anyone off the hook without giving them a lecture on what they were giving away—possibly forever. Standing tall as he talked, his audience looked small, meek, upset, and weak as they answered his pointed questions. He already knew he would never accept them back into the tribe, but before he showed them the door, his lecture continued for an hour or so longer.

Four of the most out-spoken students worked up enough courage to respond to the demands placed upon them to maintain silence about what they had been taught and how The Maya were involved in the lives of those who stayed. All four decided to lie and say they would be back one day and would never talk about what they saw here or knew. Able to see deep within the four discontented friends, Jorge knew they would betray The Maya and their tribe that very day, but he did not say it.

Looking back at Jorge as they walked toward the door, each was stunned to see Jorge apparently on fire. Was it anger? He had never before appeared to be a warrior! They believed he was not fiery enough or willing to war, so they had committed treason to the order and wanted to leave. Jorge was not a revolutionary, and they all wanted to fight and get on with the war—but not fight The Lord. As Jorge merged his mind with his soul in time, the elders aligned with others out of time. They stood and approached the departing group of malcontents while Jorge signaled his lieutenants to pat down each person as they passed and urge them to come back, but not actually saying that.

Seizing the moment when the students hesitated to leave, one elder pushed forward to block the door until he could speak his thoughts about traitors of his faith. He said without hesitation, "When you are asked about The Ascended Maya or the tribal elders, be honest! Say you know nothing! Confess that you never got any further than the first verse of *The Maya*

Word. None of you can say that you ever studied with Jorge or with Mandy, or with anyone associated with The Maya of all time. You're not that wise! You'll want to brag and boast, but that will cost you a lot—not a slit throat from anyone here, but maybe from others infiltrating your group. You're unwilling to see, trust, and believe, and that's okay with us. We never expect much from fools—like all of you. We continue to trust that God of All maintains the balance of good and evil in this world—as well as everything in-between the planes."

The elder stopped when a young woman pushed in front of him and asserted herself without hesitation. Defiant, she was no one the elders ever expected to see exit. She joined the exodus without much thought and no complaint from those who worked with Jorge. Several others gloated along with her, as Nita spat out venomously, "So you believe in good and evil? Funny, as in strange, that you never mentioned it before now. Maybe if you had told us what you do, or what you see, or what you believe, we could've met you half-way? But now it's too late! You can't change our minds. We're leaving and never coming back—ever!"

Her pronouncement was greeted by a sibilant hiss from several seated women who obviously were waiting for the malcontents to leave. All the men, however, remained quiet. They knew Jorge was not upset. He smiled as Nita yelled, then laughed loudly.

Jorge's reaction frustrated Nita so much that she raged and screamed at him, "How can you laugh when we're leaving you forever?"

A shaman standing beside the door interjected, "Because you're NOT Maya and you never were Maya! How can you assume you are leaving *us*?" He was not happy with how Jorge was handling the situation, but was wise enough not to say it.

Ignoring the elder, Nita spoke to the men she was following out the door, "We are Maya and born to the tribe! We don't believe in the afterlife that the Catholics talk about. They slap your face if we say we can fly and that the tribe will ascend again. We're mad that all of you just talk, talk, talk, and sleep a lot—instead of working out a plan to block The Church and others who are building *their* power base on top of our hard work." When none of her companions met her flashing eyes, possibly unwilling to align with her now, Nita was shocked—a lot. Unable to be calm, she shouted louder, "Why are all men so weak? The tribe is effete today because The Maya in olden times didn't work it all out and keep our records away from the Spaniards who came to bury us."

At the end of her tirade, Nita found herself without any allies left in the room—no one left to enable her to leave with some dignity. Unable to hide this weakness in her plans, Nita's voice rose to a squeak as she squealed at the backs of her departing friends, "Did you all forget that The Maya weren't wiped out? We're a tribe and able to do a lot. We haven't forgotten anything! It's in our oral history—not just a few old stories. You can't understand, because you denied your minds and your souls the right to grasp Today and entwine it with your lives all the way down the line."

When Nita paused to gasp for air, Jorge usurped her energy and speed and said with finality, "For generations upon generations the stories have been kept alive for the few who understand them—which never included any of you. You're Maya in a sense, but not of The Maya who rule even now. You're a fool, Nita, unwilling to be led by the wise of the tribe, so now you and your friends are doomed to figuring out mentally every next step. We won't hold you to what you said Yesterday or do Today. Whatever comes after Today is totally up to you, but if you betray us—by keeping your present stance, we won't let you return to the tribe or even sit with us when we conduct business; and if you ever say you knew us well, you'll be denounced immediately! Is that understood?"

Jorge's words were thought forms as they entered Nita's addled mind. He had entered her mind and followed her line. She was shocked when it suddenly became apparent to her reality that she had been released by The Maya—never to be believed by anyone else, either. She wisely decided to leave immediately and never mention that she had been unhappy with any of them. Would she make it in the world or ascend at the end without them? That is something for others to discover. She is off the spot now. She tossed the dice and left when asked to leave again.

Jorge escorted Nita out the door in order to address the group of students lagging behind the four ringleaders—apparently not quite ready to cut their umbilical cords. He said with unexpected mildness, "Whenever you meet a stranger on the street and ask him or her to dine with you, know that they know you if they readily accept or are truly regretful that they can't eat with you then. You will know instantly if they are friend or foe. We always knew who would stay and who would not, so it is unfortunate that some of you leave now without any food for thought—or even a meal to fill your bellies, because you offended those who taught you much about life. Because of your bad behavior, never again will anyone else who is determined not to learn and work hard be allowed to enter this compound's life."

The youngest present whined, "Jorge, you make us sound as if we're lazy beggars, and we're not. We're students—seekers of wisdom! All we wanted was someone to teach us the ways of The Ascended Maya. You promised to help us, but all you ever did was walk around aimlessly and never teach any classes. You said more today than ever before, but it's too late to change our minds."

With no readable expression, Jorge said slowly and firmly, "You were all unwilling to work with your hands! That's about all I can say now."

Unwilling to give up and walk away, another ex-student said, "What are you saying, Jorge? Why would working with your hands gain entrance into the past, present or future—spiritually speaking?"

The exiles were now asking questions they should have pondered before joining those in overt rebellion, but Jorge was not swayed against blocking their path back in the future. He relented only enough to say one word to each student as they passed from that place that day. Only one final thought they could use to succeed in the world was given since their work with Spirit was closing. Jorge never wavered as he said farewell forever.

Now aware that Jorge would not answer the immature student's query, the eldest elder came forward and spoke. "You have asked why all are expected to use their hands before they are considered to be Maya." Although always an extremely powerful shaman, he now felt his energy rise within as high as when he was a young man. He could see the needy and the rich, two extremes of any society, dieing of one thing or another without ever knowing why they lived, while The Maya thrived.

Rashly interrupting these power-filled thoughts, the foolish student said, "Yes, old man," but got no further with whatever he intended to say. His rudeness took away the breath of everyone standing in the path leading from the compound—except Mandy.

Mandy emerged from the shadows at the back of the crowd, as if out of a deep trance and said, "You are very rude—ignorant, too. How could you have ever hoped to help The Maya of this time or any other? You're not even able to have fun with others. You always say you're tired and depressed—trying to hide your self-conceit—what you think is to be your life. You even believe you're not like anyone else!" Prowling about the fringes of the group reassembling outside the compound, Mandy spoke out as she often did with the elders, but never with this class. She commanded everyone's attention now, not just the silly man-child. "I see that you're worth very little outside your own mind, so inevitably you never saw anything here but reflections of your own desire for power—and our seeming desire to thwart your wishes."

Sputtering and stuttering as he tried to evade Mandy, the once arrogant young man appeared unable to move more than a few steps away from her now. She swayed in place as her fingers appeared to form claws capable of shredding him into pieces. Looking especially fierce and determined with a jaguar pelt slung over her shoulder, Mandy was clearly visible to all standing in the pathway leading to the outside world. Never before had any of them seen Mandy as a Timekeeper of Ancient Mayan times nor had any jaguar totem ever appeared as healthy and sleek as hers. Some said later that it was alive, but in a trance-like state then.

Seeing terror in the eyes of the young man, Mandy purred: "Ahhh, you see my friend and now recognize a Timekeeper from outer space…an enigma you can't erase from your mind as long as you live in this time. You want to run away and tell your friends how you found us and left us because we are fakes and frauds. That thought will cause all of you great pain, my dears. If you lie, The Timekeeper will send the jaguar to find you—wherever you may be. Don't say a word about the tribe or The Maya, and you'll be fine. Instead of running back to mama or papa, go to towns and make your own living. After all, none of you are children! At first, we thought you were adults—until you refused to accept responsibility and work for the good of all. You can leave safely now, but take care to never say you were here." A hiss passed through Mandy's lips as she spat out her final words.

The eerie sound caused those leaving to sit on the ground as if they had been told to do so. Those seated cringed as if being attacked, but their self-appointed leader could not sit. It was he who believed he could teach his peers more than Mandy, Jorge, or the elders about 'Mayan ways,' as he phrased it. His feet refused to walk. He could not talk. His lips moved as if echoing what Jorge or Mandy said, but he could not speak.

Jorge had stayed his distance from them while saying good-bye to Nita and giving a few others his final blessing—not really paying attention to what was going on with the few who continued to remain behind in the compound. As he smiled, waved, or escorted dawdlers out the gate, he did not speak about what he felt now.

When the final hiss issued from her lungs, Mandy was out of gas. She felt completely beyond being able to do whatever needed to be done now. She started to remove the jaguar guard and leave the area. Jorge felt her mood change and since no one else was leaving them now, he reentered the compound. He was not so much surprised as thrilled to see how well Mandy held the jaguar in check—restrained it or had retrained it to walk safely among The Maya now. Her control was inspired.

Jorge was not that gifted, but easily existed with it. Smiling now, he turned toward the students still sitting inside the gate and said, "How can you all sit here when you want to catch the last bus to town?" Inspired anew, he was determined to be nice—even go easy on them. He could not suppress his own wonderment about how they could ever describe Mandy or The Maya without appearing weird, superstitious—and totally unbelievable. Could anyone ever describe Mandy with a jaguar on her back—not being attacked? He mumbled, "Leave it to Mandy to go over the top! She really stopped them cold. No one will say Mandy stopped by to say good-bye and—why, they're even afraid to meet her eye now."

When Mandy addressed the stragglers, they could not hear what she said. To those who could go within, they heard, "I have a list of things you have to do before you can survive and thrive. The list is easy to remember, because it contains only two things." Her words were heard, yet not taken into consideration by any of them then. Seeing a lack of reaction, Mandy laughed and walked away with her cat slinking along beside her—or was she the jaguar? Hurling her final words over her shoulder in the direction of the elders as they made room for her to pass, she said, "So be it! It's easy to see we're losing absolutely nothing when these students leave!"

As if on cue, several young women standing near the highway screamed to those sitting in the pathway—still unwilling to move, "Hurry up! Hurry!! The bus is coming and beeping. The driver's in a hurry! Let's go!"

"Better get going," said Jorge to one showing no movement. "You'll have to walk to the city if you miss the bus. Remember, we don't intend to feed you again."

Turning sad eyes to plead with Jorge, the young man said, "I can see you're tired of us, but you don't realize that what happened today is exactly what we wanted to see all along—how we always wanted to work with you. We'll obey you now!"

"No, my friend, you have to go! You want strange and weird things explained, but want no pain—and *you* definitely don't want to work hard enough to ascend with us in the end. You want to tell others what you think I mean when I speak and chat about what Mandy teaches now…." Jorge felt himself losing control, so he spoke his final words angrily, "Leave before I scream!" Pointing a shaking finger at everyone sitting in the pathway, they each felt an odd sensation, as if something had been wrenched out of their brains. Now frightened, they left without noticing that no one cried or said good-bye.

♓   ♓

Mandy's secretary, Angelina, the woman she trusted more than all other staff members here said, "What do we do now with all the work they did for us?"

Not looking up, Mandy shrugged and said, "We have no problem. Trust me."

"Oh, I do, Ms. Mandy, but we have trouble getting out all the orders as it is, and now this--"

"You'll find that we can fly through our tasks much faster without slackers badgering the artists and others with idle questions, grousing about something all day. None of our workers left—only those who want to reap what our people sow. We all have to trust and believe that they'll never hold us back again. Don't we?" Mandy smiled and affectionately poked her secretary in the side and prepared to leave.

"I guess, Ms. Mandy." Angelina hoped to delay Mandy by engaging her in some casual conversation about what had happened to the exiled students, so she quickly added, "But where are they going? What will they do now?"

Throwing up her hands, Mandy said, "Who cares?" With that she wrapped her beautifully designed, hand-woven rebozo around her shoulders and smiled.

Her admission of disinterest shocked her assistant, but Angelina let it go because she believed that whatever went on in the compound, Mandy was the only one to ask, because she knew everything—even more than the elders, or so she thought.

Mandy's parting words were barely heard in her rush to leave. "Don't worry about the mail. There's nothing of any great interest."

When Mandy disappeared with pronouncements like this, as she frequently did, her personal secretary knew it was not necessary to open the mailbox; but because she was paid handsomely to handle all correspondence and expected to do it well, she routinely set about it anyway. After all, those in positions of power must keep up the appearance of doing a good job.

As Mandy drove out the gate, the sun rose over the compound. Unaware that she had departed until they finished eating breakfast, some of the artists and all of the remaining students surrounded Jorge to check out their day's assignments and digest any remarks he might make about what was going to happen next. But before they could begin peppering Jorge with questions, they were astonished to discover new recruits standing in place of the students who left earlier in the week. Most did not wonder about how easily their group could be entered by strangers, but it was not easy for some to accept that now, more than ever before, seekers were preparing themselves for this work and pushing forward to enter their world.

The newcomers were welcomed by The Lord of the Night. When their dreams became so vivid that they knew instantly what they meant, Spirit would move them to join The Maya. After that, it took only a few minutes for the school to resume its old ways, even though its membership had changed drastically since the last weekly meeting.

Waiting patiently, Jorge stood without smiling or greeting anyone. When it seemed that no one could bear to wait any longer in silence, he smiled broadly and said, "When you're ready to work, please insert this magnetic card in your head and accept what it says." He held up a plastic charge card and proceeded to pantomime how it should be inserted into the mouth. "When the card runs out of interest OR power, you have to recharge it or get a new one. Understand?"

No one said a word, but a few were disturbed enough to wriggle around a little. Totally serious, Jorge raised his voice and said, "Do all of you grasp what I'm saying? Do you see what I mean?"

Still no one said anything, and it was becoming embarrassingly obvious that they were supposed to do something or ask questions, but no one knew what to do to impress Jorge. Becoming impatient, he said, "What do you want to do here? Are you going to accept every word I say as if pontificated by the ancient Maya?"

That stirred a few to ask questions, and the students relaxed a bit more. Those familiar with Jorge's ways knew he could easily upset a calm class, but this was not to be one of those days. He wanted them to relax and ask questions—to question what did not make sense—right then, before they moved upward or did any work.

"Once again, if you don't understand a metaphor, or you don't know what to do, ask someone near you. If they're lost, too, then we have to retool the entire school in order to help you all teach others what to do next." As he spoke, Jorge looked at each student and artist, noticing one who obviously was unsure what to do now, so he added, "You're not students here—but teachers. We're all here to learn what *you* want to do while here on Earth. We're here to help you do your best and excel in the modern world, too. We want you to use the tools that came with this birth. You are Maya—and don't forget it! That means you have unlimited use of my ideas—if you understand what I am here to do, too. Understood?"

The men quickly nodded, some even mumbled that they understood completely, but few women indicated they got it or were lost. Noticing the women's general reserve, Jorge suggested that they stop hindering their own progress—not be humbled by the presence of mere men. His words produced a titter or two among the women, but the men did not appear to appreciate it.

Sensing the best direction to take now, Jorge smiled and shouted, "You're not women and men—you're Maya! You're here to learn what you can do to help the universe produce a better world than this one—which is jaundiced. The yellow race is not to blame for this infection, but their rivers and streams are polluted and unable to produce good fruits, vegetables, and meats, like everyone else. We can go back to 'the past' and learn how to farm wisely—using water to create greener pastures, but it's not easy to convince the greedy that we must do this immediately. You're wise to listen to what has changed for the better, but pay attention to what was tried and found not to be wise. Once you understand today's history, you can begin working on it within time."

Stepping back from his position of power to listen intently to the men and women talk about their ideas and thoughts, Jorge became aware that no one present was upset or unable to win, but he knew two would leave soon. He could see them leaving, even knew their needs, but he was not going to mention it now. When a man decides to forsake his tribe, it begins at the beginning—not when he actually leaves.

☼ CHAPTER FIFTEEN

Jeanne snapped, "What do you want now?" Unsure why she felt annoyed, but thought it might be caused by the weird sensations she often felt when in this room alone. Something weird seemed to be happening now. It felt as if someone was standing too close to her—breathing into her hair, but there was no one else there. She stopped to think, 'I used to feel like this at home, but I got over it when I married and moved to Montana.'

Letting that thought flood her mind, Jeanne continued writing a list of what she had to do that day and the next. Her penmanship had slipped recently, and she worried that one day she might not be able to write legibly, but her fingers had become more nimble and ran over the computer keys with amazing speed now, so she was not worried about losing her ability to earn a living writing every day. Using her favorite pen and favorite color of ink—green, Jeanne added to her list:

Go to office—get list of people who want to move to Mexico.
Go to store—get can of walnut stain for warped drawer.
Get new container for juice.

What about the list annoyed her? Her thoughts collided in time and she stopped writing to pace the cramped space, attempting to create a better mind set—one that could finish such simple chores. Suddenly she shouted, "I get it! I'll just do it! But first I have to finish this list so I can get someone to deliver the stuff to the group."

As if arguing with herself, Jeanne wrote down one more item before folding the paper in half. She did not seem to notice that she wrinkled the paper as she stuffed it into her pocket. In fact, she did not seem to notice anything now. Her mind had slipped out of time and into space—again.

A voice within or near her ear whispered: *'In the next few days, you will get this group to move into the new house you bought with the proceeds from your work…that is all you will commit to doing here.'*

As if she suddenly saw something long hidden, Jeanne stared at the computer sitting in a box on a chair at the end of the table beside the door. How could she possibly relocate right now when she had so much to do to motivate everyone who said they would move, too?

Such views competed for consideration by her mind and soul. Distracted just enough to be taken unawares when the door swung open to admit a woman dressed in white, Jeanne watched as the woman walked over to her computer and casually placed it on the floor. Older than she appeared at first glance—her facial features blurred slightly and she was no longer as clear as she was. This woman in white maintained views seldom heard in the world now, and when she did speak, she said very little. Perhaps that is why she is greatly respected and admired by everyone who meets or talks with her or participates in her infrequent seminars.

Jeanne remembered with some embarrassment that when she first met Mandy she had not been impressed—had even felt confident that Mandy's reputed ability to communicate on many levels had been overstated. She originally went to see Mandy against her will (and her unwillingness to sit still), forcing herself to listen to a woman whose beliefs were irrational, according to many of today's theologians and philosophers. Only now was she curious enough to override such a mindset and discover why this one woman routinely upset so many men.

Most women take Mandy in stride, although almost always missing the behind-the-scenes action; so why did some men fight over her so loudly? Some said men fight because they know she is right and are afraid they will one day have to change their theories and science to agree with what she alone believes now. Others claim men fight because she will not let them dominate every conversation and every situation. Who is right?

Right then, Mandy broke into her thoughts by saying, "As if it makes any difference who is right and who is wrong."

Jeanne was not sure if Mandy was listening in on her thoughts and adding her opinion or abruptly announcing the reason for stopping by, so she waited and watched while Mandy continued to survey the office. Mandy pushed the computer with her foot a bit closer toward the door, but Jeanne noticed she paid no attention to the huge boxes filled with computer accessories. They, too, had to find a home in two small rooms buried within the thick walls of Mandy's largest compound in the Yucatan. She seemed to be concerned about something unseen. Stumbling over her words, afraid of what Mandy might say, Jeanne jutted out her chin and mumbled, "I'm sorry to take up so much space, Mandy. I'll move in with the others when they get here and won't bother you."

Nothing escaped Mandy's steady gaze as she said, "Guess I wasn't on your wave length, Jeanne. I thought you were talking again about change and how men and women differ. You write a lot about people within American society who are sequestered from the world, and how they live now. Is it any different from, say the Maya who still live within the tribal system, trying to stay away from the Mexican government and other outsiders? Is it not true that *every* man and most women and children just want to be left alone to do what they alone want to do?"

By planting this conversational seed deeply, Mandy forced Jeanne out of her inertia. She instantly realized her belief system accepted the need for change but focused on how groups viewed the same need and reacted differently toward it; but she was not about to admit that to Mandy. Instead, she said more quickly than persuasively, "I was going to try and persuade you to let me leave and live with the new group of Americans and Europeans in the other compound—not here, like I do now, but I guess I got lost in my thoughts."

Jeanne had been working hard on a plan to seek out wealthy women who could afford to help others—especially children. Being considered pretty in the fundamental way of beauties her age, she had never worried enough about appearances and station in life to capitalize on her birth rights—until lately. Since childhood she had eschewed working on people's sympathies, even though her life story was not nearly as wonderful as it appeared to be in her essays. She preferred that no one know just how lonely her life had been as a child, so she cited make-believe relatives in her stories or painted over the character flaws of those she admitted to having, and she resisted the impulse to include historical references that applied to her ancient lineage.

Interrupting her thoughts, Mandy spoke softly, while making a sweeping gesture that took in the world outside, "Why don't you sit still for a day or so and let these people put their house in order themselves—without you?"

With total honesty, Jeanne blurted out, "I don't know why, but I want to be in charge now—get them all settled quickly." As if as surprised as Mandy appeared to be now, she smiled defiantly at her old friend. They both laughed loudly!

Smiling broadly, Mandy said, "You really do want them to be happy, don't you?"

Jeanne could never hide her feelings when around Mandy. "I guess I do tend to underestimate the ability of Today's Women to arrive in a foreign place and time—a place they never even knew existed, and be okay with it right away. Anyway, I hope I'm underestimating them!"

"Don't worry! I'll talk to them, and then pick you up and deliver you to the main room, where I'll repeat once again that you bought this house for them and expect everyone to work hard—and pay you back. Meanwhile, you're going shopping."

"Oh, no, don't say a word about me owning it. I had so much trouble getting the Mexican government to lease the property back to me. I even had to take on a Mexican partner. You know that! If I say that they can buy it from me, we'll be in deep doodoo with the Mexicans—again."

"Don't worry, Jeanne. They aren't going to want to buy it from you, but it will make them realize they owe you a lot. Don't you see that?" Mandy wondered at times about the psychology used by her American friends, but never as often as when she worked with her scribes.

Petulantly, Jeanne said, "Why should they feel obligated to me?"

Mandy's deep voice rose an octave, then quickly dropped as she said, "I don't give away my things like you do, Jeanne. I have my ways, but all I want from your group is that they help The Maya and give freely of themselves. Besides, my idea is better than yours, and I can prove it! But right now, you *will* let me take this group aside and tell them a thing or two—or you'll get sick and vomit when you try to talk to them later."

She looked benign and kind as she said this, but Jeanne wondered once again if Mandy was a woman of magic or a shaman. Hearing Mandy laugh, she realized Mandy could indeed read her thoughts! Strangely enough, it made her feel better. To test it out, she thought, 'How could a man or woman of God not be able to read the thoughts of those who might harm them? After all, God created angels to take care of business here and there, and gave us enough sense to get into the best work we can do on Earth, yet we never give credit where credit is due.'

Mandy said softly, "*You* do."

Jeanne's face and neck reddened until she thought about her proposed lectures for tomorrow and the day after. They had to be delivered before she could relax, sit back, and let others take over for her.

"You don't have to worry about your classes right now. I'm going to say you're unable to teach due to technical problems in The States, and you'll be back when you're back. They'll appreciate you a lot more then."

"Oh, Mandy, you're such a good friend, but to lie in order to get people to respect you seems unwise. Don't you think it's *un-spiritual* to do that?"

"No, Jeanne, I don't. It seems to me that as soon as some people see the light and recognize God is on this side—here on Earth, they open themselves wide to greedy invaders and stupid advice. In other words, when Spirit arrives, in way too many instances, common sense leaves. You were given a brain and free will for a reason, so instead of thinking about what others might like, think about what you need right now and in the future, and how *you* have to proceed to achieve success. Be wise. If others can help you, then do what you can to help them. If they're the type who end up despising you—after taking your advice, they'll twist your words in order to discredit you and your life's work. You shouldn't help them do it! Catch my drift?"

For a second, Jeanne thought she heard John Wayne talking, but shook her head and said, "I don't know if it helps to moan and groan a lot, but I did a bit of that recently, and it was amazing how many more women came forward to help the kids then. Maybe I've neglected using a lot of other persuasive tools at my disposal, too?"

"Too? Are you saying I'm not very persuasive?"

Jeanne raised her hand and laughed as Mandy mugged and groped about the room as if lost and blind. She said, "You're the best, Mandy! You could get an Eskimo to build a summer home in Nebraska. You can sell anyone anything—and never be told off if it doesn't work."

Barely smiling, Mandy spoke with a bit of an edge to her voice, "When do I ever sell…and when doesn't my advice help?"

"Now don't get huffy, Mandy. I was just saying that you're able to talk people into doing things they wouldn't do on their own…and you get them to follow you anywhere, but it takes others coming after you to teach everyone what to do—and you never notice it."

Speaking in hushed tones, Mandy said, "I see. Yes, you have a point, Jeanne. That's exactly why we want you as our scribe."

It slowly registered on Jeanne's mind that she was being called to work for The Ascended Maya—not just Mandy. Wondering how she could answer that call and why The Maya would want her as their scribe, she glanced at her wall clock and announced that she had to leave immediately.

Mandy backed up a step or two, then said with a radiance that often came over her when she smiled, "You were chosen because you're simply the best there is! We work only with those who have been tested and proven to be totally dependable—good workers, masters of great knowledge—but not necessarily in that order."

Shaking her head in disbelief, Jeanne began laughing almost hysterically because she could neither accept such a huge role nor walk away from it. At that moment in time a truckload of worry moved out of her way so she could see the road straight ahead with no traffic to consider. She felt better for having had this vision.

"You do have a lot of work to do, Jeanne, but no one else will ever worry about it, but you. You'll continue to work as you always do—using your mind all the time, but from now on you'll sit at times during the day in such a way as to release your spine and permit the Ancient Mayan Timekeepers to dictate their messages to you, too. Your fingers' work will open a world of readers to the world you and I live in now, but you won't have to teach anyone what The Maya mean or seem to be. Leave that to me."

Once again, Jeanne thought she should either laugh or cry hysterically, but decided to turn and walk away without saying good-bye. However, a rebellious thought flashed through her mind so fast she could not follow through and do it.

"You're surprised at being chosen to be The Scribe of The Ascended Maya, but you're that good, Jeanne! We want you to accurately and efficiently take down whatever you get from The Timekeepers and publish their words at the right time. You don't have to run all over town doing research or travel far and wide to tell people why they should buy the words of The Maya, all you have to do is look nice and not spit—"

"What?" Jeanne laughed, while deciding not to do anything rash. Once again she realized that Mandy always knew how to use laughter to tear apart her entrenched defenses. She gave up thinking about the call until she could check in with her Spiritual Guides and see for herself what comes next or is best to do now.

"Yes, I want you to talk to your Spiritual Guides before you decide if we're going to be of use to you. After all, I just lectured you about doing that. Didn't I?"

Jeanne said, "I guess," without enthusiasm as she sunk into the chair she had been using to steady herself. She felt a sharp pain as the rungs of the chair back dug deeply into her spine. Although wondering about it, she said nothing in complaint.

"Why do you hurt yourself? You do it a lot, and you're doing it now. Look at you. That chair isn't a good fit, yet you keep it around."

"That's because I hate waste! When I was growing up I was told over and over again that I'm extremely picky and extravagant, so I guess I'm still trying to prove I'm not. So I hold onto chairs like this—too small for my fanny and too stiff for my spine."

Jeanne's lips parted to smile when Mandy said, "At least you know why you're doing it. I was beginning to wonder about you. After all the psychology books you've read, written, and edited, I thought you had it all together—everything figured out, and it turns out you're as bad as me—maybe worse."

Surprised to hear that Mandy read her work and wondered about her, all she said was, "You're very wise, Mandy. If I resemble you in any way, I'm honored."

"That's a stupid thing to say, Jeanne. You're a woman of today—and now a scribe of The Ascended Maya! You have enough money to buy a group home for over-privileged women with poor children—yet you want to be liked by me?" Mandy laughed loudly, but stopped abruptly when she spotted a man leaving a building across the pavilion headed towards them. "I guess I blew our cover! They're looking for us, and I had to laugh loud enough to break the sound barrier. Now they're all headed this way." As she spoke, Mandy pulled her scarf up over her hair and headed toward the door.

"Ahhh, Pedro, pleased to see you. How are things?" Mandy spoke as she quickly opened and closed the door behind her, without letting him see into the office, implying there was no one inside.

"I am fine, Ms. Amandy, but my mother is not. She wants some herbs and things, and I don't know what to give her. Can you talk to her?" The man bent over and swept the path in front of Mandy as a sign that he honored her more than his words implied.

"I will gladly visit with your mother, but I can't make it until Sunday, Pedro." Mandy watched the man as she spoke and noticed his amazement that she knew in an instant that his mother was not that sick.

Bowing and swishing his hat, Pedro said, "I will tell her. She goes to the zocalo on Sundays and makes her way home after noon. Can you visit her then?"

With a flick of her wrist, Mandy said, "I will be in the plaza and meet her there."

"Oh, I will tell her, but she may not be able to stay that long." The man shook his head as he edged away from her, wondering: 'How does Mandy know my mother trusts that other one so much? How will she react if she sees my mother talking to the witch who parks her cart near the bar?'

Mandy slid away from him toward the open kitchen door where she knew several women would be standing inside close enough to listen to their conversation. She waved as if dismissing him as she said, "Pedro, you're a good man, but you worry too much." She did not check to see his reaction, instead plunged into the kitchen, announcing with a grin, "I see you're all done with your chores. Good, it's time to leave."

Only one woman saw her smile, because all the others had dropped their eyes when she arrived. However, they all observed that Mandy's feet were sore and red. Each thought she could not walk another step before they would start to bleed.

Following their eyes and reading their minds, Mandy said, "I'm okay. I need a clean towel and some chilies…and a few things from the pantry to crush into a poultice. Can you find them for me or do I have to do it myself?" Mandy stressed her words just enough to let the women know she did not like them idling and listening in on others' conversations with her. She did not speak of it directly, preferring to display her difficult side, so no one in the kitchen would underestimate her when other men stopped to talk or walk with her.

"There are a lot of things in the pantry, Miss Mandy, so the chilies are drying outside. What kind do you want? I will pick them myself." The head cook was Mandy's chief ally in the local tribe. Very able to practice her craft as an art, she never bothered to use tact. Mandy appreciated her bluntness, even if others did not.

Mandy said, "Pick out the one you like and add another. That should be enough."

"Okay, Miss Mandy, but I like them hot and you don't."

"Heat is what we need to heal these feet, so do as you please. I know you'll choose exactly the right ones."

As Mandy sat in a rocker they kept for her beside the fireplace, the younger women milled about wanting to hear what she would do next. The older women knew better. Dismissing them with a sweeping motion, Mandy said without emotion, "I want to rest, and I want you all to help Amelia and the others—and I want you to laugh. Laugh a lot! It'll help The Healers find me here."

The youngsters were not sure what to do to please her, but when the head cook came back in the kitchen and started laughing with gusto, the others laughed, too. Amelia was not aware that Mandy had told the girls to laugh. She just felt like laughing, so she did. This caused some to worry and become afraid even as they laughed. Three young women burst into tears because they never realized that Amelia was like Mandy—until now, and it was a good thing they learned that lesson then.

☼ Chapter Sixteen

"In the evening we usually sit here and drink healing tea or *hot* chocolate, but tonight I propose we sing songs we remember or make up on the spot. We'll all dance along with the songs, too. What do you all say?"

Jeanne looked at the speaker very closely, wondering why she could not place her, yet everybody in The States said she was a big star. For whatever reason, she heard herself speaking hesitantly. "I don't sing…" A titter from some of the women stopped her from saying much more about her lack of talent. Deciding instead to lead with her strength, Jeanne announced too loudly, "I'm a writer, and some of my poetry rhymes and some doesn't, but I've never tried to put music to my words."

Joyfully jumping now, Julie shouted, "Oh, that's okay! What we're going to do is what many modern composers do. You know, they sit around or play with a guitar or piano and burble and bubble over words—to see what comes out of their mouths next. In fact, the other day I was working out on my rebounder, you know that little trampoline thingy in my room?" Julie anticipated that everyone would know what she meant and how to use it, but one glance around the room indicated that most did not know anything about rebounding, so she stopped talking.

Feeling a bit sorry for her, Jeanne moved the conversation away from singing, hoping to change the subject so she would not have to sing, as she said with a grin, "I know what you mean. Rebounders were all the rage in the 70s. Everyone had one! There were some shysters, as always! They charged as much as $500 for what K-Mart sold for $29.99."

The Mayan women said nothing, just continued smiling and shyly looking at the Americans as if they were alien beings. It was obvious that if something that made sense was not said soon, everyone would stand and leave the room, maybe never open to them again. They had only recently begun to join in and participate with the strangers who visited Mandy's compound and stayed for a few nights.

Barely smiling now, Julie looked at the Mayan women lined up opposite her with their men standing behind them against the wall and said, "I guess we sound silly and frivolous to you. Don't we?"

One man nodded, and then ten others began to laugh. The mood in the room changed immediately. Not wishing to miss out on a moment of mirth, Jeanne stepped back into view and said, "I think we've done so many things trying to get high that we've lost *our* minds, but never the Maya. Your tribe and The Maya keep us grounded, but what if after they left Earth the last time The Ascended Maya didn't return to find us again?"

Her thought ignited the women and men sitting closest to the two Americans who talked about dancing and singing and such things as women would not do publicly without their men's approval. The few Maya present thought about it in a group mindset detached from whatever anyone else inside this room thought then. Without speaking, they quickly came to a consensus, which the men could not explain. They knew what was wanted or needed at that moment in time, and at precisely that moment an unseen Mandy spoke to their hearts and told them to explore their personal creative worlds more than ever before.

The wisest and oldest woman present, who always sat at the far side of the group, close to the male elders, said with a grin as she pointed to the bottom of her feet and then her heart, "I think Ms. Mandy wants us to explore our souls more—not our soles." Her ready wit often defrayed wild conclusions that might be impulsively accepted by her clan, and today she added to that reputation by intervening when their joint meeting was about to bog down in practical thought. She looked at the assembled women and asked cheerfully, "Does anyone know what Ms. Mandy wants us to do?"

A young woman, without much of a chin, said sarcastically, "Talk, talk, and talk— then work with our hands! She never says sit and chat with nothing else to do—or to dance and sing." She clamped her lips shut as her deep, dark Mayan eyes shifted to Jeanne and then to Julie. She apparently did not intend to speak to either again.

Searching for a new approach, Jeanne said, "When you see someone happy and glowing, do you think they know something you want to know, too?"

Without reaching a consensus, the tribe normally would not act on any new idea or plan, but this clan had two sides present and both sides wanted to work together immediately on new business—or at least be heard, so one of the men said, "I think we can dance and sing and still build a great mission."

The women had decided long before that he was not very ambitious, so they merely glanced at him and discarded his view without discussion. He flushed at their rejection of his wisdom and retreated into the shadows to say nothing more.

A woman with wide gaps between her teeth from drinking too much Coca Cola in the past reviewed their combined thoughts before saying, "Ms. Julie, you want us to dance and talk and walk a lot, but that takes energy away from what we need to weave, or create pottery, or scribe for Miss Jeanne. When would we find time to eat and create more energy?"

Speaking haltingly in the most common of Mayan dialects, Julie said, "I think we can at least try it out…and if it works…we can do it again and again. If it hurts or isn't good for our feet…or nerves…or whatever, we'll forget it…I have a saying, 'If it feels good, do it again. If it doesn't feel good—forget it!'"

Julie's efforts to speak in their dialect were well received by the men, so they decided among themselves that her idea had some merit, but they would watch and see how the women pursued the dance—at least at first.

Sensing that the men did not reject her or her idea, Julie stood up and pointed to one or two of the prettiest women who now appeared ready to dance and sing. She asked them to join her in the center of the room. They did so, with speed. Once in place, without much thought Julie directed them to walk clockwise, and then said hastily, "I mean walk in the direction of the sun going around the Earth." She wondered if she had changed directions on them, but made no effort to stop the next set of instructions from slipping out of her mouth without further thought. "Put out your hand and embrace the hand of the woman to your left…then pulse in place for a count of ten…then embrace the hand of the woman on your right. Got that?"

The women glided and slipped into gear as the circle grew wider and wider as other women decided to try out the new dance, too. Each one smiled as she admitted another to the ring and felt the power surge as they realized that such a great experience had been inspired within their individual minds. Excited by the success of the impromptu dance, Jeanne shouted, "Let's appoint someone to sing!"

Three of the girls sang out immediately, "Let it be Juanita."

Crippled by shyness, Juanita hid her eyes and refused to sing alone. Coming to her rescue to keep the party moving, Jeanne said jovially, "Okay, Juanita, I'll sing first, then you take over—so I don't lose face."

Juanita continued to hesitate, so a man sitting along the wall began to chant. Immediately, each dancer entered a deeper trance. The American women said nothing since they hoped for a miracle, but did not expect to see one.

The dance-trance went on until many Mayan women started spinning in a state of rapture—behavior far different from their everyday ways. This state of heightened awareness was so seductive that several men drifted off into space, only to return to their usual daze with a thump. They then stood up and began singing as if they had been hired to entertain by the hour. As a trio of such singers sang loud enough to reach far beyond the rafters of the great room, a sound coming from the front gate stopped them all in the middle of a chorus.

It had to be the police—again. The loud thumping on the gate became clearer as the men ceased singing and the dancers stopped whirling about the room. They finally realized it was not someone knocking, but the sound of objects being hurled at the gate, as if trying to arouse their attention. Without thought, Jeanne said quickly, "Why don't they ring the bell if they want in?"

The men, being extremely superstitious—or very wise, wanted more information before they moved to leave the room. They motioned to Jeanne to stop talking and listen. Regretting the American need to fill in every gap in any conversation or concentration, she immediately did what they said.

The outbursts became a constant thunder before one of the women recognized it was hailing outside, possibly fronting a gale. She announced very seriously that it was the priests from the other side demanding payment. No one laughed. The hail continued its rampage, soundly beating the roof above them before leaving just as suddenly as it had arrived. Not a word was spoken by anyone in the room until it was over.

The first question each Maya then asked was: "What does it mean?" Within a few minutes of the storm's abatement, women started leaping into the air and spinning more quickly than before. Singing along with the men as if they had discovered yet another way to reach the gods of the sky tonight.

Moving closer to Julie in order to whisper, Jeanne said, "What's going on? What do they see that we can't see or believe? I'm thrilled that they're so happy, but nothing's gone as planned. Was I supposed to participate or just be here to witness The Maya do their thing?"

"You're an instrument of peace, Jeanne—gifted with understanding way beyond mine. I don't know what to tell you, but these women really know how to sing—and dance. Why don't we encourage them to hum and sing as they work every day?"

Thinking only a moment or two, Jeanne said, "I never thought of it before, but it'll work—at least for the weavers and potters. Writing doesn't exist in the same time or frame of mind as singing, but it's usually enhanced when someone sings in the background and you can feel their bliss. It produces stronger prose or better connections with your fingers than when you're merely doing copy work all alone."

"When you live in and around DC—never getting out of the suburbs for months at a time, you forget the joy of living an elegant, simple life. This is so wonderful for us that we found The Maya!"

"You know, Julie, I've moved around a lot, too, trying to find time to do all the things my son and I wanted to do together and apart, but this place is different from anything I ever imagined it would be. I'm still adjusting, but feel great! I want to create now! I even want to write about myself—believe it or not."

Julie wrinkled her forehead as she said, "Why not? Don't all writers write about themselves?"

Very serious, Jeanne replied, "Not me! I write non-fiction. You know—reality. There isn't time to take down self-dictation or delve into my life in order to figure out why I whine. To me, self-indulgence is for literary types who have no social life."

"You have so much to give the world, Jeanne. Why not try to produce a journal or diary that everyone can sift through and read to find out more about you and your son and all that you did to find this time and place—and why you want to live with us now?" As Julie spoke, a high intensity smile lit up her face and produced some interest among the men who sat watching the two as they talked alone at the side of the room.

Noticing that some men were putting on jackets and moving toward the door, Jeanne said quickly, "I think we better get back to our wards and watch what they're doing. It seems the men tend to lose interest in their women whenever we do."

Julie's smile widened still further, but she spoke with no emotion, "Oh, yes, they have to leave. It's late for the field workers. They didn't eat much this evening because their stomachs are so small, but in time we'll increase their capacity."

Jeanne laughed and Julie chuckled, so those who watched them laughed, too, as if they knew what the two wealthy American women talked about and why both of them willingly gave up so much to follow The Maya in time like they do. The tribe believed itself to be wealthy now because of the interest shown by rich Americans who came and went from this compound almost daily. Pointing to one of the men having trouble standing, Jeanne said, "Help the elder, please."

He immediately brushed away the helping hand extended toward him and straightened his spine. Silently looking Jeanne in the eye, he let her know he was able to lift himself without assistance. Thank you very much! She was taken back by his pride, then realized that she was just as stubborn as he was. Never quick to leave any scene, the old man lingered longer this evening than usual because he grieved his inability to dance and sing as he had when he was young.

Jeanne could read his thoughts during the brief moment when their eyes aligned in time. She knew she would forget him, but not before she wrote a word or two about his work. Approaching the elder, now walking slowly toward the door, Jeanne said, "Senor, could you spare a few days a week to talk to me privately?"

A tear ran downward from his rheumy eyes to his jagged, toothy smile as he nodded and implied that he would do whatever she liked. He filled with pride and his mind overflowed with it for a moment, but since love was the basis of his pride, it did him no harm.

Jeanne then asked Julie, "Can you see the two of us working as a team with him?"

Julie smiled, surprising her by saying, "No, I don't understand and talk Mayan."

"What are you talking about? You talk like a native!" Jeanne did not think of herself as able to speak Mayan well, other than to share a few pleasantries, but Julie assured her that she spoke well enough to work with such a man of wisdom.

Wonders and miracles were certain to happen with Jeanne around, but Julie could not help worrying about her own work—a lot. In an attempt to ease her anxiety, she asked softly, "Do you ever feel like you don't belong here—that you should leave?"

Obviously puzzled, Jeanne replied, "What do you mean, Julie? You're the most positive influence these women have ever had. You've elevated their art! And you've introduced them to thousands of people who admire them—and their art. Doesn't that make you feel good?"

"No, Jeanne, it doesn't. I want to make a difference, but being shy makes it a lot harder for me to do my work with The Maya…Why do we always have to do things that are not within our nature if we want to star?"

"Maybe because we want what others have—or we think they do it better. Just like you saying I speak Mayan better than you. You're letter perfect! I'm the nut trying to be fluent!" Jeanne snapped her fingers then and the crack caused men nearby to stop talking and stare at her. She wondered about their reaction, but did not say a word.

An older woman who kept her personal life unknown to the tribe—even though she always sat near the elders, approached the Americans and said without passion, "Do you notice how often you're caught talking to your friend and not to we Maya?"

Jeanne reached out impulsively to touch the woman's right arm as she spoke in a rush, "Oh, that's not good! Thanks for telling me. I miss my friends, but that's no excuse for misbehaving when new people appear. I want to connect with old friends and find out what each one has to say, because I fear new people will leave before I get their message or learn a lesson from them, so sometimes I forget about those closest me—and what they teach me daily."

"You have such intensity about you, Ms. Jeanne. You could lead a parade through the night with your light, yet whenever you stand up you always say you don't know what to say. Why do you do that?" The woman talked on, seemingly loath to go home as she, too, ignored everyone else to talk to only one friend.

⚹ ⚹

A few days later Jeanne decided to start interviewing elders who worked nearby in order to find out more about their lives in particular and tribal life in general. She wondered why she had never thought to write about those living close at hand—instead flying to other parts of the world as if strangers were smarter or greater in some way than the people she could easily interview at home. Once her outline was done, she decided that Wanda was the best person to work with first. She also wanted to go over her interview notes with Wanda before she did any more work with The Maya.

When Wanda said emphatically that whatever she wrote was okay with her, Jeanne panicked from the responsibility of portraying such a wonderful woman in the best possible way without reducing her luster and power by making insignificant retakes of her younger days and past interviews. When she finished her first draft, she laughed. By the time she got the final copy of her ninth draft typed, she felt wise and triumphant—but exhausted. It was now time to see if Wanda would keep her word about what was written about her. Would it float—or not? She placed a copy of the text under the door to Wanda's office and quickly walked away, hoping not to hear too quickly from Wanda, unless there was a rave review due.

When Wanda spotted the neatly printed pages efficiently clipped together, she ruffled the papers with the palm of her hand, wondering why they felt warm. Then she spotted it. Jeanne was a master craftsman! She did not hand out sloppy work to her critics and editors because they would think twice about making changes to such neat and perfectly typed pages. Perhaps this was not quite the right frame of mind to read her life story, but it helped Wanda get started.

As she read the first page, Wanda shook with laughter and delight. She thought about how weird it was to read about yourself as if you did not exist. Since it read more like a novel than a biography, Wanda was happy and intrigued to discover where her series of interviews had led Jeanne.

WWW ~ Wise Women of the World

By
Jeanne Beck

Wanda Windstrom
Weaver of Extraordinary Dreams

Asked to think about her life and share whatever was there, Wanda Windstrom sat completely at ease across from me and let her mind flash through the past and reflect on her life. At first she was tired and expressed concerns about phantom pains she still experienced in her right leg, which had been shattered in a home accident and later amputated. Without further risk to life or limb, Wanda slipped into a mood from which she could view everything as if it was taking place now. Her words were elegant as any prose I could hope to compose, so I decided to let her design this piece and fill in the blanks later. I am not taking much credit for it, so here goes, see how it flows....

"My leg wasn't healing as well as everyone expected, and I didn't believe it would be okay once the cast was removed in Mexico a month or two later, but something else bothered me more about moving away from my home in the US. I'm still unable to figure out where it started and when it will end, but let's pretend that I know, so you can write your book.

"I was too young to understand adults, yet they always assumed I knew what to do and that I would turn out better than they did. Usually you turn out just like your parents, regardless of what you intended or they wanted, so when I turned 18 everything became as clear as mud. I let my self-image accumulate a little debris, then added a bit more, until I was entirely buried by my own false assumptions—overwhelmed with what it meant to be an adult by age 24. I just didn't get it then!"

"I was sure motherhood was way beyond my grasp and singular abilities. Back then you had to cope with the terrible pain of bearing a child and delivering it to people who would never believe in it—only to have the kid turn around later and attack you publicly—after all you had given up for her! Women in their later years move every conversation around to 'the change' and how terrible it was! Always, always a horror story that ended with regret that you wouldn't be able to have any more kids. They suddenly forgot all the pain, the insolence, the ingratitude of their kids and longed for more. I didn't want to raise a child because of all that chatter, believe it or not. I tried to erase it from my mind by saying it didn't matter, but now that I've breezed through '*the change*' myself, I wonder if the pain and problems of raising children were also greatly exaggerated. What made me listen to other women? Why did they want to scare me and others like that?"

"I guess it has a lot to do with your idea of self-importance. If you don't think you have much to offer, you make a big deal out of whatever you do contribute. My mother constantly said women were stronger and more powerful than men, but everyone doubted her. Now women think they're all powerful and want to cheat men wherever and whenever they can—and not give them any respect. I know that would never have been condoned by *my* Mother!" (Wanda shook her head then.)

Question: ***What did you do for fun when you were a kid?***

Answer: I used to ride my bike over the hills and through the woods—without scarring the earth. I didn't carry on like some Hell's Angel was after me or I was evading the law. I left the trees in peace, and I always left the trail the same as it was when I arrived.

Question: ***Why do people vandalize and ruin what others want to use, too?***

Answer: I guess if you weren't an only child and didn't understand why others might be lonely, this could be viewed as a funny existence—this life. When I was a kid I could never sit down and talk with a sister or brother, because I didn't have one. On the other hand, I didn't have to share my stuff or envy siblings getting stuff I wanted. This makes it hard when you have to learn to share at school—and some never do. Get off on the wrong foot and you have to judge for yourself if you're right or 'they' are. I guess that just about explains my life.

Question: ***What are your thoughts on marriage?***

Answer: As you walk down the aisle, you might think about what you would do if the groom doesn't want you, but you don't really give it much thought and just do it, because it's expected….You're supposed to get married. When I got married, I had no ambition to be anyone but my husband's servant, possibly have the mythical child that would make us happy and content. I did nothing to improve my life outside the house. I didn't listen to what women who wanted to get ahead on the job were going through. Instead, I watched and learned a lot about how to cozy up to men or resist them—nothing about the ins-and-outs of doing business with them. I now wish I had paid attention to the men who ran the world then. Maybe I would know more about organizing this group of women and men, and do a better job than I am.

Question: *What can you tell us about this new group of Mayan weavers you are bringing together now?*

Answer: This group of artisans and shamans is so incoherent and unruly at times that I doubt we'll ever be able to do the disciplined, orderly work required to make weaving an industrial art. But my friend, Teri, thinks otherwise and is happy we are willing to try to get organized outside this clan. I wish I had her outlook at times, but then I wouldn't be me. Would I? I could not be a master weaver, either, if I had met lots of resistance to my doing it.

Question: *Why is that?*

Answer: When you set out to do something that no one in your family ever did or ever wanted to do, you meet resistance if you're a son. I became an only child as they waited for a boy to arrive, so I didn't do much of any one thing. When no longer young, my mother insisted that I do what I love—and do it quickly. That made me push myself a lot harder than if she had said, "I know you'll do great—whatever you do!" That is what lazy conversationalists and disinterested friends usually say. Isn't it? (My mother) was definitely not lazy, but she had a rheumatic heart and all the problems that go with it. I'm not saying she wasn't loving and generous and all those good things, but her pump didn't work right, so at times it took all her strength just to stay alive. There was very little juice left for anything else then. I remember those days well….

Anyway, she was a great coach. Her knowledge of fabrics, sewing, embroidery, and such helped me a lot when getting started. She sorted the wool and helped me learn to card so I could control every aspect of my art. She always referred to it as 'my art' and never let my father get too upset about all the money it took to weave a little piece. Oh, yes, those were tough times at home! Me, acting out the part of the wayward daughter, having been abused by her wayward husband, returns to her parents' home just as they fell in love—again. Looking back, it was sad for them that I returned then, but good for me. They didn't bother me much, because Dad was retiring and not happy about it. Now that I look back, he didn't really retire. He must have been fired!

Anyway we worked together getting a big loom set up in the basement—while my father fumed about our spending. He was positive that this enterprise would end with me being greatly disappointed—a lot like he was, I guess. But today I'm able to tell my parents, wherever they may be, that I'm happy, loved, respected, and resourceful. I still get my own way a lot, too, because I'm almost always right and everyone knows it!

Question: *How much can anyone expect out of life?*

Answer: After a few weeks of re-living with my parents, I guided my dad up to the attic and showed him how nice it could be if he made me a pad of my own. He wasn't delighted with my plan because it would cost a lot, but we all set to work on it anyway. Now that I think back, it had to have been my mother who insisted that I get my own apartment, so it might as well be in the same house—to save money. She always knew how to get around my dad!"

Question: *Do you think about your parents a lot?*

Answer: Whenever I go to the cemetery alone, I wander about and talk to people who are visiting, too. We don't seem to talk much sense about those we love enough to visit and place flowers on the monuments we raised, but we all feel pleased, blessed—at peace. It's a strange feeling. You know you're honoring your parents or the dead, and someday you're going to get a gold star for doing it.

Anyway, as I sit and pray and chant each day, I ask for help from my parents and others around me who have nothing better to do then than help me. I usually end up laughing. I always laugh. When my mother was on her deathbed she asked me to never marry a man a lot older than me and not to forget how to laugh—not necessarily in that order. She said it helped her live ten years longer than the most optimistic doctor ever predicted she could. I want to live as she did—minus the heart trouble. Come to think of it, my heart is sound, but look at my leg. It'll probably bother me all my life. My mother always said, 'Whatever you worry about never happens.' Maybe we're meant to slow down as we age, so we're given physical problems that make us stop and meditate before rushing around like some crazy chicken that's dead and doesn't realize it yet."

At this point, Wanda stopped proofreading and took out a notepad and jotted down a message to Jeanne to be included with the manuscript when she sent it back.

Hey, Jeanne!

Speaking of killing chickens, that reminds me of that ceremony yesterday. It was great, but killing chickens!!?? What is Mandy up to anyway? I still get a chill remembering how she put chicken blood on my forehead and mumbled something about God taking away my pain. I wasn't aware I had any pain until last night…never mind.

Stop back to talk to me when you get a chance. Okay?

Chicken-Hearted Wanda

The next day the two friends got together in the weavers' workroom to talk about the article Jeanne wrote. Their conversation got strange and weird, as it does when those who have known each other for more than this life rehash the past. Wanda said, "Whatever happened to that friend of yours who went off to school and never returned home? I think about her. She had such a sweet face—really determined to be a psychiatrist—not a psychologist. No one wanted to talk to her about it. She had to have been made of solid marble to be able to resist all those teachers trying to talk her out of becoming a doctor, because women 'are meant to marry doctors, not be doctors.'"

"I'm not sure," said Jeanne. "Someone said her name was mentioned in *Time* the other week, but I forgot to stop and buy a copy at the airport. Maybe if it gets to Mexico City, it'll make it here. Just a thought, but I'll file it away for now and pull it out later."

Wanda appeared to be in deep thought, so Jeanne changed the subject. "Wonder where Teri is? She went out this morning in her car and left me a note about her mother and father not being able to talk to her privately here, so she wanted to call them from town. I guess that's what has her in a stew—that and thinking back."

Drifting about the room as they talked, one loom seemed to beckon Wanda to work now. Her hands began to fly across the materials fast enough to prevent her mind from focusing on a single thought or about what had come into view beyond this room. Usually when she assumed this mood it was due to inner conversations, but now she looked up occasionally and focused on someone other than herself.

At such times her intense cobalt blue eyes would rivet others just enough to make them stop whatever they were thinking and tell her what they were doing—even when they did not want to do it. Wanda had a strange magnetic power and demonstrated it now—as the two women talked about mutual friends. She looked out the door and saw a young man standing in the half-light of the portico and beckoned for him to enter. He appeared to be frightened, so she stopped working on her latest pattern long enough to assure him that he was welcome, or at least that was her intention. She said in an assumed gruff manner, "As if I didn't have enough to do already, now you want to learn to weave, too. Right?"

"No Maam! That is right, isn't it?"

"What's right?" Wanda snapped.

"I should call you Maam when I talk to you."

"Oh, yes, that's fine, but you can call me Senora, too. I don't mind."

The boyish man smiled and took a tenuous step into the room as if he had been invited to stay and talk. Wanda pretended to ignore him by talking only to Jeanne, as if dictating written instructions on how to weave. She let him listen in on what a beginner must do to set up a loom. "You have to keep everything clean and organized before you sit down to weave. It's not enough to clean your hands. Everything must be clean because you'll be leaning against the loom and touching the yarn constantly. You'll even touch it with your feet. Be clean all over so body odors don't taint the cloth. Do you understand what I mean?"

Jeanne did not even pretend to take notes, instead she closely observed the young man, trying to figure out his plan. When Wanda stopped working and popped the question, she was too shocked to answer. However, the young man enthusiastically responded, "Oh, yes, yes, I will be clean always. I will not just wash my hands, but wash everything every day. I will not leave my house without washing—a lot."

Smiling in spite of her desire to come across as a stern disciplinarian, Wanda continued with less intensity, "You must also sort the wool or whatever material you use to weave.

Place it where you can reach it easily—before you begin to weave. You don't stop weaving much once you start. You have to maintain the same tension to keep it from wavering. See what I mean?"

The young man, now confident enough to edge closer to the loom, continued to sweat even though the room was now cool.

"Don't come too close! You're too exhausted from working all day in the fields to be able to learn much tonight, so get a shower and come back in an hour. I'll see if I can stop working long enough then to show you how to set up the other loom. You do what I say, and we'll both be happy."

Without stopping to look back, the young man hurled a 'Thank you, maam' over his shoulder as he raced out of the room.

Jeanne continued to think about him. She wondered what he did all day. His feet were brazen and bold and knew no fear. The thought that his feet will take him high in the Alps one day made her wonder why she picked that up from somewhere else. She thought, 'Funny how the mind skips around when you stand around with nothing to do.'

♓   ♓

As the late afternoon sun slipped behind the hedges and trees planted inside the massive walls of the outer garden, Wanda smiled as she saw her daughter approach her upon returning from a visit to Merida. She knew instantly that Thérèse was very pleased, which always made her happy. She continued to wander about in the shadows waiting for Thérèse to close the garden gate so they could have privacy.

Instead of quietly closing the gate, Thérèse threw it wide to display a huge shopping bag. She flourished it in the air as she walked toward Wanda and said, "TaDa! Here's more yarn for your mill, and there's more where this came from! I found it at the big Indian market. Wait until you see it. You'll be thrilled! It's just the right shade for the next three or four wall hangings I want you to make."

Normally Wanda resented anyone telling her what to do and what materials to use, but never Thérèse. She never foresaw problems then, because it always worked—regardless of how improbable the design might be or how Thérèse believed it would be used by others. Wall hangings, 'Designed by Teri,' always sold best and were most admired by outsiders, so Wanda seldom groused about making the changes required to set up the looms differently and teach those weavers who never easily grasp what needed to be done when new designs were introduced to the line.

"As if I need more work, Thérèse. Come, let me look at it—and you." She was not grumbling so much as mildly scolding her daughter, to let her know that she was getting a bit too close to the edge of her temper.

Thérèse always knew when Wanda was very tired, because her mind did not willingly open wide at such times, so she said with energy, "I can see what you need now! You need a cup of tea! Let's go to the shop and see who's flitted in while I was out and about doing my *own* business for a change." As she spoke, Thérèse pushed her mother through the garden gate toward the fading sun. Both laughed spontaneously as Wanda pulled the gate closed behind them with a quick, wistful look at the peace and serenity they left behind for another day. Thérèse grinned as she asked, "Why don't you let me close doors for you? It seems sort of superstitious to me. Does it mean anything?"

"It means that I get some exercise while you do all the really heavy work of pushing me around. It also means that no one is pushing me out the door—just yet. I'll leave under my own power when I'm ready to go—I hope, I hope, I hope."

Thérèse paused outside the compound's main showroom so her mother could catch her breath, if necessary. Wanda did just that as she peered through the tinted window to see if anything had changed since she last looked over the weavers' display. Her eyes roved over the large room, taking in everything—or just about everything, with one deep insightful sweeping glance rather than several brief probes. She spoke, without giving it much thought, "The shop looks great! I didn't realize you would change it so much, but you have the designer's touch."

Thérèse may have missed the point while pointing out a brilliant green, yellow, and white wall hanging that somewhat resembled a macaw in hiding. The surprising element missing was the bird's dominant shades of blue and red, otherwise it could easily be identified as a macaw by its head and body shape. Thérèse said, "I think women enjoy buying and selling more than men, but don't usually bargain as well, but since I'm the model in this family, I get to pick what we sell—and that kind of hanging sells well."

"A macaw without brilliant plumage isn't what I would normally create, but you know what leads people to open their wallets and buy now, so I'll leave it as is until you say otherwise. But why the need to do so many things in only these three colors?" Wanda squinted at the hanging as if deciding whether or not to buy it, then shook her head and said, "I really don't like it! I like nature's color scheme best."

"I know you do, but people in New York and Chicago want showcase houses on a budget or in a limited color palette, which isn't close to Earth tones, so we begin with easy designs and introduce more color as we move them into the future."

"Bah, New Yorkers are boring in their black. What do they know about color and what it does to change your mood?" Her own words soothed her, but Wanda still shook her finger at Thérèse and admonished her with: "You're always trying to change people—and succeeding at it, but you shouldn't try."

Thérèse said nothing more as she guided her mother into the kitchen that stood strangely empty for this time of day. She picked up a tea tray made up especially for them. It sat alone on the tiled counter. Examining the rose-covered pot that held their afternoon tea, and the dainty matching tea cups and saucers, Thérèse wondered, 'What if we introduce the Maya to afternoon tea? We could serve it on our colorful earthenware and delight them—as well as tourists, while pushing traditional tea service designs out of style. Would women buy it—maybe start a rush for it like we did with the evening wraps?'

Without lifting her eyes, Wanda said slowly, "I think we should start serving cocoa in earthenware mugs or making hot chocolate a new way—like the Maya of old. What do you think?"

"What a great idea!" Thérèse did not say another word. Instead she put their combined thoughts to rest as they left the kitchen to check out the loom room to see how the evening weaving class was getting along and what they might need.

☼ Chapter Seventeen

An aging American tourist spoke as if he knew all there was to know about places far from his hometown. "There are several places in Mexico that get no dough—and this is one of them! I see so much corruption down here that I don't even trust that the maid who opens the door is really a maid. Know what I'm saying?" He tacked this complaint onto his long litany about what was wrong with this trip and let a look of smug contentment sit on his face as he settled in to talk. No one else in the group of travelers seated with him at the table now covered with dirty breakfast dishes appeared willing to disagree or change his beliefs, so whatever he said then stood for all of them.

At a nearby table a shrouded woman sat with her head held high and addressed a group of university students in Spanish. They were drinking from carafes of fruit juices and pots of coffee and tea. All receptacles were pushed into the center of the table—handy if they wanted another drink. The young people watched her attentively as she spoke. "The way to stand out and make a name for yourself requires that you do two things. It's not enough to pretend to be someone whom you want to be, you have to live that life! Begin with brief statements or comments that reveal what *you* believe, then enlarge on that as you gain wisdom and experience. Some never sense when it's time to make a public confession or to speak courageously about what they believe. They think that they alone see, so they lose many opportunities to make new friends. Friends, after all, are people who agree with what you say or do, or at least let you continue to think they do and believe as you do. If no one sees you as being different from what they perceive the rest of the world to be, why would anyone seek to make you an ally?" Having said this, the teacher waited for someone to volunteer an answer.

The discontented man at the next table looked askance at the group of students and the woman steering them into a discussion on public relations. He was advanced in age and no longer using much of his mind when he spoke to everyone within earshot. "Look at them! They can't even speak English, yet plan on taking over industry!"

The student seated closest to him laughed. Mandy laughed, too, and turned toward him and gave him a wink and a grin. Their amiable response puzzled the aggressive American and made his associates uncomfortable as well, so Mandy said, "We have so many people from all over the world visiting us now that we can't afford to *not* show love to strangers, but it's difficult at times. Is it not?" Mandy spoke to the students while continuing to look directly at the offensive man who sat chewing on an unlit cigar, no longer talking. He did not know what was said in Spanish, so he thought he got away with making racist statements then, but he did not.

Mandy retreated into lecture mode again and said, "What we have in front of us now is a town about to become a super star. But…it's going to be a point of departure for many. Do you catch my drift or do I need to tell you more?" Using her hands she sketched out a ball in the air and pantomimed that they would be flying everywhere from here. Then she paused for a few moments, as though listening to someone else talking to her.

The young man sitting on Mandy's right was always willing to take sides in any debate, so he filled in gaps with what he hoped might become controversial in order to end the seminar or change its direction from where it was headed now. He said, "I think we need to be prepared to accommodate all who want to go with us, but if it comes down to building hotels and such, we're beginning to sound more like economists than philosophers and theologians."

Without smiling, Mandy said quietly, "We're workers in paradise, so we go where we're needed. Can't you see that?" She was worried, but unsure why she felt such unease when everything around her looked to be at rest. When she worked within a group of decent people who could provide a high wall of white light, she did not extend her spiritual antennae very high. So she tried to rise above this circle of protection to see if anyone was on the prowl around them now, but could not. This group was unique—unwilling to let her stop speaking to eat, so she confined her fears of whatever to what she planned to do with them over the next few days.

Lowering her voice, Mandy said quietly, "By reducing our scope of activities and thoughts, we can centralize our beliefs and gain access to what everyone here needs. For instance, if we thought the enemy of our family was going to enter the living room and take away our spouse or child, we would act different in every respect from when we expect a welcome guest. Respect the difference! But remain open to those you welcome into your home—and learn what you can from all of them."

Hands started going up, but Mandy ignored them because she did not want to interrupt her thoughts or stop channeling right then. "I see you're wondering about the difference between good and evil… You know it, but you don't want to believe that evil is possibly as strong today as it was in ancient times. You want to believe people are more likely to spot it now than in the old days, but that's not true. In fact, it was much easier to sense evil then than it is to recognize it in a friend now."

One young man nodded, and then another, but the women pretended to misunderstand what she meant. They maintained blank stares and silently sat watching Mandy. Shrugging, she tried a different tack. "When one person looks lasciviously at another, is that not pornographic in nature? Is that not a rape of intent—if not in actuality? What did the man or woman think would happen with that thought? Is not evil the intent more than the actual belief?"

"You're losing me again," said one young woman who frequently tossed her long, black hair around her head as if auditioning for a shampoo commercial. She craved attention and accepted any negative consequences of her actions, if that was all she got.

Through clenched teeth, Mandy said to the vain woman. "You have a mind and a good sense of time, so go into it now and sense what's there. When you're done, sit quietly until we ask you what you found." The students were amazed that her words came out clear and strong and as loud as if she had moved her lips to pronounce them.

Noticing their astonishment, Mandy enunciated her words and spoke just above a whisper. "I can 'ventriloquize' my thoughts. Then they become your lies or your wisdom—depending upon what is said, it's still me—this being, who created the belief. You must be careful of what you put out into space now because it's going to rebound much faster than it did in the old days—and none of you can remember how fast news traveled then."

A young man who had been dreaming when the lecture began was now alert. He intuited that someone was about to hurt Mandy, so he spoke to her alone. He blurted out a single Mayan word: "Bacab"

Stunned, Mandy said quickly, "We need to fortify our belief system immediately! I'll begin by calling upon The East to compress and make a safe spot for everyone sitting here. Can you assume that position for me, Rafael?" Motioning to the man seated to her left to move immediately to the Eastern-most point of the table.

As Rafael changed position, he noticed a tourist at the next table stand up and walk away. Without realizing what others nearby might think of him, he began chanting: "I am East of the Moon and West of the Sun and able to bless everyone." Although he thought he was praying loud enough for the genii to hear him on the other side, he was not heard by anyone outside this circle of friends.

Frowning slightly, Mandy said, "Thank you, Rafael. We'll begin every session from now on by placing the wards at each corner of the table. Rafael, please continue to work your wisdom and listen. I want the rest of you to take your accustomed positions. We'll set up a radar base now and see if we find anyone straying into our space. Quick, move it!"

Her intuition was always stable, fabled by all her students, so no one doubted that this would be a class they would always remember and would later say paid their tuition in spades. Some missed classes occasionally, and some repeatedly skipped lectures by those who urged them to move up *into* the world, but none missed Mandy's scheduled seminars on any subject she thought was necessary to help them move up and out of this life and time. Mandy's mind was a vision of time and most of the shamans in town hung around the outskirts of her study groups trying to listen in, but this time none of them was seen nearby. She wondered about this. "Do you feel anything strange, Luis?"

Without waiting for Luis to reply, Mandy moved into the center of the group mentally, in an attempt to hide her light. She was spied upon by many too much of the time, so it was not an exercise in futility to try to disguise herself now; however, she wondered why it was necessary right then.

Juan said, "I see a spy, Ms. Brown!" He shielded his eyes with his hand and looked upward into the space above them.

"Thanks for the warning, Juan. I see that we must all take cover now. This is no longer a good spot to teach."

On cue, all the students stood up and started stretching and talking casually as if taking a break. They gathered their pencils and papers, as well as the few books pertaining to their studies, and walked away. Mandy stood back and motioned to the waiter as she placed a few bills on their sidewalk table. She smiled and spoke quietly to the waiter. "Wait for me in back. When I get through with the students, we'll flee."

Not as tall as Mandy, the young waiter appeared to other customers as disinterested in everything but the money, once he spotted the generous tip. He bowed low over her extended hand as if the tip was very grand and quickly retrieved the money and pocketed it. Attached to the top bill was a note to be delivered to Jorge. He continued to act as if he could retire on the tip she left him. Obsequiously, he said, "Let me walk you to the gate, Ms. Mandy. I see the students are well behaved and eager to leave, but you may stay."

Mandy swayed a bit until she spotted a man who had berated the Maya and all Mexicans of any tribe. He was nearby and watching her closely now. For his benefit alone, she said quite distinctly, "Don't worry about them. Kids are kids! Give them a break and they can't get out of class fast enough." She laughed as her eyes shifted dramatically behind a mask she created by donning sunglasses of a purple hue.

The waiter also saw the American loitering across the street and laughed as if he were extremely happy. Their ongoing act seemed to put the spy at ease. He had previously not been aware of Mandy working there, but now was sure that something was about to happen within this group of students. Many thought he was CIA, but he believed he worked for all sides, thus he was not trusted by anyone who ever knew him.

As far as the average New Yorker could discern, Mandy was not in a hurry, but to her class she appeared to be running by the time she caught up with them. She spoke with urgency, "Let's all look sharp and get out of here fast."

"I don't see anything," whined the prettiest girl in the class. None of the men bothered with her then. Since the other women never did, the group moved speedily forward without further comment.

After a block or so of determined walking, Mandy spotted a better place to sit and begin their studies again. It was the oldest cathedral in town. Not very pretty, but it was hallowed ground. She would not be bothered once safely inside that sacred space, but they had to cross a lot of open ground to get there. Much evil could happen if they were not fully protected. Mandy said, "Juan, Rafael, take the defensive positions assigned and strut as if you're able to protect everyone in the world."

Mandy spoke softly to one and the other heard it, but the other students did not. How did she do it? The answer came to each man intuitively. God and angels use human beings, often taking over when it is time to ascend or when it is not the right day to die. These two men protected their classmates from outward interference, but Mandy was on her own.

The pretty young woman moaned loudly as they entered the cathedral, "I feel nothing!"

"Sssshhhh, we're in church! You're not supposed to be wearing shorts in church, you idiot!" The men looked at the would-be vamp again, realizing that even the most tolerant girl had reached her limit of patience and was screaming in her thoughts: 'Why is she always so loud and needy—like now?' The response came immediately: 'She shouts because she has no profound beliefs!'

No one spoke intuitively or otherwise, because they were aware the insecure beauty might start talking out loud about what she thought was not right—according to her mind. Her belligerence often upset the women and made the men wonder about their own interest in her. She had seduced two students more easily than they had believed possible—and they knew Mandy was aware of it, too.

To end the tension within them, Pablo, the youngest present, whispered loudly, "Don't look now, Ms. Brown, but the priest is coming down the aisle—and he looks angry."

Mandy turned toward the priest with a smile that was partially hidden by her very dark glasses as well as the scarf covering her long dark hair that resembled a wig even to her most ardent admirers. With a casual wave, she said, "Hi, Father. We're studying art and thought we'd begin with the cathedral and start working our way around town. Is that okay?"

The priest rubbed his fingers in the ancient gesture of greedy clerics to indicate that a fee was required. When Mandy placed a few pesos in his hand, he walked away and did not return to see if they might be defacing the church.

"See? All priests ever think about is worldly needs. They're all greedy!" said Juan to those standing nearby.

Recognizing Juan's disgust, Mandy raised her head to catch his eye. When she got his attention, she nodded in the direction of the altar and said, "Whatever is said in my name is said by me, and whatever is to be has been said. Please keep in mind that you're in the nave of the church. It's not the place to swear or criticize or make mistaken judgments about people who slave all day in the work of God—or whatever they believe they're doing now."

Mandy's quick defense of the man who would be a priest did not amaze anyone present, but each was suddenly struck by the thought that whatever was said in such a place could be heard by those who were willing to fly far and wide. That is to say, they felt the presence of angels and wondered why they never noticed them before.

"I think we have many friends with us now. Are you picking up any blips on your radar, Rafael, Juan?" As Mandy spoke, her sudden head movement dislodged the scarf used to loosely capture her mane-like hair, letting it cascade down over her shoulders and beyond. She pushed her sunglasses upward to her crown to better control the flow of her hair, thereby insuring that if any sunlight did filter into the cathedral only the purple rays would enter Mandy's thoughts through her crown.

After completely viewing each area of the cathedral, they paused for a moment and prayed intently. Once the entire perimeter of the cathedral was cleansed in this way, they entered each adjoining chapel and repeated the ritual. Mandy said nothing until they cleansed the chapels, the apse, the nave, and wherever else she led them. Without looking at the Baby Jesus and its crown of plastic flowers, she said, "Do you see how the gold has lost its luster?" She was sure it was not the same as it was the last time they met in the cathedral, due to a recent theft, but the students were unaware that anything evil had happened there.

"Oh, my God of All, look at the way the Baby Jesus sits! It's not the same! Someone has stolen the golden babe." When Angeles uttered this profanity, she had intended to merely shock her closest friends into a spiritual awakening. After all, she was considered to be the most pious among them. But calling upon God of All in that way caused everyone to shudder and watch her closely as she mutely pointed out more gaps among the cathedral's golden treasures.

"I don't believe it!" Juan yelled as he entered the chapel right then and spotted the empty space where the gilded baby Jesus normally lay.

"Don't touch a thing," commanded Mandy. She lifted her hand and said she had to leave immediately, but they must call the priest and report the theft.

"You will be suspected if you leave," said Rafael. His words fell on Mandy's back as she prepared to flee down the aisle toward the side door.

"We never met! The priest didn't see me. He got the money from one of you, and you all live around here. Remember, I wasn't able to accompany you here today, so you all entered the cathedral to work on your art assignments—without me. Remember me in your prayers!" Mandy's parting words ended as she opened the door just wide enough to slip outside.

The sudden bright sunlight blasted Mandy's eyes and reduced her visibility immediately. Unable to focus for a second or so, she could not see what was ahead of her just beyond the glow. Just enough time for evil to subside, collide, or take her to another time, but Mandy was not willing to acknowledge evil. She put up a fight and left the city that night.

☼ Chapter Eighteen

"Whatever you do or wherever you run, there is always going to be someone who bothers you. I know!" Wanda spoke emphatically as she glanced toward two men sitting in silence, staring at her as she talked to a few weavers. She assumed the men did not understand what she was saying since they spoke Mayan and she was talking in English, but their laughter indicated otherwise. Startled, she wondered if they had known all along what she was talking about to the weavers. When neither man spoke, Wanda dropped what she started to say and began again. "I think maybe we can find a common tie in all this work if we put our heads together…but, remember, we don't want to mix the tribe's work in with the other. Know what I mean?"

The two men stood and began speaking in rapid succession, one right after the other, without any break in the flow—from one to the other. "You okay, Miss Wanda. We were much afraid you wanted to blend one tribe into the other—and make one clan from ten of them—and that is not allowed. Each pattern describes much that cannot be allowed to be lost—The women do not all realize this—and are willing to let you do whatever you want—We have been angry at you—and now we see that we were wrong—You can work with my wife and my family now—and mine."

Echoes of the twin versions of the same words ricocheted around the room and all the women smiled at them. Wanda knew that no one wants to go against kin, but some of the youngsters were willing to rebel if it meant they could learn how to weave as fast and easily as she did. They wanted to be in her classes, regardless of any flack it might produce at home. She said with a smile, "I'm sorry that you worried about *my* motives and plans. I want to emphasize that I don't wish to change anything that is Maya. I'm merely trying to use the Mayan colors in a new kind of fabric that will help others who are cross, I mean angry or don't feel good. I'm not going to give away the history of the tribes."

The men moved as if to leave, but the women created space for both of them near the window they usually kept closed to their fathers and husbands who gathered outside to escort them home. Seeing the women willing to accommodate the men, Wanda announced with a smile that she hoped would work wonders: "Open the window and let the men listen to us. We have nothing to hide. We don't want anyone thinking we're doing something evil or unwise, when all we're doing is learning how to weave and move into our minds and time to create new styles."

In their eagerness to watch Wanda's fingers fly over the threads that she had spread across the loom, the young women ignored her remarks and asked to begin weaving and talking together again and forget about the men. However, it was apparent to Wanda that this was not the consensus of the group. She could feel someone in the room was too angry to let her begin her work again, so she said, "I can feel—no, I can see—one of you is mad at me! What is this all about? Why are you here if you're that angry at me?" She turned her head and her eyes riveted on a woman sitting near the back and glowering at her.

Having succeeded in gaining Wanda's full attention, as well as reaching the ears of the men present, she spoke loudly without hesitation. "I see nothing to be gained by making new designs. We have memorized how to make tourist belts and small purses, and we can weave them quickly and sell them easily. Why should we do something new and different—just because you think it will sell better?"

In a flash of insight, Wanda saw several women agreed with her critic, but she was not about to let their discontent grow beyond a murmur, so she said with some sarcasm, "I think you've gotten too wise too soon and too tired to—"

Before Wanda could finish, one who agreed with the angry woman retaliated and said, "How can you say she's tired? She is young!"

Wanda casually raised her arm and wiggled her fingers at the two women to indicate she wanted them to leave. Her good-bye was so casual that it took the other women a moment or so to realize Wanda was not about to argue with her students. Unwise and ill-tempered weavers would not be trained in her ways until they obeyed her lessons and worked as she did every day.

As the rebel gathered her things, those who had been willing to seize attention and go up against Wanda, too, shut up and did not move a hand to help her pack her bags. The much chastened woman left the group, unable to understand how she had let her mind and temper ruin her life plans and cost her many friends, when all she wanted was to be noticed as being the best weaver of them all. Her cohort hung back, making no move to leave, pretending that the message to leave immediately was not meant for her.

"When one person claims to be the best or worst at what is taught, they need to blend into the group rather than call attention to their work. We're like a club of artists, thus subject to petty jealousies and rivalries, so whenever that happens we all have to refocus on our ideals to insure that we become a group such as those known in the classical world of Europe as a Guild. I like the concept and think The Maya have used it all through time. I almost said, we Maya, but that is a slip of my ego and not permitted. I feel so very close to all of you here that at times I think of you as my tribe. Please forgive me when I do that." Done talking, Wanda lowered her head and appeared to make the sign of the cross on her chest, but she actually did not.

Wanda sat for a few moments praying over her work until she heard words drifting toward her from somewhere she had never been before. A deep-pitched voice said, "We see nothing wrong in saying that. You are Maya! You are strong. You are a woman of tomorrow." As the words flowed over her from above, Wanda lifted her face to look out over the room. She discerned that there was still one left who would cause further disruption before long, but she proceeded to teach and not mention it then.

During her lessons on weaving and life in general, Wanda often prepared tea and asked others present if they would like to take a cup with her. Usually, no one joined her, that is, until several weeks after the expulsion of the star weaver. Those who stayed obviously felt more comfortable and willing to try something new and perhaps discover what Wanda, Teri, and Mandy saw in such tea.

One breezy afternoon a week later, a few of the students pulled together in close harmony when a Mayan maiden said, "I see strange things when I drink your tea, Miss Wanda. What does it mean?"

Since Wanda was already in a trance, she easily saw them all and could talk to one or two at the same time, without missing any opportunity to weave a new dance. Her mind was not engaged very much, but she felt a mental jolt whenever this young woman spoke. What did it mean? She said aloud, "I don't know what you're experiencing, Juanita, but you are able to see many things. We've all seen that." Wanda deliberately avoided confirming what the girl had seen when drinking tea because she preferred to encourage them all to share their visions now.

Without blinking, the teenager said in muted tones, "I now see visions of the night when I look into the cup. I see a jaguar standing in the jungle outside the compound looking in at us now."

Wanda hummed and then said, "I see. What else is outside the compound?"

The girl brightened at this show of respect from her great teacher and immediately reentered the trance scene. She sat in silence for a minute or so before speaking of what she could only see in her third eye. "I see a man with a bow and arrow. He's trying to kill the jaguar! He's not very nice… I can tell that because of how he stands. He doesn't do the dance… He's a white hunter who kills for fun."

Upon delivering this revelation, the young woman came out of trance and did not look directly at Wanda. She appeared frightened far beyond anything she had experienced in the past while in trance and could not settle down. She began to shake. Wanda and two elders immediately reached out to steady her and then asked her to look at each of them. As she did, her mind settled down and she was released from the spell. She never drank tea after that.

Whatever the young maiden spotted in the distance was approaching them, and Wanda had no idea what she might have to live through again to exist, so she asked the weavers to leave her immediately. Bustling about to clean up what was not already in good order, the youngest weavers squealed with joy at being relieved of such chores. The elders were much too concerned to do anything or to leave, so they let Wanda do the necessary cleansing rituals.

"You will not be left alone, Miss Wanda. We will roll up a few towels and sleep on the ground around you and guard you." The elder who spoke had been rejected earlier in life by the tribe when it was discovered that she was barren. She never forgot that men wanted children more than they wanted to war, so she worked on her art long and hard, finally creating something useful to fill the void in her heart. Her art was creating sheeting and table linen more beautiful than anyone ever produced in the Yucatan. A master of her craft, as well as serious about what she alone saw in the distance, she said to Wanda, "Sheeting may not be as pretty as what you teach the children to weave, but it's stronger and lasts longer."

Not sure where this master weaver was going with this, Wanda nodded and spoke as if she understood completely what was said between the words. "I know, Rosita, but it's not colorful enough for Today's young to desire to learn it first. White, or ecru on the same field, is a challenge to the eye—only the most gifted weavers can master it. That is why it is so prized by collectors now—it's so hard to produce by hand."

The artist humbly bowed her head, closed her eyes, and said prayerfully, "Thank you for saying that, Miss Wanda. I often forget that I am no longer barren—without a purpose in life. The tribe needs me now, and I am here to show others that they can be loved for their art, too—even when it's different from what some believe is the way of God in art now."

Looking into Rosita's eyes, Wanda asked quietly, "Is art the way of God to The Maya of today?"

The woman looked at Wanda in amazement. How could she not understand such a simple fact of life? Wondering if perhaps she worked and worshipped differently, she said, "What do you believe art to be, Miss Wanda?"

"I think it's an acute state of activity in which you can see into the immediate future or present and the past—easier than into the future and beyond…into the higher spiritual levels that become you, you, and you in your present mind." Wanda was amazed to hear herself describe art that way. Never before had anyone asked her such a question, and never before had she talked in that vein.

She wanted to hear more, so she blocked all rational thought and opened her mouth to speak. Words poured forth. "We work in cloth because we're experts in human nature. We know people are vain and want to eat off fine linens, and dress in the finest patterns and colors we can weave. We weavers sense these needs and play with them and mix them into our work just enough to sell others on what we do well, but we never use our work as others do."

This statement or thought wave was not clear to Wanda, but the sages standing around the room nodded in unison. She was amazed that they understood what she said in a daze. She ignored her own rules of conduct and fired off questions to them without waiting for answers. "What do you ladies see in space? Can you share it with me? Do you dare talk to me as you talk to each other? I truly am here to do my best work and hopefully ascend with the tribe when it's time, but do you understand what I'm saying now and why I always work as hard as I can?"

Wanda stopped and said nothing more. She waited minutes that stretched into an hour before a woman who was cleaning up the tea things said, "I see many things, Miss Wanda. You are not like Miss Mandy—yet you are. We are simple people who have always worshipped God of All—and not let anyone take away our lives in time. We don't like the government, or the people who move against us now, but when we aren't afraid of them, we do no harm. We try to negotiate sometimes, but only evil intentions fly now. We want people to see that peace is achieved when you no longer want things. We want to try to live more simply than we did before you arrived, but it's not easy in these times of corporate societies."

Wanda could not help but notice the steady improvement in the woman's diction and vocabulary as she opened to all present and spoke from her heart. She recognized that this woman had previously not talked much in English, afraid to say what she thought, but once she overcame the obstacle erected by her pride, she was able to leap into leadership easily. It became even more obvious that she was a university graduate who knew a lot about economics and politics. Without registering any appreciable degree of change within her brain, Wanda could hear herself say, "You speak of economics and social dishonor a lot. Do you not?"

"I am not as you think, Miss Wanda. I am not a weaver. I try, but you should know that by now. I spy upon Maya who try to live as we all should and claim that they always do." After dropping this bomb in the center of the room, she dropped her head and left them gawking at each other.

As the door closed, the woman who wove all of Mandy's white garments cried out passionately, "I did not know, Miss Wanda! I did not know she was not a weaver—that she is here to spy!"

"I know you didn't know. I didn't know she wasn't a weaver, either. In fact, I'm sure she's not the spy I feel watching us at times. I think someone close by, one who listens to us and wants to change what was is trying to make us the scapegoats for her beliefs. That one is the spy! But she isn't going to be able to continue. The real spy is now aware that we're closing in on what we're all here to do and that we're about to make a breakthrough. Did you notice it, too?"

The two women who had refused to speak thus far now nodded as if imitating the bobble-headed statues that low-riders favor and place in the windows of their souped-up cars. Both smiled and rapidly spoke words too foreign for Wanda to logically comprehend, yet intuitively she understood what they said. The older of the two ended by saying happily, "We see many things, Miss Wanda. In the crowd around you now are women who want to be better than you. They want to steal your designs and take credit for your work. We remembered them from other times, so we don't let them cheat now. When they come to us asking for help after you're done lecturing or demonstrating, we don't give them the right thread counts. We limit them on purpose, so they don't hurt themselves—again."

Entering into an even deeper trance state, Wanda squinted a little at the group of women working to cleanse the room again and said very slowly, "So we have all woven cloth together—in another place or was it another time?"

Everyone nodded enthusiastically, laughing at the same time. Through tears, the oldest woman spoke, as if for everyone, "I can see you never thought about it before, Miss Wanda, but it's good that you didn't see it until now. We are here to help you teach the young weavers, along with the elders who were lost a moment or two in space. We all want to renew everyone's interest in the universe. We know The Ascended Maya will arrive over time to look in on us! We don't want them to wonder if we'll be able to make it to the next destination—or lose our way again."

Wanda checked that the door was bolted and all the windows were tightly closed, before she cautioned all not to say anything more. She left her mind while one of The Maya working in the room caught her hand and led her to the couch where she collapsed into time.

Later she described this time away as taking only a few minutes, but for the women standing by it was measured in hours. When Wanda finally opened her mind and eyes to what was going on around her, she was not upset by what she saw, just puzzled at how dark it was outside. All she could frame in her mind were questions, no answers. "How long have I been out of this world? Why did I go away?" She spoke a few more words before the Mayan women who had been guarding her body exploded into a frenzy of activity.

As Wanda came out of trance, they did not doubt that she had walked with God. Each woman knelt down and bowed her head and touched her right arm. She was a powerful wheel and they were clay. She now shaped them into a new arm of Earth's work and a new mind in time. They would work as a team and use this dream, but no one else on Earth was to know what their work might be.

Speaking hesitantly, Wanda said, "I see nothing…I am nothing…I have come to you from a time where there are no minds…I see deep hatred building in this community…It must be removed immediately—this evening. No one may leave the compound until it is weeded out…until we can see who feeds it…Do you all agree?"

Everyone silently nodded in agreement, so Wanda continued. "I can see nothing now…I feel like I lost my feet. Do you have any socks I can use to cover my toes?"

The woman who wove birds and flowers like no other, but almost always remained silent during class, said soothingly, "I have exactly what you need. Thyme made into an ointment. We will massage it into your toes, then put them into white anklets we wove for you—just in case."

"Thank you for all you do; but what do you mean—just in case?" As Wanda spoke, she looked deep into each woman through their right eye. When no one offered an explanation, Wanda refused to let them rub the thyme ointment into her toes until they told her what they knew and she could not see.

With resignation, the eldest said, "We are here to help The Maya on this side, but we're not of this tribe. We're elders, and respected by each of the peoples you are used to and know, but we're not like them. They know we're not spies, but we notice a lot. We are here to mend the ladders—again, and help them ascend."

Staring into both eyes, one-by-one, Wanda laughed when she suddenly saw someone standing in the shadows. She shouted out merrily, "I see you! You can't hide from my mind. So you decided to come back with me from the other side. Come on in, Mandy, don't look at me that way."

No one reacted as Wanda thought they ought. Some of the Mayan women yawned and dropped onto the makeshift bed they had prepared for her, while others lay back wherever they sat and quickly entered a deep sleep. She was amazed that they could sleep so easily! Such sleep is a gift that sages over time often request, but are usually denied, even after many lifetimes spent seeking it.

Her version or vision of Mandy glided into the light and said mysteriously, "I see you're wise enough to bring me into this time with you, but I can't weave and help you do it. Let me provide you with protection and not be detected again."

Wanda wondered aloud about the predicament she was in and why she could see visions so very different from the ones she had when she lived in The States. Right then this Mandy of another world said matter-of-factly, "You're in a different world now, Wanda. You *must* be able to see that every day. Mexico is not the poor country Americans wish to believe it is. In reality, it's the richest nation on Earth. So much has been preserved! Mexicans will be able to live on minerals and other gifts long after other nations cease to exist. They have the gift of prophecy and need nothing from us. You are here to help you alone—not help women find your home. The Maya won't stop and ask you to fly, but at times you might be able to join in and exercise with The Maya who exist in this time. It might even produce a high that you'll want to renew every week or two, but don't get too used to it."

As Mandy faded, Wanda shook her head and the women who were drooped over the bed or slumped on the floor awoke once more. The younger of the two women who always spoke in rhyme, and at about the same speed, so as to appear to have only one voice, said in Mayan, "We can see you are fine and able to walk in time, but are you able to do what we do?"

With a grin Wanda rejoined, "I think I should go to bed without eating, but we have to watch a movie this evening, because we need to see who is watching us and who is trying to act like The Maya. Do you catch my drift?"

"We know what to do. You only have to dim the lights, and we open our eyes wider than you did just now. We made a pass over the group earlier and saw one who never laughs. Laughter is the way to open the mind and grow in Spirit, so if one refuses to accept fun or laughter or other gifts of the Holy Spirit, we watch them. This is going to be so easy! We want you to be able to run when we yell, 'Fire!' That's all you have to do." The message came through to Wanda as she sat in a state of shock. It entered her mind in a block, so she could not detect which of the women said it, but knew what to do.

Suddenly Mandy popped into view again and announced in the tongue of everyone, "Let's go watch 'Lawrence of Arabia' and see what everyone is up to."

Wanda shook her head and spoke, as if only to herself, "Now what are you up to Miss Mandy?" When she heard no reply, she followed the women out of the room and through the courtyard. They all laughed as if having the time of their lives—which they were.

☼ CHAPTER NINETEEN

Thinking first about the future of their work within the tribe, then talking it through to the best conclusion was Mandy's usual modus operandi, but Wanda and her weavers were not as into mystical views as those who worked with clay, or even those studying to be Spiritual Scribes. She was not aware of the weavers' *backward views*, compared to what others worked on in the compound, until one day when Mandy left the potters' class with little to say.

After Mandy left, Julie stood at attention and said to the now-silent room, "I think Mandy wants us to use our initiative and intuitively follow whatever comes to each of us through the veil. What do you think?"

At that exact moment Wanda was standing on her tiptoes outside the potters' studio window peering in at the class, trying to get Julie's attention. She heard only those words and became so intrigued that she entered the classroom to check out what they were creating, rather than just waving for Julie to come out and talk with her privately. As she walked in, several women sat with closed eyes and others mumbled or prayed or appeared to be doing nothing. Wanda thought it quite odd, especially when she realized that Julie was no longer there. How had she disappeared in the short time it took her to walk from the window to the door and enter the room? What did it all mean? As if reading her thoughts, one of the potters looked up and smiled, so she quickly said, "I think I better leave now."

The radiant native potter spoke slowly. "No, please, do not go. We're just preparing to do new work—and Miss Julie is working in air. She's here—just not like you see her most times, you know."

Wanda panicked, worried that she was supposed to know something that everyone else took for granted and she could not figure out. Indeed, this was a very weird situation to be in. Was everyone crazy—or just her? She was able to visit strange places in dreams and see visions, but were they doing even stranger things? It had never been easy for her to ask questions and pry into others' lives, because her upbringing counseled against it, but this was fast becoming a day when she had to pry and find out more about The Ascended Maya and this tribe.

Now standing at Wanda's side, demonstrating how she had levitated, Julie said, "I felt this strange prick of pain in the palm of my hand and then suddenly I was flying!" She said the pain subsided immediately thereafter and went away for good as she flew about the room. Flapping her arms now like a sea gull, Julie seemed able to gain enough lift to elevate her feet a few inches off the ground—not far, but more than Wanda could comprehend as humanly possible.

All Wanda could say upon witnessing this miracle was, "I feel faint." She immediately regretted having said it because all the Mayan women stopped what they were doing to peer into her eyes. They appeared to be struck with total disbelief. The woman standing next to her said with wonder, "How can she be a teacher of The Maya if she cannot fly, Miss Julie?"

Julie smiled reassuringly at the women and said to her stunned friend, who now appeared ready to bolt from the room without saying good-bye, "I don't know why we fly, Wanda. I really don't. But we can fly here in the compound, and I guess I always assumed you and the weavers flew, too."

Without stopping to think about her choice of words or intent, Wanda blurted out, "I guess I got into this without really knowing what *it* is."

The Mayan women silently condemned Wanda in the past because of certain strong views she maintained, and now because she smiled and could be happy without knowing what to do if the winds changed and everyone had to leave, as if on a whim. They all wondered: 'How would she save herself now or at the end of time? How can she teach the weavers to ascend, if she can't?'

As if in response to their psychic bombardment, Wanda turned hastily as she reached the door and said, "I feel so strange now. Can I sit down and talk with all of you? I can't seem to understand where I am or remember what I came to ask you, Julie. Maybe someone can explain what's happening to me…"

Several women hurried to help her sit down near the door so she could catch any stray breezes that might pass that way. The first woman to reach her was able to free her hands of clay as she eased her into the chair. Another patted her arm and spoke softly, "I think you must rest, Miss Wanda. You worry too much."

Nodding in agreement, Wanda said in a hushed voice, "I think I've just had a great shock, and I feel weird confessing all of this to you now."

All the potters, including Julie, waited for Wanda to assume a more comfortable position before they resumed working as they had before she entered their space. Julie now stood behind the lectern shuffling a few note cards as a signal that today's lecture was about to begin. Her lesson was not the one scheduled for that Tuesday afternoon, but it was one the potters and Wanda would never forget.

Sometime later, the room darkened and Julie became aware that the tropic rains were about to descend. She opened her eyes wider at that moment in time and saw Chac, The God of Rain! It lasted only a second, if that, just long enough to produce a huge laugh that bubbled up within her chest and crested. The oldest woman present was also looking into time at that moment and noticed Chac, too, but she did not laugh. In fact, she was frightened by the sight!

It was then that Julie flashed intuitively a signal to the women in the back of the room to latch the windows and doors. Straightening her back, she took in a deep breath and proceeded to relax as much as anyone can while continuing to stand in front of a crowd. Once the women secured the room, they prepared themselves for a long sit.

After a few minutes of quiet, Julie spoke clearly, enunciating every word. "In previous times, we did not allow men to enter the work we do. They grew upset with us and disgusted with each other to the point that they could not stay out of trouble, so we decided to share our power with them... We gave them a game plan... We asked them to kill enough game for each day's needs. But they soon turned it into another contest, then into a sacrifice, and now—whatever they like. We could not say a word about it since we gave the game away then, but that was then and this is now."

⽊   ⽊

Meanwhile Mandy sat within another room inside another world fighting to find her way into their day as the storm descended on the potters' studio. Tired of struggling against her bonds, she decided to tune into what was being said elsewhere within the compound where she was held captive, unbeknownst to the teachers and women who believed in her work. In this cell-like room she intuitively felt the Earth move for a second or two. The tremor was so remote that she did not worry about it shaking the buildings she had painstakingly built over the years. She knew that it foretold a storm that would wreak havoc out in the Pacific, not here on the Yucatan peninsula. Her mind balked at not being allowed to be upset about being imprisoned against her will, and her body strongly resented the confinement. It wanted to walk and talk and move about as if it was in charge of the lot, but it was not.

Mandy had to turn over her work on Earth to others, and then leave in spirit without any sense of what she might need in another space and time. Mandy grieved that she could no longer plan her next move. Right then she was teased by the thought that plans are what get you through tough times. That is when she began to fly. She felt the exhilaration of sudden elevation and leaving the room without any sense of doom.

The wind whipped dust and debris into whirligigs outside the pottery studio's windows while Julie stared into the center of the room—at no one present. She stared until she could feel the sense of impending doom being removed from her mind. She thought, 'I wonder what I'm feeling now? Could Mandy be in trouble?' She could not speak to those sitting at her feet, smiling up at her as they waited for her to continue telling her story.

"When you're able to feel pain and sorrow—having lost much of what you thought was your life work, you tend to sit within your mind and fret about it a lot, but don't. Don't waste a moment on what is over and done! Move forward! Go for it! Head immediately toward the next door and see what happens. If you lose your momentum, you can't spin as easily or as fast as you could before you lost faith in your work. Remember that!"

The women blinked at Julie as if to signal they understood what she was trying to say. One even winked at her sister as if to say, 'I told you Julie was okay,' but nothing was said aloud and their attention remained unbroken.

"Okay! Now that we're able to see and feel a storm brewing, and no one is home to worry about, let's start humming our favorite song."

No one hesitated to follow Julie. All present parted their lips a bit and began breathing out and then in, making sounds indicative of incredible inner strength. At first their humming more closely resembled a string ensemble tuning up than it did a choir uniting to sing in harmony. Quickly, the combined voices achieved a pure G, and the group was elevated into space and time. This time it happened much more easily than in times past, but its reoccurrence could not be taken for granted by anyone present. Whenever it happened, the potters rose to their feet and bounced slightly, keeping their thighs parted an inch or two. Normally they would laugh and cradle their hands within that gap, as if the sky was raining coins and they intended to catch them, but this time their minds were instead transported into the next world. They did not notice the storm passing overhead or who was surrounding the nearby town.

When the wind subsided the first time, the folks in the nearby town went into flight mode, rapidly moving toward Mandy's compound to seek bread and shelter. They were not without alarm because it was very, very calm. Many were now calling upon the Mayan elders for help. The oldest elder said, "The wind has moved to the moon."

Even the children could find no fun within the mass exodus from the village. They were upset because their parents were obviously afraid. Children know what signs to watch for, and what they saw then indicated that something was very seriously wrong. Normally when Mama or Papa was angry or upset, the other was not, so you wait until later to ask for whatever you want. But when both Mama and Papa are upset and afraid, you know something terrible is happening, and your life might change—a lot.

The children ran ahead of their families once they realized the tribe was running to seek help from Mandy. The villagers did not know her real name, but the superstitious among them always showed fear of the woman in white whenever she entered town. They often made the sign of the cross and mumbled prayers of deliverance while quickly moving away from her, but Mandy never seemed to mind. She always smiled and inwardly sent them a small blessing.

When the vanguard of children arrived at the compound they discovered the gates were closed—maybe even barred, so they waited and wailed for someone to open a side door and let them in. Only when the last villager seeking help arrived outside the gate did anyone inside hear them and open the door part-way at the side of the huge gate. The wait seemed long to the young. The worried teenager who opened the door asked, "What's wrong?" She tried to intuit why such a large crowd was gathering outside the compound, but could not make sense of it.

Shouts pierced her ears: "We're afraid." "The storm wiped out the *abacero* and we have no food." "The grocery store is the only place left with food. The crops aren't in yet. It's beginning to storm again." "We don't know what to do!" "There shouldn't be so much rain now." Their combined fear alarmed the would-be sentry, but she knew better than to let anyone enter without seeking permission from her superiors. Now afraid, she closed the door against the crowd as they pressed closer. Some yelled obscenities.

Eventually, the elders persuaded the crowd to stop shouting and ask the girl quite reasonably if they could enter and take cover from the huge storm that would soon arrive. She pulled at a metal shield that covered the small barred opening embedded halfway up the huge panel of the gate and said with as much authority as she could muster, "Wait here. I have to ask what to do."

The women were patient, but the men could not control their fear as well. One old man raged that these women were all rich and had so much that they forgot how to be humane and didn't want to feed starving children outside their gates. Several women chastised him to prevent the harangue from starting all over again—the ever-present insistence by men that women are trying to change the world and not let them in on it.

Almost five minutes passed before women emerged from the compound's kitchen loaded with trays of food for the town to eat on picnic tables placed under the trees for the use of tourists and clients. They motioned for the teen attending the gate to open the door once the food was tastefully displayed. She opened the door with great care and quickly stepped aside so as not to be pushed back by the crowd outside, but no one rushed. The village shaman led several men through the door and up to the head cook and announced, "We are sorry to bother you, but our village has been hit by a huge storm—but you were not."

The women arranging the bread and bowls of fruit and other food looked up at the trees surrounding the compound and silently prayed. They knew the sentinels were keeping watch and that the guardians required an immediate offering for sparing their lives, but they would not make it in front of the villagers.

Sensing the true mood of these men, the cook snapped, "We also heard the wind, but we got busy working instead of worrying about it." With her wooden spoon upheld as if it was a lance, she advanced toward the women and children's outstretched arms barking out commands left and right. "Sit under the trees! We have plenty to feed you. You can eat and leave—or stay and dance, but you have to clean up after yourselves and rake up the leaves. There is little else you can do for us, because we're always busy taking care of our property and our business—not standing around talking all day."

The cook glared at several young men who appeared unwilling to sit down and obediently eat her food. One whispered that she looked mean and nasty, but everyone else knew the cook to be a wise and generous woman, so they ate her food without saying anything disparaging about it then, which was no easy task for some who sat at that table.

As the day progressed the unexpected feast disintegrated into a communal siesta. The town leaders asked what they might do to repay the women for their hospitality and were told to pray. This stunned all who had entered the compound earlier with fear lodged in their minds and a belief that they might soon die.

The oldest villager sat busily cleaning his teeth, unfazed by how few he had, when he heard what was later called a command to pray. Slurring his words, he voiced his community's reaction. "We pray—every day, and even more on feast days. I pray more in a day than all of you pray in a month."

Still in action, the cook was moving among the villagers handing out whatever remained in her kitchen. Upon hearing what the old man said, she stopped doling out food and said defiantly, "You say the same old mumbo-jumbo every day, old man. You think you're blessing and thanking God, but you aren't!" Since the head cook's voice was loud, she was heeded more than ever before, so she took center stage—bristling and laughing and cajoling as she pushed the men to work harder for The Lord than they had ever done before. Her words were powerful and totally new to the villagers! They had to work hard to understand what she cared to share with them then.

When the men finally appeared organized enough to continue working as she ordered, the cook glowered at the young women holding babies, but then grinned at each mother and said pleasantly, "I think all of you need jobs you can rely on when times turn hard. You think you're safe from harm because you're married and have a baby, but you aren't. You have the hardest path of all to follow. That is why you have to laugh—a lot. If you don't create an opening and stay open and happy, your path in life will collapse."

The men refrained from boasting now and later some admitted that the cook was honest and good, even if she did have too much to say. They did not enjoy listening to a woman take the news and spread it about without first asking them what to do with it or who was highest among them. Instead, she led and they followed, if they wanted to eat the treats that came from her domain.

Following her lead was extremely difficult for one ram in this flock, but the other sheep set aside such scruples long enough to eat better than normal. This man was enraged that his tribe ate and listened to a woman who was not educated in the ways of his clan. He went from family to family saying, "I think the cook is trying to run the show. Don't you?"

He did not understand the basic principle that when you give willingly and sincerely to Spirit, it is abundantly returned to you by the universe. What he did understand, however, was how to turn a bright day into a time of darkness. He ran his mouth to such great effect that by the time some families reentered their homes they were unhappy with the women who had fed them and resented how they lived. One man denied the cook and others respect and would live to regret it, but what about the families who took what was given and later turned on those who sacrificed for them?

♓   ♓

All the while the cook and her crew fed the refugees from the nearby village, the potters sat on the floor in the studio with Julie and Wanda praying for a better day. No one there was eager to leave to serve the people of the town. They did not like them, because they were never given any credit for the work they did in building the local economy. The local women clashed with them repeatedly, and the men said their art was indecent. The tourists, however, sought every pot they made and ordered more—which really upset villagers working outside their compound who called themselves potters and artists of Mayan times!

As the day ended, Wanda sat in trance and envisioned a man. He was carrying Mandy. He could not hurry, but seemed determined to take her someplace where she could rest and relax. He was not attempting to rape her, but he held her mouth shut. As the romance of the vision subsided, Wanda stood and spoke rapidly in an old Mayan dialect to those seated beside her. "I see Mandy being taken to a cave. She's not able to walk. Her mind isn't equal to the time. Her mouth is being held shut by a man. He is tall. He is Maya, but not one of us. I can't see his face."

As she spoke, everyone stopped exhaling to better hold onto their last breath for as long as it would take Wanda to tell them more about the vision. When she did not speak, the women gasped as if in unison and all said: "What is he doing now?"

Wanda motioned to them to be quiet. She stared into middle space as if a movie was being screened on the wall. Her eyes quickly moved sideways as she watched the man go into the cave, then come back without Mandy. That is when she saw it was Jorge. She wanted to scream his name, but could not. She wondered, 'What's going on?' but did not speak. Her mind zoomed toward Jorge and Mandy and she eagerly watched to see if there might be a chink or slit in the veil where she could enter and pretend to be with them. Finally, as if asking a reasonable question, Wanda said, "I see Mandy being given shelter, but I don't know where she is. Will you all go to dinner and leave me to figure this out?"

First to respond, Julie let out a whoop and said, "Let's eat! That is, if there's anything left after the village was fed."

The women surrounding Julie and Wanda were astounded at her response and asked in various ways, "What do you mean -- leave?"

Suddenly realizing that she was using her outer mind and her inner eye at the same time, Julie relaxed just enough to tell the women that a huge storm had passed over the compound while they were working. It did not damage the compound or any of the gardens, but it leveled the village grocery store. No one asked Julie how she knew this when she never left the room, because they knew she saw such things easily. It was Wanda who held their curiosity in bondage. They had no previous knowledge of her ability to see visions and interact with them. As they watched her pray in good faith with each breath she took, Wanda's life and work rose in their esteem.

A young woman who did not realize she should not touch anyone in deep trance, patted Wanda's arm and said, "We'll come back and see that you get something to eat."

Julie immediately issued orders that the girl was to be taken to the washroom and rinsed off with running water. She was told to not talk about what she had seen or heard. Unable to understand what she might have done wrong, the young woman kept mumbling, "I only touched her arm. I didn't do anything!" But no one agreed with her. It was the time of her menses and instead of the usual outflow, she was made more aware of her error in assuming too much about others in a state of grace, because she did not produce blood that month. She never forgot this lesson. She was regular ever after that and went on to produce many children at the full moon.

Julie always felt unsure when it became necessary to assume leadership, especially when Mandy left without leaving instructions or directions on what needed to be done immediately or next week. Since Mandy insisted that it was critical to include everyone within a group, if they wanted to do something new, Julie decided to ask the elders gathered at the back of the kitchen what steps to take next. Nothing like this had ever happened to her in the past, so Julie eyed the head cook and the oldest elder and said slowly, "What do you think we should do about Wanda?"

The oldest wise woman said, "I feel Wanda about to reveal something we can't see—something crucial to The Maya, something we must agree upon as worthy of our combined ambitions and energies right now. We need to do whatever she says, so we should sit with her—be with her when her eyes open." She spoke slowly so everyone would agree and not grumble or complain—and be ready for whatever Wanda said—and do it exactly as told. Although Wanda had never been fully accepted as being one of The Maya, because she could not fly, she gained esteem among these wise women because of her dream work.

⣎ ⣎

As the sun dipped below the Pacific rim, it was already the next day and a long way from where the potters sat and pondered Wanda. The wise woman who kept track of time and such things let out a sigh because it took so much effort to get all the women to sit in silence for even a short time. Since her end time was nigh, many younger women were eager to fill in and do her work in hopes that she would consider them equal to keeping time after she was gone. She never encouraged them, because she intended to give the keeping of time to whoever stood at her right side when she died. She knew that only the most patient and thoughtful stayed with the wise until they crossed over, so she had no worry about who would receive her gift. The group that lived around her, however, worried much and constantly talked about what will happen at her passing. On that day they would come to realize that she was the one who kept them all from entering a new day—without appearing to delay anyone in any way. She alone held them back, but they were not to know that until they let her go.

One of the women who would be a Time Keeper, if only in her own mind, took to wearing stylish creations woven with black and white instead of the usual brilliant hues of the tribe. She believed herself to be the anointed one who would take over when this elder passed. Rehearsing for her self-appointed leadership role, she casually said, "Let's go into the next room and see if we can catch something decent on TV."

A potter who rarely said anything outside of the studio spat out angrily in the direction of this woman she knew to be unwise, "Bah, her and that TV! We're needed by Mandy. She wouldn't call a friend to watch over her if she wasn't in trouble now." Instantly, the group broke apart to make room for her to stride between each side, headed for the room where Wanda had been left standing an hour before. The remaining potters followed her lead, staying several paces behind since it was obviously her day to decide what they were to do now.

The wind died down and remained perfectly still as the kitchen staff and several elders stood outside the potters' studio door watching the woman who immediately followed the woman who knew what to do. She spoke in a loud whisper as though a news reporter witnessing a great event. "Wanda is about to speak. We haven't missed anything. She's weak. They will bring her tea as soon as she can sit down."

The crowd inside and outside the workshop maintained total silence as Wanda turned toward them and said without a smile, "Within a week…She will be asked to speak at a large dinner party where the men outnumber women…so that means she is into something political now… We're not to say a word about this or to speak her name… She needs to gain enough strength to withstand their attacks… She's okay for the time being… Jorge is not going to let anyone near her who might hurt her or give her another job to do." A sense of calmness seemed to settle down over Wanda then. She waited a minute or so before addressing the crowd again. This time she spoke in her normal voice. "I can say that she is okay, because I saw her that way." Without any thought about the group sitting on the floor waiting for her to sit down, Wanda added, "You'll notice that I did not mention her name…"

The elder who had led the kitchen staff to the studio in time to hear Wanda speak of the vision and what it meant said, "We want *you* to tell us what to do next."

"I think we are to work diligently…Work to clear out the air somewhere…I don't have any sense of where she is going to attend this meeting…but she's in need of energy— and needs all of us to work as if she is here among us now."

"That's easy," snapped a woman who suddenly appeared just outside the circle of light cast by Wanda's mind. "Mandy's in the back room of the warehouse. She was locked in and left there by some men this morning."

The elders whirled about the sneering woman, hissing as if they were geese about to attack a snake and eat it alive. She did not flinch. Her mindset was such that she gained much satisfaction from watching others work hard to accomplish what she could do easily, and then deny them feeling any pride in accomplishing what they had labored to do. However, she was now out of her element, unaware that she would never again be able to talk to such women. She continued taunting them and laughing as she related what she watched strangers do to Mandy earlier that day. The elders formed a circle and began to dance around her. One even tried to spit in her face. She laughed even more and said, "You amaze me, you silly geese. You don't have more power than me! I'm studying to be a great Mayan shaman—able to do anything any of you can do—and I can do it without even trying!"

The spiteful woman pointed at another who often sat beside her at the potter's wheel or in the kiln area, as she jeered and yelled at Julie, "You think you can change the way we make pottery, but it'll never happen! We are Maya!! You have no right to change our art! You're not Maya, just another pathetic woman without a man who wants what we have. Why don't you go back to the United States? A bus is leaving in an hour."

Silence descended upon the potters as the hateful woman hurled her curses in their direction. They all looked to Wanda for guidance. She immediately reversed the flow of power and intuitively told them to do whatever they wanted; she was with them all the way. The frenzied mood that had propelled them all to this studio was now directed at the screaming woman they agreed to hate. Her hair, which was no longer the color of a modest Mayan woman (bleached in a way that suggested she used sex to get her own way) attracted their attention first. They pulled at her hair and pinched her cheeks as they pushed her outside and around the outer courtyard. By the time the native women finished chasing her about, she was intimidated by the elders' wrath, but not afraid to scream at Wanda and Julie and several others: "I hate you! I hate you all! You think you're better than we are, but we are Maya! We are the tribe!! You're trying to be Maya and will never succeed. You'll see!"

The oldest elder cast her eye upon the evil woman who denied their abilities and their place in the tribe. She did it in such a way that the would-be shaman was unable to speak for the rest of her life. How it was done is a mystery to some, but one among them could slit a throat as easily as kill turkeys, and never leave a trace of blood. The police never heard about it because no one heard her say she was hurt.

The elder who pushed their common enemy toward her fate told three women standing beside her, "See if Mandy is in the back room like she said. If she is, free her. If she isn't, put this one in there to brood." This wise woman apparently disbelieved Mandy could possibly be imprisoned, but then again she was not as high in the sky as others of the tribe.

☼ CHAPTER TWENTY

Working through the night, the weavers produced a lot of cloth but did not feel as if they had done enough when the van backed up to the loading area to pick up the order and drove away with it later. Their artistry was cherished more and more everywhere, but some who lived or worked in the village near the compound were churlish about it. They said it was making women stronger than they were intended to be, that it did not help others thrive, because none of the weavers shopped locally for supplies or even gasoline. The tribe was not able to reach a consensus or compromise on these local problems, so they asked Mandy to return and resign her post or take over the work of the weavers. She did neither.

"The day is over when a few profiteers can rape the public and take a huge chunk of change back to their own homes and not share with their villages," said Mandy to the women who greeted her after dinner the first night she returned from an extended trip abroad. She told her friends that she would not stop living her life in order to decide what one village must do to keep up with the times; however, in the next breath she proposed that Wanda and her crew stop everything they were presently doing and review what could be done to help the nearby town to either accept them or leave them alone. Gesturing to indicate that a wide gap in communications existed, Mandy said, "You must be stepping on a lot of toes for so many to hate you this much, so place yourself in space and see what you would do if you were in their shoes—since, in fact, your fates are linked. Think about it. You'll not be able to do much more in this compound without recruiting people from town to do work that demands too much time away from the production line—or all of you hate to do."

As Mandy stood and stared into the faces of the weavers, she saw many were upset that she appeared to be siding with the villagers now. Because these women did not wish to believe they were annoying others, they were exactly who Mandy must reach now, so everyone could get back into their own best line of work again without tribal interference. Smiling at each pair of eyes, Mandy said, "You don't have much time now to put up and take down displays and keep the counters clean, so what do you think will happen when more orders come in—on top of all that you already have to fill?" She kept smiling as she pushed her point deeper. "I think you all realize that sooner than anyone could have ever imagined you will have to hire men and boys from around here to help you build a larger headquarters. What do *you* intend to do about it now?"

No one spoke, so Mandy rose and said a prayer of thanksgiving and immediately closed their impromptu meeting. She quickly walked out of the work room, leaving Wanda to comment on what she wanted her crew to do, but no one listened because they preferred to sulk and complain. Extremely annoyed that they were not interested in erasing this problem immediately, Wanda shouted at the women preparing to leave, "Stop this nonsense immediately!" Since no one had ever seen Wanda this angry before, everyone stopped moving or worrying about what Mandy would do next and listened when Wanda demanded, "Sit down and listen!"

Wanda spoke with no attempt to soften her words as she paced back and forth like a nervous cat—crossing the narrow, raised area known as 'the stage.' Her heart was racing and she suddenly felt out-of-place, unsure of her future with this work. She tried to sort through her jumbled thoughts about why artists would willingly abandon their work when told they should consider hiring people from a neighboring town. She felt their strong resistance and wanted to immediately find out why, but decided to talk it out and share what they all did so well before she explored what upset some of them.

Continuing to pace, Wanda started throwing questions out to her audience of students who owed her a lot and had to decide now if they wanted to leave her classes forever or behave like adults. In as calm a voice as she could muster, Wanda said, "Do you see anything different about our work? I mean really, truly, totally different? All I see is color and shape and a definite wave of energy conveyed to the public this way, but maybe you see something I don't see? Maybe you're competing with others who aren't ready to accept what we can all be?"

Stopping to look directly at each woman before she spoke again, Wanda was delighted to see the elders were on her side—for once. This could mean war with the group split along the lines of young versus old—each wanting their own way, but she knew how to prevent that, or so she thought. She said softly, "I think we have a split opinion, and what we can do about that is write on the board what we all want to see happen before the next war or tidal wave or general confusion reigns again. Okay? Now what do you want to do before the men or whomever you think is in power take us backward a few steps?"

As she said this, Wanda felt pressure at the base of her neck, as though a powerful ally had come through the veil and was taking over and talking through her to everyone now, especially her. She had wondered what she had to do to stress the importance of continuing to work even while they listened, just in case this ally was not the kind of being who loved to weave. Pleased to be a channel of a royal being of The Ascended Maya, she still worried because she had received no clue that this would happen. As the importance of this assignment sunk into her mind, Wanda began to stagger under its weight and feel faint. She only managed to say aloud, "I feel faint…need to sit down and rest…Are you able to sense that you're draining my energy—not helping us do what The Maya want done?"

The group watched Wanda in silence now, stunned that she could no longer stand nor could they. Sinking deep into the chair she used only during visionary work, a strange odor permeated the area—as if a lightening bolt had exploded in the next room. The smell of ozone was so strong that several got sick with worry and apprehension, but no one attempted to leave or speak of their anxiety.

Wanda's eyes became shades of steely gray as they narrowed just enough so the light could not reflect their true blue color. She appeared to age as she sagged on the stage, but no one else was looking at her now. Everyone had instinctively turned inward, away from the stage, so as to protect themselves in the event someone who was not of God came through the veil. Speaking in a much deeper voice than anyone expected, Wanda said with a slight lisp, "I am able to talk to you today because you're all afraid. I feel that you're not ready to do what you came to Earth to reveal, so we will all work in this way until you're okay. Do you feel okay—well enough to pursue new work?"

Hearing an ancient Mayan princess invoke American slang, Wanda wanted to chuckle but she could not because her throat was no longer hers. "Superstitions abound in that town, and you are surrounded with hate and jealousy, too—and that terrible by-product of your new world—competition among friends. You say you are not capitalists? You are, but you are not aware of it now because you say you're artists who weave in the ways of the old days… We want you to earn a living—and share it with others, but in today's world you believe your art will be cheapened if you don't demand more and more while doing less and less that is useful and beautiful. You all want to be paid more than all artisans were paid in the past, and you want it stashed rather than used now. You're paid more than all weavers everywhere, and they once had enough to live on as you did before you started this consumer's feud!"

Wanda returned from time to her own central mind and felt her neck snap with the impact. It hurt—a lot! What was said was only in her mind, or so she thought, until another rush of energy blanked out her mind again. She had time only to say angrily, "I see nothing about this place that is significantly changed from the past, but all of you are too proud of your work…selling it at prices high enough to spread your wealth over the entire tribe around you now. If you don't share what you're doing here, a war will erupt and someone will come and take away your pay, your materials, maybe kill you. Do you understand what I'm saying?"

The women sitting in the front row shivered and cowered with the importance of this new work, but many of her words did not register on their thoughts then. Most appeared unable to smile; however, Wanda spotted six elders willing to submit to the demands for more power to be downloaded so she could continue channeling the visiting Maya from another time. She asked each elder intuitively to release enough energy so she would not implode or have to let this Maya go. The energy requested was given to her in spurts. She could feel it enter her spine and declined none of it since it was indicative of their minds. She wanted everyone to know what was happening and grow along with her—but not attempt to channel The Maya until she knew how it worked.

A high pitched voice said, "This town needs you more than you're willing to explore. I feel you all need to go out from this compound which shelters you and do your personal business once a week in the nearby villages. Begin to seek out the men who hate you. Study what they do to each other, and then watch who sells out first… See who wants your money enough not to remain loyal to what they decided as a tribe—which was to sell nothing to any of you. When you look at them—think power! Give them a sense of what you've developed so far—and that you're going to do more and more work than they can imagine. Hint that they are wise to always take care of you, but remember that you need them, too, because they are warriors without any ties to the outside. They may not realize it today, but tomorrow or the day after they will awaken and want to fight like Maya. Be aware that they can help you here *and* there, but only if you align with them as a tribe now."

As Wanda channeled the final words, she felt her spine realign and watched as she stood and moved as if ready to leave the scene. The elders immediately felt electricity ebbing back into their worlds, too. They then gifted Wanda with a great ability to confuse the world, while getting the weavers to work without confusion. The wise women and the weavers made it happen, but it appeared to the uninitiated that Wanda was able to find the path and lead all the weavers into another dream—at last.

♓ ♓

Keeping her eye on the cook and the women who had been waiting with her in the living room for the weavers to make their evening appearance, Mandy spoke to a few of the weavers as they trailed Wanda into the room. "Well, ladies, I see you've had a long discussion about what you intend to do about the nearby clans. May I hear what it is, or do you intend to keep us all in suspense?"

A young woman, among the first to enter the room, said with quiet confidence, "We know what to do." She seemed elated as she took a position behind Wanda and projected her approval of what had been decided.

Waiting for Wanda to approach her and the other elders, Mandy thought, 'Wanda is truly doing great work with these women.'

The staff member who usually attended to Mandy's needs when she visited the weavers' compound approached and asked, "What can I do for you, Miss Mandy?" She was not standing directly in front of Mandy, but she blocked her view of the other room.

With a motion of her hand toward the next room, Mandy said, "I saw something just now flit through my peripheral vision. Can you see what it is?" She continued to wonder about it until her aide returned to her side.

"I find nothing, Miss Mandy," she whispered.

Now on full alert, Mandy noticed that her assistant made no attempt to join the weavers or move closer to Wanda. Instead she moved away, even from the elders. 'I wonder what she is into,' thought Mandy.

Although it was merely a thought form and not uttered aloud, Wanda picked it up quite easily now and decided to check it out for herself as well as for Mandy. She walked toward her mentor as soon as the other elders took seats against the wall of the living room to watch whatever might take place. Before reaching Mandy, she said loudly for the benefit of everyone gathered there, "I think we should bar the door and not let anyone else in. I want to be sure we have things straight before we're quoted in today's paper."

Wanda's decision instantly alerted Mandy that the leak they had spotted only a week ago was from the woman who always tried to know when and where Mandy traveled and would arrive here. No wonder there was always just enough work to do and just enough things to check before she was safe in her berth every night. She did not let on that she caught the warning. Instead, she addressed several women standing at the back of the room. "I think we can safely lock up, but make sure the dogs are put outside to run—in case the unwise try to pry."

The ever-vigilant aide looked a bit miffed as she stood her distance slightly apart from everyone else, but then brightened and said, "I can check it out for you Mandy. I'm not involved in any of this. You all can do whatever you want, and I'll let out the dogs."

Barely able to soften her impatience with the would-be traitor, Mandy said, "No, Gloria, just relax. The women at the back can sweep the pavilion and sic the dogs on strangers or peeping Toms if need be. After all, we women are all alone this evening and no man should be out and about bothering anyone now. They know the rules!"

Immediately several women dashed out the door and shut it with a slam. The dogs were not vicious, but trained to respond to anyone they did not recognize by smell. They knew the scent of every resident and worker who belonged in the compound. They picked up on strangers' hair and body odors first and seemed to know that the smell of the crew working with cloth was very different from all others because they were extremely clean and had lanolin on their hands. Their scent was very different when compared to men from the surrounding area.

A few minutes after the dogs were given their freedom everyone could hear them barking and running after someone outside their walls. A shout, followed by cursing, was heard in the distance, but no one listening to the wise women speak cared, except the one who had wanted to run out on them.

While the dogs did their job efficiently and effectively, an elder moved away from the wall and stood at the front of the room. She peered out over the heads of everyone seated and said, "I see nothing, but I feel that there is a force among us that has opened a portal to the evil of men—and those who care nothing about our work." She bowed her head, then suddenly raised her arms to the heavens and shouted, "Traitor! We will know who you are by tomorrow! You will not do your evil work against us again."

Mandy watched as panic ran randomly through the group, but did not say a word. Wanda grinned when she sensed that Mandy also knew who the spy was but said nothing. The group began to run itself, and neither mentor stepped in or commented without permission from an elder. Finally, one of the weavers stood up and pointed toward the roof and cried out, "I see what you see, too! I see a fly on the ceiling. It's unusually high. It's drunk—or is it on drugs?" The weavers, as a group, whined in such a way that it made the blood of the wise curdle and others worry, but no one left the room.

A blonde woman experienced difficulty trying to maintain her balance, due to one leg being in a cast and her crutch falling, but managed to say, "I'm not Maya, but I'm able to see something out there lurking around, and someone in here giving them information about our work. I can feel it, but maybe it's not true since I'm not Maya."

The oldest elder stood and announced, "I am Maya! I know who is Maya and who is not. You are Maya! Never assume that you are able to feel the work, yet not welcome to work with us as a Maya. You are of Earth, but not of the work? You know what to do now! Try to smile and look deeper into the future than you usually do, then speak to us of what you see."

Thus encouraged, the blonde, one-legged woman said loudly, "I see a woman and a man embracing... He is not of this land... He is not of this work... He wants her to cheat on her clan... He's holding her hand, but looking at another woman in the back of the room. He's a liar and a cheat... She doesn't realize that he doesn't admire her or her plan...that he loves someone else."

The weaver who had assumed command of the group suggested, "I think we can let it go now. Don't you?"

The oldest elder walked toward the door and reached as if to open it and immediately expose the man seen in the vision. She was not able to follow through because Mandy stood up and smiled as she announced tomorrow would be a great day—one of amazing discoveries and explanations of things now secreted away. The weavers' leader changed direction then and suggested they quickly recap their business and go to bed and dream of what will be.

Mandy's mind was already far away in time, but she remained seated in the mistaken belief that no one would notice her leave right then. All the elders, however, saw her leave. They smiled at how easily she did such things, because she trusted them to take care of her body now. They alone knew of her dangerous work this night on the other side.

⌖ ⌖

When the dawn opened to another day of rain and the knowledge that few tourists would be out and about, the weavers decided it was a great opportunity to put their new plan into action. They had decided to pursue a strategy that included lots of shopping in the nearby villages, at least until everything they wanted to do as a Guild was done. Hopefully, the natives were equal to the work they would do as a tribe, too.

In three bliss-filled hours, the weavers bestowed thousands of American dollars on businesses in the nearby town. The merchants were so excited by their sudden abundance that they invited several weavers to stay and see what else they could do for them if they only had computers. The weavers were not deceived, but pretended to be.

"When you have access to the internet, you're keyed into this century," said one young man as he tried to boot up an old Apple computer that he was manipulating with a bent screw driver. He was pleased to demonstrate his knowledge of 'computerese,' if not the techniques needed to become the most computer-literate person in his village. This eager young man wanted to be the leader of any group they might choose to work with and claimed to love technology of any kind, but admitted that he was not very good at math or science.

Standing beside the owner of the now crowded auto parts store, watching this fellow try to connect with the internet, Wanda whispered, "With no real need for more business, we're trying to decide now who should go to tech school and learn about computers, so we can handle more weavers as they arrive."

A merchant who was unwilling to see anyone else succeed with these women in such things said loudly, "I see no one in this town ready to go to a technological school." He alone wanted to lead and make plans for marketing their cloth and such and was not interested in broadening the town's horizons on the internet.

Even louder, the would-be computer guru shouted, "I can do that!" Now excited, he chattered about having been denied jobs in Cancun and other major employment centers because he was Maya. He had seemed confused about trusting outsiders who always abused his people and wondered why the central government gave tax credits to others for taking away their ancestral land. He centered on wanting to learn something useful that would help his tribe survive.

Appearing at Wanda's side, as if by magic, Mandy said, "You're a good man, my son, but are you able to study for hours before going to work?"

"Ahhh, Miss Mandy, you know how much I love electronic stuff! I built this computer out of old parts. Can you not see that I'm able to take apart many things and put them together to work better? Is that not a sign of my dedication and concentration—and hard work?" The young man beamed his smile to Mandy and confounded many present by displaying a dimple in his chin. Where did that come from? They all wanted to know about it. "I've had this dot on my chin since birth, but never had any reason to smile—until now, that's all. Oh, Miss Mandy, can I go to the university?" He pleaded as if his life depended upon it, and it actually did.

Mandy could see far into his future right then and said, "You'll meet many people in Merida who are quite different from you. You won't have to do much to get good grades, but you will have to learn how to interact with many strangers. You'll have to set aside your superstitions in order to become wise, but that doesn't mean you forget Mayan teachings. It just means you'll hide your wisdom whenever you're with those filled with pride." Mandy said this last with a grin aimed at the crowd around her.

"I can do that!" shouted the young man as he stood up and knocked over the stool he had been perched upon when they arrived. First, he hugged the women and men of the village, and then wiping his hands more carefully, he gingerly shook hands with Wanda, before he dropped his eyes and asked Mandy, "Where do you want me to begin? What do you want me to do first?"

Mandy laughed heartily. It felt so wonderful to see a brilliant being released from his past so quickly. Both sensed that he would be a great shaman of the Maya one day. She did not have to ask anyone in the past about how to help this man today. The path opened and the past closed as he stepped over the threshold of the little shop and walked into the sun to greet the other merchants, all of whom were eager to tell everyone in the town that he was going to the university in Merida. No one ever doubted that Mandy could do whatever she said, except those she paid to work for her.

Not particularly interested at the moment in stimulating the local economy, but wishing to socialize with women of the nearby clan, Mandy visited her favorite rest stop in the small town. Within a very short time young women arrived in groups to stand shyly along the side of the cantina as Mandy sat and drank Coke directly from a bottle. She did not use a straw!

The elder sitting across from Mandy shook her head and thought about how she was always doing something equally as undignified. Someday she would tell Mandy that proper etiquette dictated the use of a straw when you drank your weekly CocaCola with friends in a cantina or at the bazaar. She sat and glared at the teenagers who might otherwise do something rude, suddenly realizing she would never have that conversation with Mandy about what proper Mayan women do in public, because everything had changed—even as she kept watch.

First one teenager, and then three more, who had been drinking Coke the proper way, threw away their straws. Several young mothers did the same. One young woman continued sipping on her straw, seemingly detached from the inner circle of women gathered in the cantina, as if in a world of her own, as Mandy watched. Dreamily she said, "I propose we all go home and prepare marvelous dinners for the men who love us." She then looked happily from one friend to another, but no one smiled back.

One young mother said good-naturedly, "You think only about men!"

The other women continued talking about cooking and household chores, comparing their work to how much energy their men burned every day praying and planting and doing whatever it took to raise their food. They all agreed that their work at home preparing it was not nearly as difficult as what the men did to get it there, and that caring for the children was extremely easy, too. In the end, they agreed that women everywhere had to feel that same way about men and children.

Mandy wanted to laugh, but instead let it settle into her back so she could think about it when she was alone. Right then the Mayor approached Mandy and the others relaxing under the tiny cantina's arbor and announced loudly with great self-importance: "I want to say that today has been a brilliant, beautiful day for our town!"

Without checking to make sure he could hear her, Mandy said softly, "Thank you." She did not like the Mayor, but did not intend to offend him again. In the past whenever she addressed him too casually, he would get upset—but not today. Today, His Honor The Mayor, was elated as he counted the change jingling in his pocket as he walked among them.

Bubbling over, he announced, "I feel like Santy Claus came to town." He was very sweaty after prancing about the town, so The Mayor ordered a Coke, intending to drink with them, but no one was willing to give up a seat. He looked around as if his feelings were being abused again.

"You can sit here, Mayor," said a woman leaving to take care of her children who stood gaping at him with toothy grins that revealed gaps. She did not look back, but they all heard her laugh as she walked away. No one wondered why.

Wanda chose this moment as her time to arrive. Looking at the Mayor who was still sweating profusely as he teetered on a chair too small for his rear, Wanda waved her hand to indicate that the heat was getting to her and said, "We're lucky all the stores were open for business…It's a dark and gloomy day—and hot. Is it not?"

The happy Mayor waved as if he could change the weather with his magic hand as he said, "We've ordered this day 'specially for all of you at the compound, Senora. We want you to come back soon—not wait for the rains to come again."

Wanda spoke first, but a weaver echoed her words, and then several others from the compound chimed in as if in chorus. "You look great today, Mr. Mayor. You're doing a great job," and so on and on, ad nauseam.

Amazed at his warm reception from these women, but unafraid to accept their recognition of his many wonderful attributes, the Mayor stood up and bowed toward Mandy and Wanda and left them all in a daze. Never again did he ever openly oppose anything the weavers did at the compound or comment about their work without using the most effusive and enthusiastic of compliments.

☼ Chapter Twenty-One

"Thank you! Thank you! Gracias! Gracias! Thank you and good-night!" Teri shouted to the crowd of young girls gathered around her in the largest room of the weaver's compound. She was a star willing to share her beauty and her wisdom, but none of the women wanted to hear about it or believe in what she said. Her motives were as pure as she could make them, but she was unable to shed her reserve when it came to talking about men, thus the older women present saw through her vague explanations and refused to accept her. 'When will I ever learn?' she thought as she took a bow and turned away from the crowd. 'When will I learn not to talk about men I really like, but don't seem to know?'

Mandy lifted her cup to Thérèse and said, "I see you're physically tired, but mentally stimulated, Teri. You need to take a nice warm bath, get back on your spiritual path—so we won't keep you out late tonight." Turning toward the audience, she added with a laugh, "But *we're* going to party!"

The older women sat back in their seats and watched both women, without sharing the same enthusiasm Mandy projected to all present. Since the local women were never sure what Mandy might do next, but had paid to hear Teri Whitfield speak on the subject of relationships, they were unimpressed and a bit disappointed to see her leave. They now watched Mandy with anticipation, but also some dread about what might happen next.

Without thinking about the audience, Teri bowed her head and mumbled something seemingly not important enough to say aloud to the crowd, nevertheless it immediately changed everyone's mood. This too-thin woman suddenly appeared to be radiant and happy—not at all like the brazen woman who said only a few minutes before that *she knew* what men wanted and what men meant when they said they wanted sex.

Later many would relate to their family and friends that Teri had been aloof at first, 'talking dirty, too,' and then she magically changed from that persona into someone else, as if taken to a different place in time. It was said that a diffused light rose from her body or descended around her head, depending on who described it.

In reality, the air radiated a kind of glow around Teri's head as she stood still in the center of the stage trying to put the microphone away. Her mother recognized immediately that she was being transformed once more into the saint for whom she had been named. It always amazed Wanda that others did not seem to notice the change as quickly as she did, but that was not the case now. This group of native women was more astute than most Westerners. They witnessed the transformation as it took place at the same pace as she did.

Teri cried to the teenagers sitting around her, watching her through adoring eyes and mouths wide open, "I feel faint." Spotting a chair behind the podium, she moved toward it as several girls jumped up to help her sit down.

Wanda pushed her way toward the dais, saying, "Let me get through to Thérèse," just as the world-famous model staggered across the stage, rather than strutting her stuff and displaying a rude runway attitude.

A catty woman or two murmured, "Any mother would do the same, but not someone who's just a friend." Other women may have wondered about Wanda's behavior, but they said nothing to indicate they knew about the rumors circulating almost daily in the tabloids about these two famous American women of today.

"I'm okay. It's just the same old thing," said Teri as her voice faded away. Her body had not changed as far as anyone else could see, but she moved sluggishly and talked as if she were lost in a fog. Wanda always tried to shield Teri from crowds whenever this happened, but was not able to do it now because Thérèse chose to speak out. "I think we need to talk about life in general, ladies. I was unable to speak earlier due to prior commitments." While saying this, Teri completed a total transformation from super model to what seemed to be her alter ego, Sainte Thérèse. That is how Wanda described it to Mandy's friends later, but could it be explained as easily and simply as that?

Gently waving her hand, as if riding in a regal carriage in a grand and majestic caravan down an urban parade route, Thérèse slowly stood up, eventually curtsying with great grace, ignoring the fact that she was wearing tight denim pants—not an elegant gown or a humble habit. The teens surged around her as she admitted in a soft, hushed voice, "I feel very different from the woman who was with you a few minutes ago. I really do exist, and breathe and work like this."

Always able to command attention, regardless of what might happen next, Mandy changed her plans and announced: "Now, ladies, please be seated! We have something grand to share with you tonight. We're going to have a trance-induced chat with a lady much revered by many of us, Sainte Thérèse of the Little Flower." Pausing dramatically, she then asked the crowd, "Are you able to join us—or not?"

Since Mandy was party to many weird and strange affairs, the girls in particular were not about to leave and miss anything that might happen, but several of their mothers stared in disbelief and mumbled to each other that a super model could never be a saint. Able to hear their mutterings across the room, Mandy said with assumed sympathy, "I can see why you can't imagine God choosing you, or a woman of great beauty, to work for Earth, but it happens—more often than you can imagine, and it's happening right here tonight. Please sit back and relax and breathe easily, so we can all hear what Sainte Thérèse wants to give to us to remember this day."

A young girl, speaking aloud what many others might be thinking, said in awe, "This is already the most amazing day of my life. I will never forget it—ever!"

Mandy smiled and beckoned for the child to come on stage with her. Although frightened to be singled out by one regarded by The Maya as mighty, the girl bravely walked to the front of the room and stood beside Mandy as she said in her deepest tones, "You see one who at an early age can speak for the tribe. She is able to pick up positive thoughts—not bothered by what worries adults. This young woman is a translator or trance-interpreter! This is a blessing for her—and for us. Please, don't worry! She's not going to read your minds—at least not now. Wait until we're done tonight, then clean up your act—fast!"

The room resounded with laughter. Everyone seemed to relax as the little one moved away from Mandy, bent on leaving the stage immediately. Mandy held her back and invited the elders to join them and fill in the gaps left after the previous presentation. When the shuffling of positions was completed, Mandy said seriously to the audience seated in front and below her, "I think everyone has entered the room or is on stage who can help us with this transmission, but please leave if you can't believe… We can't let one soul sink our work this evening. Please leave without being asked!"

Everyone in the audience looked around, wondering what was happening that Mandy wanted someone to leave immediately. Without a trace of her usual smile, Mandy said more slowly, "I know you want to do your work alone… and you think you have little time and energy to spend on others or what they have to say, so please leave without any excuse… But remember, you won't get help from others if you don't help anyone but yourself." The crowd grew quiet enough to hear Mandy jokingly say to an elder sitting behind her, "I see we have a spade in our deck of hearts, and she's unwilling to leave, so we'll have to change her mind."

With that said, a woman in the back of the room smiled at Mandy and the elder and held up her hands to show they were clenched in a symbol of prayer.

Unaware of this silent exchange, many women present were taken by surprise when Mandy announced with finality, "Okay! You're all ready for Sainte Thérèse, so we'll wait patiently and quietly until she's ready to speak." She sat immediately on a chair that seemed to materialize out of nowhere, but actually had been hidden behind the stage curtains where Jorge was sitting—unbeknownst to everyone but Mandy.

Thérèse stood up easily, but slowly. She looked over the audience, then at Mandy and the elders, and finally at Wanda. She smiled sweetly at each person before she spoke in very subdued English with a French accent. The teenagers were immediately alarmed that since she was not speaking Mayan or Spanish they would not know what was going on until the lessons were published much later. To add to their confusion, Thérèse announced humbly, "I will now speak in my native tongue, French. One able to translate will talk for me today." With a motion toward the little person still hovering at the edge of the stage, she said, "Please come forward. I need you to translate into Mayan, Spanish, and English everything I am about to say… Please do not be shy, come forward and let me use your gift of tongues for a minute or two."

The audience separated into two groups—one believed everything immediately and the other was so afraid that they complained about everything not being done properly. Without much thought, Mandy asked one of the women at the back of the room to go outside and look at the moon. She left the room and the mood changed immediately into one of great expectation with no signs of rage. No one felt the change more than Thérèse! She suddenly spoke louder and clearer, and what she said was easily translated by the anointed child. It appeared that this girl was being asked to translate everything for everyone! Her abilities were never, ever doubted again, because every person present was able to immediately hear Sainte Thérèse's message in their own tongue. Speaking simply, she captivated the mood and minds of all the women in the room—as well as Jorge.

"I am so happy to be here with you in Mayaland. I love to visit, and always enjoy how much you accomplish with so much fun! I love you all! You are happy, never glum, as we so often are in cold, cold France. We love to eat and dance and feel grand, but have so many enemies! I cannot begin to tell you about them all!"

The Maya immediately felt her pain and sorrow, but refused to believe she could possibly know more about hatred than they did as a tribe. Intuitively they knew she was right when she said life was forever and each tribe has its day to ascend and rule before leaving Earth, letting go of its hold when it is the next tribe's time to lead the world in their own way and ascend once again.

"The day is over for the American way! But they will not admit it until someone ascends and leads them into a better belief system than they have now. We know that one of them will know what to do at the end, but some will want to stay as is and decay and eat up whatever they have saved. It is never easy to admit that you have not done well with your inherited state. It's true of us, too. We wasted our wealth and power until people rose up and annihilated the state…I have no power. I am not a saint of the wealthy or leaders of France, but I plant seeds wherever I please. I truly do love the United States, where so many roses grow, but we all know that land is being taken for granted, being wasted to build things that will not last more than a century—if that."

Thérèse stopped speaking and waited a moment or so before getting it across without saying a word that she wanted to be alone. The elders said nothing. They acted as if this were not an unusual request, because it was not. Mandy often spoke this way, as if they were all part of her family and need not worry about the strange things she said about her country and the world or what was in the universe above Earth.

Sighing, Thérèse indicated that she had more to say. "I think you and I can work as a team, but we need more gardens. We need to plant roses all over the Earth, but we must be alert because the Japanese beetles will always kill them if they can. Do you dig what I mean?" Thérèse alone smiled until a loud chuckle erupted from behind the curtain and floated out over the audience. Startled, she said in a somewhat confused way, "I'm not saying the Germans will rise again and take over France, but I do advise all to watch their alliances and flanks, and remember it happened in the past and is doomed to happen again if we don't work for the good of Earth."

Mandy was surprised that Thérèse was teaching big political issues rather than her usual brief message delivered in measured tones about doing small deeds and letting such work take root to produce good things in time for others as well as yourself. As if now confused, Mandy said, "May I ask you a question?"

"Yes, please do. For me this is such new work—strange business that I'm not sure what to say—or how much to say. Everyone, please use whatever helps, and ask me whatever you like…"

Thérèse's voice trailed off without actually stopping as Mandy said, "Would it be better for us to begin a new kind of life in another country like Peru or Colombia—soon? We're running out of space where we can do our work and not be disturbed. Everyone is running here and there trying to reproduce whatever we do and making excuses for it, as if we're the ones who aren't Maya and they are…" Mandy was unable to continue speaking because what she said did not make sense to her.

She felt swept away while listening to her words blend into new views and things she had never thought about until she heard it now. It was her eyes that first registered and recognized what was happening as she scanned the room and spied someone beaming ideas at her without any desire to leash her power. As soon as it became clear to her entire being what was going on, Mandy said crisply, "I'm sorry, Thérèse. It seems we have errant powers here and there. It's important that everyone understand that what I just said was not coming from me or my Higher Self or my Guides or The Maya, but from someone who wants to speak to you and use me to get through to you. Please pardon us for a moment or two."

Quickly moving toward the back of the room, Mandy stopped suddenly within a few feet of a woman from Peru who smiled as Mandy said forcefully, "You're welcome to join us, Josephina, but don't use me as your tool when you do. Understand?" Mandy spoke without thinking about why this woman was present or what she wanted to convey to the women present.

Ignoring Mandy's tone of voice, Josephina said playfully, "I thought you might want to keep it light tonight, Mandy, so I decided to fight. I couldn't pass up such an opportunity! So many tiny minds inside so many mature bodies—and all products of this time. I want to get through to these girls and young women that we can do something about the world right now—but as you said, the only one listening was you!" Josephina continued grinning at Mandy until she laughed, then she added, "See! It's not good to honor models and forget that we are mothers. We are who will lead the countries of today—not some thin-as-a-stick, sick model with no idea that what she does is wicked--"

Mandy held up her hand and asked for peace in her usual way, until she was able to carefully review what Josephina was thinking about. Within seconds, she decided to stop it! Her own power was now in place and able to move against this woman who loved to feud in public and then make up in private, so she said peaceably but with determination, "I think you might find a walk in the moonlight more to your liking, Josephina." Mandy motioned to her old, old friend to leave and wait for her outside until the crowd left.

Having made her point, Josephina nodded amiably and said, "I think maybe I'll find the moon to be a better audience than yours. The air in here is stifling and I feel a cold spreading through the room. I don't want to catch anything when visiting you."

Mandy walked back to the front of the room as Josephina edged toward the door. As she approached the dais, the young girl (apparently still translating) said loudly: "Thank you, Mandy. You're so eager to help me, but truly I need nothing now. We are all able to turn our lives into a garden and a place of power, but so many of the very young do not realize that now. Why?"

No one spoke, so the girl added, "You need to know what to do when you're able to move into adult shoes. You know you can go barefoot through your youth, but as adults we don the shoes of the world and move about its business. That time has arrived. You must know what to do."

Right then a young Mayan maiden seated on the middle aisle stood up and began whirling about as if assigned to lead everyone in dance. The elders on stage clapped their hands as though it was rehearsed, and Thérèse came out of her trance just as more women and girls joined the impromptu dance—twirling and whirling, letting their dresses fly wide like wings rising from their sides.

Mandy smiled at the group's change of mood and leaned toward Thérèse, as if to straighten her collar, in an attempt to block others from hearing what she was about to say. "It's not over, Thérèse. You have to stay. You have to get your work out to the government now. We know your way is not one of war, but you're here to train soldiers for another day.

Jeanne D'Arc was not mischievous or weird, praying to win battles to free enslaved minds, but today she and her ways are seen as profane—not equal to what science can do. Spirit can leap into meetings and take over for weeks in Mexico, but not anywhere else right now. You've seen it happen before. Do you really want to leave now?"

"You're overwhelming me, Mandy. I have not thought about anything said because my mission is to speak to children about God. I have strayed far from my usual work today, but I will know why it happened once I get back to chapel and can meditate. You can work and pray and dream all day, Mandy, but I have to maintain my belief in small ways always. I need to be able to fly to my work—a lot. It's my way to visit each person who prays diligently for me to intercede in the way the world strays today. I must go now."

Mandy did not ask Thérèse what she meant by intercession or how she worked, because she was confident that one day everything would be known to her and everyone else present. Until then, she would continue to pray and work as they all did that day.

☼ CHAPTER TWENTY-TWO

Whatever happens now is not just good luck. Remember that! You're here with us—not merely traveling a road far from home without anything computing, renewing, or moving, but doing what we are all here to do…

While watching things come into the atmosphere, as if from some far-away planet of today, do we sense anything about to happen? No. We don't even look around. But if someone calls our attention to a hunch they have or an article in the paper about someone trying to change the way we want the world arranged, we get upset. It takes only a moment of dismay to make us all a bit crazy.

If you're reaching to close the book now—and not read another page, think back to what made you sit and relax and join us in the first place.…

When the day is over and the book you are reading returns to being only paper and ink, do you realize how much labor went into the writing, making the paper and pen—or a computer? No. You grow without knowing. You assume without doing, and you move without doing anything—or so you believe when you stall.

Today, as you sit and labor with us—or not, think of one single thought, that's all…

Jeanne's eyes followed the next line or two of text as she muttered, "What will my editor do with this? I bet he takes it out because you're not to assume readers accompany you as you write." Scanning the screen further, she saw a line appear as if coming to her through time. It was a visionary thing—not really happening—or was it? She said, "Maybe I should turn off the computer and see what happens when I reboot?" However, she did nothing to change or stop what she saw arriving through time. Her hands did not roam over the keys, nor seek to remain idle in her lap, rather they played grandly over the keyboard as if coaxing something to appear that would align her notes with whatever was taking over her work now.

'Let me see,' she thought, 'I can almost make out a design. Yes, it's a huge wing—multicolored, like a brilliant rainbow—but only one wing. Hmmmmm, I think it's Mayan by the way it's configured. I have no idea if the Maya today admire angels as spiritual guides or know what they mean to others…but The Ascended Maya always find a use for whatever Christians and others insert into their work—not necessarily what the *missionaries* or emissaries intended or meant.' A chuckle interrupted her thoughts and she mumbled, "Let's see what happens if I print off a copy of this icon or wing and put it out to dry on the counter. Maybe one of the girls will stop by and want to know what it is—or tell me why it appeared?"

The printer chugged and sighed and produced the brightest piece of art Jeanne had ever given birth to during any of her writing frenzies. Totally amazed—somewhat mesmerized, she looked at the art with great satisfaction and wondered aloud, "Why would this angel's wing show up on my computer? How did it get here?" What made it so extraordinary was that she had never mastered the art of merging computer graphics into texts, and she knew nothing about graphic design—could not successfully download many materials sent by other authors and teachers if on a disc or attached to a file. So she knew this vibrant-colored symbol or whatever had to be used immediately—but where?

Peering over her computer and out the window, Jeanne noticed Wanda standing in the doorway of the studio located directly across the pavilion from her. She watched Wanda smiling and nodding to herself, saying something that no one else could hear. It must be amusing, as well as confusing, but that was all she could read of her friend's thoughts from this distance. She wondered about it for barely a second before she returned to her own thoughts.

As minutes passed she entered a trance-like state of rapture unlike anything she had ever experienced before. She wanted to see if anything else would appear as magically as the angel's wing, so she reentered the text that she typed right before the wing appeared on the screen. She wondered if anyone else ever had something similar happen when they worked with angels.

Slipping away from her muse, Jeanne prepared to dive into her writing when she caught sight of Wanda waving and motioning for her to come over and visit. She did not want to leave just now, but she could not easily refuse since she appeared to have been staring at Wanda for quite some time. With no socially acceptable excuse at hand, Jeanne stopped typing and went to see what Wanda wanted.

Moving across the central courtyard that separated each casa, Jeanne looked from one friendly face to another, hoping they would intuitively know something about the paper she clutched in her hand, but no one seemed to notice it. Some did, however, wonder how she always managed to look so pretty when she paid so little attention to her appearance—even her hair.

As she approached, Wanda called out loudly, "Thanks for coming over. I have something you just have to see! I can't believe what happened. I was walking around the office and happened to turn on my computer to check out what designs we might use when the next class is ready for new work, and voila!, up pops this design—an angel's wing, or I miss my guess. Isn't it beautiful—and unusual?"

Shocked, Jeanne said nothing as she brushed past her friend and entered the area where Wanda shuffled through her reports daily while pretending to tend to the part of art she hated—paperwork. Without asking, Jeanne went straight to the weavers' computer and looked at the screen. She sighed and said sadly, "You have exactly the same image I have on my computer." Realizing she sounded rude, and wanting to be excused, she laughed without mirth and climbed onto Wanda's high chair, leaving her to find a perch that suited her artificial leg almost as well as her throne.

Paying no attention to the slight—imagined or otherwise, Wanda cried, "Don't you see! This is a message from The Ancient Maya!" She failed to realize that Jeanne had the same image printed out and was holding it in her out-stretched hand. When she spotted it, she slipped off the other stool as if her foundation had been blown away. Stammering, she said, "How did you get that? Did you e-mail this?"

"No, Wanda, I didn't. I got this vision while I was writing a new book about helping yourself enter meditation to do any work that requires a lot of concentration. It just popped up on the screen and I printed it off, without thinking about where it came from. I may have used up every drop of ink in my computer printing it out." Jeanne dropped the picture on top of Wanda's desk to better compare it with her version before adding, "I guess we can ask Spirit what to do, but maybe we should just sit on it and wait to see what Mandy thinks…or see what happens with Julie?"

"That makes sense, Jeanne, but I'd like to be able to use this design right away to weave a blanket of some kind. Imagine going to bed every evening with this beautiful angel wing covering everything! It would transport everyone high above our usual dreamscape—make us all wise."

"I don't know, Wanda. I get the feeling it should be on the cover of my next book, but maybe it's meant to be kept in a secret place and only shared with a few? What do *you* think we should do with it now?"

"Like I said—or you thought—or whatever, we should wait and see what others think—then use it immediately."

Appearing confused, Jeanne turned around to look directly at Wanda. This small, deliberate motion made the room move around—put her in a bit of a spin, but she did not stop to think about it. She was already moving rapidly upward into the stratosphere.

Wanda was sitting motionless when she felt a long length of rope drop into her lap. She looked at it, then at the ceiling, before realizing she could keep Jeanne from going too far by yanking her back to Earth. She said, "Is it all a dream," as the door opened and one of the Mayan elders who helped manage the compound, Leon, hurried into her office.

"I need help, Miss Wanda. The storeroom isn't open and there are tourists all over the place. They want me, and they want Mrs. Jeanne to talk to them immediately. Their books aren't what they expected or they're amazed at what they say—I can't translate. Do you know where she is? She's needed immediately! Someone said she came here." The elderly man spoke to her chest only, without looking around the room to see if Jeanne might still be there.

Without smiling, Wanda waved the man away saying, "I'll get her for you. Go to the side door and open it as wide as you can so the key will fall out of the crack in the wall. Go! Do as I say." No longer afraid of her, he ran toward the store instead.

Wanda called out to what appeared to be an empty studio, "Okay, my lady, we have to move. You can't float around gloating over this wonderful news all day. You have work to do. Seems you've already said or done something to exorcise the press, so we better get ready to handle it."

As she spoke, Jeanne lightly descended into the high chair and sat there. Her mind seemed to be in another time. She did not frown or clown around as sunlight suddenly shone into the room, directly into her face. Wanda could detect no lines on her face, even though the light was extremely bright. It was as if Jeanne had had a facelift without ever visiting a surgeon. It amazed Wanda, but she realized they had no time to lose if Jeanne's fans were to be appeased immediately. Pointing out the details of the angel wing Jeanne had copied earlier, she said, "Look at that!"

Jeanne did not seem to remember anything. She asked hesitantly, "Where did you get that picture?" Without taking her eyes away from the design, Jeanne reached out to take the paper as Wanda pulled it away from her.

"No, you have work to do, Mrs. Jeanne! There are clients to see, readings to give, people to amuse. Go do your work, then we'll talk about what happened." There was not even a hint of amusement within or around Wanda's mouth as she spoke.

Likewise, Jeanne appeared serious, but continued to sit as she said, "I don't get it. I was feeling just fine when someone yanked a rope around my throat and made me come back immediately or be hanged. What's going on? I'm in no state to read for anybody. I'm too sick and tired to hear their complaints and what they want from God. I just want to go back where I was."

Ignoring her plea, Wanda pushed Jeanne out of the chair and toward the door. Laughing with great humor, even though not happy, she said, "Up and at 'em, my friend. You have your work to do and I have mine. We can't let these tourists down. Think about this—when you can command the kind of money you demand now for a reading—and don't do them, you let the tribe flounder, too. Then we can't buy all the supplies we need—and I want that new loom, so go out there and do it for the Gimper!"

"Don't make me do it!" Jeanne begged dramatically as she moved on unsteady legs toward the door. Once she caught the doorjamb, she felt more secure but still not ready to walk across the veranda and greet the hoard of tourists waiting for her in the storeroom area.

Unable to hide her alarm behind a laugh, Wanda said, "Let me hold your arm."

Ready to take Jeanne by the hand to steady her, a man suddenly appeared. Looming over them, he said, "Don't worry, Jeanne. I'm here now! We're going to do this together." As the tall stranger moved out of the glaring sun, Wanda realized it was Jorge. She was amazed to see how tenderly he took Jeanne by the hand and led her out and across the courtyard toward the noisy hoard.

When the crowd of tourists, made up entirely of American women, saw Jorge, they were apparently so overwhelmed by his presence that no one spoke to Jeanne. She sat down without ceremony and began laughing, rubbing her ankle as if she had sprained it and the pain was so great that all she could do was try to laugh it away. The crowd accepted that explanation immediately.

Quickly and deftly, the crowd was given a lecture on The Ancient Maya and the gifts they left behind, then Jorge spoke to those standing closest to him about what he was doing personally, but no one in the back of the store heard him. Due to his extra attention, the happy women left with many purchases tucked inside their purses, with even more being shipped home by UPS. They were so excited to have met Jorge, *The Phantom of The Maya*, as described in a recent issue of *Time*. He appeared to them to be worry-free, unconcerned that they might not understand his mission and/or be interested in it, because he did not need the help of those who were interested only in their own welfare.

)( )(

Meanwhile, Wanda sat in the weavers' office examining the colorful angel wing and only now noticing what was printed across the bottom of the page in a grand hand:

Angel of The Maya. Thinking about which fibers and threads she would use to reproduce the many different hues, she casually put away her paper work and carefully locked the studio door, even though she had never locked it before. She then slowly walked toward her comfortable living quarters.

The day was over before Wanda left her bungalow and entered the public sitting area next to the main kitchen. She was not looking for anyone in particular but delighted to see that The Scribe was talking animatedly to Jorge and Mandy. Whatever they were saying was not to be repeated apparently, because as she entered their charmed circle the subject changed immediately to other things, and Jeanne closed her eyes and said nothing to her in greeting. Somewhat offended by the cool reception, she tried to hide her feelings by apologizing. "I'm sorry. I won't bother you all now. I don't wish to interrupt your conversation. I was hoping that you were talking about the angel wing."

Each participant in the aborted conversation appeared surprised. Wanda could see it in their eyes, but when no one responded, she prodded her friend and said, "Don't you remember the copy of the angel wing you brought over to show me this afternoon, Jeanne?" She looked for any sign of recognition from Jeanne before she glanced at Mandy and Jorge, but nothing seemed to register on their faces or in their eyes. Peering more closely into Jeanne's eyes, Wanda was amazed to see that her pupils were very tiny—not dilated as they had been when she descended from the ceiling in her office a few hours earlier. As if leading a small child, she said, "Jeanne, don't you remember me saying I got the exact same picture you got when I opened my computer to see what designs I would use in the next class?"

When Jeanne did not respond, Wanda feigned being tired of standing. She looked across the room at a recliner and inclined her head in that direction to indicate she would give them privacy to continue their conversation. As she did this, Mandy suddenly moved to pull herself up and out of the chair where she sat between the other two and motioned for Wanda to sit there instead.

"No, no, I don't want to interrupt you. Please, Mandy, I'll sit over there and eat my dinner and leave you all in peace." Wanda said this while making an undulating motion with her right hand as she pointed toward a tray of food sitting on a nearby table apparently reserved for her.

Mandy's response was to bob her head and say emphatically, "Oh, yes, you need to eat. We'll move over there to be with you. Go ahead, eat."

Now fully recovered from what she had so recently perceived to be a snub, Wanda said, "I was so excited by the news of the wing that I just thought you all were talking about it! You really should go on with your conversation and not worry about me. My food is still hot and one of the girls will carry it for me."

Ignoring her attempt at polite conversation, Jorge said jovially, "We want to hear all about this angel wing." He then went straight to work moving their chairs and placing them around a small table away from the kitchen workers who were beginning to eat their own late suppers at the tables placed outside the kitchen door.

When they were settled enough to resume their conversation, Jeanne asked innocently, "What happened this afternoon, Wanda?"

Peering over her glasses, then back at her food, Wanda decided to let it slide until after she was done eating, but immediately heard herself say, "Don't you remember anything that happened then?" Her question was asked without any trace of impatience, but it seemed to imply that Jeanne was lying. So without hesitation, she tried to edit or otherwise change what was implied, but could not.

Relaxing further back into her chair, Mandy said quietly, "Jeanne is at peace now. She's been working hard on so many projects that suddenly something snapped in her mind, so she's not able to work as she did. Right now we all need to go back over her life history and piece together what she did to receive this ability to write for hours and hours—reading others' lives simultaneously. She was trying to write about it when something happened to her mind today. You were there, Wanda, but apparently you didn't notice anything unusual."

Startled, Wanda said with a little laugh, "Mandy, I was there all right. She was okay until she levitated and a rope dropped into my lap and I had to pull her back." No one apparently saw anything strange in what she said, because Jorge motioned for her to go on and review all that happened. "I was—Well, let's go back to the beginning. Maybe you can figure out what I did wrong or she did right, and how it ended up with Jeanne changed for life."

No longer smiling, Wanda continued talking and her face glowed as if a candle had been placed directly under her chin. Seeing this flickering glow caused Mandy to look within and seek another place to enter and pray. Her mind opened to time then and returned to the present only when Wanda related that she had been holding the rope that apparently kept Jeanne grounded or attached to Earth, when one of the business managers opened the door and said he needed more supplies—or Jeanne was wanted by some tourists. She forgot which. He did not notice Jeanne and left immediately upon being told where he could find the key to the storeroom.

"Wait," said Mandy. "Why would he have to ask you for a key? Why would he barge into your office looking for Jeanne? Do you ever assume leadership over the store? What's wrong with this picture?"

"You know, Mandy, now that you mention it, it was strange how he came in without even knocking. He was upset and said he couldn't help the tourists because he needed supplies and the supply room was locked. I told him what to do to get the key—so we better move it again. Don't you think?" Without waiting for any explanation or more questions, Wanda removed herself from them and hobbled toward the cook who was seated at the head of a table where her crew was eating and talking boisterously about the day's events.

Perhaps her prosthesis was not attached properly or she was in pain, no one knew for sure—not even Wanda, but when she returned to her seat beside Jorge, she looked scared for the first time in any of their memories. She spoke hesitantly. "The cook said Leon left right after he talked to me and never went to the store or came back for dinner. What do you think, Jorge? Is something wrong? Did I harm you or the project?" Her mind refused to yield to the pain, so she struggled to stand still while mumbling that she had to do something to her leg and would be right back.

Jorge said firmly, but gently, "Don't leave us just yet, Wanda. Can you stand the pain long enough to talk this out?"

Wanda laughed at herself, and they followed suit, but not without sending her a word of blessing. She said with resignation, "It's nothing. My leg just slipped a bit. When I put it on this morning the stump was apparently swollen and then the swelling subsided during the day—that's all, nothing to it. I'll just pull it off and put it under the table now, if you all don't mind—but remind me not to get up too fast."

No one laughed at her attempt to make light of her pain. Instead, silence reigned until Jorge said, "I think the spy is gone, but we need to stay vigilant. I felt something wrong at lunch and wanted to talk to you and Jeanne about it, but the events of the afternoon were indicative that everything was going great, so I completely forgot about it. Maybe we *are* in trouble, but I doubt it."

Wanda said with finality, "I can see nothing in the immediate vicinity." Her great ability to see into the future or into time was never doubted or second-guessed, so Jorge and Mandy employed her now to embark on a mission involving delicate conditions.

Jeanne added without conviction, "That's good to hear." She seemed sleepy and showed signs of becoming weepy, but she did not attempt to leave them.

Mandy pointed to a picture on her place mat that depicted a resort, but it was clear Wanda was confused, so she said, "What happened to you, Wanda, was a gift. We have to go back to the beginning and bring Jeanne up to the point where she looked at her computer and saw a beautiful angel wing come across the screen. Apparently she sent that picture to you via the internet without realizing she did it." Pushing the paper mat toward Wanda, Mandy smiled and added, "Let's think about all this, then get together later and discuss what happened one more time."

Without hesitation, Wanda could see them meeting later that week at their ocean villa—hidden from view and enemies of The Maya. That was the best she could offer, so she decided it would suffice until she could figure out what to do about the mysterious artwork Jeanne placed in front of her face that day; but before she could close the door on the day's events, she said, "I have a copy of what Jeanne printed out. You can keep it, but on the original she gave me I added, in some sort of script I've never used before, the words: *Angel of The Maya*. Why do you think I did that? What do you suppose it means?"

Whatever was said then was never repeated by any of them, but the mood of the group changed from a blue to white hue and spread throughout the entire room. All gloom lifted and sunny thoughts sifted through every mind present. Some of the cooks even admired the work of others, while some became less despondent about never rising above the level of being admired only for the way they scoured. Could one picture produce such changes in the mood of people unaware of its existence? Yes, but it will not be explained here and now.

☼ Chapter Twenty-Three

A tourist at the back of the room shouted, "Do you ever wonder about who is trying to get through to you when you channel?"

A gasp arose from some, while others tittered—a lot. To mend the embarrassing gap, someone spoke through a guffaw, loud enough for everyone to hear, "I think you have to take some things on faith. Don't you?"

Instead of looking at the woman in the straw hat seated in the back of the room, beaming a message meant for her alone, Mandy said in a voice other than her usual one, "I am making a statement now! I want to look great, and I want others to think that I'm a New Age thinker--"

The woman who was rude enough to interrupt Mandy in the middle of her lecture registered dismay. Her face changed hues from rose to ruby red as she attempted to speak out against her again, but she could only sputter. It was too late to hide her lack of enthusiasm and interest in what was being taught, so she said nothing more.

Smiling at everyone else, Mandy began to laugh, but stopped abruptly and said, "I think I may have overstepped my boundaries just now, but then again, this woman is indecent and not at all nice."

Immediately a hush fell over the crowd, but a smiling man standing beside the intrusive student, apparently related to her in some way, yelled, "How'd you do that, Ms. Brown?"

Everyone's attention was being drawn away from her planned lecture, so Mandy decided to let it fall apart and teach from her heart, which seemed to be bursting now. Pausing to take a deep breath, she started out softly. "I think it's all about projection—something in a person's mind that gives him or her the ability to accept what someone else says or thinks. I think your friend is deeply embarrassed now, but doesn't regret what she said, so it lingers among us now, so that becomes our lesson for today. Anyone else see that—yet?"

Some seemed to be thinking more deeply than when she lectured and expected no reaction from them. One of two nodded their heads as if they understood the change in mood or what she was saying now. With no further encouragement, Mandy spoke in a voice difficult to imitate, yet it was that of the woman who was still sitting in the back trying to get others to leave with her. She said, "I feel so weak. This woman is *not* going to take my mind away, even if she can read it. How does she do that?" No one laughed at Mandy's accurate mimicry of the brat disguised as an adult.

Several men had been leaning against the back wall, pretending to be interested in whatever she said. They now moved quickly toward the rear exit, but just at the precise moment they reached it, the wind blew the door open, scattering papers in circles around the room. The crowd hushed and the men in black did not leave.

"I see we have invited the wind." Mandy spoke through a big grin, then did not say another word for a minute or more as she swayed back and forth, seeming to dance with the power of the spirit within the air. Finally, she spoke so softly that some strained to hear her better, yet everyone clearly got the message. "Think about it… when you get angry, you begin to seethe and twitch, maybe even wrinkle your nose and twitch your lips. Your hair may even stand on end a little bit. Whatever is bothering you and moving you from a rational mood into madness is going on outside the lines of your inner vision, but affecting your heart physically. You feel your temperature rise, if inclined to get hot or just enlivened a bit if you're the placid type. As you feel these physiological changes, you give up energy—displacing the atmosphere around you. You could measure the displacement if you had access to equipment used by rocket scientists and others for such tests, but why bother? You know you make an impression on your aura as well as on others nearby—but these changes are not welcomed by others unless they set out to enrage you."

No one looked up while jotting down notes in books held on their laps. Those trying to take dictation from Mandy could not, because she was not willing to slow down or repeat what she said. After a few minutes she stopped and said, as if impatient with someone close at hand, "Why not just listen and take in what I'm saying, rather than splitting your attention between me and what you want to remember? Why not give your full attention to what is being taught now, then sit in meditation later and remember what's most important to you? Then you can jot down what you want to review every week or two." Mandy's words tapered off into an almost monotone drone as her mind projected toward the student living within each of them how to ace any class.

While speaking, Mandy examined each man present. The one sitting beside the woman who had started this unique experiment was going into a deep trance. He had told many he was unwilling to do anything new, so he twitched a little as he meditated before letting fly an idea that only Mandy could pick up. Sufficiently blocked by ego, he was able to speak, but did not. She spoke in a soothing voice directed at him alone. "You're able to pick up every thought your friend projects, and it makes you upset…Yes, that is exactly the impression she wanted to give everyone. You, however, got the brunt of her negativity and sent it to me. Do you see that yet?"

Every other person present, including the Mayan men and elders who usually assumed a neutral position relative to whatever was taught in such classes, shook their heads as if to indicate they were lost—unable to follow her thoughts. Leaning over the edge of the stage, as if talking to musicians seated in the orchestra pit, Mandy said sadly, "I guess we better begin at the beginning then—if we can."

No one responded, but the room was quieter than before this latest thought was projected toward them all. Mandy left the stage to circle the room as best she could. She walked in and out of the irregular rows, stopping occasionally to push or pull a chair into line to better concentrate on her presentation. As she passed each chair, she paused long enough to look directly into each student's right eye. Her talk projected compassion yet seemed to be playing with their attention rather than urging them to accept anything said.

Back at the podium, Mandy addressed a question to the woman who started the uproar among her traveling companions and even now continued to try and control what was going on around them. "Why do you attend lectures or classes on subjects you think you shouldn't listen to or believe in?"

Looking chagrined and upset at not being able to speak quietly on the side against Mandy, as she had planned when she began this mission to change her man, she suddenly realized that Mandy easily picked up on all her thoughts. She could not successfully employ her usual strategies because she never played games out in the open—choosing instead to quietly undermine others while appearing to agree with whatever they said. This revelation was startling enough to make her want to leave for America immediately instead of returning to Cancun that evening.

Facing this enemy up close and very personal, Mandy showed no mercy as the woman maintained an attitude of being very reasonable and easy-going. She said sternly, "Speak up, friend. What are you so mad about? What has upset you so much that you would give up sitting on the beach to accompany those who wanted to see me and supposedly learn what I do?"

Without a thought as to how insulting she may sound now, the unhappy woman said, "I—I think—that you're too much of a lady to do this kind of stuff. I mean—you being upper middle-class and all—just like us, and I don't think you can be a Mayan and speak like the wise—and you shouldn't even try."

Mandy said nothing and let the ugly American's whine end the session as she projected healing thoughts toward everyone present, although only a few *sensitives* felt it then. As the day passed, this misguided woman's venom was diluted enough that even she was able to leave the compound as a friend of Mandy and The Maya, but not then.

How did it begin and when would it end? No human being could answer that question to Mandy's satisfaction, so she decided to peddle Jeanne's latest book and use her friend's revelation of Spirit, as channeled through the Holy Ghost, to teach rather than go into trance during lectures and possibly place her life in jeopardy twice.

This day ended with tourists and 'wannabe' students of Mayan culture buying every copy of Jeanne's book that Mandy was willing to 'auto-graph' or inscribe with a thought about the buyer or someone they knew, before they boarded the bus and headed back to Cancun and their usual hedonistic pastimes. As the last tour bus headed out of the compound, the elders approached Mandy while she talked to her staff. They asked to speak to her alone in the back of the lecture hall. She was not sure what was wrong, but knew someone was upset and wanted her head.

"Aaahhh, Miss Mandy. Thank you for coming to our council. We are not afraid of what you started today, but what might be said about The Maya. We do not want these people telling their friends how we work and what we do. Can you understand that? And we want you to stop talking about how you work, too." The old man was almost blind so he gently reached out to touch Mandy's chin and her cheek before stroking her head as if she were a favorite pet. He did not say another word, nor did any of the other elders, but Mandy could hear inside her mind everything they wanted to say and why.

"I can see that I've overstepped the boundaries—again. I'm not as wise as The Maya who have lived always on this side. I'm not a woman of Mexico, and I'm not exactly an American, either, but I do repent and always change my ways when I have wronged or upset an elder—especially one so wise as you, *anciano*." Mandy spoke softly and sincerely as she bowed deeply toward each of the elders. "I have offended you all and I am sorry for that, but what was said must be said—by someone. You all can do it much better than I, but you don't want to appear too forward, and you don't like to talk to others without possessing a perfect understanding of their language, so the true work of The Ascended Maya is being introduced to the world by impostors who are not of The Maya or the tribe, and they never hesitate to freely transform our lives into lies to make a few dollars."

Mandy could not stop talking and realized that her lips were uttering dialects not easily remembered by the elders, as if to assert the truth of what she said. This amazed the men, so they let everything she said or did during the day fade into time, in order to concentrate on what she asked each of them to do for The Maya now.

"Why is it necessary for a friend to assert herself or himself from time to time to reaffirm that friendship and wisdom are woven with the same thread? Don't you see that we are all weavers? We are all scribes? We are all potters? We are women and men without exception now? We are all Maya!"

The ancient one nodded his head and peered into space as if able to see something in the distance. He said one word that no one heard before his mind was transported in time. The other elders began looking up toward Venus and asking for help and wealth and power and whatever was in their worry line at that time. They did not stop praying until Mandy asked them to go into dinner and eat at her table.

After a long, relaxing dinner, the elders prayed together, and even invited the women and men who lived or worked in the compound to sit down and chat with them. As the evening progressed into the deepest part of night, a song began to play on the lips of several women. They started to hum as a few remembered the words to old, old music. Some of the elders sang along with them then.

Mandy believed that this change of heart was inspired by the anger left in the room by the American tourist that afternoon. That woman was not at will to give up her spiritual path, but she had. She left that day without a will of her own, or so she would say later, but that was not true. She started lying again too soon after being healed by The Maya of the anger that had festered in her mind all this life.

The women continued singing and praising God and The Maya who always lived within their minds and they asked for help in cleansing the room of its dark mood. The gist of their work was that the American tourist who was not acceptable to The Maya had left behind a cloud of darkness which needed to be removed immediately. It was no myth to them that her image existed within the room and mocked them still.

Suddenly Mandy started to dance in place. She asked two women to take her hands to prance and dance along with the song being hummed and sung. These maidens were eager to show off their feet and how lithe they were on their toes as well as their abilities to create beautiful dresses—and no one ever backed away from dancing with Mandy. The dance, weak at the start, became a vision from the past. As more moved into the dance, they closed the circle. Everyone had a partner to the left and right as they emerged into a depiction of the night watch that exists in outer space.

Mandy crooned to the room and to the sky above them: "If The Maya of ancient times have eyes, let them show us the way home tonight." She was unwilling to perform a weird ritual or be the only one willing to keep the room free of evil beings who might try to enter the tribe, but she kept that to herself.

"We are all here," said the man known as 'The Scribe to the Tribe' until Jeanne arrived from America and challenged his career. He never appeared angry or upset about it, but his words written or spoken often betrayed him. The tribes' scribes did not always work as they did in the past, so Jeanne often accepted work that other scribes refused. Mandy was curious about why this scribe now chose to address the elders in various dialects, as if asserting his calling to be *The* Scribe. He stated in several different ways that he had always wanted to be a scribe, and then he asked what he had been leading up to for ten minutes or more: "Why was I given such a responsible position by The Ascended Maya if everyone on Earth could be a scribe, too?"

Having spoken his mind—finally, The Scribe sat back and waited for an answer to enter his mind from an intuitive source. Instead it came through a man who often channeled wisdom in the way of the tribe of old, although he did not speak in a particular dialect so much as a mixture of Mayan idioms. Acting as a channel, he delivered the message from Spirit with no attempt to embellish it. "You will be told, but not until you are old." Since his work was always respected, he was usually terse.

Just then a young man who had been admitted to the work and socializing of the tribal elders for the first time that evening spoke out eagerly, as if asked to deliver a message to the assembled cast. He almost shouted, "I want to cleanse this room and those people dancing who are unable to sense that evil is about to be done--"

An elder well known for his ability to read the combined minds of groups quickly reprimanded him. "Wait! You're young and not willing to listen to anyone. When you have added ten years to your age, then you may be allowed to speak with such power, but not until then, and if you don't study and listen to the sages, you'll never meet with us again." The elder was never doubted, even if his message disagreed with what others might say, because his psychic abilities had been proven to be superior to everyone in the nearby tribe when he was very young.

"I see everyone!" shouted a woman from the center of the dancing group. Her head fell back and she could not center it over her shoulders. Her body weight shifted just enough that she had to be supported by dancers on either side.

"What do you see?" asked the woman to her right.

"I see the world! It's not like you think. It's not white or bright. It's blighted and without life. I can see a cloud of darkness headed toward us out of Africa. What can we do to make it dissipate—keep it from creating a life form that will not produce life in the future of time?"

All the dancing women stopped immediately and stood their ground, letting their arms fall to their sides. A keening sound came from one woman, then another and another, as if someone had died. The young man who had been chastised only minutes before spoke out again and asked what had happened to take all the joy out of their dancing, causing them to grieve.

The ancient elder who had remained silent most of the night said, "You are young. You think man can do anything he wants—and that when his time is over he will call home and be transported out of this world. That is not true of The Ascended Maya we work for—and maybe one day will permit you to work with, too."

Leon, an elder and one of the compound's managers said, "I feel we shouldn't give away our power to tourists—like happened this afternoon." He pulled out of his medicine bag a bejeweled ring he had hidden earlier in the day. He now declared it was given to him by the evil American tourist who wanted him to give it to Mandy as a token of her esteem.

"You are a thief, Leon! You're going to be doomed—never able to ascend again if you keep sneaking around stealing things," shouted one of the women who attempted to leave the group of men she had caught staring at the women again.

"You will be damned, Leon," said the elder who loomed over the guilty-looking man, preaching rather than trying to help him stand.

"I'm not a thief! That woman asked me to help her because I understood what she wants from men. She wants men to honor her—give her whatever she wants without always questioning her motives. She just wants to be seen as the most wonderful woman on Earth." Since Leon was talking with his head bowed low over his chest, he did not notice that just about everyone was laughing at him.

Mandy moved gracefully into the middle of the room and raised her hand in the sign of peace. As she lowered her arm, she smiled at each of them while listening intently to discover who within the tribe was dishonest. Now raising her right hand with index finger extended, she began slowly turning clock-wise within the circle of dancers that had gathered around her. Everyone, including Mandy, watched as her finger stopped and pointed at Leon's face. Everyone in the room including Leon knew what it meant, but he did not have the grace to accept its meaning. Instead, he lied until he was escorted outside by one who served as a security guard when necessary. The elders were left to decide what to do about the expensive ring and how to chastise him in the way of The Maya, without humiliating him before everyone in the nearby town.

As dawn's light streaked across the eastern sky, couples who had remained throughout the entire judgment process left the group to make love. They did not have sex as frequently as others alleged, but tonight they would try to create children who would benefit from their elders' advice. It was a tradition among The Maya to first desire a child, and then produce it—rather than the casual insistence upon 'accidental births' or determined scheduling of motherhood as practiced in America.

Later that day Mandy asked the cashier in the compound's store, "What do you think will happen when this woman receives a beautiful basket with her 'lost' ring buried inside its lining?"

"I think she'll believe she lost it when she was shopping and that it came back to her in a very unique way."

The cashier was not known for her beauty, but recognized for her clever way of putting thoughts into words, so Mandy pushed the basket toward her and said, "Would you select a nice card and prepare a note—and sign it for me?"

Shaking her head vehemently, the clerk replied. "I can't. I don't know how to write. I say things that the elders write down, but I'm not a scribe. I can't write."

Mandy realized only then that she was asking this trusted employee to become a scribe. She willed her present mind to shut down as she went within to read this woman's mind. Without hearing anything wise, she mumbled, "I see…." She then stood still a few moments before pulling from inside her blouse a long chain with an amethyst pendulum attached to it, as well as an engraved locket.

Fondling the beautiful piece of gold jewelry, Mandy said, "This locket came to me from another trusted employee. I believe it bears the same name as you use today, Anita. Why don't you try it on? If you like it, it's yours."

Placing the locket and gold chain on her palm, Mandy watched as Anita gasped, "Where did you get this, Miss Mandy? It was stolen from me a long time ago. I have looked everywhere for it—for at least three years!"

This simple statement amazed Mandy as much as anything she had ever heard coming through the veil. Her mind refused to understand what was stated, flying instead to what was implied. Without thinking, she said, "Nita was a thief! We never doubted her—and she was a thief. We gave her access to our power, our books, our computers—and now I discover she was a thief—while investigating another theft. Can we ever be through with all of this greed and evil?" Mandy dropped her head into her hands and appeared to cry.

"Don't cry, Miss Mandy. We are Maya—not gods, or even wise people, or people who have no faults. We are human beings plagued with the sins of the Old Age. We have to work out of it now—quickly—if the words said last night are to be taken to heart." The humble woman said nothing further as she closed the gift basket and waited to see what would happen next.

"I see many things, but never thieves… Why is that?" Mandy spoke as if she was amazed that anyone could take what another achieved, earned, or been given as a gift.

"You are gifted—and many take credit for what you say. Is that not theft? Do you not wish to accept your gifts?" Anita said this very slowly with a shy smile as she threaded the locket onto a black satin ribbon and placed the beautifully carved pendulum on the gold chain, ready to give it to Mandy.

"Let me take that locket and bless it for you," said Mandy when she noticed what Anita had done.

"No, thank you. I will bless it myself and wash it in the river with my clothes and such. Water is best to remove whatever may still be attached. After all, it hung about your neck a long time and must carry some of your aura now, too!"

Mandy felt her neck prickle and itch in several places. She pulled the chain off the pendant and tossed it into the flames of the fire they maintained to amuse the tourists when demonstrating how the average middle-class Mayan woman of today still cooks for her family. Within a split second of watching the chain disappear, Mandy took Anita's locket and threw it in the fire, too.

Stunned that Mandy would throw the locket and chain away, but afraid to complain, Anita mumbled, "I loved that locket so much. It was a gift from my mother. She got it from someone who loved her. It was very, very old, and now I'll never be able to give it to my daughter." Tears ran from her dark eyes, but she did not speak again of her sorrow.

After a few moments, that seemed to stretch into minutes, the sad woman and two of the cook's helpers watched as Mandy reached into the center of the fire and pulled out the gold locket and held it firmly in her hand. She moved to place it on Anita's neck but changed her mind and clenched it to her chest instead. The two scullery maids and Anita crossed themselves, very worried about the intensity of the burns Mandy sustained saving the locket for future generations to be amazed by its sudden rescue from the flames. With a hint of her usual grin, Mandy then said confidently, "It's safe! You can place it around your neck and wear it without worry now, Anita, but don't wash it unless you're washing your neck." She noticed then that the women were trying to check her hands for burns, so she held up her palm and said, "See! Nothing was harmed. I have hands of asbestos—as my favorite chef always says."

The sun, apparently unable to stay away from center stage, blazed a path across the glass countertop right then and ended at Mandy's extended hands. "You see! The sun is greater than any heat we can imagine or appreciate, but it would never burn my hands. It might burn my face or my back, but never my hands. Think about that!"

"But Miss Mandy, that is because we are always busy doing something with our hands when we're outside," said Anita as she wrapped the little gift basket in a cloth woven by Wanda's assistants.

Without thinking it through, Mandy blurted out, "That's the reason we work! Imagine that—and we have lots to do today, too. Thieves have taken enough of our time and energy to complete two years of work on ten Mayan women. Let's get going and get this package to the *turista's* hotel in Cancun—before she goes home!"

When the women realized that Mandy intended that they deliver the package, the cook's helpers laughed. "You trust us to drive your Jeep again, Miss Mandy? Remember the time we landed in the ditch and didn't get home with it all in one piece like you asked?"

"I think you learned more from that one accident than ten years of driving carefully without ever getting a ticket. Go and find out where this woman is staying—and don't forget to tell her when you find her that she left her ring on the bathroom sink."

"You will lie to save the tribe, Miss Mandy?" asked the youngest of her admirers gathered around her now.

"Yes, if it takes a lie to make a woman decide that she's not perfect and has nothing to lose if she believes in God and a tribe—then I'll lie every time. But make no mistake about it, I am not a liar! I just bend the truth now and then." Mandy did not smile until the three young women left her behind the counter to run the shop until another clerk could take over. Once relieved of such duties, she laughed long and loudly about their great delight and pride in accepting the keys to her Jeep—again. She could feel how thrilled they all were careening through the village and speeding to Cancun.

As soon as Mandy felt totally calm again, she said softly to herself, "I think too much has happened in the other room. It needs to be cleansed immediately." Before she could put thought into action, an American tourist hailed her as the 'head honcho' and marveled that she was willing to wait on customers, too.

Unable to attract her total attention, he added with humor, "Hey, you! What are you doing to these native women anyway? They drive like crazy! I thought the Maya were supposed to be modest, unassuming women, but I was almost run over by three giddy females who don't know how to drive." As he talked, he extended a chubby hand across the counter top to Mandy and grasped hers as if it were the handle of a pump that needed primed vigorously before it would work. Then he added as if an afterthought, "Guess you're the one who gave them the keys."

Something about his voice or manner stopped Mandy from ignoring his boldness. A feeling seeped into her conscious mind that he was someone out of her past, so she immediately extracted her hand from his sweaty grip and thought about what she would say once he recognized who she was.

"Don't remember me—or do you, Mandy?" The man's question was almost inaudible, so it did not attract any attention from customers checking out beside them.

Slightly breathless, Mandy said, "Yes, I do." She felt trapped, but was willing to wait to see what this man planned to do instead of giving him an edge.

"I think what you're doing in Mexico is great, but why sacrifice yourself when others can help, too?" His tone was flippant, rather than annoyed at her indifference.

His identity still escaped her, so Mandy said casually, "I don't think one person's mission is something that can be shared with people everywhere, but *if* it would help The Maya climb out of the past and into the future, I guess I'd get in line and seek admittance to the game—again." While talking, she gripped the edge of the countertop. Only when she felt a cramp in her hand did she realize that none of the tourists standing nearby were willing to break in and pay for their souvenirs and fabrics while she talked to the handsome stranger. The shoppers seemed mesmerized by his smile. She then realized he was pretty enough to be a movie star or a male model. Young women stared at them openly now as if they were actors on a stage, so Mandy eased her grasp on the counter top and possibly on the situation. She turned and smiled at the eager women and asked if they needed help.

Not wishing to lose his place in line or her full attention, her nameless friend said quite loudly, "Oh, I need help! I want to pick up one of those bolts of fabric Teri set aside for me. She said it would be in the back room and that you know how great a need I have for it now that I'm redecorating my New York apartment. The upholsterer keeps bugging me about it."

The women swirling around him were not sure if he was buying something they wanted, too, but they appeared willing to wait and see it or just stand in his light. Inspired by how the women followed him into the storeroom, Mandy thought they might be able to create a rage this way and have all of America begging for native fabrics as if they were made of rarest silk. She signaled to a man sweeping leaves outside the front door to come in immediately. He arrived at her side without breaking stride, happy to do anything inside rather than work in the sun. She said, "Pedro, summon Wanda and her weavers, please."

As Pedro paged Wanda over the public address system, she spent a few moments smiling and talking nonsense with the tourists about the weavers and potters and their art, while continuing to search her memory for the name of this man who was soon to become their best client.

"Attention! Attention! Will Miss Wanda and her staff meet with Miss Mandy in the showroom immediately? Attention! Attention!…" the announcement was broadcast in oratorical tones all over the compound several times, until even the tourists became aware that Pedro enjoyed the sound of his voice—not intentionally trying to annoy everyone.

Glancing at the time displayed on the wall clock, Mandy motioned to the mystery man that it was almost time for lunch. He signaled back that he was hungry and would wait for her to clear the crowds away if she would go to lunch with him.

When the grand inaugural announcement that would become a trademark of the weavers' compound in Quintana Roo was finally finished, Mandy turned over that day's work to Wanda and wandered off with her long-lost friend without mentioning to anyone that he was not interested in purchasing anything woven by the tribe—at least not then. Unable to put off the inevitable any longer, Mandy asked, "How are you doing?" without sensing that she was being repetitious.

He spotted it immediately and thought that he was about to score. "I'm just fine, Mandy, but you seem to be coming apart at the proverbial seams. Is seeing me again like this what's upsetting you so much?" He tried to capture her hand as he spoke, but she put it in her pocket for safe keeping.

Mandy felt confused, unable to clearly share her views, so she spoke softly to keep him away from her face when she answered him. "Yes, I guess it is. I don't remember when we last met or what we said then…It seems to be gone from my memory…What was I to you anyway, if you don't mind my asking you as a friend?"

'Hurt' was the first word Mandy found to describe the strained look in his eyes. She was embarrassed at not being able to mend any long-held belief systems he might be clinging to relative to her or her work, so she suggested that when they were refreshed she would drive him to a beach where he could relax and sit by the sea.

This suggestion made him sadder and he let her know it immediately. "I hate the sea! Don't you remember that I get red as a lobster if I even step on sand? I can't believe you have no memory of me."

"I think I see you in another view—but then again, I think I see you in another room, too. It's hard to see into the future and still remember the past. Don't you agree?" Mandy spoke without sensing that she was not making any sense to him.

"I can see that you've had some kind of serious psychotic episode, Mandy, and it's going untreated down here. I want to take you back to New York tomorrow. I can get the best psychiatrist on Park Avenue to help you get back on your feet again. You've had a hell of a time here, I can tell." He spoke slowly without taking his eyes off her face, as if he could control her with the force of his will.

Looking at him intently now, she saw many fine lines that could easily be erased if he meditated even for a short time each day. Without thought, she said slowly, "I can hypnotize men, my friend, but I don't wish to advertise that to you now or ever again, but in the past you weren't aware that we were not the best of buddies. Isn't that true?"

"You're crazy, Mandy! We were an item in the old days. Everyone invited us to every event advertised in *The Times*. We were seen everywhere together, and when you up and disappeared, leaving me there…Well, I was driven to drink—I swear." He looked as if he was sincere, but his words came out as so much drivel that Mandy now found him offensive—not at all persuasive, so she let him have it with double shots. "I guess I do remember you—now that you describe it that way. You were somewhere on the way from one relationship to another, as I recall, but that was a long time ago. Why try to find me now? What's up?"

"Try to find you? Mandy, you're all over the papers now. No one wants to believe that it's you, but I always knew it was you! I haven't told the others, because I wanted to find out for myself that it really, truly is you. Once I got here it wasn't that hard to figure out that Mandy Sheriden is now Mandy Brown of The Maya, as the press likes to describe you. So it's with great sincerity that I say you have to get out of here fast, before you totally lose your mind, your career, and everything you ever had."

Mandy smiled sweetly and picked up the check placed beside his plate by the young waiter. "See? Here you pay up front—then you sit and enjoy yourself and know that nothing more is expected of you. Know what I mean?"

Upset with what he could not control and with this woman who did not seem to recognize him, he shouted, "No, I don't see what you mean! What a stupid idea! You chase away paying customers by giving them the check before they have a chance to eat."

Mandy winked at him and said, "Think about it."

While he thought about it or acted as if he was stunned with the changes he detected in her face and body, Mandy tried again to fill in the blank where his name should appear. It still did not register, so she decided he could not have been a friend in the past or she would have remembered his name by now. That click of a mental switch led to her decision to get rid of him immediately! Her favorite way to get rid of men who offended her or other women or just became pests was to dominate the conversation—have definite opinions, not listen to what they said—even if by some strange chance it was interesting. She could not control the smile that crossed her mouth when she said in her thoughts, 'It always works with jerks!'

"I can't seem to get your attention, Mandy. You do seem to be cognizant of what's going on around you, so let's just zip back to New York to see what's happening and visit this psychiatric friend of mine? You used to know her years ago, but probably can't remember her name either, since you've slipped quite a bit."

Mandy smiled as if tasting some delicious delicacy hidden on her plate of mildly spiced tortillas, slipping deeper into her mood. Quietly she said, "I know who you mean. We had a dream class together when I was 23 and thought I was clever. She went on to work in New York while I puttered around in LA and other places for a decade before joining her there--"

"See! You remember, but have selective memory. You just want to keep me guessing and make me upset--"

"No, Ronald, I don't!" If Mandy was surprised that she suddenly could fit the name to the face, she did not indicate it and continued to talk without guile. "I remember what's important, like who helps me, but I don't bother with the flotsam and waste that might otherwise tie up my life, or at least tie me up in knots for years. I'm free down here, and I work very hard, but you wouldn't know about that!" She threw down the dare along with her white linen napkin, but he refused to pick it up and run with it or go the whole nine yards or any of the other nonsensical things he said before arriving at his point of departure. The time was here when they could get mired in mutual declarations of hate if fate did not step in again, so she sat still and let him continue bragging about things she barely remembered as interesting goals before she stood and indicated she was through with lunch and wanted the waiter to take away their plates.

"—so you see, I'm doing great, and believe me, I have my share of women—always, but none of them is as wonderful as you were then. Believe me."

About to erupt in laughter, Mandy spotted Jorge crossing the patio to where she was standing and her 'gentleman caller' was still sitting. She waved Jorge over, but he ignored her as much as possible while attempting to conceal a smile that was now as obvious as a new decal on an old shower stall. (Who writes this stuff?)

"Oh, yes," said Ronald as he glanced toward Jorge taking a seat at a table near the gate. "I remember him. He used to be some kind of a clerk in New York—or was it Jersey?"

Amazed that Ronald would condescend to lie about another man, Mandy said sourly, "How would you know Jorge? Apparently, you have no idea who he is or you would never suggest that he was a clerk or an illegal alien when I lived in New York—or that you and I were ever an *item*."

Ronald turned his full attention to Mandy and attempted to smile as he said snidely, "You had him on the side even then. Didn't you? You used to act like you never noticed him watching us—like you didn't even know him. You never said a word because you were going at it with him after I left you! What a mistake to worry about you and whatever happened when you moved down here! Meanwhile, you're shacking up with that slick character, acting like you found some new religion, so you can con gullible, generous Americans like me into buying your junk and your bunk."

Mandy held up her hand, smiling at his lackluster bluster. She was not upset, because his spiel was nothing new from what others said who also claimed to have known her way back when, but she was extremely interested in what he had to say about Jorge. Had he been around her when she lived in New York? If so, this was really BIG news! So she said as sweetly as possible, "Ahh, look, Reginald--"

"That's Ronald!! As if you don't remember!"

"Ahh, yes, Ronald. What I'd like to get straight is how well did you know Jorge—and where did you meet him?"

Suddenly finding that he was interesting to this mysterious woman, whom he barely remembered and did not recognize at first, Ronald began to pontificate after deliberating over each word until she was ready to scream. Mandy held her temper in check and let him eke out each word. It took awhile, but she realized he had never met Jorge nor ever talked to him. His tenuous recognition was based on a hunch that Jorge was some kind of spy who passed himself off as a clerk, a waiter, or a drunk—using many disguises to get close to Mandy. She was thrilled by his disclosures, if not with him, but said little—only an occasional hmmm, just to keep him talking.

Finally, Ronald folded his beautiful, hand-woven napkin and surreptitiously checked to see if the waiter was watching before placing it in his pocket. He was startled when Mandy whipped it away and presented it to him as if a lavish gift. He was not that embarrassed, but he should have been. That napkin ended up costing him $50 by the time Mandy was done selecting souvenirs for him to take back to Cancun for whoever was waiting for him there. Being cheap, in addition to being a thief, he bought only the work of beginners from the various craft classes, but she charged him as if he purchased the master craftsmen's work.

Once Ronald left, Mandy was able to relax for the first time. Spotting Jorge sitting under the sentinel tree, she headed over there immediately.

With his usual urbane charm, Jorge said, "I see you had a handsome visitor."

"Yes, just one among millions of New Yorkers who miss me very much!" She was emphatic, but not smiling.

Jorge knew her well enough not to take anything she said seriously when she was in a mood like this. However, he was in a mood of his own or he would have snapped back with something in the same vein, rather than changing the subject. He appeared to be peering into the far distance—able to see someone approaching them. He said quietly, "Did he want anything in particular or just playing the fool as usual?"

In an effort to hide her amazement at another crazy turn of events, Mandy adopted his attitude and pace and said, "He claimed he just happened to be vacationing in Cancun and decided to 'motor over' and check to see if Mandy Brown was indeed Mandy Sheriden, whom he claimed was so very attached or attracted to him in New York."

Unsmiling, Jorge said, "And were you?"

Thinking, 'What a strange thing to say,' Mandy was not swayed from her determination not to share what had happened until she knew something new about Jorge, too, so she said, "Funny, but until I arrived the first time in the Yucatan, I was always known as Amanda Sheridan—not Mandy Sheriden, and I *never* thought he was a hunk—ever! What if there is a Mandy Sheriden living in New York? What if she was once attached to Ronald—or is it Reginald?"

Jorge jumped in too soon with: "Ronald." He immediately realized that he had tipped his hand and Mandy would pounce on it and wheedle him constantly until he told her all about what happened in New York way back then.

As he knew she would, Mandy with a hint of a smile started in. "Sooo, you knew Ronald, too? Interesting! He said you were a spy—that you watched us a lot. Is that true?"

In an attempt to end this trail of thought before it led them away from today and what he wanted to say, Jorge stated loudly, "No, I was not a spy! I was an emissary from the tribe."

"Oh, no you don't, Jorge. Ohhh, no you don't. You owe me some explanation about years past. I never got it all out of you then—about who you were and why I met you when I arrived here, and what happened before I arrived at your door. Come on, what's the real story?"

Jorge grinned and said, "Now that would take a book. Wouldn't it?"

Excited that Jorge might reveal what had to be said sooner or later—maybe even how he worked with The Ascended Maya and why, Mandy grabbed his arm and attempted to jump up and down while staying seated beside him under the huge ciba tree. With great enthusiasm, she said, "When do you want to start writing the book?"

"Not now. I'm too tired. There are too many people to feed and too many to keep on their feet."

Defeated by his tone, but unwilling to let the subject drop, Mandy said sadly as if about to cry, "You mean—keep on their toes. Please, can't you at least tell me why you were in New York when I lived there? Please…."

"All right, but that's all—and no more wheedling about the past. Understood? If you don't accept this with my limitations, forget it."

Jorge looked sterner than usual, so she did not push her luck and said softly, "Okay, but you have to admit that I have a right to know what happened back then."

Shaking his head, Jorge said, "Not really. We always know what we have to know and forget what is no longer of any use to us, but today you got caught up with thieves, so everyone who ever stole anything from you or you never noticed was a thief appeared so you would know them—and you did. You've grown much wiser over time, but you still ask questions—and that is not allowed. You know that."

Mandy did not rise to his bait. She sat still and waited for Jorge to continue.

✺ Chapter Twenty-Four

Seeking out a villain is no different from spotting a flaw in a beautiful glass vase. It takes clarity, plus a brilliant day and watchful eye to spot either, or so Wanda thought. Groping for a catchword or a phrase she could use to expose the spy who had disclosed her ideas before they were developed enough to explode with color, she knew for sure that one or two of the Mayan students were not who they pretended to be. They were not nearly as accomplished as liars as some Americans preferred to be while visiting them.

After one full sweep of the minute hand, Wanda began chanting about the day The Maya were betrayed. Indeed, she had revealed to a few that she had visions, but her mind was not able to sow seeds in times seen. Beyond that admission, she never told anyone she had the ability to initiate events in different cities and in various countries that would cause the world to sing again. Her mind was open now, so she let The Maya, as in olden times, come close and work within her.

As Wanda chanted, her fingers plucked and pulled at threads she wanted left at the corners—not to be used for quite some time. As she watched herself weaving, a crowd of fascinated Mayan girls surrounded her with their dark, intense eyes wide, wide open as if they, too, saw a vision of someone other than Wanda weaving on the huge loom at the front of the room. Not wishing to call this much attention to her personal work, Wanda said loudly to her students working on their strap looms nearby, "Please don't interrupt me for a few minutes. I'm going to rethread and need to pay close attention to what I'm going to do next."

When no one said a word, the Mayan women crept closer to better observe how Wanda prepared to weave. They watched as she worked silently pulling out some threads and inserting different hues in what might appear to be a random fashion, since she did not look at the threads as she pulled them from a bag at her side.

Seated among the Mayan women was one who could interpret dreams. She was much admired for all that she learned from the visions of those who actually had the dreams, but did not study them seriously. This shaman's work was not what most wanted to do, so they admired more than envied her ability to work on dreams without interruption or interference from any of the men. To be revered by The Maya of all times and the men seemed the only way to get ahead, nevertheless, few women wanted to learn anything new.

"I can see thread not being used…It's sitting in the back of the room. Please get it for me and put it on a spindle here." Wanda directed no one in particular, but one woman rose immediately, as if in trance. She went back and returned with a long skein of yarn that she began working into a more pliable form. Without glancing to her left or right, Wanda said, "That will go right here."

Each weaver was busy memorizing the size and color of each thread, as well as the configuration of the loom, without seeming to work that hard. When eager to learn, most of the American students worked differently. They usually started out asking so many questions that if Wanda stopped to answer them, her thread of thought would break. The Maya were raised to never ask rhetorical or unnecessary questions. They felt it was rude—so they listened intently when trying to learn something new.

To incoming students who wanted to excel and learn how to weave in the way of the Maya of ancient times, Mayan weavers appeared wiser and friendlier than the others—never rude to students from other nations and tribes. For this reason, newcomers sought them out whenever Wanda was not present or was busy at her loom, even when they might gain greater benefits from studying those who did outstanding work but were too officious to be appreciated by anyone nurturing a good opinion of their own work, too.

"When you're able to pull out *that* paddle, please don't," said Wanda without giving it any further thought.

None of the Mayan women would touch Wanda's loom or attempt to change a pattern, but they were aware that at least two women had changed how the pattern was laid out. As a group they wondered if Wanda would want to know about it, but individually decided not to tell her until asked.

"Make sure the warp count is right!" Wanda spoke while leaning away from the loom, thus inviting some to look more closely at what she was working on now.

One woman said very seriously and a bit too loudly to be believed by everyone in the crowd gathered around the loom, "I can see something you need to take out. It's not going to help the work flow. It might even create the wrong wave."

Wanda said nothing. Her students watched with total concentration until finally one whispered she knew what it was going to look like. Since Wanda appeared not to be listening, working silently as she usually did, the group relaxed and eased back to talk quietly among themselves as they watched her fingers fly up and down the fabric coming into view. Suddenly, in the middle of a sentence spoken without much thought, the talk stopped and Wanda tuned in just in time to hear one hapless girl say to another sitting close-by, "I know she did it. I watched her!"

"What did you see, my child?" Wanda spoke as if she had been listening intently to everything being said by everyone around her the entire time, because she had.

Intuitively, the group tightened its grip on what was being processed mentally, hesitating to admit they were no longer thinking about the pattern being woven—once again, even forgetting to work with Wanda intuitively as she carried over and pulled through brilliant threads quickly hidden within the intricate design. They broke the spell cast by Wanda and permitted stray thoughts to divert them from their work.

Understanding the problem, Wanda eased back in her seat and softly asked everyone, "What were you saying? I didn't catch the name of who you saw touching my loom." She was smiling sweetly, as if it was no big deal, but the Maya knew that the time had arrived to reveal to their master what had been bothering their minds for days.

An elder, wishing not to have a childish woman berated in front of everyone for something she did not understand, spoke up. "Miss Wanda, I have seen something—several times. I have watched and waited until now to tell you these things because I wanted to be sure nothing bad happens to you. We need to be sure that you're safe and secure—always. We're not here to learn about the patterns so much as help you pick out the colors and bits and pieces transmitted from those ancient Maya who are said to be lost in space." Wanda, staring into space, looked amazed as the elder added, "Do you know what we want to do next?"

Squinting, as if looking into the sun, Wanda smiled easily, as though it was common practice for her to stop and discuss such things while weaving or teaching a class. Since her mind was no longer overpowered by what was being channeled to her, she recognized for the first time that work was always easier when the Mayan weavers gathered about her. In a flash, she realized that she became fatigued—unwilling to stop and talk or teach when surrounded by people who were uninspired or doing poor work, and especially those who had too much to say about themselves—not like now when all the weavers willingly worked harder than any other new students in her memory to learn old patterns and correct bad habits. Assuming the American students did not know what the Mayan elder said due to a language barrier, Wanda chose not to reveal that she had her own spies and body guards protecting her and the work.

She adroitly changed the subject and directed the students at the back of the room to put aside their work. She told them to take a break and enjoy doing whatever they loved. Some lingered over their looms, but prepared to leave. Meanwhile, the Mayan women sitting close to Wanda were not excused and grew restless; some appeared to be upset that they could not leave with those they judged to be undeserving of a break. They were unaware that the elders, who never moved from their places standing against the walls, knew there was an enemy nearby. None of them knew if she was Maya or not, but they surmised she was not.

How can you look into the sea of belief systems and achieve a clean start with just one? Watch your heart! That is what The Maya do so well, but they were struggling to teach this to the present generation—until now. The heart harbors resentments whenever you are upset, which produces envy and jealousy, as well as the work you most desire.

As students continued to file out of the room, chattering about their reprieve from weaving all afternoon, the elders moved closer to Wanda. Watching their movements and picking up on their thoughts, she felt a sudden release of tension among them when the door closed after the last student passed through.

The weaver who usually spoke first said, "Miss Wanda, we see many things. We notice a lot. But most of it's not serious, so not nice to repeat. But we want you to know everything now…But we don't think you would like us to tell you about everyone we meet…" Her voice trailed off when she noticed how silent the room was now.

Unsmiling, with her mind open to whatever might be hidden among the Maya, Wanda took the fabric she wove the day before and placed it on top of the work she had been setting up for today's class. This was her way of demonstrating that no further work would be done by her that day. Letting her smile find its way across her mouth, Wanda finally said, "Thank you all. I'm so happy to have you all on my side—and I say that with pride. I have to admit that I'm not aware of anyone being unhappy with me or upset with what we hope to achieve, but I do sense at times something strange—something wide of what we want to do here and now. Do you all feel it, too?"

The elder who usually spoke for all the weavers said, "We are here to help you prepare the work for the public, Miss Wanda, but we're also here to protect you from whatever is out there." As she spoke, she pointed toward the world beyond the studio. Everyone's eyes followed her finger pointing to a woman standing outside the window laughing and imitating Wanda walking without her right leg.

Wanda said only, "I see," but the women were pleased because she knew immediately what had to be done and knew that they, too, were unhappy with people who behaved badly and showed disrespect to their teachers and elders.

Without dropping the hand pointing toward the plaza, the elder said, "We're not pure, and we're not without many problems. We also are very poor, but we would never discredit your talent or steal your work and ideas in order to gain power over you or anyone else—to get rich. That is not the Mayan way!"

Several women's eyelids drooped as they peered intuitively into Wanda, without appearing to do so, since this is not permitted by the elders. Wanda was to be given total privacy as the shamans watched to see if the woman outside their lives was aware she had been spotted by those she claimed to idolize the most—Wanda and the women elders of the tribe.

After a moment or so of deep intent, the Mayan weavers realized they had time for themselves and did not have to move away from what they came to do that day. The gates opened and several of the tribe stepped into time. The women left behind laughed loudly and heartily so Wanda could collapse and walk into time, too. They sat and talked about many things, including men, remembering to laugh loudly every now and then.

Once the room was thoroughly cleansed, the elders prepared to walk about in the evening with Wanda now suspended between the youngest and strongest of the maidens. She was now inhaling her first full breaths since falling into the deep trance. She smiled and the elders began chanting simultaneously the mantra Wanda had introduced earlier in the day. It ended in the most unusual way, and they could never speak of it again!

Instead of discussing the mental processes that erase memories of an event, they simply accepted that they forgot it. It happened more often than ever before to each of them, but not nearly as often as The Lords said it would occur when it was time for The Maya to assemble and ascend.

"I feel okay, really!" Wanda spoke as if out of breath and only now able to relax and get her mind aligned in this time. She was still entranced, but in such a light trance that she could dance and walk as usual, so the elders decided it was time to appear in the dining hall and drink the sacred chocolate that gave them all fevers. It was used as a cleansing drink, not something that can make the Earth speak.

It turned into just another working day for Mayan maidens in other worlds—not the kind men enjoy. Speaking to the women closest to her, Wanda said, "If we see rainbows and skies full of rain tonight, we'll know more about the enemy who is trying to defy the odds and defeat our cause." She no longer thought it odd that she spoke Mayan to one group and Spanish to others almost simultaneously, but the younger women questioned how any human being could change her mind so easily—and do it constantly. Wanda became a legendary woman of wisdom to them then.

Once outside the weavers' studio, having made sure that the hasp and lock on the door were secure, Wanda turned to her friends as if nothing strange had happened to her or to them and said with crisp good humor, "Let's eat dinner in the living room—by the fireplace. Won't that be nice?"

Immediately, one elder knew what to do and why, but the rest had to be led. They walked toward the dining hall after wandering by the open kitchen door and yelling out "*Hola!*" to friends and foes alike, waiting only long enough to see someone grin before they entered the wing with a large fireplace.

Speaking in English, because she wanted to loudly announce what the weavers and elders intended to do next, Wanda said to the first servers they met in the dining area, "I say, dear ladies, could we impose upon you all today? We would like to take our food into the living room. Will that be all right?"

Hearing the unusual request, the head cook immediately surmised a mystery was afoot and she wanted to find out as soon as possible what part she could play, too. She smiled, waved, and shouted to the elders to go and help themselves at the buffet table and feel free to take their plates into the living room. The rest of her staff stared in amazement at her willingness to permit something normally forbidden, but they said nothing because it was not like Wanda or their boss to do something that crazy without a reason, because neither of them was a lot like Mandy yet.

As the last of the elders and Mayan weavers trailed into the living room with their heaping plates of aromatic food, Wanda closed the doors, pulled the curtains over the windows, and motioned for someone to light the logs in the fireplace. Everyone else stood for a few minutes with plates in hand, waiting for Wanda to tell them to get comfortable on the floor and not stand on ceremony.

When the flames began leaping out at them, a few women fanned themselves as if unable to stand the heat. Wanda laughed in such a way that they immediately caught on that it was not an ordinary fire, rather a cleansing tool for all to use in a ritual later. Maya of today are unable to talk much about fire because many tribes do not keep the old ways; however, such traditions are kept alive among the weavers, who often pretend they know what to say *until* they say and do exactly the right thing—as though they had given it a lot of thought.

Wanda addressed the now quiet women watching her every move: "Working on the warp and weave of cloth produces many views of what life represents to you…Don't think we're all going to become rich, so it will come to be. If you wish for riches and then see them come to you, remember that it's a miracle! Which means you owe the universe prayers of thanksgiving for at least three miracles then!" She did not notice the look of relief in the eyes of three women, but felt something move beyond her mind in time.

The freedom of Mayan women is not known outside their inner circles, so anthropologists have often and loudly asserted that Mayan men run the tribe. It has never been that way since olden days when the men traded and spied and lost their pride in battle. They eventually were left behind, so their women took over and led them to do more and more of the work of The Lord rather than live in constant regret. If they had not led the men then, the Maya of today would be as dead as many of the other tribes seem to be now.

Working with the falling logs, pushing embers around, caused some sparks to fly out of the grate onto the skirts of two young weavers sitting too close to the fire. They hurriedly moved to safety as the elders laughed, but no one was really amused, because it was not a good sign. The elder who most often spoke of omens and such things when they chatted in the evening spoke to Wanda, but included everyone else, "I see women upset with you—unhappy about what they do. They are trying to set fire to your work. There are at least two doing evil to you now." Everyone was now riveted on watching the fire, because this elder was always the first to speak. She could hear Spirits talk before a thought even entered the door and moved around the room as it did now.

This thought wave moved as if it were the sun rising and setting on the tribe. The elder who usually spoke next said, "I see only two women! They hate to be told what to do—never think they need to be corrected…They hate you, Miss Wanda! They do not want to work as hard as you. They want what you have without working their whole life to earn it. Their hands are not callused enough to produce good work, but they refuse to work harder."

Out of turn, another woman interjected, "We're going to see them leave, but not before they try to steal your recipes, Miss Wanda." She then turned and addressed those who had laughed at her choice of words. "Yes, *they* say 'recipes' when they talk about our work—as if they're not talking about stealing our patterns from ancient times. It's like a code for them to talk about cooking when they're really talking about weaving."

One of the young girls whose skirt had been singed burst out with: "You're right! They talk about cooking every night. I never listen because I don't need to know what kind of mutton or whatever kind of lamb to cook tonight, because we always eat beans and squash at home."

Everyone laughed as it simultaneously flashed upon their inner screens the fact that each of them had witnessed such things, but had not put it together until now. Tonight they would put all the pieces together and rid themselves of whatever hampered their work individually and as a guild.

Another woman who was also not an elder said with wonder, "Mutton is old wool, and lamb would be the finest pieces of yarn we have carded."

Suddenly Wanda realized the elders were holding back—not concerned that the younger women were talking out of turn without their permission. This was indeed an amazing breakthrough! She was determined to not speak, but listen to what others uncovered as they wove the pieces of the mystery into a complete tapestry.

"As if that is not enough," said the weaver who was always upset and in a rush, "I get up every day and constantly run into that one who always talks about cooking and about what she had for breakfast—but it's not on the menu. Cook would never put such things out for us."

"Now we're getting somewhere," said the elder who normally would have spoken earlier, if the usual line of progression had run its usual course.

A woman usually blind to what the tribe wanted her to do, but recognized as a scribe by many not as wise as she about the tribe, asked another elder, "What say you about this today?"

The elder hesitated, as if she doubted what she was about to say, then said with certainty: "We can all stop now! We have no doubts at all about who is spying and why, but I would like to talk to Miss Wanda about it, before I pass my judgment on to you."

The other elders stood up and circled about her, asking what she intended to do about those who would feel left out if everyone left the room without saying a word. She was not sure, so they convinced her to settle her mind and tell what she found inside time.

After expressing extreme doubt about the suitability of talking in front of young women untrained in the ways of the ancients, she finally agreed and said very slowly, "I have never worked with women who have not converted."

The elder who usually complained about anything that was the least bit out of the ordinary or appeared to be weird, blithely said, "Don't worry!"

This reversal of roles was immediately noticed, so no one spoke until the oldest elder said, "Miss Wanda, you are very quiet. Have we hurt your heart tonight?"

Suddenly laughing, Wanda said, "I'm fine. In fact, I'm so happy I can't even find the words to explain how I feel. Do go on and forget that I'm around." She spoke as if she believed they could forget she was in the room and not of the tribe.

Those assembled did not forget Wanda's presence or worry about what she might say later as the room darkened when they decided all the women and girls present should stay and pray with the elders. No one really expected much to happen, because so many were new to the ways of The Maya, but it turned out to be one of the most fantastic nights ever witnessed by Wanda in her many lives.

☼ CHAPTER TWENTY-FIVE

Mandy stood talking to Wanda in the doorway as they watched women and men dancing and flirting and having fun in one of the weavers' workrooms that had been cleared for a celebration. Smiling, Mandy said, "There's nothing wrong with your hearing, Wanda, but there is something you should realize by now—about what you see in visions."

Wanda did not understand what she meant, so she waited for Mandy to elaborate or expand the thought, which she did. "I think what you see in visions is watered down when you translate it—or perhaps you're not really working with The Ascended Maya?"

Having dropped her bomb, Mandy laughed and patted Wanda's back as though she were merely teasing—not serious in her intent, but her eyes betrayed her seemingly playful actions. Anyone watching could easily see she was breaking bad news to a good friend.

Instead of responding, Wanda walked across her office to rearrange a curtain meant to screen her view of the outside world. Only then did she turn to speak. Mandy meanwhile pretended to read the spines of several textbooks arranged on shelves behind the desk. Suddenly wary, Wanda decided not to change the subject and instead said, "I don't know what you mean, Mandy. I've been seeing things all my life, but only lately started picking up on The Mayan Timekeepers. They come in a hurry—flow through me in a strong surge and then leave me exhausted. Do they do that to you?"

Still facing the wall of books, Mandy said, "You know what I mean, Wanda, but since you say you don't, I'll say this: You've been able to interpret your own dreams and visions without any problem for years, but you're not able to keep up with this new generation."

Definitely annoyed by what Mandy said about her interpretive and visionary skills, Wanda did not attempt to water down her response. "What new generation? You don't mean Gen X or whatever silliness marketers dream up—do you?"

Without her usual grin, Mandy said quickly but firmly, "Today there are many 'out there' working harder than you who want to travel to the stars and deliver messages that you can't understand, because you're not interested enough to study or work with The Maya."

Wanda spun around on her good leg to face Mandy and began gyrating her hips as though doing some kind of weird modern dance that required no rhythm or skill. As her hands moved awkwardly over her face it became apparent that she was doing the worst possible imitation of a hula dance, but Mandy refused to ignore what needed to be said. Her mood neither changed, nor did she even smile. Her refusal to respond as prompted caused Wanda to stop dancing and permit that thought to drop. Deciding that Mandy was way too serious and not ready to end her lecture, she intended to leave without waiting to hear what Mandy said about her latest efforts in making spiritual connections with The Ascended Maya and others.

As Wanda started to rejoin the party, Mandy stunned her by saying, "Watch out, Wanda! You're not going to be able to stand up to the pressure if you don't let up on giving away your power to everyone you meet now." Her response was to walk out of the office, so Mandy added, "You don't have the energy now to do all you came to do—but there is a power you can use that requires nothing of your physical body. Do you want to lose it? You can, you know."

Once headed out a door, Wanda normally could not reverse her progress without looking clumsy, something she tried to avoid, but this time she stopped and turned around easily and walked back into the office, slamming the door on revelers who were unaware she was even there.

Slamming the door did not reduce the pressure on her temper or give her an excuse for losing it, nevertheless, Wanda shouted in a slight Irish brogue: "I don't see why I have to be berated by The Tribe every time I try to do something new! Don't they get it yet? That if you can't move on a dime, you lose time!"

Mandy smiled a little at Wanda's naiveté before renewing her attempts to explain the ways of today's tribes. It took very little to convince Wanda that she did great work, but it was never easy for her to accept criticism of any kind. This was not the first time she had been reminded that she tended to push the tribe to appreciate her work, using methods she had grown accustomed to in the outside world, refusing to accept that such prodding and pushing did not endear her to many—especially the men.

Not famous for being patient, either, Mandy's smile tightened. Just before it evaporated completely, she said in a very reasonable tone, "Wanda, you have to realize that a coalition is always necessary when introducing new ideas in order to keep them out in front of the audience. They then assimilate into their own belief systems what is accepted by others present. Usually you reach consensus by bargaining and giving up what you thought you owned in order to gain the support of others. Consensus takes time! It's not easy to rule a tribe, but the ancient ones want you to stop and do what you can for yourself—then worry about those who come from afar to study your art. Can you see that now?"

"No, I don't see why I can't enroll students with art degrees directly into seminars and classes, so we can afford to buy materials we need to produce Mayan art. I'm being practical! These people want me to do spiritual work only—"

Wanda stopped because she suddenly saw that she had bought into a new deal, never realizing its full impact on her life until right now. Shaking her head, she said with reluctance, "I guess I really don't have any ability to see what lies ahead of us…I even lost my own way! How can I lead others in the new days ahead when I borrow ideas that are dead?" As she spoke she dissolved into tears, dabbing at her eyes with her sleeve.

Mandy was not watching Wanda as she said solemnly, "I don't think you ever bought into their lies, Wanda. There were several women, and at least two men, working on you to get you to change your mind, so they could sell work you all produced all over the earth at a huge profit. You can do that if you want, but they can't. Do you understand now? The Maya aren't impressed with The Suits. They looked into their hearts and saw dire needs not yet met inside their vests. They saw men and women so stressed and full of dread that they couldn't talk without repeating themselves constantly—even shouting as though the elders were deaf. These people stooped to being derisive about the age of some elders, as if they were wiser because they were half their age. Did you notice that?"

Wanda snapped back sarcastically, "No, I never notice anything, because I'm an artist! I'm not very smart, and I trust others way too much. Isn't that what everyone says about us?"

Recognizing the arrival of Wanda's nemesis, self-pity, Mandy patted her back and said softly, "Don't upset yourself over this, Wanda. We have many miles to go and have to drive faster than time to get around the next bend. Hold up your head and tell everyone you're going out tonight, then meet me in an hour at my Jeep. Pack a small bag and hide it in your purse." Mandy chuckled as if the size of Wanda's purses was a long-standing joke, but Wanda did not respond as she had hoped. She was unhappy and fully intended to demonstrate how much, so Mandy quickly said, "Don't forget, Wanda, this is your life. If you like, you can leave the tribe—again, but remember it's been your way to avoid change and never expect others to work as hard as you do."

Seeing no reason or vision to explain why they had to drive off into the night and stay away for a day, Wanda became even angrier and screamed: "I don't have to go anywhere tonight, and I'm not going to! I have my own life to live—and my own gifts! If The Maya want me to give up my art for a farthing, so they can tell others that my ways are not theirs—and I have to change, they can forget it! I don't want anything from any of them—I never have. I can read the stars and know who's out there and how far! Can you do that?"

Shocked by this unreasonable act of passion, unable to fathom what led her old friend to attack now, Mandy said nothing and walked into the washroom behind the office. She peered into the mirror above the sink where the students rinsed materials or washed their hands. Staring into her eyes, as though hypnotizing herself, Mandy reprogrammed her mantra as a way of clearing out any stray thoughts that might get in her way now. Before Wanda could wander away, she decided to let fly a few more ideas and let them sink into her friend's mind—before they went on this drive into time.

"I see you have a lot on your mind, Wanda, and your leg is bothering you again. Yes, you have the gift of vision, but you and everyone else can see only what you're able to accept…We want you to open your mind wider—and wonder more. We want to help you see more clearly, so you can prescribe what we must do as a tribe, but you have to be willing to do your part, too. We can't break the rules for you. We're not allowed to take over another person and use their gifts against their will. You have the power to refuse to help and go about your business—whatever it is, but The Ascended Maya will translate it as a desperate attempt to control their work here on Earth. You will not be despised for dropping the ball, but the local tribe may tell lies about you if you leave without a better explanation than you now have in mind."

"What explanation are you talking about? I'm not going anywhere! I have my art, my looms, my work, and my students, but the tribe always wants to tell me what to do!" Suddenly Wanda decided she was not being treated well by The Ascended Maya and the tribe, and she resented it—and them.

"Tut, tut! You're filling up with self-pity again. That's not like you now. You've got a personality that knows what to do to follow your nose, so let's go. Let's find out what you have to do to open up to more than whatever you saw before." As Mandy spoke, she washed a dish that she found sitting in the sink and put it on the rack to dry. She wondered why anyone would place a dirty dish there when it was easier to leave it in the party room.

Unable to drop that thought, she looked down at the debris she had wiped out of the dish and placed in the garbage. A spark ignited her mind and lit up the scene enough that she could see what had happened here recently. Now on full alert, Mandy noticed everything and knew instantly what it meant without having to reason it out. The unwashed dish had traces of peyote on it! Someone had attempted to poison Wanda, using her favorite dessert, but fortunately she had not eaten much because it tasted odd. Who wanted to taint their meeting, maybe even kill Wanda? Why would someone who had access to the mushrooms want to do that? Unable to pull in a picture of who placed enough peyote in the brownie to poison Wanda's mind, Mandy turned hesitantly toward her and said, "Something is clouding your future, Wanda. I can't see who is involved, but I know it's someone new, someone who is trying to take over your work. Can you see who it is?"

Sitting in her swivel chair, without any sense of what was happening around her or in the next room, Wanda tried to answer Mandy's question but could not. Her words were not slurred, but they contained rancorous thoughts expressed incoherently and loudly in disagreeable tones.

Wanda was clearly not herself, which gravely concerned Mandy. She thought back to the events of earlier this evening and mused: 'When did this first become noticeable? How did I miss the symptoms until now? All the signs were present that Wanda was not herself… She never talked so adamantly about her work—not like she did just now…and her sense of adventure always saves her when self-pity rises above acceptable levels set by her mind… For Wanda to argue about taking off with me to visit The Maya on the other side of the Yucatan or the other side of the world is inconceivable…Why didn't I see that before it came to this?'

Right then Wanda started choking on her words. All Mandy could make out was "Feel sort of hazy. Do you think I ate something that made me sick? I feel like my throat is closing." The croaking sound of her choking resounded in Mandy's ears as she contemplated what a gong might sound like when hit by a rubber mallet.

Hearing a gong bong nearby, in her mind or middle sky, Mandy said, "I can see you, Wanda. You're tired of all you've had to go through with this group… First, you had two women steal your patterns, then you had to demonstrate to the Mayan elders that you weren't who they thought you were, indeed much further up the ladder, and then these sales types came in—bamboozling you with talk of profits, not realizing you were a prophet… Thank goodness you're among friends again."

Her pupils dilated and her neck twisted, as if straining to swallow a large pill, before Wanda croaked, "Mandy, I don't know who you are—really. I can see you, but I can't figure out what you do or how to work with you. Am *I* being heard or are you just listening to what's coming out my mouth?"

"Here take this water and drink it all in a single gulp. I want you to go into the other room then and casually walk around the room until you come to the one who served you the brownie. Act natural and mention that you're not able to stay because you're feeling nauseous—want to throw up. That should alert whoever is trying to stop you from interpreting our work." Mandy opened the door and let the party noise explode into the office and bounce around the walls as she handed Wanda off to the first person standing beside the door. Wanda immediately went to work as directed.

Taking up a position in the doorway where she could watch Wanda's progress through the party, Mandy watched as several weavers rescued Wanda just as she was about to collapse or slip on something spilled on the floor. She said little to her friends, instead profusely thanked two women and a man for helping her earlier in the day. Immediately Mandy telegraphed to her, 'Which one betrayed you?'

At that precise instant Wanda swayed and flayed her arms every which way before suddenly correcting her gait and walking straight toward the punch bowl. Mandy thought, 'It's a miracle Wanda can even walk. The Maya are able to sense it, too.' She continued watching the group's mixed reactions to Wanda's strange behavior.

The dancers opened a path just wide enough that no one would bump Wanda as the music stopped. The musicians bowed and clapped as if she were the belle of the ball. No one resisted applauding or saying how good she was at her art, except the women who were often unwilling to follow her instructions. Then they, too, started clapping and shouting praises at Wanda.

Mandy came up beside her friend then and directed her toward the exit. She thought, 'How could they tell that Wanda was in a dream? You must be Maya to see or believe it.' As they stood at the door for a minute or so, Mandy laughed in an attempt to conceal the fact she was tracking bigger game. Waving merrily at the emcee, she shouted to everyone: "Thank you all for taking care of the party! I have to run a few errands on the other coast, but none of you has to leave. In fact, let the games begin! Please eat, drink, and dance until dawn—and don't forget to eat all the food. We don't want anything left over!"

Acting as though she was leaving the compound alone, Mandy surreptitiously watched Wanda walk home. She could not ignore the fact that her friend looked totally exhausted, maybe sick, so she called a young boy to escort Wanda to her door with instructions not to stay or bother her. He was quick to do so, returning almost immediately to ask Mandy if she needed anything else. Her mind no longer on full alert blocking viewers from her work, she said nothing to the boy, but he heard everything. His intrusion into her space was immediately picked up in her inner world. She was now aware that The Ascended Maya shared a life here and there, and were deploying more than little boys around the compound and in the villages nearby.

⋇ ⋇

Knowingly she blocked the driveway and left the car idling to indicate she would leave soon. A crowd of young friends strolling by decided she was not going to leave without taking along a few things they would gladly help her deliver anywhere. As they tramped into the main office to see what Mandy was doing, Wanda quietly slipped out of the shadows and into the back seat of the Jeep under a tarp without anyone noticing her. The little boy who was training to be a spy was close by, but even he missed her escape. He was miserable and cried in frustration when the men later called him to task for his lack of attention to his single mission.

"Put that in back. The backseat's already overflowing." Mandy said this as she locked the doors with her remote keying device. Having said the trunk was open, but it was not, first one and then another tried the rear door, but no one could open it.

"Don't worry about it. I have a spare key somewhere." She then fumbled in her pocket and produced a ring of keys the Mayan boys admired a lot. In their estimation, anyone with that many keys had to be rich and important to have so many things that needed to be locked up. When the music from the party increased, none of them heard the beep of the electronic key opening the lock. The door sprung open at Mandy's touch, and the men shook their heads and asked each other, "What manner of person is this Mandy?" No one had an answer—again.

An hour later, the village far behind them, Wanda came out of hiding to sit beside Mandy as she drove down the lonely dark roads. With nothing better to do, the two women began to laugh about the party. What came over them? You know. Women traveling together down a long dark road are bound to laugh at men. Neither mentioned what happened earlier or how Wanda had been taken by surprise by a Maya. Why? Because they knew it was inside their minds—locked away until the right moment to be enlightened. Nothing clicked yet, but when they found the key it would open their eyes immediately to the woman and man who betrayed not only Wanda, but Mandy—again.

"Mysteries make us think! We need to continually work on our powers of discernment. Studying the pictures of places unseen, yet remembered, can jog our minds a little in time, but if we see something and remember it for weeks and months, easily replicate it, that's a sign of keen abilities—a rare and great gift." Mandy talked easily to the woman about to fall asleep beside her—again.

Shaking her head as if to clear her thoughts, Wanda roused herself just enough to say, "Why would anyone want to poison me—and with peyote? I don't hurt anyone. In fact, I'm trying to help the tribe get beyond where they are in art—and force every other tribe alive to respect them now…so we can move up the search for those leaving Earth with us."

Mandy listened and wondered, but said nothing as she drove with ever-increasing speed toward the other coast, following the moon and hoping to keep up with it until she reached her home.

⚹   ⚹

An elder sitting in Mandy's living room, drinking hot chocolate from a cup of many colors created by one of Julie's student potters, said to no one in particular, "Without the ability to see into the future, we're doomed to worry about what is coming down the road that might ruin all we have ever done. We need to be able to see, so we can avoid a collision—or accept its inevitability without fear."

He was unafraid of anything he saw in visions or dreams, or so he said, but she was afraid. Without a trace of rancor about what this Mayan shaman had said previously about her work, Wanda said, "I see things that make me stop and wonder a lot. I stop the visions at times because I'm afraid something may overtake me, like those people at the other compound. They got into me without my noticing what they were doing or that they were enemies. If I try to fly and find myself in space without a base, how will I know who to trust—and what is right?"

"I think you're able to fly fine now, but you stop it—a lot." As Jorge spoke, he winked and gestured at Mandy to convey to the cook that he wanted something to eat, since she was usually very hungry after being in trance all day.

Unaware that Jorge and Mandy were communicating their desire for food rather than more talk, Wanda whined a bit more. "I think you might be right, but the speed gets me. I could just scream at how fast they jet me through time. I'm only getting used to it, but I guess I would be of more use to all of you if I did believe nothing will hurt me in time--"

"That would not be wise now, Miss Wanda," said an elder who usually was unwilling to speak up in any group of this size and intensity. This change in his behavior caused a few men, as well as Mandy, to look at him and wonder what he was up to now. When he said nothing more, they added a few thoughts of their own in hopes that he would continue telling them they were either right or wrong in their assumptions. They wanted to know what he thought, but he remained silent after that.

Wanda spoke to him. "Thank you, brother, for all you do. I feel quiet inside. I'm not Mayan, but I feel like I am Maya at times and," but before she could finish her sentence, several men jumped in and admonished her, which made no sense to her. She was told to be Maya and not let others influence her to forget or not recognize it as fact. She was told to delve into her own work and not worry about what others scattered over the Earth might want to buy from the tribe. Her response now was to feel wounded that the elders said so little about her personal work. She withdrew inside her pride until one of the women sitting and watching everyone said Wanda's art was so perfect that anyone would know at a glance she was Maya.

This statement went directly to Wanda's heart and she blurted out her pain. As she revealed how miserable she felt when no one commented or complimented her on her designs or how well she wove cloth or how many students conducted seminars in other countries—teaching the old ways now. The elders were stunned and amazed. They thought as one: 'How extraordinary are these Maya born on foreign soil!' But nothing was said aloud.

The mood changed then and some of the elders saw that Wanda's foot was swelling—a lot. They started praying that she would not have to lose that leg, too. Although concerned whenever her 'good' leg ached or swelled, she paid little attention to it and was unaware that anything was wrong with her one and only leg, so it was a shock to hear that the main artery of that leg was blocked—a lot.

"We see many things, and this bad peyote was meant to block your brain, but it did not. Instead it moved blood down into your foot, and then it was not pumped out again as easily as it went in. We will put a poultice on your leg. You will be as good as new," said a toothless elder who was unable to talk without lisping a lot.

Tears welled up in Wanda's eyes and began to pour over their rims as she shouted without thinking about others who might be sleeping, "Thank you! Thank You! Thank you all! Without you around me, I know I would've lost this leg, too. What will happen if it ever comes to that?"

All the elders remained silent. No one wanted to mention that it had happened once, and she had adapted to it. Instead they prayed and asked God to create faith in her mind over time.

Their silence reminded Wanda of how tired she was, so she left them to climb the stairs to a room with a view where she went to sleep without worrying about what others might want from her somewhere down the road. For now, she could see her future was not a problem—at least not for a month of so. That was her view and her own interpretation of the vision—not what The Maya expected.

In addition to being an artist, Wanda was a perfectionist and accustomed to greatness—and being recognized for it. So for her it was unfathomable that she would ever give up working harder or seeking to become greater until she was either dead or rising with everyone on the other side.

✵ CHAPTER TWENTY-SIX

"Thank you all for the wonderful gifts you've gathered for the Maya. We'll deliver them in a few days and offer up something that you'll feel in your bones rather than in the usual way--" Teri couldn't say anything more for fear the tears hanging on the ends of her heavily made-up eyelashes would trickle down over her cheeks and ruin the illusion of her 'natural' beauty.

"I want to add that the Maya of the Yucatan have benefited very little from the surge in tourism in their area—in fact it's hurt them a lot. Many Mayan youth are now tempted to pursue capitalism, and we know that is not what works best when you're just getting started in your art and there's no one to buy your work but family and friends. We admire the industry of the Maya, but we also admire the way they keep their home fires burning and do what they can to keep the old traditions alive within their families and clans. All of us here would be crushed if a bomb hit and took away our electricity, for example, but not them. We think we're so advanced, but we're far more dependent on others than the Maya are, yet we've been far less interested in making our country safer for our families, until recent events forced us to do so, even so many give no thought to what might happen if a natural or man-made disaster struck our lives."

⤖ ⤖

'Teri looked fabulous,' according to the morning paper, and quoted her as saying she was going to remove herself to a tribe where she could spend the rest of her life working on promoting their work rather than her own career. That seemed to please many people as they drank their tea or coffee or walked around their office, but some were envious enough to scoff and say it would never happen and, besides, Teri sounded Anti-American—like a communist. That was meant to sever all connections to her, but lies never break ties made of love. Friends come through the veil to rescue you—over and over again.

Setting aside the newspaper, Teri pulled out a battered notebook and opened it to a fresh page. After a moment or so she began jotting down notes she intended to flesh out later, before she spoke at the Governor of Yucatan's mansion. Her girlish scrawl was not easy to read, but she had no interest in making it easy for others. She wrote:

> *At times intelligent life dims and no one appreciates those willing to start over or recover from whatever held them in bondage in the past. For this reason, the Maya are not willing to give up tribal life—at least not now.*
>
> *On behalf of the Maya and myself, I am not telling you what to do or asking for much. I, we, prefer to live and work and do what we're able to do—every day.*
>
> *When I can sit and look at what has been done, then I will congratulate the state and celebrate. But until that work is on display, so to speak, not just talk about what will be done—or worse yet, what we need to do, I…*

At that moment a man approached Teri and laughed loudly enough to interrupt her thoughts and stop her work on the speech notes. Glancing up at him and then looking down at her notes again, she did not acknowledge his rudeness or nearness. The man knew his attentions were not wanted, but he denied his sensible side that urged him to walk away and opted to follow a winding, windy path and did something stupid instead. Speaking loudly as if she were elderly, hard of hearing, or possibly did not understand English, he said, "What was a beautiful super model like you drinking or smoking when you decided to run away to live with some godforsaken tribe that doesn't even have running water?" She continued to ignore him, so he moved closer to her table.

Several men also waiting in the airport lounge reserved for elite passengers jumped to their feet. Suddenly, Teri was the center of a passionate defense orchestrated by unknown men. They were dark-skinned, yet their skin was more olive in tone than Asian Indians. It was then that she realized who they were and relaxed because she recognized them as Arabs who lived on her block in the Village. They had talked to her several times when she walked her neighbor's dogs. Their defense rested before anyone learned more about Teri than they already knew, and just as an airline agent opened the door to the jetway and asked everyone to gather their hand luggage and board first class. Airline personnel avoided looking at her directly because they knew she was angry and not likely to stay quiet about their lack of security and/or interest in the safety of women passengers traveling alone on their airline. Perhaps looking down and away, never meeting her eyes was their idea of tact? She rapidly jotted down a thought about that:

> *Upon arrival in Houston, the elite deplaned and no one complained to the airline about the rudeness they experienced along the way. After all, it was first class and this is as good as it gets—so it had to be great. Right? After all, we can only imagine what the herd in the back had to put up with during the flight??*

Teri wrote more in her diary, but scratched most of it out. Unhappy that her trip had become weird and conflicted, she added in the margin in her signature green ink:

> *But what can a woman traveling alone expect—really?*

As the plane rose into the sky and pursued a general southerly direction, Teri relaxed and accepted the material world for what it was and what it meant if she ever returned to it again. Picking up the plane's phone, her first words to Mandy were to the effect that she was excited to be leaving the plastic world she had created around her façade—able to finally use her mind for something other than making money.

In this reality, Teri was still bewildered by her sudden decision. For a minute or less she looked into time and visualized a garden of roses outside a chapel where a group of nuns were talking about something that had to be done. Her thoughts continually changed from the obvious to the arcane as she daydreamed on the plane. She was not in Mexico, as far as she could see in the visions, yet Europe was not obvious, either. Maybe it was really France she was being guided to travel to and make her home now? Why? What was ahead of her? Who would she talk to about getting a house and garden in the country? Where would it be? Could she live happily ever after now? What about running water?

Her diary slipped to the floor and the flight attendant picked it up carefully so as not to appear to be reading it. She made no comment and Teri wondered about how this airline compared to what she normally used—until now. Why did one country nationalize and another privatize their airlines? Obviously they all wanted to rob the public and gain financial advantage for one man or one clan or whatever. Not wishing to remain actively involved in political games, Teri encouraged her mind to move out of this line and into time. She left her body safely strapped in a leather seat as she lifted off into the sublime—unfettered, to walk in her own world among the clouds.

"I think I can see you," said someone in the clouds around her. Teri could not identify the voice. It was quite high, had a heavy accent, as if the speaker was a French national. Since her mind was lost in time, she trusted Spirit would assist her in safely reaching her destination and help her do whatever she was called to do there, too. Her trust in God produced a rosy hue around her body while it rested within the plane, and several passengers complained that the smell of roses was too strong for them to appreciate and wanted it eliminated immediately.

At that moment, Teri transpired into Thérèse and no one present recognized her departure or arrival, except her mind. Would she become a new person when she arrived for a brief stay in the Yucatan, before settling wherever The Lord guided her to provide for a little tribe of children who had been orphaned in time by women who believed tourists would take care of all their needs?

As the plane jetted to its next destination, Thérèse took Teri's place in first class. She was serene, undisturbed by the service or whatever anyone else might do around her. Unaccustomed to jet planes and modern conveniences, Thérèse sat and watched with great curiosity—entranced by everything she saw. She marveled inwardly at how others seemed to be in constant motion—unable to relax, always needing something, unable to converse, often uttering curses. She observed these things, but did not worry about what they might mean.

Noticing the notebook laying in her lap, she put it inside the handbag that bore her name on a tag. She thought, 'As a servant of The Lord, I am to go where I am needed. This woman has asked me over and over again to help her, to do something through her that no one else has ever done before... I am a humble servant—not a great saint... It is going to be very difficult for me to work as she did in a view that is not of my own time... I wonder how we can change so easily at times and then we cannot move beyond our work on Earth until God finds us another place?'

The plane landed and Thérèse continued sitting until the flight attendants entered the compartment to hastily pick up whatever had been carelessly discarded by the first-class passengers. The first one to notice Thérèse still sitting as if in trance panicked because she distinctly remembered this seat being occupied by a very beautiful and famous model—or was she in another seat? The stewardess peered into the face of the woman to see if she was sleeping or sick or possibly dead and saw only the pallid complexion and slight bloom on the cheeks of a woman who obviously never actively pursued life in the sun. She told the others that this passenger was about the right age, but definitely was not a model! No one knew who she was or when she got on the plane, and that really worried them all.

The pilot pulled the attendants aside to debate what to do with Thérèse since they had to take off almost immediately for Houston and return to their own busy lives. When the first-class steward tried to interrupt the captain, he was ignored, but when all three attendants started talking as one—ignoring him, he decided to make an executive decision and assert his authority immediately, or so he thought. Deepening his voice, he demanded that someone explain what was delaying their deplaning and why they were complaining. Without waiting for an explanation, he expressed disappointment that they were so easily upset by a woman obviously content to wait quietly on the plane until everyone else got off. Since he was in command, this passenger had to get moving right now and they had to stop their nonsense. He could see she was no ordinary woman, but he did not recognize her. Speaking slowly now, with as much sincerity as me could pretend, the pilot said, "What seems to be the problem, ma'am?"

Thérèse directed a radiant smile at him and the pilot thought she looked familiar—maybe a famous actress, someone he had seen on the screen. He quickly moved to unfasten her seat-belt and help her to her feet, which released everyone else to do their work and leave him to manage this odd woman.

"I feel strange," said the passenger who was no longer young, but definitely not old, either. She appeared regal, like someone used to ruling or had a lot of money—really old money, maybe her only claim to fame.

As the pilot escorted the seemingly-frail woman toward the door and the jetway beyond, he said, "You look a bit pale."

"Thank you for helping me. It will take time to acclimate myself to this world."

The pilot absent-mindedly agreed with her because Mexico, in his estimation, was an alien planet he never wanted to visit. He did not say it, but Thérèse knew he did not understand Spanish and did not wish to learn, thus he felt insecure. She was also somehow aware that his habitual ways and mores were different from Mexican men. He saw them as shifty and believed they felt the same about him. As she continued to explore his mind through time, he continued gently pushing her out of his area of responsibility and onto the jetway where someone else from the airlines would take over and get rid of her. He was quickly growing tired of being considerate to a woman who would never be interested in him. He wanted to have fun, not escort an old frump.

The strong hands that stretched out and rescued Thérèse from the pilot were very brown, and her nails were not carefully manicured, but love and competence exuded through her hands. This woman was not just doing a job, she loved her work, so she was finally able to relax and laugh.

⊁ ⊁

As days passed in Mexico, Thérèse sunbathed and worked in the weaver's compound without experiencing any major problems adjusting to her new life. At first she felt the compound was far too open—not quiet and private enough for her to feel safe and secure, but the Maya respected her. They would never offend anyone as kind and lovely as she. Her extreme modesty was also noticed. No one mentioned it since it was their way, too. At least they were all supposed to behave that way.

When Mandy finally arrived she found Thérèse sitting in the outer garden feeding a pair of blackbirds who heckled and hectored her for more and more popcorn than she was willing to feed them on demand. Mandy was elated that Thérèse had arrived to work with the tribe, instead of her old friend, Teri, the super model. She smiled and opened her mouth to say 'Hi!' but said instead, "What do you say when you're not sure what you'll find out?" Thérèse responded by looking at her as if they had never met. Mandy wondered about it for a second, then decided not to worry and just act as if this is exactly what she expected to find.

Thérèse vaguely recognized Mandy as an old friend, but was not sure which plane she was on then. Her feet seemed to be standing on solid ground, but she noticed only then that her heart was pounding loudly, so she must be back on Earth!

Not sure how to respond to the vacant glance her words induced, Mandy shifted into her higher mind and said, "Dear, dear Thérèse, how wonderful to see you again! I would like to take you to my home today. You are long-awaited, but we won't leave until we've eaten and talked about what you want done here and now."

Thérèse blinked, suddenly recognizing Mandy. She laughed sweetly and said gently to this woman of The Maya, "I see you're as brown as the Maya now. No one would ever believe you're American, and I think that is exactly what you set out to achieve. Is it not?"

Caught off-guard, Mandy smiled and stumbled over her words until they caught up with her thoughts. "I thought, I mean, I was anticipating that you would be tired—not able to do much at first—not as much as you want anyway. What I guess I mean is, that we're all eager to get started, and no one knows what to expect, but we're ready for anything and hope you feel the same."

"That sounds promising, but I'm not sure exactly what I came here to do. Do you know?" She was so sweet and unique that Mandy started thinking they should not leave until she had more time to get to know her new, old friend better, until Thérèse whispered that she wanted to move quickly into the countryside—away from the spies.

The startling disclosure that there were spies operating in the weavers' compound now came as a shock to them both, but only Mandy knew what it meant. She decided not to stop to eat now, instead put on an act like she would stay for at least a week—not leaving immediately. Arranging with an intermediary on the housekeeping staff, she stated she wanted her place thoroughly cleaned and then have her bags brought in from the car—not the other way around. Everyone on staff was pleased to see she was not leaving—at least not immediately, but it turned out to be a ruse Mandy often used.

Removing a rose from the vase beside her chair, Thérèse adjusted its stem and felt the power of anticipation and change, but not the hour it would bear fruit and she could once again see within her heart the consummation of this holy gift from God. The work of an entire day was done in a moment, so there was no reason to sit in the garden any longer. However, Mandy did not wish her to alert anyone to what they were planning in the event someone was watching them now.

Mandy sauntered toward the pool, then back toward the wall, and then toward the parking area where her Jeep sat. As soon as she determined how many seconds and steps it would take for them to depart in haste, she said loudly to Thérèse, "Let's check the mailbox and see if anything's come in."

Thérèse was not surprised when Mandy took her arm as they walked toward the gate, urging her to move toward the Jeep rather than the mailbox. She gave no thought to things left in her room or what she would do without them as she moved with hesitant steps, closed eyes, and hands outstretched, as if being led blindfolded toward some pleasant surprise. When she finally opened her eyes to see what existed beyond the gate, Thérèse noticed immediately the pungent smell of rotting papaya. Why? What did that tell her about the compound and its staff that was in stark contrast to how they treated her since her arrival?

Mandy opened the passenger-side door and encouraged Thérèse to sit down in order to better admire the Jeep's interior. Quickly closing the door, she appeared to leap over the hood and jump into the driver's seat without any hesitation or circumspection. What gave Mandy such energy? She never asked questions.

As the engine fired up, Mandy quickly ran through the gears and picked up enough speed to race down the lane. Once on the Federal highway, she realized Thérèse was not strapped in—safe from any sudden stops. Her alarm immediately dissolved into laughter, because they were in no danger. She was now in the presence of a saint!

☼ CHAPTER TWENTY-SEVEN

Note: Thrifty people seldom think about what they're doing to save and reduce waste, but if they start noticing what others do, they usually shake their finger (mentally or figuratively) and begin feeling different about themselves, too. Knowing this, why would you judge others?

Glancing over her hand-written notes, Jeanne thought about her upcoming meetings with men who would be taking part in their new production. They wanted to spend lots of money advertising before anything was even ready. She was positive they were wasting precious revenue accrued by the busy fingers of the Mayan women, so she spoke up and made a few men angry and unwilling to listen to her explanation of what The Ascended Maya wanted her to do, and them, too.

Speaking out, as if someone else was in her office, Jeanne said, "I lost my mind!" Prone to talk to herself, she even argued at times if it served her purposes, because as a writer, she believed her own beliefs were not valued until they appeared on paper and were read by others. She often talked out her thoughts before writing what hung together best, but this time she was not composing—just talking. "I don't see how these men can spend, spend, spend, and never get anything done!"

Wrinkling her forehead while looking in the mirror, she laughed at the image of great worry and concern she saw there. "I do look like an elf!" She said it without conviction, pretending it was as funny as when the men said it at meetings. Speaking to the image in the mirror as if another person, Jeanne smiled and said, "If you want to clown around, wear makeup!"

Amazingly, she felt a sudden surge of inspiration and the urge to put pen to paper and write another syndicated column about life in The World of Tomorrow. She was looking for a comfortable place to sit and write for a few hours when she heard voices outside her door. A couple was arguing, so she waited for them to leave before letting herself slip into the state of mind where she could write without having to edit much. They were now standing outside her window, talking heatedly and growing more animated than is wise for lovers trying to hide from prying eyes and ears. Thinking about an image from her own past love life, Jeanne started laughing. She wanted to yell and tell them to stop hiding their true feelings and just be themselves, but realized they probably could not expose themselves now. They were probably married or had accepted proposals from others. Was love what made *The* Maya wise? They were not like people hiding without reason from what others might think or say about their lives.

Twisting her hair between the fingers of her left hand, Jeanne watched as she returned to a time many years earlier when she, too, flirted and wanted men to hold and care for her, because it seemed the easiest way to live then. She knew now why she felt that way then and hated to agree with those who believe it is merely a stage in every woman's life—and just happens. What else can explain that once through menopause most women never again think about men that way—perhaps do not feel as much rage, either? Men in their teens are not urged to give up their freedom like women of the same age, so they appear tougher, more independent and confident. Later, women want that kind of freedom in their lives and force men their own age to pursue younger women who will, in turn, give up their dreams to feel secure enough to have children.

Her mind ran down a long list of stories she had submitted in the past on the many aspects of love. This one would have to be different or it would not get past the censors who read every page she sent to the local papers for distribution here and in The States. How to write without offending the elders and others who wanted society to remain as stable as possible in a world that was slowly going to pot?

A voice from somewhere in time said, "You'll feel fine if you move down a few lines and let the introduction write itself—after you're done with the entire work of art."

When The Maya arrived in time, they usually did not announce themselves to Jeanne when she was alone. She often felt weird—slightly tired, as she sat and scribed or dreamily did as she was told from somewhere in time, but her recent work was totally different from what she wrote in The States. Many of her perennial critics said it was taking on a new flavor "due to being translated from Spanish." She laughed at their sophistry because she still wrote everything in English and translated nothing.

The voice spoke again, a little less softly—a bit more directly, about what she needed to do immediately, but her hand refused the pen. Jeanne watched as she stood and walked to her computer and opened a new page, observing as she sat and placed her hands lightly on the keyboard. She was further amazed to watch her fingers rapidly type—not stopping to make corrections. It all happened as if magically! She knew what was being written only after it was typed; however, nothing remained in her conscious mind, instead it was stored in some other world.

Within half an hour the essay that would become her syndicated column was written, and she was amazed at the results! No one could criticize it as illogical or too anecdotal, because nothing was said about any individual. It was as if the entire society merged and she wrote about everyone from a detached, very wise perspective. She did not describe one person having trouble after a birth or a single woman, living alone without a man—wondering what a husband would have done if he was there, or an old man who no longer felt he was wanted by his children. Instead, she visualized everyone living together as one single life. There was very little anyone could criticize about this work. In fact, even her super critical, editing mind did not want to change it!

Jeanne suggested to no one physically present in the room, "What if I wrote like this every day?" As the answer spiraled into space and appeared to rotate in her mind, she fought dizziness for a brief time before writing at the bottom of the page:

Work as if you will never be able to speak of all you must do and be. Say only what you need to say to get others to obey, or listen, or work as they are paid to do. Never take upon yourself the burdens of others! Let them surface and work alone until they admit that only God can help them with whatever.

Shaking her head slowly, Jeanne said, "That seems harsh." She opted to not review anything until she could see the entire picture, because the urge to write was surging through her again. How many hours would it take to get everything scribed? Should she write until she felt faint with hunger or thirst?

The inner voice responded with: "Write until Spirit provides nothing more." A lot more poured forth, but Jeanne felt she could not find the words to put it all into thoughts. As she trance-formed she wondered how her work arrived at this stage without any formal training or education in the way of The Ascended Maya. The answer arrived immediately loud and clear: "You are Maya!"

Hearing the words, but not understanding their meaning, she wondered about the importance of being Maya—having heard it said occasionally about people who were not born of today's tribe and not exactly the type you would readily identify as being wise when you met them outside this world. Immediately, Jeanne began typing again...

The exterior of a woman or man is not what you think it might be, rather a ruse to get you to stay away or come closer. Can you approach a man busy at work? You can, but his interest in you will be greatly reduced. Only those who are dense would seek out such a person to listen then.

Jeanne laughed as she reread the prose, then let her fingers continue typing as before without any apparent signals from her own creative mind...

When a woman wants to meet a man, she goes inside her mind and thinks about all the men who ever abused her, and then too often decides to quit working at being her best person.

Jeanne did not readily accept this idea, but let it stand as is and continued to watch her fingers dance across the keyboard...

What I see when I am with new people is not their personality but the image they project. However, they are unaware that their personality shows through even when they do not wish it to appear.

She immediately noticed that this line was not as spontaneous as the previous seemed to be, so she stopped and looked at her hands and wondered about the words. When nothing more appeared, she moved away from the computer and let it go to screen-saver mode. Her eyes were not open wide, but she noticed an image of a person standing alone at her window—on the other side. Was it one of the lovers? Had they fought until one left the other? She could see nothing distinct, so she decided to peek and find out who was out there...but then thought it would be nosy to peek. She often carried on such debates in her mind.

Finally, she spoke to the overall view rather than the small woman she saw standing on the verandah just out of ear shot. "Hmmm, I wonder if I should take my umbrella or not?" Without another thought, or so she wanted to believe, Jeanne pushed the window outward and spoke to the woman standing nearby. "Are you okay? I didn't realize anyone was standing here when I opened the window."

Her lie was over and done with before she saw the woman's smoldering eyes leap into flames and penetrate her mind to easily confirm that she was lying and had wasted her integrity stooping to do so. Feeling more than a bit chagrined that she had lied for no good reason, Jeanne said, "Won't you come in?" Jeanne wanted to make amends, so she smiled sweetly.

The young woman shot back a look filled with hatred and disrespect. This was weird—a reaction unlike anything she had received from other young Mayan women. Her lips collapsed into a grimace as she stared back into the insolent face before her, but she did not budge from her perch nor close the window, instead choosing to wait for the other to either speak or leave.

As time moved silently toward what is often referred to as the future, but not by the Maya of this time, the woman said nothing. Jeanne felt the pressure of her own societal upbringing urging her to end the silence. She felt compelled to speak, until she remembered what she had written only a few minutes before she noticed the woman standing outside her door. With those words in mind, she remained silent and watched the woman as though she might be a thief. The power of this negative thought forced the woman to turn and walk toward the dark side of the pavilion.

As her eyes followed the woman leaving the compound, appearing to be headed toward the village, Jeanne thought, 'What do you suppose she was up to?' When no answer came to her mind, she began putting her work away and thinking about that day. It had been so strange that she had completely forgotten what the men suggested at the meeting. It seemed long ago, before she started writing in spirit, before she became preoccupied with the woman lurking outside. Perhaps she was once again diverting attention from her work so as not to deal with the meeting? In the past she often suffered from what some called 'writer's block' when faced with an unwanted problem or an overdue assignment. Normally she explained it away as not organizing her time well, or writing without a legitimate cause, or having no interest in what had to be said to be paid. What was the reason now?

The day ended before Jeanne closed her office door and locked it. She told others that she locked her office because her computer might be stolen, but it was really because of the inner work now being given in stages that she wished to protect from prying eyes and spies. She was unaware that the hate-filled woman was back, watching her as she said to the heavens: "The way to become a scribe is not as easy as it seems to be."

Seeing something in the corner of her mind, Jeanne walked toward the kitchen where she thought Mandy might be hiding out from tourists and others. She was happy to see that her hunch was right once again. She shouted as she opened the door, "Hey, Mandy! What's going on? I heard a couple fighting outside my office earlier, then later the woman—at least I think it was the same woman, was lurking outside my window. When I asked her what she wanted, she gave me such a look!"

Mandy gestured that she did not know what to make of it, either, indicating that Jeanne should let it go and forget it. Her shrug suggested it was nothing, but it was. In fact, Mandy immediately began to shiver and shake, thus alarming the women baking bread for tourists to take home with them the next day.

A tour guide walking into the kitchen right then said with grave concern, "What's wrong, Miss Amanda?"

Not wishing to express her concerns with a comparative stranger, Mandy forced a smile and said without conviction, "Nothing, Emanuella, just a pain in my side—my liver, I think."

The bakers made noises as if Mandy said something funny, but their eyes never left her as they casually blocked the tour leader from moving closer. The woman intuitively understood that this was none of her business, but she wanted to see what was going on in the kitchen, so she spoke to no one in particular. "Did you ever think about how much the women in the nearby villages envy all of you—living here like you do?"

Immediately Jeanne saw it all and knew what was wrong, but she acted as if such an idea had no validity and was of no interest to her or the others. She shrugged and replied quickly that Mayan women are very gifted but modest, and no one could say one clan had it easier than another, because it was not the Mayan way to boast or compare what you owned or did in your home to others.

At this rebuff the guide rejoined her group standing nearby, even though she obviously was unwilling to end the discussion on that note. They could barely make out what she said to her clients waiting outside, but instinctively felt she was being rude again. All the bakers nodded at the same time, as if having reached a consensus of opinion. They continued measuring and sifting flour—doing whatever with it, as they watched Mandy and Jeanne walk towards a bench under the sentinel tree in the herb garden, apparently intent upon watching the night arrive in quiet contemplation and prayer. Right then Jeanne furtively asked Mandy, "Do you think she might be a spy?"

Barely moving her lips, Mandy said, "No, I think she's here to rescue someone… that man you heard her talking to wasn't a friend of hers or mine. She wanted him to stop bothering her—or she wanted him to leave. It was definitely not a lover's thing." Mandy's face brightened with a smile that lit up the area around them, then said a bit louder, "She's not a spy, but I think she wants to write. She wants to have access to you and what you do—maybe even get into your computer, but she doesn't know how to pursue it. Because you can really write and are much admired by others, she hates you, but she isn't crazy."

Shaking her head, Jeanne mumbled, "Jealousy and hate are everywhere now. You think you can escape it by moving out of The States, but it's always there—staring you down, wanting your career, but not willing to do the work. When will it ever end?"

With a chuckle meant to end such worries, Mandy said, "You don't want it to end just yet." They sat in silence for a few minutes, until both intuitively decided what they would do about it the next day.

☼ CHAPTER TWENTY-EIGHT

The years went by in a rush and the tribe trusted them very much, but there seemed to be an awareness that everything was being done to prepare for a single great event—not to create a way of life that might compare to what The Ascended Maya had lived once. What was the reason for all these women and men working together, if not to prove that The Maya were ready to move?

Speaking to the director of her newest settlement, Mandy said, "In the next few years we'll open to news of The Ascended Maya and what their calendar reveals—or not, but we know there will be many men and women unprepared to ascend at the end. So what can we do about them?"

"I think we should continue to act as we do and work through the patterns actually being used, then see what people do with it before we do more." Wanda talked as she passed her shuttle back and forth creating a new piece of woven matter.

"You may see things in the weave that we don't, Wanda, but what if we all look at it and miss the way we're supposed to behave?" Although Mandy appeared to be speaking rhetorically, she expected Wanda to respect the intent—not how it was said. Mandy often regarded her own inner visions as being esoteric—not founded on work that will come into fruition in this world. She wanted everyone to love and use *their* intuition as much as possible, too, so she taught through thoughts a lot. It never was quite the message others wanted from her—or the present Maya, whom the world seemed to idolize now and even tried to mimic at times.

Looking quite serious, Wanda applied a new thread to the intricate web of yarn displayed on the loom. Her hands never shook and her mind seldom wandered, but she waffled a lot when discussing time—like now, so she asked, "What do you and the elders actually do when you sit and talk for days?"

Mandy tried to sidestep the question to avoid talking too much, but Wanda was not easily diverted from any thought she wanted to pursue, so she said, "What do you want to know?"

Pulling an errant thread out of the way, Wanda said, "I want to know if you talk about levitation and such--"

"Stop! That's not what we talk about, Wanda. What we're doing now will be given away soon enough. You might not like what we do, but it's easier for someone of your hue to see into the new 'future' than people of a darker hue who aren't as able to sense what they came here to do." Mandy stopped speaking in order to look into the mirror across the room to see who was talking through her then. She saw a dark-skinned woman peering back at her without any idea that she had been spotted by Mandy.

"What are you actually saying, Mandy?" Wanda stopped weaving and speaking when she noticed Mandy was not listening—again. This time her attention was diverted by a form or vision or something not terrestrial. Mandy had always had a strange way of walking into the future or wherever it was she went at the oddest times, but lately it was becoming more and more her usual behavior. As she sat and waited for her friend to relate where she was, Wanda wondered aloud, "What is she up to now?"

Without much thought Mandy returned to the idea that had caught her attention when she identified the woman in the mirror as beckoning to her to do something new and said, "What happens when you leave your mirror image or your life work and do something different—totally new to you?"

Not sure what her mentor and friend meant, let alone expected from her, Wanda said nothing and continued weaving, however, her fingers were no longer as nimble as they had been before she opened this last door.

"I can see you're not sure what to do next, Wanda, and at times I feel inside my mind that all of us are trying to combine the old ways and the new time—and not doing it right. What did you find out when you went to town? Tell me, are they doing anything really new?"

Sudden changes of direction during their conversations never stunned Wanda. She was now used to Mandy instantly entering Spirit during the day, while physically sitting in front of her seeming not to breathe, nor was she surprised when Mandy suddenly opened her eyes wide and delivered messages to someone nearby about their personal life. Since these messages were not always as flattering as people wanted to hear and share with everyone there, they were disliked by those who were not likeable. Since no one else was in the room with them now, Wanda sat and relaxed and waited for Mandy to clear the air or give her some news about what she wanted to do next. She suspected it might be a new style of weaving, but could not imagine what could be done that was not already in stock.

"Wanda, I can see round and round the next week, and you're not happy with what you see."

Before Mandy could say more, Wanda laughed and shouted out, "You bet your sweet bippie I'm not happy!"

This shocked Mandy for an instant, then she talked non-stop. Her words overlapped and precluded any interruptions possibly uttered by her friend, because if they were not heeded when given, they were never repeated. As was their custom, Wanda listened and took notes, but this time she also marveled about how her work would change ever after that day.

⋊ ⋊

Wanda spoke slowly to the weavers gathered around her loom to watch her create a new pattern only she could see. As if in deep trance, she spoke slowly and softly—with unusual clarity. "When you move the shuttle or move your feet, please realize that you are doing a new version of the same old dance."

The youngest woman in the group asked her, "What do you have to do to enter this vision and see this pattern, Miss Wanda?" She was not very tall and had to stand on her tiptoes to see the total design as it grew ever more glorious. Her teetering motions did not disturb Wanda, but caused other weavers to move closer to the front of the room each time she almost toppled forward off her tired feet.

After a minute or more, Wanda mumbled, "You can walk all day and not see a single thing happening to anyone nearby…or you can stay at home and see the entire universe at work."

When nothing else was said, the Maya wondered about it and the Americans talked non-stop. This difference in cultures that produce such artists was never more apparent than when Wanda combined their classes as she did now. Wanda felt often as not that she could never be an American again, because she could not chatter like they all felt compelled to talk whenever they faced any problem. Instead of meditating and hesitating, the tendency of the American students was to leap into space and try to take over the class, without any idea why they should be put in charge. The pressure to ascend was great among them, but not recognized as a way to move into time. She really wanted to help the Americans do better work spiritually, but most of them assumed they were there to assimilate Mayan designs into their own lines and beat the tribe to the cash others would lavishly spend on such fabrics.

Denying their own humankind, some Americans said, "The time isn't right for The Maya to move ahead." These skeptics usually left without any new designs in their minds. Wanda noticed that these disjointed thoughts were entering in and leaving more quickly as she bobbed and weaved into the early evening. Finally, she announced quite casually to the class standing around the loom, "Go to dinner and stop back later if you like." She did not stop to see who might stay and watch her work instead.

The students moved toward the back of the classroom when they realized they could leave without being discredited. However, once everyone moved back and started to disappear, the Mayan women gradually moved forward to stand behind Wanda exactly as they had previously. None of the women of the tribe left the room then. Why?

Whenever the weavers worked together as a group, the Mayan women worked feverishly for days and weeks until it was done. The Americans, however, were always eager to leave whenever any teacher implied it was okay to go. The vital difference within the two tribes was that one thought they knew a lot and the other believed it was not wise to assume they knew anything about time.

Working in the gloom—in the shadow of the loom, Wanda said very little, preferring to let the women stand close and observe her as she wove this color or that into the intricate pattern. While perched on her stool covered in sheep skin, she often felt it quiver or shake when she did something she should not do with the wool—according to that sheep. Wanda often wondered if anyone else felt such things, but she never asked. Instead she sat and watched as her hands flew across the loom without any design in her mind. What mattered most was Wanda keeping her mind as clear as possible all the time she worked. If she let a pattern get etched into her mind too deep, she made a huge mistake—choosing the wrong color or missing a weave. This seldom happened, but when it did, she stopped whatever she was doing and did not work for days after that!

The elder who sheltered the weavers from any intrusions of spirits not wanted around them said, "Wanda, what do you need us to do today to help you tomorrow?" She was not very tall, but her voice boomed in such a way that all the women shook and worried about what she really meant.

Wanda said, with a trace of a grin, "I believe we've accomplished a lot today, but we need to profit more in times when we can work peacefully without anyone whining." The Mayan women did not smile, but one or two moved their feet just enough to indicate they caught the insult and agreed with what was implied.

"If you want to weave and your teacher is not a believer, you have to learn everything in your head, but here we have lots to do and few hands can stick to a plan. What do you suggest?" As Wanda glanced toward the elder, she discovered she was no longer standing where she had been positioned all day. Wondering why she had moved, she said nothing and offered to answer general questions from the students instead.

Several young women wanted to know if the thread was to be dyed before or after the work had been decided upon. She thought that was very astute and answered in a way that cannot be revealed today. Her teachings were never said to be done in the way of a lecture, as in the earliest days of her work in Mayaland. Now it seemed to just flow and grow as she moved the shuttle or moved her feet. She did a lot with her good left foot, but someone usually had to help her with the work her right foot would do if it had not been lost.

A thought of the past lingered in the room now and someone laughed at it. It was the elder who dared laugh. She was suddenly standing in the back of the room, opening the door and ushering out someone in thought. Her back was not fully visible. It was black, as if in a deep shadow. What was going on was not questioned, but who was being removed and why? The weavers moved closer to Wanda when the elder's laughter stopped and the door slammed shut. They all heard her shuffling her feet as if they needed to be cleaned before she came forward again to watch the shuttle move and the fabric grow.

When a breeze came through the closed window, stirring the wind chime high above them in the rafters, the weavers laughed with ease. Some were elated because they knew an angel had arrived to see what they were doing or maybe to protect them from whatever. Nothing was said by anyone present. It was how they worked and prayed that brought these women to the attention of those who closely guard groups like them.

Angels are not as you might think them to be, but then who knows anything? Who can describe a tribe of Maya without losing sight of what others said when they tried to describe what they believed them to be? We know nothing of what we are going to be, either, yet we assume it will be something we have already seen. Such thoughts wove in and out of the group until the energy exploded into a red rose, suddenly revealed in the middle of Wanda's design—as if by divine intervention. The aaahs and ohhhs of the weavers were peaceful sounds to The Ascended Maya who were also flying about the room and guiding one or two more to move outside of their minds.

The weavers' awe-filled sounds impressed upon Wanda's mind that it was time to end the session and go to bed. She would not eat dinner with the women and men of the tribe tonight because her feet—both of them—wanted to meet someone in her dreams. Wobbling a bit as she stood for the first time in a few hours, the women began singing a sweet song that St. Thérèse would have led if she had been with them then.

They sang with blissful whispers, "We are the women of the world…We are women of God, and how God lives now…We are prayers…We are here to help…." The song did not translate from the French as well as the rose in the center of the woven design, but its power was present, nevertheless. Wanda felt it and shivered a little and watched the women now hurry away to see what their children had done while they, too, were busy in school. They took away with them anyone who wanted to stay and talk a while longer.

As the weavers filed into the kitchen and helped themselves to stew left simmering for them to eat, Thérèse asked, "Where is Wanda?" She was not wearing her usual dress of white, rather a light-blue silken robe. She never wore the cloth they wove, so the women were unsure if Ste. Thérèse was the same woman who greeted them every day or just an illusion that only they could see. To be sure, they prayed to her anyway and asked for favors from both sides.

An old woman who was no longer able to weave, but still remembered colors better than any of the others, spoke softly. "Begging you to understand, Ste. Thérèse, we are humble servants—not able to know the ways of God as you do…" Her eyes lit up as she spied a few beings beside Thérèse and assumed they were angels, too. No one else could see into the future as well as she, so she alone knew she would be leaving soon. Her daughter had no clue about what would happen; however, she felt sure her mother would be gone before the new year arrived.

"Thank you, Rosita. You are so kind—and so gifted. I worry about you because you're so used to being of service that you can't let go of work. Why not sit with me during the day and let the others work in clay or weave and not be too concerned?" Thérèse was not smiling so much as letting her lips part and remain that way all day—an expression of peace implanted easily within everyone she met.

Rosita said, "You're so wonderful to me!" She had no intention of taking Thérèse's advice, even though she truly believed the woman to be a saint.

"You're a powerful woman of the tribe, Rosita. You know everything! You're going to have to trade it or give it away…You have more time left than you will ever use, so why not relax and sit with me every day or two?" Thérèse talked without raising her voice high enough for others to hear what she said, even though Rosita stood at a distance from her.

Shaking her head, without intending to negate her reply, Rosita said, "I want to do something for you, sweet Thérèse. I want to make a beautiful design full of roses that will circulate all over the Earth, and whenever anyone sees it they will sense how to heal themselves. Can you help me do that?"

Thérèse did not answer, instead she asked everyone present to stop whatever they were doing and bow their heads and thank God for all they had, so they could choose food and know it was good. When she finished this simple grace of her own making, the weavers left the room. Only she and Rosita stood in the way of the cooks then. No one said a word, but the head cook was not prone to let any of her workers alone. They might as well have been in a tribal circle, not heard by anyone around them. The noise was not dense enough to stop the onslaught of doubt that arrived when women try to make up their minds alone. Aware that the cooks were staring at them, Thérèse ceremoniously shook out her sleeve and settled the matter right then and there.

The old weaver said to the saint, "I will stay with you half the day and work with Miss Wanda at night." Rosita had not thought about the decision and seemed unhappy about it within. Her aura changed just enough to be noticed by some, but only the cook prayed that everything would be okay—and her soup would boil now.

"When you make up your mind, but it doesn't come from deep within you, you get sick if you follow it all the way through to the end. You must let Spirit guide you, Rosita. You may be scared of what lies ahead of you, but you're not to be afraid! There is a guide who has been waiting all your life to help you submit and ascend at the end. It's no secret! Just know that God doesn't let us vegetate on this planet without anyone around to help us. We always have Spiritual Guides! Some come and go, while others sit and wait until we're ready for what they know—and they help us then."

The old woman smiled as if she saw something ready to radiate information and satisfaction enough that she would follow the plan. Her aura retreated back to what it had been in the past. Her golden hue was bright enough to light up the room, but she chose not to do that now. Time enough later when she was ready to cross over to give her spiritual gift to someone who deserved it.

Thérèse sat with her back to the stove area, unaware that her robe was about to catch fire when Rosita saw it happen in a flash. She shouted, "Watch your dress, Thérèse!" As she spoke, a spark flew out of the fireplace, crossed the hearth and landed where Thérèse had been parked. She had jumped at the shout, so the spark hit the floor and died instead of landing on the fragile silk and burning through to her slip.

"Indeed, you are very gifted, Rosita! Where did you learn to use this gift? When did you submit to it?"

Not sure what Thérèse was implying, Rosita immediately believed it to be a lie. Her mother had told her such dreams and 'visions of the future' meant you would die soon after they began appearing, so she tried for years not to see such things. Now she was resigned to the fact that this year would be her last one on Earth because she saw visions almost daily now.

Thérèse prodded, without stopping to think that others in the room might be disloyal, "Are you afraid?" Slipping off her robe, she placed it over the back of her chair. Immediately, without speaking, Rosita slipped to her knees and prayed without stop until Thérèse left the room.

The cook asked twice, without stopping her work, "What did she say to you, Rosita?" Her fat hands were stirring two pots at once, but everyone knew she never talked to herself when she did more than one thing.

Rosita said to her oldest and best friend on the kitchen staff, "I'm okay. I just thought I was going to die, that's all."

"You thought you were dying?" The cook erupted into laughter that shook her full belly and forced everyone else to laugh, too. Infectious laughter is like that, but the cook was unaware of her precious gift. She told everyone she liked to laugh because it made food taste better!

When Rosita motioned for her friend to go outside with her, no one else spoke, although they all wanted to know what had happened. The cook did not want to stop working, but she did. Once outside, the two women embraced and cried loudly. An elder sitting half-hidden under the arbor, yet able to see whatever happened on the verandah, said with satisfaction, "The Holy Spirit is descending on them again."

When the cook finally stopped sobbing she appeared to be in dire stress and needed an immediate answer. Finally she managed to gasp, "What do you want?"

Rosita appeared bewildered and said, "What do you mean?"

The cook was not smiling as she said, "Don't waste my time saying 'What do you mean?' An angel walks into the kitchen while you're talking to a saint—and you wonder why I know you'll get whatever you want?" Long ago the cook had figured out that her own power was greatly enhanced by her close association with those able to see into the next day and those who worked with angels.

Sitting in silence, now unhappy about telling her friend what she knew about the fire, she finally asked, "Do you think I need to ask?" Rosita wondered, 'What if no one understands, or they abuse me for being a witch because I see things?'

"Don't worry, Rosie, I know lots of men who live off such visions—and they aren't dead yet. In fact, they're fat from talking all day about what they see in the future—never doing a thing about it, but no, not you! You're afraid! You don't want anyone to think you're evil or going to die, because you're afraid. Wake up and face today, Rosie! Accept that you're gifted! You have amazing gifts, and you know what to do with a loom, but this worry sickness has robbed you of your weaving. Now you want to stand around and die as soon as tonight. Why?"

The cook continued to rant and rave, leaving no stone unturned in her ramblings about what they had done together in the past working for the good of the tribe, but she never once mentioned Mandy. Why?

☼ CHAPTER TWENTY-NINE

Some tourists, calling themselves 'seekers,' sat looking at Mandy as if seeing her for the first time. She was talking about the ancients and how they left this sphere to do business with those on the next plane. As she described it, it was not supposed to be a long stay away, but it lasted longer than most are able to comprehend today.

"In the oceans of time and tide there are no waves that can't be controlled or left to grow old, but some try to do too much while here. They begin by moving in increasingly larger scenes, visualizing themselves becoming seas, watching themselves swell. Egos seem capable of doing the same thing, but usually they're held in check by others who wish them to excel. Now consider this: What happens when a group of people decides they can enact laws and tell others how to excel?

"First, realize that they are NOT Maya. The Maya would never tell you what to do or how to get beyond who you are now. The way of life prescribed by the Maya of this time isn't the same as it was in the distant past, because it wasn't given to them directly by those who ascended. It was derived over time. The wave of people who left Earth back then didn't intend to leave behind no teachers or wise people to train those who couldn't get it into their heads that it was time to ascend again, but it happened! Today and Tomorrow, the tribe will once again gather its own kind and make up for all that was lost, but it will take years for many to realize that it's all about time."

When Mandy stopped talking, the few Americans in the group waved their hands. Other nations were well represented, too, but the Americans always wanted to be told exactly what happened and why. If Americans only wanted to be told exactly what needed to be done to connect with The Maya of old, what happened then?

Appearing to be in trance, Mandy said, "We want to embrace all who come here in good faith to view the end of the last millennium and greet the new one, but this is not the time to speak of things you want to discuss now. We find the decisions not yet made that will enable us to walk into space. We can and do expect spaceships soon to circle the moon and go out about a mile or so further than they do today, but that's because we see ourselves limited to a shell now. As a people, we truly believe this is the only way you can travel in space."

Directing her words toward a man who appeared to be astounded, or perhaps more like a movie actor trying to project his objection to what was said, Mandy added, "You don't have to accept anything! You can leave your path at any time—no one will say you're doing anything wrong. We're in this world to learn its ways and then go back to where we lost our path—or travel into the light and find our Spiritual Guides and walk toward the next time."

Mandy asked everyone to hold a picture within their combined mind of what they all wanted to do in time. Instead, the class laughed as a man dressed completely in black stood up and exclaimed that he was already in heaven—surrounded by so many beautiful women! The women laughed, but Mandy did not smile. Receiving neither a nod nor a smile from her, he sat down and let others assess his actions. Only then did his condescension and lack of respect become an issue for some—an issue all would have to work through soon.

As peace returned, Mandy said with a slight smile, "Women don't want men to stand up and cheer because they're beautiful or wise. They want to be accepted as one of the guys!"

One or two men prepared to leave, disinterested in pursuing that train of thought. The mind leaves your work first, then the body grows extremely tired, and so on until you must depart for one reason or another. The men left shortly after Mandy said she would go no further without a new lesson plan prepared by the group within an hour.

The attendees sought rooms or alcoves off the main auditorium, making it difficult to see who remained to do the assigned work, but when they returned to greet Mandy again, it was an entirely different workshop than what they entered less than ten hours earlier. With a smile that encompassed the entire room, Mandy said, "Thank you all for quickly going to work and sensing within you what *you* want to do. Arguments are limited to what should be talked about first."

While Mandy talked the group energetically grew stronger, in contrast to being pulled apart and shrinking in size previously. Several Mayan elders filed across the back of the room, standing with straight spines aligned against the walls. That freed up everyone else to be able to move in an instant. Feeling it, Mandy said without a trace of any accent, "We need anchors or we'll lose our place when we move into space."

Reportedly Mandy's nasal twang upset a few attending the seminar because of her reputation as a fabulous financier who left the world to do even better. This outdated concept created the wrong image, but it often brought individuals to this work who would otherwise have been lost in time, so it was allowed to circulate—until now.

"We're making a statement today about the work we can all expect to do once we're through talking here—and actually doing something about our lives in time. I'd like to mention that I'm not the same person who arrived in Mexico years ago. I've changed drastically! Whenever I look back to that time I can't remember what I was like, but some of you remember that Mandy Sheridan better than the one talking to you now. Why? I think it's because we all have this need to decide things, and once we make up our minds, we hate to change them—even if it makes no sense to think that way."

A strong breeze or wind sprang up from the center of the room. No one moved. Some felt it as a warm breeze and others shivered and huddled as if caught in a blizzard. What did it all mean?

"I see we're surrounded by angels—here to help us do whatever we can to preserve this womb. Yes, The Ascended Maya say that in the end of time the Earth will take back all that it lent us over the years, and then forget us…but will anyone who ever loved Earth be able to forget what she gave us this birth?"

As she spoke, the murmurs and chatter of a few grew louder. The Mayan elders stood as before, not acknowledging the rising excitement. Instead of requesting silence, the elders provided insight, and a mirror, that accurately reflected what the wise do whenever given such news. They were not shocked? Who would be able to spot it, if they were? The elders stood out from others because they listened with every bone in their bodies—not partial attention to how something may or may not work. They waited to figure out what they would do with new ideas until safely back at home base.

"I'd like to express my own thoughts now—not what is given through access to another world. I would like to draw upon my own intelligence, but it may not happen since this workshop isn't mine and wasn't given to me to talk about my life…. In the future, if you're a guest at any lecture, wait until the speaker is done talking before you form questions about it…It's a sign that you *are* listening—not merely defining the limits of your mind."

Whenever Mandy paused to take a sip or gather her thoughts, many in the audience fought for her attention, just as small children in American schoolrooms might do. She did not like it, but usually said nothing about their lack of interest in what was provided. In no hurry to channel what was in the ether or to talk about herself, Mandy let her mind settle on one thought at a time and spoke without any idea that it was not usually told to outsiders by a Mayan elder. Somehow, whatever she said was absolutely necessary for this group to become one and be able to ascend together at the end of time.

Pausing to finish her drink, Mandy rose, raising her hands in a pose described as Messianic by movie producers in LA. She did not smile as she said, "You must not assume that everyone loves you." Her stature was now great enough to interrupt whatever passed through the group as she walked toward flowers in pots meant to demonstrate what Mayan artists create with clay and paint now. She gestured toward the altar constructed of cement blocks—not at all interesting to touch, pointing out an eagle feather and the candle that provided the focal point of light. Her wish was to still the minds of those consumed with the idea of lack—especially time, but it did not work.

An earnest young man in the front row demanded, "Please, Mandy! Tell us what you did when you left your job in New York!" He just did not get it! He was trying desperately to figure out what kept him shackled to this group when he wanted to either lead or leave—with no in-between.

With raised eyebrows, Mandy said, "You've not written to me or seen us on TV or in taped lectures, have you?"

He said nothing. He could not talk! He tried to engage her, but could not follow what was going on, because he was not familiar with her mission. His glib cover story was exposed so easily that most of the others were stunned into not speaking again or asking about Mandy's past. However, a few men still wanted to talk about anything rather than what was scheduled for discussion at that moment in time.

An unhappy woman who looked to be a hundred or more pounds over her weight limit stood up and said, "If you were able to do it all over again, would you still go to Cancun and travel with a man you never met before?" Was she shedding her own doubts about men now? No, she was trying to comprehend how Mandy could not realize that men were after only one thing—sex. That was where she stood in the past, but wanted to rid herself of now. Her mind shouted at everyone that she was totally out of sync with the work of that week—and not ready to start over. She did not get it and tried to cover her ignorance with questions seemingly unrelated to this work.

Smiling, Mandy said, "We all came here today, to this place, to work on what holds us back from moving ahead with people we don't love—working harder than ever to evolve beyond classes and self-taught beliefs about what The Maya of old are here to teach us now. So, are you right to worry about my life? No! In fact, my life isn't your worry ever, but it does call attention to the fact that we all have more work we need to produce right now—maybe another book or two?"

Mandy could not control her need to laugh, but she stopped laughing when many in the audience grew animated and started yelling that they wanted to read whatever she gave to the press or to a scribe that would help them decide what to do in their own lives now—based on what she had lived through. Their views were not news to Mandy, but a subject she did not enjoy talking about. Her mind was not lost in time now. She was able to write her own books in her own way. Many present did not recognize her ability to scribe or produce art with the tribe. They comprehended only that experts were teaching such things for her. Was it a lesson she must yet learn?

Back at the podium, Mandy waved at the audience and said, "When you entered this room, you left people outside who serve your needs and help you find peace in a country that many of you see as being beneath you. What do *you* actually do? Do you leave them or do they remove themselves from you in order to help you succeed and feel better about your life?"

Without another word, Mandy sat down and began reading a report that had been placed on the lectern earlier. Not even mumbling an excuse, she began scanning the material as though unaware the audience was sitting, staring in amazement, wondering what they should do. Finally, a man stood and said loudly, with an expression of grave concern, "Are you okay, Mandy? You don't seem to be on target today. You're not looking at us like other teachers or someone who is Maya. What can we do to help you?"

With a flash of a grin, Mandy laughed loudly and quickly stood and asked if everyone was now ready to begin working? It caught some off-guard, but the Mayan elders laughed and kept at it until the entire room caught on to what Mandy was up to now. She had to stop talking and pay no attention to those behaving badly before everyone noticed that they were not ready to work. She did not have to do that again! Softly addressing the crowd, Mandy said, "Now that we're all ready to rise within and remove our thoughts from the process, let's pray."

The audience sat until several women stood and prayed along with Mandy as if they knew what she would say. The prayer was not one they memorized in another place or time. It was made up in space—or so many described it later that day. How many could now pray as a group and not stray from their truth?

Mandy knew it would not be easy to teach people who wished to be unique and did not want to give up control over their work or what they thought they might be, so she sat and laughed until she sounded a pure G, as if she had been singing rather than praying. The prayer ended in a resounding "amen!" Tranquility and harmony were finally established within the group. After that Mandy's work easily won over the poor of spirit, helping them move ahead further than they had ever gone before, but it did not seem to succeed as well with those who were tired of doing spiritual work. To them she said, "Today, we're going to give you a choice.

You can either attend lectures or go out and about and shout to the Earth what you know and what you want to do when you get home. You can shout at the natives, too, since many of you don't think they can hear you grumbling about what you have that is so much better than what they have." The audience sat still for a moment before the room moved enough to let everyone realize something was about to shake them up for days.

An earthquake is not usually appreciated, but since this one happened immediately after praying for the World of Today and The Maya of old, they all sat and wondered about it. Could it mean something more than the fact that the mountains were climbing and the seas were declining? No one spoke and the elders stood firm and protected the walls from falling down.

Mandy did not sit back and suggest they rest, instead she urged them to stand and move towards the rear exit—preparing to possibly leave the building. Casually she said to those willing to sit and listen, "Do you realize that in the past few days we've been given every kind of weather system to study, but only this one scared everyone?"

When she said nothing more, some ran, leaving her behind. Each time someone not in line with time left, those who remained found greater attunement and were more able to absorb the meaning of ascension in their histories and previous lives in space. What did all this mean? What was going to be seen now? No one answered Mandy.

Several men wanted to leave immediately and never attend another seminar with Mandy. They took their anger away with them, thus learning nothing that would ever again disturb their life stories.

One woman who was unwilling to leave the auditorium announced, "Women seem better able to rise to such occasions!" She spoke as if she represented the entire world of women, but her eyes revealed her thoughts enough to expose her true self and what she was now trying to do. Her thoughts about sexism were usually reversed. She did not see herself as sexist when she described men as the enemy of women over and over again. Her words got through to the others present and they started to enter the workshop again. What worked for her then was to believe that women were better than men, but this belief would not help the group ascend at the end!

Totally at ease, Mandy said to the attentive audience, "Some of you can't understand why we stopped talking, yet many others left without saying good-bye. That is because it's not their time! They're not ready to work with the tribe—again. What we want to achieve immediately is a consensus among us about what it takes to humiliate our minds enough to look into time and review our mistakes—before we make them again, and to listen willingly to what others have to say—with wisdom enough to know what's wise and what's not going to fly."

No one smiled now. Instinctively they moved closer to the point of admission to the work of The Ascended Maya! The elders could not decide who was ready and who was not, but Mandy could see. She prayed that one more would leave immediately so everyone else could work together and not waste yet another day. She said, "If you're all ready, we can take a break and get some chocolate or just sit here and pray." She watched to see who would bolt for the door and saw only one man wanted to leave. The women with him urged him to stay, so she motioned that he should leave. Smiling and extending her hand over the heads of several people sitting between them, Mandy said, "You can go, Nathan. No problem. You're not feeling well, but when you're feeling better, find someone who can show you the road through the jungle to the stele that has a story or two to tell you. Later you can tell your ladies what you experienced there."

Not actually shaking his hand, she nodded that he could leave. That was not what one who had accompanied him wanted to happen! She snarled under her breath that he was a disgrace. Mandy erased her comment before it was heard by anyone else, but she remembered the thought even as she said, "Now, let's pray for peace and happiness and the ability to accept what comes to us in this place."

It was never Mandy's intention to pray all day, but it seemed to be a common belief that she led this group in so many prayers that no one could remember any of them well enough to repeat them to others when they met again. She did not tell anyone how to pray because she never prayed the same way twice, and since no one present would be praying with her this way again, she sent a wave of energy to each and every one present who was willing to work with her now. After a few moments, she said, "What happens when we pray? We release envy, jealousy, hatred, and grief…Don't use the same words over and over again, unless it's your personal mantra."

When the angelic presence appeared to be leaving them, the elders stopped praying and left to find something to eat. This suddenly reminded Mandy that others were hungry and needed to eat, too. Her own day was usually spent in partial fasting—not eating or drinking enough to affect her stomach. She often asked her stomach and heart to care for her mind as it traveled here and there, in order not to suffer hunger pangs. Today, however, nothing was normal! Mandy suddenly felt the need to eat almost as much as the two women who grabbed up large paper bags they had packed for themselves and intended to take into the garden to eat now.

A woman who seemed afraid to say anything she had not read in a book said, "Can we eat what we brought to class now?" She was not happy, but she was definitely meant to stay with this group, so Mandy tried to include her in a big smile. It did not seem to get through to the two friends, so she sent them thoughts of love. Then she heard a word or two trickling through from above that she should stop and eat lunch with these women to find out what they do for a living. Shocked by the idea, she never doubted what to do. Looking directly at the two women, yet including everyone else, Mandy said, "I'll join you for lunch outside, after I go to the cafeteria."

The two friends seemed afraid others would want to crowd in and eat lunch with them, too. They said in unison that Mandy could find them under the 'big, old, ugly tree' standing near the gate to the outer world. They both pointed at the sentry tree. No one else agreed with them that the tree was ugly—or so it seemed.

Mandy showed up later and talked with them for a few minutes about their careers. She did not linger because she had made up her mind not to spend her free time with people she did not like. Her Spiritual Guides often helped her do what was best for her, even if it was not always in line with what The Ascended Maya prescribed.

☼ CHAPTER THIRTY

Theory and practice—two ways to learn business administration, but neither can be accomplished in a day.

How to know what is romantic notion or what can sail on the ocean? Sit and dream of traveling—seeing things or doing them. What so many amateur voyeurs seek when on vacation is a little peek at what the natives seem to be. If such a sight fulfills their idea of what is real, great! If, however, the natives turn out to be ahead of such people, they run home and hide it, saying they don't like that tribe or nation or state. Their pride can defeat 'their' tribe. You may find respect in this world or the next, but it happens when you work on what you need to do first. Remember, you're not the best—yet!

When the idea that a person can cherish another more than they love themselves first came into existence, it was seen as a foolish dream, but today it's the epitome of what people strive for all the time. If you truly love someone more than yourself, you martyred your mind and consumed all of your time doing nothing to prepare you for leaving this air. Why?

If a psychiatrist can't help you get well, is it because you're so hopelessly upset and out-of-sync that no one can link you to your home in time? No, but you might discover that the doctor is out of line. What if you accepted the teachings of someone who leaned too far to one side? What if you were sure others knew more about a subject than you, so you did nothing and discovered later that they misled you? All of this could lead you to reminisce when you leave this existence. You would say: "If I could do it over again, I would do this or that instead of what I did." Instead, why not find out what you need to do on this side and in your main life now that will help you leap out of this world and into time?

This is not a treatise on what it takes to have faith, but a book about what you will do when you are able to move into the future and look around—before returning to your hometown....

Jeanne sat staring at the computer screen. Her fingers refused to type another word. She was not sure if this was where she was to begin 'The Book' or even if this was 'The Book' or just another Introduction to 'The Book'. Her mind was unable to make these ideas fit neatly into the work she once created seemingly on her own, so she held her fingers over the keys and let Spirit direct her writing, just like she had done all this past year—waiting to see what would appear. Indeed, her prose seemed superior to what she had scribed in the past, but not quite as good as when she worked hard to edit her own work and put it together in ways she had been taught in the schools of her youth. This was not proof that she could or would be asked to work for the tribe, but she was now willing to learn how to devote her entire life to being their spiritual scribe.

Work progressed in the village established by this group of famous women. Each contributed more than ever before to others, but it was not coming together quite the way they wanted. It was not perfect yet!

Utopian ideals survive! They seem to arrive and disappear every half-century or so, but no one in today's world wants to be told what to do, nor do they take to instruction well or listen long enough to produce communities that will sustain them for more than a few years. The need to live within your means is such a foreign concept to most Americans that they charge into such groups expecting others to pay whatever they are used to paying for common needs, without regard to how much money they might be wasting. A village cannot thrive if everyone wants to be in charge, but no one wants to supervise spending or lies.

With a long list in hand, Jeanne set out to go shopping in the nearby town, clearly forgetting that her only way of doing business now was to barter. She lost her way all day and was not able to decide what she wanted to trade. Her hands and feet were unfulfilled when she walked the last block back to her parked car. Without a list, Jeanne might have done business differently, but probably not. Her mind was still in the ether and out-of-sync with her vision. She needed to down-shift and slow her thoughts—a lot, as she headed home. Since it is not safe to drive down a major highway in such a state of mind, she exited onto a side road that wandered in and out of the path of the main road every few miles.

Finally, her eyes opened! She laughed with joy at being able to do nothing but drive. She wondered why she had never done it before. Driving absentmindedly in and out of the jungle and nearby villages, a thought arrived out of time that a Spiritual Scribe can have no ambition about her own work. This concept was so stunning that she was unable to assent to becoming one then. Her mind rejected the idea that she would have to forget all the usual themes and all the beliefs that existed within her life, using only what was dictated by others whom she would never meet in person. This defied logic and everything she had ever been taught or believed in or had seen. It was unwise to become a spiritual scribe full-time, according to her mind.

After traveling at least an hour without any thought of where she was going, Jeanne suddenly stopped the car, got out, and started walking. Her mind was lost in time. She was not aligned with what she normally did during the average day. It seemed as though she had nothing to do and no place she had to be right now. No one at the compound expected her to return empty-handed or say she could not find any bargains in the huge open-air Indian market, so she had to create a more plausible excuse than just not being able to swap worth a darn.

As the sun set, the night breezes began to rise and cool the air just a bit, but not enough to grab a coat or a rug to pull over her. She returned to the car and sat there, wanting to do nothing until another car came along and forced her to move over or move forward. That is what she wanted, but her mind would not permit her to sit still. Jokingly, she said aloud, "Why do I let you control me every minute of the day and then dream of things you won't believe?"

Smiling as she listened to her thoughts take form, Jeanne was amazed that what she said was not what she thought when her lips parted and she started to speak. Without thinking about meanings, she said, "What does it mean to channel or dream?" She waited until it was apparent no one was going to advise her intuitively, so she might as well move on down the road and head for home.

Within a minute of moving at her usual speed—always faster than the posted limit, she spotted a donkey standing beside the road. She decided to slow and wait for it to cross in front of her rather than block its path. However, the donkey decided not to move and stared back at her. She shouted with no mean intent, even if her words were rather rude and offensive to the donkey, "What is it about you mules that you never do what you're supposed to do?"

The donkey's owner sprang from the bushes beside the road and hissed at Jeanne for talking to her pet as if it did not know what was said. Her words were coarse and quickly dispersed, but Jeanne knew instinctively that she had to do something to erase the offense or be banned from visiting that area again. Intuitively she knew that the curse would work if she did not do something and do it immediately, even though she would have scoffed at such an idea a few months ago. She had come to know better after computing all that she had seen and heard outside the compound and around the nearby villages when someone gossiped that Mandy was a witch and not allowed to live in the area any longer.

Thinking about the curse the girl uttered with such force, Jeanne shivered until she felt a hand rest on her left shoulder. It was not heavy, but cool. She described it later as "Like an angel standing there, telling me to hold my ground." Without any doubt, she made up her mind to do something about this nasty child. She got out of the car, but just as she started to walk toward the girl, the donkey brayed and scared both of them apart.

They both jumped and then laughed at the idea that the donkey saw something they did not see. In a flash, the girl stared at Jeanne and noticed a halo or a strange light radiating all around the strange woman's head. It was obvious to this pious young woman that an angel was with her now, so all she could think to do was appease the gods and keep this woman from leaving her. She stammered, "Would you like to come to my home? We have plenty of food, and you can sleep in my hammock. It's a beautiful place. Won't you come home with me?"

This sudden invitation so startled Jeanne that she was unable to quickly arrange a suitable lie that would not offend the girl more than she already had. A mere moment later she felt herself holding the reins of the donkey as it traveled over a path through the jungle, leading her back into at least the last century. Her legs dangled on either side of the donkey's rounded belly and her toes dragged in the dust when she forgot to hold her legs out straight. She felt like laughing, but she did not.

"You will like my house," said the girl without pride. Her easy assurance that life was good on the other side of this material world was very interesting to the journalist who resides within Jeanne even now. She wanted to see what would happen next, but was a little concerned that in another hour everyone at the compound would wonder where she was.

Seemingly unaware of what she was thinking, the Mayan maiden said, "We have a wire so you can call your family, if you want to."

Their disjointed conversation was no different from many others she had with those who lived in the rural areas and practiced the old Mayan ways, so Jeanne rode on in silence until she heard herself say, "Thank you, but how do you have a phone line out here? It seems miles from civilized ways—there are no poles anywhere." She said this without looking up to see if this were true or not. Her eyes were riveted on the girl's hair, wondering about its sheen and how long it might be, instead of being concerned about her final destination and if she would find a good bed and be allowed to survive the night.

The girl said nothing and pulled on the reins and politely asked the donkey to hurry a bit more. Fully aware that this was not an elegant way to travel if you wanted to make a great first impression, Jeanne was amazed that when she arrived in the clearing at the end of the trail she was greeted as if a member of royalty—not as a tired, middle-aged writer of books no one here could know about. Because she was surprised, her eyes were unnaturally dilated. She tried not to look directly into anyone's eyes until they adjusted.

The first person to greet her was obviously the head of the family. He said with great respect, "How are you? Thank you for coming to our home. We are ready for the fire to be moved into the center of the yard so we can roast a chicken and a bit of another animal that you will like better well done."

The man speaking would normally not tend the fire or cook since Mayan men do not do such work when women are around. Apparently the spokesperson for the clan, his speech was very sophisticated as he extended his invitation for her to stay and eat dinner with them. There was no way Jeanne could leave right away without offending everyone in the clan and possibly re-enforcing the threat from the curse still hovering in the vicinity of wherever her car was parked in the bushes out-of-sight of the main road.

As the evening progressed and grew toward midnight, Jeanne wondered repeatedly if Mandy knew this man and his clan. She had said little since her arrival because she wanted to find out who they were exactly, what tribe of Maya they were descended from, as well as what area of expertise they were striving to repeat.

When the fire was pushed into the background again, her host said with great dignity, "I feel content and happy within, Miss Jeanne. We have heard of you in the village, but never thought you would get our message, so we could meet like this."

Jeanne took in the man again, making mental notes about his age and whatever she could make out as the flames disappeared. He looked to be about 50, but who could tell when skin is not wrinkled and hair is not gray? The Maya work hard and eat very little most years, so poor nutrition often robs them of height, but does not diminish their intelligence or spiritual power. Musing over what he said, she realized verbal recognition of his statements was not necessary. However, since she was curious about what they wanted from her, as well as why they sent out thoughts as spies do to capture others, she asked each person to explain why they had done it. She was no longer amazed to learn that they had chased her in spirit for several days or that it was their thoughts that prevented her from being able to barter in the market. It is just something you learn to live with and accept when you work as The Maya do on Earth.

"Two times we have prayed for help. Two times we have met someone related to you," said the woman married to the leader of the family. She was not stout, but plump compared to most of the other women. Her breasts protruded just a bit further than many of the other mothers, but no children appeared to beg her for favors while Jeanne sat with her by the fire.

Jeanne did not ask more questions, but watched to see who did what and who would eventually tell her about their life on this side of the universe. As she sat quietly, they thought as one. She could hear what they said. Without signaling that she understood, she said, "What do you mean by that?" She wanted them to tell her as much as they could or would without her saying anything about her life, since this was the easiest way to conserve energy and be able to remember later what was said now. She seldom took notes and certainly would not do it here, because it was not helpful when getting people to talk; however, she had to be able to quote them verbatim without losing the thread of their various conversations.

Finally willing to talk, an elder spoke to everyone, as if sitting on a far-off cloud. "We are Maya! We see many things and we hear much within our tribe, but none of us knows how to fly… We are tired of not being able to swim in the ocean without wearing fins and webbed feet to please tourists who are not aware of the tides, but we do it to make money for the tribe… We sometimes find people who cannot swim jumping off boats to see animals and fish in the sea. Why do they do that?" Suddenly a smile split his face in half and his deep laugh erupted and flowed over all, thus encouraging everyone to laugh along with him.

Jeanne resisted because she wanted to see what would happen if she acted as though she did not understand what he was saying. A light flickered above her head and stayed there until the man stopped laughing and spoke more slowly in lower tones. He was unwilling to talk about his family or his home, but asked questions about hers. This definitely was not what Jeanne expected, nor what she wanted. Her mind overflowed with what she wanted to write about tonight. She wondered how she would be able to present this man's life in the best possible light, in order to relate his philosophies without forgetting that he was not asking her to recognize him as the great teacher he was.

Without thought, Jeanne blurted out: "I think we can sit here and assimilate a lot of what we're like, but it's very hard for me to do that when I work in The World constantly! Can you tell me something about meditation—how you use it, and most especially about The Ascended Maya?" She recognized too late that she had created a barrier between her mind and the men. She was no longer talking like women talk to them, let alone the elders of a clan. She was not following the ways of the Maya or the English or anyone they had linked to in the past—and they were aghast at that.

Raising her hand as if to ask a question, then dismissing her gesture as if realizing it gave away her age, a young woman said the men did not want to talk directly to Jeanne, even though she was a unique woman. The Maya still resist the Mexican school system, but more and more use whatever is provided, letting their children go to the sixth grade with others who may not be Maya, hoping to beat the government to its next attack.

The young woman apparently looked older than her age, so it was indeed strange that she would speak to a stranger at such a meeting, but she did. She spoke hesitantly at first, saying: "I would like to live in New York City," and then rambled on about a movie she had seen on TV in the village. Her mind was mesmerized by what she could not visit. Her mind in time wanted to assimilate much more in order to do a lot, without reducing her family in status, but her ego self saw only the glamour, not the work it would take to leave her family and move to a huge city just to earn money.

Thoughtlessly, Jeanne blurted out, "You don't want to leave your family! You want to see a lot and do what we in the United States call 'travel.' We don't actually leave our homes or anything we love, we just visit other countries—look around and then go home and think it over. You don't really move or stay away, you just *travel.*"

The group murmured, and she was amazed at what she heard. They had never re- alized that Americans stayed behind in the Yucatan and Guatemala only when they were touched by grace or were running from the law. Realizing that many people just came to look around and see for themselves what was on TV or they had read in a book or a magazine amazed them! She said without any doubt and no thought, "You're very deep individuals at work within your clans, but Americans have no families! They leave home as soon as they can. Some try to find strangers who might like them or make them feel that they're wanted, but many live by themselves and never go out except to make money."

An elder who had previously said nothing, but had admired the way Jeanne looked on the outside, said to her, "That's hard to believe, Miss Jeanne. We admire Americans. They're like grown-up children—just not as nice. We would like to advertise what we do here, like you and the others at your group houses do, but we're afraid Americans will come and stay—and never leave."

Not unaware of his stares at her dress and hair, Jeanne did not reciprocate with a smile. Instead, she almost glared at his stare so he would know she was not flirting with him or any man—or going to do something silly or weird—at least not then. Out of sorts, she snorted, "What do you do? What do you create? What can we do to help you men? We're able to deliver the goods and use the internet for good—and we do a lot of educational work, too. We're always looking for ways to help the tribe live better—if that's what they want. You can use us or not, but we're happy to be of use to The Ascended Maya regardless of whatever you think about us."

The snicker emitted by the group was so unexpected that Jeanne stopped talking. Her eyes were not open wide enough to discern what caused the laughter, but she knew something was going on beyond her—out of her range of sight, so she sat for a minute or two while they laughed uproariously about something they saw but she did not. When their laughter merged into a pure G, Jeanne felt like she was leaving her body and floating into the next view—able to see what the future held for her with this group, too. She was amazed to see that this family would be paid tribute by many living in the United States. This clan would create a new way of life that could be taught in a few months to any pilgrim willing to submit to living it. Her first thought was of those who had lost their minds to drugs, and then she saw men and women who had achieved great jobs and suddenly lost it all benefiting from such rehabilitation more than anyone else in the world. She suddenly laughed at the idea and landed back in her own lap.

"You are amazing, Miss Jeanne! We are so happy today! How can we explain what you are going to help us do? We never thought of opening our homes to the Americans who tramp through the jungles without any care for the animals and plants and trees living here. We never thought about the money being wasted on cars and houses and bars because people no longer know where they fit in or who they are, even when God speaks to them—in what-ever way God speaks to Americans today. You are a genius, Miss Jeanne! You are inspired by the Angel of The Maya!"

Stunned that they all knew intuitively what she had to leave her mind and flow into time to see, Jeanne felt strangely renewed and reborn—able to see that her mind was not helping her any more. In fact, her mind was blocking her view and holding her back! Since her mind was little use in communicating what they would do together in the future, Jeanne sat on the only available seat and did not think again. Her feet normally were unable to fold over and under each other when sitting on the ground, but now she felt the need to fold her legs like that and did it easily.

Seated in the lotus position, she acted as if she were a visiting fakir sent to teach them a lesson. She smiled with ease and said with great humility, "The crossover of other cultures within their own country makes Americans hunger for a society that is fair and honest—as good as when it was founded. Most who stray far from their luxurious homes in search of another more promising land can't see that it's not easy to recreate a family—let alone a clan or a nation of your own. Today's Maya are ancient compared to people where I once lived and called home. Our work here isn't going to be easy! No modern American wants to work very hard or very long. The easy path is always preferred! Few want to do the difficult work of practicing to become adept—at anything. If you can't do something fast and perfect the first time, you move on and do something new—and devalue anyone with talent who does what you would love to do, too."

Everyone laughed at the absurdity of not working hard to master what must be done to be what you came to be. Everyone looked at Jeanne now as if she were telling fantastic stories—letting her imagination pad reality, but she was not. As her thoughts intermingled with time she began to prophesy and talk about the new life and what it would mean to the tribe, but they told her even more about those times because they arrived that night.

☼ CHAPTER THIRTY-ONE

Speaking to the backs of the girls and women gawking at the commotion outside the weavers' studio, Wanda said, "We're not going to stop and talk about what just happened! We're going to work right through it!"

When the looms stopped moving, Wanda always acted as if she need only speak to get everyone weaving again, and it usually worked. Wanda pointed at a man standing outside, but within their line of vision. His mind was wandering outside the lines, or so it appeared to her when she said, "You'll find out later that it isn't something you have to live through…You'll be amazed at how much work you get done while others idle—unwilling to get on with their lives."

The younger women laughed when the man suddenly turned around as if to say he could not figure out what was going on or was unable to fathom where he was. Their ridicule was not loud laughter or a bitter titter, but it was powerful enough to stimulate a sudden burst of growth and maturity in some of the women.

A weaver who usually stood at Wanda's side watching for changes as they occurred in her work, so she could alter the next day's patterns and lessons to include whatever wisdom was imparted then, said, "You have to know when to act if you're going to help some-one—and more importantly, you have to know when it's best to let them take care of it without any help."

Always working a day ahead of the group, Wanda was finding it increasingly more difficult to keep things running that way. Several women were expert weavers when they arrived to sit at her side and watch and learn from her and other artists in the tribe. However, they, too, were now being eclipsed by several women who were determined to be great teachers, rather than great weavers. Teachers were given greater dispensation when following the rules laid-down by Wanda than those learning the trade or expressing themselves in their own way through this art form. The teachers also received more energy and steam. They worked even harder when others became fatigued from all the talk and alterations made in the work from one day to another. This was meant to test their faith and persistence when working around others.

As the women returned to their work, the commotion outside the loom room ceased, but entered another building nearby where others were not as willing to ply their trade as the weavers were that day. Disruptions happen, but not as often to those focused and busy working on a life pattern and able to share laughter.

When the day's work was put away and the floors swept of lint and such, the women slipped into the lean-to room attached to their classroom to enjoy refreshments Wanda kept there especially for them. The chocolate was always hot and the cookies were usually great, but nothing was more appreciated by her students than hearing more about the world in which she and many of the other teachers had worked before they came to Mayaland and decided to stay on and work with them.

"When I used to drink warm tea, it would go through me so fast that I'd have to stop work and go to the pot—a lot." Wanda sat and smiled at this silly little ditty while the women laughed, so as to keep her talking. She suddenly wondered why she would talk about such a thing with so many more interesting topics available to go over and teach or share emotionally or whatever. A surge of adrenaline rushing to the surface of her mind or brain or whatever caused the eruption and she almost shouted: "This talk of pot has got to stop!"

Wanda could feel her eyes roving over the group and coming to rest on a young woman standing outside the inner circle, yet still within the room. Her mind was apparently not in line with this time because she listed things she wanted to do or teach, and then suddenly her total attention became riveted on a single word that plunged her into the deepest concerns she had conceived so far. Adding by way of explanation, Wanda said, "I mean, we have to do something about this craving for pot and recreational drugs and such. I can see that many young people are being blocked forever from ascending because pot blocks them. It seems to reduce the amount of stress required in order to achieve and strive to become a success. Ambition leaves with the use of such drugs! You can see them—standing around, content to watch others work, like that man this afternoon who wasn't working, wasn't helping, just standing there—wondering what was going on."

Knowing that Wanda's moods often made deep or sudden changes, the women did not smile or say anything to contradict her. Still, they were unprepared for what she was about to say because it was unrelated to anything they had ever discussed. Without hesitation, the weavers backed into the loom room and sat down as if ready to hear a lecture. It turned out later to be one of the greatest moments any could remember about this time, because it imparted truth, mood, and the ability to see into what they all could do to improve themselves and their communities.

At a little after seven the weavers left the studio to return home or go to the washrooms before entering the communal dining hall; only one stayed behind to talk to Wanda privately—the woman who had made Wanda think a lot about pot. She said, "I see you are aware that I use. I was trying to hide that I've abused drugs a lot… I really like pot, but I've cut back to using it only once a day now… I like it because it helps me see colors in their fullest range. It always inspires me to do better work. Without a bit of pot, I'm not able to concentrate and bring my full creativity to a project--"

"Stop, Stop! Enough! You're extremely lonely and upset and the pot isn't helping you relax and learn the ropes fast. In fact, you're dropping out of this class. So much for your big talk about being inspired—able to go higher than others who work a lot harder than you'll ever work."

After pushing aside Wanda's rocking chair attempting to flee what she believed would be an attack on her need for pot, the would-be weaver sat down heavily and started rocking furiously. In a voice not her own, she managed to say, "How did you know?" Her mouth refused to close and remained agape. She looked like a clown-face painted on a fun house entrance that invites people to walk in and look around, then leave when they have seen enough. Since her mouth refused to close, she had to let Wanda speak her piece or leave the room looking extremely weird.

"How did I know? You don't move much, Maria! You sit around as if this is it—despondent and blue, tired and listless, not like a turned-on artist or even like women working alone at home. You're out of it most of the time! Is this really what you want? Is this all you expect out of life? Are you ever *really* interested in anything? Is the drug world so great that you want to stay in it and let them make tons of money off your habit? Why do you work to support what will never work for you?"

Maria laughed disdainfully. Her lips flapped more than they relaxed as she laughed, but she spoke with greater clarity now. Sneering, she whipped out, "You think that marrying is any different than using pot?"

Realizing that Wanda did not follow her line of thought, she added with disgust, "You take care of men so maybe they'll share what they do with you—not go out and talk to other men who want them to chase women—then they come home with such an attitude! Suddenly, you're the reason they never got ahead. You're eating up their money! You don't know anything!! You're stupid if you think a habit like pills and pot is more destructive than-
-"

"Enough! Enough! Every woman learns about men—some sooner than others, but it's our world, too. So stop the pity-party and get on with what you came to do—and we'll all have enough! We women can do whatever we want and make men respect our game. They may play rough, some act like that because their mothers urged them to be tough, but you don't need to wear blinders or spar with men to get action. My advice is: Be yourself and make them come to terms with what you are instead of singing the blues about what you would do if you were in charge."

With a mocking grin and an obscene gesture, the haggard young woman yelled back, "How do *you* do that? What makes *you* such an expert? You have a college degree and think you're smarter than me—better educated, but if you really are, where are all your men? Where do you spend all your time? What do you do for fun? Let me tell you. You hide! You don't go out or go to parties or ever relax."

Wanda smiled softly to deflect the anger expressed in the woman's voice, as well as her words and behaviour that struck her heart. Instead she interjected, "You must have missed out on the lesson about how one leg cuts back on how many men want to dance with you." She had not intended to dabble in self-pity, too, but if it cleared the mind of this woman-child, she would use it. "I don't dance or drink as a matter of personal choice. I'm an artist and a teacher; and believe it or not, you interest me more than any of the men in this town."

"Oh, no, you don't! I know where you're going with this. Way too many of you Americans think Mexican men, boys, *and* girls are toys you can use for sex and never have to answer for when you return to your stateside friends."

Shock registered on Wanda's face as pain etched its way across her famous face, but she spoke without anger, "I'm not homosexual, Maria… I'm trying to help you understand how many women don't have the same needs to procreate as most men. I'm content to see my seeds go unused and watch others succeed as mothers. I love you and the others, as if you are my sisters and brothers—and some as if they were my daughters and sons. Is it of little use or no good to love and trust, yet live alone? I think it's the only way to survive today. You've got to live in this world until God calls you to whatever reward is allowed, then we move into the next view and work there, too. So whatever you do here and now is going to help—or not what you become when you're no longer here."

Wanda's words were less coherent than usual because she was in a trance speaking a dialect she had never encountered until now. She tried to channel rather than translate, but her mind was watching the conversation as if she were sitting on a cloud waiting to jump in and interrupt Spirit. Unable to contain her mind any longer, Wanda exploded with: "Are you trying to say that you were molested or raped as a child?"

Maria nodded because she could not raise her eyes and look into the face of this great woman of the tribe. She felt humiliated and ashamed!

"Were you molested by someone who gave you pot afterwards? Is that what got you started?" When Maria nodded again, Wanda screamed as if in deep despair: "What kind of man would do such a thing to a woman like you—and get away with it? Who did it? What's his name?"

Maria held her breath for a very long moment before she started sobbing out her story. Her voice was just above a whisper and what she said tore at Wanda's mind more than her heart. "I was a child—only 11 years old. She wanted me to go to the store for her, because she ran drugs out of the back of her house. I wasn't supposed to know about it—or that she was into men and women, but everyone knew it, so no one said 'don't go near her,' because that is not our way. She caught on that I didn't know anything about her kind of sex and I wasn't willing to admit that I wasn't grown up—I always wanted to be big then."

Wanda grabbed the arm of the chair so Maria would stop rocking. The need to settle Maria into a pattern of relaxation and laughter was so great she asked God to materialize and show her how to help this woman calm down immediately. Instantly, or so it seemed, the office door opened and a woman entered without stopping to knock. She looked as radiant as a Renaissance saint. Wanda gasped with relief that it was her daughter, instead of another. Thérèse was knowledgeable about The World and would know what to do in an instant or two.

"What's wrong? Are you in trouble?" Thérèse bent over the woman sitting in the rocking chair and said nothing else for almost an hour. Her long, long hair did not touch the chair as it flowed outward from her shoulders and created a tent under which the three of them could pray together and keep their energy between them better. Couples and groups passed by outside Wanda's office chatting about what they had eaten or what they would do later as the room darkened and the energy dimmed within the teepee created by the three women praying then.

As if she had been waiting for a sign, Maria leaped to her feet and announced, "I'm free! I'm able to be me! I feel so great! I know I'll never use pot—nor let anyone's hands offend me again! I'm wonderful! I'm a new person!" As she jumped up and down, Thérèse smiled gently at her mother of this time and thought about nothing else, or so it might appear.

Wanda suggested, "Let's go get something to eat and talk about this later." Her suggestion was not adopted by the others.

"No, if the miracle is to continue, we must offer something in thanksgiving," said Thérèse.

"Of course!" Wanda spoke with finality, but did not forget to bow her head as she slipped down on one knee as easily as if she had done it for years. She extended her hand toward the woman she believed to be healed from her addiction to pot. She knew Maria was still fragile in the world of thought, but had nothing more to say, so she waited in silence for Thérèse to pray.

Softly, Thérèse spoke as if giving a benediction or prayer of thanksgiving. "You can say anything—at any time, but it must be said with deepest appreciation that God is saving you to do something better and wiser than you've ever done in recent times." The light shining from within and around them increased then.

Maria mumbled, "I feel so much that I can't speak. I want to pray, but I can't. I don't know how to say a prayer that counts. I'm not worthy of anything... I don't even have a bed of my own—and no one loves me..." Since self-pity was raising its ugly head once again, Wanda nudged the woman, but said nothing. Her stern look stemmed the whining and Maria returned to blessing and giving thanks enough to maintain the healing of her heart. When done praying, Maria mumbled, "I guess I do make a lot of excuses—and no one likes that. I know I don't. Anyway, I want to say that from now on--" Wanda nudged her again. "I mean that from now on I'm going to laugh more and work harder, and I won't be last to get my assignments done, and I'm not going to make any more excuses ever again! That will be very hard for me, because I've been lying to myself since I was 5. I never accepted that I'm Maya. I'm not going to be ashamed to be a member of the tribe anymore. I want to be as tall as I was when I was 13—not bent over with shame, trying to hide from everyone I meet, and I'm going to succeed! I'll give all that I make to God--" Again Wanda nudged Maria's elbow.

Since what she said seemed to displease Wanda, Maria stopped talking and rethought what she was saying. When she resumed praying aloud, she said, "I mean, I'll tithe. I'll give ten percent of my pay to people who need it more than me, and I'll go to church every day and pray."

When she said this, Thérèse mumbled a prayer under her breath that seemed to be exactly what was needed to end their meeting, but before anyone could move or speak, an angel swooped into the room and stared down at the chair where the young woman cringed in fear. Excited and overwhelmed, Maria screamed: "An angel! I'm being greeted by God!"

She then fainted and did not come back to the present for almost an hour. Where did she go and what did she do? No one on Earth knows. It was obviously a radical change from what she had experienced in the past, because no one after that ever talked about what happened in the courtyard that morning. Instead, they gossiped about how Maria made a new start and got a big heart!

Now, whenever Wanda greeted her daughter, she bowed her head and said nothing until spoken to, as if she also worshipped this woman proclaimed to be a saint by the Maya. At such times Wanda looked to be more alive, but not nearly as vibrant as usual. Why? She assumed it was because Thérèse required some of her energy, but that was not why she appeared to fade when they met. The wave of the future is such that it takes a bit from whatever you are doing now and adds it to the past, then makes up the difference. You have to see the future as a tapestry you can read to make the quantum leap into space, time, and faith, but most cannot.

☼ Chapter Thirty-Two

Shaking her head, Jeanne reread the notation in her journal. It was exactly what she wanted to do, but she was not happy with the conclusion as scribed. Taking one last look at it, she decided it would have to do for now.

> *Thinking about doing something new or thinking about what to do next is about the same thing. If they overlap, you have to work fast if you want to combine the two and use what you do to make life easier on your mind.*

Through the years of her very successful career, her personal life had often stalled—even got off-track a few times, but she always worked hard on her hidden fears through it all. She had left herself open to only a few men, because all wanted to change her. She owned a house or two that she loved to rearrange, and then she had adopted a son who always shed joy in her mind. Finally, she married a man who brought her great grief. After she arrived in Mexico, she had opened to Jorge, and then other men, but now was aware that she was not wanted here as much as she was at first—or so she thought.

The day began in a most unusual way, she was not able to pretend any longer that her end was near or that she had to leave Mexico immediately. Using such threats is how she often drove herself to do something new, but all she had to do was change her mind! This was a time when she felt it was necessary to decide whether to stay in Mexico or move to LA and write for *The Times* every day. What to do? Who to talk to about this new venue? How could it benefit The Maya and her other ideas about progress?

As her fingers dashed across the keyboard of her latest state-of-the-art computer, Jeanne thought, 'What I need is a new kind of editor. Someone who'll listen to me first—and only then point out how to make it really pop! I don't need a reader or friends to say this or that is wrong or right. I need someone strong enough and smart enough to say this is what needs to be said and whether or not I'm doing it right.'

Unhappy, or so it would appear to strangers passing nearby, she was neither upset nor filled with fear. In her mind, it just had to be a great year! When Jeanne was upset or not quite in sync with her own views, she often realized that this day or year was not conducive to sharing her innermost fears, so she would shade her views and wait for a better time. Maybe later today or another day would produce a better time to bring out her dreams and make headway with them then? She often struggled mentally this way, rather then checking out the chart created by an astrologer in the past. She used that chart only when her plans were drastically delayed or she could see no other way to make headway. She often wondered why she even bothered having her chart done?

As the day came to an end with no one entering her office or calling, Jeanne realized she must be wearing 'that face' again—the one that said 'don't disturb me unless the building is falling down.' She laughed at the thought, because she did not really feel like that most days, but it let her get work done. It was not easy to write while living within a community brimming with life and constantly trying to include her in whatever was going on. Her mind would slip into the past just far enough that she could whine or cry and look as if she were unhappy—filled with regret that she could not participate then—yet she did not really regret anything.

To Jeanne, looking back was like taking a warm bath, it helped her relax. Usually, when she looked into the future her anxiety level escalated to a point where she felt jittery and maybe even a bit unhinged. A practicing psychologist diagnosing such a patient would say this is to be expected when you move into other views, but not what practicing psychics described or diagnosed now.

When Jeanne lived in the United States with her *handicapped* son, she often felt as if she was there to enlighten the world about his plight, assuming others did not care about her and what she did as long as she was able to keep the outside of her house looking neat. She was seldom far off the mark in her editorials and hometown views, according to letters received by the Op-Ed Editor, so she imagined she knew all about her neighbors, as well as those who lived further down the road. She did not! Jeanne left that life without knowing she made a mistake, thus she was now being urged by her Spiritual Guides to move back into that lifestyle to better understand what she did not comprehend in the past.

She thought about it—a lot. Continually wondering if it would be okay to skip LA—just explore it in time and figure out what she had done wrong in the past? Did she have to actually reconnect and do whatever with whomever she had forgotten or did not meet or talk to in-depth—once she sensed they needed her then?

It was not easy for her to write and go inside The Ascended Maya as their scribe when her mind was in whirl about other times, so The Maya came forward and talked to her with The Lord. Their pronouncement was astounding to her alone. The Maya proclaimed in a combined echo of time: "You are not going back to LA. You have lived so long in simple states that you cannot appreciate what they do, how they speak, and what in their view is art and style. If you went back you would be too miserable to continue working with us. It might be that God intended you to miss the point, so you can't stay on Earth any longer. We will not impose upon you or anything you wish to do. Instead, let us propose that you stay with us another day or two and then move into a new 'you' that will do whatever this *you* plans to do." Their voice, loud and strong, not deep in tone, reverberated throughout her mind the rest of the day.

Jeanne felt spent, bent under the weight of the meditation that produced such a lot of thought and doubt, until an angel of The Lord ascended from the wishing well that stood outside her door. She saw the angel rise while glancing out the window waiting for the mail-carrier who was late.

The angel did not sing or play a harp. Its wings were multicolored—not white, and when the angel smiled she saw a rainbow of color radiating outward. The angel was multilingual, so anyone could understand every word as easily as she did, but no one else got the message or spotted the angelic messenger announcing: "You will stay in Mayaland! You will work hard and play your part. You will one day take away with you from this place many who are afraid and unwilling to work hard now. You are going to write about The Maya and life in these parts from your heart—not from *research* or talking to science majors who play at art. You will not do anything you do not want to do, but you must talk to others every day and lecture more using the messages channeled through You for *you* to use, too."

Her future did not appear as clear as she had hoped it would, but she was still amazed that only a few days earlier she had been content to sit and do whatever came through to her to do. She had dabbled quite a bit then—written a few ads for the boys to place in their school yearbooks or whatever, shipped books out to the villages for the children to read at home, and now she was sitting and talking with an angel about LA! Miracles do happen every day, but some days you cannot deny it because they change your mind.

Not exactly spoken, she could still hear messages transmitted through time and space some way: 'The time limit for being sublime is very brief now. You must move immediately or all is lost to you.' This much Jeanne already knew. She was willing to begin work immediately, but she wondered about Mandy. What would happen if she did something so unique that Mandy did not want her to teach it or send it out?

Just the thought of it caused an angel to fly in and begin lecturing her in midair. The messenger was not as tall as the angel who rose from the wishing well, but was nice and bright—very light. It announced: "You are now doing your work and Mandy is not. She is doing her own work and doing it alone. Do you have to do what you are given? Yes, you asked for work, and it has been agreed that you can do it, so if you don't do it now, it will be ungood—or whatever you say."

It was the first time she ever heard an angel stumble over a word and was stunned by it! Would it change the way she wrote? What would happen to all the channeled work that had been so challenging to scribe originally? Would it continue to pile up, as it did now, or would it be published for others who possibly understood it better than she did? Who was *really* using her now, and why would anyone want to use a scribe when TV and such things reached millions more than the written word? Would not that cause the world to reflect more and live better, without having to be lectured to a lot?

When Jeanne was upset or unable to type messages as easily as when writing in trance, she usually wrote in a notebook using a pen, so she took up her battered notebook and golden pen while thinking about her past. How much work had she completed over the years? Her thoughts ran to men and women who came through for her over and over again, helping her widen her view of life in this time. It was not an easy plot to develop or talk about, but she felt it was time to write about her own life as if it were a novel. A book that would explain what had caused her to leave the world and follow her own path back. The story would jab out the eyes or 'i's' of those who advertised themselves as wealthy and wise—in control of everything God ever created in the form of fossil fuel. She was sure that was what she wanted to do next, but was it wise? Would it cause too many problems for the tribes?

Since you and others in this community of weavers, scribes, potters and other artisans can read the future, can you see if Jeanne will leave this compound and work with others who view her writing as a form of art? How else can she find an editor who will not sacrifice substance for what is nice or inoffensive to those who pay the price for what is published? Jeanne is not as able as you to see into her future because she clouds her mind. Are you able to do any better now?

During the hour Jeanne sat in this deep meditative state she tried to write what she thought, but many others came through the veil and talked about what they would like to do with her, too. That is when Jeanne spotted the fatal flaw! Why did she have to be a Spiritual Scribe anyway? Why not take off the rest of her life and write whatever she liked or wanted to say?

Right then laughter erupted in the ether. After a few moments a voice, seemingly one of many, spoke to Jeanne: "Mandy said the same thing! You're about to merge lives and propose to do something the world needs now, but it doesn't want you to do it."

This added mystery was too much for Jeanne to chew on without food, so she roused herself from her reverie to go to the kitchen. There she placed a chair beside the unlit fireplace and sat in what she thought would look like a brown study. Her thoughts were not about what she had done or who she had to meet tomorrow, but about the editor she must find if she was to do her best work. At that moment in time, an editor walked into the kitchen and stopped in front of her and said with dignity, "What do you want to eat, Ms. Jeanne?"

Jeanne stood up and said eagerly, "Are you by chance a reader, Louisa?"

Somewhat baffled by this response to her direct question, Louisa squinted through her deep-set brown/black eyes and said without smiling, "Yes, I am. Why do you ask?"

Astonished at the speed her life was proceeding to develop this new view, Jeanne flushed with embarrassment because she had assumed the head cook's apprentice was not well-educated or well-read. She never expected to find someone in the kitchen who read a lot or to any advanced degree, thus she was properly put in her place and unable to hide her mistake.

"I see you don't believe me, but name a book—any book! I will tell you about it. Why I hate it, or did not read it, or why I love it!" She spoke without moving to serve Jeanne dinner.

Flushed, trying not to blush more, while staring into Louisa's penetrating eyes, Jeanne said softly, "I'm amazed that you're a great reader simply because I can't imagine how you find the time to read. You're always busy and don't seem to ever get away from the kitchen—ever. When do you find time to read?"

Suddenly she realized that this had to be the absolute worst time possible to discover she was a bigot—and an arrogant one at that. Why had she not realized it before? Her thoughts were confusing because she was extremely unnerved by this view of her mind. Fortunately, grace came through and guided her quickly through this moral morass without further need to stumble over her offensive ego.

"I read when the others go to sleep. I read in stages. Sometimes I can't complete a book before it has to be returned, but I've read everything in the local library. When I travel with you and Miss Mandy, I gain access to libraries other places, too. I'm looking forward to when we move to Cancun soon. I think I'll find many new American books to read there—and more time to read, since you and Miss Mandy will be out lecturing and working—not at home as much as you are in these outposts far from the ways of the world."

Absolutely without thought or anything to say now, Jeanne continued staring into Louisa's deep eyes. She was wise enough to remain silent if she had no substantive thoughts to share or only weak arguments to offer, but having been initially programmed in The States, she still felt the urge to make some kind of excuse and whine. Right then she witnessed another miracle! She had kicked the habit! She did not speak or make a movement—or even laugh.

When Jeanne did not move or speak, Louisa took this opportunity to attend to the stew she had been putting away when interrupted by the lonesome writer. She did not want to stay and chat, but Jeanne looked very upset and blue as she wandered about the kitchen—puttering with this and that. When she felt it was safe to speak, Louisa casually mentioned that she did not realize what she said would come as a shock to her. She did not realize Jeanne had no idea Mandy was thinking about leaving this compound, let alone going back in the world and lecturing a lot, so she thoughtlessly asked, "What do you want to take with you to Cancun, Jeanne?"

Louisa was unaware that 'all of Jeanne's ducks were *not* in a row,' as Mandy often said. Her present position was not that of cook to Mandy and the other elders, but it was the only role she played with Jeanne since they met, so that is how she appeared to Jeanne until a moment ago. She walked toward the dining room, as if intending to leave and not come back.

Jeanne quickly retrieved her scattered thoughts and mumbled thanks, but was still unable to think clearly. What had happened since morning that brought about so many humbling experiences now? Was it a warning? Was she so ego-driven that she did not notice what was right in front of her, circulating through the rooms daily—able to be used by her, too? How did she ever get to the point where she forgot to look into the hearts of others—instead looked only at the parts they played and assumed she knew what they meant? Who can write and be admired—let alone make a difference, when she uses formulae instead of delving into personalities and others' hearts? Without that you merely turn out interpretations of what everyone else writes or talks about.

The day ended without anyone realizing Jeanne could see around the next bend. She would never again have to break into her heart. When her mind leaped into time previously it turned sour seeking power, but now she sighed and said to herself, "Thank God, I was put in my place today by some other estate—by other beings. Able to see that all I need is right here in this community—which I seem to be leaving."

✿ CHAPTER THIRTY-THREE

Working a loom or shuttling people across town on a bus, you notice a lot or get lost in the crush. You need patience and cannot rush. You have to know when too much is too much, but other than that you manage different kinds of life work with about the same amount of drain on your thoughts. I know the difference between loving my job and not, but it comes from years of doing one thing or another until I found out what I wanted to do always.

As Jeanne finished typing this thought out, she stared at the computer screen and looked back through time to her past. What actually happened to make her upset enough to leave the world of Corporate America behind—to never again look at what she could have been when it was all over and everything was out in the open—with no one to tell her what to do every day or ever pay nearly as much? Did she really want to know why she stayed so long in one place? No! She knew she did not have anything to compare with this life anywhere else. It was peaceful and good to stay where you were until life generates a better place to work and develop your voice. Jeanne had always felt her writing could easily speak what was in her mind, but now her thoughts seemed fuzzy. Why? She knew she had changed, and she could do something new, but was not sure when that thought would occur to others, too. As she mused, her fingers began to slowly move across the keyboard again.

When you have a voice in politics and social outlook, as well as how people play or pray at times, you feel good about yourself and your life, but you may not realize how many others hate you for being so capable. Today is a time when many sit on the sidelines shouting profanities at others as if they know them or are related in some way. They are not! How few really enjoy what takes place in sports today and is meant to entertain? How many faint when an idol is carried out of an arena writhing in agony? The Romans never fainted! They made fun of them! The Romans

When Jeanne sensed a line of thought differed from any other she had ever written, her mind usually stopped to admire or to wonder why it came out now. This was such a time. She found herself interacting with someone who seemed to be just beyond her life or her mind—not very far away in time. She wondered about her past and lives she may have lived as a Maya, but never thought about being a Roman or living such a life, so these lines caught her attention immediately.

As the day dwindled into dusk, all of her syndicated material was sent via e-mail to editors everywhere and Jeanne was left alone to think about what it all meant. She returned to the lines mentioning Romans and what they did to their idols then. How could she write with such certainty? How could she be so sure it was not all in her mind, but her lifeline? How did it compare to her sense of being Maya? These thoughts ran through time until others somewhere beyond her life picked them up. A decision was made by those who discuss what is to be taught about The Ascended Maya.

♓   ♓

When the elders and some weavers gathered after dinner to chat about their day and this and that, Mandy suddenly moved toward the back of the room and surprised everyone by inviting a woman of the tribe to address the group rather than herself. The chosen one was a Mayan teacher of many times who recognized that her ability to channel was quite different from what everyone else present practiced, but not so different from what is done in China and Japan now. Her lessons were often described as Buddhist-like—not from the wave of Christianity that circumvented the globe today. Her ways were quite different from how she was raised. Angelina was a Maya from Guatemala, not very tall, but her braids were often arranged in ways that made her appear to be just a tiny bit taller. This day she let her hair flow down around her face instead of dressing it as she usually did. It looked pretty, but seemed a bit weird to see her with unconfined hair, as if you had caught her wearing no clothes—too personal to witness or mention, so no one admired her long black hair then.

This teacher spoke in English, but with a difference, as she said, "I have lived in many times." Her speech was not wavy or accented as when most speakers translate text from Mayan or Spanish into English. Everyone was amazed because this woman had never spoken before in any other language than her own pure Mayan dialect. She was known to be very skilled, having mastered several art forms before joining the weavers in this remote community; however, her personal life was not known to anyone here. When she stood up to speak everyone paused and looked at her in silence. They waited expectantly for what would follow her prayer. She said humbly, "I am able to see into the future…and I can look back. But without anyone here who was with me there, what good is it to search such memories now?"

Pausing, Angelina waited for this wisdom to sink into the minds of those resting or waiting to speak next. When one person, then another, acknowledged they were listening, some even nodding agreement, she spoke again. "You'll find that if you don't look back and realize what you had, you may not believe you did it and will try to do it again now. That is why *we* are Maya from birth and why many on Earth, who were also Maya along with us in the past, don't remember it and wish to change the way they live today. They come here and never leave, or they visit and change so much that no one can talk to them about religion or whatever. It's what they found within themselves when they visited Mayaland that caused them to change their minds."

As Angelina moved toward the center of the room, a few men looked at her with lust. This strong, out-of-place thrust of power was immediately felt by Mandy and others standing outside the perimeter of the circle. She and others wanted to leap in and crush a few skulls or at least throw them out, but there was too much love present to do anything right then. The women watched these men and without saying a word decided they would never again enter their compound and sit among the women or dine within their walls or seek out wisdom from them. That would be punishment enough.

"I feel pleasure and pain from phantom worlds that no longer exist... Is that the way to begin the new day? Should we try to rebuild? Should we try to redo the pyramids and prepare for the day when we will use them to hold meetings and ascend with the wind? What can we do to get through to the next generation and the ones to follow that The Ascended Maya are always here—always able to help everyone who can use their views."

This teacher did not stop talking about The Maya until she digressed and mentioned how she had been urged to look at The Scribe—a lot, but not talk to her. She said she watched this woman from another country work daily without talking or walking or starting conversations with others, yet she seemed to know exactly whatever needed to be discussed in morning papers all over the USA. Her tone was normal, but her words exceeded the vocabularies of most Americans they knew. They all wondered who Jeanne really was.

"This is a time when our people must survive! They have to keep their minds and hearts open to time. If no one exists to teach what comes after this, we all lose the future. Especially since we say the future doesn't exist. What can we do to help the tribe realize it's able to work alone, or with other groups, or just as it does now with each person working alone in their home—not telecommunicating what is going on within them?"

Each question became a statement without need of an answer. Angelina stopped often and let them think back on what she just taught. It was not easy to take notes and listen to her wisdom, so the wise did not attempt to write. The foolish and the inane tried to explain what was being said to anyone sitting within earshot whenever she paused. This rude behavior annoyed Mandy and the others protecting the group from outside intrusion. They had not contemplated such behavior would occur during the meeting, but it had to be curbed. Speaking from the back of the room, Mandy said just loud enough for the teacher to hear, as well as those sitting between them, "Please repeat that last sentence. I'm having difficulty listening. There's an undercurrent of consent—even understanding, but it doesn't help me work intuitively."

The women who talked whenever possible looked somewhat hurt, while others were shocked that Mandy took responsibility for reducing the noise. Smiling now, Angelina repeated her last question. "When a wise woman or man comes to see you, do you serve tea?"

One of the women in the rear of the room said, "We serve chocolate."

Everyone's mood lightened and laughter allowed all to settle down and conceal the fact that some present would no longer attempt to interpret Angelina's work now or later. The diversion worked.

"Today—almost every day, look at the world where you were born and think about what changes came to be once you understood that you would survive and stay for more than a few days. What changes made life so different—not at all like when The Ascended Maya lived on Earth and erected pyramids meant to stand until a few reappeared and needed to uncover the facts of their ascension?"

No one asked for an explanation, yet a woman or two down front turned to strangers sitting beside them and asked what they thought about it, apparently making casual conversation about things they did not understand. They were gently rebuffed until the room was aligned and everyone could hear what the wise came through time to say that night. It took quite a long time to get it in line, by Mayan standards, but record-breaking speed for Americans.

"I see many think we aren't whomever we seem to be…that what we are is based on the ways of our mothers and fathers and their ancestors before us. Our genetic structure is no different from what you would find in any group who lived in the same place for a very long time. The world shrank enough to force some clans to uproot and move to another place. They made the United States a place of immigration rather than deportation…But now it's happening there as well. The Earth can't produce men and women who live well with each other if they have nothing whatsoever in common. If you look at all the diverse people of Earth, you see some who prefer the desert, others the mountains, and some the sun. What else?"

The group was silent. No one had a word to say. Taking this as a sign that The Ascended Maya were now able to speak through her and work in this world, Angelina made an arcane sign and pushed her hair beyond her facial boundaries. She swept it back in a way that emphasized her profile. She stood with an elastic band poised to hold her glossy black hair in a tight bun resting on her nape. Doing this accented her hawk-like nose and the way her head seemed pointed toward outer space. She was not aware of changing, but others noticed when her aura turned a different hue.

Fully alert, ready to work on what Angelina had been asked to do here on Earth, most sat ready to listen now. Some were still unwilling to remain motionless or stop doing their work, but even they finally settled down and became still.

With eyes closed, Angelina opened her mouth wide and words sprayed over their heads. "I see that it's time to go into the mind, because the air is rare. I will help each of you climb with me. You must not let your mind become afraid or scared…You are with me, and we are not alone. We are in your home…Think of it as a launch pad…one from which you can see into time whenever you are so inclined. We will hold our minds in space and time, clinging to no one else now. Drop this belief system and assume that you have found kindness and wonderful beings…who are helping you now."

Everyone appeared to realign their spines, backs, heads, and necks and assume the uniform appearance of men and women able to sit for hours without moving much. This was not an illusion, rather the conclusion of hours of practice during past lectures and classes when some had been unable to pass this particular test. The test once passed, the group was asked to imitate the teacher and get into a position similar to the lotus seat taught by Swamis to attain freedom of thought.

As Angelina watched, many struggled to cross their legs or keep their necks straight. She walked from one to another, prodding here and there to help some assume the proper position—usually a touch was enough. Finally, Angelina assumed the position she needed to achieve to talk about life as it was.

The spirit of the group rose and entered into a singular mood. It was not an ethos or a way of life, rather an episode most would never again assume in this life. It was a precious memory, but not the first time they tried to do something this wise. In the past this group had never gone beyond the first lesson planned—into the next session, before falling apart into individual lies and lives, but now they moved more quickly than classes before them into the real work. This made Angelina very pleased and happy to be there, but would she be able to teach them?

"I feel very capable of reaching out to everyone here. Do you feel the power, too?" She did not expect anyone to react to what she said, but several hands went up as if they were on fire or had the power. They knew what she meant! This was a sign she did not expect to find, and it ignited her head as if it were a beacon to The Ascended Maya.

With hands stretched toward the heavens, Angelina prayed, "If I have ever offended any of The Maya, please forgive me. It was not intended. If The Maya and God of all on high are not loved by me—and my entire belief system, please don't speak through me today. I will not grieve if it's to be that way, but please show me what I have to do to be a teacher of The Maya and work for the tribe." Her prayer seemed to be a prelude, as if she were praying to The Maya and to God on High, but it was not. It was her way of offering all their work without asking everyone to advance with her.

All present had to accept ascension within their minds and swear it was true, if they were to move on, too. Without asserting this prayer and other statements that followed, the group could not have continued to be tutored by this woman and others who started arriving out of the gloom. Whenever one present thought something, it ran around the room in a circle or two. This was not good, so a thought was sent out to stop thinking and let the teacher do her thing. Once accepted by all present, they could use the wavelength produced by that single thought to open to this woman who appeared to be in deep trance—no longer aware of anyone being there.

Angelina said, "I see many people. Many armies coming here to wage war. They are not Maya—yet they are. They have lived in other times. Existed in a different climate, but they are Maya! I see it! I believe it! The way of the Earth today is made up of many who once lived within the circle of its outer-most limits. It was never as it is now. It is going to return to what it was when we came to Earth as our home base. We can't stop it! Some hate that our star will return to its own space and time when we're no longer able to use our host and must leave Earth. We will bless her for all she did for us here. Today, we salute the world and its people, but we love Mother Earth more. Say this with me…"

She stopped and dropped her arms, but kept looking up at the ceiling and the world beyond her vision and appeared to laugh. Her mouth lifted and puckered like a bright red rose bud as a pearly note came from her throat. It was a long, long tone that sounded as if she were keening in the key of E, then nothing else for a long moment, and then another sound rose and several others could be heard over time. The tone she emitted was not eerie, but the group could not get into the same mood and repeat it, because someone among them now thought it was weird. This broke the group in two, and then into three separate parts. One group would never remember where it happened or who was in the room then and who left with whom. The other two groups would never again gain entrance into this room and work with this teacher again. It happened before, but usually not at this advanced stage in the work.

Angelina did not stop and watch them fall out, instead she continued to channel and wail: "I am Maya! I see into the future and into you!" Then very quietly, she said, "Please don't sing now—hum and keep the sound open in your hearts. I will teach you what to do later…Please block out the rest of the community with sound. You can join me intuitively on the next level as we chant."

The room was humming and the sound was numbing, so three men left. They could not stand the way everyone ignored their work and did not listen to them. Mandy helped them out the door, assuming they would leave the community immediately. She was not going to miss this movement into the future or into the past or wherever it would take them without being there then, so she gave each man a bit of a shove and pretended to watch them head toward their cars, but she did not. Only her shape remained in the doorway. They left wondering about the community and why they had not caught on that something was going to happen that would exclude them and their versions of Earth as it would be until the end of time. Their movements outside did not bother the group inside, but the men in their cars—once on the road, felt the Earth move—a lot!

After Mandy removed these men from the group, no one else moved to leave or behave as if unable to breathe deeply, so she moved into history, proving to her mind that she was Maya from birth this time, but not in the space that today's Mayan tribes willingly saved. Her days were not numbered so much as limited by the way she was raised; however, she had work that would help the world of the Maya of today and many others who would come after her. This was why she was not a member of the tribe as it existed in the Highlands or Yucatan since her first day on Earth. This thought produced another bubble in which she suddenly felt a deep ache for her mother and father of Earth who were not to be with her when she ascended at the end with a group she was able to work with on Earth now. Instantly, she felt her parents' presence at her side and never worried again about who they were or why they had not understood her then.

The day ended with more women and men becoming aware of their heritage. They would help others when they surrendered their bodies in time to the magnetic waves of The Ascended Maya. The perimeter of the room was not wide enough to accommodate The Maya, plus all the minds and bodies present during the long discussion about the Romans and how they gave the Maya access to ideas based on the calendar they brought back to Earth several years later—unlike how Americans gauge time now.

The group's work erupted with the power of a volcano and forced several men out without an explanation or need for one. "When you're unafraid, pray! If you're afraid and unable to find your way, pray! If you can't live with one person or another, pray for guidance and the ability to find a home of your own or a way out of whatever was planned for you." The tone of Angelina's words, more than content, seemed to implore each and every student to pray more, but she did not insist on it. Her hair now looked different and many admired how she had interlaced it with flowers. Her aura was extremely bright and shiny—like a painted halo in a Renaissance piece of art. She saw no difference, but felt intuitively renewed and able to work with those given to her to tutor or excuse them from doing any further work with her on Earth.

Finally, Mandy stood and walked toward the front of the room and asked everyone to clap loudly as if they had been greatly entertained. They did not need any explanation, but one man was amazed that he alone was unable to clap his hands or stomp his feet and praise God. What happened to him was so rare that only Mandy and Angelina could help him move into the next view. Mandy, although unafraid, was unprepared for the channel to leap over a chair to stand in front of the man and grasp his head as if about to cut it off. He fainted then, but she helped him regain his mind in time. It was very strange! Mandy was reminded once again that each has a special gift. One can see into space and another understands time, while simple facts elude both.

Within a moon of that meeting two men met in the afternoon and stood together without talking, yet still conversing about life on Earth today. They decided it was time to dig out a bit of the mountainside and begin once again to build a pyramid of clay.

☼ CHAPTER THIRTY-FOUR

"Thinking about your future?" Jorge spoke softly to Mandy as she stood beside him lost in thought. They were looking down a mountain to a valley where one of their outlying compounds spread out below them in the early morning light.

Mandy appeared to be leaning against a tree without actually touching its trunk as she replied. "No, I was wondering about where we'll all go when life is over on Earth. Will we be taken to task for all the scars and implants we produced over the years in our attempts to remove and restructure what God amply provided for us—so we could live well without much effort?" When Jorge remained silent, she added, "I doubt that God has been watching us very closely, or we would have been chastised long before this... The Maya believe Earth is provided for us for only a few hours and then we must leave and go into infinity without any way of coming back. I know that much, but how to live it and not worry about when it's the right time to leave is what bothers me."

Jorge said nothing, but put her thoughts to work by placing them inside another dream designed to see what they might do as a group or as one or two working together. Silently he asked God to help them create a life plan that would not become effete or useless to pursue. That was about all he knew to do.

If life produces nothing for you, it is not your problem once you ask God without any personal ambition to show you the way to live your last days on Earth. But what about all the women and some men who want to do a lot now because the end is in sight? Will they be able to do all that is required in the time allowed to be on this planet, or will they go to their 'deaths' worried that they did not finish what they started here? Who will help those still reaching and striving and trying to create something new? What about the Maya who refuse to heed their elders now and listen as they did when they were children? Who could be so thoughtless as to believe they were savages because they are poor in the wares of this world?

As Jorge stood beside Mandy and thought, a breeze from the bottom of the valley wafted the aroma of Mayan coffee, baking, and such things as people prepare in the morning hours at homes everywhere, but seldom in Mayaland. What was the real reason for all these changes in their behavior now?

Mandy stood tall, listening intently to the song of a bird sitting on a limb somewhere above her. She followed the lyrics and heard within its song that she was so good at her job and so strong in her words that many Maya emulated her now and tried to do what she did almost automatically. They even ate food she enjoyed, rather than what they grew at home. Alas, she had not helped them as much as polluted their wealth. This was not a good thought! She wilted a bit and began to transform into a new kind of woman, one who did not want to do as much for others as she had done in the past. The bird ended its song right then with: 'Why do we change when all we have to do is be ourselves?'

Thoughts of The Ascended Maya and the tribe were uppermost in the minds of the two old friends standing on top of the mount without touching or speaking. They stood for a day or more this way. No one knew where the two shamans were or what they were doing, but no one sounded an alarm because it was not unusual for them to disappear without saying where they were going or when they would return.

When the sun rose the day after the amazing sunrise illumination of their minds, Mandy was still standing very erect. She listened intuitively to the bird sitting among the branches above her, hoping to hear its wisdom once again. The bird sang its usual song, but this time she heard no words of wisdom. She noticed that Jorge did not smile as usual. They both knew they would not be teachers of this world much longer and were struggling with their ever-growing anticipation of leaving Earth forever. They knew the day was approaching faster than anticipated when it would be necessary to break away and leave everyone to do whatever they wanted to do, too.

Glancing at the man standing beside her in the shadow of the great Ciba tree, Mandy said, "What do you say to our going back to the village and seeking out someone who still knows how to prepare a good, old-fashioned Mayan breakfast and eating it before we return to our work?"

Regretfully, Jorge declined her invitation, saying he could accompany her only as far as the village. He wanted to fast and relax one more day in order to discover whatever *facts* could be garnered from The Ascended Maya about the upcoming Earth changes, as well as figure out who would take over their work within the tribe and their compounds all over the world—not just those nearby.

Reluctantly, Mandy walked into the village alone. She did not sense danger, which made her nervous. 'First, the bird didn't sing words of wisdom this morning, and then Jorge decides to stay away another day. Something isn't right! I can't find my mind to figure it out and I can't stay in time, either. What is going to change and make it difficult for me to move?' Such thoughts occupied her mind so completely that she remained aloof from what was going on all around her.

She silently moved through the village, watching the children walk to school. Her own son, if she had had one, would attend a village school of love, unable to spend his days at home with her learning the ways of The Maya of ancient times. Why did the Maya have to change? What was being taught now that was so much better than what they knew in the past when it came to weather, for example? What had changed in their minds that made them uneasy with what they saw on TV and hoped to be? Too many things were not as they needed to be or should be, according to the views she accessed now.

Her head drooped, her shoulders slumped, and her steps faltered. The villagers were not sure at first if it was Mandy as she approached an elder who suddenly appeared and stood waiting for her in the square. The elder wanted to speak to Mandy, but could not produce enough saliva to say one word in Maya. Her thoughts turned inward and she could see that Mandy was burned deep—not feeling well, because she had been hurt. No one but this woman standing in the sun, greeting everyone as they came to town, could see the hurt. This blind woman comprehended what others could not see or believe. She alone saw how others' anger and the intensity of past encounters left Mandy vulnerable to thoughts of what she had to do now. The blind shaman knew what she had to do, but would Mandy let her do it? Could she remove the spell in an hour or two? Her random thoughts produced a stone in Mandy's path that caused her to stumble and fall toward the blind woman who grasped her hand tightly as if to steady them both. Shaken awake, Mandy said to the blind woman holding her hand, "Come little sister, I have hurt you. Let me take you to the café for a cup of hot chocolate."

The old woman did not appear stunned, upset, or hurt, but she mumbled something under her breath that sounded like a curse. Without thought, Mandy led the woman to a bench beneath the tallest tree in the zocalo where they could sit in the shade and not do much. The tree would keep them from feeling hot and humid until the sun moved to midday, by then they would be far away.

The village square was not far from the mountaintop where Mandy met Jorge and stood for a day, but she might as well have been on another planet. The zocalo was busy with its mundane affairs—not at all quiet enough to say prayers and be heard by those who rush to your rescue if needed. Mandy felt strange. Pain is illusive and the woman seated beside her was not a scribe or an interpreter of words, nor the usual tribal elder, but she seemed to be able to breath in rhythm with Mandy now.

After a few minutes they stood and began walking about the village. They did not stop to eat breakfast or lunch. Some said they talked together, but most thought they walked in silence. It was an event no one wanted to forget once that day was over. A kindly old man approached them with water once and let them drink from his cup. He never wiped that cup out again for the rest of his life.

When a teacher noticed the two wise women walking around the town, he suddenly realized it was time to teach the children how to rise. He could see it coming and knew at once that it was the time foretold in ancient books hidden away until now—still inscribed in the way of The Maya—not to be shared with anyone who would steal or destroy them.

As the day ended and the sun set over the mountains to the West, Jorge suddenly appeared out of the air directly in front of the two women and asked them to dine with him. He was not famished or tired, but they were. He could see Mandy no longer needed his prayers, but wondered who was helping her now. She looked different—much warmer than is normal after walking and working with someone of the tribe. Her skin seemed to change color as they parted—more and more like the skin God had given her at birth. She was now as fair as when he first saw her in the city of her birth. Mandy had obviously arrived at some point in inner time. Was she ready to return or ascend or whatever? Jorge's mind could not imagine or cogitate more. He was stunned—unable to talk of what he meant to say, so he walked quietly along with them to a nearby restaurant in the heart of the town.

Around the patio where the three elders ate their dinner and prayed, the trees bent and listened to their whisperings while warning the town not to peek or scan the secluded space they provided to hide the Lord of the Night's work. Trees cannot see? Trees witness all of man's frailties and report when asked. For this reason, the trio sat and asked the greatest tree what they could not see themselves. The tree was pleased to help them and did such a great job that it grew another inch taller and shed some unwanted leaves when they left.

Within a day of this meeting of the three magi, the villagers realized their town was in need of much paint. The buildings were not white enough to attract the eye of people passing by, nor clean enough to please God and the angels who fly in the night. They worked quickly, because they wanted the Magi to come back.

Working on their own themes, processing what they alone had to do in dreams, the three elders walked out of town into the countryside that night without anyone aware they left the zocalo. How did they do such things and why were the usual questions left in the minds of those who did not study time. For students able to at least understand the theory of relativity, they know it is not easy to do but is possible.

For a few more days Mandy and Jorge appeared to be busy doing what they usually did—talking to everyone as if there were no problems anywhere else. The folks in the compound located deep within this valley heard first what the two shamans planned to do, then the next compound or two reviewed what they told them would happen soon. They all looked forward to receiving a great review, too. However, it did not go down that way. What needed to be done immediately was entered in the long count that some do not understand, and those who saw these things and did what they were told were asked to lead the way back.

When you fail basic training—unable to listen intently or keep your mind in line over time, you never get beyond wondering why, or worse—whining. Such people sit and ask lots of questions, but never accept answers suited to what they want to hear, so they whine even more. If you hate to be told what to do and whine all the time, why not stop and listen to the wise? Forget about asking questions—listen and show respect!

The forebears of today's Maya were the first to be left behind the last time. They were unable to find their way back to the first step of pyramid creation. Unable to remember what to do when the sun was hot or when the sun was not, they became obsessed with the fundamental concepts of their remembered religion, often forgetting to honor God.

These fundamentalists were determined to remember the old ways, even if unable to ascend. They insisted that the doctrines written down and previously taught by those who had ascended were to be accepted literally now! They insisted that actual human hearts be given to God in a way consistent with the pages of their gospel. They knew this was right because they were God's chosen people! They killed outsiders without thinking it might be wrong. They wanted to be strong and dedicate their lives to God, so hearts had to be beating and pumping so they could ascend to God and not burn in hell. This interpretation of the doctrine was such an amazing alteration to their previous faith that many Maya left such places, running as though the Toltecs attacked and won. They did not believe in such things and knew instinctively that the ascension was not just another ritual, but a belief system that needed to be kept alive in one's mind if it was to endure and save those who came to be after the last ascent.

The belief and knowledge that they could fly was not long held by the tribe once the ancient wise ones left the tribe behind. Where did they go? The wise assembled in groups of ten or less—flying to a mountain where they could ascend as a tribe; however, no one alive remembers that time. Only those Maya deemed to be lost in space are able to retrace those days and place that knowledge into the minds of those who can now walk in time.

It was not difficult to select a group to ascend with then. You studied with them for many years, strived to have normal family relationships, even when not related by blood, because a difference in group mindsets is necessary to block the growth of superstitious beliefs. The combined mindset of a clan is usually enough to gain ascendancy, but some families were unable to ascend because they were led by those with no belief or faith in God of All.

The way to understand a group and its unique dynamics is to study and accept what they do together. Who do they listen to and follow, as well as work hard to emulate and recreate? If they select a bad model, instead of heeding those who are highly regarded in the ways of Today, they will go nowhere in time and never know what they missed, regardless of how many around them are gifted enough to ascend and survive in other times.

The way of their Bible was such that The Maya knew immediately when the one they needed to follow arrived. They knew it would be the same man who told them they would ascend once again and do what they were asked to do—work alone for God only. Just as a bee works without a life plan (or so the lazy and useless believe), The Maya work on whatever is at hand, refusing to be taken from their land.

This is not a superstitious mindset, but a way of life that needs to be shored up every few months now if today's TV-programmed mayhem is to be kept at bay. One clan recognized quicker than most tribes how the anger and greed of actors and malicious news views creates havoc in the minds of teens. They began moving their villages and such out of the range of such godless pastimes, even doing away with satellite dishes loved by some. It is not good when a clan's individual mindset is infiltrated within the home and children accept directly what outsiders say is best for them without testing its usefulness to the family and tribe. Television belittled the tribe and took away their pride in designing their lives, so it was stopped—believe it or not!

♓ ♓

On one occasion Mandy and Jorge were called into a village to settle an argument that began over a goat seen grazing daily at a nearby home instead of roaming around the hills. They knew the seriousness of settling such disputes before all could work on ascension. If the mortal mind is upset and unable to understand the sacrifices necessary in this world to move beyond it and arrive on the other side without any scars, much is lost. So Mandy and Jorge set up tribunals to judge minor cases when they interrupted the daily life of families and clans, thus negating the need to take them to a magistrate where they would have to hate each other for days and weeks until the case was settled unhappily for one or the other. The villagers could now take their problems to one person to be heard almost daily, and if that wisdom was shunned, they could then go to a trio of elders appointed to listen and pass final judgment. All had to abide by the triumvirate's decision or lose membership in the tribe. The only time to take mundane or trivial matters to the magistrate would be when the problem involved those who were not Maya.

Within weeks of this resolution to change the way the tribe would govern, the towns and villages held local meetings again—no longer trying to run the country beyond them.

A message sent from the Federal Governments said they could do anything they wished provided they informed the countries that did not love them enough what was decided—and that it would not cost them anything. Were there problems when a decision or law was implemented elsewhere? Very few! Outstanding problems not settled to anyone's satisfaction usually involved the common good and taxes paid by every neighborhood. Since only the government could pave the main roads and put in sewage lines to the tribes, it was decided that the Federal government would be made to pay for such public works and help in small ways or let the mud slide—as it had in the past.

Work in villages surrounding the compounds increased. Neighbors prospered more than villages that resisted Mandy and her people settling among them. In time, these traditionalists started rumors that Mandy used magic when she was pleased or worse when she was upset. Their lies entered the atmosphere and poisoned many minds. Too many now blamed Mandy if anything appeared wrong—large or small.

Mandy felt hurts and slights burning away at her heart the day the blind shaman helped her cry and find an out-of-the-way healer who made an incision, removed her scarred heart and replace it with another filled with enough love that it would never again be damaged that way. It was done in less than an hour!

The decision to leave the villages to the people who ran them was not a decision made on Earth, even though it appeared to be, so it was adhered to gradually, not immediately. You must have noticed that no one accepts immediately that you know what God means or says, but most people will listen to common sense.

Without disappearing many days from the usual world they lived in then, Mandy and Jorge changed once again. They were blended into a marvelous work of art. It first arrived created in clay, then wood workers did their thing, and later weavers created a new line. The scribes described it as a colorful blend that enables everyone to meditate and reach inside their souls to find The Maya working for them on the other side of time.

☼ Chapter Thirty-Five

Whatever the day or hour, there is always something that needs to be done and cannot wait another day, but when you realize that day-after-day you are doing work that never ends, or there are no friends around you now, it is time to move. With that mindset in place, Wanda thought about another life in which she could live without the people now dependent upon her and her patterns and all the work she did whenever coerced to weave a huge mural. Her wall hangings were being copied by others onto huge commercial looms in the States—without paying royalties to her or the tribe. An act of the faithless that left a bitter taste in her mouth and much anger when she saw Mayan wonders recreated with huge mistakes.

Her friends were not aware that she was unhappy there, but Thérèse saw that her mother was no longer working as happily with people of her own kind. Wanda did not like to impose upon others when her language skills came and went with the breeze rather than remaining fluent as a Maya who knows many dialects.

In the years of work that went into the birth of this home on Earth, Wanda was always too busy weaving to see what others might be doing on the side. She was not burnt out, just not as happy doing her thing as she had been in the past. Waxing enthusiastic when new classes walked through the door, eager for her to teach them Mayan weaves, now drained her rather than boosting her personal power. Her life was no longer as interesting to her or her family—perhaps because she had not been back to The States in several months—or was it a year already since she visited Tucson? It was getting harder to remember her own life events before another began in the Yucatan, but she felt she had to do something new or everything would disappear and she would not be remembered here or there.

Was this the panic of seizing immortality, the drive to be remembered by members of your tribe? What made people build monuments? What made anyone want to do something that would last long after they were gone? What tasks survive and provide an impression of what you gave this planet when you walked the Earth? Wanda did not feel deserted, but disconcerted to find weaving was the only art she could leave behind to impart the art she was born to create. This upset her because she wanted to get away from everything and everyone and start over. Her heart was no longer in teaching more and more students and weaving for the public. She was suddenly tired of it all!

As the Sabbath beckoned, everyone moved to an open space created by Mayan elders outside the village where Mandy and Jorge had established a great settlement of weavers. As Wanda and Thérèse walked toward the anointed spot where everyone would meditate, they saluted the parish priest with a joint wave that he thought very charming. He smiled a lot, but never went near the women and men who worked all day with determination and dedication to build a huge family of nations. He stayed away, in fact, but not because he was afraid of them. His own life was enhanced at times by the coins some families left behind at his chapel, and he secretly believed they all did more for the world than he did. He felt that way often, but never let it show in his faith.

Wanda spoke haltingly to her daughter, who seemed to be lifted and drifting along on the air currents that swept across the road, while she stumped steadfastly toward the group assembled in the clearing. "What do you think the dear father really thinks of us, Thérèse? He never stops by to talk. Do you think he believes we make pagan sacrifices or are not God fearing?"

"I think he knows who we are, Wanda. He may not be able to put it into words, but he knows we're here to help the tribe and, after all, he is Maya, so he wants us to help—but not upset his Church or call attention to his lack of work. He likes it here as it is, but he's now afraid that some Monsignor or Bishop will visit one day and tell him he has to move. No, he's not afraid, just not able to experience his faith—yet." As Thérèse spoke, her face glowed as if a candle had been placed behind her brow. The light shone outward through her face—not toward the back of her head. The glow, so wondrous that her mother could only blink at the vision she had then, mentally filed it away for use next week in a new form of art she would start.

They walked or glided over the roads until they arrived at the space in time where no one they knew could tell if they were talking or not. Instead of a crowd standing in the sacred space, as they had anticipated, a house appeared. While walking toward the house, it turned into an inn. Both wondered if it was a mirage or had always existed there. They had learned from experience that anything could happen in Mayaland and usually did.

When they reached the front door a mother with a child stopped to look at them, then beckoned Wanda and Thérèse to enter the inn. They felt no sense of forbidding then, but later remembered it was strange that an Indian woman would ask them to enter but not send for someone to wait on them. Instead, the young woman took her child by the hand and led her to another room, then returned wiping her hands lightly on her snow-white dress without leaving any fingerprints behind.

In the center of what might be the dining room there were tables and chairs set up for people to dine or lounge about. The flooring was highly-polished ceramic tile that tapered away from the center of the room and became raked earth in the style of most Mayan family homes in the area. Wanda examined a chair she thought needed rockers to be complete. She wondered, 'How can this be?' She was in sore need of relief from pain in her right leg, thus happy to see a mirage or fantasy or reality present a chair of any kind and hoped it would be offered for her use now. Her lips could not smile away the frown caused by pain, thus she quickly got across her need to rest. To settle into the chair without undue wear and tear, Wanda had to adjust her fake leg, but once seated the rocker fit perfectly—as if custom-made for her.

In the time following their arrival, the mother and child appeared to have disappeared, unable to hear them talking about the appearance of a Victorian rocker in the middle of a wilderness. After a few minutes they inspected the ceiling and noticed that the wood was neither rain-stained nor old, and that the thatch was done in a pattern not normally found in this area. The ancients had used cane and such in ways long forgotten, but in modern times the palms used were not as weatherproof or perhaps were not woven as tightly, and the pattern steadily changed over the years. Water often drained inside houses once the roof went through a hurricane or two, thus Wanda and Thérèse surmised that this house was newly thatched in the way of the ancient Maya. But who in this area lived unknown to them until now, and why were they given admittance to a room where no one else was present?

Before the day was over, strange items appeared in the middle of the great room, along with even stranger apparitions that were very aromatic and smoked a lot. A large brazier already afire popped up out of a mist, but no one else arrived to make this vision come to life. Things seemed to just spring into existence, with Thérèse and Wanda the only witnesses. If two humans see the same thing come to be, is it a mirage? They wondered if it was yet another Mayan wisdom quest beginning in time.

Suddenly an old man appeared out of the smoky air, apparently determined to meet them there. He had walked from a nearby village not identified on any map the average tourist might buy. This elder was the epitome of wisdom and had many things he could teach, but he was unable to talk. Having lost his tongue by accident when young, only those who listen intuitively can hear what he says. He chose these two women above all other students and asked that they be sent to him immediately. That is why they arrived exactly when he expected them! He identified them as new pupils, even though they did not know him. Why? The way of life is not open to the mind, nor the mind open to time, so much happens that continually amazes initiates.

While their work progressed into the early dawn of the following day, the villagers avoided the strange building that suddenly appeared in their midst. They stayed away and worked on their plots, doing chores at home, and sending their youngsters to church school. They had no wish to call attention to the fact that they did not understand the ancient one they wondered about privately but never in public.

This shaman feared no one! He never spoke, yet they felt he was not mute or he would have said so. The fact that he could not speak was not known since he never said anything to people he met wherever he went. His feet directed him here and there where merchandise awaited him at the side of certain roads. He picked out what trade goods he wanted and left the rest for others. Everyone assumed he spoke a dialect so ancient that no one in their clan remembered it. Strangely enough, they always forgot to think about him after he was gone.

Without anyone to tell them what he did and what he intended to do, Wanda and Thérèse assumed he was wise and would guide them back to their minds, time, or whatever it was they left behind to join him now. He said nothing at first, but decided it was unkind to let Wanda and the saint wonder about his tribe—The Maya of all time. He spoke not in words but with gestures and inclinations of his crown toward them or toward the ceiling or toward a wall. His head seemed to beam messages to them that they easily channeled. As they sat in front of him, it was necessary to change position when he changed the direction his head beamed wisdom.

This sage had no name, because he had no need for a name. He had no way of telling others what he had been called in the past, so no one knew, but he wanted to share his last known name with them now. He knew it was Ezekiel and that he was a member of a long-ago tribe who visited the shores of Yucatan, and then could not find the way back in time to reach their ancestral home. He told Wanda and Thérèse that he was not allowed to repeat all his story, because it was forbidden to do so; however, someone always existed who could tell the whole story or give permission to teach what was usually forbidden.

Ezekiel was a teacher—not a storyteller. He reached them intuitively as no one else had done since Mandy shared the vision of where they would live in the Yucatan years before, as well as what their roles would be as time moved toward its inevitable end in the United States and around the world. This shaman appeared elderly, but his mind was quite young. Although he never traveled beyond nearby fields, he was wise about how the mind reneges on what it sees and says it will be. They all laughed at how easily he stripped away their own false pretenses and worries that never came to be.

After a few hours, Wanda started to unleash her leg so she could feel the earth with the stump of her leg. The old man indicated with violent gestures that her leg was not to be pulled apart because it had become one with her body. She laughed at the idea, but suddenly felt a sensation that made her believe her leg had been reattached. He said her leg would carry her far and fast and never again give her pain—that she could now dance a jig.

Without thinking, Wanda laughed at the idea of dancing a jig—as if she had ever wanted to do such a thing. The shaman then revealed she was the long-ago leader who brought the Celts to this country, and she alone knew why weavers were so highly esteemed that they were never questioned about what they would do if enough yarn was not produced for their use. She knew it would always be provided by The Ascended Maya!

This information and wisdom was not relayed in the usual way. Normally they could not think this way because his sentences were so deeply etched and incomprehensible to human minds most of the time, but information was now arriving in their minds as if downloaded by some giant cosmic computer run by The Maya.

When Wanda and Thérèse left the magus and walked back down the lane toward their home, they saw workers building an addition onto the weavers' compound to accommodate the potters who produced art that coordinated with the products of their looms. That is when they both knew what they had to do!

The density and intensity of the old man's revelation was far too difficult to relate to others, so they did not repeat anything he appeared to teach them. Is it not amazing that a saint and a weaver could meet someone who could change them completely in a single day? To discover one now deaf and blind to all that was said and done in the usual way of the mundane world of today, and the other would never endure pain in her scarred leg, was just too much to explain. The methods used were described later to some members of the tribe, but no one else entered the flame and gathered the wisdom taught that way. It amazed the local Maya that this elder spoke to Americans! They shook their heads in disbelief because many had begged the old man for any instruction—over and over again, and he had merely shuffled away muttering under his breath.

Their combined work quickly moved forward. Wanda was no longer interested in returning to The States to live or even visit. She moved and walked in a totally new way, too. In fact, many doubted she had a prosthesis or lost her right leg! She never experienced pain again and her brain was never lame when it came to recognizing the merit of her work and how much she was needed in this provincial town. She now knew they would remember her long after she was gone and unwilling to visit in spirit again. Her work was her monument to posterity.

Thérèse acted different ever after, too. She was totally removed from the gossip still bandied around about her days as a famous model. She 'just didn't get' whatever was meant to hurt. Thérèse smiled and paced with style and grace back and forth across the tiled verandah all day as though modeling serapes, rebozos, and such, never aware that it seemed a bit strange for a saint to do now.

Ever humble, Thérèse's knees were no longer able to bend easily, so she stood about or walked through the compound with quiet dignity to the chapel built especially for her needs. Daily Thérèse taught whatever small lessons the young women and men needed. Her favorite work was in the garden! Since her knees were arthritic, she had to instruct others on the art of loving roses, so they would grow abundantly even in the shade. She was ever watchful of everyone around her and constantly assured all who came to visit her that she was not a saint, but they knew better.

☼ CHAPTER THIRTY-SIX

The thought of moving away from Mayaland was not present in Mandy's mind until she saw three men leave 'to make tons of money,' as friends said about them. Those who left never, ever thanked those who taught them. Each group dispread and dispersed throughout the world once classes were over and awards handed out to the best artists. This had to stop! Why? The Ascended Maya said so.

The Maya watched how Americans worked and took upon themselves some of their motions, as well as how to use the computer to produce better art. What The Maya admired most about computers was how they could be used to converse with folks all over the Earth, but they were unhappy with what many students did with them instead.

What too many students admired most about the computerized world was their increased ability to buy what they would never use or give to anyone as a gift. Many students, regardless of age, did not wish to continue their previous automatic response to daily life. They wanted to drop the dispirited and desperate lives they lived as average Americans of their particular generation. To their credit, they did not try to authorize buys or give away secrets of the tribe, yet far too many continued to buy everything they thought they wanted, even stealing if they could not arrive at a trade of some kind to get whatever they coveted. This unsettling development ended the initial stages of work created by Wanda, Julie, Jeanne, and others who had come together to help promote the work of The Ascended Maya and their descendants left behind on Earth.

After weeks and months of litigation with corporations in the United States over copyright laws and such, Mandy decided it was necessary to move into political venues throughout the world and take a stand for The Maya on both sides of the veil, but she was not able to persuade many artists to adopt this view, too. She found them more interested in whining about lack of support than willing to go out and work hard to get what they thought they deserved today.

Within three days of the last rain expected that season, Mandy packed up a few things in a very large suitcase and walked out of her apartment in Mazatlan. Silent about where she was going or what she would do with the work she prized enough to pack and take with her, Mandy was determined to work in ways the tribal members had never seen her follow. She was not herself—as they were wont to say. Walking out on a large family is not as easy as leaving one or two people or a small group who never understood you anyway. What transported Mandy into the world was a mission for *them*, thus she was not afraid of being far away or out of touch for days.

⊁　⊁

Speech writing was Jeanne's assignment. Her work as a teacher changed dramatically to accommodate this new mission. She stopped training scribes and secretaries to assist people of high estate and began writing weekly columns once again. This time they related what she saw in Guatemala, the Yucatan, and regions forgotten by various heads of state and their administrations. This ambition of Jeanne's dated back years, so she dug into it with great force of will now. Her mind leashed her spirit—or was it the reverse? Anyway, it worked for Jeanne. Her syndicated columns were immediately sought by newspapers all over the United States, then South America, and eventually the entire world.

As some said, her future was assured the day she returned to writing her old column; but she was not working for the usual reasons. Fame is not a game for people of good will. It may happen to those who work hard and are associated with excellent work and honest attempts to help others. However, no one can enjoy fame for very long. Seeing a woman receive much favorable attention causes many to hurry to make sure her head is not turned; however, Jeanne never worried. She was in no hurry to gain fame as a world-beater or even as a leader, so it happened almost instantly.

Since Jeanne lived hidden away somewhere in the mountains of Guatemala or on the Yucatan plains, no one could find her and bother her with witless questions and interviews. Even so, some fools tried to write contrived stories about her, but lost out in the end. Evening news shows seldom ended without a quote lifted freely from her work, and in time they sometimes even gave her credit. Jeanne continued to enjoy e-mail forwarded with her words highlighted and identified by members of the tribe living everywhere now. She laughed, even stored some away, saying she might write a book someday and refer to them, but said it without any real enthusiasm. Diligently Jeanne crafted her art and continued to search for the perfect word to place in polished phrases so as not to be misinterpreted when translated into more languages than she kept track of now.

Meanwhile, Julie threw pots wherever she traveled. Working with Mayan potters, waiting for any excuse to make busts of Mandy and the others, her work changed dramatically over the years and was not what it was when she arrived in Mayaland issuing orders on how to pot and use today's clays, but it was not that different either. Her hands were tougher—strong enough to easily use the forge. She had no need for a man to do the heavy work of smelting and molding brass and gold or whatever was required to create a great statue, an ornate image, or even a bust.

⊁　⊁

At the same time Jeanne left her compound for parts unknown, Julie stood up in her studio, waved, and collapsed. Two Mayan women were first at her side. Then someone stood over her and cried. It was not an angel. It was the woman called, Thérèse, who could not believe others had not paid attention to the needs of this great artist who always wanted to do her own thing, but yielded to the will of the tribe. Thérèse heard Julie praying and was about to answer her prayer in her small way when apprised of her sudden collapse. The two women kneeling at Julie's side were the first to hear Thérèse say softly, "You are able to stand up, Julie. You know what you want. Go to the next view and look at you…What are you?…You're an angel locked into this face and body for only a short time…Try to move now …" Whatever else she said to the corpse-like body of the artist was not heard, but within a few minutes Julie stood and looked about her as if nothing unusual had happened and immediately left the room.

Julie walked into the kitchen and talked to a cook washing clay pots. The same pots she had taught the local children how to make over and over again. She casually asked if there was any juice left from breakfast. The cook looked at her closely, then gently pushed her into a chair next to the work table where she had been adding her home-grown herbs and spices to a pie of some kind. She told Julie not to move fast or go very far, just watch what she did with the jars and pots that she and the kids had produced for the communal kitchen. The cook laughed whenever she said 'kids' because it was such an American idea—not what they taught. To the Maya, children are little adults—not to be compared to young goats, always frolicking and getting into trouble.

The cook pushed a spoon and bowl of lemon chicken soup toward Julie before leaving the kitchen. She instructed her not to let the pie burn in the hot oven close by, but Julie was so lost in thought she did not notice the pie was overdone until she smelled smoke. This failure to pay attention made her nervous and upset, because she expected every job to be done perfectly. She had been asked to take charge of a simple task, but abandoned her post! Such thoughts were so disconcerting that she hesitated to call the cook and tell her the pie was burnt. In an effort to create less trouble for the harried cook, Julie decided to make another pie.

The flour was already sifted, and sitting nearby were all the spices and herbs required. She did not quite comprehend yet that the leavening sitting in a measuring cup ready to be used must have been left there for that purpose, too. Carefully measuring and using a spoon to level all the elements of the new pie, she thought about life and its many lessons at the same time.

Her mind reflected back to how she worked as a child. How many mistakes had she made using the kiln before achieving the reputation she now enjoyed of never misfiring anything—a miracle she had come to expect. She heard a voice in her mind, as if from a very far distance, 'If you don't take great care measuring your life work, it gets lost in the fire. You aren't very far beyond your youth, yet are tired of life. You can commit professional suicide by seeking work that will not lead you to new gains for YOU—the eternal soul of the *you* whom You are now.' Julie sat down and stared at the dough as it appeared to rise between her fingers, as if it were alive and kicking. She suddenly realized it was alive, just as everything she made in clay was alive, too. 'The clay has life or it can't be used. Paint is a living organism by its own definition or it can't be used as glaze.'

Without further worry about what must be done, Julie pushed the dough onto a pie plate and gingerly placed it in the middle of the hot oven. She did not add more fuel, afraid that this pie would burn, too. She would watch what happened to the pie. 'When you are put in charge of someone else's art, you don't take as much care as when you make it yourself.' The thought created a tidal wave within her mind over time. She firmly believed that the basics were being overlooked, and she was not doing as much good work as she could. Her energy recreated in space a pile of clay sitting and waiting for her to work immediately. She would start fresh and model clay using her hands only—sorting out what art she wanted to keep and fill her home. Her sacred space should be great! She would recreate it wherever she stayed, even if only for a few days or weeks. Hopefully, she could root in time—and stay for years. The time it took Julie to think through this one single thought was just enough to create a great pie eaten by the tribe that night.

The cook never revealed to anyone that she had set it up to teach Julie a life lesson. The lesson took and created a greater artist than the one who had fainted—unable to go any further down the wrong path.

When this artist rose higher as a destined, major creator of modern Mayan pottery, she was accepted by critics in the United States and everywhere else as the best woman of this age to produce works of clay. That is when she switched to brass and copper, leaving clay to others to use or play with, until she was summoned by the muse of clay that day.

When Julie started back on her path, doing what she did best, her mind rejected plots to keep her potting as she had in the past. She asked Mandy to recall the men promoting her pottery as their own in attempts to gain admiration and acceptance for work they could not produce without her help. When it was truly their turn on Earth to star in art, other such thieves convinced many to esteem what others did in order to defraud them. Their work would be spotted centuries later as fraudulent—not produced by the hands of this great master of clay.

With Julie busy at her art and Jeanne writing as a recluse would do, the class of students studying to be shamans dropped dramatically to only a few Maya who continued to work on the side while creating families and such ties. Each compound was busier than ever producing the work of apprentices now turned into masters. The affluence that such recognition brought to many artists produced a noticeable difference in production from days gone by, but something was missing. The missing presence was Mandy. She no longer stopped by to talk about The Maya and being Maya in this time.

Mandy asked Jorge to encourage more elders to abandon their old rituals and practices and begin teaching these students about The Ascended Maya and such things. It was a great way to use what she knew and move ahead, too, but the men were unwilling to follow in her footsteps now.

As time persisted in keeping men at a distance, Mandy eventually gave her work to others who appeared ready for it—but as it turned out, they were not. Her work doubled in size and complexity when she gave away work she could easily do alone. She finally realized it when her personality said it was time for a change. Her mind seemed years away from accomplishing what she was willing to give up or accept then. At times, especially when dealing with imprisoned egos that preferred sitting in bars and passing time with fools to talking with God and listening to their inner guidance system, her innate wisdom failed her. The time for change arrived and only a few of the tribe were ready to levitate and move higher. Would it take a major earthquake or national disaster to change the ways of these Maya?

ᛝ   ᛝ

In the eyes of the world, Wanda and her daughter were often seen to be Maya living in this time. They were so immersed in the language and dialects of various elders and others who passed through their compound that they now taught lessons in humility to priests, who truly believed *they* had given up everything to serve God.

The work of Earth's weavers has never been given enough respect, and the people who use fabric to create clothing, gifts, and works of art are valued even less, so Wanda set her daughter to the task of creating respect for weaving and woven art of every kind within the mind of the crowds gathering around them now. Thérèse moved many to see within cloth what they never noticed before, but the average woman would not pay for what was handmade by the Maya at great cost when they could more easily buy rip-offs elsewhere for less.

Affluence eluded the weavers, but would arrive years hence when other women once again fell in love with thread, cloth, and fabrics to cover their nakedness, as well as their sofas and beds. That would be a great day—not expected for a few more ages, however. What a shock when it appeared with the great light of the 21st century! Men and women no longer wanted to sit and watch others work, they wanted to create and love life, too.

What happened? People expelled the framers and re-arrangers of the news, replacing them with their own minds taking charge of thinking about change. The world became a safer place when children were raised with wisdom and kept in their proper place until they respected the human race and the faith it takes to become great.

As this world changes, some remain as is: scribes, artists, weavers who work with cloth of many designs and colors of the rainbow lost to no man or woman even during times of decline. Why? The world cannot figure out what is happening at any point in time. It loses momentum when many think something is amiss or a mess, but not nearly as much as when people think they have it made!

☼ Chapter Thirty-Seven

Surprised to find a draft of an essay among hard copies of her work from last week, Jeanne pored over it as if someone else had written it—not she. She decided the essay was probably best suited to sending over the internet to others who generally agreed with her writing while adrift, but it would never fit into a syndicated column, because it was about the ways of The Maya of all time—not about today. It seemed wiser not to advertise that she had seen the other side of life or that time was her main study now. Instead, acting if she were editor of a mainstream paper, Jeanne pushed back in her chair and slowly read what she wrote a week ago.

Quickly groups dispersed all over North America while others went to the ends of the Earth to work together with other tribes to solve common problems. Each outpost was connected by the internet and such, able to do more than ever before to teach time and handle the repercussions from such discussions. It was a great time to be alive, and The Maya of the other side were busier than they had intended to be in this century. They didn't realize it would happen this fast? Yes, they never believed Americans could leave so easily.

The wave of work done in the United States was just enough to create a state of mind in which time could be taught. A few were ready to leave by month's end—believe it or not—a time of deep discussion and much love, but not a joyful time for those who cannot or will not leave their toys behind.

Worldly boys and girls are busy playing games daily, complaining, and buying dubious treasures stolen from other cultures. For them, it is not a good time for their world to end. However, it is a great time for those who work to ascend in groups of eight, coming together from many places. They meet on the internet, pretending to work with single men or women of time. Their work is good, but not as great as some would like it to be—nor as easy.

Keeping balanced without moving as fast as some wanted was challenging. Encouraging the backward to keep working challenged The Teachers and others most. The wave of time is such that many are able to climb and elevate their minds for hours at a time, but no one has yet ascended or can demonstrate how to levitate or move a body through space and time. The methods taught are condemned as backward and difficult to use. The human brain is equipped for processing thoughts, not inspiring thought.

The world is not aligned into a single religious conviction, but Christians are easing up on the idea that they alone know the road home. That huge belief switch is all that is needed, apparently, for the entire world to shift and do its work without hurting the minds and religions of others. The work of Jesus Christ can be summed up in one word—love! Why then is so much blood shed for love??

The Maya converted first! They moved into the work without any thought because Christ was in their minds all through time. Actually, theirs was not a conversion, just a change of systems. The way The Ascended Maya saw Earth, as well as the missions and system set up by The Church, is unlike Mexicans who defied the Church at every turn. The way of The Maya was to go inside the Church and see what worked. It seemed fine, so they took what they found, but they did not change what they believe or how they behave in time.

In the world that exists around missionaries and believers of only one religion or another, many must change—immediately or be deemed Godless. In the ways of the world you cannot change anyone or make another do what you want. If you want your work to last, little will get done if you do not do it yourself—and then incorporate what others will accept.

"Try it! Give yourself a test, then rest," is what The Teachers said, but no one listened to them in the beginning—again.

As Aztecs of ancient times learned in Mayan villages, The Maya are firmly established and widely respected as being the wisest of all. The Aztecs and Toltecs hated that image and tried to erase it, but they could not. The early migrations of The Maya into what is today Southwestern United States is not understood even now, but it will be known that the Anasazi left when chased, not because they lost their faith or wanted to leave that place. Why would anyone move, unless chased or it is no longer fit to live in?

The race to create a new faith is so great today that single, solitary minds constantly dream up new ways to pray. Why? Ego-driven, hoping to be missed when they leave this life. A few will remember you or many, if you are truly a great man or woman—over and over again. Why not be content to live this minute and just do it?

The world as it exists is not found in a book or story about women and men who found a new way of life, but a lot of information is hidden within the written word—unseen by those who live in dreams. Is your work impractical or unworthy of you? Why? What does the potter produce? What does a weaver sell others? What does a writer really understand and sell well?

Within the confines of work that is Maya, Mandy labored to convert her mind to accept that it was her time to work for others—not to sit and enjoy the fruits of her past labors. She made friends wherever she went—still forgetting to collect money when out gathering funds, but she was happy—which was the essence of her message—and the most difficult one for The Press to accept. Equal numbers portrayed her work as false, using the same old phrases… "It's not true!" or "It's a front for a labor/communist organization!" or "Unable to liberate women in the US, Amanda Brown fled south." News of her views was seldom positive, yet she erased such traces of hatred when interviewed by those who wanted to bury her.

The way of faith is such that you do hate and are even tempted to be rude, too, but you try to accept what people are, what they do—and laugh it off. That was Mandy's preferred tactic anyway.

Through her years in the Yucatan, Mandy did not cry very often. More often than not she casually laughed at Mayan ways of today that either did not help them get ahead or kept superstitions alive, but she did not say, "Don't do that!" or "What are you doing?" Instead, she laughed it off as too trivial to worry about. Rather than complain about such things, she petitioned God to resolve them. If a problem remained, she either befriended the person hurting her or others or ended the relationship then.

- When you blame women or men leading a town for everything they ever said or did, it is difficult to accept that they are as human as you.
- Do not expect fame and fortune to visit those who give up all they have to rescue you, even though some do.
- Why expect men and women to befriend you because you always give them whatever they want?
- In time people expect you to act out the role of the parent/provider, so they can act like children.

Try to see that when children move into the world they are no longer small in stature or innocent in mindset. Going to college can prolong their dependency upon their family, but they still become adults—sooner or later. Do not set out to mother or father a person over the age of 21. If you have not seen your sub-adult lately, you do not know what helps, nor how to defend them, if necessary. Instead of expecting more of them, do less! Realize it is a blessing to help another mature—not evening up old scores.

If your sons and daughters do not enjoy playtime as children, you produce adults who play with toys and pursue foolish plans instead of working and providing for a new generation of your descendants to arrive safely on this side over time. Whatever is skipped will be covered later, according to psychologists you quote, but most who quote do not deny their children anything—especially toys.

To many men, Mandy represents women unwilling to believe in them. She does not see that as news or anything new, but admits that too many women are afraid to say they feel the same way. Some change when they notice men still want Mandy to be with them, in spite of what she said about the mores of the USA.

When women stopped pretending to be men and began asserting their own ways again, the villagers noticed tourists were not as boorish, pushy, or ignorant of their ways as they had been when women were conceited and racked with insecurities, too. It will take time, but Americans will dress better, eat less, and act like adults visiting friends when they travel, rather than behaving as rowdy teenagers with no idea what it means to arrive on time or drink without passing out.

The ways of The Maya are not the same as they were in other times, because there is no apparent need to dwell on the fundamentals of the religious aspects of the ascension…and so it is with most living in this world now. When this world begins to change and begins to feel strange, you can leap to the next one—but only if you know you can ascend at the end and know how to make that leap into time.

Within each piece of pottery and woven tapestry is a lesson written in time. What do you get from it now? It is not talked about—rather felt. If you cannot move in your own groove and see into time, at least know others can help you. Why don't people imitate Mayan tribes now and forget the messages of the past? They don't know any better, either, but now you do.

When a Maya majoring in anthropology suggests that you do not know what you are doing, tell him you are ahead of wherever he is trying to arrive, because you have discovered time.

That will really blow a mind or two and release you from paying attention to them again, but it is best not to upset the science of the mind so much that such people give up and lose touch with what we are trying to do here: Land in a line in time ready to leave this world behind.

What happens when one person suggests a radical idea and it is immediately rejected by others? You do not read much into it before you give it up, too. That is why we waited in a back alley after you were through working out changes in your mind to give you this message. You are finally ready to study time once again.

The goal Jeanne was striving to achieve while working in time was so unique that she could not find a literary agent who would represent her. She could not find anyone who wanted to accept that nothing is complete—and that nothing is what it seems to be. Her stories were criticized as not romantic enough and seldom inspired great thoughts. She had to agree about the lack of romantic dreams, but that was all. Her channeling produced reports on what she found at the edges of time, thus reason enough to drive her work underground. When The Ascended Maya proposed that there was a way available to live better that others were ready to grasp, her words rose out of limbo and were read avidly by people all over the globe.

As one person spoke to many, or to a friend-of-a-friend, who understood work on time, the books, leaflets, and sessions Jeanne previously recorded of Mandy's teachings were sold all over the world. It was no fantasy! It was a deliberate change in what people believed to be their work in this world now.

The day Jeanne decided to leave the compound never happened. She found peace within this way of life that coincided mentally with her desire to serve others who were not as bold as she—but wiser, so all could be fulfilled. This was not to be a lasting change? Do not believe everything you read.

♓   ♓

Jeanne rearranged her entire life, gave away all she owned in other places, and even accepted her son's unwillingness to live with her in Mayaland. She was glad he could live his own way—accepted by others without her intercession. She loved her adopted son, who was not as handicapped as most thought, and wanted him with her, but Mexico is not hospitable to those who have trouble with simple math. Merchants often survive by cheating and cheapening such people. Brian had too much fun and was too happy to remain forever young, but he never ventured into the world without changing the life of others he met along the path. Whenever the car with Montana plates arrived at the compound, many Maya averted their eyes and examined him from hiding, but when he left, they openly asked him for his blessing.

What a life he and Jeanne had had, including the opening of the first play Jeanne staged! Brian loved movies best, but the theater gave him a bonus. He was able to choose stage plays and help create sets because of his legacy. His birth father was never known, but his adopted father was a movie star who loved him enough to leave him a trust fund that took care of him so well that he did not have to rely on luck or love from others.

The days and weeks and months in which Jeanne worked and did her 'stuff' were not so much luck and work as faith and trust. She had put aside enough in her early days to take them into the future without any cares, but she had not been interested enough to guard her funds then, so they dwindled enough that she and her scribes had to work harder to save the future. Their work paid well, but not as much as most people thought.

In the weeks following any visit from Mandy everyone in the compound around Jeanne would be as busy as the proverbial Mayan bee—and never angry if someone stopped them while they prayed. However, over time each personality asserted its desire to have his or her words and wishes recognized above all others, and most grew defensive about any critical analysis of their work. That meant it was time for Mandy to come back or Jeanne's son to visit and change the dynamics of the entire compound!

Without saying much, Jeanne surmised who did what and why. No one else could read minds and write at the same time, as well as commit to the time needed to edit wisely, always giving credit where expected—yet not expecting any in return. Only a few respected the written word enough to write it over and over until it was letter-perfect. Those few were hired to write and work in political life. The title 'Scribe' was conferred upon only the best writers. It was never given to those who only took dictation from others working in life situations. To a few the exalted title of 'Secretary' was bestowed, indicating that a woman or man had many confidential duties, only one taking dictation and insuring it was accurate. Secretaries were paid more than Scribes because their work is recognized more on this side of the veil. However, Scribes are remembered long after Secretaries are fired or retire.

Those who resided with Jeanne and others in compounds throughout Mayaland watched as many of the young left and returned over-and-over again with money and tribute, plus things they learned that were previously unknown in their old homes. These fresh insights did not hurt the tribe. In fact, it liberated parents from having to support so many that they had little time to bless their own lives—having to work constantly to feed the family until they died.

The work of this guild was such that some of its writers and scribes traveled to other parts of the hemisphere, visiting here and there. In Altoona and Philadelphia they saw many things supposed to be strange to them, only to say immediately that they already knew about it. It turned out that they changed the people they visited, rather than the other way around—and everyone had fun!

In The East and West of the United States the fringe elements clung to the coastlines, separating themselves from middle-class norms of the past. Elements who refused to move to other views became stagnant, usually controlled by braggarts, but The Maya with their special way of looking at time did not notice any difference since the world is not divided into spheres. They saw this world and the next about to collide, unless people prepared to give up dirty air and polluted water, and cleaned up their garbage dumps and such. That was all The Maya wanted from the rich and famous, and it upset them the most! To have reached a pinnacle of performance only to be outdistanced in time by a very poor tribe was not what made people excited to live in this time. The few who did grasp what The Maya could do were afraid to say so. When a man or woman spoke out, he was admired and she was stared at long and hard—not much had changed.

When people blend their lives, then divide them over-and-over again in their minds, they do not notice change. When they blend and try to come back together again, they cannot take their minds off differences long enough to stop talking and let their personal views subside so love can take over and heal everyone. What a war produces is toys for the old boys. What love produces is toys for little boys to use when they work at home, but it can cause war, too. What to do about a home in which children are not wanted and 'adults' are so infantile they cannot be happy alone in their own thoughts for an hour or two? We will not bother to go into that now, but Jeanne may.

What Jeanne does, as well as any scribe for teachers of other times, is write what is dictated about this world and the next. It is not easy to be a scribe and succeed, but Jeanne was a success long before she arrived at this station in time. Although she was willing to let people suggest much and do less, she always did her best—even confessing that she never released anything to the press that was less than her best and been edited many, many times—even when it was scribed.

The way Jeanne lived at home and abroad was about the same. She was not tense or nervous to meet others face-to-face. In fact, she was so relaxed in political circles that she was asked to run for Congress in the United States. Because it was such a compliment and done with love, Jeanne refrained from telling them that she no longer cared what they did there.

As weeks and months and years disappear from a mind and enter time, does that mind find out more about love? Is love made the primary issue in order for you to sort out how you inner-act with others who travel back or forward over time? Could Mandy help Jeanne accrue more work, do more work, or write more? No, but she always seemed to inspire each and every writer and scribe to try harder.

The distance between two people is all it takes to create space, but any gap can be bridged. It can also be blocked—a lot. What happens when one scribe decides the work must be perfect and other scribes are satisfied with whatever was said and write 'stet' instead of questioning it a bit? It happened only once.

It came to be that a group Mandy had set up to work on a specific project ended with members hating each other when they discovered they could not recreate the mood she originally produced so easily. This group expanded when one or two left to do their own thing, only to come back later with hat-in-hand asking to be forgiven for their hasty moves and moods. They expected those they left behind to have grown as much as they had and quickly said so. This class was not doomed, just a lesson learned about what not to do if you want to last in a group.

Any group dedicated to producing the written word cannot succeed if they never laugh. Members must decide and then abide by their decisions on who scribes the work, who edits the material, and who does whatever it takes to get the work out without mistakes. Once you ask two people to do the same job, you set up a study in dominance—and one usually leaves. In groups, each participant is equal or able to contribute, or they are not part of the group and leave it bit-by-bit, if not suddenly. Consensus, getting people to participate and cooperate in an endeavor that takes more than three trying to achieve a goal is an art form not appreciated in Today's world.

As Mandy learned more and more about this world, she was better able to move into the next one. The local Maya were inspired to teach others who came to their shores, but no one was ever again given the same kind of welcome as Mandy when she arrived in the Yucatan that first time—headed for a grand reunion with her friends from the past.

☼ Chapter Thirty-Eight

Speaking only to Thérèse, Wanda whispered, "I think maybe we should leave the compound now." She looked tired and a bit out of sorts, but not angry. She no longer smiled constantly as though she had to project happiness. Her energy dipped more and more with every chore, yet everyone meeting her believed she was happy and thriving in her art.

"You need a vacation!" Thérèse spoke without a trace of humor. She was emphatic enough to make her mother turn and stare at her, trying to frame a reason why she could not leave.

"You know, Thérèse, you might have the solution to all my problems! I don't feel out of sorts so much as constantly annoyed. I feel put upon by others—always tired. What I need is to let someone else attend to my wants and see if that helps. What do you think? Do you want to go with me?" As she said this, Wanda spun a bit of flax between her index finger and thumb, so preoccupied that she could not put it away.

"Why don't you go alone to a state-of-the-art spa and rest for a week or so? That would take care of all that ails you and give you a lift." Thérèse spoke without feeling it was the right prescription for what ailed her mother.

"No, that isn't what I want. The spa idea is great, if done right, but most of them are just cashing in on a fad. I would love to go to some safe place where natives watch over you and let you sleep all day and call you to supper and feed you the best of food, and then you go back to bed again--"

Thérèse's giggle interrupted her thoughts, so she stared at her until it subsided into an amused whimper. Her thoughts had been disrupted by the way Wanda moved restlessly about all the time and she had assumed the worst—that her mother was once again depressed, but it turned out she was just bone-tired.

With a touch of acidity, Wanda said, "I don't see anything funny about any of this, but since you do, please enlighten me!"

"Oh, Mom, you're great! You're just tired and really want to take a vacation, but feel guilty about leaving us. Why didn't you say so?"

Hiding a smile, Wanda spoke hesitantly. "I guess I didn't notice it until now. It just crept up on me and took over, and I didn't have the sense to know it was time to rest. Now I'm way behind in bed time and find myself a bit more cranky than usual." At this point, Wanda started to cry.

Without any idea what would happen next, Thérèse said, "What can be wrong about taking a vacation now?" Stunned she watched her mother collapse over nothing—or so it seemed to her.

"I feel so useless. Right now I can walk out of here knowing that within a week everyone will do whatever they think I'd expect of them—and never miss me."

Amazed to discover her mother once again lost in a haze of self-pity, like the old days—not like recent years, Thérèse spoke with abruptness, demanding attention. "You're not going to be missed if you keep acting like you're miffed! Get used to it! People come to study with us, then they go on doing their own thing. We're not here to make them dependent on us, and we're not here to build a cult. So life happens!"

Whether or not Thérèse was exasperated, she gave the impression that she was no longer happy and more than a bit disgusted. Wanda said nothing, continuing to sit and stare at the bit of floss wadded between her finger and thumb. Several minutes passed without either speaking when they heard a knock at the back door. It was most unusual for anyone to try that door since it was wired with an alarm that has to be disengaged before you open it or risk frightening everyone in the area. Wanda wondered, 'Who would use that door?' as she rose from her rocking chair. Thérèse moved swiftly to look out the window, then disarmed the alarm. She was elated to see Mandy had arrived and obviously did not want the others to know she was home.

Bursting into the room, out of breath and smiling, Mandy appeared to be the only woman alive living a great life. Her face was radiant, which explained why they were feeling a bit down. The agreement among them was that when one of the 'partners' needed more energy, they could draw from the others without warning, but they better have a very good reason for doing it! No longer afraid or dismayed or worried about her old age, Wanda felt young again—eager to find out what was going on and what would happen next.

The day ended without anyone in the compound seeing the three, but rumors circulated among the tribe that Mandy was seen driving through the village headed for home—and that news arrived hours ago. The question being bantered about the kitchen now was, "Why would Mandy change her itinerary and come back now?" No one ever figured out what Mandy would do next, but they loved to try.

Twice the three friends started to leave the loom room, suggesting that they were able to change and go to dinner and let everyone in on their plan, but both times they decided it needed more work. The room where the weavers met appeared unoccupied because no one could spot their candle.

When midnight arrived, a student weaver decided to slip in and open her loom to explore designs that might come to her if she worked in the moonlight—different from working in sunlight. As she crept closer to the workroom she realized someone was inside. Mumbles were interspersed with laughter—not faked chatter or a laugh track, either. She wanted to stay and listen, but was afraid she might be busted for lurking about the compound after dark without permission or a good reason. After a few minutes, when she heard nothing more, the maiden knelt down and peered into the room through the keyhole. She was surprised to see that Mandy had arrived and not told the rest of the clan. It had to mean something new was going to happen soon! Her first thought was to leave immediately—be obedient to the rules that stated never pry into the lives of others, but her second thoughts ruled. She decided to listen intently and find out what would be announced tomorrow—or not.

As night ended, the three friends were still hunched over from sharing laughter as they discussed various political factions and their lack of action. The young woman hiding outside felt a chill and was suddenly afraid, but unaware of what caused the chill. Right then Mandy spotted a movement outside and stopped laughing. Rising to her full height, she walked to the door, checked outside and saw the little woman creeping away. Angered that anyone would disobey the compound rules and not make their presence known, Mandy quietly closed the door, wondering: 'Is she a spy?'

Immediately a chill entered the room through the closed door. They all *knew* now what was about to happen, so Mandy quickly and noiselessly returned to her seat. The angel stood taller than a huge man, but was graceful in every way. It was not as tall as the ceiling at the center of the room, but stooped to enter the door. How it managed to appear and disappear was not something they wished to debate, but it did come up for discussion once. Because the angel appeared several times within the past few months, as well as now, it had been discussed. The reason was now being announced!

The angel said: "YOU ARE NOT WHO WILL MAKE THE EARTH WORK. YOU ARE TEACHERS AND AIDES. YOU ARE NOT HERE TO TELL THE WORLD WHAT IS OUT THERE, BUT YOU ARE TO WORK AS YOU DO TO HELP THOSE WHO ARE ABOUT TO ARRIVE IN TIME TO TEACH WHAT TO DO IN TIMES OF GREAT DESPAIR."

This great messenger of God did not stare at anyone, rather encompassed them all with the impression or image of great care and concern—if it is possible to describe a radiant countenance that only appears as human to human beings. When the angel spread out wings that seemed to be suspended above its back, the colors of The Ascended Maya radiated outward in such brilliant hues that the first rays of sunlight coming through the shutters made no impression on any of them.

Without hesitation, the angel furled its wings after plucking three feathers from one. Each was given one plume as the angel pronounced over them: "YOU WILL USE THIS FEATHER WHEN YOU ARE ABLE TO PRAY UNDISTURBED IN ANY WAY."

The three women nodded, then knelt as if being knighted while the angel did whatever was required. The silence was not golden. It was pearly and echoed over their world. They felt strange, loved, yet able to do anything God wanted. This was in stark contrast to those who wished to use their minds or follow their hearts rather than call upon God.

The angel spoke again. "WHEN THE SUN IS HIGH, YOU WILL LEAVE HERE AND TRAVEL TO ANOTHER PLACE. YOU WILL TAKE AWAY FROM THERE THOSE WHO ARE WORKING WITH YOU. ONCE YOU ARE TOGETHER, GO TO A PLACE WHERE THE MAYA ARE WAITING. THEY WILL TELL YOU WHAT TO DO."

The Maya? Surely, this was not about the Maya of this time—was it? Wanda thought it first, then the other two, but the question was not the same as they had had in mind when the angel arrived. Was it?

The angel stopped talking or whatever it did to communicate messages and began illuminating each woman with a radiant wave of heat that seemed to sear her hair and shoulders. At first they felt a strange pain in their shoulders, then it hurt even worse, but they did not complain. Experiencing a shock to their minds, they suddenly felt feathers sprout around them as wings grew out of their shoulder blades and that general area. It was weird, but they loved it!

"YOU HAVE EARNED THE WINGS OF THE MAYA! YOU WILL HAVE TIME TO GROW, BUT YOU MUST NOT EXPOSE THESE WINGS TO OTHERS WHO DO NOT BELIEVE. ONLY WHEN THE MAYA HAVE ARRIVED WILL YOU KNOW WHAT TO DO—WHEN THE TIME IS RIGHT FOR THE TRIBE TO MOVE THROUGH THE SKY."

The women continued kneeling and feeling the wings surround them with colors equal to a very bright rainbow. The hues represented the tribes of the Earth, not easy to erase from the retina once etched there. The three suddenly realized their kneeling position was becoming a painful experience. Wanda was the first to move, and then Mandy stretched her neck until her halo fell off. The women looked at each other and started to grin. What would it take to keep these women from laughing and having a good time when together? The answer is: They were chosen because they know how to rise above the worries of everyday, to laugh and have a good time regardless of what they had to put up with from others.

The angel switched from radiating bright light to emanating a soothing glow that dissipated when the women began to move about the room. The image of the angel disappeared, but the holy light did not leave them right away. The entire room glowed intensely! Only then did they notice that the loom was filled with glorious cloth. It was as if the three had worked continuously through the night to produce a multi-colored cloak. It was bright and huge, able to cover an angel who might like it, too. They carefully removed the cloak from the loom. It needed no trim or hemming. It was a miracle! A mysterious message they would stabilize and relay to the tribe—after they did what had to be done first.

⧗ ⧗

First light was usually enough to rouse most living in the compound, so three lights and ten bells were too much to ignore, even if you stayed up all night as Wanda, Thérèse, and Mandy did. The trio met in the kitchen, as if prearranged, at ten-thirty. Mandy measured out cocoa and a bit of chili, enough to make a huge pot of cocoa. The cook was not amazed to see them making chocolate that way, but she was stunned when they motioned for her to join them in the room set aside for small conferences of major consequence. She walked with pride out of the kitchen, but immediately felt stupid when she did not know which door to use. Her pride slipped enough then for sense to arrive and save the day, thus enabling her to pray with them.

Within an hour or so of preparing the pot of chocolate, the quartet left the conference room but did not use the door or windows to exit. They ascended within a group of angels and flew to the United States. The cook had never been to that country and believed it to be corrupt and evil—extremely dangerous, based on what she read in the papers and saw on TV, but she was thrilled to see abandoned ancient places The Maya had built there. Eager to visit what was once her tribe's home, she zoomed in and looked at the Gila River first. She was in charge of the trip now, but never suggested that The Maya were the greatest tribe. The thought was carried within each mind. At times pride still survived to such a degree that everyone had to be humbled for their own growth. Being aware of a weakness usually strengthens or eliminates it.

The four women relaxed and talked once they got back to the conference room, but not as chatty as usual. They could neither say anything negative nor guess at final outcomes. Each thought expressed was brilliant! Every stated belief essential! Each expressed her own thoughts and work in ways not requiring correction or amendment. Their work together was so great that they hesitated to leave the room and move about as they normally did with others.

The cook spoke without realizing that it indicated how much she had changed in a very real way. Louisa said, "I feel so much pressure across my chest." Spreading her hands across her apron, she grasped at the strings attached to the bib and pulled at them while working out a new idea. Suddenly she threw the apron into a corner, stood up, and announced, "I am the leader of this group, and we are going to have a meeting!"

Wanda laughed and Mandy grinned because it was exactly what they wanted Louisa to do now. The problem with so many spiritual groups they worked with was no one took charge and did the work as a leader must. They had been stymied when it came to producing leaders to handle all the work needed to be done before The Ascended Maya arrived, but now they had one woman ready to move and do whatever had to be done to get her friends moving in time. There would be others who would stand up and put aside pride and personal lives to do what was required, but Louisa, The Cook, was the first one to take up the work when placed before her. She did not realize how hated she would be at times, but The Cook could stand up to heat and pressure and do whatever it takes to get meals out at exactly the right time. Louisa said, "Getting ready for The Maya will be no different than preparing a great banquet."

Without speaking, Louisa summoned her staff to remove the now-empty dishes. She was no longer interested in telling her crew what to do about dinner and whatever, but remained nearby in case she was needed—so they figured it out themselves. They followed her rules, used her recipes, and discovered more about life than they did when she told them how to work.

When the tribe assembled again, Mandy and friends told the men how each would begin working within on their next assignment, but had to frame it in such a way so as not to anger each woman. Why? Women do not like to watch other women rise in fame. It fans the flames of jealousy and pettiness among them. If one ascends, it seems to condemn the vanity of others.

What can a woman do about pride and evil minds that defame those who try to do something new? Mandy would say, "Ignore it. See yourself as a good woman—unafraid of what evil people say. Once you're perfect and able to move out of here, you'll laugh about your enemies. They're not friends, but in the end they help you more than most friends to become the best you can possibly be."

☼ CHAPTER THIRTY-NINE

Without thought, or so it might seem to passersby, a group of women left the compound and entered a bus headed for the nearby city. They left their tribe behind to shop, maybe even buy, but no one was prepared for what lay ahead of them all.

The day started out sunny and bright on the outside, but someone was plotting to undermine the women, so it was necessary for their leadership to determine who was doing what and why before they lost all they loved. At times the group was unaware of anything being said or done that was evil; however, at other times some recognized fear or a tide of energy sweeping through the community and troubling everyone standing in its path. Eliminating negative influences was a way of life for some, but the average personality cannot comprehend and use it successfully to live better once such an event is over and done.

Mandy was not a personality of these times, rather a woman of destiny. She was able to intervene in almost any affair without being burnt or hurt personally. What did she see when they met that day? What had she already heard? Her thoughts were not diverted by gossip or outrageous superstitions that held some Maya captive to the point that they could not believe in God or accept the new work of Earth. Since she was aware, Mandy used whatever she possessed to bolster the work of The Lord.

While this clan could not see or believe in a new parish until it appeared, Mandy prepared new teachers to train their children in the way of God—not in the ways of today's idolaters. They were given just enough money to not want a lot, and were taught how to use time wisely and what to do when someone tried to stop them from doing well, too. These simple lessons were taught in a block of classes identified as Ethics. Mandy did not stop to think about teaching ethics, it came to her out of the blue. She did not stop to wonder if it was the best course, either, or if she should teach something else as well, because she *knew* what had to be done and did it!

When seers doubt what is sent, someone else has entered and is using them who cannot contribute much or wishes to stop whatever is being taught. That is not helpful when building a community and putting into place old ways that can be retraced to the past today, so Mandy did not bother with people who merely played at channeling, pretending to understand her and others who worked for The Lord. She was not averse to others receiving messages from God or their Higher Selves, just wary of many who diverted such work to enrich themselves. At times her work could not move ahead due to bad experiences people had with other scribes or Mayan clans who sold their culture, claiming to understand all that was being sent by The Ascended Maya, even though they never knew them.

ⵋ ⵋ

As the day progressed, the women left the city—without meeting anyone sent to teach them a lesson. They wondered aloud if this trip was meant to get them alone somewhere outside their homes. This rumor reached Mandy just as her car neared the bus. She sensed it as she drove along side and looked at the women inside. They were not talking loud enough to be heard by others nearby, let alone someone driving by their bus, but Mandy's inner ear clearly heard all they said. The why of what had to be done to save the tribe from something evil was then provided by her inner mind—or intuition.

Who was in danger and why? That was what Mandy wanted to find out in time. Once she knew who to rescue or change or help in some way, the tribe would be safe. Until she could hear or see an image of the traitor and know what to do, the tribe was in danger of losing this evil-doer and everyone who believed in her. 'Aaaahhh,' thought Mandy, 'The field has narrowed down to someone who doesn't live in town, a woman who can take away a few who work in the compound now.'

This group by itself could not investigate the mystery or worry about it because nothing was open to their view. Only Mandy heard words of intrigue while visiting the communal bathroom at the compound. Words that at first did not worry her—but now seemed ominous clues about what she had to do and who was working against her and the crew. Her problem was how to remove suspicion and doubt that she was onto what the evil ones were trying to do now. She decided to set up two women as enemies, then see who would use this group to cover their evil work.

At first this idea was too devious and unpleasant for Mandy to easily understand, but she soon realized it gave birth to concepts that in turn changed the lies of Earth into words she could use one day to prove her case about who needed more than just a belief in what was being taught and done by others not of Earth. This work is hard on the physical body, especially the electrical system, so Mandy could not do anything else while working on such problems. Thankfully, it was not so difficult that she did not receive thoughts and information generated by her own experience or that of her Spiritual Guides when she entered into meditation now. Just as Mandy arrived in time at the place where the tribe might collide, she reached out the car window to wave as she shouted to the women seated above her: "Don't get off the bus!"

The women on the bus peered out at her and saw for the first time that Mandy was passing by and going to park her car and maybe join them. They were delighted to see her and yelled back greetings. She did not return their laughter, but smiled reassuringly to indicate nothing was wrong. She signaled the bus driver to follow her to a spot down the road where she would enter the bus. Her unexpected visit was unwanted by a few, but everyone else was oblivious to their concerns and greeted Mandy with open hearts.

As Mandy pulled over to park, she phoned the compound and told a young man to come and get her car and drive it home. He was not upset to leave the women and children immediately. He welcomed an opportunity to drive her new car. He loved it more than anything he had ever seen on Earth, but was not envious or jealous of Mandy. He knew the car was not hers, but on loan from a movie star. It was a huge Mercedes in exactly the same color as the hair of a doll in the store where the Maya sold their wares. It was loved by all who sat in it, and had already acquired a history of being very mysterious inside. The Maya believed in many things, and mysteries initiated shamanistic work within their minds, so the elders loved to sit in the Mercedes and dream. They never left before a vision or healing took place. The limousine was seen to be a throne of a great Mayan god—not a piece of metal that would rust away in time.

Jumping onto the bus, Mandy stood on the second step bobbing her head and watching for those who tried to catch her eye and those who avoided looking at her directly. An easy test, but one many forget! Mandy followed the old ways of combining her everyday five senses with her intuition to discover what was going on in the usual world of others around her. Use of this intuitive system died out by the end of the twentieth century and was replaced by an egoistic-based belief that people can manage their images and do whatever they want without being caught in a lie. Unable to sense how harmful it is to be untrue to Spirit, some do not see it sap their inner strength until it is too late to save their wealth, health, or fame.

Mandy prayed as she greeted women seated at the front of the bus. She held a bouquet of roses Thérèse had arranged for her to use whenever confronted by enemies. The power, beauty, and aroma of roses combined can remove one or two enemies, proving that you cannot live and work hard within a group and develop a cabal, too.

Wishing she could skip this trip, Mandy stood in the bus's stairwell a bit before gradually ascending into the group's mood, which seemed happy now. She smiled and remained still to help the group elevate their volume and mood a notch or two higher. Her life was operating on fast forward—not looking back at what she had. Whenever this happened, her mind often strayed outside the lines of today. She was willing to stay inside the lines provided to examine how others were infringing upon her designs—now and then, hoping to gain her fame or whatever.

As the bus picked up speed, Mandy said something to the driver that surprised her. With eyes wider than usual, she looked in the wide rear-view mirror at the women seated at the back of the bus. Her mind was now severed from time so all she spotted was an unsmiling woman trying to hide her chagrin. The driver looked back, too, and surmised that the young woman in question was anxious to meet a lover and was not sure if she could keep the date or not, but she was wrong.

Since the bus held many lives, driving faster than the speed limit was not advised, but it zipped through traffic anyway, moving through the limits of time to arrive at a sacred spot within half an hour reel or real time—even though their destination was hundreds of miles from where they started this trek.

In the way of women always ready to play, the young disembarked and ran toward the *cenote,* or sacred spring, to examine everything there, while their elders stood watching and waiting for what would become their fate. When two younger women did not follow the others and remained behind with the elders, Mandy realized she had forced their hand, but it was not time to act. How could she coax them to ignore their suspicions and behave as usual, so they could be analyzed in time? She smiled and asked them to join her in helping the others locate a spot shallow enough to wade and cool off without slipping into the *cenote's* center and drown. Obviously believing that Mandy fully trusted them now, they bossed everyone around them until they, too, were truly enjoying the water and had completely let down their guard.

When a woman starts throwing her weight around, you know she is upset and believes her work will not be done right by others. Once a woman of determined mind realizes the job will be done right and on time, she usually turns down the heat and turns up the charm—unless it better serves her purposes not to be nice. When women band together and decide to usurp the work of a higher being, supervisor, or life counselor, they merely succeed in removing luck from their work for a very long time.

When Mandy started out, unsure of her calling and how she felt about the Mayan women who were unwilling to share their tribal work, a few angry women took her to be a fool, until she was highly respected by their men. That was the last time any women within the tribe tried to undermine Mandy—until now. That memory had slipped into the distance, but was about to be revived by those who did not remember that time. The Mayan women were unaware what was happening, because time has a way of restoring what you do not remember. This is, after all, an existence in time—not an experience normally desired or given divine limitations such as wings.

When Mandy and her closest allies grew wings and sat in them for hours, they felt waves of energy emerge in their brains in a way that erased many days where they had had little faith. They then saw only what would work or what was about to happen and what they would do better than ever. Negative vibrations and waves were swept away in time. Their computerized brains sought only positive connections—over and over again. Would such a lack of balance create wave shortages or blackouts one day? Who knows, but it was not Mandy's problem when she stood in the *cenote* and prayed nonstop.

Whatever Mandy said to God while wading in the sacred waters was not converted into words that others close-by could overhear. Water was the chosen medium because of its spiritual connection to Mayan thoughts about human birth. She chose this way to help women see into the future and recognize what they had to do next. Several commented that from the moment they entered the water the haze around the pool had disappeared. A mist hovering above the spring lifted immediately for some, but not for everyone.

Mandy began singing a romantic song that upon leaving her lips emphasized her hips, lovemaking, and sex, so she danced. This did not surprise the wise, but the younger women were shocked—a lot. Working as a clan produced a view that Mandy was so virtuous that she could not understand average women and their thirst for men. It was not what she said or did, but what some who pretended to know Mandy said that hurt her most. The current propaganda meant to sell her out stated she was a harlot of old and unable to bear children, so she wanted other women to avoid men and not have any fun or children now. This lie hurt the work of The Ascended Maya, so it had to stop!

When the last two women joined the group, on the sly they took several young women with them to the other side of the *cenote*. Mandy watched without turning her head or following them with her eyes. Attuning her thoughts to these women, the tune she carried had nothing to do with what she said next. In fact, it was a ruse meant to confuse, and it did.

Working on her body movements—appearing to be in a light trance, Mandy danced closer to those who stood alone or aloof from her friends. She watched them move closer together whenever she approached, so she held out her hand and asked their ringleader to dance with her. The woman blushed, a sign of deceit that anyone wise could easily read now, but most chose to believe it was caused by genuine embarrassment at being singled out. Mandy wished she had not been given a sign to dance with The Divine and could instead watch the woman's friends while they danced together now.

Even with her enemies close by, Mandy was unworried about what this one might do as she coaxed her to dance. This left one less person able to produce a vortex that might hurt her or her work, but more important, it divided the women into two groups that divided again and again—many times, until all was revealed and Mandy could work on the problem in her own way now. To start the process, Mandy said sweetly, "What are you trying to do, Miriam?"

Waltzing to a tune in a grand ballroom is not the same as dancing life away in a sacred place. Life is not the issue in time, but what you do with it is. You either progress in your world or not. Whether you believe it or not, you have chosen the spot where you will stop. What you do at the end when you are through here is not revealed until you are ready to leave and begin receding into another force field.

Since Mandy did not appear to be talking about life, Miriam, the ringleader, smiled and said loudly, "I'm not as clever as you, Mandy… I don't dance with women usually. It's hard to get in step with you… I want to sit down."

Mandy was not alone in recognizing the sarcasm as hatred in this obvious attempt to badger her with lies about her personal life and what she did with women and men, but she did not bite back. Instead of leaving the water and the dance to sit on the bank of the spring, Mandy speeded up creating circles in the water. Diverted, her mind easily followed a line straight through time, but the woman dancing sloppily at her side became dizzy and could not stop herself from falling into the deepest part of the *cenote*. She then screamed, "Mandy, save me!"

Miriam's close friends and allies were shocked that she did not ask them to help, but instead called Mandy to rescue her. It was their first sign that they could no longer follow her as their leader, even though they willingly left Mandy for her.

Mandy did not rush about or even shout, she merely stretched out her hand and motioned for Miriam to stand up where she was and catch her balance. It was obviously embarrassing for Miriam to discover that she was not over her head any longer and could easily wade to shore, thus avoiding waves created by her own panic attack. Not wishing to lose face, she started walking backwards to demonstrate the depth and dropped off the ledge into the center of the sacred well and disappeared.

What made this woman go in the wrong direction? Why did she walk into the pit with eyes wide open? She was unable to spit on Mandy or steal followers she had believed could easily be used to do her work, so she chose to drop out. Some women do that rather than fit in or produce good work. They attack and attack and stab in the back, but when found out, they leave and never come back to see what they could not see previously: They were never needed!

The women who had isolated themselves with Miriam did not move to save her. They appeared in a daze—or perhaps they thought Mandy would save her again? Everyone else blamed *them*, including the police, for not going to the rescue of their friend. Mandy was standing on the shore when Miriam left for her final destination. How did Mandy leap so high and move so quickly to get so far away from her? You would have to ask the Mayan woman who witnessed it all.

When Miriam was pulled from the *cenote* later, police and others pried into all of her lives, including the one she seemed to live within Mandy's compound, as well as those she maintained on the outside. At first her intimate friends eagerly volunteered information when asked, but later when they discovered she was not who she claimed to be and had infiltrated the compound in order to write for the tabloids, they receded into the group surrounding Mandy. Miriam had been into cults, trying to create one so she could claim later Mandy had taught her how. Her motives were all very complex, but no longer interesting to the Maya who stood behind Mandy and sided with her while the police decided that it had been a fatal accident and nothing more than that.

The local tribe had been unaware that there was any need for concern about their work in that area or that someone wished harm to Mandy and her work. Once discovered and discussed, they felt it was caused by neglecting their prayers or following their own advice when Mandy was away. Often as not, they had neglected Mandy in their thoughts and prayers, but now vowed it would not happen again. She was not deceived or willing to let the lesson go up in smoke, nor give up on what this tribe needed to learn.

⊁   ⊁

As the women scattered, they formed opinions more and more diverse about the woman who drowned in the sacred *cenote*. Mandy felt hurt anew when they portrayed her as being unable to save her. She felt diminished by something that was not of her work or could have been done by anyone on Earth. For this reason, she started holding meetings on the sly with a few women at a time to talk about the day they went out to shop and ended up with a woman from the community committing suicide instead.

The thought of suicide was repugnant to everyone in the tribe. They preferred to say it was an accident or fate—not a woman taking her own life. For that reason, Mandy did not reveal that Miriam gave up her life for reasons unknown to anyone but those who were with her at the end. Instead of saying *suicide*, Mandy spoke of God alone knowing what happened and why. This effectively prevented others from criticizing the seasons or God's reasons. This suited the tribe, but produced a group who wondered about what Miriam had really done to be taken away by God that day.

Once the tribe moved beyond seeing it as suicide, but still unwilling to believe Miriam was a foreign emissary, the elders asked Mandy to pray with them in a nearby cave. The waves of terror and the flames surrounding suicide were not forgotten, but the elders agreed that Miriam chose to leave this world rather than face her own judgment here and now. She was unwilling to admit that she had lost the game of life, instead she assumed Mandy had stopped her, thus she made one last attempt to discredit Mandy before she left. Such hatred is not easy to overlook or mistake, but it passed through the Maya unnoticed because no one in the tribe believed anyone wise could hate Mandy—and they were right!

The tribe, not weakened by this lapse into the past, continued as usual as days passed into weeks. Some spoke of a time when Mayan maidens leaped into sacred *cenotes* because they had no other way to live as honest women, which displaced the joke previously accepted by outsiders that maidens were forced to leap to their death for religious reasons. It was not what the tribal elders set out to do, but it became unusual for any Maya to repeat that lie to outsiders again.

☼ CHAPTER FORTY

Working on a new project produces new views that either produce a better group or rip apart whatever existed previously. A new group committed to working with Wanda and her daughter, Thérèse, formed shortly after the death of Miriam. She had attempted to steal the best of whatever the weavers taught by Wanda had produced, and since Wanda had been teaching her art, as well as producing new designs with ancient patterns and colors for more than three years, all this intrigue and mystery was just too much for some of her students to understand. However, most of the Mayan weavers knew what needed to be done immediately and began working on a new pattern in time.

Never again would they try to understand women who arrived in their lives for a short time from outside the tribe. They would remain content within their own lives—not envious or jealous of Americans and others, because they could see few ever stayed with anything long enough to master an art or even become friends with their work. For those reasons and others, the elders finally realized that few could receive the spark needed to create the art of The Maya who taught through Wanda and her daughter.

Thérèse taught by walking about a lot and smiling sweetly as she lectured, without seeming to do either. She shared her thoughts simply or talked about whatever she was going through, but some women broke down and fell into depressions as a result of her ability to strip away what frightens the mind in this life, or worse, uncovers lies residing inside minds. Meanwhile, others appeared to be walking on air after meeting Thérèse anywhere. Just how different her teaching style was, and how much it was mocked was not known until 'a departed woman' tried to teach the same way in Arizona and was asked to leave town.

That rebel never got over Thérèse's mastery, nor could she leave it behind. How can one woman talk and walk about constantly—teaching without any apparent thought, and not appear to be strange and incompetent, while another doing the very same thing is impeached as being unprepared by all she tries to reach? The answer to mysteries lies in the lives of each person in time. If you have no doubts about tomorrow, you may not live as wisely today as you otherwise might, but at least you would not be surprised when the end arrived—or so some say. What is wrong with saying, "Study the future only if it will help you live wiser today than you otherwise might?"

The growth of psychic work within their community accelerated after spending an hour a week working on it diligently. The subject captivated Americans more than others, thus it immediately became necessary to add more such courses—ten to be exact, to teach the ways of the mind and time—and how to step into one and use the other. Unfortunately, most of these devotees were after only one thing—personal power, even though they claimed to want to help humanity because it sounded more reasonable or wise. The power to help others is not something you can foretell since it is measured in how well you listen now and follow up later when you are tested to see if you can do whatever is given through others to you to do with them then.

If you work in a shop where tired customers come in upset and demanding satisfaction or action, and you step up to the counter and talk to them, perhaps introduce yourself and your products, you may be unaware how much help you give others without payment. Never fear! You will be well paid if that patron turns out to be an angel disguised as an irate customer out to give you a blessing. Why would a business not treat every customer properly the first time or be afraid when an angel stops by? That was a lesson Thérèse portrayed on stage and in role-playing games to impart wisdom to her students before they started group study on what would come up for review later.

What could they teach a group of graduate nurses about caring for others? It was not their intention to teach them anything, rather inspire professionals to reach deep within their souls and pull out whatever patients needed from them, as well as work things out with people sent to them as tests. The nurses did more than most groups who came before them, but they were not able to elevate their minds high enough to practice on the side or permit themselves to levitate into space. The Mayan women, in awe of their healing gifts, envisioned their education and wondered why they were not happier with their work. This, in turn, amazed the nurses—even the few aides who accompanied them. The wonder of each group as they met others was offset at times by envy and jealousy lodged in individual minds. It became more and more noticeable that the Americans were growing old and tired before their time, without knowing anything about the other side. Why?

When asked to lead and you refuse, you lose enthusiasm. You do not exactly lose your mind, you lose time. You do not lose or gain femininity or masculinity by standing up for yourself, but you lose it if you try to run over others who are equally determined to work everything out in their heads. Most liars are unable to laugh at their mistakes, instead preferring to accuse and blame others for their problems.

Working where people were not judged by clothes they all bought on credit, but what they created, brought shame to too many Americans. Nothing positive is ever gained by blaming others for what you do not wish to change. When the way of life in America became depraved, no one assumed it would change or that they could change minds by walking in lines beside others to the next time. By diligently ignoring the international discord and the lack of cooperation sweeping the nation, as well as forgetting to provide the basics required for their own lives, the old world collapsed—and no amount of spin could reproduce it again. Some worried once they realized it was a time of change within the Mayan tribes, too. Why?

Opening to the next world, or entering your heart, is not as difficult as living the life you are asked to act out every day by a mind that is distrustful, upset, or nervous, and unable to quiet its own thoughts. In these times when one woman celebrates her life, ten envy her. It began innocently when one woman talked about her life of charity and giving advice to only one—and then ten more. At first glance she appeared to be so wonderful that others thoughtlessly wanted her life right then and there, which caused many to hate everyone, because they had been forgotten during the love feast that enters the lives of any two who share and forget that they are there. Hating to be forgotten, even if they did nothing to deserve anyone remembering them, they created a maelstrom.

What can a woman much desired by men learn from Maya living on mountainsides and hiding from soldiers at times, even now? They can vicariously discover that men are not always as great as they would like to believe they are, and strangers are not apt to run off with them to seek a marriage bed when they can easily have whatever they want and flee when the deed is done. You see? No woman in the tribe worried about the men in their lives. They worried about men who entered their villages intent on raping them and their children again. Women of the world did not automatically think of rapists when they saw soldiers, yet many feared men they knew well. Everyone noticed that their groups were dehumanized when would-be terrorists wearing official uniforms walked through the villages and towns to look around.

Why would a government expect people to fall into line and submit to public humiliation when its own officials steadfastly refuse to fulfill what is expected of law-abiding citizens? Americans could not figure it out and were issued warnings to follow ever-changing rules without creating negative waves in political circles, but they would not listen. The way Americans wanted to live was no longer officially condoned, so many found they could no longer pray and foresee their futures—unable to know what would continue and what would be thrown away. As a result, many forgot how to pray and look beyond today, preferring to ignore everything they did not like about the present and try to leap ahead in time.

Studies of psychic phenomenon interested Americans more than the Maya who lived on the mountainsides, but such gifts and art held a certain fascination for all who studied with the Maya intending to help men and women find peace again. If each mind could move into time and mend one broken fence from within, would they do it? No, was the answer most Maya here from other times believed now.

The group often said, "If you don't have strife in your life, you invent it." That was how they looked at Americans driving big cars and building lofty buildings in an attempt to be less sad. The Maya did not wish to say they could not comprehend American ways, but it was true of them, too. Earth produced many people able to unite now, but Americans withstood all efforts to help them rejoin other nations again. It was not that America was indifferent or unable to move into a better time frame, but its people were ignorant of what they wanted—assuming power was the only way to build another day.

When a new leader arrives and sweeps away the mores of others who came before, not many follow him or her to the end. What happens to reformers? Normally they are assimilated into the crowd and either live long—forgotten or die without saving themselves. A few reformers live on in the memories of others, but no one who did a lot to change society is remembered that long.

⤬ ⤬

As you sit and enter your mind more often, try to prove that this writer is insane and unable to relate to you today. Whatever flits through your filters then is the memory of others who came and went in the past. You are reminded now that no one changes the minds of those who believe they have great power. Look no further than the pretty girl who has been raised on praise and cannot imagine doing anything to earn her own way. Soon she becomes a woman eager to be the wife of anyone with money who is willing to let her forever be a daughter, rather than a woman who can lead her family.

Suddenly, in the midst of the compound, strife arrived in the middle of a session about life here on Earth and how others cannot gather sufficient energy to expand the world. Students decided they would not take such a lesson sitting down, instead would explore it more. They could not decide what to work on as a clan, so they ended up working alone—and that taught The Teachers a lot! They discovered that people of this plane cannot expand, because they have no plan or desire to work together again. Each man and woman who wanted to do something great also wanted to star. No one wanted to help others star! Yet most had started these classes stating emphatically that they wished to help others more than anything else in life.

The power of sermons issued by this group of teachers was intense! Once a week ten of the elite would enter the group and teach nothing but truth. This blasted away several students each week, but most who could take the heat were better than ever. Why did it take the pressure of honest men and women preaching, for students to realize they were not doing enough to change in time? We are all what we believe! If no one says you are unwise to do this or that, you might grow to believe you are the same as everyone else. That is not true, but some never study psychology or anyone other than themselves, so they do not understand the society in which they dwell. If you had a lesson or two a week that swept you off your feet, would you want to review what you had to do immediately or leap into what might arrive in weeks to come? As The Teachers left to rejoin whatever community they were drawn to help next, they would only say, "Think about it!"

Did moving from compound-to-compound and town-to-town produce anything new? Usually it gave Mandy time to think about her life and how many she left behind who assumed they knew her—sure that she would return to them again. She did not want to work on this mindset now, but since it was there and not exactly shared with anyone else *down there*, Mandy moved through it before she did more work.

If she was caught unprepared or others did not share what they expected, completing her portion of the work was not easy. Some women expressed shock and dismay at the way she moved in, did her thing, and then left quickly. She did not stop and ask if they wanted anything from her, instead she gave what she had and left in a hurry. It made no sense to those who wished to remain sad or dwell outside a state of bliss, but it taught a different lesson to those who persisted in wishing to be what Mandy seemed to be—powerful, respected by men, not needing others. Some women never got the message or were unwilling to listen and learn, but it helped those who were eager to help others.

Who benefits from free lessons in life? No one, if the message is believed to be unworthy. If you want to take a missionary stance and attempt to change the Maya on Earth today, you will find some will listen and buy into what you say, but most will not. Why? They, like you, cling to what they know. Americans are apt to believe that buying a lot sets you above those who do not spend much or own a lot. Does that make sense when what you spend is borrowed money? Deep down you do not believe that what you buy on credit makes you look great to those who already own such things. Do you?

When Mandy and friends began insisting that no one could join the academies or take classes unless they paid cash, it seemed strange to people from other places. Many believed the change was initiated because Mandy was stashing the money and not paying taxes on it. Untrue, yet accepted readily by those who do live that way. When you are crooked, tough, disharmonious, you cannot see how women like Mandy and the rest would give up a flat or two in the States to live as they do in Mayaland today. After examining their shoes and hairdos, some Americans insist Mandy and her many friends gave up far too much, while others said they cannot be straight. Why? They claimed cash is out of style and never used by the rich and famous now and said they cannot imagine how anyone can live like that. When too many women descended in waves from the United States thinking that way, it became necessary to teach what The Ascended Maya advised as absolutely necessary to ascend within a group again.

When outsiders tour Mayaland—drinking and dancing half-clothed in village streets, what message are they transmitting to the natives? They obviously are not there to learn from The Maya or the tribe, so nothing is given to them! Those who stand on the sidelines never win the game, but some may enter the game later. Who would bet on a talker who does nothing—but plans to get in shape for the big game? Not many people would risk it, but reportedly angels often take such chances.

As days and weeks advanced into months and became the time of their lives—never to be repeated again, women and children aged gracefully and advanced in gradual stages to become the greatest artists ever seen in their hearts. While their hearts burst with love and contentment, others came and went without learning much from what was taught. How could Maya who never took classes easily complete exercises that others had to study and practice long and hard? It comes down to what you are given and what inspires you—but then again, maybe it is more? Regardless of what you decide, inside *Western* minds the individual matters most—not the tribe.

Forget where you were born! If you live long with others who support you or take you down with them, you either become enemies or friends; and whatever background you lend to a group in the beginning changes into whatever your life with that group becomes. If you want to create a great country, let one group lead, then sit back and let another group do the same, but remember some people never want to give up power they think they won. That will end in misery, but it can be averted by energy workers converting hate into love.

The lesson The Ascended Maya want to leave behind concerns healing scars visible from other stars, as well as reducing noise produced by humans that hurts the ears of many generations here, and those who visit Earth soon, provided the present population does not lay waste to its own life. Noise and music, as well as love and lust, are polar opposites to people who study such things, but when *you* are into one or the other, you may not notice the abyss between them. What to do about music and views of love that are not soothing enough to lull you to sleep or settle your turbulent mind so you can calmly enjoy this life? Cut back on the intensity and romance will reenter your mind. Everyone wants to feel great, and people love to see others in love! The emotional program installed at conception includes the need to be part of whatever work is going on around you. What else does a human want? Human beings want to abide with God—believe it or not.

Whatever The Ascended Maya teach within the minds of humans living in this time, they do not rule or take over their controls. The *Word of The Maya* is not a mindset or belief system or anything other than a release of energy into wisdom to live by now. It is a study of Time, because Time is how Earth currently exists. What others say about you or you wish to tell them is not true unless you live that way and believe you will continue to live that way. Whenever you think a single thought that differs from what you originally accepted as true, you create a new belief and a new way to be you.

⋈ ⋈

Wanda's weavers loved her and worked hard with her daughter, too, but were unwilling to let them alone when they were relaxing at home, thus it became necessary for them to leave the compound, as well as the nearby villages and town, to move about the Yucatan peninsula from time-to-time to meditate and do their own work—alone. Did that present serious problems for those they left behind?

What would suggest a serious dependency problem exists? When you hate others because they move away or someone loves you only when you are near. You probably know someone who prefers being alone at home but continually laments about how much they need a man or a woman in their life. Why lie? Why not admit that you always want to do your own thing and hate to share? Because it sounds selfish, arrogant, even stupid when applied to the lives of others who have accumulated much and are happier than you are—or are saints.

When you want to accumulate something—anything, you usually look to those who have more than you. That is the first false start! It often leads you to a broken heart. Once you learn to exist on your own—not bothered by things you once believed you had to own, you are almost home. But what to do about the moments before you leave this existence and are living alone within your mind? You need only slip into deep meditation or contemplate the navel from which you came—and you are in!

The pride that some tribes perpetuate limits their views of others who are different. When sufficiently able to understand that there are other religions, they cannot tolerate them, choosing to believe they are 'the chosen ones' who alone know what follows this life. What many seekers in Mayaland do, once they find religion again while visiting Mandy and friends, is try to sway others *at home* to do as they say or believe then. Cults are not worthy of the mind that cultivates them over time, but provide a lesson some apparently need to learn from time-to-time. This time it is men who want to start new religions when they merely believe in themselves.

What Mandy did was simply talk—and then walk. She also laughed a lot and seldom reacted to what she read or heard talked about on the street—at least not immediately. She made total sense to most folks, yet at times she was quite blunt and thought to be unkind by those who did not want to work with her or anyone else. The enemy of her life was not someone she taught or tried to reach, but her mind. It tried to tie her down and keep her in one state continually. It dogged her to do more for the group closest to her rather than work with others *out there*.

⋈ ⋈

Writing her own life story was not for Mandy, but Jeanne made a plan to do it when she found time to write about the lives they all lived now. The biggest problem she foresaw in writing her bio was that it would have to begin either at Mandy's end or begin with a new version of who she was once it started. Mandy's reason for not writing was simplistic, "No autobiography is worth the time it keeps an individual away from living right now." She finally agreed that it might help their scribes, writers, and teachers to study her life. Since Jeanne was all of these rolled into one belief system, she seemed the ideal candidate to ghost-write a book about Mandy; but would it be a deep analysis or merely helpful to those who already know her?

The work of writing about life is not easy if you cannot ease your mind every day or two and just be you. Since Jeanne was used to writing for weeks at a time—doing nothing else, she could move into the proper mood and supersede the work of a scribe in order to dictate at the same time. This was easy for Jeanne to do! She was amazed when her mind skipped about and played, because she wrote more than ever before when relaxing this way. She still had to free herself of professional responsibilities to find computer space and time to do everything without erasing her faith, but that was arranged.

The tribe was eager to talk about Mandy at times, but unwilling to mention her to anyone from the outside. Why? They knew more than Jeanne about the ways of inter-lopers—and some tourists were there solely to make trouble for others. The Maya, always respectful and kind to strangers, even those they do not like, do not say much about either extreme in their personal lives. If you are invited to the village of a Mayan man or woman, accept at once. You will never be asked again if you pass up that opportunity or are disagree-able, thus you will never understand them. You must visit the tribe and let today's Maya talk to know who you are in time.

What kind of walk converts an enemy into a friend? One accompanied by talk that hits the spot wherein you live a lot. If you are tense and nervous—never friendly, and try to interview a member of another group, you will become upset and unable to discover anything great in what they say. Instead of hating others, wishing to expose them, try living within the same view they use and divide your mind into two different lines. Live with the enemy in one time line as you live with your own kind in the other time line, then measure what can be compared.

Anthropologists often resent amazed tourists who, without reading a book they have written on the subject, theorize and make comparisons between various dialects and tribal extremes and immediately see the same things they labored to discover. The difference is ego-bound. They often respect only their colleagues who agree with them usually, hating advice from those who might know more than they without studying the subject much.

How Mandy arrived in time and knew instinctively what to do put many Maya into orbit. Anthropologists hated her, too, for what she was permitted to explore. She became more interesting to some men because Jorge did not judge or say much, aside from professing love for what she was. Their acceptance preceded her leaving and finding someone else over time, but it also helped the Mayan tribes understand that help is where you are and where you have been—not what you think might be. Anthropologists now get apologies from tribal members rather than holding meetings with their elders who alone know what is going on around them. Why? Anthropologists and many others did not approach the work of The Maya with prayer and thanksgiving, instead treating artists as if they were day laborers.

Faith produced in a day or two working with youth is greater than whatever you can imagine now. Why would the faith of one tribe and youth of other countries be easily explained in these places? When the youth of the United States invade Mayan space they usually show no respect for the tribe or for themselves. A too prevalent attitude displayed today announces that Americans are great and others are not! Male students' behavior often depends on the local price of beer and the sexual ease of the girls who follow them. Is it really true that "boys will be boys and want a lot of toys?" If so, the cultures crash—not merely clash! Such a view of men is not the way of the Maya. Too often Americans interpret their culture as if truly amazed that anyone would choose to live the way they live today. Such missionaries want to sell American wares and culture everywhere, but often fail because they visit and drink themselves to sleep—unafraid the Maya might be depraved or dishonest. Is it wise to trust luck and others to take care of drunken American children? Perhaps they are safer in Mayaland than the USA, but what American will admit that now?

Without much thought, look into your mind and view what we are working on within *you*. Are you within the same line as the author or scribe? Are you able to transcend these words to know how this book ends? If so, you know then that this is not the end of the work being taught, but the beginning of another vision.

✺ Chapter Forty-One

Two men stood with their backs to the rear wall of the lobby, both boldly staring at Mandy and Jorge sitting in the hotel's small restaurant directly across the hall from them. Mandy mentioned their presence to Jorge without raising her eyes, just as he looked directly at them. When Jorge denounced them as spies, Mandy laughed and bent across the table to straighten his tie and tweak his cheek as if he was saying something very funny or childish, rather than acknowledging that they had a serious problem.

Lifting her cup of hot chocolate to cover her mouth, Mandy spoke softly into the cup that they were in trouble. That is all it took! In a voice that did not reach people at nearby tables, she asked for help immediately—and an angel came to their rescue.

"Are you ready for dessert?" asked the angel with a smirk and a jerk of his pen as he began writing furiously on his pad. They had not asked for service, so they knew he had been sent to assist them or to deliver a message.

Rolling his deep, expressive eyes, Jorge said, "What would you like?" He touched his tie with his left hand. Worn only to meet the Press, he impressed everyone else, too.

"You can see that I don't need dessert, but a nice sherbet would cool us off. Don't you think?" Mandy said this with a wink to the angel masquerading as a waiter.

Working up enough nerve to send them into the future without anyone else knowing they left the café, they knew the angelic waiter had it in him, but his nervous tics suggested that he did not have a lot of confidence that he could pull it off easily. He managed to say with complete aplomb, "I would recommend that you look at the menu and see what else we have. The sherbet is not very good today."

Having told them to look in the menu, they each took one and turned to the last page. A map had been traced over the page of desserts. There were several letters they had to remove cautiously, before handing back the menus to him. When neither could lift the letters without being observed, the waiter said he could gladly wrap their desserts 'to go.' They agreed readily, since they really had to leave.

Once the angel left them in full-sight of everyone in the room, they noticed a few patrons were also eager to leave. The dynamic duo looked into each others' eyes and thought: 'Are they angelic messengers or warriors sent to protect us? What should we do if the emissaries of the evil-doer get to us before we get through the front door?' It was all very reminiscent of the first time they met, but years had added fewer things to fear, and neither could move quite as fast as they did in the past. Thus, they decided to sit tight and not take flight into the night just yet.

When the waiter returned, he gave them a styrofoam box and little bag, without saying what was inside either parcel. It appeared to be what they had not eaten, plus dessert, but it was neither. Mandy could detect from how the bag was packed that it contained several things they could use when they escaped.

Ignoring the waiter now gaping at them, Jorge said to Mandy with a grand sweep of his hand, "Would you like to freshen up before we go?" He did not appear to those nearby to say anything strange, but he knew she never used a public bathroom unless she was very nervous or about to leave on a long trip. His comment put her on full alert that they would soon be leaving Earth, or at the very least, this part of the world and would not be stopping for quite some time, so she stood up readily and motioned that she would be back in a flash.

When the waiter saw Mandy leave the lobby, he brought the check to Jorge and chatted while clearing away some crumbs from the table. The two men in the lobby continued their silent vigil, trying not to act as if they were CIA. They hoped others thought them to be old friends, which actually was true, though each stated emphatically they were not.

When Mandy did not return from the bathroom in the time allotted by the two spies, one wandered down the hallway leading to the rest rooms. He did not look back or he would have noticed someone intended to hit him over the head. What happened next was interesting. Mandy came out of the ladies room, stepped on a cat, it screamed and flew into the restaurant making all the diners laugh. As a result, no one heard the man being clubbed or the noise made as he was dragged across the hall and put into a broom closet, where he was gagged and left to dry out.

While that was happening, the other spy straightened his stance as if at full military attention and listened intently to the silly gadget he thought was hidden in his left ear. He was laughable by anyone's standards, except the CIA's, where he was looked up to as an agent of many *stagings*. He had not lost much in the years since the Bay of Pigs but his hair. His toupee did not hide the latest invasion of baldness growing ever wider and deeper across his skull as he cupped his chin with trembling hand and started mumbling. His face flagged down diners and wait staff alike who noticed his red face and ever-increasing anger. Why did the CIA want either Mandy or Jorge? They did not! They wanted to meet with them or follow them to see what they would do if asked to spy on Mayan tribes. It was assumed by CIA leaders that neither Mandy nor Jorge was Maya, so they led with a false premise that was bound to get everyone into a lot of trouble—but not for some time.

Mandy smiled at Jorge across the café, indicating that she would wait there rather than return to the table. He stood, while she sauntered toward the bar. When the CIA operative did not return to his post, Mandy leaned against the bar and watched the spy who was left behind check out what had happened to his guide, thus his cover was blown forever. He was never again seen in public places in that ratty toupee. It ended up in the trash, where he ended-up flat on his back. As he recalled later, he slipped on a wet rag as Jorge hurriedly passed him headed toward the lobby.

Mandy and Jorge laughed as they passed by a group of women and men smiling into their drinks, sharing stories of pranks they had pulled on their guide earlier. No one appeared to notice them leave until they were gone. Once secure in a car waiting for them near the hotel entrance, the waiter clapped his hands above his head for someone to come and clean up the table because he had the rest of the night off.

♓   ♓

Whenever the tribe met in secrecy, it usually meant someone was getting a new assignment. Today, however, they met in private to go over what Mandy and Jorge would say when they visited the United States. This was not something Mandy enjoyed, but she submitted to it—even asked what she must do. Her Spiritual Guides always took care of her, but angels also seemed to be involved now. That would change the way the entire mission was run. Angels and such are not above human beings, but the work they are assigned is not to be countermanded by others. When an angel asks you to do whatever, it is not wise to advertise that fact or forget to do it quickly.

When the The Ascended Maya existed in ways that go beyond Today, they sent emissaries to view Earth as it grew, but some of them stayed and never left. Jorge was described as being one of these Mayan beings, but he was definitely human—and a man who could find his own kind in every time. Jorge loved to walk and stroll about towns, and he loved to talk to Mandy and others when they were not blocked or upset or whatever, but he usually stayed in his own thoughts most of the time. His work was not difficult for him, but it demanded his total attention. It was not to be done when others were nearby, so he waited for this group to leave Mandy and he alone.

Walking through the next room to escape those seeking to release tensions with women, drinks, and other flings, Jorge noticed that nothing had changed much over the centuries for some of them. They fit right in with the American way of life today—loafing and playing, instead of working all day. Some elders were shocked at how quickly the recent civilization collapsed without anyone realizing it was gone, but Jorge was not surprised.

The next time Mandy saw the waiting man she thought was an angel, he was helping the captain of their luxury liner—piloting it into port. Of course, pilots are very often angels in disguise! She was not sure why he was there and what he would do, but she knew something new was due soon. Her hands moved automatically across the keyboard as a message from Jeanne suddenly appeared on her laptop computer screen. What was happening behind the scenes in her area of expertise that needed to release energy enough to send messages to her and Jorge this way? Working on these messages was never easy because Mandy had to decode the words before figuring out what was intended. She took this one apart and put it into prose that made sense and taught a lesson that was not what was originally meant.

Jorge normally was unwilling to stay aboard ship whenever it entered a port, but he was now content to sit with Mandy and wait for what would happen next. Smiling at the purser and others, he loudly announced that he was staying away from Aruba, not bothering with it because it was polluted. No one on board thought he was rude, but some wondered, because they had heard strong sea breezes kept Aruba clean.

Jeanne's note was terse and appeared to agree with what they were trying to achieve; but did it agree or not? Her prose was practiced and easy, so Mandy only had to labor over what was actually said and why it was being sent then. Her mind could not find the lesson in time, so she left the ship and went into port to meet with several people she knew as a teenager. They were vacationing on Aruba, but had arrived only an hour before her ship docked.

Within an hour of meeting them, Mandy was locked into the mindset of strangers prying into her life to find out why she was doing so well these days—captivating the minds of political factions of all kinds. She was news, and they wanted to be seen with her, too, but not with Mayans, as they incorrectly referred to people of the tribe. Her close affiliation with the Mayan tribe was something they repeatedly mentioned as not wise to advertise. She was advised to stop talking about them, instead take her money and run away as fast as possible.

Mandy laughed at their repeated references to money, because she had none. They did not believe her and said she had to have unlimited funds to be seen all over the world with so many different heads of state begging her to stay and give them the benefit of her legal and financial advice. How could she be less than a financial success if she knew what to do and others were so impressed with her that they avoided heeding Galbraith's messages from the past? In the way of a great economist, she kept her true thoughts to herself and projected what they said, repeating what they believed would happen next. It always works with egotists and non-believers and keeps many from getting upset and unable to work things out in a stable, economical way. Her method was called 'dispensation' by some, but it actually was relocation without dispensing any wisdom available then.

After all the passengers headed for shore with Mandy, Jorge returned to his stateroom and waited for the angel to arrive. It was only a nanosecond in time, but an hour passed according to the stateroom clock. For some reason, Jorge was not able to turn off the shower and needed a plumber quickly. The angel appeared to be the most capable plumber on staff, so he was dispatched to see what happened. Meanwhile, the captain left the ship, prepared to relax on the beach and visit the casinos when he put his mind to it later. The last to disembark were reluctant to leave because the ship seemed to be listing, rather than standing tall in the water.

When a passenger spotted the captain drinking a glass of something straight at a nearby bar, she asked, "Who is manning the ship?" She was quite concerned and sought out her traveling companions to complain about the way the ship was going to sink and the captain would be drunk if they did not hurry and get him back on board.

The captain was not afraid to go on shore during brief visits, but today he was uneasy about leaving the boat high and dry. The other night, just as a beauty called and asked him to visit her and talk things over in her stateroom, he had felt a warm hand pressing on his chest. When he arrived at the buxom blonde's cabin, she was not there. He pushed this memory around, trying to find a better place and time to meet her without arousing his crew's suspicions, but it was never easy. Without saying much, he usually acted angry about how the ship was serviced or said he needed a walk on the beach to think about what had to be done before they sailed for another ten days. The crew bought his story today and sent him merrily on his way without further thought.

When women returned to report the Captain was drunk on shore, sitting at a bar in a casino not far from the pier, staff realized he was not clearing his head, as he had said, and was obviously not very angry, either. It is never wise to tell lies, but the captain was so used to lying that he had skipped over thinking about the repercussions of doing what *he* wanted versus abandoning his post. After a few moments of doubts and thoughts about possibly losing their jobs, the head purser met with the steward to discuss what should be done about the ship and the captain, too. The steward went in search of the man who had assisted the Captain as he piloted the ship. Unable to find him, he wondered how they could contact him immediately, since it was obvious they could not move the ship without someone sober on the bridge.

Just as a bridge spans a river only if designed to do so, this crew was not able to leap the gap created when the power structure was breached. They wandered about looking for someone to assume authority or for a chore that would keep them out-of-view until order was restored. Unfortunately, no one followed the written orders that cover such a situation. Why? The crew was not sure who was in charge or if the boat would even sail when it was due to leave port, so they rattled around the ship boasting about being panicked by this turn of events, instead of working to restore order. For reasons not deciphered in print at this time, the minds of each employee (never having been *real* sailors) collapsed, thus enabling one mind to take over and tell them what had to be done now. That one mind dictated that they sack the captain and get rid of his advisors, but a mutiny was averted—or was it?

When Mandy returned to the ship she learned that a mutiny of a corporate-type had been executed while Jorge remained in his cabin waiting for someone to repair the shower. Without any announcement that a higher power had taken over the ship and everyone on it was about to witness something weird, she knew what was happening. Mandy approached their cabin door just as the ship lurched, then steadied as if it had hit the dock. Speaking in as reasonable and reassuring tone as anyone could muster when a ship is listing to port, Mandy said, "Would you look for the Steward and see what's happening?"

Smiling, Jorge said, "No, Mandy, *he* is with us. We don't have to worry. Everything will all be over in a few hours, so sit down and use your smile *and* your sense of humor to try and figure out just what is going to happen when we get back."

Mandy did not sit down or smile. Instead she walked about the suite looking at each and every single thing fastened to the wall or screwed into the floor. Her mind was not lurching so much as reacting to all the work going down in this ship that she had seen instantly. Her own life was definitely not going to end here, but she was not sure why she had to sit in the suite and watch everyone else evacuate the ship. She handed Jorge a crossword puzzle that was halfway done and said, "Work on this…"

Speaking to her back, hiding a grimace rather than his usual grin, Jorge said, "You can do this easily!" He could not laugh at what was happening because he felt a stab of pain in his shin and suddenly realized the bed was not made and the strap that held the mattress in place was not secured well enough to keep it from moving as the ship plunged up and down. He watched as the mattress separated from the frame and box spring.

An envelope addressed to both of them fell out, so Mandy picked it up and handed it to Jorge, miming that he should read it aloud—loudly. He chose not to do so. Instead, he scanned what was written before handing it back to her. She detected an urgent message hidden within the words, but could not see what was in-between the lines so easily. Now upset that the ship was to be sacrificed to the tide, because they had to leave this work immediately, she realized in a flash that everything was going just the way the angels wanted it to go now.

Quickly walking into the passageway, Mandy and Jorge saw immediately that they were the only passengers left on deck. Since arrangements had already been made, all they had to do was get to the atrium where someone would rescue them. This was all they got from the message, but it also implied that no one was left on board to help them with the assignment given at their last meeting with The Maya of other times. The ship continued to list to the left and then right itself, as if to say *it* was okay and were they going to stay or go?

When the news was reported later, the Head Purser was quoted as saying the captain was unaware of any danger to the ship when he left the helm. It was meant to excuse his odd behavior, but it caused a huge rift and ended the career of a few men who had become used to drinking beer before going to work and while on the job. They left luxury cruises without a second thought and entered into a new view of Earth. They had to settle for less money, thus unable to drink as much or work as little.

What can be enjoyed when the ship of state is sinking fast and the captains of industry, along with those once trusted, can no longer lie to save what remains of their life and times? Why salvage a ship when there are many others better than it still afloat? That was the rationale the company used then, but later its charter was changed to reflect that what was done once is not to be done again.

☼ CHAPTER FORTY-TWO

"When you're able to do anything you want, why would you limit your horizon to sitting and doing very little—except getting mad at those who do act?"

Jeanne's question, which was more of a statement, hung over the auditorium like a dark cloud. Too many women in the audience were unhappy and refused to follow her leads or even use reason to solve problems now. She repeated herself before letting her challenge linger in their thoughts as she resumed her place among women of many faiths who did not look at her straight. Billed as the keynote speaker, she had not led with a joke or a story funny enough to cut through the chill produced by what had been asked of women of all faiths prior to her taking over the dais.

The wave of animosity was so great when Jeanne initially walked into the auditorium with Wanda on her arm that she was alarmed. She was not used to people rejecting her before she opened her mouth, especially when she was an invited guest and a paid speaker. It was apparent from what was said immediately before she appeared on stage that the crowd did not want her to speak or do any work with them now.

It felt strange to be back in New York, surrounded by so much pain, ignorance, and sorrow—barely concealed by the shallow patina of Big City arrogance. The negativity was too obvious to be mislabeled as: misplaced distrust or lack of love. The locals were timid in their attire, resorting to all-black clothing rather than adorning themselves with whatever color turned them on or accented their sex appeal, but their individual behavior was anything but shy. Later it was described far and wide as rude, crude, and lacking in cultural sophistication, but that was then and this is now.

The cloud of sadness created by the somber shades of black worn by the natives blighted the brilliant auras emitted by those seeking to raise the consciousness level of their city. It was apparently not an exercise many wanted to accomplish, but someone had arranged for women of different hues and faiths to come together today and talk about religions that did not exist any longer for any of them.

Wanda pondered what could be done to improve the assembly's attitude and mood to enable them to fixate on peace long enough to stay on the path of the Divine and enjoy the good life as they defined it. When Jeanne sat down at the end of her speech, Wanda stood up and clapped, but only a few other women stood and applauded, too. Less than one percent of the audience approved of what Jeanne said they had to do as a group. She was unable to project why she was afraid of these women and the sub-adults some brought with them, but she recorded their angry hatred and animosity toward everyone seated on the stage. It shook her mind! The audience sat as if cemented to their chairs—sitting on their hands. No one moved or applauded, other than the few who saluted the bravery of Jeanne for stating publicly what was needed today.

Jeanne saw images of beings standing up while others sat and slumped in their chairs and wondered about nothing. What could she do to spark their hearts and move them to open up and take part now? As soon as the panel sat back in their chairs, Jeanne laughed because the entire meeting was so ridiculous she could not stop her mind from revolting. She had to laugh! She laughed as hard as anyone alive has ever guffawed. It was such a shock to the old crows in the crowd that they started to laugh just as hard. Suddenly the room broke in two equal parts in a final attempt to create harmony from afar. Gloom could not ruin the day! The remainders of the day spun out of control and ended this meeting that had no beginning or meaning now.

Asking friends who knew many of the people who had planned to attend the meeting, Jeanne said, "What just happened in there?"

"They don't believe in God, for one thing," said Thérèse.

"And they don't have any faith at all," added Wanda as if completing her daughter's sentence for her.

As if she now understood why the seminar could not have ended any better than it began, Jeanne said, "They want it all, but don't believe anyone can star—unless they work alone." After a pause, she said softly, "If only we could open a vent or create a wave, or do something to help those being betrayed by ideas out of line with Today!" Talking without apparently understanding what she was saying, Jeanne said, "What do you propose we do when you take over?" Obviously deep in trance now, she peered at something in the distance approaching her quite quickly. Eyes narrowed, she automatically sought her reading glasses, but said nothing about what she saw.

As if the meeting's agenda was up to them to decide, Thérèse asked, "What do you all want to do?"

"You know, Thérèse, this meeting needs something we can't quite see, mainly because we don't wallow in a state of disbelief—or not enough to grasp how deeply depressed these women can become if left to their own thoughts and self-pity. Way too many are suffering from minority paranoia, for one thing, and we have to do something about that quickly or we'll be contributing to their becoming even more uncivil." As Jeanne spoke, her eyes twitched in a weird way, appearing to move from side-to-side, without actually moving or doing anything unusual.

Her two friends observed her for a moment or so before Wanda said, "I see you're having a vision, Jeanne…and here we are talking right through it. Why don't you sit and live it, then tell us what to do?" Wanda's words were spoken at the same reasonable, relaxed pace she adopted since losing her leg. It was as if she were coaxing her friends to relax or not panic now.

Thérèse raised her hand in benediction and said she would speak once again. She would talk about her life of ease and how many times a week she had had to have her nails done and her hair tweaked and her feet soothed, and how the migraines never stopped then.

This strange admission caught the other two off-guard. They suddenly realized the pain and sorrow Thérèse had endured over the years. The boredom she had never shared before. During the silence that entered their conversation a napkin unfolded on the table, seemingly by an unseen hand. It revealed a few easy-to-read lines. *"What do you do for those who take upon themselves the work of the entire human race, but first must submit to their bodies' demands?"*

With a flurry of her hands and a blush, Thérèse said hastily, "I'll do whatever comes through! But you two have to sit with me in front of everyone. We'll talk as if we're on our way to a great party in LA as soon as we leave New York. We'll out-dazzle them all by beginning with a fashion show. They'll have to admit then that color needs to be added to their lives immediately! We won't sit by and let them die within their minds. We'll admit them to the holy places of the heart and the open spaces of the mind so they can go home and teach others how to meditate and live for the day."

As Wanda stood, she pointed toward a shop that appeared to be celebrating its grand opening. "Let's go to that new boutique you're always talking about and see what they can lend us to demonstrate how to change your aura with one quick stroke of brilliant color. It may even turn out to be fun for everyone!"

"I think the proprietor is an angel!" Thérèse spoke as she bravely approached the store and walked in as if she owned Manhattan. Plopping her huge purse down near the chair where her mother would sit and watch her model, they all started talking at once.

Once started, Thérèse reverted to her old career path without hesitation. She did not notice the proprietor standing straight and tall, as if he had been a super model, too. When she spotted him, she wondered if he also posed for magazines that create images of whatever is the rage and implies success, thus encouraging fans to pursue fashions and fads in order to appear to have it all.

Without smiling, yet radiating light everywhere—piercing through their auras, the proprietor said, "Thank you for opening my shop!"

Without smiling or taking her eyes away from his middle brow, Wanda said, "You're a real angel!"

"I'm an angel for now, but I can appear to be either a woman or a man. I'm not like you, Wanda, I need someone to look after me and take care of my physical needs." He talked with expressive hand movements, as if to indicate that he needed sexual tasks done for him and desired someone immediately. It was all quite strange, out of a dream, so no one bothered him with what they saw, since they believed he was lost and unable to find his way to the top.

"If you help us, we'll help you when we return your clothes later today." Jeanne spoke in a manner far too brusque for someone begging—totally unwilling to pay even a small deposit on the very expensive clothes and accessories they intended to borrow and model later.

The man stopped talking in order to stare at them. He looked more closely at each, as if someone was standing behind them. Nodding to that image or view or whatever he believed was there, he encouraged the women to check out the racks of clothes that best expressed the colors of their auras.

With a sigh of relief, they noticed there was no black outerwear anywhere—and only a few pieces of underwear appeared as old-hat as that. The young/old man pulled a dress off the rack in front of the mirror at the front of the store, then another and another. He handed each woman a dress to try on, saying with a smile, "We intend to crack this town wide open with the best light show possible—Help these sorry souls brighten their minds and move into a better line in time."

Silently, each woman twirled before mirrors in separate dressing rooms, but anyone could see that a new day was emerging as the past moved out of black in Manhattan. It happened just like that! No big deal!!

When the trio reassembled mid-salon to await the owner/designer's close-up inspection and decision about what was needed to accent each ensemble, they saw for the first time that they each wore something unique—not noticed before because they had been captivated by color. Each ensemble highlighted and delighted specific women from other times—merely suggesting, not actually in a costume.

Speaking to Jeanne, Wanda said, "I see you're the warrior and will protect everyone under attack." She pondered why Jeanne was best-suited for such a role? Right then it popped into her mind—not to leave, that she was the one most in need of the services of a warrior if she was to help Thérèse heal the waves of energy being displaced over this space.

"When you have enough to eat and drink—and good air to breathe, you can rise to your highest sky," said the angel without pausing as he seemed to fly from one to the other helping them with jewelry, flowers, or whatever to complete their plumage. He did everything possible to align their bodies with the spirit of the outfits so when they returned to the synagogue and opened this afternoon's work they would win everyone over immediately. This was not an easy task to undertake, since most participants were positive that they did not need to learn anything new about fashion or love. Unless they were changed in some deep and meaningful way immediately, the audience would continue to react in a negative way to everything taught by women they thought were not famous enough to be respected or to study with now.

As if reading cue cards, perhaps rehearsing the lead-in to her speech, Thérèse said, "We've chosen a hallowed place to conduct this meeting, yet so far the light remains faded—not prismatic, which certainly doesn't help us all appear charismatic now." Then, as if addressing a loud crowd milling about the back of the room, hesitant to return to their seats and sit quietly, she added, "What do you think we should do to project beauty and love?"

As the empty room filled with spiritual beings representing The Lord, Thérèse's rehearsed words were heard by those there to listen and learn. Others strolled into view or left without speaking. Within half-an-hour the afternoon session was reconfigured, the theme changed, and the furniture rearranged. It was a daring and unusual experiment for those working in Spirit to visit such a place without being invited, but they were willing to help—even participate in a lesson on visualization. That work opened the afternoon session and led into talks about missions the three women had completed in Mexico, Peru, and Colombia, too.

As the audience reassembled after the lunch break, it became obvious that many women were no longer willing to sit in the seats originally assigned to them. They moved to seats with better views of the stage or moved to the rear with their bags arranged around them as though ready to take flight at a moment's notice. None of them looked happy.

Wanda stood first and dazzled those nearby with the radiant hues of her purple dress and gorgeous lilacs woven through her silver hair. She stood mute, letting the lilacs an old friend mass-produced do their work. The lilacs easily passed as the real thing, except they did not introduce allergens into the room. Even so, several women in the room sneezed and complained about their smell. Wanda smiled at that and totally relaxed into a great mood. She laughed and waved at women in the front row as if sharing something funny. Others, unable to comprehend what had changed, stared at the stage in amazement and became silent. The vision of gaping mouths and fingers held in front of painted lips was more than Wanda could handle in a sober state. She laughed even louder, then asked the audience to let go of their stress and laugh along with her, even if they believed fate would slap them later if they laughed or were happy now.

Laughter rose very weakly at first, but finally burst through the tension until it reached the back row. Their happy sounds lit up the room enough to highlight the podium and make it the center of everyone's attention. The audience elevated its own mood—and no joke was made about it later. Afterwards many would try to emulate the effect, but it was not possible without a divine comedian of some kind warming up the audience and encouraging them to laugh.

As their work centered on Earth, the reason for the meeting became clearer. Women in the front were first to notice how Wanda's friends were all dressed. They watched closely to see what Wanda did with her cane when ready to leave the raised stage and were shocked when she threw it away to create a special effect half-way through her presentation. She stood tall, free of any obvious need for support from anyone or anything around her. Her declaration of freedom created an image of belief in action that inspired one or two in the first row to stand and clap and yell 'bravo!' and ended only when the last person in the back row laughed. Wanda laughed at that! In fact, Wanda laughed almost continuously the rest of the afternoon. She firmly believed that Spirit is something you can never know how it will strike your heart and mind, so she advised everyone to just accept your part.

Woven within the work of the trio was a workshop they asked everyone present to attend. Each woman was asked to select one of three different angelic roles needed to heal family situations or work atmosphere where fear is present. One role followed the tasks laid down by Uriel and those who channeled the word of God like angels of Earth and those who worked with angels in time.

The selection process was easy for the group seated at the front of the auditorium, but seemingly impossible for the women who huddled in the back, so they divided the audience into three sections. The front of the room was designated as Uriel's domain. The people at the back were appointed guardians of the group and would assume the role of Michael, who guards souls from attack when under the spell of God and letting love take over their hearts. Once a role was accepted, they could not easily leave it behind or ignore it. Surprising even Wanda, the women at the back of the room were open to being guards or guardians—willing to learn more about Michael and what he controlled. They listened intently to everything Jeanne said.

As the afternoon progressed, Uriel and Michael did their work in the guise of two human beings, Wanda and Jeanne, while Thérèse enacted Raphael imparting wisdom and healing to all, within an hour or so of praying together for the first time. Some were merely amazed, while others were in a complete daze, but no one present was ever the same afterwards.

"If you want to do something—make a difference," said Wanda, "Put on your best suit of clothes and go forth and wage war against *your* thoughts! Who cares if no one understands you—just do it!" When she said this she was standing, not sitting, with both feet so deeply implanted in the floor that her movements caused the stage to shift a bit. Her body experienced a tremor that went up her 'good' leg and down the shaft of fabricated materials of the other leg as if it were flesh. Standing even taller now, Wanda began dancing a jig! Everyone was amazed to see her moving with such grace—dancing with such energy all over the place.

A universal thought emerged, 'If she can dance, why can't we?' Their dancing began as a jig but the music playing quickly turned into a hora. For the very first time, everyone understood its meaning. This is not a gloomy time for anyone alive! This is not a time to be upset or downhearted about those who have fled. This is a time to rejoice and follow the Lord anywhere! Everyone danced because they had shed the morose mindset put in place long before the seminar arrived in time. Time shifted and they were lifted into new and better views of what they could do for Earth, as well as how to create a life without much strife.

The view of the East River is such that you have to stand on tip-toe to see the water. It will always be there, but nearby areas blighted by man-made industry can be changed or rearranged. A few observers suddenly became inspired and saw the river needed trees to reach into it and screen debris and whatever else was not good for it and the city, too. Trees were needed immediately, and the women of the city suddenly saw the need. They were not lazy or indifferent to beauty, just used to what was or had always been ugly. They forgot to improve or conserve trees and see the city as the world sees it today. The dance would stop, then begin again and again until everyone was spinning and laughing and going within their minds deeper than they had ever ventured this life.

The seminar ended before Wanda realized their attire had to be returned and the audience had to go home. Right then a psychiatrist approached her and Jeanne at the podium and invited them to dine with her at her home that night. Her practice was not limited to the women who lived near her office on Park Avenue, but many boasted that they paid her huge rent. She was friendly, not at all nervous, so they decided to accept her invitation to eat steak grilled on a high terrace overlooking Central Park while checking out the sky.

When the jubilant trio exited the brilliant yellow cab and walked toward the entrance to the building where John Lennon and Yoko Ono had once lived as man and wife, they departed a bit from their conversation to say a prayer that he would be there, and he appeared! He came through to them and spoke of something not known about his home in Liverpool, England. They each felt his pain and sorrow. He wanted to speak about something he wanted done, that it would be done in another way that day, but he was gone before they could reassure him that all was fine.

They knew then that within the day and night that followed New York would have a party like no other. It was to be a gala of great vision and foresight, intended to last all night without revelers getting upset enough to ignore ethical behaviour. Merely contemplating the event produced a hilarious, yet somewhat somber mood as they considered the great and small. They deliberated on their mission's impact as they strolled and chatted, working out a plan to revitalize a city that had helped them all grow.

As Thérèse peered at the park spread out below her, she said to their hostess, "What views you have!" She leaned out over the railing, not thinking about anyone who might be looking up from the street far below. Suddenly rain became noticeable—even to her, so they went inside before it dampened their enthusiasm. The rain came and went while the group stayed glued together drying in the huge dining room. They sat in sweet contentment, eating and drinking something sweet or sour depending upon their whim, but no alcohol was served.

When the friends realized the psychiatrist did not intend to ask for help now, they admitted that they were mystified about why she had invited them to her home. Her response was to laugh, then smile as she revealed how she had met Mandy at the airport in San Diego three months earlier and promised her she would look after her friends when they came to New York for this meeting.

This truly amazed the merry trio, because the invitation to teach today had been delayed or not received until last week. They all wondered aloud, "How did Mandy know that?" Without any further doubts about the psychiatrist, they discussed Mandy and her grand plan. Her plan is one of epic proportions—one that needs every woman alive to buy into it to transform everyday life into a work of art capable of changing the Earth. Their conversation ended when each said the same thing simultaneously: "Mandy does her part and always makes it look so easy—so why can't I do it, too?"

Without thinking, Wanda stood and announced that the party was over and they had to leave immediately for Mexico to see what could be done to improve their water. She spoke easily, almost jokingly, then waited for someone else to speak. You see, only one channel can speak at any given time.

☼ CHAPTER FORTY-THREE

A clan convened to talk about providing suitable proof that the Maya, of today and always, could help the United States learn to live better with *what is* rather than *what they want*. Willing to beg, borrow, rape and pillage to get whatever they desire or think they need, Americans appear to be losing battles everywhere, especially within their own families. Could Mayan spiritual guides or shamans, with their total lack of regard for the material aspects of today's world, help them now?

These elders never mentioned leaders by name, because they do not matter to them. Leaders of any country are selected not by name or reputation but by a bloc much like themselves, so their own group's work gets done first. To them, the group of leaders meeting in Mexico was no different from others meeting in the United States, except that they based their existence on faith—which when compared to people counseling Americans now is very different. This conclave ended with a consensus that reduced everyone's work, yet prepared all present for their future.

The question under discussion was: "When you can look into the future and see yourself as you really are, is it a mirage or are you always the same—regardless of whatever part you play today?"

When one faction rules independent of all others, everyone else must obey their rules. As a result, friction is activated again and again until someone moves out of their range of authority or someone new takes over and rules. The Maya are no different now than when they ruled in the past, except now they do not have the benefit of the ruling class's inherited knowledge. That caste was defeated by other rulers and tribes who succeeded in trashing their great work as mathematicians, bringing shame upon them all. That view of Mayan history is not shared by scholars in the United States, even though many laugh and say it is. That is why The Maya want to help Americans avoid losing their integrity and earning a bad reputation for doing things their founding fathers never condoned nor would have permitted if they had continued to reign.

The Ascended Maya see history about to repeat itself and want to stop the bloodshed. Without much thought, the elders met a lot. They sat for many hours without seeming to need to relieve any physical needs, but they were human beings! They believe anyone can control the mind to let go of bodily functions at times. However, most people who seek such mind control do not realize the wisdom of waiting for portal days to work in spirit when they wish to move up and away from a place where they are no longer able to produce anything new or worthwhile.

When the elders met that evening, they started out praying for the United States and other places. They asked for the faith needed to take everyone by the hand again and lead them through the maze to do whatever needed to be done without expecting anyone to respect anything they did. They needed a thick coat of skin to withstand the barbs and cuts that would be handed out by those in the United States who acted as if they never needed help, yet took whatever they could get. Because of their grasping arrogance, many of the wise were willing to sit back and let America collapse. The Maya were not!

This group of elders always met in a room dense with the scent of incense and such, but when Mandy appeared, it disappeared—leaving behind only a bit of dust and the hint of copal. The elders refrained from using much incense when she was able to do business with them, because she had bad lungs. They could not risk losing her due to asthma, so this room was chosen since it was airy and cool due to the high roof made of woven palms. The exterior appeared to be a relic of the past when kings and queens ruled and were the all-powerful teachers of the tribe, but it was not. The tribe was alive and doing well without anyone knowing why it was moving ahead now, thus some in the tribe wanted to retrace the line and find out why.

"If you take time tonight to go back over time, you'll lose today," said Mandy without a smile. She always kept them 'in the moment,' as the New Age sages like to say, unaware that this comment revealed how The Ascended Maya participated in the work they wanted to do one day, too. Mandy was eager to pass along classes on how to meditate and enter dreams without losing any of today, but most New Age students or *seekers*, as they often call themselves, were not quite attuned to the mood of the moon or able to touch the outside of Mars. According to Mandy, they did not believe in what they sought, merely tuned into the mood. She expected to one day teach some *seekers* how to move up and out—to levitate and rise so she could end her connection to this birth. That was her goal, but members of the tribe not from the other side did not wish to help Americans as much as she and The Ascended Maya.

Without saying a word, Mandy listened as complaints about what the US would try next were lodged over and over again by several different men. She did not comment, brushing aside whiners who complained that the tribe resembled America more—more than ever before, and would have to take responsibility for their own countries' behavior before they complained about how the United States was run now. Her reaction was not taken as intended, but it got through to the ancients on the other side that there was a war of sorts going on now and Mandy needed help combating their old enemies once again.

Only when the room darkened to the point where only people sitting close by were visible, and the moon was high, could the group chant and celebrate its ascendancy and what it meant. Sages can speak of the past without regret and without concern that what happened once will not occur again and take them into a tunnel in time that might end with someone being pushed off a cliff or taken apart to get to his or her heart. They all repeated several times, "The enemies of the state were not as profound or deep as those you could not see, but no one believed it."

Mandy stood then without speaking to whomever appeared to be leading the meeting. She walked over to a woman whose mouth was moving but seemed unable to speak and asked her, "What do you think, Grandmother, of this plan?"

The old woman awoke from a deep trance and spoke in Old English—not a Mayan dialect. Only Mandy, Jorge, and a few of the men could readily understand her. Everyone became instantly alert because this old woman never used words other than what she had heard since birth. She normally spoke in a dialect so old that others in her tribe had trouble deciphering it, so few ever asked her to speak of what she knew or heard from the deep. Her first word was not discernible by anyone, but when it became apparent that she was speaking English as spoken in the 16th century, the wisest of the wise realized she was a member of the tribe trained to remember that time. She was immediately revered and asked to talk without fear.

"As you walk into the future of this country, which is very great, we want you to remember that The Maya are a tribe…so are many others who now must be content to work very hard. We are all Maya! We do what we do because of the distance in time and space and the way you live today. You have no way of holding in what you find in time. For that reason, we are not going to show or tell you what is happening in space and time now…it would erase the faith of those who must live through it in order to climb and ascend now and again.

"The way you act and talk is recorded in your mind, then downloaded at the end of a life, but in too many instances today it is not fit to be downloaded. The universal mind is being corrupted and the main thrust or drive of personality is lust. It is indecent and not worthy of good people to watch and try to understand what lust has to do with love." Right then the old woman's back sagged and she cried. Motioning that she no longer wished to talk, she appeared to be watching something going on within her mind that made her very sad. She was unwilling to speak of it then.

Again, Mandy stood up and addressed the woman with her unique, direct style. "Grandmother, you are who must talk about the future—a lot. You are to dwell with us for many months…then plant the seeds of what we will be. You are going to need what you see, and we need you to intercede for us and help us to breathe better than ever. We need you now, so please reconsider and take us with you to the new view of what is happening around you—and us, too."

Prolonged pleading was unnecessary to get the old woman to talk again. The group melded when it realized that it was Mandy who gained this power for them—not one of the men. Though it was noted, some did not want to call attention to her, so they inched closer to the fire in the center of the dirt floor and listened better than before as the old woman quietly talked to Mandy.

"We are not to plow the earth or move into condos, yet we help others take over our land and plow under our altars. We need to know why we let this happen and prevent them from taking over our minds…but first we have to stop the fires! We must not pollute the skies…doing what we did in the past to survive. The ancient ones knew how to build huge fields out of watery places and harvest great crops, but we never farm that way any longer. Today we do what we have done ever since then. We must change back to how we farmed with water and very little earth, or we will lose our children to the drunkenness, lust, and corruption that surround them in places like Cancun.

"The devil worshippers of other faiths try to say we are like them, but we have nothing in common. The Catholic faith implies that God is wise, but has enemies who try to take over his place. We do not defile God in any way now. God is and gods exist, but we are not gods… We are able to call upon angels and tell them to work for us, but that must stop… No one again must challenge God and say, as many do, that a devil has as much power as God or his family… or that a devil will take us away from how we are made and make us do something evil." At this point the wizened, old woman held up her arm and extended her hand as if asking to be excused from the burden of speaking words she could not easily interpret. Her mind was exhausted from trying to translate and she wanted to lie back and rest for a while.

Whatever the test used in the past to decide if this member of the tribe was best suited for such memory work was not recognized now even by the Traditionalists. They believed men were always the bearers of great beliefs and implied that her messages were too garbled to mean anything. They objected most to the news that how they farmed now had to change. They mumbled that it was done the way it was done because God ordained it and said it was to be done that way always.

Within a few minutes of the last transmission, the woman collapsed as if in a coma, but many recognized that she was deep inside a dream rather than in an ordinary trance. She thrashed about for a minute or two before going into a dream. She returned as they sat and watched the fire and talked about what she said earlier.

Producing translations in dialects far and wide across the Mayan tribes was not something Mandy could do easily, even though she spoke naturally in a dialect that most Maya could use if they combined only a few of the many lines into one. Her version of a universal Mayan dialect did not include Spanish or English, and her accent remained American with a nasal quality that intoned much more than what others taught as pure dialect. She laughed at the idea that language could be taught from a book or computer, but had no idea how she got her skills or *gift of tongues*, as the priest once described her strange abilities to others.

While working on her thesis in graduate school, Mandy lost most of her desire to read and write what others opined because she recognized by then that they knew nothing, too. As it turned out, her entire life had been preparation or introduction to working for The Ascended Maya. She was not wise or willing to strive, so she bailed out of her career and life outside? She proved herself in the United States long before her mind opened to The Maya. She thrived and rose to the top of a profession not designed for women of any time, and by all accounts succeeded in that life and made a lot of money; but when given the opportunity to leave The World, she took it immediately. Why? What made Mandy run?

"I think the United States is unable to maintain its pace in the race. I think it can change in ways that will benefit the common man and woman who have a life plan, but too many are lackluster and lazy to work at change." Mandy looked at the elders, but stopped talking because she was no longer speaking Mayan. They did not know what she was saying and she was not able to translate it. That shocked her—a lot. It was as if the words came from someone watching and hovering over her, but not her own Higher Mind. She could not say why she was thrilled by this voice, but she was.

Smiling confidently, Mandy said in a slightly altered tone, "I'm a native of these parts and have shed a few hearts in the past—only to arrive back here in a time when the country leading us is hate-filled and ready to sacrifice lives as easily as make up excuses for it. Nations love blood sports, but not in the ritualistic sense we followed, until the Toltecs used the ruse that they were meant to rule and we became pawns in a game played to win what they alone wanted to gain."

Moving closer to Mandy, Jorge said little except to ask two men not to talk. He was fascinated by this change in direction and wanted to remember every word, because if he could not, Mandy was in such a deep trance that she would forget everything and not be able to discuss it later.

"I see myself as a woman of the world—a woman of deep inner conviction, but not happy with what I find around me now… I want to clear the air. I want to purify the water so air can help us leave this planet as it was… I want to help others realize that Earth is merely a generous host—not a destination where we stay forever." Mandy stopped then, as though lost in thought. She no longer translated the message for the men. These words hurt her mind more than she was ever hurt before. What had she done to return again and again—not to have ascended to a higher plane by now?

After a few minutes, Mandy spoke again, but this time in a dialect everyone easily understood. "I am here to teach you what to do so you don't have to come back. I volunteered, so to speak, to be here, but I'm not willing to do it again. I've lost interest in what goes on within this group, too, because it's not willing to do more to purify the mind and control bodily wants at this time… I want to move into another role and model it for a few hours—see what I find. I did it when I submitted to the call to visit Mexico—and later Yucatan, and decided to stay as I am today. You can visit a new place and not feel a pull of any kind to enter that world, but I always knew, even when I lived in the United States, that one day I would leave for a better life."

Mandy was not surprised at what she said, but Jorge was shocked. He did not realize until now that she would never again be a citizen of the country she had dropped into when she came back to Earth this time. That rarely ever happened. Perhaps this was a dream that would complete the path she had established in the past?

The elders formed a circle by holding up their hands one-by-one indicating they understood what Mandy was saying and recognized her as being a Maya who was not of this time. The news amazed only a few present, but the outside world remained unchanged and unaware of what was happening here. Mandy said, "When the Earth is clear of all that was taken away or blasted out or corrupted, it will shake itself off like an old dog flinging its fleas into space—never to be bothered by them again. We might like to think about that now, but why? Why would anyone buy a book about the Earth shaking, people baking or being thrown into the fiery furnaces of volcanoes and such, then go out and create the same life plan again? Why?"

As Mandy sighed and looked at members of the tribe who sat on their haunches as if about to spring into action, she thought about the first time she met some of them. Nothing was what she thought it was then. It was much better to be inside the tribe and able to talk as a friend, rather then be a strange woman who related stories about times lost to recent Mayan minds. She wanted to sit still, but the impulse to talk and the need to see what else might be disclosed now impelled her to work harder than ever to open her present life so members of the tribe could see inside it.

"I'm not a native of my birthplace. I was not raised in a traditional way by anyone assigned to watch over me then, but I was able to rise above the expectations of the family assigned to me this time. I first introduced them to my beliefs about the age of six when my mother flew to another place and sat at the right hand of an angel who shared my life plan with her. She was never the same after that—unable to worry, yet frightened that one day I would lose my mind or join some cult or not love Christ a lot. Her fear was always that I would not be able to handle the power that comes to those who are loved by man *and* by God. She often saw power as evil, but never revealed to me what she feared. It was her belief, by the way, not based on what the angel said when she was warned not to stand up to any man again—to let her home be one of love for the one who would one day be her only reward. She wasn't happy to have to submit to the temper of others to avoid any splits, but she did whatever it took."

Tears dribbled down Mandy's cheeks, but she seemed strangely pleased. The men rued that many women might have received such messages about their children and were not respected, either. Everyone moved ever closer to the center of the room as the fire grew higher, rather than wider, thus making it safe to do so.

"What do you suppose happened to the mother of my youth? The woman who arose from her bed was given a life she could handle, yet it was never grand. Her life after that was one of study, but she never again lost her sense of humor or her positive viewpoint. No one could rock her solid foundation of belief in helping others and the ability of God to heal *anything*.

"My mother was ignored by her fathers and mother who went before her, but a grandmother or two often visited her before she crossed over to be with a brother on that side of the world. Her mind was always strong and brilliant. She had several children beside this ward, but they seemed unable to accept that the world was not as impressed by them as she was, so in the end they left her to run after those who would hurt them as she never did. Her life was one of little encouragement and many delays, but it made her confident about what she was going to do—one day or very soon. The religion surrounding her birth was meant to help—not hurt, but she never got into it as deeply as others who were committed to it. Instead, she wondered why God was never mentioned when people tried to prove their belief in Jesus Christ and his resurrection—and that anyone who believed any different from them would perish in hell—without any possibility of rescue from the one who created them—God of All. This was never her way! At age 12, the church elders were upset that she questioned the theology they accepted as being not only correct but the only way to live. Was she a genius or just a woman ahead of her time?"

No one moved. Everyone sat as if meditating or wondering what Mandy would say next. All the men and most of the women had opened to time and understood the language she spoke, so no attempt was made to translate for the few women who refused to learn English. They were forced to listen within, but found the message intended for them, too, as Mandy continued her story or whatever it was to each one.

"I wasn't wanted, but my mother always said that was due to the Great Depression and its affect on her and her family—not that she didn't want another child. She was unable to carry several babies to term before my arrival, so when I stuck, she dedicated the fetus of me to God to use in whatever way he saw fit. She dedicated her life to saving mine and gave up many things—including nourishment needed for strong teeth. Her life was blessed for all she did in good faith then. The money situation cleared up the day I was born…My father declared that I was child of greatness, because I came out of my mother's womb laughing. You see, I was born at home in the middle of a storm, so he was able to be present then. He said over and over to me and to her that I was his lucky star and had to be watched to see how far I would go. He continues to watch over me… He is Maya by faith, but not of the tribe we celebrate now."

♓   ♓

Working on her mind in time turned out to be easy, but the tribe was not into it as much as Jorge and the few who always wondered about the lack of background provided on Mandy and her childhood. She was unlike anyone they had ever worked with, but her life prepared her to be a scribe and an artist, as well as someone who could weave and remember stories about other times.

Mandy could do many things without any problems, but usually she computed for The Ascended Maya. What did she work on within her mind over time? The Maya do not and will not talk much about it, but give out much work you can use, ignore, or grow through, too. What Mandy did was not unique for a child of 8, but extremely difficult for an adult. The fact that she arrived and survived in a world outside Mayaland proved to all present that she had to be pure Maya—back again!

Mandy was not always greeted by Mexicans as a friend, which puzzled her until she realized how distant and different they were from the heads of the tribe she slipped into so easily now. Other tribes teach and heal, but nothing like The Ascended Maya. Many in recent times are jealous of Mayan past history and try to change bits and pieces of it, but they cannot sell that to The Maya in charge of keeping the tribe's wisdom in such a way that it cannot be destroyed again by flame.

The ancients had more to give than scribbled stories designed to glorify an emperor or his lady, but such work paid well and attracted many scribes of that time. Today that basic wave of energy is being used to understand the calendar—again and gain ascendancy over this plane. That work takes precedent and transcends whatever the Mexican government says or does to offend The Maya over and over again. The root cause of the differences between them appears to be taxes and what the Mexican people believe they are owed from the past, while Maya of today do not believe they benefit enough from said taxes. The conflict is never about a lack of faith or the belief systems of their race.

When peons fled from haciendas all over old Mexico, many wandered into territories ruled by The Maya since ancient times. They were not wanted because they did not understand what it meant to be Maya. The Maya insisted they would not be able to stand up to the torture, pain and sorrow, and lack of physical comforts that Maya must submit to or die out as a tribe. Those dejected by this rejection hated the Maya and passed it to their descendants who are now in government and hate the Maya as if recently offended by them, instead of the reverse.

Jews all over the world are offended easily when they fail to recognize they are at the apex of another life and that it is time to recognize that the Messiah lives inside the mind. The world must take this experience and realize it is a gift. It will take two worlds that currently exist as if they are very different to merge into one clan that existed from the beginning of time. Can it be done? The Maya are not Hebrew, but they are as alike as any two tribes can be. What would The Maya of other times do today to heal the breach between the twin heroes? They would say, look to the Popul Vol and understand what it means—not necessarily what it says. Why? It was written by a scribe who was a Hebrew then, and the text is as benign as anything found in the Torah now. The work of one time is not always the same as it was in the past, thus it is proper to vary your work in ways that change when your mind moves and makes new waves.

Today, as in the past, the book you read is not about what you said or what someone else thought or anything you have seen. It is a ledger of what you must do to leave this world. Our only request is that you meditate and pray while learning how to find your way home.

Jeanne Beck, Scribe to The Ascended Maya

☼ Chapter Forty-Four

"When you are ready to leave and no one else wants to go,
Do you stay or do you venture out alone?"

The question was posed to each woman seated in the auditorium, plus women and men scattered throughout the country who were participating in the seminar via a link patched into the computer sitting at the side of the podium where Jeanne presided. She was laughing and happy, very content to be with all present but most pleased that there were people 'out there' who also want to do what she does and do it at home alone.

Jeanne's work proved to some that they could tap into their inner minds or Higher Selves, as well as the universal well from which ideas spring forth constantly, or activate a mental editor who knows what to change or not include or what to write and study when seeking new work. She was continually evolving as a mentor to other writers who could not work as spiritual scribes because they let too many others write through their minds and use their hands now. Always able to express herself, Jeanne was always helpful, but some men were not as well-developed spiritually or had too much ego to accept what she taught, so it was women who had trained with her to become spiritual scribes who led the class today, and they did it with finesse. These women were recognized as stars long before they were given much credit by publishers of such art.

"What can a woman do at home to prove she can work on her own?"

Two men moaned and complained loudly that they were being excluded again. They were not happy! Jeanne smiled—then laughed! They were not used to being overlooked by the dominant group, and did not like it. Still smiling, she lectured on the use of gender specific pronouns and how it still confused too many women and most men when 'he' or 'man' was used to address an entire room, group, or clan. When she finished, all the women clapped and the men laughed—except one who wanted to leave then and would do so before the next session began.

"When you know what you want, do you act immediately or do you think it through before making a move?"

Such questions preceded private readings for attendees within the room. For a brief interval some who were connected via computer also received private help. These readings, sittings, or reviews were not done as a Spiritual Scribe might do them. Instead, Jeanne spoke directly from her mind, or so it appeared at the time, and included genuine news about the future of that person, too. She was not aware of slipping into the mood and methods used by oracles of all times who reported what would go well or not, but everyone else noticed it. Many afterwards told their friends how much they would accomplish and when, citing what Jeanne had said. It surprised no one at the seminar, but later some lost friends as a result of sowing seeds of jealousy among those who refused to believe that they could ever achieve anything worthy of their envy.

"What happens when *you* lose friends who never again speak of your kindness or wisdom to others—or to your face?"

Hands flew up all around the room. Instead of asking for their thoughts, Jeanne indicated they were to pick up pens or pencils and write whatever came to their minds right then and be ready to compare it to what she would say next. It was a most unusual way to demonstrate how much you pick up from others simply by watching them in a public place while contemplating what they will say or do next. She was not afraid of what they would say, but surprised that the exercise was included in this seminar.

"What do you see in the center of your brow when you look in a mirror?"

Everyone, wherever, wrote while Jeanne stood firm—not thinking about the answer. All finished writing quickly, compared to the time it had taken to respond to the first question. What these students did not realize was that Jeanne would not supply any more answers, watching instead to see if anyone else picked up on what others thought. It was such a great day that many finished without realizing how close they came to being oracles on a par with those who used to work in the Everglades and throughout the Florida peninsula in the days of the Mayan prophets and such.

Since the room was lit with candles, their soft light helped some fight the desire to stay in their right minds all day, refusing to experiment with what was left for them to use again. At first most thought about the same thing—men. Yes, even the men thought about themselves first. The men did not venture to ask questions about women until the room was electrified with the news that women must seek out their own kind and make friends of them on this side. If they did not do this, they were doomed to never being truly admired or given help in overcoming worries, thus forcing them to covet men. The men resented being categorized as unable or unwilling to help women achieve any degree of competency in whatever they wanted to be, but honest men did admit that they hated to have to stroke anyone's ego and listen to others moan about what they went through.

Friends, one after the other, left the conference together to share a meal far better than one eaten alone at home or in a car parked outside a fast-food cafe. Jeanne wondered why so many in The States and other places chose to eat alone rather than widening their connections and friendships—at least while working with them. She made a note to explore that issue more, perhaps address it in an upcoming essay for her syndicated column. While thinking along those lines, she realized the Maya were unaware until now that the Americans had been afraid to speak to them at first, but willingly sought them out now to learn from them.

Dining *al fresco* is common in Mexico, so it was seen as the norm by some to eat outside now, but too exotic for others. Those who hated bugs and dogs and cats and such living beings were not pleased to find them roaming freely about cafes and restaurants, but the Maya did not notice them unduly, treating them as they treated others—with tolerance and respect. The way Mexicans tolerate such feral guests amazed most New Yorkers, as well as their relaxed attitude about unwinding over their meals. They were used to restaurant food being fast and tasteless, served with the appearance of sterility and cleanliness. The freedom to unwind during a meal was not appreciated until later. It became the most enduring lesson learned by those bound in mental knots now. They were given an opportunity to dine with others who willingly shared their thoughts or to sit in their hotel rooms and eat alone. Much was learned from that!

As Jeanne packed away the laptop and other accouterments of her trade, she thought, 'What a waste of time to sit all day and talk about yourself and what you do to students who want to do exactly the same thing—no questions asked!' She was unwilling to share any more of herself now, but had to say more if she was to continue in the teacher's role assigned by The Maya of old. Her laughter was not heard at the dinner table the first few nights, but after that she moved up her talks and did what came to her naturally well into the night.

Typing and talking while her fingers scribed lessons and such was a spiritual gift, as far as Jeanne understood it, but some students said she had previously programmed the class work to appear that way. It was a shock when Jeanne realized that even some of her personal clients who had studied with her in the past believed she moved her mouth in sync with her typing—faking that she was a scribe of The Ascended Maya. Her mind balked then at helping such people reach higher, because they offended her, until she remembered that teachers must rise to *their* highest level and not advertise their superior knowledge if they are to lead and help students progress as fast as possible today.

While typing out words channeled for her own highest good, as well as the higher good of the group, Jeanne realized that most present thought channeling was magic and not of God. She sighed and thought about how she could get them to accept that the Holy Spirit readily provides such gifts if you pass all the tests. To her it had been easy to advance to the level she worked at now. She willingly gave up whatever was unlikely to inspire others' confidence or might become a lie over time. A few readily accepted that she had a very special gift and was doing something truly extraordinary, but the majority chose to believe that anyone could learn to type rapidly while reading simultaneously what appeared on the giant screen. "Like Vanna White on steroids!" Originally said by one man and repeated by others without questioning how she could type and field their questions and comments as they popped into their heads.

It was not until later, when they attempted to reproduce the same work, that some discovered how little they understood Jeanne's work and what she had given so freely to them during her seminars. Even fewer realized that they did not meditate to a deep enough level or believe Spirit was great enough to circumnavigate their inner life to produce what their minds could handle and benefit from over time. Most were afraid to let go because they did not have any belief system in place or trust that God was in all they know and do and would be, so they lost the essence of her class.

Jeanne fretted and fumed about how people could watch her work and doubt that she was downloading information from The Ascended Maya that she could never create in her right mind, but then she thought about the process that produced this mindset and saw how many problems needed to be addressed immediately if these seminars were to help people ascend at the end. She thought about how many people do not listen because they are trying to block what they believe is evil, even if it is not. 'How many turn away from TV or movies when they realize how much animosity is being reproduced for reasons of greed rather than to entertain them? What happens when you accept synthetically-produced portrayals of evil meant to remove your self-control and unleash lust or fabricate reasons why you should hate others?' Realizing that this indoctrination occurs daily on a seemingly random-selection-basis all over the world, Jeanne wondered about those who initiate such thoughts and create evil plots for the public to watch. 'Is it seen as evil by them? How can that be wise? Why is it allowed?'

Quietly and quickly, Jeanne worked on what she had learned so far from her students and seminars. She sensed that most of the men meditated to deeper levels than the women, which surprised her. Why? She wanted to believe women did more spiritual work on a regular basis than men, but the idea that men meditated more often and deeper than women was something she had to accept, based on what she saw clearly demonstrated in class-after-class. Few of the women meditated long enough to reach a state where you can safely handle the huge electrical charges needed to channel universal sources through and into your present state of mind where you alone create, but most of the men could do it. She was also surprised at the outcome of a simple survey that women authors primarily wanted to make money while men wanted to write something worthy of a literary prize or be remembered long after they were gone.

Putting her mind into time would take out a few of the why's that appeared whenever she did something new, so Jeanne worked on what to do once the retreat was through. She foresaw at least three students able to do more work as Spiritual Scribes and several others would easily move into a world where they had never worked before, but that just was not enough information. She wanted to know who would make it and who would not, in order to encourage the stars to take yet another seminar. Shaking her head, she smiled because she knew this would not happen. No one on Earth judges the righteous and the bright or the bold and the brave with the right mind. What you judge is what you do not like or believe will not be of use to you. You quickly signal your dislike, using subtle cues and some not so subtle that 'you don't impress me.' Jeanne smiled as she realized how much she was learning about her mind by analyzing the behavior of everyone else.

The ending of the retreat was easily achieved on Friday. Jeanne simply assigned readings, as well as a few problems for students to do at home and return to her via the internet, but she knew few would actually follow through and do these assignments the way they had been taught. Was it too much to expect anyone to return to their favorite haunts and continue writing what came to them through their inner-views? She decided to leave that up to God.

Assigning questions without any thought as to what effect they might have on those who attended the retreat merely to observe what their rivals might do next, Jeanne discovered, strangely enough, that the homework affected ringers more than those who came hoping to receive some psychic gift they could use later, rather than work at whatever as they did in the past.

♓ ♓

Working at the retreat did advance her own plans, but Jeanne was unaware of it until she returned home and spotted the scribes all lined up, with smiles in tact, wishing her a warm welcome back. She was delighted to see their hand signs, as well as how they had painted the hand of an ancient Mayan Scribe holding a fine brush on a box. They said with enthusiasm that it would be her new logo! She felt, rather than thought, that the symbol was exactly what she would use if her work was from the world in which the Ancient Ones existed and would live in next, but she did not believe that it was.

One scribe who was very capable in the technical aspects that all writers need to master said, "Let's paint it on the back of a book and see if it scans into the computer as well as it looks here." She lifted the box and traced the hand with the quill pen onto another sheet and scanned it. It printed in full-color as if the original had been in color. The group was shocked, and Jeanne realized it was truly her logo to use and take with her wherever she would go and whenever she worked as a scribe of the tribe, but never applied to what was penned with the help of her present mind and friends in time.

The next day Jeanne greeted her class of scribes with the words: "When you feel time slipping away or you feel upset or betrayed, stop and look within."

After a brief speech, if anything said in Spanish can be brief, Jeanne answered questions asked the previous night while they all dined at her home. A few had decided that Jeanne was no longer going to help them as much as she had in the past, yet they could not figure out why. They were the first scribes to realize that classes would never be the same because Jeanne had moved up two levels while teaching at the last retreat. She now worked the way of Mayan Scribes from another day.

After taking a warm and fragrant bath to relax her back, Jeanne walked into her sitting room expecting to enjoy an evening of privacy and classical music, instead she was surprised to find one of the scribes sitting there quietly waiting for her. This mother of three children said, "What gifts you have been given, Miss Jeanne!"

Unable to hide her chagrin from this woman of a nearby clan who had never accepted her work like most of the tribe, Jeanne said, "I'm surprised to see you here now. What's wrong? Are your children sick?"

"I have come to see you because you've changed, Miss Jeanne. You don't seem to be so happy as you were when you left. Why, if I may ask, did you do it? What is wrong since you returned to us? You still do the classes that we want and need to get secretarial jobs, but you seem to be—out of touch with us now."

Without hesitation, Jeanne stated emphatically, "You come here every day to learn a trade, and I understand your needs, but I've been with authors and writers who want to make a huge difference in what this race of individuals does next... You want to change the way you live in the future—to have more 'stuff' than you ever had before, but I worked with women and men who want to leap into time! Can you understand that I want the experience to continue—not just channeling how to help one person behave in the world so she can get a better job or work out of her home if she must?"

The woman glared at Jeanne and spit out, "You're afraid of us!" She hurled the insolent words at Jeanne without even bowing her head or lowering her eyes.

Unsmiling, Jeanne moved toward the door and said firmly, "Get out! I will not put up with insolence or thoughtless women who too easily adapt our work and become evil employers of others. You're way too bossy to ever achieve a peaceful state of mind, so get out! Move on! Take whatever you've absorbed so far and don't come back."

Her unwanted guest looked upset and refused to leave or speak. In fact, she moved further back into the chair Jeanne reserved for her own prayers. The chair was too big for the tiny Mayan woman to sit comfortably, but she recognized it as Jeanne's seat of power and wanted to see what it felt like to be so respected by others. Whatever she felt caused her to jump immediately out of the seat without a smile or look of triumph. In fact, she was overcome by dread! Jeanne continued to wave her out the door, which did nothing to allay her fear. The energy locked inside her heart was enough to cause an apparent heart attack, but she was too shocked to talk.

Realizing that the situation had gotten totally out of hand, Jeanne absorbed the extreme heat coming from the woman's body. She genuflected and reflected it to another standing beside her. As Jeanne often said, "Angels know what to do, so always keep them close-by when doing something definitely not of this world."

What Jeanne saw in a flash was that this woman was no shaman, yet eager to become one. She wanted to gain power in order to rule others and believed this would happen if granted spiritual gifts that enabled her to see into the future. Now she was blocked from ever doing that! Her faith in God was not where she left it when she came to study with Mandy, and later with Jeanne and the scribes. She lost her faith along the way by becoming smug about what she believed to be true. That pride grew and she became conceited when other students sought her out to do readings. Everything was lost because she could not cross the bridge named vanity and self-conceit. She failed the test and lost her gift, so she collapsed, and then she laughed.

Since her laughter sounded rather maniacal, Jeanne threw a pitcher of water in her face, wiping off the excess with a damp towel dipped in a thyme distillation. Thyme: the herb that provides work in time. When the woman woke with her head on Jeanne's lap, she was embarrassed to discover that she had merely collapsed—not been elevated in Spirit as she had believed would happen when she laughed and let go of her grasp on time. Jeanne explained that her laugh was false—not what would open the mind to flight. "Cackling doesn't increase the oxygen supply needed to enter the space behind the brow and elevate the blood pressure." She went on to explain everything to a woman unable to understand what was said until one of her own many questions about love, life, and whatever was answered.

Jeanne had no clue about what to do, so she asked whomever it was who came through to help a woman who wanted to do shamanic work: "If laughter helps us elevate our minds, what does hate do to us?" The answer came in a deep, resonating voice from somewhere within her mind. It was so alive with energy that she felt the need to write down every word immediately—not stopping until the last word was printed out. Opening her ever-present laptop computer, she began typing rapidly:

I am not able to confirm it, since you want to see it written, but you are going to experiment with this in several different ways. You will ask others to do work you are done with and watch to see if they gain as much from it as you do from helping them.

You will ask your ego-self to follow the instructions given by someone in each and every class, then get back to us quickly with what happens next. You will meet with shamans who are not like you, as well as work in other avenues of faith. First, get out of the way what they want from you and then work with all of them on Earth. Yes, you will travel to the Himalayas. You will work with an Eastern European monk, and you will do something for India, too, but not Japan. You will never go there again.

Jeanne's mind wandered and her thoughts separated. She lost the thread of whatever was being given to her now, yet words appeared on the page and seemed to pulsate rather than enter her brain when she stopped to think. Without any ability to reason or sound out words, she applied her old work skills and continued typing as if copying what had already been written out in time by another scribe.

I am not going to do anything that will harm you, but you could short circuit your mind in time if you do not let your body unwind and relax more. Get rid of this woman who is not able to help. Send her into town to speak her mind, but first make sure she cannot libel you and the family. Before you put her out, take her into the bathroom and wash her hands, then give her time to think. She will become aware that what she learned here is going down the drain then.

This will be her lesson: "Never seek out a teacher when you believe you know everything, because you will resent the teacher and end up with less than what you brought to the class."

We are not going to spy, but please move this woman to the other room and come back without haste when she is put away. We do not wish to continue writing like this with so much negativity existing in your space. In fact, please wash your hands—and laugh, as soon as you get her out of the house.

Jeanne quickly moved to open the bathroom door, pointing toward the sink outside her bathing area, she told the woman to hurry and cleanse her hands because she had to go to bed now and wanted her to leave. The Mayan woman did not leave without whining that women always have to please men before they can do anything without them. Jeanne ignored what she assumed was a blast meant for the elders who were predominantly male. Since the woman was reluctant to wash her hands, Jeanne poured hair conditioner over her extended arms and hands, motioning for her to rinse it off and leave quickly. She told her firmly not to come back again.

The unhappy woman snarled at Jeanne, "Working with you is the best thing I ever did for that man, but do you think he respects me? No, and he laughs at you—at all the scribes! He says you all need men, and if you were married and lived as we do, you would understand why he has no use for women without men who have their own houses." These words were barely out of her mouth when her eyes darted about the room until she spotted a framed picture of two happy men standing side-by-side hugging a woman who was smiling directly into the camera. With a jolt, as if hit by a cattle prod, she realized Jeanne was loved by men and must have someone in her life now. This was so shocking that she withdrew her mind from this space in an attempt to look into Jeanne's future to see what these men would do for her soon. She was unable to see anything. That was all it took to convince her that she no longer could read spirits or do magic as she had done on the sly for a long time. She felt doomed!

"You can leave now—and don't look back in sorrow. You have enough typing and computer skills to work for a local politician. Maybe one day you'll run him the way you want to run me." Jeanne spoke without any doubt it would happen.

With Jeanne obviously able to witness scenes no longer available to her, the woman left the house without worry. In fact, she felt the release of a lot of false thoughts and doubts she had accumulated about Jeanne—including the rumor about Jeanne and Mandy being witches.

Once alone, Jeanne washed her hands and wiped down the chair and much of the bathroom with a damp cloth to take away any traces of the angry thoughts left behind by the woman who had visited her without invitation. She decided to never again give free readings to any of them! It was not the way to make people recognize the value of the gifts of The Holy Spirit. Her Guides insisted her time was far too valuable to give work away, but she had to learn it the hard way—always. From that time on she charged for her time and let others figure out their readings so they, too, would do some of their own spiritual work.

As she moved to secure the door, Jeanne noticed an envelope sticking out under the door. It was a gift of money left by a grateful tourist she could not remember. Amazed that one woman took so much, and another paid for it! "What does this mean?" Jeanne asked the room at large, and in a flash she realized that this is the way the universe operates when it is in balance.

That thought etched a smile so broad and deep across her face that she went to bed and did not get up for two days and several hours. She was missed by some, but unable to know it happened. When she finally rose to go outside to greet the sun, she discovered that her powers were so much greater than she had believed they could ever be! In dreamtime, angels surrounded her on a faraway cloud and announced that she had been tested to find out if she could be beaten by those who are testy, selfish, rude, and pushy, too. Laughing heartily at the memory, Jeanne returned and took the shower that ended her life as it existed before the seminar. Her reluctant return to the scribes' compound moved her into the world of dreams—a place unlike any other!

☼ CHAPTER FORTY-FIVE

"When you look into the future, you see into *You*…Your Higher Self, and what you can do. You sometimes align with others who will be waiting when you arrive at that time, too, but what happens if you adjust the present you—this small, egotistical being you see in the mirror? What happens if you adjust this personality that exists as is, because you saw something while in trance that you want to be immediately or don't want to happen at all?"

Wanda stopped talking long enough to look directly at each weaver's eyes. Encountering the unsmiling stare of one who always sat in the back, her voice wavered as she added, "When you find yourself in the future, as you see it, it's not easy to resist changing it a little bit--" She stopped again to look into the mind of the sullen weaver and was shocked to find the woman was not alone. She was not sitting and listening without any thought! Instead, she was surrounded by a huge group of teachers in spirit who seemed to be weaving her thoughts. Wanda had never seen anything like it in all her years of working like this, so she immediately asked the woman to address the class.

Without hesitation, the woman stood very erect, then slumped forward as her mouth twisted and opened in a grimace—nothing came out. Since this was the first time she had ever opened her work and knowledge to the group, everyone turned to look. She was not very tall or wide, but definitely not Maya from birth. Little was known about her except that she easily kept up with their artful weaving, and her fingers often bled due to overwork. She insisted upon doing too much work every week, as though seeking something no one else here could achieve. When she finally spoke, it was a monotone—adding only a bit of flourish at the end when what had sounded like a positive statement became a question. Most of her words poured out as if she were reciting or reading from a boring book.

Wanda rightly assumed that her function was to merely channel the thoughts of the large group of teachers surrounding her—not to speak for them. Everyone else was stunned when the dour woman said loudly: "I am the portal to another life. It is not a surprise that other weavers can see into these rooms and do what we do, because they make use of my eyes and my hands all the time… I am a useful vessel—a virgin since birth… But I am no longer willing to change my life to suit them and do what they want now. I am afraid of what lies ahead of today. I see nothing but clouds, and I worry that my mind will not be able to handle all that is said now. Will someone take this burden from me and let me go? I want to move across the Earth and do many things while I am able to do them…" She paused for a few moments, then added with conviction, "Are you aware of the indecent exposure now occurring everywhere? There are men who prey upon innocent women and children this way! Are you aware of the offenses they commit? Are you going to stop it?"

Her last words seemed incongruent with what was moving through the group, so Wanda stopped the woman's tirade by raising her hand to her brow as if unable to accept what was being said. As she waited for the young woman to stop channeling and take a deep breath, Wanda prayed about what had to be done to stop her talk.

Within a moment or two after asking God what to do, angels arrived in the room and took out the spiritual teachers to talk to them within a cloud that now permeated the crowded room. The smoke that created the cloud was such that some smelled incense while others thought something was burning outside. In the end, nothing burned and nothing was learned about the group of teachers who channeled through this woman and wanted to use her then.

Straightening her mind to begin lecturing again, Wanda felt a tug at her spine, but otherwise she was not harmed in any way by the intrusion produced by the woman who sat in the back of the room. Since the spiritual work done by this woman was not the same as what the other weavers were there to learn, she could not turn her work over to anyone else to pursue another career or a different life. Wanda smiled and said a prayer of grace that gently covered the face of the disappointed woman as she sank to the floor and lay very still.

If others in the room felt anything unusual within their minds, they did not speak of it. If anyone of faith was upset by what happened, they did not say it then or later. The woman eventually left the group, but the effort it took to remove her was greater than anyone expected it to be. The question that haunted Wanda was: 'Why did it happen?' Everyone else accepted it as fairly routine—something they did not have to worry about, but they were wrong.

♓   ♓

In the days to come, The Ascended Maya unburdened the tribe of several who lied too often and swept away a leader who could not stay away from children at play. Other than that, it was as if nothing ever happened that related back to today, but there was one major change. The change arrived in the evening as the light was leaving. When the sun went down the afterglow was not as bright as it might have been. The sun was not as clear as usual in summer rainy seasons, but it cleansed the homes and the rivers, as well as the areas where the clans got their spiritual work assigned to them.

Mandy had been contacted immediately when Wanda saw the discordant weaver overcome by what could only be described as an infestation of beings who wanted to take over her work in order to pursue their own agenda here on Earth. They had since discovered that the woman had been a medium of renown, but none had seen her work until then.

In response to Wanda's letter asking what to do with this class, since the spirit that initially presided over it disappeared, Mandy wrote back: *In time of trouble, review what you did in the past.*

When Wanda read that, as well as, *Working on the spine can help align the mind in time,*" she felt her spine realign.

She felt increased waves of energy flowing within her back and her smile returned! She was ready to tackle whatever work remained undone—until she read the following lines and everything settled back into the past: *You must leave—go to another compound immediately! Do not act as if you are racing about. Move quietly out now. Do not look back until you are given a sign that everything is ready in time.*

Scanning the rest of the letter, Wanda accepted that she must pack quickly and take only her daughter with her, and that both must act like they would return in a few days, so no one would ask them how to use the computer and such now. Later she would contact the weavers from a safe distance—at an undisclosed location, and give them orders to remove all the trash in the compactor and in the pails at the back of the compound and have them hauled away and burned immediately.

The thought that someone from outer space was able to infiltrate their world and work through them had never entered the minds of the weavers and scribes who worked together in this region to develop a better line of communication to the other side. Their work was unusual, to say the least, but it was never perceived by any student as being dangerous to pursue.

What really happened when Wanda spoke to the weavers about the temptation to change today based on a visit to the future? She knows now, but is still unwilling to put it into a few words. Instead, she wove a circle into the woolen fabric she had been weaving when the letter arrived, and did not remove it from the loom. The circle protected her loom and the room from intruders better than anything else she could do right now, but would it stop or block evil thoughts from weaving in and out of the room? She thought not, but continued to do what she could to protect herself and the compound from those who would try to harm them in time.

Wanda wanted to believe that the school would be safe from harm once she was gone, but she had no confidence in that because things did not make sense in the legitimate way logic is used today. Could it be that her mind had spun out and left her in a time long gone by, then picked her up and dropped her back in the same spot? That was when Wanda realized her life *was* a surprise! The idea of being asked to help women and children had not come from her mind! In fact, this thought caused enough chaos that she had moved to block it—only to find it was now lodged in her mind. It was rattling around as if trapped and seeking an exit until it became embedded and unwilling to leave.

⼽ ⼽

As days and weeks passed and neither Wanda nor Thérèse returned to check on what the women, children, and men were doing in the community of weavers, the only thing produced in large quantities was noise. A time shift, as well as the evacuation of Wanda and Thérèse, caused a void in leadership. One leader wanted one pattern taught, while another thought it was time for everyone to 'do their own thing' and not ask for any more help. Their combined absence exposed the plans of many who always intended to pursue life outside the tribe. They now prepared to move out. Meanwhile, the men who support the weavers until they can support themselves were unaware of any changes. It was not a great time to be the scribe who takes down all that is said or needs to be changed when Mandy arrives on the scene.

The guild's work was outstanding, and its leaders were able to succeed, but several weavers became extremely rude—very pushy, and did not wish to wait until others decided what should be the best course of action to follow now. They wove whatever they pleased without first gaining acceptance of their designs—pushing others to accept what they believed helped the tribe most. Without Wanda and her daughter in charge, consensus was ignored as a tool to help the entire group adopt a new life-style. Instead, they bickered and bit each other until everyone's work faltered and no one was sure what was best to do next.

As their time working together drifted, the rains declined and the mists of summer lifted until autumn was visible in the near distance—a time when they should all prepare for Christmas business as if Wanda was still here. The guild decided to split into two working units. It was not a great way to work together, but at least they worked and got beyond talking constantly behind one another's backs.

With the decline of time and the unified design of work yet to be discovered—still sitting in the middle of the group-mind, the weavers decided it was not a good idea to align with any other tribe. They also decided to keep new designs to themselves and work on them secretly without telling anyone else what they were doing. This 'secret mission' made some feel better about work in general, but it failed to sell them as a guild or sell their clan's combined work to those who paid for the supplies. Failure to please the tastes of the buying public leads to the demise of any product line over time, but these Maya were convinced they could do whatever they wanted because it fit the way they viewed today. Were they right?

That month ended and the time when the tribe permits adding new ideas elapsed, too, then Mandy arrived. She was not tired and she was not remiss in what she thought was business, but she did not appear to be her usual self. As she talked, her eyebrows crinkled so much she appeared to have only one eyebrow. She peered out from under it into each person's eyes as if studying their hearts and souls at the same time. When they discovered she was in no hurry to leave and intended to stay until they did whatever they did together all day without any stoppages, they worried—a lot.

This guild was not unique in being unable to link to select leaders for very long. However, they had always respected their responsibilities when teachers left their classes to them and were ahead of other clans when it came to understanding the crass nature of tourists and other buyers who wanted whatever they wanted 'right now,' with no care about costs to the tribe or the nation to supply their demands. These weavers were unable to take away the emotional pain of others, but they felt pleasure in taking away the mammon of the children of lesser gods who tried to despoil their lives. Tourists came and went, most taking away as much as they left, but some stayed behind.

As more and more of the world's people came to visit the compound and stayed on in the local environs, the villages grew and became quite good at ending many of the games being played on other stages. If a temporary resident wanted a house with a maid, they paid handsomely for it. If, however, they were willing to work and make a commitment to the church or the village, they were given a room in someone's home and their housework was done by the children, and parents when needed. This had never been the way of the Mayan world, but it helped many learn to pray properly and meditate instead of vegetating in a state of mind where alcohol removed time.

When Mandy appeared this time, without warning, via the early morning bus, those present were shocked to see her dismount without any luggage. They had forgotten that she kept everything she needed in her room at each compound. Most preferred to believe instead that she loved fast cars and never traveled as others did. Such a mistake caused some to lose a lot.

As usual, Mandy requested all the financial records and business plans be produced quickly, but she also wanted to examine the hands of everyone who worked for The Lord. Some were unsure what she wanted to prove, and the guild split down the middle talking about it. Their discussion was meant to be a diversion, but it worked against them. Mandy decided to check their money situation first!

Mandy noticed that one weaver had withdrawn more than she had ever earned and could not pay back what she stole over one pay period—let alone ten, so she was expelled immediately and no one yelled. Because no one rose to her defense, the woman's shame was much greater, and it taught everyone a lesson—Mandy only had to glance at the books to spot if anything was wrong. No other women were willing to lose such a great life in order to supply a lazy man with booze and drugs.

Within a fortnight Mandy was surprised to discover that nothing remained of the original clan. She had been unaware that over the years many joined this group, and then left when they learned enough—or so they thought. She watched more closely what was talked about now, as well as those in charge this past season when no teacher in spirit or flesh had come forward to help them. She was displeased with what she heard and saw, but did not immediately make any changes or even comment.

Without a doubt, Mandy made the men nervous and the women worry. She was not alone when working out a plan to change the compound, but most of the weavers believed she always worked alone. Her first change was to move a few key weavers to other compounds, hoping to erase any ideas they added to the original plot to enable 'others' to land in the middle of this guild and take root.

The way *others* work when entering such a group is to infiltrate—then deny it! The denial response was now so automatic that Mandy only had to speak or ask a question and someone denied it immediately, had an alibi, or tried to blame someone on her staff. It was unpleasant to hear such nonsense, but she was used to it after years of working in corporate America. Her main objective now was to set up a computer file containing the names and addresses of sages and where they could meet or be seen or helped, so she could leave soon and dream.

Technically, Mandy was not into weavers' work, so she recalled Wanda and Thérèse. She was sure it would be safe, once she erased everyone lacking faith in them. This was done before they began creating from scratch a new class of weavers who could reach into time, as well as teach others who could not work out designs.

A guild logo contains the names of all the weavers in that clan. However, this clan changed dramatically after Wanda and her friends moved into cyberspace to improve the way designs were given away, so Wanda created a new design for those who were not members of the tribe and were not interested in working on time. She dropped elements of ritual or color, but the group she left behind never knew it. They passed their designs to Maya who quickly spotted the difference! This conflict in design grew until Wanda was once again mistrusted by many Mayan elders. They preached that she had changed their clan's luck or misused their designs for personal gain.

As the weavers entered the loom room and sat on the floor, they did not immediately look up at Wanda and her daughter. When they did, they were shocked to see much love in their eyes! It radiated from them like rainbows over time. The weavers knew they did not deserve such respect and were conscious of it, but Wanda was not. Her eyes were open only to the light beaming down on the heads of students she remembered and wanted to teach. However, Thérèse, bowed her head, sighed, then cried. Her mind was tormented with worries about those who thought their guild was condemned and they would have to go home, unable to work again as they had.

The guild's work was good, but not perfect. As the original patterns were duplicated, each copy lost a line or two, until the work was less and less defined. Blurry copies were hidden in the safe rather than the originals, and renegades could not explain why they were upset and unable to work as they had in the past. Without any thought about what evil they had wrought, Wanda smiled and looked at them now.

The day was over before Mandy stepped into the loom room to talk to the guild about what they had to do immediately. Wanda was no longer smiling. She was thoughtful, wondering how so many students could have wandered so far from base without any idea of where they were going. She was unsure if they believed her so much that they did whatever she said, or if they were lazy and acted as if they misunderstood in order to avoid working harder to weave more perfectly.

Words flowed from Mandy as if she were a scribe writing and reading wisdom simultaneously. However, she was not talking when the Angel of The Maya pushed open the door and limped in as if walking with a cane. The women screamed and the men moved out of the way. Mandy was safe where she stood, even though she had been unaware that the great angel was nearby.

Apparently it is the way of God to take on faith whatever *any* group prays for all day. Angels had been enlisted to help The Maya, but they were not the same as *The* Angel of The Maya. The Angel of The Maya is such a huge being that no one ever forgets or questions what is said. The weavers wreathed in pain, as if waiting to be judged harshly.

Later, a child remarked, "The angels didn't do anything until more came in the room—right after the big angel arrived. The walls couldn't hold all the electricity. My Grandmother said it was a time when everyone in the same linage could see into one another. Grandmother said the angels were given assignments and the means to complete them immediately, but they weren't given time to do them then. I don't know what it means, but she told me to remember what she said until I am very old."

Wanda was upset by the vision of angels standing in the middle of the room because she had nothing to demonstrate how well everyone had used time in the past. She cried and her eyes overflowed with fear about what was needed and could not be done immediately. Everyone else present thought she was overcome with Spirit rather than fear. If they had realized their faith was not what accomplishes a lot, rather the work of their hands, they might also have been stunned and cried. Instead, they reveled in the idea that angels arrived to save someone in their tribe!

One weaver said later, "It wasn't the same as seeing a miracle or whatever, but it came close." Angels work for those who are close to The Source and able to know what course is best for a certain person, but they do not usually enter groups or move individuals to act. Spiritual Guides do that work—not angels! Individuals in any sphere can contact God through their own inner spirit and use their spirit to guide them to the next event or next destination or to get something mundane done right away. However, some abuse this power, without considering how much time it takes The Source to produce a list of stars to help you wherever you are. Mandy knew how very necessary lists were when teaching children, but had forgotten it was necessary to create lists when you want work to continue as is into the future and are not present to see everything is run in accordance with your wishes.

Angels came through to the women and gave them work. However, they were not the angels who deliver messages. They were God's warriors, personified in the tribe as eagles able to fly at any time. Such members of the tribe always deliver God's warnings, but were not recognized by the weavers as such when they first appeared. Several elders later reported they saw a woman, looking like a queen, arrive that fateful day, but did not see where the *queen* went and which meeting she attended.

When several weavers bowed and prayed to the angels, they were reprimanded and told not to pray to anyone but God of All. They heeded the command ever after, but others still pray the wrong way even though it is not correct to do so. After that day, all the weavers helped women and children in the neighboring village by giving cloaks and blankets made of wonderful linen and wool. These gifts reportedly had no lasting effect on anything they did because the angels had angrily demanded it as a means to cleanse their work. The Angels' message to the tribe was loud and clear: GET BACK TO BASICS AND FORGET THE TRASH!

While Mandy visited Wanda and Thérèse, they washed everything they found around the compound, and the clan colors were changed to indicate that no foreign strangers or *others* from other times or other spaces were welcome in their town. By the end of the week Mandy and Wanda were heartened by the weavers' work and how they did chores, but not Thérèse. She could not detect any change in the way the weavers prayed. She believed they continued to chant without doing much spiritually, assuming it to be *the right way* to pray when you wanted to move to your everlasting or eternal life. Thérèse wondered, 'What to do now?'

Working on what you want to accomplish without requesting help is most unusual—probably not the best way to move into another day, either, but some of the tribe were practicing voodoo kinds of thinking, hoping to create fear in the minds of those who did not pray *the right way*. For this reason, Mandy announced she would cast a demon into a stream to see if it would sink. Her announcement was greeted with many stares and outright laughter from some tourists staying at the compound, while the Maya sought one who was unable to sleep at night. They asked that the demon be removed from this weaver immediately so she could resume her work and the guild would not be weakened by it again.

Mandy looked at the sleepless weaver and smiled. She knew immediately that this woman would lead her to The Dreamers! She decided to act out the part of an ancient prophet and cast aside the woman's mind to help her move into work she could do at home for a month or two before moving back into the guild. Sitting on the bank, Mandy asked the woman to wade out into the middle of the nearby stream and look toward the sun—but not directly at it, as she was tempted to do.

When the sun blinked—as many described it later, the woman disappeared into the water and remained completely hidden for an hour. Because the water was only a foot deep, this mystery was never explainable to anyone without faith. However, many others knew instantly that she was able to do work assigned to her, change her daily habits, and live happily ever after—as Mandy moved to the next level of work she came to Earth to pursue. Mandy became a Dream Weaver within weeks of this scene! The woman who could not sleep, now sleeps every night as if a child who plays very hard.

☼ CHAPTER FORTY-SIX

Thérèse sat back and relaxed as she opened her mind to time and introduced the thought that she would like to do her own work instead of working for others and helping them move up in the world or to the next plane. She was not fat, but when compared to the trim body she had shared with millions of people in underwear ads over the years, she was pleasingly plump now. She no longer dined on parsley and thyme and very little food as she used to eat. Now she ate eagerly at the feasts prepared for her in villages and towns where she was invited to speak about her life changes, as well as why she was now Maya rather than whatever she had been in her other life.

Most Maya did not question the ability of a French saint to enter the mind and body of such a worldly woman and work through her, but many others who knew her as a super model could not accept it—at least at first glance. According to old *friends*, she had never been interested in anyone who could *not* advance her career or whatever she wanted to do, thus it was too much to expect such a woman could become totally altruistic now. This lack of acceptance was not a test of her will's power, rather a review of the years that caused her to spill a few tears now—about then.

Thérèse looked at a few pictures taken during her youth and recognized for perhaps the first time that back then she had always been afraid and responded by acting older than her age to fend off men who wanted to take advantage of her immaturity. If she had only known then how futile it is to get upset and worry about what will happen when life just is, she could have made millions guiding young people's lives. She didn't do that, never wanted to do anything that reeked of manipulating what people think. Was she wrong?

In the movement of the tribes and towns surrounding the compounds, the Maya remained strong, yet many young people and some adults now longed for the material world they saw too easily to completely ignore it like their elders. The old ways decreed that you do not pay for what you can do yourself, but it was getting easier to pay money for tribal needs instead of donating work. The young people did not look upon tourists as angels or think The Lord was giving them honest work to serve them, as children in distant villages once believed. They did not realize God did not give *others* bounty and such because they lived great lives, but let them take whatever they wanted and ignore all others—and only God knows why.

When the Mayan tribes united and supported a scribe or ten of them without manipulating their work, they had it made, but it took many developmental stages to be able to do this. What would one Mayan tribe do with ten scribes who wanted to paint pictures as created and used way back when? The Maya prized these artists above all others, and the elders asked them to create calendar art that proved to the people of today that the ancient steles told more than dates and names of places, kings, and such. They had not wanted descendants to forget the work a tribe must accomplish to accrue the energy needed when a group ascended and ended this confinement in time.

The most outspoken clan or tribe was not catty enough for those who watched over them. Their scribes worked hard to avoid politics and had the decency to see into the past without saying much about it, but the cast of characters hidden away in the mountains and throughout the peninsula were inclined to be too chatty for their own good, thus it was arranged that they would never get together to talk a lot. This division was created so fewer clans would dissolve or be erased later.

When the artists started painting and sculpting in the native ways of yesterday, strangers visited and asked them to make art that appeared to be created in the past so they could sell it to gullible collectors everywhere. The few artists who did such things were obviously not committed to The Ascended Maya and were told to leave the tribe or lose their pride and commit to doing menial tasks making what would not last, instead of being admired for their own art.

As the days, weeks, and months of Mayan studies continued, they worked to build communities of students who previously had not worked with anyone other than close family members when studying Earth. Those groups departed first! The very first group to ascend was one so ancient that it was able to sway trees with a single thought, and since they were all so advanced in age, no one noticed them leave.

Working in the fields or standing around outside at noon, seemingly unaware that the sun was burning their skin, was not a lesson The Maya wanted to review again, but it came to life anyway. Aloe was not used to build new skin or a new belief system in the past. It was not the same as yuccas harvested to enrich other faiths while enslaving them, more like a blend produced and used then. Hemp then was good for nothing but dreaming and never used by men with families to feed. It produced no good fruit, and nowadays police hunt you down if it is found anywhere near a compound. To avoid The Law and being bothered even more than usual, the Maya banned it from ceremonies and their surroundings.

Someone preached that if you could stop the fall of someone who wanted to eat and drink and drug until they could no longer live sanely with others, you would automatically ascend in the end. Whether or not this was spoken by an elder or by someone passing through, no one knew, but this is what they all decided to do: Walk through their fields and carefully weed out plants that might cause another to die or linger forever in a mind unable to find time. These herbs would then be combined in a certain way to produce antidotes, but only one knew what they would do.

That one person was not Mandy, but she knew who would teach the next two classes about ascension. She found the elder who knew these herbs and how to blend them, and she helped him reach others so their mission could change from developing artists, weavers, and writers to producing a better world to live in now. Everyone agreed they needed to start with the drug addicts and adulterers first, but it would not work if everyone involved did not recognize how difficult the work would be initially—before it could command a demand.

Once people were healed of addictions and could think straight long enough to tell the world about their success, the Maya knew they would be overwhelmed with visitors and The Press—something the elders dreaded, but were willing to live through to enable many to ascend with them at the end.

At first no one found the work easy, so Mandy helped the elder preach instead of teach. The work of reformulating the herbs, as well as the law, had to be ratified now and argued about later. They usually worked in these areas by testing and testing, then thinking through issues of cost, but this was not what they would do now. Instead, The Maya located on islands and in countries overseas gathered in one central location for an hour to three and were given plenty to eat, then they were fed some of the seeds and some of the blends to determine if they had good dreams or not. If not, they placed that weed or plant or seed in a bin to be removed and checked again by others.

Whenever these select groups of teachers and workers of The Lord met, they often prayed that nothing they ate would upset their minds and bodies. Since they had great digestive tracts and were praying not to be bothered, it could be that they were able to use things that might adversely affect those not so strong, but it worked! The tests passed the inspection of those who cared enough to visit, so the governments did not care what they did after that.

With millions around the world existing without income, and no social reform undertaken to give the poor more than what they had or knew before addiction, governments turned away from Mandy and her players to attend to their own business. They did not wish to commit more soldiers to a war that continued even now with the Maya, but at times they raided a village just for the sense of power it gave some of their men. This evil did not fit into the schedule of Mandy and her clans, so they complained—often and loudly, which seemed enough to get local soldiers and others who thought they were powerful to leave the compounds alone and not molest anyone outside their houses.

What the Maya never expected was foreigners planning vacations to visit and sit with them, hoping to find ways to help family members who were virtually useless due to addiction. Haunted parents came in droves from all over America to study with The Maya for hours—praying and passing out from fatigue and pleasure at times, without getting the power to ascend or heal a child. Changes were then made by The Maya! The tribes began to think beyond where *they* had been and started admitting strangers into their towns and villages in order to better help them. Although the weavers feared strangers would pillage their villages again, they decided to permit longer visits. The angels said it was time to open the minds of the heathen—let in the light, and let them find better lives than they had when they were grounded the last time around.

The first compound remodeled to help addicts advance to the stage where they were no longer afraid was completed in August and dedicated the following May. It was not obvious to anyone in charge then that it would become a way of life for The Ascended Maya to use now. Many came to Mayaland abused and afraid to do anything new, but left the compounds thriving—able to drive, sing, dance, and use nothing that lingered longer than it took to learn new ways of living today.

The in-crowd became aware that someone was doing something new in Mayaland, but the local establishment was not aware of it. This was great for waves of New Agers who wanted to share and give to whomever, but hard on the Maya who were unused to people who did not work, preferring to sit and talk.

When philosophers think, they usually do not help others much. Much work was sitting undone until it was added to what the Maya already had to do to care for their own tribe. It was not that the Maya hated doing this extra work, they were afraid their children would become as lazy as these latent adults were. This worry opened their eyes to the need to teach such people to work harder and develop the habit of taking care of their own personal outerwear and underwear—and not block toilets a lot.

Mundane thoughts were the first talked over and moved through by all addicts. After that they discussed what had to be done about drugs they brought with them and had to be removed before anyone else knew about them. Police do not reason that addicts are people who can be cured, preferring to suspect them of outrages in every village and town that they previously ignored. The idea of thieving, murderous addicts running loose caused some concern throughout Mayaland, until villagers learned compound gates were locked and guarded every night. The Maya felt even better when informed there was a head count several times a day and every night, and anyone not in bed or around the head was expected to be in bed within an hour of the last bell. Anyone who did not obey the rules was dropped from the program—and that was that. No future admission permitted, since there were literally a half-million people waiting to enroll a few months after opening day.

Witnessing people arrive at the compound drunk or drugged, dead on their feet, unable to eat or have fun, and then several months later seeing them working their minds and helping others was enough to interest governments. They were asked to stay in the background and give the group homes some slack, and they did that. With the help of the United States government, as well as the connections Julie maintained within her crowd of artists who worked with galleries all over The States, the police did not bother the compounds and towns around them, unless someone reported they had been robbed nearby. Police used that excuse to walk around the compounds and 'investigate what was going on,' even though they never took away a single stray that way. The police did, however, often bring back someone who had slacked and walked away, trying to hide during the day instead of working hard. The police enjoyed rounding up such truants, because it meant a fast payment in cash when they made their delivery to the office of an associate who worked for Mandy and Jorge.

Jorge was recognized more and more as a judicious world leader of Mayan tribes. He seemed to grow and enlarge, becoming harder, but he was not the man others believed him to be when he entered a plea. He was never upset, because he was always aware of what would be, yet he acted as if this or that detail was absolutely necessary to complete a case or a cause when, actually, he was playing with time.

When no one could locate Jorge or Mandy and other elders, it was assumed they were traveling incognito and unavailable for interviews, or possibly on a trip to study something new, because most never knew when they stepped out of time.

How can you step into a new life and out of time, as if it were a coat or a robe? You must be Maya to find out!

☼ Chapter Forty-Seven

Jeanne mumbled to her friend and fellow scribe, Mandy, "What a treasure!" She lifted up the tarp covering a statue and realized it was a piece of Mayan art that was unbroken, chipped, or damaged in any way. She was so rapt in her attention to its details that she did not notice Mandy's reaction.

With one swing of a hammer, Mandy came down on the statue and broke it into two huge pieces, then several smaller ones. It did not crumble. It held together in lumps as it would if made of today's clay rather than clay used in antiquity. Stunned that this statue, which she had thought to be perfect, was now a pile of rubble, Jeanne said angrily, "Why did you do that, Mandy? It was so beautiful!"

Unsmiling, Mandy replied in anger greater than what Jeanne felt, "It's an abomination! It's useless and a mockery of the work done by artists asked to save the human race. The Maya tried to store in clay all that could be said about that day. It's being erased and others are being paid to save today! What the ancient Maya left behind about how to ascend again is no longer available to study and learn. It was hoarded by British explorers, boxed up without thought and sent wherever. What didn't arrive wherever in one piece or several was thrown away then! The ancients can't use those engraved symbols to reach us now, but at least we can stop this wave of traitors who produce tourist goods and sell them as ancient artifacts—and we're going to stop them now!"

Still rambling on about intellectual thieves and counterfeit art, Mandy stomped out of the room. Jeanne realized she had never seen anyone get that upset about the theft of relics, and she never realized until now that Mayan art and architecture was a way to teach future generations how to ascend like they did when a pyramid was built. It was not just a fabulous way to decorate tombs and temples, as everyone said.

Within an hour of working on the mind of a blocked artist, Mandy discovered other pieces of sculpture meant to imitate art created in Classic times. Scouring the warehouse, looking into nooks and crannies she thought might conceal counterfeit art, she found dozens of statues. Her temper was not in its usual mellow mode, but in high gear and not going to downshift for quite some time. She furiously smashed every object she found that was not divine or done by an anointed artist of this time.

No one saw or knew what Mandy did until Jeanne wrote about it in a column that circulated around the world. It eased Mandy's mind that many who thought they bought genuine Mayan artifacts would now see they were fakes and might refuse to be taken in again. She wondered, 'What became of false art? Is it sold to others to get rid of it, hoping the next buyer isn't strict about checking provenance?' Greed does not end when wisdom begins. It usually takes millions to discover it is not the way to work together. Art can crash in value so fast that anyone investing in fake artifacts is truly working without a net and taking too many risks. What hurts is that this world cannot benefit from the work of artisans who work in clay the same way as scribes did in ancient times. Their work was lost when the counterfeiters' work was tossed—never to be put together again until such time as every single individual desired to ascend. Quickly, artists decided to get back to their work and work together to ascend.

That was the plan, but how can anyone hope to ascend at the end when so many others are afraid to meditate or even pray, let alone go into time and work together on a line? Lines extend from one planet to another and help everyone create their own art—or life, as it is often described; but it is not the same as life that exists in this solitary place called Earth. It is different and MUST continue to live until it can move up a step or two, possibly move into a new venue. Earth is not the top of the mark, but it is the top of a line of people who have heart. If one drops out of line, does not do what was taught when the end of time arrives, possibly others lining up later will not be able to move as fast or do as much as they must, either. Usually Mandy said nothing about it, but when asked, she once said, "Eternal life is not about sending power through arteries to extend the heart's life so it can pump for years and years longer than ever before."

Today, and every day since Mandy flung the hammer that destroyed the counterfeit artifacts and expelled several artists from the compound, she lived in fear that someone would assemble those pieces and create what would end all the fun human beings have ever had. She was not worried about her own art or books, but about what others would not understand and possibly repeat without knowing what they must do individually before lessons on ascension appear and can be used.

Thinking about the article she wrote about the burst of energy on Earth and how Mandy walked into a gallery and discovered the work of their artists was not suitable to be shipped to others who willingly paid much more than it was worth, Jeanne smiled. Writing in her very next column, she said, "Why wouldn't artists create what their patrons expect?" She included a long and detailed record of certain masterpieces and how they were made with the blood of ancient artists and survived due to the greed of men and women who killed if necessary to possess them. This was her best writing, but she had to run it by Mandy before submitting it, or be branded a traitor for not backing her friend in matters related to the tragic loss of Mayan art and books.

Jeanne waited a few hours before approaching her friend and mentor to show her the essay. Mandy glanced at the first page and commented that it was arranged without margins. She did not read it, but said it was plain to her that even Jeanne did not realize what was going on around them now. It appeared that Mandy was fuming, but she was not. Her eyes were ablaze with energy never before seen by anyone who had ever known her. Mandy had changed—become more dramatic!

During the weeks ahead, whenever Mandy seemed to be in a rage, she left her compounds and traveled into the countryside around them to talk to scribes. She was not upset with the scribes, but she found a few romantics who had to either move or go back to basics and stop wasting their revenues writing trash that would never help people survive until they could ascend in a flash again.

Scribes were not upset by Mandy's visits, but the artists were concerned that what they created might be confiscated or altered to suit Mandy's tastes. Most artists were not upset by the art projects assigned them, but some wanted to expand on them and recreate the work in other ways, using different paints or rearranging the installation of the statues and such. Mandy ordered them not to change assignments and not create anything new until she knew what was taking place *below!*

This arcane reference to another place—one that sounded ominous enough to make some Maya shake in their sandals, did not deter the theft of Mayan art. That was the goal of some artists who joined Mandy's compounds saying they wanted to study The Maya and how they ascended at the end. Their paint and work was confiscated and put into a kiln at a higher heat than required so it would explode, thus eliminating what The Ascended Maya did not want. Artists whose creations survived these firings proceeded to study and work on ancient Mayan art until ready to take down new lines and place them in clay again, so others could use them in daily studies.

When some elders wanted to fire up this special kiln or set its contents aside for Mandy's arrival, many artists vehemently disagreed. They were upset enough to suggest they would leave and work outside the lines on their own time. Tribal elders recognized that The Maya's work would not be harmed by student artists who moved into new venues or tried new lines of communications or made other friends, but they dreaded the suffering that would occur if those who built the art program to this point chose to walk away—just when it was about to pay.

When working on her own art, Julie stopped throughout the day to pray. She could not understand why some who studied Mayan art would decide to duplicate it rather than let it enter their minds and use what it said to them then, thus she was amazed and upset when Jeanne wrote about what had taken place in the Yucatan. She faxed a list of what she taught there and how many students were trained in her ways. The list was not what she wanted to send, but the only thing in place that made any sense to her brain. Julie, as an artist seeking perfection, worked for years and years before her hands' performance matched what she saw within her mind over time. She was neither a showman nor a shaman. She promised nothing, and she asked nothing of others.

When Jeanne gave up her life in The States to teach The Word of The Maya and *their way* to artists who worked in clay, she was unwilling to do it for nothing, convinced that such work must pay for what she did and those who lived with her, too. She asked for little and moved into this venue without any thought of gaining more wealth, yet she was a millionaire many times over now. All because she did not care what others thought or did, and worked hard to move into the spiritual world of artists.

Spirit provided Jeanne with proof of what could be done with art, often speaking to her as others used her hands. Artists taught classes that Spirit is great and good, and you can do whatever you want, as well as how to use everyone who comes before you when you paint or use clay. Some artists refused to let their hands do the work without mental interruption, as taught, but most improved enough in their expressions of love that they gladly paid for the compound's upkeep and all that surrounded it, in order to meet over and over again and eat as a family or go about the villages without being molested.

The work of a group of scribes was confiscated before Jeanne knew there was a problem in Mayaland. This made her mad! She was very unhappy to learn that she had trained people to work as scribes in clay and they had used this art for display purposes only. She was most angry that friends and confidants never told her about a new group forming with the intention of doing her work. It was a secret society that exacted silence from its members and was unwilling to share its esoteric work with others in the tribe. This group was not only Maya of this birth, but several were even recognized as Mayan leaders by the outside art world. This made Jeanne even angrier! She was not afraid, because Mandy could erase the problem by dramatically stating twice that no more work would be assigned to this world if the artists did not clean up their act and live in bliss.

The ancient tribe was not always contacted when problems arose, but the work of scribes and artists now moved through the inner workings of their universal mind without anyone noticing it. The tribe could exist in 'the mind of the many' at times, but it took a jolt and a leader's anger to move it out of the mist and, unfortunately, prove angels are not always ready to take over, when needed on Earth, the protection of God's work. Angels *are* greatly outnumbered, or so it seems, but the real reason they are not around when you need them is that they are not often assigned to this *dream*.

When a man or woman plots to bring down a clan or another personality before they can produce more work, it hurts the entire tribe. One person cannot act and interact with others without using the group's energy, thus it hurts everyone if this infected member of the body is not amputated and removed immediately when discovered.

That is why Mandy was crazed by this mission—unable to stay within the walls of the artists' compound very long. She could not sit without pacing the floor and talking to The Lord. She raved about the mission that was lost, as well as the cost to the people who prayed and meditated to bring about all the work that had to be cast off. Her thoughts were verbalized. She even screamed at times, but no one heard her. The walls of the office reserved for Mandy when she was in the vicinity were deep and wide and able to withstand an atomic blast, because God existed within these walls, or so she said. Mandy was not yelling at any particular person or even the tribe. She shouted so God would hear her prayer. Her prayer was verbal because she *knew* it had to be heard above all others. Words mumbled and said inside the mind might get to God in time, but she wanted help right now! Her plan was to yell until she could feel nothing unwell inside her body or mind. This spell lasted a long moment, but was deep enough to be heard in other parts of Earth.

The moment Jeanne's syndicated column arrived on the steps of the local Archbishop, he wept. He was afraid, too. He had been able to find only a few remnants of The Maya in Spain, and was afraid the ones they found were unable to help The Church. His work was to see to Earth and help The Lord of All find those of great faith and save them. He felt that call rather than heard it, but many were not able to maintain his ways and were swept away by his changes. They fell from grace and caused many to disbelieve in God because God had been explained to them as being like men. If the Archbishop defamed God or did something strange, he should be taken to task, but it was not like that. His mission was to change the way the Bishops behaved and taught through the missions now in place. He wanted the people to adopt compassion and live as Christ taught and lived—not like Christians lived and taught now. His work was not spoken of much because he was not liked by many in high places—including the Vatican, nevertheless, he was a great man.

When Mandy walked into a mission chapel or church, she stopped and looked for the spot where God taught. This spot is usually near the main altar, but can be found in a chapel if more people prayed there than any other place within that sacred space. The thought that some ran to church to be free of negativity did not escape Mandy. In fact, she often urged artists and scribes to go to mass at least once a week to pray and meditate and do whatever appeared with parishioners who met there. This was not an order, but it seemed strange for someone in her place and her race to ask them to do that.

ℋ ℋ

What will last?
Who cannot go into space and move into a State of Grace?
What is wrong with the human race?

Perhaps it was the last question that brought the rain? Water spread across the plain. The Yucatan is famous for lightening stopping clocks and igniting fires at unlikely times, but this rain was very strange because no lightening accompanied it. It was gentle, coming in three brief interludes, as if the world was being blessed or christened.

Jeanne stood in the rain and saw in a vision that Wanda was upset and tired, too, but she did not complain about what happened to the art she taught. She was still amazed that Mandy was able to instantly expose a gang of thieves others believed could steal anything, get it through customs and deposited in Geneva safes where it could live for ages—and never get caught.

Meanwhile, the Archbishop continued saying his prayers and feeling graced by God. The Bishops did not see life as he did, but they felt waves of electrical energy ignite their faith in God, and they gave better sermons after talking to him.

As The Date passed without anyone saying it changed them in any way, Mandy realized it was the rain that changed everyone. No wonder the god, Chac, was so revered by The Maya! She could not understand why she changed and could now see inside the mind of those who once ruled the tribe, but she knew the universal mind was not the same as the sages of today described.

Everything changed to comply with the plans of one who could not be an anthropologist, yet condemned everyone not trained to work as he did. This man harbored evil in his mind and never took time to weed out egoistic thoughts until that rain came and changed the way others viewed his work. He left the Yucatan and never became as famous as he planned. Unfortunately, he did not take all the evil with him that he sowed by claiming The Ascended Maya did not do all the things as reported. He implied it was magic or chicanery, and many unfortunates believed him.

What can change the minds of those condemned to believe such men? Nothing! Either you believe and move into your integrity or you lose it. It is not up to someone else to save you gracefully, but it has been known to take place. Calvary appears as the cavalry, if you are prone to martyr your mind over time. If you follow that path, be prepared to let others take whatever you produce and change whatever you say later. Be upset and blue—or fight for what you believe you came here to do!

♓   ♓

Mandy slipped silently into a room full of artists talking about how some had abandoned their classes and taken their art away to be completed in New York with several others. She was chagrined to see how many present envied those who left this work to do what they called *their* art.

"What can we do to become famous, too?" moaned a woman who was famous for her constant complaints and insistence that everyone compliment her work while she said nothing beneficial about theirs. She abruptly stopped talking when she noticed Mandy was obviously unhappy, and then acted as if she was trying not to laugh. This strange juxtaposition of emotions frightened her enough to stop complaining, but no one worried that her performance art was over.

Her audience sat and waited for what she would rant about next, but it never happened. Instead, Mandy stood up and looked at the artists with a smile playing around her mouth. It never spread further, moving from one side and then the other as she wandered about the outer circle of friends, looking at their teacher's art to see what she was teaching them. Their instructor had been working up to the moment when Mandy made her presence known. She was given no time to moan or groan or make excuses for how she had ruined great students. It had been decided that this class would be retrained if they were to be retained to do the work of increasing this world's energy to a level where they might aspire to move higher and ascend at its end.

When their teacher stood in silence, students became aware Mandy was in the studio and began to wonder what would happen next. No one expected to be given time to get over the work that had been destroyed or be given new worlds to work within, but some still had hope. It was not to be!

Mandy stopped beside the table of each and every artist and did her work. She placed her mind into time and let her hands move the clay or use the paints in ancient ways. When it took too much to alter what an artist produced, based on this teacher and her moods, Mandy destroyed the piece and told the artist to pack up her things. It was always a woman who was told to leave, because women are most likely to fall under the spell of those they admire. This teacher defamed The Maya with her lack of faith and loss of bliss, but the men were not without condemnation. They might have been allowed to continue *if* they had not altered the art to suit their own hearts.

Several women and most of the men were able to be retrained, thus retained, but most were asked to leave immediately and never come back or list the school on their resumes. Most were afraid to ask Mandy what was wrong, but the boldest asked what she did to gain such a bad reputation that she could not save her art or her career. This one was stubborn, but Mandy did not mind since she mumbled a lot and seldom ever spoke out of turn—and because this was the first time she ever said what she felt.

Without frowning or smiling, eager to end the class on the hour, Mandy said, "You're not an artist—yet. You may become an artist in a day or two or never, but today you play with clay and let a teacher dismay you with distorted stories about the old days. You have no faith that time is able to be identified and displayed in clay, and that histories can be combined into lines to be saved and then read when it's time to study them in depth again…You just don't understand art!"

The women silently sorted through the tools from the state-of-the-art equipment provided by the school. They would miss all of the computer expertise, too, but had no clue about that then. Such people take for granted any help given. They wander the Earth looking for those who will give them whatever they want. Such takers are never seen as a loss to givers when their relationship ends.

The one without a clue about what she had to do to improve was a mystery to her teacher, too. When relieved of all responsibilities within the week, the teacher did not speak about what happened to her class then or later. She was retained to show tourists how to make sure they never bought fake Mayan art, because in her mind that was all she was fit to teach now. She recovered eventually and found a store in town that paid more than Mandy. She left and no one missed her. She had worked her way into the artist's compound, but lost her artistic abilities by showing no respect for what she was paid to teach. It was 'like normal' in LA—but strange to the Maya working diligently and praying over the clay and using whatever paints were on hand.

☼ Chapter Forty-Eight

When the wind moved through the guardian trees stationed around the perimeter of the compound it left a message. Here is what it said:

YOU ARE ABLE TO DO WHATEVER YOU WANT AND STILL GET TO THE END WITHOUT BEING ANY DIFFERENT FROM WHAT YOU WERE AT THE START.

"What a strange thing for a tree to say," whispered a weaver to others standing beside her trying to read messages posted on the bulletin board. She could not understand why trees were guardians to begin with. Who appointed them? Who knew what trees said? She asked questions instead of opening her heart to the sun to see if it would speak to her, too.

As the day progressed, several weavers stopped to read the message Wanda had written on a three-by-five card. They admired her penmanship and writing style and so on, but they did not get the point or absorb the thought. Others tried to read something into it that was not intended and talked about it with those eating just outside the kitchen door. That is when the head cook got upset and began to shiver.

"I've never seen a denser human being than that one," said the cook as she raised her index finger above the kitchen stove to point out a blonde woman standing and talking to a group of Americans as if they were toddlers learning their ABC's. The cook reached over and threw a lid on the floor. The clatter broke the spell of the powerful enchantress over her charmed crew. The cook saw her as a venomous snake and thus renamed her—the Blonde Adder.

She had no clue why an Englishwoman standing nearby exclaimed, "The Blonde Adder—the perfect name for another BBC creation!" No one in range dared laugh, but the name stuck and was used over and over again throughout the week. How does one woman, or ten of them, enter a mission and sleep and eat with all present, yet never partake of their wisdom or art? It can happen, and it did happen…but we are getting ahead of what the trees said and what they meant.

The trees planted or growing around the compound walls stand as guardians over the weak and infirm, helping them learn what normally takes years. When good people occupied the seats under these trees they often found themselves uttering profound wisdom, with no doubt about what it means or who will do what and when; but when fools or evil-doers tried the same thing—nothing happened. The trees did not bend, creak, speak or think for them.

The women studying with the not-so-young, blonde 'guru' came from huge cities overrun with people seeking fun and, thus, had not developed wisdom. They eagerly invited others to teach them rather than go within. The synergy needed to ascend never happened within this group, but few noticed it and wanted to leave her. Those few who left went without a speech—leaping the compound walls, running through the villages, never to return to Mayaland or speak to those who shared their wisdom there and then.

Following her own teaching for a week, The Blonde (what most men called her) was unable to figure out what happens to her and others torn apart from the havoc they experience and probably initiate in any relationship they have with men. She blissfully taught her students that they could have anything they wanted—without doing anything to earn it, because they deserve prosperity and need only believe it wholeheartedly and unreservedly to manifest whatever. This dichotomy was humorous to those who were either unaware of the tragedies that followed those who believed her theory or were not concerned about Americans outspending everyone alive with credit extended by those who believe they will repay them with interest one day. This dilemma did not exist when they arrived at the compound fresh from Cancun, but was alive and growing when they left! None of these women sensed what they lost that week—what they tossed away so carelessly when talking pseudo-seriously in hushed tones that lacked conviction, totally concentrating on what their false prophet taught them.

Within a week of the police delivering a local man to prison for stealing from his neighbors, another thief arrived who was not associated with the tribe. This thief claimed to be connected to people in high places and able to help the tribes accomplish much more than they ever did before—without any in-fighting. At first everyone was suspicious of his claims, until he mentioned his Rolls Royce and his mansions in Asia, Western US, and Rio. These far-distant dream-like realities apparently sealed the deal. Men came from miles around to make friends with a man they deemed to be a scoundrel, but able to make lots of money—fast. Yes, he made a lot of money quickly, but they lost a lot more before he left their villages.

When this man arrived in the area he crossed thoughts with The Blonde as she strolled to the village to shop, accompanied by her group of admirers and students. They met within an hour, not realizing it had happened before. 'In another time they decided to arrive in this world as a couple—lovers unable to discover the world without each other.' This fated meeting was described by her as 'instant karma' or 'soul discovery' or whatever sold better, and he agreed.

"Love is my only vice," The Blonde said too often to the women at her side. "You need only love a man with all you are to have a relationship like no other," became her new mantra. Upon meeting the mystery man face-to-face, she immediately directed her students to amuse themselves doing whatever they enjoyed, and she would meet them later at the compound. They were *not* happy to be dropped for a man and were unwilling to fall back to entertaining themselves, so they wandered after her—watching her meet, eat, walk, and talk to this very mysterious stranger.

The Blonde did not recognize him from a past tryst when they had met briefly, but before many hours passed she was holding onto his arm, then his hand, and then leaning into him to hear his every word. Her new beau was not immune to using sexuality to seduce, either. He held her close, but with a bit more reserve. He was as dark as she was fair, but not handsome in the way of Today's male models. There was a dark aura above his wavy hair piled in a pompadour—swept back as if imitating Elvis in his youth. The man was not tall, but carried himself as if he thought he was.

After parading around the plaza half an hour, they visited a café to sit and relax. She followed behind as he strutted toward a table, only to slouch toward another table, and then walk into a wall. This stopped The Blonde dead in her steps. She laughed when he smashed into the wall, without realizing what had happened. This was not the reaction he sought! He snapped a curse meant only for her, but since the word was rehearsed so often in moments of bliss, he acted as if the shock of the collision had caused him to say it with such passion now.

How do women of these times meet men destined to betray them? According to a verse written by The Blonde Adder, "It is a person's worth that determines what they seek, what they find, and how much they learn this time." Can it be said that she needed him now to be able to see around the next bend—or did she need to learn a lesson from the past again?

By the time the sun set the women who were frightened to be out at night had returned to the compound and were relaxing at the kitchen table where the cook presided and related her life lessons to those studying her art. This group claimed to love cooking, but she was not hoodwinked by what they said or did. The cook always gave each would-be protégé a test that quickly proved most knew nothing about mixing flour and water or how to feed a man or his family. These women had no idea that she did not deem them worthy to be taught by her, so they bragged about how much they paid to visit this far-out place.

Standing at attention, the cook bowed from the waist once, then twice, while several helpers bowed their heads over the ovens, stoves, sinks or wherever they were working. The visitors sat, stared, and asked rapid-fire questions. They totally missed a tremor while discussing being kissed and made love to versus achieving personal bliss.

Recognizing the naiveté of these American beauties, who resembled the youngest children in the tribe, she worked on this idea a lot and decided to not hold back any longer. She would teach them what she planned to tell her very last class. These vain idlers were astonished at what she said, but afterwards some leaped and bounded through the air while others clapped rhythms on their legs and chairs as if children just released from 'Time Out' and suddenly given permission to be happy once again.

After a few days away from The Blonde Adder, who according to the cook "just didn't add up," the group was forever lost to her charm. What is more, they were determined to prevent anyone else ever admiring her as they had! These ex-disciples of the famous guru worked side-by-side with the Maya doing chores they could handle and even asked for more. The cook was pleased that Mayan peasants and women of the world were so easily pleased simply working together. At times they even blended herbs better than she did! She took this to be a lesson much needed and not to be dropped until she mastered it. The Head Cook's adages were repeated over and over. She emerged as the mother hen these lonely women came to Mexico to follow. Her chicks even walked as she did, without realizing it.

Mandy stopped by the kitchen for a short visit and was amused to see how much these women were imprinted with the Head Cook's ways. They would never be the same, but they did not know it. Would the wisdom taught now take hold and stay with them when they returned to The States? Mandy did not know, but Wanda had a vision about them.

Wanda could see some of these over-privileged women opening a kitchen within a group home meant to help those who grew up in slums overcome the ways of the world and learn to eat more than French fries and pizza every night. Her vision was cemented into place when they left the Yucatan; but before that happened, they had to know what would become of their old leader to understand the overall plans for their new lives.

Their deposed leader, The Blonde Adder, was always happy—never sad, when she met a man she liked. However, by the end of the third date, she was usually frazzled and upset. This affair was no different from all the others she flitted through in the past. Several women who accompanied her to Yucatan heard her squeak to him: "I want it now—not tomorrow. I'm not some floozy you can toss when you get tired of me." Her pouty rant was meant to be a poem—not rhythmical, but what she had in mind at the time. It exposed how unhappy she was with whatever he proposed. His plans took a dive after he ended up with her in his lap, so he wanted to take over her work. At first she thought it would work—for her!

Once they realized how little sex it took to divert this gringo from his work, most of the Mayan elders spotted his ego's insatiable need to advertise and make grand statements about his life. This was now an easy call for the elders, as well as others who know the psychology of love and business between men and women who exist in a time and space where love is becoming extinct by the week. This knowledge remains a mystery to women who become mistresses when they want to be a Mrs.

Thoughts flit by in an instant, but anger lingers. The man in the vision was so maddened by his lover's words that he did not consider how his statements would be taken by those nearby. He snapped too loudly: "What you need is a slap on the back, low enough to jar some sense into your brain—right now!" His lack of control and this display of hatred cost him the business he planned to confiscate while in Mayaland, so he took what he could get wherever he found it and worked on a change of plans.

The Blonde Adder was wealthy enough to afford a luxury car she seldom drove, and never interested in others enough to support any cause other than her own career, so he moved first. Waiting for the right opportunity to help himself to her wealth, he was delighted when she said, "I think you're very abusive to women, whereas I want to help women and children harmed by abusive men. Maybe that's why we met? Maybe I'm supposed to create a foundation for battered women and children to teach them how to live without men like you?"

Opening his eyes to their widest extent, he laughed and checked her out more closely. He noticed a tear sitting in each eye, just waiting to subside or explode, so he attacked her past. Her life would become his history. It is easy to do! He simply echoed whatever she said—parroting every word a few moments or minutes later, and she never noticed nor realized that he was manipulating her into revealing what she normally hid from prying minds. She was frowning and sorry-looking when he started his final campaign, but exploded into smiles and pulled him close to her after shedding a few tears. Sighing as if the world she once knew was gone forever and there was no one left to comfort her now, she invited him to say something nice.

He put his hands around her face, squeezing just enough to appear to be caressing her cheeks and caring only for her. Right then she glanced away at a group of strangers watching them with smiling interest. She flew into a rage and tore herself from him, then quickly walked away! His grasping hands left red marks on her face that caused the crowd at the bar to gasp when she walked toward them. She, however, was unaware that he had left a red tattoo on her neck. She added to her anger the negative feelings she harbored towards peasants, tourists, and others she branded as 'lowlifes.' Disgusted with everyone at the bar looking at her with pity or derision, she described them as 'vulgar lowlifes' in need of lives of their own. She threw a bag of tortilla chips into the air, and when it landed, she stamped her size ten, four-inch spiked heels all over it. No one really cared, but some continued to savor the moment as others shook their heads, trying to decide how to describe this to the tabloids and gossips around the bars. As a result, no one was prepared for what happened next!

The Blonde Adder was about as upset as she usually got after a few glasses of wine, but her ex-beau was shocked to realize he had produced a bruise on her fair face. Add that to how disheveled she looked and it was cause enough for the police to question her, if they were on the ball at all, so he hurried after her and begged her to share a table in a nearby café and have a cup of tea with him. He often affected a British accent, knowing it excited the snob she tried to be, but it had no effect on her now. In fact, she resented his condescension—suddenly saw it for a phony ploy that had cost her a lot. All traces of a smile were gone as she plunged into her purse and sorted through what she usually stowed there. She pulled out a small gun, but was not prepared to use it. She just wanted to be sure it was there, just in case she could shoot him and get away with it.

How well had they loved each other in the past to meet in the present and not make it last? It was obviously not the time and place to reunite and make love based on faith. Each participant in this tryst was a cheat and unwilling to give up stealing from those who were naïve or stupid enough to want to be rich and famous overnight. They both used their unique takes on beauty, as well as their work in past lives, to gain acceptance from their public over and over again, but this was the last day of their last play and the confidence act was fading fast.

Sitting at a table waiting for whatever passed for tea in these parts, as he was wont to say, he grasped her hand and held it fast. Having noticed the impression of a gun against the side of her handbag, he was sure she would use it if he tried to do anything she did not like, so he sat still saying nothing while reviewing his plans. His latest convoluted plot was to deceive her once again, but make it stick this time! He figured out how she would set him up so he would never again have to work to make a living.

Interestingly enough, The Blonde Adder thought the same thing! She was very interested in using his contacts in many places to convert his work to cash, so she would never have to work again.

Greed sets the stage for need to take over. Any plan worked out in that state of mind will prove to be bad for those who follow it. For once, these thieves were not going after others to make money, but planning to rob the other of what they valued most—money— money that did not belong to either! Money is picked up easily anywhere in the world where industries are downsizing and executives are hiding the money fast.

To buy more time, the nefarious duo talked briefly about the fight that reunited them, smiling at the waiter until he thought they were in love. That is when she felt her hands grow cold and he felt chilled to the bone. Neither understood why they were suddenly cold, since the ice in the pitcher of sangria had melted, thus the need for tea.

What was the reason for the sudden chill? At that moment an angel stepped into their space and cleared away all who sat too near these scoundrels. It was easily accomplished—seemed to be the perfect time for everyone to rise and leave, but one American stayed. That one refused to listen to the whispers and urgings coming from within his mind and soul to go now.

How to get a human being to leave when everyone who can hear God has left the building? That single thought drifted aloft. It was the same lesson taught by the ancient Maya many times over time. What to do when one person refuses to flee danger, unwilling to leave until everything is over? How do you get one person or sheep, as Christ taught, out of danger in order to save his soul and his life work?

This one lonely American refused to pay attention and leave when the waiter placed the check at his elbow. When he did notice the waiter pushing him to leave, he was not happy and became determined to sit, until he discovered no one else was left in the café except him and the two lovers. He did not want to order another dinner or stop the help from leaving now, so he stood up and walked toward the entrance with his cash flashing. His bulging wallet did not escape the eyes of the spies, but the tourist did not realize he was being watched.

When the last man to leave finally walked out the door, a large group entered the restaurant. They immediately decided it was too empty at mealtime to be any good and left. The two pseudo-lovers were thinking of assassinating each other until left without any cover. They decided to follow the drunken American who had been flaunting his cash. Each wanted to work on him privately, but realized only one would appeal to his sexual tastes—whatever that might turn out to be.

Hurrying, they could see where the tourist was headed, so they took a shortcut through a store and ended up walking down the street directly in front of him. As if trying to avoid a puddle, The Blonde Adder stopped to pose. Sticking out her hips, she ran her hand down her calf, smiling as the mark almost knocked her over. He did not recognize them from the restaurant and was immediately interested as she flirted more openly–wiggling her hips and rubbing her rump as she pranced in front of him.

At the corner he got a look at the man beside her and left them both without smiling back. No man of any worth is interested in taking away the woman of a man of high birth—even if she is not, or so the tourist thought as he sat alone on the edge of his bed an hour later. That narrow escape was not the result of a mistake in judging women *or* men, but due to the way he was programmed. One stroke of character saved him from imminent death.

When neither conspirator could work alone as originally planned, they decided this was the way things had to be for now. They also decided to build up their appetite for others by having sex before they approached anyone else. Obviously, sex is not the best way to communicate, but they used it so often they believed it was.

The Blonde Adder, unable to satisfy her own demands with this man, glanced at his hand and motioned for him to do something he did not want to do. Shaking his head and sneering, he said she was unable to satisfy him, too, and indicated she should open her mouth. Making mutual excuses for not being able to produce an acceptable sexual response that satisfied the other, they realized it was because they were eager to light a fire under others. The seed of greed was planted more deeply than lust. This was definitely not a good time for those with money to be nearby, unless they had a sense of what they would do when they died.

Imagination can play with thoughts and produce pictures that are not true. Mirages and wishes are produced by the mind and the eye all the time. If you look at someone and believe they are handsome or pretty, they are beautiful to you, even if they are not. You may believe someone has a lot of money and will support your dreams, when they are deep in debt—looking for someone to take care of them. That is how these two lost the art of love and all that it imparted. Lust left them in the dark! They had to form new plans or return to the cities of their choice without any loot. Apparently, there was nothing more to make off the lambs she had raised to shear and slaughter one day. Her sheep had moved away to greener pastures while they played in the maze.

The amazing thing about this couple was that they were able to fight and get back together almost immediately at night. They did not appear compatible when strangers first met them, but after observing them holding hands, acting like lovers who could not wait to get under the covers, few doubted they were the genuine article. The acquaintances they cultivated were not actors who recited parts learned by heart, but everyday people seeking adventure and romance—thus primed to be targets.

Operating within and around the atmosphere of Mandy's compound was too restrictive for The Blonde Adder. She announced that she had a vision when she arrived the first day with her adoring supporters. She claimed to have talked to the trees about it and it had come true. She planned to talk about it at a village café that offered poetry readings by anyone able to prove they could write in the air or in rhyme. Standing beside the podium in full regalia, she threw kisses, accompanied by a dazzling smile, at each and every man and even some women drinking alone at the bar. She was confident of the outcome, because it was a well-rehearsed and practiced routine. She was not prepared for what happened next!

As she repeated her latest interpretation of wisdom given to her that first day by the Guardian Trees, a Mayan busboy slipped on a piece of greasy chicken skin in the kitchen and screamed as he landed flat on his back. His shout let everyone who was aware of such omens know that a god or an angel was alerting them to a fraud going down now. Immediately, elders stood and surrounded the crowd. As they looked over the tourists, watching The Blonde do her psychic act, professing to understand trees, they knew what would happen if she were interrupted, so no one spoke then.

Whatever you say in a public place to many people is analyzed right before your eyes as it enters your ears. If it does not compute or is unwise to do, many leave immediately. So when this woman held all the men mesmerized, as if they were lovers to be, the bartender did not worry about what she was trying to put across or pull off. He should have worried, but he did not.

As their world expanded and then drastically contracted, a man stood and walked toward her saying he believed her. He was a shill, but no one realized it. He asked her what she thought about several investments he wished to make, he was aware that rich millionaires use psychics all the time. She was unwilling to recommend anything, but with a bit of coaxing from other men who were also interested in ways to make an easy profit, she let slip a few funds. Infected with the fever of greed, many men asked then what would pay off enough that they would never have to work again.

With sweeping gestures, she announced one stock fund and then another, until she finally said all stock funds are good, but just not as great as the one that would announce gains tomorrow at ten times what Magellan Fund made. The men hesitated to accept this tip—at first, but investing is based on faith and since all of the other funds recommended were proven good buys and already on the rise, they all pushed their intuition aside. One man standing at the bar mumbled to another, "How else could this stupid blonde bimbo know what stock to buy, unless she was given a tip by God?" His crass remark guided the reasoning of those who began writing down NASDAQ initials for individual stocks and trying to remember the rest of her advice—especially about that last mutual fund. They went outside to call home or borrow cell phones and place orders for the rest of the evening. Some laughed about it later, but no one laughed then.

Working on impressing men and women drinking at the bar, her shill, an ex-lover, asked her to name stars. She was startled, but he assisted her in a way only a Maya could spot as a fraud. He used the sign language of the effete—making waves with his tongue to get her to 'read' what he wanted her to say. She was relaxed enough to be able to quickly read his signs, but not fast enough to hide from the Maya who called the cops.

When the first police officer entered the back of the bar, the shill did not realize the act was about to be broken in half. Someone tipped The Blonde off, so she had time to collapse as if in a trance that would not release her from its dance. She was given a chair in the audience and the shill returned to being unknown.

There was no plot as far as the crowd could see, but one Maya realized that lives could be changed in adverse ways by how this woman played on everyone's thoughts. He sent a message to The Ascended Maya and asked if Mandy could come by his office the next day. Angels often deliver such messages, but not this one. It arrived in a flash in Mandy's mind as she was preparing for bed. She saw Jorge clearly and noticed that he was unhappy with what was going down somewhere in town. He was the one appointed to watch out for tourists who were well-heeled and unable to hold their beer, so he was often away and up very late.

As the vision of Jorge faded, Mandy opened to what was happening to the villagers as they walked home. In spirit she walked up to one man and whispered in his ear that the blonde woman was not what she pretended to be. He repeated it out loud and several friends immediately said they agreed with him. This started a loud discussion about her scheme to get people to invest in a scam. Her scam came undone in half the time it took her to put it together, but some never listen and lost a lot due to the plot.

Why do some always lose and a few always walk away better off? How do people know when they are about to do something dumb? Winning is a way of life or a way of thinking about yourself, caused by heeding your own inner guidance, advice, and hunches at least once in a while.

When the Guardian Trees closed their leaves that evening they smiled at each other because two evil people would soon be leaving and no one from the tribe would have to hide their money for quite some time. The Maya were spared another expensive vacation plot hatched in another spot. They survived by heeding the waves of electricity that came into and circulated through them as it did through all humans now and then.

When the police picked up a dead American woman the next morning in town, no one knew who she was or who had attacked her during the night, but some whispered that she looked familiar. That clue caused one woman to suggest the victim was one of the lovers who sat in the plaza yesterday. Another said she had hugged an evil man for dear life then. The police were wise. They listened for a few minutes and then called up Mandy and asked if anyone who looked like this blonde was missing from her compound. She reported immediately that no one was absent who had been present when she arrived the previous evening, but she was not sure about the week-long guests.

Working through the guest list to see if anyone was missing took only a minute because the cook was at her side in an instant. She was prepared for such a call. She knew it would happen the moment she spotted a blonde hair rising in the air and falling into her dinner. To her, this was a sign that God was shaking her head to make her listen, but she did not. The cook expressed her doubts and thoughts while Mandy listened. The cook then inquired of a member of the disbanded group about The Blonde Adder.

Gossip spread throughout the compound like a wild fire. The Blonde Adder was dead! She had not been with them very long, but her followers or whatever they thought themselves to be were shocked because they had all been so very close and now could not remember anything about her. Her family was not notified, because no one knew who they were. The local travel agency was given the mission of contacting someone in The States to let them know her body lay unclaimed in Mexico. She was officially identified by the American consulate's office, using the passport left behind in Wanda's office, but that was about all anyone knew about her then.

"This past week was just awful!" moaned Wanda. "I haven't been able to sleep well, and the trees keep talking to me whenever I sit under them … I wonder what they can see that we're missing?"

"Let's go and talk to them now." Mandy smiled then and exchanged wisdom intuitively with her friend. The two sat for several minutes under a huge tree, feeling a hand resting on their shoulders. Each woman felt the pressure with a sense of endless ability to endure all tests without rest. They blessed the trees and the water and the seeds and asked that the rain be able to wash away all stains. The tree was not able to bear down more, but gave them a sign by dropping some very dry leaves into their laps.

"I will always cherish these leaves," said Mandy. As she placed the leaves in her hair, the tree seemed to tremble without moving its trunk. Mandy felt power surging through her and overrunning traces of her brain waves. She almost had a stroke, but was able to reduce the overload in a minute or so. That should have been enough time to change the mind of anyone else on Earth who was working on self alone.

Wanda did not speak, sitting in deep trance until a sigh escaped and she could stand and proudly walk away with ease. In fact, she appeared to be leading a band of trees or an army of civilians to fight in some huge battle. Stopping suddenly, her stance was one of a great man, but she was still Wanda.

When the police found the man last seen with The Blonde Adder, they discovered he was not the lover passersby had noticed in the plaza. He was rich enough to get away and not be bothered again, while the thief made his way to a virginal place—ready to spend money he had burgled before cutting her throat. Since she was never willing to leave home without her charge cards and check books, it was easy to lift them and do whatever he wanted, because, after all, he was now a rich American traveling in Mexico.

Classes started once again in the compound and a few of the soon-to-be-forgotten guru's students were unwilling to leave them. They tried every ploy, but could not stay. Would they, too, come back and live with Mandy and Company and do something new one day soon? Who knew? Only trees know such things!

☼ Chapter Forty-Nine

Talking to a friend visiting from The States, Thérèse said, "When a new spa opens you don't think about all the people who will make a living off of it or how many lives will be enhanced by it, but we do. We want the greatest possible exposure to people who need our healing efforts, yet don't realize it until they feel better, too."

Thérèse had not intended to talk about their spa plans until everything was in place or at least funded, but when her old therapist stopped by to visit and explore the life of an average Mayan wife, she could not keep quiet. In fact, she exploded with enthusiasm! Her present life was going great, but she thought it would be more wonderful if she could have her own village to manage, and be able to live as she did when she was in charge of the compound every now and then. She was never bitter, nor did she regret giving up her career, because looking back all it seemed to entail was standing around for hours and hours acting indifferent or as if she had a bad attitude, which too often stuck to her—just to call attention to outrageously expensive apparel she modeled while dreaming about doing something useful. Her dreams did come true, but at times she still wanted to do something more for others.

The life of a saint is simple and easy compared to what happens to your mind and spirit, not to mention your body, to model underwear. Thérèse no longer had to diet or eat only celery and apples all day to stay in the best possible shape for a particular camera angle or to sell whatever to people who thought she was stupid for modeling it. That lifestyle led her to become too self-absorbed and insensitive to others, including the public who loved her poses. Working daily to sell herself, the money accumulated so quickly that she never thought much about wasting what she made in a day on something that would never interest her again. She had been very foolish and vain, but worst of all—not interested in anyone else. However, her soul never languished because her mother nourished it with thoughts and prayers, even when she stopped caring.

Wanda never let on to acquaintances in her adopted hometown her true relationship to the famous model, until they moved away. When it became obvious that Wanda and Thérèse were never as they seemed to be, many of those left behind were deeply offended. Why? They had always connived to know all about Wanda and Teri, going behind their backs because they loved gossip more than loving others outside their family alliances. Today the American Way is to look, watch, ponder—then make assumptions based on offbeat pictures taken in strange places. To think Wanda and the super model were lesbian lovers was a lot more interesting for neighbors to talk about than recognizing them to be devoted mother and daughter.

It was never easy for Wanda and Thérèse to work together every day, but not as difficult as it would have been if they had not lived and worked with others since Teri's birth. Although Teri is a saint now, regardless of what measuring stick is applied, many refuse to believe she was born in The States or ever modeled bras. Folks deny her past profusely at times and got upset when articles and pictures of the old Teri appear with wild guesses made about her life today. *People* magazine and other tabloids that gossips love to read had her on a revolving account. Every few months someone there wondered what she was up to now? Thérèse never denied anything, because she only read about her work among the Mayan tribes now.

Among the Maya, Thérèse was accepted as a woman who did whatever was necessary to help another find the path to his or her spiritual source. They did not find her quaint or fascinating or as strange as The Press painted her to be. She laughed about the media fiction, but not much. She chatted about local news, but unhappy if any was about her. At times she talked about how she was given this instruction or that lesson by her mother or others, but never took credit for teaching anyone. Her relaxed style and teaching methods were lauded by Mexicans and Maya alike as an example of how women should behave who are saints, but she felt like a fraud whenever they introduced her as a saint in public or discussed her asylum among them with great awe.

Memories of life in The States receded from the front of her life to the back of her mind. She never thought about her past life unless another tabloid attack was released with no thought about how it might damage her present life. The last time the rags put out a bulletin of sorts about what Teri was supposedly doing, they said she had been deported from one country to another for consorting with the enemy and causing a disturbance when she got drunk. Since this was so out of character for Thérèse, friends and followers of her work throughout the world did not believe it. They bombarded news bureaus with e-mails demanding to know who wrote it. Unfortunately, too many Americans bought the lie and bought every article they could find about it.

Beauty salons and businesses that cater to idle minds who want to get rich quick were the first places to settle into the daily habit of discussing how Teri/Thérèse lived now. Many doubted she was able to change people's minds in other countries, but children and teens still wanted to believe beauty was the key to winning everything they dreamed about now. Teens were most interested in her past, which effectively ended Thérèse's plans to never again grant interviews to Americans seeking news.

With articles circulating about her life as it once may have been—glamorizing that existence, she enlisted her best friend, Jeanne, to fight back. She talked to friends about how to handle slander and vicious gossip with dignity and truth in hand—resisting the impulse to be snotty and slap various tabloids with law suits. Jeanne scribed her thoughts that began to appear in lengthy articles that never reached the kids who were implanted with seeds of grandeur based on what tabloids and TV portrayed. How many children are given such rags to read by adults who believe them? We cannot say, but we know Jeanne could not make a dint in the way most Americans viewed her friend. As time consists of only what you do or know, Jeanne sat and thought a lot about what her own work was doing for her as a person. If no one believed the facts she released about Thérèse, how did they evaluate her work? She decided to find out!

When their work arrived in *time*, she was sitting on her verandah looking at the Mayan women stamping out a fire. She was not concerned that their feet would be burnt, because they knew what they were doing. She thought: 'Confidence comes from watching others succeed and doing it yourself.' That flash of lightening-fast recognition resulted in her igniting with the idea of producing a video that explained their life among the Mayan tribes and working for The Ascended Maya. Their spokesperson would be Thérèse, because her work would be seen as most unique and attract many teens to PBS instead of MTV, for maybe the first time since Mr. Rogers died.

This was not exactly how the video turned out. Many women wanted to share only what they did best, not what they were learning and trying to master. They argued relentlessly that it was not good to share the great effort it took to master a trade or how long it takes to create a piece of art. They thought it could not help them sell work that supported their lifestyles. Mayan women could not let go of the pride imprinted in their minds—having existed there since the last time the tribe survived by ascending into the clouds—leaving their enemies behind for another time.

Whenever Jeanne wrote a script that did not deliver the message she intended, she rewrote it and did it over and over again until it was letter perfect, according to the critic who resides in her mind. But when she started to write this video script, it was written by a master and arrived in Final Draft form. She did not want to change anything because it fascinated her, but she wondered if it would fit the public mind.

⚓ ⚓

When the team of photographers arrived in the weavers' compound, they were in awe of the colors and patterns produced there—at first. Then they diluted and adulterated its purity with their ideas of what the producer expected since he was funding their crew and expecting everyone to win an Oscar for him again. It was not turning into the kind of movie Wanda had in mind or envisioned in time, but since it followed the script Jeanne produced, it could not be all that bad—or so she thought.

As the crew made its rounds to check out the nearby towns and villages, they were astounded to discover the women and men working in the confines of the weavers' compound lived better and were much more content than Maya and others living nearby. Theirs was not a primitive lifestyle, but they did not watch movies and TV, preferring to eat like peasants left behind from ancient times. The Maya were happy to relax and talk about their day as the sun went down and the moon rose into the night. They were happy—which was too much for this crew to handle well, too.

The tools used by the crew filming the Maya and the weavers—and later Thérèse working on her plans to build a better venue, were not suitable for the way they wanted to work now, so they moved looms constantly. Some weavers had to stay away from their work all day in order to make room for the booms and lights and the shades. The Mayan women did not admire these men because most were sloppy in their dress and appeared to have too much dirty hair. The Mayan men also believed they were not respectful enough. They did behave badly—drinking and drugging, but the worst was their constant use of foul language without regard to women, children, and elders present.

Styles clashed—a lot! Tempers soared whenever the temperature topped 85 degrees Fahrenheit. The crew learned to stop and eat together as the Maya have done since ancient times. The men began to laugh more, not swearing at each other as much, and feeling better in weird ways. This was not the first time many minds from the outside felt a spiritual change while here, but it was the first time many expressed what they felt so graphically. The crew talked a lot about how relaxed they felt working with natives who were not what they expected.

The Maya are not humble servants of others, but someone in the past spread the rumor that the Maya did not work as hard as Americans, so Hollywood studios were not sure if they had to supply laborers to do the work behind the scenes or not. The diligence and artful ways the Maya worked around the sets surprised them all so much that one or two Mayan men were hired to work with them when they moved out. With everything done as soon as needed, the crew learned they were the ones being watched and studied.

The difference between a Mexican and Mayan man is not so much a thought process as a difference in culture. They are not alike and they often fight when thrown together, but inside each man is a way of looking at life that is not very different. When it differs, they fight to the death rather than take the other's part. This conflict in interests is causing more and more problems for The Maya than ever before! Mexican governments have wanted the Maya moved out of Yucatan into neighboring lands, but this is not to be, yet the government wants it done immediately—and then not so frequently, and now not at all. Why the changes of heart? They cannot do anything about 'The Mayan Problem" without upsetting their national economy. American tourists, in particular, used to ruling and getting things their way, profess to love the Maya and their ancient cities and culture and expect them to be there when they arrive.

Once the money was in place, work on the movie left no time for what they usually did. The cast included Jeanne, Julie, Wanda, Thérèse, and a friend from The States—a famous New York psychiatrist who chose to remain nameless. Her role was to narrate views of their lives in the United States compared to what they did here. Only a partial profile was ever shown of her, which lent an air of dignity to each scene. Since she preferred not to be known as a 'media expert' and be bothered by reporters and such whenever something went wrong in countries south of America, she chose anonymity even when working alone with those filming the documentary. Her lines were pulled from several scripts approved by the crew, who were apparently intent on cutting out all the best parts, but it was still a good fit for her.

As the crew aligned to produce a fluid style, discarding many that would have suited this Mayan tale better, some felt compelled to give it the kind of treatment MTV viewers recognize immediately. As a result, Mayan music suddenly became much more important than originally planned. They made recordings of various musical groups within central Yucatan, but none communicated what the ancients wanted to say. As a result, it was not easy to compromise, yet it was absolutely necessary for the project to move ahead and not fall behind. Finally a group of decent men who played traditional instruments accompanied by a woman who played the flute better than any woman ever could were chosen to be made instant stars. The flutist was beautiful, and for that reason only, she was chosen to front everyone else. In a white dress she stood out from the musicians who sang at times. She did not.

What happened next hurt no one there, but it changed the world and made it a kinder and more decent place in time. What does the mind want from time? Peace, serenity, a sense of decency, and honor help you now and when you ascend at the end. All that was present then, but later it was not.

Working with a screen crew, in addition to producing CDs with the musicians and singers was not easy, especially when your experience and expertise is technical writing that evolved into a syndicated column. Jeanne was not happy with what she had to do daily to produce ever-changing scripts, but she got her way more often than not without anyone realizing it until it was too late to dilute the messages she scribed and inserted into the final work.

Her work would become far more dangerous to pursue in the future if Mandy was seen on TV, so she stayed far away from the compound during the filming. The crew was never aware when she stopped by to watch them working within the compound or in town, because she was a master of disguise. She was unwilling to play a part because her reputation might taint its eventual reception by the general public, aiding those who might want to harm the beautiful reputation of her friend, Thérèse, the saint. Mandy helped everyone, but in ways not usually mentioned now. She stayed out of the way of the public, but most Maya knew when she was there. After all, she was their mentor and they loved her for how she could talk to *anyone* as if they, too, were the same as the shortest, dumbest man or woman alive—and get away with it. She acted the same with everyone—giving everyone the same respect, which is a gift, according to the elders.

What went down the last day of filming was remembered long afterwards. However, no one proclaimed a miracle or said Thérèse was a saint until much later. Such an event was a pleasant way to end the production and begin another, but most present were not listening as Thérèse worked that final set.

Thérèse was so accustomed to film crews working around her that she ignored this one when she stood and walked toward a child to help her stand and walk and never use her crutches again. It was an act of faith when the child forgot her fear and clutched Thérèse's hand and walked with her down the path. Instantly, the child chose to never again limp. This miracle was featured at the end of the film, but no one in the States believed it actually happened that way. Critics and clerics alike said it was staged and the crew should be ashamed of doing it. For that reason, the film did not make Oscar history or reach most of this world's theaters. The Maya, however, treasured the work because it was unlike anything they had ever seen in this time frame or line of time.

When you perform in accordance with a script, you live within your mind and forget what you would do if you were thinking and talking it through. You forget that you would not remember a lot of what was said and would not be easily convinced that you were merely an instrument of God, thus not really important. Actors often succeed in doing great things within the minds of those unable to think easily or quickly, but they do not realize the total effect or such results when the pieces are put together and the cameras are rolling. They forget everything then. Afterwards they may try to remember why people idolize them for one film and hated ten others they thought were much better. Was it the director or the Divine working within them and outside the lines?

Once the DVD was available to view, the public might look at Jeanne, but stared longer and harder at Thérèse. Very little was said about Thérèse's old life style now. This was a miracle come true for Thérèse, and even the crew realized God truly does move you to do things you could never do alone—but does it in very odd ways.

If you have trouble getting a message across, you might think the best way to get people to pay less attention to you or your body or what you do all day is to write a book or act a part that demonstrates your thoughts and how you live now, but that did not happen here. They were too pure of heart, too honest and good-natured—much too hard-working for critics to rip everyone apart. Because they strove to improve the human race—far too ideal to be real, as some say today, it was just too much for the average person to emulate, so they did not try. It took a lot of effort to rip out their hearts and discuss their bodies, so the average person forgot or ignored this work, unless they got it.

Working on parts and acting out their art had not been easy for the weavers. They lost pay and lost time much needed to prepare for the biggest art fair Mexico City had ever produced to showcase Mayan art. Once the crews were gone the weavers rushed about and worked into the night, but they could supply only half the number of tapestries and fabrics they had planned to display. The weavers did not recognize that the few works they sent were so strong and beautiful that they thrived in the absence of many lesser works scattered about them. Since the tapestries sent were produced by only a few of the masters, Wanda worried that the younger weavers might lose heart and walk away from their art, but it made them work a lot harder!

Working on how they lived daily, while trying to impart a sense of responsibility they felt in their hearts, was the easiest task accomplished while the crew worked with them; but after everyone left, it was not easy to regain their old comfortable ways with each other. Jealousy was more obvious. Some envied that others' art was included in the final production and theirs was not. It took much time and effort for Thérèse to ease their minds, but she did. If she was not ready for new work in the past, she was ready now. However, along the way her plans changed. She finally knew what she wanted to do the rest of her life! She wanted to specialize—teaching life and after-life skills to children.

☼ Chapter Fifty

Thinking back over the last few years, laughing at the excuses many gave for giving up, Mandy sat in her room working on a dream or two she received last week. Her review was within her soul—not what she did when admitted to this elite group of dreamers. In the past she would sit in trance and stay at the dance until the last song was played or the last drummer went home before opening to work displayed in her dreams, but not now.

Working in the state of existence next to this one is not easy, especially if you are riveted on greed or need, instead of what you must achieve to make this a life you will not want to relive. Mandy was not happy with her work in New York, but because she left it unfinished—never returned to it, she lived it out in various ways in dreams about that time. At first her work was repetitious, then it was easy, and finally it became boring enough that she found herself snoring. This then made her laugh because it indicated she had ended that life and was ready to do something new.

Whatever you do in your mind, you are working on it now. You work as you smile, read, study, and eat, but you still hope to do something new, too. Why? We are given so much to do inside this time frame that trying to do it all is not fun. You might try to live selfishly—alone in a house, never bothering with anyone else, but you would have to live to 110 to finish all the chores you promised God you would do before you were through. If, however, you decide to immerse yourself with people of Earth and get into whatever they do and how they live now, you might leap ahead and be through with all you came here to do ahead of time. What happens to You then?

As weeks turned into months—a year passed without any new ideas created on this side of the veil to aid the tribe. Mandy finally realized she was alive to complete her own work before she left Earth and something was not done well enough for her to ascend and end this birth now. She sat in silence for a time, only then realizing her mind was a transitory state that wanted to explore her fate. Everyone identified her as a shaman of the tribe, but she never believed that line. Her own mind rejected such salutations all the time, because she was not born a Maya of today's tribe.

In the weeks and months following the outburst of energy that produced a new group able to help The Healers on Earth use herbs, Mandy was unable to thrive. Her energy level plunged! She was not as willing to work with others as she had been in the past. Jorge was not around much, but when he stopped by once or twice, he was rebuffed. He thought she did not understand what was going on, but chose not to impose on her what he believed it might be. Jorge was unable to know when she would end or when she would begin a new life again, but he could see she was about to do something he would never achieve—be free of all that was in her mind and leave it in time.

Working on her own divorce from the life she knew in New York, Mandy found a string or two leading her back to an attack. She followed them to where she had been molested as a child, but not serious enough to worry about now, yet it was something she could not escape—being a woman of today. It had to be. How else could she have understood what every other woman on Earth has to go through? This memory was not unique or easy to keep, so she cast it out and wondered again why so many men eagerly hated women, only to want their attentions over and over again. This was not a life to explore the ways of men, but she had no wish to let it happen again without working it out on this side for a little bit.

As the days became a week of decent sleep, then ten days of feeling great, each morning she had no need to run to town or answer letters from friends and others, instead she slept more deeply than ever before. That is when she realized it takes at least ten days of great sleep before dreams are worth being analyzed again and again over time.

Within ten weeks of the day she began studying her dreams her way during the day, many abandoned their efforts to see her. She had become 'a recluse,' according to them, but the village understood she had to be left alone to do her dream work. Americans everywhere did not wish to give her that much time alone and demanded attention—even threatening whatever they thought would intimidate her to pay attention to them. Mandy never again worried about the abuse that comes to those willing to live in time, because she was not a recluse or out of her mind. She is Maya and living through a universe that others outside this world cannot see into or believe.

Without any doubt now, Mandy suddenly arrived at her headquarters one afternoon in the month of June with a friend in tow and a dream she wished to let go. This friend was a man who had once lived with her in the city during the old days—before she moved to Mayaland. He was not a friend in the way of many who claimed to be friends today, but a man of integrity who was deeply trusted by everyone who knew him. This man could provide her with the ability to flee time the very first time. He was an engineer and able to provide her with work she would never want to give birth to on Earth because her mind hurt when she now used math. However, this was not to be the man who would eventually take care of her wherever she might rove, rather a man who posed no threat to her and helped her with computers in her work.

He was not the same man others thought they knew, but a man from another time who worked through his Earthly work and was now trying to figure out why he was here to do another time. He could rip computers apart and put them together easier than other men because he knew what was at their heart. He was interested enough in putting them back together again that he often worked in stages or for days, never complaining about the work. He was able to invent things that others got patents for with amazing speed, but he never pursued that life, either.

To Mandy, he was the grandest of men and she spoke so often about him that way that even Jorge was just a bit jealous, until he discovered the man was not someone who would ever love her as a man. Men seem to cling to such emotion even when they are free of the gravity of this world, but Jorge rose above it more and more now.

As work continued within the compounds scattered about the Yucatan, Guatemala, South America, and in central planes, their group expanded and moved into a new plan. It was to make a movie about how Mayan shamans live now, without actually saying they planned to produce such a film. They would disguise the entire cast, so they looked different than they actually do, so others would not flood their countries trying to imitate whatever they said to the Divine now.

The movie would not be ready for filming until every man and woman portrayed agreed it was what they taught or fought or worked with a lot. As their plan of a play began to work out, groups came together for a month or so of intense work. The movie was ready for screening without loss of integrity due to haphazard filming methods and editing done at disconnected stages.

During the time it took to write the screenplay and put the scenes together so it would play well, Jeanne kept busy doing publicity work intended to pave the way for the public to learn about The Ascended Maya, while having fun and being entertained doing this semi-documentary. The Hollywood crowd insisted it was necessary to turn it into an action movie that stands out from religious and philosophical films of other ages, because The Public is incapable of understanding metaphysics unless blatantly displayed and spelled out in images graphic enough that even a child can get the message.

The joke they never caught was that action takes place between the pages—not on the page you are reading. The work these executives chose to ignore was what was being explored, so they were dumped by The Maya. Then someone, somewhere, suggested they talk to a Frenchman about producing and directing the film. This was not as dumb as it sounded to Maya who did not understand French films or their beloved mimes, but their final choice turned out to be a man who was both British and French, who merged the material so it could be easily birthed.

The filming began on a Yucatan beach and ended in the mountains of Guatemala. The plot centered on Americans who wanted to fit in as Maya and work with those who lived this life since birth, but could not. They taught the wisdom of Earth as it existed in their books and labs, but the Maya resisted. When it comes to thinking, then telling someone else what to do, Americans believe they excel at it. So these folks were amazed that they could not get anything through to the tribe that way. They eventually sat down and actually did the work required—hoping that sooner or later someone else would want to do it for them. This possibly makes sense to audiences not born in America, but hard to sell to the paying public that Americans do not work at what they talk. If that basic bit of wisdom could not be put across easily, the movie would be a fiasco costing the Maya money they had put aside for the end of time.

These tribal concerns entered the light beams of Earth and circled the globe, so without delay Mandy stopped dreaming and trucked to a spot where crowds were awaiting the filming of a day of lovemaking and such. She stopped everything with a single thought: 'What will it say about the way the Maya live today?' She worried that they were using sex to sell or worse, the other way around. 'What does it take to create a mind and body in time? What comes together when someone decides to host another soul? Would it become a lesson on what Mother Earth is trying to do with us now?'

As Mandy reminisced about how she had come to realize the tribe was just a tribe until it went inside, the crew of Indians who had adopted them decided to film Mandy praying and talking out loud, so as to show the public there is a God. Others did not understand what they were trying to prove and disapproved. Mandy approved, but she refused to do it.

When it became obvious that no one could do what Mandy did, and no one else was willing to star in her part, she was asked to consider standing about in rooms and dancing in halls, even eating with the Maya in dining scenes. After careful consideration, she decided it could not harm her or her mind in time to lend her energy to the film again and again, but she would not idle for hours while they fiddled with wires.

When it became known that Mandy consented to sit in and watch what they did, the elders dropped their initial resistance and joined her in a scene of revelry, and then in a scene where everyone wanted to make her queen, but she would not let it happen. This scene was what several women vied for, but only an actress with heart could do it without falling apart. It was very tiring to go into the middle distance and romance nothing but your own life plans.

To prepare to do her life as a role model, Mandy had to do this work in her own time first. As a result, the play moved slowly until one day some groupies thought it would be fun to produce a cartoon. There drawings were never a part of the art they produced in LA, but they were very much a part of the art of the ancient peoples who still lived in the hearts of these artists and even some of their scribes.

Without any appreciation of Mayan art or any desire to do something wild and new, the group asked the old friend of Mandy if he would create a computer program or example of what they could do in an hour or less to show what The Maya know. He was blessed, so he felt the immensity of it immediately and decided not to do it. This was an unexpected disconnect that Mandy felt inside her head, before the film crew asked her to help them persuade this man to reinvent himself again to help them. She refused.

"When you want someone to do something for you, always present the benefits of your plan first—then what it takes to get it done. Wait to tell them what mistakes you've made or what you can't comprehend or why it's not working. Now, go back and take this approach with my old friend, maybe he'll be interested then in being employed again and want to be your friend." Mandy's smile as she talked hid many thoughts.

Since time dragged everyone down between shooting one scene and the next, the Maya walked a lot and talked very little. They were unable to plant seeds, even if the crew had not trampled their fields, so some onlookers thought it was okay to talk about The Ascended Maya—in order to help them out. They said this to elders' directly, and then betrayed them as well later that day.

When it came out afterwards that some of the victims of set gossip were wise men and women of the tribe, the elders decided it was time to end such talk once and for all. They announced that anyone talking out of line or lying would be put in front of a tribunal and made to tell what they did and why they tried to sell out others without knowing they were doing wrong. This rebuke was totally unexpected, yet not seen by the rich and famous as helpful or aimed at them. The tribes started something that ended many media careers for those who pretended to be friends of The Ascended Maya or the tribe and used whatever was said against them.

Jealousy and envy follow the rich and famous around, but some covet it more than anything else associated with being a star. Why? They want attention which only a parent can provide at any time. Without anyone to give them advice, they often seek out people who are so overpaid they will never help them get into a better frame of mind. Envy is taken for granted and expected, so when stars of that realm come across a boss or a woman like Mandy, they are very cross when she does not take their lead or says something they do not want to hear. Deep green shades of ego came into play during the making of this movie. They were so intense that many wore sunscreen and put on purple glasses to resist it, while others laughed at such vain attempts.

Whenever laughter preceded a filming sequence the group found it much more interesting than what they had explored previously, but if the group sat and listened to cursing or worse, they were less able to produce anything worth using. Since the director was a good businessman, he decided no one would begin work until a good laugh descended upon them from the clouds above. That was what the tribe generally waited for when in town, too, so the command was easy to explain to them.

Within ten weeks of filming the first scene, the entire cast was able to adequately explore their dream of making a movie together and get across what they had developed in their separate minds. Would it help to insert a plot into the work and talk a lot? Maybe not, but they placed that thought into the mind of The Scribe, so she was constantly busy trying to tie in their thoughts with lines that made sense to others who had never spent any time in spiritual retreat or working through things on the other side.

As the entire crew bonded and grew into a close-knit family, willing to stand up and defend anyone who did anything that was offensive to them, the entire industry discovered that it could learn a bit from this. The most powerful asked the Indian crew to film ten more movies for them, too. That crew's success was contagious, because it was a blessing from the ancient sages.

When you sense you have learned something new, you send energy to friends or authors who helped you by using their wisdom then. If you connect to a thought or write a poem that speaks peace to another mind in time, you are blessed more than someone who used that same wisdom to conduct a piece of business. It always pays to, at the very least, thank God immediately, even if you can never resist doing it your own way.

♓   ♓

Working on the story as a play, and then a screen version, was enough to seal the bargain for those who worked with Jeanne and her scribes. Several of her aides left for LA and were planted among the people who produced scripts for outsiders. In this way they could and would control the depraved in whatever they set out to produce today. Regardless of what a producer or artist might want to do with art, it has to stand up to what it was made to do—entertain and help others who cannot read and understand its depth as well as its profanity.

When an author is unable to talk to her public about her art, is she less of an artist? Speeches and interviews were turned into ceremonies held in other areas of the country, but Mexicans expect artists to say very little about themselves, which pleased Julie immensely! She continued to study with Jorge and others, exploring the world of oratory, so as to teach what she could see.

In many ways, the Maya of today live in the old ways, but give us a break and let all of us see what has changed since we arrived in our time. Did you accept what you had to do or did you greedily need everything your *friends* bought to make you envious of them? You may not realize that living as a scribe or an artist within a tribe means giving up your pride, but it does. You cannot hide your thoughts and work much when you are in the center of a room full of others doing the same work as you are.

If you try to hide your light, someone might describe you as shy, which might be true, but you may be resisting acceptance in order to say people do not value art as highly as those who crack jokes or laugh at others and create wide waves of anxiety. You would be wrong if you decide to change what God provided your personality inside your mind. Always, all ways, be yourself! Be shy or nervous or whatever when you accept accolades and you will become famous. Today too many congratulate themselves constantly, so you will be noticed immediately by everyone who counts as being the least intimidating and the happiest of all heroes.

When the day ended and the last cartoon was printed, a group of artists asked Mandy's friend, The Computer Geek, to have dinner with them. She was unable to attend, but was told later that he was so much wittier without her around that she would be a better friend if she let him go out and about without her. She was not offended by such remarks because she worried that her insistence in channeling whatever whenever it came through to her could be offensive to friends who were not as natural as they might otherwise be if they were not providing her with time to work.

Working on the side and dreaming as much as she might, Mandy was unable to see into the future of Jorge and what he was going to do tomorrow. He was a man of great stature and many blessings, so she let him stand as is, doing his own life over without benefit of her clan. She was never offended if he reached into his bag of tricks and removed clues about the future or made fun of her, too, but she would not let anyone who was ignorant of their mission ever do it again. Her own work precluded fools, and she planned to leave them behind as soon as she could move ahead.

☼ CHAPTER FIFTY-ONE

Jeanne's hands paused over the keys as her mind wandered or wondered—depending on how you describe what goes on in the mind of a spiritual scribe. She sat and thought about nothing so as not to intrude into what would come through, but then thought she better not stay on the computer long because she had to get her teeth cleaned. That thought roused her immediately and she began cleaning up papers and things on her desk. As she moved to stand, she felt a hand constrain her to the chair.

There was no one in flesh involved, but she felt it was important that she do what she was being asked to do and do it fast. Her hands began typing so rapidly that she could not read what arrived through time. Settling back, she let it spell out exactly as it wanted to appear on paper. She had grown used to this kind of domineering spirit, but never aware of how deep it could take root within the mind of others, too.

> Working in compounds throughout the countryside gave this group of American women much to do. They learned to whisper—rather than shout and laugh or pout, but some still wanted out. They resented not being given spiritual work by The Ascended Maya or being allowed to lead others of their linage or line. They believed it was a way to keep them outsiders, but it was not. The reason was—they too easily tired of working hard over long periods of time without support.

> The Maya Way of Life is not one of great delights and many surprises, so for those whose moods are up and down following such pursuits, they grow dull after a few years. Some sought to be proclaimed saints or at least women martyred for their work. Fame and/or martyrdom is not what anyone claimed they sought when classes formed, but art makes many demands on spirit and mind at times and can lead to lives lived far away in time. Those who stuck it out were able to ascend in the end without thought, but those who left the faith never figured out where the others went.

> What The Ascended Maya expect from a tribe is the ability to enter its way of life with a spirit that promotes harmony and good will, without taking away a lot of the daily struggle the tribe would otherwise give up because they worked too willingly or quickly in the past. The ability to be free of Earth or associate with those who can spiritually enter a column of energy was not extended to those who came to Mayaland and worked for a short time and then asked to leave.

Work that leads to ascendancy is not granted, gifted, or given to those who are merely interested in doing something different while on Earth, because they obviously do not believe spiritual guidance is readily available if you ask for it—or you master a task.

What can men or women who choose to live without the benefit of spiritual guidance do in Mayaland? They can meditate and connect to their personal line of faith and listen. What then? They must make up their minds to use any help and guidance given—and actually follow through and do it.

Right then Jeanne remembered she had a dental appointment, but before she could move away from her computer, her hands took off again, this time on a rant of some kind.

The medical establishment would not intentionally fail to help those who prevail over the bad habits of their own humanity or seek help to withstand the effects of a stress-filled life, but what about others deemed to be health care experts, too?

Medical standards are not so high that you have to leap over tall buildings to make it into medical school, but they do require extreme dedication and inspiration if students are to actually become certified as doctors. The same is true for dentists, too, but dentists differ totally from physicians in what they are prepared to do. One is heavily regulated and the other is not. One makes more money than any other health professional working now, yet faces the highest level of suicide—and the other does not. One works constantly in the face of impending death and the other does not.

Dentists of the islands and continents use wisdom when pulling teeth that are decayed and unable to be saved, but most other decisions are mixed with what they want to do with teeth they save. On any given day one man is told his tooth can be saved and will last and be just as strong as it was, while another is told that saving that tooth is not the best way to proceed. What creates the difference in diagnosis? The amount of money the patient is willing to pay the dentist that day.

Interestingly enough, the greedy do not badger the dentist nearly as much as the doctors they trust. Why? Decide for yourself and you will discover that one is expected to be perfect and the other is not liked from the moment his work is discussed—so expectations of satisfaction are not very high.

What can 'we' do about those who cannot save your body, your mind, or your soul and expect you to help them live better than you do? This is not a decision you must decide anytime soon if you are wise and live with a tribe—and are very young; but it is very unwise to put off deciding if you cannot afford to pay for insurance, which unfortunately will not be there when you reach your declining years.

This world was established in the past for those who maintained a tribe that considered and worked with each member all the way through to the end of old age. Now many have opted to disband tribes in order to let individuals decide what they wish to do for themselves as a people without family or kin they can cling to at the end of time. What would you do if you had no one to support you, pay your salary, or employ you now? Would you be able to live the same as you live this minute or would you have to cut back on what you spend—and demand?

If you discover that the way you live today is extravagant—not a way of life you can sustain all by yourself, you may save more than ever before or put aside enough to buy a house and secure a car. But what if you do not? You will find that when that last check is cashed and you are expected to pay for everything you buy on credit that you will sink into debt of another kind. An obvious deficiency caused by your own lack of wisdom, or in some cases, a sign of your innocence about how things exist. Be aware of what time brings or takes away today.

Jeanne felt a bit of pressure building up in her mind…was it worry over money?

> *While working in the compound store, noticing what other artists were paid as a result of laboring all day, many decided art did not pay enough and moved out. Some, however, discovered they could set up shop and duplicate each and every piece of Mayan art many times over and be paid a price for each fake piece that was almost as high as the original could bring in. Their thieving ways resulted in a loss of artistic thought. Renegade artists are paid so well that many cannot produce as much from original thought after greed enters their dreams of mastery.*

> *What about a doctor, dentist, or artist is alike? Each has a creative way of working for pay, but if they forget to tune into why they chose their profession and what it could do to help their tribe, they end up richer than others of the same degree and acceptance, but not in ability to build toward the final day when this life fades.*

> *Should you be able to see a lot of work in a degree or three? If work is not good enough for you, what did you expect? Most likely you assumed others did well or would not have gotten far, but you could be wrong. Become aware of what it takes to get ahead without making huge mistakes. How? Do it yourself. If you do a great job and know what you are doing and why, you expect others to maintain the same degree of control within their professions as you do when you seek help from them with whatever you cannot do alone.*

> *Consider what a smile does for a face and compare it to what a wallet filled with dollars does to a character that is not great. Regardless of what you thought, neither lasts as long as the character that enables a person to achieve the same degree of acceptance without a lot of cash.*

When her fingers stopped typing, Jeanne sat back and reviewed another manuscript close at hand. First, she looked at what others who had reviewed it wrote in the margins. Her words were rubbed away some places and some wrote in suggestions, but she no longer resented such misunderstandings about her work. Being a spiritual scribe is the top of her line in time, but on Earth it is a destiny that requires fortitude and skin as thick as a walrus's backside—if you are to succeed and work with The Maya.

Although Jeanne seldom disagreed with what was said in interviews with strangers inquiring about her work, she did not speak in terms reporters could learn much about her daily work and style now. Her lessons on Earth were not the same as students who worked with her, but they were unaware of it until someone announced they were as good as she would ever be. The assurance of the youthful few, as well as some experienced elders, was such that they still thought she could not scribe for The Ascended Maya, but she scribed for them anyway, without the uninitiated knowing why.

She knew why many were not told about some of her books until they were out and about and in public use long enough that outsiders also wanted to join The Ascended Maya, whom she scribed or knew so well. The Maya never asked what the public would buy or why. Instead, The Maya assumed it was time to take stock of what Earth had delivered to millions of people living within their tribes throughout the south of Mexico and nations below.

Stopping in mid-stride as she paced, reading page-after-page in amazement, Jeanne read something she did not remember writing out.

When the The Maya of the outer skies led the tribe in ancient times, the tribe did not have to ask for directions or take classes on what to do next in order to ascend at the end. Today everyone lives far removed from the existence of that time, so they have to be given work that will enable them to leave this Earth again.

The Mayan tribes scattered over Mexico and Guatemala tried more than once to establish a time when they could work with their youth and begin educating older members who were willing to dedicate their lives to keeping the wisdom alive, but it did not work out as it had in the past. Today the world is a place where many erase their existence and produce a different fate than what they came to Earth to pursue or use. The use of drugs and alcohol occupies so large a portion of the mindset guiding the American spirit that many cannot climb out of it in time to escape their end. This produces fewer women and men able to believe they can ascend to God of All in the end—rather than wait around for another time.

The ability to ascend is discussed much everywhere. Too many believe it to be a psychedelic type of experiment and intimate that time can be found if given enough time. Their thinking is incorrect! They behave insanely at times, but at least they talk about what too many others forget—the study of time.

When this world began ending its plans, people were not aligned inside the general mind to do something new. Too many cry and worry now, calling out to those above that God surely will let them escape, if such a fate is allowed. They fail to realize that the universal mind contains every escape route available in time.

What can a Maya of today's tribe teach a man or woman who is unwilling to meditate or pray? Not much, but it occupies their mind and elevates the tribe in time and space. If no Maya can work with those of another time or inside their own minds, the tribe loses much of the energy it needs to convert its own unified-field work.

Work is not the way to get ahead, rather how to build an image of what you can do while on Earth. If you have never succeeded at anything or always wanted someone else to lead, you will be the slave who builds a structure others will use when their day is over, and they will not remember you much—if ever. You may never be confused with being one of the architects, builders, or bosses developing the pyramid that produces work needed to ascend, but without any thought about when it is finished you can still cash in on it. Bear in mind that you have to stick it out to the end, be there on the last day—ready to rise and pray, and then work at your highest level until you are carried away with others ready to fly then.

What to do with those who will never live to see the day when the pyramid is apparent to the naked eye and people can travel into the sky? You will never see it happen because each and every human being has the ability to change before the last day and become a spiritual being eligible for the crossover to God of All.

What you may not realize now is that many of the religious lives you think are extreme are prophetic of what will be. You may not realize that you have many lives, too, but one of them will be remembered, and hopefully it will be your best one so far. If not? You will be demeaned—maybe forgotten before you leave.

When you are ready to date steadily and marry someone very friendly to you, do you wonder if they will at some time take over your work and do everything you direct them to do? If so, you will be taught many lessons, some of which will steady you while others will rip you apart. Your heart is not to be put on an altar and given to another. If you do that, you will be cast down the stairs of that altar because you are unable to give your life to God.

Jeanne stopped reading and sat—stunned, unable to think straight, but it lasted only a minute or so. She knew something momentous was about to happen, so while preparing her mind to accept messages out of context—perhaps out of time, she pulled out her keyboard. With a jolt of energy that squeezed her insides from the spine outward, lines jerked into place on the screen. Indeed, she felt very strange, but glad to be alive and able to scribe.

> *Work on what you want to do and you will find the crew who worked with Mandy, as well as many others who worked for The Ascended Maya, will not be the same when their days are over on Earth as when they arrived ahead of this time. They are changed in ways that cannot be explained in one day, but in 52 years or more you can see The Mayan belief system is not unique.*
>
> *If you wrote out everything you saw in a week and added what you did all month, you would find you do not survive for a minute at a time but longer as you climb. When you are a baby of several months you do not know what it takes to get your dinner right away, so you whine. If you are 22 and still crying for whatever you want, you are not driving straight to the top of your mind, instilling wisdom and learning how to care for children. Indeed, you are stuck in the life of a child and not able to see into time.*

Jeanne never intended to pursue work on an essay about children reverting to childhood in old age, so her mind wandered over time until it spotted the clue '52' hidden in the text. Usually, her mind paid little attention to the many adventures, ideas, and work others pursued on Earth without thought to what they induced in the mind of her readers within this time. Jeanne believed she was merely creating pieces that linked various beliefs and philosophies, and taught in a novel way that entertains the mind. She was unsure if the world would or could understand what she planned to do next, but her thoughts were converging into an idea to write about the groups disbanding throughout Mayaland in an effort to live their individual lives again—or one last time.

Suddenly realizing the time had finally arrived when most women and some men she worked with daily were able to let the past sit as is while they retired into whatever they wished to do in time, Jeanne prayed that her friends would not be disturbed if she wrote about their past lives here this time while building her own memoir.

What does a writer see and describe? How does it differ from what a scribe does? Jeanne was not interested in discussing such differences or in portraying women who worked as writers and spiritual scribes. She did not enjoy describing how she typed and produced letters more effectively than using a stylus on tablets of clay or brushes daubed on animal skins that had been tanned to a degree of pliability so the seams did not destroy story lines. Her delight was seeing into another's heart and telling the story each woman brought to the Yucatan, along with her unique plan and work here, before leaving with full knowledge that life was better on the other side of this life.

Working a short time within her mind, and then putting those thoughts down on paper with a pen, Jeanne credited each and every woman and man who romanced the work of the Yucatan and Guatemalan Maya now. Since she loved only those willing to let others grow, her list was quickly downsized. She hoped her work would herald a new age when artists would stop working for pay and pick up the old ways once again. Her New Age was certainly nothing like what others on Earth claimed it to be, because she saw so much further into the *future* than others who wrote about the *past*.

As this work ended, Jeanne once again became accustomed to the climate, noticing how the heat and humidity adversely affected what the computer wished to contribute. In a flash—just like that, Jeanne snapped her fingers and decided to move to a place with less humidity. This move, of course, produced a lot of discord! She did not expect anyone else within the tribe to move, too, without knowing what could happen to them outside this world. She was willing to take the risk and make such a break, then await what happened next.

The best way to chronicle a sage is not to write about what they ate or how they told their life stories, but to observe and report what appears to be their most important work. With that in mind, when Jeanne's essays circulated through newspapers they were never thought to describe a New Age so much as discuss what had been overlooked or forgotten and was now remembered by those passing from one age into another.

Was the final curtain about to descend? Jeanne believed the Earth was just about the same as it had ever been, and now The Ascended Maya were once again trying to help this particular world ascend into the sky with them and dwell with God of All again. Would her stories of women and men who had successfully moved into time help others ascend? She would never know unless she risked taking it upon herself to show nations what was being done in the Yucatan and other such spaces that exist today.

If you write about the wisdom of sages of this age, as Jeanne does, you would not own a home for more than a year or two so you could have privacy enough to get your work done without interruption. She was secure enough to write and not compete with 'The Whisperers,' her term for those who thrive on gossip produced by idlers living near people who work hard and cannot bother with them.

What one woman thinks and does is not valued the same as what another writes, so you have to fill in spaces and divine the truth about what probably happened next. When Jeanne finally wrote her life history, she did it without thought. But before that happened she had to understand why it took 52 years to complete one Mayan calendar cycle. Each thought on the subject had to align in a time line that taught one aspect of The Ascended Maya, as taught on a particular date on the calendar filled with art. But in this reality, Jeanne did not see the total picture until her unique book of essays about this new age was free of her estate.

The life Jeanne willingly subscribed to was not devoted to seeking wealth or even seeking out the wisest men and women of the tribes. Her life choice was to sit and work hours and hours apart from all others in order to fulfill her art. As she wrote then:

> *The soul of a writer is not the same as that of a spiritual scribe because one is not surmised to be wise. A spiritual scribe is given a gift when he or she arrives at the end of an assignment with everything appearing to be in its proper place—unchanged in any way from the way it was dictated the first day by the wise.*
>
> *For that reason, this scribe and everyone else who challenges their minds to study time with The Maya will benefit from the last chapter or episode of this work. Those who skipped from the beginning to the end, just to say they read it, will gain nothing. What you can do now to help is sit and read your limit, then pray. If that is not enough to gain wisdom, share what you read with someone living with you. You need to understand if you are afraid of a friend—not if your prayer for wisdom is answered. Fear is the reason we are working here. Fear limits your mind now, if you refuse to study what you alone can do to find time.*

As Jeanne read these lines, her hands slowly moved across the computer keys one more time before they stopped writing about scribes and writers and others forever. Her mind fulfilled its time and thought about whether or not she should write a will and give all her work to others or make it a way of life that would stay alive as it is today. She did not think about it more—remaining meditative enough to know that with a skillful will and a trustworthy administrator she was better off creating a trust.

> *To trust or not to trust is not what you want to talk about when your work is over, but you must learn to trust and forget that life is full of surprises if you do not read ahead and surmise what mysteries might arise in time.*

Sitting still now, Jeanne's hands dropped to her lap and she laughed. She wondered aloud: "Is this the final chapter?"

'No!' was what she heard from somewhere close to her heart. Tomorrow would bring another episode. She would *know* then why it had to be now—and not another life or another time that the art ascribed to a woman unable to accept such work in her youth would surpass what everyone else presented as being the living end.

✿ CHAPTER FIFTY-TWO

The words appeared stiff and unyielding to her eye as Jeanne scribed. She wondered why. Glancing around the room, empty except for her active computer, she said aloud: "Nothing really stands out and yells to be changed, but I feel like something isn't right—and I have to fight it." She stared at the words inscribed on the screen and wondered what was wrong. This essay was going places she was not prepared to write about today.

White and black, red and blue—opposites to you—all in sharp contrast. This work is not in sharp contrast, if you can find the thread weaving through the pattern that teaches you how to accomplish what you always wanted to do in the past. Which is? Be you as You came to be—not as others rearranged you when you tried to become who you are.

Even if that thought was not expressed well by those gathered in the center of the room, it remained the theme of the seminar. It was repeated and discussed much in several different dialects, then translated into a number of languages, including Dutch, but it was always about love and accepting what you are as a human being and what you can achieve before you leave this planet.

Whenever the discussion was devoted solely to the efforts you, the individual, can make within your soul to develop your place on Earth, each group was unified in belief; but when it got down to how to work and create as a group—who would do what, factions formed every time. Groups went into various studios off the main room and either sat and looked around or watched and complimented the efforts of the teachers and students in the other rooms who attempted to recreate a day in the life of the compound where they were staying.

It was never the same wave of energy or the same people working with them, so The Teachers did not enjoy their work as they had in the past. Those who worked in the villages and towns and compounds were not sure if their foreign visitors got anything from these seminars, but later they were told thousands were inspired by this work to do more at home than ever before.

The difficulty in working on your own life as you read or talk to another is never as obvious as when you try to take notes and listen at the same instant. When you scribe, however, you are pushed to write down every single word, and whatever is missed remains missing—not to be added later as an afterthought. When teachers write out their lesson plans, they leave gaps for students to fill in when they get that far. In their hearts those gaps are not so great that you cannot trust fate to teach you all you need to star.

What you are and who you will be are not the same? They are if you integrate what you read, write, and think—then live that way. If not? You are scattered to the winds. Fate is fickle! You may be able to do something new and then maybe not. You need to sit and dream as you work on you for a week or three at the center, then return and recreate a break and walk into the next view of you knowing what to do then.

The future is not difficult to view if you can read and write and integrate thoughts, but if not, you will not move easily into a new view of you. Work on a way to interest You in whatever you are doing, then learn how to open your mind within time wider than ever before. Once you can visualize the sky and what exists in your mind, you are open wide enough to step into another view of YOU, but it is wise to wait until you know what to say and how to open to those who will interview you there.

When you cross over into the next view of You, try to remember that you want to leave Earth forever. Say it one more time with us now and you will find that when asked on the other side of time that same simple question, you will answer it correctly this time.

What to do with facts that stick as if glued to you—that take you back to your past? You have to erase thoughts of gloom and doom if not meant for you. If, however, you produced an evil place or humiliated others who were good to you, you might want to make amends before being made to do it or made to live this life over again. You will find it is not difficult to apologize, unless your mind is truly out of line. If that is the case, then talk to a psychologist and get straight, or pray for several days and listen to what God has to say. Either way, you need to talk and then listen to what the wise think will help you pass this time.

Working in the way of a teacher, a spiritual scribe, or other artists is not the easiest way to work and live high, but it pays well if you are truly unique. If you are not unique? Life is never as happy as you think it should be. It is not easy to live your life as well as those you copy or berate. If you are tired or upset about what is said about those who are unwell, you will find the love of being a part of mankind sells well and heals hearts.

Staring at the lines on the computer screen, Jeanne could see her hands rapidly start typing again without any thought from her.

I am not able to type much more about the world of The Ascended Maya because it is all about time now. The world cannot absorb more than its share of what it needs to know to ascend at the end. Too many have no idea that we are about to fly and that they could have joined us if they had only figured out time.

When she read that the time to fly or flee or leave had arrived, Jeanne was thrilled! Her eyes moved from the screen toward the sunny plaza that was always lively at this time of day. Speaking to whoever was near her in spirit, she sighed and said, "What will happen to this place in the end?"

When she finally calmed down, she still worried that something would go wrong when others examined her work. She had learned to accept that her words seldom made sense to those who had no ability to live in time or communicate in other ways now, but she knew these manuscripts were absolutely necessary for anyone ready to fly now. The ascent would be enough to take many away from today, but what happens to all of the people who stay? Her hands flew over the keys as she read:

> *The Maya were unable to raise the entire tribe in other times, so they do not worry about what happens to those who are content to stay. You must be willing to go! You must be willing to go as fast as you can and ascend rapidly, even if you cannot see around that bend in time. If you experience any hesitancy you will fall off the cliff of conscious existence—unable to lift. You will stay here and live this life over and over again until another time arrives when The Ascended Maya can help you move out of this space and time.*

A voice from somewhere spoke into her ear:

> *What took so many years to complete will be effete if you do not feel it in your own mind at least once. You—the ego self, have to get it together fast enough to transcend whatever you fear will be your end.*
> *Once again, dear friend, you have worked for us and done your share, but others must now read into it and through it to believe as you do, if anything new is to appear through you in the future.*

Jeanne was stunned when she finally understood what she had written so quickly. She wanted to continue to scribe for The Ascended Maya, but would it continue to come through as this work arrived or would she have to live in another existence in order to be able to scribe for The Maya once again?

Nothing more transpired, but Jeanne could sense a new life was about to arrive, and she was not ready for it to happen just now. What could it be? Would she be another man's wife or would her son arrive and decide to live with her as a scribe?

Working her mind, not paying attention to the crowd outside her office as it grew larger and louder than it had when she started to write, Jeanne was surprised by loud knocking on the outer door. Since her office door was open, she looked out at the empty hallway. No one was there!? She was baffled. Who was knocking on her door and where were they standing?

Suddenly an angel appeared and Jeanne felt as if she were being lifted from the spot where she had been working on her computer. Her thoughts were not on what she was doing or where she was going, but wondering about this huge being who was able to so easily pick her up bodily. She felt strange and wonderful and wanted to laugh, but was afraid that was not what was expected of her.

The angel was not as large as it was full of energy. It streaked from her office, carrying Jeanne outside without anyone else seeing it happen. She was a burden to no one on Earth—certainly not a burden to this being from another world, but she did weigh more than this angel was prepared to take on right now.

Later Jeanne described it this way: "As my body lifted into a parallel universe, I intuited that I would never again be the same woman who had lived in the United States and Central America—burdened with worldly concerns. I was free of all philosophy—except my belief in God, that remained. My past life as a wife swept by my eyes and I laughed to see my

Steve. Then such great love swept through me as my mind centered on Brian, my son. He wasn't handicapped, out-of-sorts, or upset in any way. I was amazed at how tall he stood with others arrayed all around him in shimmery gowns."

Whenever Jeanne tried to relate what took place then, her mouth would move but nothing came out. She could not describe how the sounds emerged from her in the strangest places or that her navel seemed to be the center of all that was synergized into this one life and kept everything in its proper place. She had felt so very happy and well then that she was ready to die and leave her life in this time, but it was not to be—not then and not now.

♓ ♓

When that fate-filled afternoon ended, the group reveling in the plaza outside Jeanne's office stopped by to see if she had finished whatever she had been writing and found she was not in her office, but her computer was still on as if she were nearby. They decided she must have gone out for supplies or to take a shower or otherwise refresh herself. Due to their great exhilaration over their own activities, they quickly forgot to look for Jeanne after that.

Working in her own orbit, unable to talk to anyone out loud, was not what Jeanne hated about the steps taken to wrench her from this life into another. 'It's the speed!' She felt disconnected and unable to steer her image into lines such as others had reserved for themselves in time. It was then that she suddenly realized she had survived the trial ascendancy and would not have to stand in line when she left again.

For several moments or whatever it took in that time and place, Jeanne thought about the meaning of not having to wait in line while everyone else who died at the same time seemed to wait in line. The angel came to her then and said she had worked out her own way through the lines and would not have to go back and relive or redo any tasks. This was such a wonder…Jeanne almost fainted! Was this enlightenment or was this the meaning of life? The angel shook her and told her to arise and talk to the group gathering in the dining room. They were waiting for her now.

This was not how she expected to end the work she did outside of Earth, but she left it behind immediately and went into her office bathroom to see what she might find. She was stunned by the image in the mirror! Her face was no longer lined. She was radiant! An extremely benign smile was etched into her skin without evidence of any other lines. The image reminded her of Mona Lisa and what it means to be so changed spiritually, yet remain outwardly the same as the day she came to this place.

When she finished examining her face, Jeanne felt her body snap to attention and her feet move in place. She was marching in place when someone or something erased the memory of what had just taken place. Raising her arm in a snappy salute, she asked for permission to remember at least part of the dream or whatever it was. That mission ended with her being granted only one memory out of billions. She knew for sure she would end this life without any fuss or bother to others, and that made her extremely happy. To end your life without troubling others meant many things to her that would probably change over time, but such a great thought at that moment in time!

Euphoric in ways not staged—unknown to her before that day, Jeanne walked out and left everything as it was. Because she continued to write in her mind, her computer continued working, even though her essay had seemed complete enough to leave as is. Pausing at the door to wonder, she said, "Will this wisdom be lost, too? That always happens when I talk about such thing to strangers—or try to teach someone else."

♓ ♓

The days ahead were marred by nothing at all. Jeanne enjoyed the most delicious meals and had the most fascinating conversations with the most gifted individuals on Earth. Everything was just fabulous! In her mind she could sense others were more, rather than less, surprised at her physical appearance than by what she said, but she did not worry about it or anything again.

In her thoughts she could lift off and fly away, so she would sit for a bit and think about it, and her mind would fill with helpful advice for whoever was lucky enough to be nearby. She helped many students this way and remembered every conversation and every life story, as if it were meant to be told again. Writing took no time at all to pursue, complete, edit, and send out to editors who were delighted to use it exactly as it arrived. Jeanne felt so blessed that she laughed all the time!

To have been pushed into the world through a small tube within a woman who was unable to let her pass easily was not the dangerous part of living this life, just the introduction to it. What came afterwards is what makes all the difference in this world. When others tried to do what they thought was her work, or what she gave them to do, or what they believed she must do if she served The Lord, all came together later.

Long after this day was over and everyone in the compound was much older, Jeanne remembered the Angel of The Maya and the beautiful wings that wrapped around her, safely enfolding her as they flew to another place and time. What happened then? Her mind could never talk or write about it. Grace and the glorious faith that arrive over time were all that remained of that fateful encounter. However, she often sought out those who appeared to have survived death and listened as they talked about the long lines of people ahead of them when they crossed over or visited the other side for a short time. Her advice to them was always the same: "Live your life to the fullest and enjoy every day as you pray and meditate in-between the moments. Don't be upset by what was at best a vague idea of what life was meant to be. Instead, be *you*!"

"Be *you*," became Jeanne's mantra. She said it whenever she left a group or met anyone unable to love the ego self. She whispered it to all who doubted they could make right decisions or felt overly-concerned that others would not love them if they followed their own path. To talk to others about The Ascended Maya became her only work. She wanted to worry about those who missed the point entirely, but finally let even that go, hoping they would read between the lines and do what came to them intuitively later.

When Jeanne's essays were collected and put into a leather-bound collection, issued to those able to conduct classes on their own in compounds all over Mexico, the Middle East, and places in-between, she spoke directly to the reader—giving each individual a bit of her energy through time.

Was it possible for a spiritual scribe to write only what was given to her by The Ascended Maya—or was she writing from her Higher Self? This was argued often, but no one knew since Jeanne was unable to talk about her life inside the work and continue to be honored as Their Scribe by the tribe.

When The Ascended Maya finally arrived in time, only a few humans remained to be swept into space. If The Teachers and other willing helpers had not done whatever it took to announce it was time to ascend or had not assured everyone that the ascent would be easy if you meditated longer than a day or two at a time, or they had not taught everyone that life was better when you prayed, there would have been long lines on Earth waiting for The Maya when they arrived.

After she left Earth to explore whatever, work was never as difficult for Jeanne. Never again could she say she did not know what life on the next plane would be like. She was now confident enough to talk about what everyone can do within their own minds to conquer time, but she seldom spoke of it. When lectures intruded into her time and space, she readily left her books and went on stage, but always with regret that she had to stay away from work that was in all ways more important. Being a spiritual scribe is not a celebration of your own writing or your own style, but a tribute to the many lives in which you wrote well enough to do it once again when The Ascended Maya needed you to help the tribe ascend in time once again.

Whenever Jeanne sat and mulled over her work, she often reviewed one particular piece....

> *Working on this manuscript, as well as working in ways that come to me when I am alone, I feel The Lord is greater than anyone can ever imagine and that we cannot do justice to the way we are made and how we are arranged. Best to give a few broad hints and know that the wise will need nothing more than a whisper to love what is written, and realize that fools will not buy into anything unless it is widely advertised.*

Suddenly struck by that last statement, Jeanne realized how much she ignored the mundane aspects of her daily work now. Without people talking about the work and advertising it, few in the world would be aware that it existed and able to use it. If the wise never buy unless given good reasons, who has to buy into it first? Certainly not the fools who listen to ads, since no one is beating that drum much now, so it must appeal to those who are adventurous and try what others are afraid to read. Unfortunately, most adventurers never talk about what they read. Humming, her fingers started typing out a resounding message....

> *Today we are unshaken in our belief that The Maya of other times have arrived and have communicated with the tribe that exists in this time as a part of the human race. We are also sure that the Angel of The Maya will care for this scribe and her work and help it flourish all over the Earth, but not when it is expected or looked at as art.*

It was obviously time to stop writing and sit back and laugh, but Jeanne's hands kept typing line-after-line. Nothing made as much sense as she thought it would. She asked, "What could be wrong that the ending is so long?" Her mind responded, as if able to discuss it, 'because this saga is not over.' With that thought in place, her fingers took chase after the impulses flying through the universe for her to produce now.

There are many stories out there that you can take to the stars. Read what you wrote in a few instances and realize that it is very necessary to believe women can work and pray and live together as we exist—angels of another place and another time. We are Maya! We are alive! We exist in time and space as if this really takes place.

⧓ ⧓

The paper was the wrong size and the laser was not set. Each delay made the waiting women more eager to read what Jeanne just typed, but it was not to be. Instead, men would read her work and say it was good, but women refused to sit back, relax, and accept it as fact. That is the reason the tribe is still led by men, even though women are rulers in the way of The Ascended Maya.

Stunned once again that a simple seminar could go into an area that was not to be covered right now, Jeanne watched as her fingers took off and started typing a message for the waiting crowd…or was it for her eyes only?

The Maya do not exist? Are you able to read this? What changed within your brain to let you learn the rules of grammar well enough to read English or whatever? Your mind is made the same way. Waves of energy produce the ego state known as 'you' every day, so behave in a way that is intelligent and capable and explain these pages to 'you' now.

Once this was read, the computer got over its fit and the paper slipped in-and-out of the printer without any more blips. Everyone present was now without any doubt about the integrity of the work they witnessed Jeanne scribe in front of them then, but in time enemies would survive who would lead others to doubt it ever happened. Jeanne now handed out a blazing red paper with black print that said:

When you are ready and can move into the future, will you? This is the only thought you actually have to work on now. Once you know, you will be able to ascend at the drop of any kind of bomb or whatever alarms you now. You will be at peace and able to let humanity end its time—or not, without getting upset.

When Mandy arrived in the United States as a woman of destiny, she found a willing family and a life plan that seemed to work then, but she changed spiritually and became the prototype of many women who would become Maya. Are you Maya, too?

☼ Chapter Fifty-Three

Somewhere in the heart of the Yucatan a woman stood in front of a room full of tourists, Maya, and devotees of her moods, and yelled: "Good news! We're going to the top of the world and not stopping until we get there! What do you think of that?" She did not sense, at least not yet, that her efforts were unacceptable, nor did she sense she was mistrusted by some, so she spoke enthusiastically, as if the crowd needed to be humored or put in a better mood, and entirely missed the point of their meeting.

Her well-orchestrated 'pilgrimages' to the Yucatan were always given great consideration, because she was a woman who could harm the Maya if she was unhappy. Her reputation throughout the tribes was what she proclaimed herself to be—a self-made guru, so she was always introduced and described that way. She never caught on that the Maya did not agree, let alone believe, that she was a guru or teacher or saint or anyone great, because she looked down on all of them. Why admire an ancient tribe and look down on its descendants? Her reasons were based on the assumption that the Maya of today could not know that she was a mess inside her mind. How could she trust their wisdom if they failed to notice that and never told her how to erase it or ease her pain?

This woman called herself Cassandra and claimed to be a direct descendant of the Sybarites. She was not popular with residents of Mandy's compound because of her work, not her personality. Her book and lectures based on creating love and luxury were no better than what anyone else who had ever read a book or two about life had produced so far, but Oprah and others thought she was a star. Her critics generally acknowledged, grudgingly, that she was better at promoting meager work than most of her birthright and age, so they shrugged her off as a passing fad. Her talent was tagged as love of self-promotion that was acerbated and exaggerated by her ability to enlist people to follow her lead and travel far and wide with her. Her charismatic power led her to believe she possessed a mind able to understand The Ascended Maya and tribes guided by them.

When Cassandra left the stage, moving toward the pavilion and adjacent dining room, a crowd of women followed behind to ask her questions about those who were weaving and working in clay all around the compound that day. She brushed away, as if so many flies, anyone who asked questions she could not answer, but lingered long on whatever implied she was wise and others would be wise to follow her advice. As she sauntered into the dining room her entourage decided to sit among those already seated. This struck her as rebellion or rejection of her as a person. Anger welled up and filled the spot she had previously described as where God resided within her mind.

Anger barely reached her brain when Cassandra felt pain streak through her head and pull her skin and body violently to the right side. Her mouth drooped sadly to the right and tears traced patterns in her makeup as they ran to her chin. This self-proclaimed guru had a stroke, just as the last of her disciples walked away from her to take seats near the stage. As she went down to her knees and then the ground, several onlookers thought she was throwing a fit. Fortunately, a Mayan man went to her prone body immediately and lifted her head and cleared her mouth. Her tongue twitched and ended up hanging over the side of her lips.

The Great Cassandra, as she encouraged her closest allies to call her, was not a woman of means, but she always dressed with a flair that implied she had much money set aside. The staff's desire to help an ailing guest overruled any consideration of how she would pay for medical assistance at this stage in her illness, so an ambulance was called and arrived ten minutes later. Without much thought, the medicos lifted and strapped Cassandra to a gurney, ready to drive her to the local hospital for evaluation and diagnosis, but before they drove away they wanted to be paid. Her students were not able to come up with the necessary sum, so one of the men asked a cook what they should do.

With dramatic gestures indicating that she felt someone among the guru's cadre should step-up and take over, Louisa, the head cook, said, "She must have taken out insurance for this trip. Get her purse and see what kind she has."

When no one moved to assume that role, Louisa looked into the huge bag Cassandra always carried in her left hand. As she touched her wallet, Louisa felt something hot lying beside it. Her hand barely touched the object, but she recognized immediately that Cassandra had concealed a stolen artifact made in ages past in her bag. She screamed because she realized it was a fetish of the type that is never to be removed from a grave because it was made to protect the tomb from such thieves. Her heart beat so rapidly that she almost had to stop talking in order to calm herself.

Rattling off prayers and mantras—anything she could think of that might protect her from the rare object's power, Louisa could still feel someone enter her and take her over. As she felt her control fade, she looked up and spotted a tall man telling everyone what needed to be done. In an instant he, or was it Louisa, led all the women in prayer and got them to move out of the medical crew's way. His staring eyes penetrated the emergency workers minds deeply enough that they trusted it was okay to take this woman away and she would pay. This miracle of faith completed, the medicos moved Cassandra into the waiting ambulance and left in a rush of squealing tires and sirens.

Only when the ambulance left the compound did the cook realize this man was not like others she had met outside her tribe. Peering at him through slitted eyelids, she spotted a rainbow around his head. That did it! Dropping to her knees, Louisa began singing a song of praise to God of All. The other women trained in the Mayan tradition joined her. As for the rest, they sat in silence looking sad until the native women who slipped into a comatose state when the strange man entered the room came out of trance. Each asked others what had happened to the stranger, but no one knew.

Louisa asked one of the elders who arrived at her side just as she opened her eyes, "What can we decide about such a man visiting our tribe?"

"You have been visited by an angel of The Maya once again," said the elder without smiling or looking away from her radiant face. "You are to be blessed…but what is this?" Spying the fetish lying on the floor beside Louisa's right leg, the elder knelt to get a better view of it. Upon closer examination, she jerked her arm away and stood up to her fullest height of four feet five and began praying fervently in a loud voice.

Shocked to see the fetish beside her—not in Cassandra's purse where she left it, Louisa mentally reviewed placing the purse and all its contents on the gurney beside Cassandra. She could not remember what happened after that, but she was no longer afraid of the fabled object. Wagging her finger at the elder, Louisa said handling the fetish was not a problem for anyone who was Maya. It had triggered Cassandra's stroke because she had either stolen it from another thief or taken it from a sacred place.

News spread more rapidly than a forest fire that Cassandra and her followers had hidden ancient relics in their luggage. Sacred or otherwise, ancient artifacts are not allowed to leave the tribe, let alone Mexico, so local police arrived and began searching everyone down to their garters and spurs, as someone wryly said on the side. The guru's students laughed then, but never again after that. Every one in Cassandra's crowd was searched twice and given the impression that they would be tried for thievery if they took or bought anything, anywhere that was not from a reputable store.

Many trinkets were added to the pile of relics, enough that the police began to perversely enjoy the naïveté of these women. They were not amused so much as repulsed that tourists, calling themselves pilgrims in order to take advantage of those who entertained them in the usual way of the Maya today, were common thieves of the shoplifting variety. The question raised that day was, "How many others in the past were guilty of something like this?" No one present knew, so the elders asked Mandy to work on it in her own unique way.

Mandy was summoned and she arrived just as the police were leaving the compound. They said they would be back again the next day to continue their interrogations, but she did not wish to stay in the presence of the police since she was not sure these men were honest in their thoughts, either. Whenever she detected the presence of even one person unwilling to do their work as stated and paid for by the State, it set off alarms within her art of divination and often caused pain in her heart. Exiting her Jeep, Mandy watched the police drive away and felt such a stab in her heart.

For reasons not shared with those sitting around her at the large dining room table, Mandy asked every tourist to recall where they traveled in the days prior to arriving at her compound. She was not impatient, but she wanted them to respond quickly, to get to the root of what was about to happen. Listening to the first few women list events they had participated in was not that interesting that she failed to notice out of the corner of her eye a slight movement at the center of the room. Mandy had anticipated that something strange was on the way, but what it might be was a mystery she needed to solve immediately, if she was to help everyone present. The chatty tourists were not done talking themselves out when one woman sighed as her head drooped until her chin rested on her chest. She was the first to drop off, but not the last. Many others could not relax, so they were asked to stand at the back of the room.

The dining room staff was now closing in on her, so Mandy laughed and pushed back the family of man intent on watching her work. She asked servers to get a glass of water for everyone to keep some moving—not to encourage static electricity. As they left the room, she watched to see who was filled with thoughts of doom now. When she saw whose aura was black and whose was blue, in a sense that has nothing to do with outer appearance, she asked them to leave and help others do something they believed needed to be done in another room. To remove all those present who could not pray, lightened her psychic work immediately, but no one else knew that then.

Creating a triangle with her fingertips in front of her face, Mandy projected an image to those gathered around her that she was thinking deeply and very concerned about something they could not see or comprehend. Intuitively, she decided to take care of the tribe there and then and not wait for someone of another estate to appear. No one present told her an angel had appeared in another way earlier, but she suspected something of the kind had happened or was nearby.

⧓   ⧓

Within a day of Mandy's meeting with Cassandra's entrapped disciples, as well as people she trusted, the thieves decided to leave Mexico and visit elsewhere in the future. They recognized that Mandy and Company's work in these compounds was proceeding too quickly and efficiently for them to demonstrate effectively that the Maya of today had no artwork or belief system that would benefit from others' financial backing, without using ancient artifacts as collateral. These outraged, so-called 'Friends of the Maya' decided they could find better ways to preserve more ancient Mayan art than was available in Mexico and began working in another third world country.

The Maya, as an international tribe, were not pleased to hear this news. Their pride in a way of life that only a few Maya actually created now was so great that many of the tribe became so offended that they could no longer tolerate the incivilities of intrusive Americans and others like them. They wanted all outsiders expelled from the compounds and elsewhere, and no work shared with anyone who was not born and raised there. Fortunately, many more elders stepped forward and pointed out that Mandy and her wonderful teachers were all Americans and would have to leave if such an edict was created and obeyed.

It was a day and a half of great movement within the compound before the police arrived back on the scene and asked for help determining who was stealing from the tribe, and the elders were ready for them then. The tribe decided to work it out through Mandy, so the elders asked her to tell the police all about what was going on in other countries around them now. Thus Mandy related to the police and other officials present that the best way to stop such illicit trade was to advertise that innocent, or at least gullible, tourists were constantly being defrauded by cheap-Jacks selling pieces of Mayan art meant to replicate what had crumbled and rotted long ago. She told the police to notify all the international networks available to them that all collectors and museums should scrutinize any art recently discovered in Mayaland because they had fallen pray to false art. She explained that what today's experts believed to be authentic Mayan artifacts had no historical or religious value! Its value was in its creators' brilliant attempts to recreate ancient Mayan art and insert personal lines of thought about time—that was all!

Nonstop, Mandy hammered out the message to the detectives present that the Mayan art smuggled now was indeed lovely and interesting, and would probably develop a devout following among collectors in the future, but it was not reclaimed or stolen art from the past. It had all been created recently with the sole intention of defrauding the greedy and those who will never know the difference between brass and gold.

Mandy also educated reporters who gathered around her after the meeting. Her message to everyone present was that unscrupulous artists trained in ancient ways were passing off high-priced modern art as trash dug out of a mountainside or a Mayan grave. She emphasized that only elders of the tribe know the difference between what was used and made in the past and what was very skillfully created weeks ago. As the meeting disbanded and many of the press surrounded the elders, Mandy spotted flaws in the way they restated what was said and intended, but she let it stand since it was a grand plan and required everyone's help, if they were to ever undermine the other side. As time permitted, the angel (who was able to come and go without seeming to be present) visited Mandy and the elders frequently, helping them win their case without letting on that The Ascended Maya were behind it.

Meanwhile, certain of the guru's 'students' unwittingly asked this angel of a man to go to Geneva and seek out a bank where their organization maintained a private account. They were confident that the Swiss would recommend them to others who were always looking for ancient Mayan artifacts. Their plan was not quite weak enough to collapse when one laughed, but the angel was unable to stop laughing, so their work collapsed amidst his laughter.

Some tried to stop the collapse but could not, because laughter opens the diaphragm wide enough to let you fly. Suddenly everyone was flying high and able to see the world was just a piece of the sky. They had no idea or desire to find out why it was important to save ancient artifacts and keep them where they were found, but they did realize it was wise to agree and declare such relics to be immensely valuable only to The Maya.

The newly-elected leader of the crowd once led by Cassandra chose to publicize that such art is needed by the Maya of today to help them survive and live as a tribe. He went on to say they were forming a consortium to locate and return all such art to the Mayan tribes. When the others finally settled down and worked on his plan in more depth, the angelic man moved to turn it over to them. He said he would fly within the day to Geneva, Switzerland, to find out what had to be done to enter Cassandra's dummy account, assuring them it would be used solely by those dummies who constantly try to cheat others out of taxes and artifacts. Prepared to speak and talk at great length, if necessary, no one thought he would have any trouble convincing the Swiss, because he was tall enough, broad enough, and light enough to be believed by anyone—anywhere, at any time. Unbeknownst to them, all he had to do was open his lips and whatever language was required flowed out fluently, so in time he left them without any trace of money left in Cassandra's Swiss bank account.

ℋ   ℋ

The Maya's faith had been tested and found to be strong, so some elders decided it was time to show younger members of the tribe how to fly—and do it without their constantly asking them questions. They pondered starting out using laughter, but decided to instead develop a romantic notion they felt would sell the idea of voluntarily practicing the intricate steps that lead to ascension. The only problem was that this plan had to be passed by tribes who were unable to dance and rise now.

Because it originated from a powerful wave started when a woman stole a sacred object, their final and grandest plan was built around a deeper understanding of human nature. That one act of treason against the beauty of people who had feted her and given her growth work was such that it could have changed the way the tribe lives today, but it did not. Many do not see beauty, let alone comprehend art, because they have rejected clean living or doing anything new or wondrous, too. Art seldom pays when a person steals rather than creates it.

While all this was being worked out in a flash, Cassandra's followers who had been abandoned in Mexico grew restless and wished to do something to help their fallen guru. She was now isolated in a hospital room waiting to be sent to the United States for advanced medical care. Separately, her followers began to grow up, mature, or bloom as many do when faced with an emergency or two, but as a group they continued to act like wayward children. They clashed so much and so often that they never reached a consensus about anything. When one woman stood up finally and said she was going to change her reservations and fly home immediately, ten others decided to go with her; but the rest did the opposite, just to prove they could do whatever they wanted, too.

Perversity and adversity do not co-exist. You cannot be perverse and admit that you are in need of another, as when you are poor or down on your luck, so their group split. Within minutes of the final break-up, several left never to return to the Yucatan. A few lingered and asked what they might do to sell fabrics and pottery created by the women of the tribe or within the various compounds. Most of these followers of the fallen guru were not really evil, nor did they want to be seen as thieves by anyone in the tribe, but they continued to create evil thoughts about others whom they thought tried to boss them around.

Working in such varied places, many created stories about Mandy and tourists promoted them by constantly asking: "Who is Mandy—really? How does she arrive at split-second decisions so easily? What kind of man does she live with now or again?" This need to discredit any human being superior in any way is not a good way to live together, needless to say, so the elders announced they would pray over the fire that night and the hangers-on were included in the event. They were delighted to be invited! They had traveled to the Yucatan with dreams of seeing many strange things, but instead ended up being caught with stolen artifacts and deemed to be thieves by the Maya. They hoped their original dreams were about to come true tonight.

The ceremony arrived with fleet feet and the Mayan guide of the women remaining from the disbanded group permitted them to sit close enough to the spot where the elder in charge would talk. These few women were not allowed to move once the fire rose higher, so the elders decided they must learn how to be Maya and survive the fire or immediately move out of the circle into the darkness.

When asked if they were Maya, the women all said 'No,' and then looked at each other with uncertainty. These stragglers were a motley assortment of child-like women who dressed alike in jeans and T-shirts, with long hair that neither distinguished nor adorned any of them. They were not alone in wondering why others could ever mistake them for being Maya.

The oldest elder stood his ground and pointed to one of them and said emphatically, "You are Maya! You are a member of the tribe. You will rise!"

Murmurs arose from younger Maya seated around the fire, but not from the visitors. The tourists did not realize it was a strange pronouncement to make over a blond woman-child who was unable to think beyond her next meal or if there was a masseur nearby. The elders seated nearby looked at her more closely. Suddenly they clapped their hands and spoke in whatever dialect they understood best. They approved her and she was transported in her mind to another time. Since the young woman still sat as if meditating deeply, others tried to imitate her pose but were not proclaimed to be Maya by the elders.

What does it take to be Maya and rise to the sky? You may sit and wonder, or read through what Jeanne scribed or Wanda wrote in her journal, maybe study what Julie etched into her sculptures, but you will never know from their work what it all means unless you, too, are Maya. You cannot imagine what it is to be Maya if you never existed as a Maya in time, so do not even try.

Here is a simple test to see if you are Maya...

- If right now you are trying to figure out what to do with your life because it is not what you thought it would be, you probably are not Maya.
- If you cease to exist at times and awaken to find you are able to do what you once believed to be impossible, you are Maya.

Many artists came to the compound to work on Mayan art and watch time fly with Mandy and the tribe, then went back to wherever they came from and lived about the same as they did when they started out, but they were different somehow. The Mayan tribes of today are no different than those that existed right after the last great wave left Mayaland long ago, but they will do something new soon. The Maya are going to trade and produce more art than ever before and, as a result, contribute more taxes to the governments under which they seemingly do not exist now.

What would make such a change necessary? Why would the Maya submit to it? The Maya know when it is time to go and when the old must die, and why, but *the world* is in another orbit and needs to be placed on notice that the time has arrived when those who are ready to go can leave and be free.

This work is not an excuse for living a certain life plan or knowing what to do with your mind—but how to find the way back home. Once every so many centuries a sign appears indicating that it is time to ascend again—and someone has to lead it. What to do then? Why not read through what was said in the past and submit to its wisdom? Unfortunately, many cannot. What happens to the pride of countries that exist in time for only a few minutes before they disappear in a flash or crash? They had a chance to do it all, too, but decided not to leave time behind.

This is not to say that Atlantis is not out there in space, but to say they tried to recreate it in the United States—but it was not permitted. The way they arrived in time was specifically abandoned as not suitable for them to redo it, but they tried anyway. The Maya, however, do not let members of the tribe ascend until they are able to connect with a few who can launch a plan big enough to encompass the entire hemisphere and move it somewhere beyond this time and space. This plan is now in place!

☼ CHAPTER FIFTY-FOUR

As the old shaman gazed fondly at a group of children gathered around his knees, listening to the breeze with him, he said, "When the sky is bright at night, you can see Venus with the naked eye, but it's not always possible when the skies are darkened by clouds, as they are now. If you sniff and look into the wind, you sense that something is there, but you can't see it. You can't catch it, either, but you sense within your nose that there is something in the wind. Use that sense now to tell me what you feel."

"I smell leaves," said a laughing boy sitting in the second row of children circling the shaman. Because he could not see into the night and was afraid of the dark, he tried to hide his fright by laughing all the time. The shaman laughed, too, frightening the boy a bit. The boy thought, but did not say, 'How could this wise man know so much?'

"You're afraid of the night, my friend, and that is all right. In fact, you must be aware of darkness and the light if you are to learn what to do with time. You must learn much and go forth and teach others everywhere, but that is not your role tonight. Tonight you will listen and not say a word to your mamas and papas about where you have been. Can you all remember that?" As the shaman spoke, he looked deeply into the eyes of each child.

The adults who had intended to stay with the children faded away. They were ushered out by elders and told to go home and come back tomorrow. The elders promised their children would be a bit different, but infinitely better behaved than they were now. What parent could resist such an offer—and from a shaman of the tribe?

The old man sat back on his heels for a moment, then stood and raised his arms to God of All high above him and everywhere around him and beneath his feet. Speaking in an exalted way he proclaimed: "The existence of God is not what we are here to study! We each know God. God is not to be challenged by us…or ever talked about. No man can answer for what God has planned, but we can do a lot to help God get on with the work of Earth…God is good… God is Spirit…God works through us like the wind. We can't know what God is or why God exists in our minds, because we aren't still enough—and we don't listen…but we can try to be as good as we can be all the time we exist here on earth." The shaman never smiled during this long introductory speech. He was now torn between taking each one gently in hand and leading them toward the altar and blessing them right away, rather than lecturing about time first. Being an obedient servant of The Lord, he yielded to The Divine and talked about time.

"You can sense, each in your own way, that there is a reason for being here… You know you have a mother and father, and many aunts and uncles, and a tribe to support your lifework, but it is The Lord who will come for you when you are done with this world… Now is a time when one world collides with others that no longer work as well as they once did … The path is open for women and children to make a move to establish their own lives in places where they were not allowed in the old days… You will all be leaders! You will know where to go if the Earth moves or blows up in places or becomes too hot… You will give directions on the ascent at the end… Can you remember all that I say now?"

All the children lifted their heads and nodded solemnly. The shaman was struck by the thoughts he had channeled through to the children—and in great awe of it all. How did it happen that children would be the ones to take future people to the next level, that all he had ever done would be wasted or destroyed if he did not teach the young what to do now? He was impressed that he had been the one selected to begin such lessons but wondered about the next lesson and the lessons after that. 'Would there be a leader among the Maya to teach the young what to do? Who was strong enough to lend his energy to others to use to help them rise above the tide of these times?' He closed his eyes and forgot where he was until he felt a surge of energy and a vision emerging in his mind from out of time.

He was surprised! The leader was no man he had ever met. It was Mandy with some women standing at her side. They were being given assignments to work on the people of Earth. He suddenly felt insignificant and sad that he had never worked with her. He felt strangely alienated from the work of Earth and sensed that he had to find Mandy and work with her now; but what about the others who had resisted her influence? He knew he would not bother with them again.

As the night left the sky the children sang and danced their way into a new belief system, without realizing it was taking them to far away places then. Their soul work was cemented in place as they stamped their feet and clapped their hands. Whenever they met again or were asked to sing or dance, that Spirit would emerge and take over their thoughts and words. This was the plan and it was grand, but would the children be able to carry it forward for their clans?

When a group of teachers and the men guarding them as well as the children emerged from the forest clearing, the worried mothers and fathers ran toward their offspring. The women cried and laughed at the same time, but the men acted as if they never doubted anything would happen. The difference between the men and women was that the women expressed what the men felt and tried to hide, because the women were not upset and the men were. How different things would have been had the women admitted they had a part to play—a role in which they starred, but they never wanted others to know they were great until the play was over.

♓ ♓

Working on Earth, doing work that keeps you grounded enough to hang tough is what Mandy always planned to do, but did not always achieve. At ten that morning, she stopped by the village and talked to one man only. This man easily understood what she wanted to do and asked her to stay and build a model of what would become an academy for the arts dedicated to the work of Mayan children. She agreed that it was a good idea, but thought more work needed to be done before it could take root and grow.

Within hours Mandy called a friend in Canada and asked her to do something for the Maya. This woman then called many others to do the work of building schools and medical centers with a few men who were not Maya, either, but of the same faith. Mandy felt her job was done then.

As weeks passed and years climbed within the mind of a group called The Maya of Earth, the old work diminished and new work began in other worlds. Mandy said nothing to Jeanne, and Jeanne did not speak to any men about her work, and so it went—on and on, until they were supported by what is not seen or believed by most people to be, because it is not about what seems to be or about the ways of the world today. These women sensed within themselves that they held the key to whatever was going to happen to the world. However, they were never free of the belief that they could not achieve anything easily.

When this group of children confirmed in the Mayan faith began chanting and repeating that chant whenever they prayed, older generations who had been unwilling to remember or study the old ways discovered they intentionally were not given much work. When adults realized their children were brave and earnest, unafraid of the world beyond them as they were, they responded when asked to reconsider what they had done in the past and open to doing more work at home than they ever did in present times. Parents listened to the wisdom of these children and to their spiritual guides or shamans. The time they previously spent listening to their children whine or refuse to do chores or go to bed on time was now spent in meditation or enjoying their leisure time with friends. Everyone won something!

Working alone at home was condoned, but not to the extent that tribal ways of today would collapse. They still needed to unite to be able to supply communications, utilities and such to people used to such conveniences once again. The clans were asked to select tasks that would help people elsewhere live as well as they did. Their simple way of life provided them with time outside, as well as time inside the home to do whatever they wanted to do alone. They were told to use their trades to help the tribe and not get lost in ambitious plots created by others in the outside world. It was a test of their mettle as a tribe, but seen as odd by Maya who live in mountainside clans.

If you can raise enough beans and corn to feed your family, are you not doing enough work? That was the traditional wisdom, but Mandy and the tribal elders talked about providing schools so everyone would have more time to spend with God. Who could argue with that? The fact that many had lost their eternal souls trying to complete that same mission in times past did not release them from trying to do it again now. They learned more about faith from what went wrong when they worked away from their home base than others who stayed…thus a few saved many from such pain.

The mission was to design a way of life that permits elders to sit and do very little once they end their careers or they are ended for them. Each member of the tribe would contribute enough throughout their prime years to enable elders to sleep, dream, or meditate—doing less than they ever did in this world, so as to be prepared to ascend at the end. Daily work was not to be so difficult that you were broken in body and mind doing it, but it could not be so easy that you might expect children to do it along with you. Work was what you had to do to share your life with those who once took care of you. The concept was nothing new in many nations, but it was strange and alien to the present generation.

Working alone at home was what most serious, educated women wanted to do, but it alienated them from new friends too much to be acceptable as the way to move into the future development of the tribe. The world needed men and women of good faith to produce the best moods and the best attitudes, but they were unable to feel great if they never interacted with others of faith. This is easy to remedy, but it takes time to teach those who have declined in years beyond their prime.

The elders of the world were restless, feeling upset, unable to relax. They wanted the young to admire them, but fought constantly among themselves most of the time, too. They had come to hate retirement so much that it was of little benefit to those who had worked the most. They wanted to have the fun they believed they missed when young, but never enjoy themselves even now. Toys of all kinds were sold and given a whirl for a day or two, then cast aside with pride. They could not feel smug about spending so much on what was merely a waste of time.

To gain appreciation for what someone did for you when you were a child is to discover what you can do for others—plus all the children of the world. If you cannot bend over and touch your toes, you probably cannot adjust much to what a child sees and loves. If you cannot stoop to see into the eyes of the youngest members of the tribe, you probably cannot criticize them fairly, either. They exist and they see what is, but you are who is responsible for what they do until age 21 or 22 in America, or many years younger elsewhere. By then adults should be able to live independent of your control and constant support. To deny this is to advertise that you are not wise.

♓ ♓

When posters arrived announcing that the tribe would finance a scholarship created to support one life plan, several mothers and many fathers asked about it and wanted to know if their children could go to college now. According to many educators, the way to the top is with a college degree in hand, but this was different. It backed earning a certificate of proficiency to be awarded when you demonstrated you knew what you had been taught to such a degree that you could pass judgment and tests created by elders who were outstanding at what you wanted to do with your life, too. This was different enough from what most believed to be taught in universities and cities of the world that the Maya argued among themselves about the need to do it now. What happened then remains a mystery, as well as how it became history.

Women entered the university system to learn how to teach reading, writing, and basic mathematics to the tribe, because it seemed the best way to blend raising a family, being at home all day—and doing something great for the tribe. Men wanted to teach, too, but felt the need to teach children well into their teens or until they could accept their kind, yet tough love. Mayan women wanted a way of life for boys where they could take a wife and not have to worry about paying for her life-style, too. It could be done, or so they said, but they did not actually know what to say to their sons after the age of 17 because their men took over then, if not before. Some young men, however, had no one to tell them what to do as men and floundered until they met a woman they could love. If they chose a wife wisely, they were prosperous, healthy, and well loved. If not? They usually spent their pay drinking their lives away or went into politics or drugs.

If you have no one helping or showing you what happens if you do not follow the rules, you might learn life's lessons by breaking into stores and homes to see if they take you to jail or not. This is okay, because this is how the elders were raised? Not true, but many let a generation or two learn lessons without the benefit of wise men and women stepping in and helping them win the game of life without waging war.

When a woman meets a mother and her child, she may wish to live that way or not, but she has a model either way. If a woman is happier now than when she was as a child, and others are aware of the difference, they might wish to follow her path, particularly if they are unhappy in their homes.

What can you do to help women learn what is wise in love without being molested over and over again? It is never wise to take upon yourself the mind of the unwise, misdirected, or evil ones, but you must if you are to trap them and remove such deviants from the path of children. The tribe was not as negligent as many others, but they, too, have problems of betrayal of faith involving children now. Why? Too much time spent loving the lustful feelings displayed on the pages of magazines, movies, and TV screens every day and all night. Elders cannot erase what has been etched into the mind, but they can replace smut with a better way of life more easily achieved than what exists on TV.

♓ ♓

When the poetry started flowing again everyone listened to what others said within, and the old tribe was free to go. Once again that was the promise—it would happen. But when, was the question asked of every wise man and woman of the tribe?

If you can write a line or two of what flows through you each night, sleep on it or maybe dream of something unique that completes the thought: Are you wise? Men and women debate such issues every day in the same way they previously argued about what to pay for a car. Their spiritual work has become more arduous, but they are able to change the way they feel about themselves and heal their minds.

The work of Spirit is not as easy as earning a living—unless you are doing more than you are built to handle. The work of the body is easy if what you seek daily works properly and keeps you alert to what you have to do when you are through. The mind, however, loves to order the body and spirit around and sever the lines of communication with others of its own line. Why? The mind is not going to remain with the spirit once ascension occurs. It has only this time to rule, but wants to stick around for another life.

If you could not change your profession, what would you say about moving into a new way of life for you and those you support? Would you balk at working harder so you could have it easier later? Would you say you were forced to throw away everyone who was once associated with what you used to do? Would you decide you had worked a long time and were ready to retire and do so? If so, what do you plan to do next?

The wave of energy needed to help a huge group ascend will be the challenge of the next few seasons and will not be finished even then—just getting started. What can you do to help your clan boom and zoom? You can work hard, always do your part, and insist that others do the same. You can also open your heart even if others do not. You can always do something new and listen to what others tried to do before you, too.

♓ ♓

At the end of another busy week working with the children, the shaman said, "We are here today to teach you, using waves of thought. If you want to move into a new line, you have to open to doing this work, too." He always left them wondering if they had said or done the right thing or done their lessons right, without actually suggesting they might have done better than they had. He was not creating a sense of guilt, rather the realization that Maya are not going to change, nor would you, if there is no lesson or pain involved. What the mind loves most is to remind itself constantly of what you said you would do and compare it to what you actually did. Therein lies the lesson and possibly the pain of living today.

The old man looked at each young face, smiling through ripples of wrinkles, winking at one or two before he began again. When ready, he held up his hand and ticked off on his fingers the lessons. He said, "Lesson One – Don't worry about what you're doing now but about what you said you would do, and now have no interest in pursuing. Lesson Two – Don't sit and think—move and believe." If the children did not understand, they did not show any sign of it, so he continued.

"Physical labor is always the end of the line for your spine if you don't align your mind with time… Money problems are a definite way to analyze your mind and how well it adjusts to what you have… If you want everything you see, you're indirectly asking for too many things without accepting that you can rest and feel blessed…. If you have enough today and want to save for another day, you may be afraid to say it out loud because you don't trust others that much." Since the children did not appear to get this lesson, he put it aside with a wave of his hand, indicating he would talk with their parents and those who teach them, so they could pass it down later.

After a few moments of deep thought, the shaman looked up at the sky and said, "When you look at the sky and see Venus rising, ask God to take you on high when the time arrives. It's that easy! You can do it if you leave your mind alone and live in your own home without any sense of frustration or hatred around you…You'll live as long as it takes to get you to where you can decide if you want to ascend in time or stay for another life…. Once that decision arrives at the office of the controller of this life, you will survive and do more or you will go with The Lord and end the confusion you feel when you put away a completed work of art."

As the night deepened around the circle, the old man stood and shook himself. With arms extended toward the sky, he spoke to the children and adults sitting or standing around him. "We are here and now ending this discussion of existence—and what it takes to live in these times…without telling you what you will do… because we can't be you. Fill in your blank spaces…ease into your mind over time and sense that if you ascend at the end of this existence, you're free to be all you can be—and never again feel this small.

"As we part for the time being, I ask each of you to say a word or two about your day. God willing—and you're allowed to say that out loud—it will be done…You will be amazed at how quickly you spot miracles everywhere now!"

Author's Notes

There are few things in life that fly off your fingers and into the hands of others without much flurry and worry…but this book is such a miracle. It had an easy birth due to the loving administrations of the folks at FemmeOsage Publishing. It is hoped that the world is as ready to accept this wondrous art form as they were. Eternal thanks to publisher, Lynne Klippel, for her generous support and work, as well as her husband, Larry Klippel, who provided all necessary technical support.

Angel of The Maya is one of a series of books that follow the lives of amazing women and men who survive in our minds and hearts through time…drawing attention to all that is fun, mysterious, and Divine about our lives. It is my hope that you will continue to enjoy the adventures of Mandy and friends as they arrive in time.

Ruth Lee, Scribe

WANT TO LEARN MORE ABOUT MANDY AND FRIENDS?

Start off by visiting **www.AngelofTheMaya.com** for any updates and announcements about happenings now, and then enter the domain of Ruth Lee where all things are possible, even the impossible at **www.RuthLee-Scribe.com**

- To learn more about The Ascended Maya and their work, check out "The Word of The Maya," as scribed by Ruth Lee.
- For some biographical information on The Scribe, Ruth Lee, check out her book: "The Making of a Scribe ~ *How to Achieve a Life You Can Write About.*"
- The further adventures of Mandy and how she came to live in Mayaland are explored in "Within The Veil: *An Adventure in Time.*"
- All of Ruth Lee's books are available at her web site and bookstores all over the world.

WANT TO LEARN HOW TO MEDITATE?

A good place to start is…
www.MeditateWithRuthLee.com

www.ingramcontent.com/pod-product-compliance
Lightning Source LLC
Chambersburg PA
CBHW080722020726
47503CB00010B/2757